THE
MALTA
EXCHANGE

ALSO BY STEVE BERRY

COTTON MALONE NOVELS

STAND-ALONE NOVELS

THE
MALTA
EXCHANGE

STEVE
BERRY

MINOTAUR BOOKS
NEW YORK

THE MALTA EXCHANGE. Copyright © 2019 by Steve Berry. All rights reserved. Printed in the United States of America. For information, address St. Martin's Press, 175 Fifth Avenue, New York, N.Y. 10010.

www.minotaurbooks.com

Library of Congress Cataloging-in-Publication Data

Names: Berry, Steve, 1955– author.
Title: The Malta exchange : a novel / Steve Berry.
Description: First edition. | New York : Minotaur Books, 2019.
Identifiers: LCCN 2018050884 | ISBN 9781250140265 (hardcover) |
    ISBN 9781250225658 (international, sold outside the U.S., subject to rights
    availability) | ISBN 9781250232564 (signed edition) | ISBN 9781250140272 (ebook)
Subjects: | GSAFD: Suspense fiction.
Classification: LCC PS3602.E764 M35 2019 | DDC 813/.6—dc23
LC record available at https://lccn.loc.gov/2018050884

First Edition: March 2019

10 9 8 7 6 5 4 3 2 1

For Elizabeth,
My wife,
My always

ACKNOWLEDGMENTS

Again, my sincere thanks to John Sargent, head of Macmillan, and Sally Richardson, who always has nothing but kind words. Then there's Jen Enderlin, who captains St. Martin's, and my publisher at Minotaur, Andrew Martin. Also, a huge debt of gratitude continues for Hector DeJean in Publicity; Jeff Dodes and everyone in Marketing and Sales, especially Paul Hochman; Anne Marie Tallberg, the sage of all things paperback; David Rotstein, who produced the cover; and Mary Beth Roche and her innovative folks in Audio.

As always, a bow to Simon Lipskar, my agent and friend, and to my editor, Kelley Ragland, and her assistant, Maggie Callan, both of whom are wonderful.

A few extra mentions: Meryl Moss and her extraordinary publicity team (especially Deb Zipf and JeriAnn Geller); Jessica Johns and Esther Garver, who continue to keep Steve Berry Enterprises running smoothly; and Rachel Maurizio, guide extraordinaire in Malta.

Ten years ago I dedicated *The Venetian Betrayal* to my new bride, Elizabeth. She was then a novice to writing and publishing, but a fast study, evolving into a first-rate editor with a keen eye for craft and story. She's now half owner (with the incomparable M. J. Rose) of 1001 Dark Nights, a publishing and marketing company focused on the romance genre. She is also executive director of International Thriller Writers, an organization of over four thousand members, 80 percent of whom are working thriller writers.

So this book is for Elizabeth, an extraordinary woman who has not only made my stories better, but made my life better, too.

It is not necessary to believe in God to be a good person.
In a way, the traditional notion of God is outdated.
One can be spiritual, but not religious.

It is not necessary to go to church and give money.
For many, nature can be a church.

Some of the best people in history did not believe in God,
while some of the worst deeds were done in his name.
—POPE FRANCIS I

PROLOGUE

SATURDAY, APRIL 28, 1945
LAKE COMO, ITALY
3:30 P.M.

BENITO AMILCARE ANDREA MUSSOLINI KNEW FATE WAS ABOUT TO overtake him. He'd known that from the moment, yesterday, when partisans of the 52nd Garibaldi Brigade blocked his route north and halted the German convoy that had been aiding his escape toward Switzerland. The column's Wehrmacht commander had made no secret of the fact that he was tired of fighting and intended on avoiding the advancing American troops with an uneventful journey back to the Third Reich. Which explained how a downed tree and thirty ragtag partisans captured three hundred fully armed German regulars.

For twenty-one years he'd ruled Italy, but when the Allies took Sicily, then invaded the mainland, his fascist associates and King Victor Emmanuel III seized the opportunity to strip him of power. It took Hitler to rescue him from prison, then install him as head of the Italian Social Republic, headquartered in Milan. Nothing more than a German puppet regime—a way to maintain the illusion of power. But that was gone now, too. The Allies had stormed northward taking Milan, which had forced him to flee farther north to Lake Como and the Swiss border, only a few kilometers away.

"It is a calm day," Clara said to him.

There'd been countless women in his life. His wife tolerated the mistresses because divorce was not an option. Mainly on religious grounds, but what would being the ex-wife of Il Duce do for her?

Not much.

But of all his dalliances, Claretta Petacci held a special place. Twenty-eight years separated them in age, but somehow she understood him. Never questioning. Never doubting. Always loving. She'd come to Como of her own accord to join him in exile.

But fate was working against them.

The Russians were shelling Berlin, the Brits and Americans racing through Germany unchallenged, the Third Reich in ruins. Hitler cowered in a bunker beneath the rubble of his capital city. The Rome–Berlin Axis had collapsed. The godforsaken war, which should never have been fought in the first place, was drawing to an end.

And they'd lost.

Clara stood at the open window, wrapped in her own thoughts. The view from their lofty perch was of the far-off lake and the mountains on the other side. They'd spent the night in this humble house, their room adorned with a plain bed, a couple of chairs, and a stone floor. No fire burned in the hearth, the only light provided by a bare bulb that shone starkly against the whitewashed walls. His life had been, for a long time, a cascade of luxury and indulgence. So he'd found it ironic that he and Clara—who once sought solace in each other's arms amid the opulence of the Palazzo Venezia—had found themselves in the bed of a peasant's cottage amid the lonely Italian hills.

He stepped over to the window to stand beside her. Dust lay thick on the sill. She held his hand as though he were a child.

"Seven years ago," he said in Italian, "I was an interesting person. Now I am little more than a corpse."

His voice seemed doom-laden and apathetic.

"You're still important," she declared.

He managed a weak smile. "I'm finished. My star has fallen. I have no fight left in me."

Of late he'd stayed more and more angry, belligerent, and uncharacteristically indecisive. Only here and there had his magisterial rage emerged. No one cared anymore what he did, what he thought, or what he said.

Save for Clara.

The cloudy afternoon loomed clammy, the air filled with the sound of distant gunfire. The damn rebels were turning the countryside into a shooting range, flushing out every element of fascism. Below he caught sight of a car winding its way up the narrow road from Azzano. He and Clara had been brought here to the house in the wee hours of the morning. Why? He did not know. But two bearded partisans, wearing peaked caps with a red star and toting machine guns, had stood close guard ever since.

As if they were waiting for something.

"You should not have come," he said to her.

She squeezed his hand. "My place is with you."

He admired her loyalty and wished his Black Shirts possessed just a tiny percentage of it. The drop to the ground from the window was about five meters. But he imagined himself standing much higher, on the balcony at the Palazzo Venezia, in 1936, extolling Italy's grand victory in Abyssinia. Four hundred thousand people had thronged the piazza that day, their reaction wild, ceaseless, and hypnotic. *Duce, Duce, Duce,* they'd screamed, and he'd breathed in the warmth of their mass hysteria.

What a tonic.

But so little of Caesar remained inside him.

He retained his trademark bald head and paunch stomach, but his eyes had yellowed and seemed more and more haunted. He wore his uniform. Black shirt, gray tunic, breeches with red stripes down the sides, jackboots, and a plain gray forage cap. Yesterday, before he'd been taken by the partisans, he'd donned the greatcoat and helmet of a German private in a foolish attempt to hide.

That had been a mistake.

It showed fear.

Some called him a buffoon, others *an adventurer in power politics* or *a gambler in a high stakes game bathed in the past.* Europeans had proclaimed him *the man who made the trains run on time.*

But he was merely Il Duce.

The Leader.

The youngest man ever to rule Italy.

"I await the end of this tragedy," he said. "Strangely detached from everything. I don't feel any more an actor. I'm more the last of the spectators."

Some of that depression he'd felt of late crept back over him and he fought hard to quell its spread.

Now was not the time for self-pity.

The car kept groaning up the steep switchbacks through heavy stands of cedar and fir, its engine growing louder as it approached the house.

He was tired, his face pale, and he needed a shave. He was also unusually untidy, his uniform wrinkled and unkempt. Even worse, he felt at the mercy of events. In a state of panic and flight.

No longer in control.

The car came to a stop below.

A man emerged from the driver's side wearing the pale blue uniform of a Luftwaffe captain, the brown of his collar tabs identifying him as part of the communications corps. Since yesterday only the disheveled, disorganized chaos of the partisans had surrounded him. He'd witnessed their lack of authority at the Dongo city hall, where he'd first been taken, none of his inquisitors really knowing what to do with him. He'd sat in a room thick with talk and nicotine and listened to Milan Radio proclaim an end to fascism, and that every member of the government should be detained.

Imbeciles. All of them.

But they paled in comparison with the Germans.

He'd delayed entering into a pact with Germany for as long as he could. Hitler was a brute, *Mein Kampf* gibberish. He both disliked and distrusted the crazed Austrian. But ultimately public opinion became too strong to ignore and, in 1940, he'd finally succumbed to war.

A horrible error.

To hell with those Aryan bastards. He never wanted to see one of their uniforms again.

Yet here was another.

The uniform entered the house and climbed the stairs to the second floor. He and Clara stayed by the window, but they turned as the bedroom door opened and the uniform entered. He waited for the man to click his heels and offer a salute. But no sign of respect was shown. Instead the newcomer calmly said in Italian, "I wish to speak with you. Alone."

The visitor was a tall, thin man with a long face, large ears, and a sallow complexion. His black hair was slicked back and a clipped mustache brushed a tight-lipped mouth. Mussolini mentally sorted through all of the desperate elements of the situation, looking for options. For the past two decades no one would have dared rebuke him like this. To be feared authority must be absolute, with no boundaries. So his first inclination was to tell this newcomer to get out, but the vacuum of uncertainty that surrounded him overcame his pride.

"Wait outside," he said to Clara.

She hesitated and started to protest but he silenced her with a raise of his hand. She did not object any further and simply nodded, leaving the room.

The uniform closed the door behind her.

"Time is short," the man said. "The Committee of National Liberation and the Volunteer Freedom Corps are coming for you."

Both were trouble, the latter especially since it mainly comprised communists who had long wanted Italy for themselves.

"The decision has been made for you to be shot. I've managed to get ahead of their emissaries, but they are not far behind."

"All thanks to your fellow Germans, who abandoned me."

The man stuffed his right hand into his coat pocket and removed an object.

A ring.

He slipped it onto his left third finger and displayed the face, which contained five rows of letters etched into the dull, pewter surface.

$$\begin{array}{l} \text{SATOR} \\ \text{AREPO} \\ \text{TENET} \\ \text{OPERA} \\ \text{ROTAS} \end{array}$$

Now he understood.

This was no ordinary visitor.

He'd dealt with two popes during his time as supreme leader, Pius XI and XII. One was more accommodating than the other, both irritating. Unfortunately, to govern Italy meant having the Catholic Church on your side, which was no small feat. But he'd managed to contain the church, forming an uneasy alliance, one that was also now coming to an end.

"I'm sure this ring is familiar to you," the man said. "It is just like the one you stole from the man you had killed."

More clarity arrived.

After founding a hospital on the frontier of Christendom dedicated to St. John the Baptist in 1070, a small group of Europeans became the Hospitaller Brothers of St. John's of Jerusalem. Their current label, after over 850 years of evolution, was obscenely long.

Sovereign Military Hospitallers Order of St. John of Jerusalem, of Rhodes, and of Malta.

Talk about vanity.

"I speak for His Most Eminent Highness, the prince and grand master himself," the uniform said. "Who asks you once again to relinquish what you possess."

"Are you actually a German officer?" he asked.

The man nodded. "But I was a knight of the order long before there was anything called the Third Reich."

He smiled.

Finally, the shroud had dropped.

This man was nothing more than a spy, which explained why his enemies had allowed this envoy to come.

"You say people are on the way for me. To the partisans I matter not. To the Germans I'm an embarrassment. Only to the communists does my death have value. So tell me, what can *you* offer to deny them their pleasure?"

"Your tricks yesterday failed."

He was sorry to hear that.

He'd first fled Milan to Como, following the narrow, winding road hugging the lakeshore, motoring through dozens of tiny villages hunched beside the still water. Cernobbio, Moltrasio, Tremezzo, Menaggio. Usually it was an easy half-day journey, but it had taken much longer. He'd expected five thousand Black Shirts to be waiting for him. His soldiers. But only twelve had shown. Then a German convoy of thirty-eight lorries and three hundred battle-hardened soldiers appeared, moving north for Austria, so he'd forced his way into the caravan hoping to make it to Chiavenna, where he planned to split off and head toward Switzerland.

But he'd never made it that far.

The bastard Germans sold him out in return for safe passage.

Thankfully, he'd brought along some insurance. Gold and jewels from the Italian treasury, along with stacks of currency and two satchels loaded with important papers, dossiers, and correspondence.

"The partisans have some of your gold," the man said. "But most of it was tossed into the lake by the Germans. Your two briefcases, though, have vanished. Is what I want in one of them?"

"Why would I tell you that?"

"Because I can save your miserable life."

He could not deny that he would like to live. But even more important, "And Clara?"

"I can save her, too."

He stretched his arms behind his back and thrust out his jaw in a familiar and comfortable angle. He then paced the floor, the soles of his boots scuffing off the gritty stone. For the first time in a long while, strength surged through his bones.

"*The illustrious order will never perish,*" he said. "*It is like virtue itself, like faith.* Is that correct?"

"It is. The Comte de Marcellus gave an elegant speech in the French Chamber of Deputies."

"As I recall he was trying to obtain the return of a large tract of land that the Crown had seized from the knights. He failed, but he did manage to obtain a decree of sovereignty. One that made the Hospitallers their own nation within France."

"And we have not perished," the man said.

"Much to my good fortune." He glared at his visitor. "Get me away from these partisans and we can talk about the *Nostra Trinità*."

The man shook his head. "Perhaps you haven't gleaned the gravity of your situation. You're a doomed man trying to flee for your life with every lire and ounce of gold you could steal." He paused. "Unfortunately, that effort failed. They are coming to kill you. I'm your only hope. You have nothing to bargain with, besides giving me exactly what I want."

"In those two satchels you mentioned, I have correspondence the British will not want public."

The man shrugged. "That's a problem for them."

"Imagine what the knights might do with such incriminating information."

"We have excellent relations with London. I only want the ring and the documents you stole."

"The ring? It's but a chunk of metal."

The uniform held his hand up. "It's much more than that to us."

He shook his head. "You knights are nothing but pariahs. Thrown from Jerusalem, Cyprus, Rhodes, Russia, Malta, now you huddle in two palazzi in Rome clinging to a glory that has long since vanished."

"Then we have something in common."

He grinned. "That we do."

Past the open window he heard the grind of another engine.

His visitor noticed, too.

"They're here," the man said.

A sudden resolve came over him, bolstered by the fact that Holy Roman Emperors, Napoleon, even Hitler himself had all been denied what he'd accomplished.

Defeating the pope.

This man being here was concrete proof of his victory.

"Ask Pius XII what it felt like to kneel before me," he said.

"I doubt that happened."

"Not literally. But figuratively, he knelt. He knew what I could do to his precious church. What I still can do."

Which explained why the Vatican had never outwardly opposed his grab for power. Even after he'd attained total control, the church had continued to stay silent, never once using its massive influence to rally the Italian people into revolt. No king, queen, or emperor had ever been so fortunate.

He pointed at the man's ring. "Like you, I take my strength from Constantine the Great. Only he and I succeeded where all others failed."

The car outside arrived, and he heard doors slam shut as people emerged.

"Tell your grand master that he will regret not saving me," he said.

"You're a fool."

He stiffened his back. "I am Il Duce."

The man in the German uniform seemed unfazed, only shaking his head and saying, "Goodbye, great leader."

And the emissary left.

He continued to stand tall and straight, facing the open doorway. How many times had he sent men to their deaths? Thousands? More like tens of thousands. Now he understood how helpless they felt at the moment of their demise.

Footsteps pounded up the stairs.

A new man entered the room—wiry, black-eyed, black-tempered— holding a machine gun. "I have come to set you free."

He did not believe a word, but played along, "How fortunate."

"We must go. Now."

Clara appeared, entering the room and stepping toward the bed, searching the covers.

"What are you looking for?" the man asked.

"My knickers."

"Never mind them. There's no time. We must go."

Mussolini gently grasped her arm and motioned for them to leave. Was she aware of what was about to happen? He doubted it since, as always, she seemed more concerned with him than herself.

They descended to ground level, left the house, and climbed into the rear seat of a tattered Fiat. A driver was already behind the wheel, and the man with the machine gun did not get in. Instead he stood outside, on the right-hand running board, pointing his weapon inside.

The car ground slowly down the steep road toward the village. Behind, on foot, came the two guards from last night. They all rounded a hairpin turn at a walking pace, but the Fiat picked up speed as it straightened out, the tires hissing on the damp road. The man perched outside ordered the vehicle to stop directly opposite an iron gateway, which formed a recess in the narrow inclined road about five meters wide and two meters deep. The gates blocked a driveway and hung between two large concrete posts, the extending walls about waist-high, curved inward, and topped with bushes.

The man with the machine gun sprang off the running board and opened the car doors. The driver emerged. More orders were yelled and the two other armed men took up positions, one above, the other below on the road. Trees and a sharp bend kept everything out of sight from the houses down in Azzano.

"Get out" came the command.

An agonized look formed on Clara's face, her eyes darting about like a frightened bird's.

Mussolini exited.

She followed.

"Over there," the man said as he waved the muzzle of his gun toward the iron gateway.

Mussolini marched straight to the wall and stood against it. Clara came and stood at his side. He would not make the same mistake as yesterday. He would not be afraid. When they recounted what was about to happen, they would have to lie to make him a coward.

"Benito Mussolini, you are a war criminal. A sentence of death has been proclaimed as justice for the Italian people."

"No. You can't," Clara screamed. "You can't do that."

She hugged his arm.

"Move away from him," the man shouted. "Get away or you will die, too."

She did not flee and the man pressed the trigger.

But nothing happened.

The assailant rattled the bolt and tried to free the jam. Clara screamed and leaped forward grabbing the barrel of the machine gun with both hands.

"You can't kill us like this," she shrieked.

"Bring me your gun," the man hollered.

One of the other two guards ran over and tossed a weapon. Their assassin released his grip on the gun Clara held and caught the offering.

Mussolini realized this was his moment.

Energy filled him.

He made no move to run or defy.

Instead he swept back his jacket with both hands, thrusting his chest forward like the jutting bow of a ship. Past the three men who'd come to murder him he saw the knight in the German uniform walking down the road. Casual. No hurry. Unmolested by the other three. The uniform stopped and stared at the scene. Good. Let him watch.

"Magnus ab integro saeclorum nascitur ordo," Mussolini called out.

He doubted any of these fools spoke Latin.

Only the knight would understand.

The great order of the ages is born afresh.

The machine gun erupted.

Clara was hit first and dropped to the ground. His heart broke to see her die. More rounds came his way. Three thudded into his midsection. Four more found his legs. His knees buckled and he dropped to a sitting position.

His eyes stared across at the knight, and he summoned what little strength was left inside him to say, "This . . . is not . . . over."

Blood spewed out his mouth.

His left shoulder dipped and he slumped to the wet cobbles. He stared up at the cloudy sky, still alive. The smell of cordite hung heavy in the moist air. One of the guards stood over him, the barrel of the weapon aimed down.

He focused on the black dot.

Like a period at the end of a sentence.

The gun fired.

PRESENT DAY

CHAPTER ONE

Tuesday, May 9
Lake Como, Italy
8:40 a.m.

Cotton Malone studied the execution site.

A little after 4:00 p.m., on the afternoon of April 28, 1945, Benito Mussolini and his mistress Claretta Petacci were gunned down just a few feet away from where he stood. In the decades since, the entrance to the Villa Belmonte, beside a narrow road that rose steeply from Azzano about half a mile below, had evolved into a shrine. The iron gate, the low wall, even the clipped hedges were still there, the only change from then being a wooden cross tacked to the stone on one side of the gate that denoted Mussolini's name and date of death. On the other side he saw another addition—a small, glass-fronted wooden box that displayed pictures of Mussolini and Claretta. A huge wreath of fresh flowers hung from the iron fence above the cross. Its banner read EGLI VIVRÀ PER SEMPRE NEL CUORE DEL SUO POPOLO.

He will always live in the hearts of people.

Down in the village he'd been told where to find the spot and that loyalists continued to venerate the site. Which was amazing, considering Mussolini's brutal reputation and the fact that so many decades had passed since his death.

What a quandary Mussolini had faced.

Italy languishing in a state of flux. The Germans fast retreating. Partisans flooding down from the hills. The Allies driving hard from the south, liberating town after town. Only the north, and Switzerland, had offered the possibility of a refuge.

Which never happened.

He stood in the cool of a lovely spring morning.

Yesterday, he'd taken an afternoon flight from Copenhagen to the Milan–Malpensa Airport, then driven a rented Alfa Romeo north to Lake Como. He'd splurged on the sports car, since who didn't like driving a 237-horsepowered engine that could go from zero to sixty in four seconds. He'd visited Como before, staying at the stunning Villa d'Este during an undercover mission years ago for the Magellan Billet. One of the finest hotels in the world. This time the accommodations would not be anywhere near as opulent.

He was on special assignment for British intelligence, working freelance, his target an Italian, a local antiques dealer who'd recently crept onto MI6's radar. Originally his job had been a simple buy and sell. Being in the rare-book business provided him with a certain expertise in negotiating for old and endangered writings. But new information obtained last night had zeroed in on a possible hiding place, so the task had been modified. If the information proved correct, his orders were now to steal the items.

He knew the drill.

Buying involved way too many trails and, until yesterday, had been MI6's only option. But if what they wanted could be appropriated without paying for it, then that was the smart play. Especially considering that what they were after did not belong to the Italian offering it for sale.

He had no illusions.

Twelve years with the Magellan Billet, and a few more after that working freelance for various intelligence agencies, had taught him many lessons. Here he knew he was being paid to handle a job *and* take the fall if anything went wrong. Which was incentive enough not to make any mistakes.

The whole thing, though, seemed intriguing.

In August 1945 Winston Churchill had arrived in Milan under the cover name of Colonel Warden. Supposedly he'd decided to vacation along the shores of Lakes Como, Garda, and Lugano. Not necessarily a bad decision since people had been coming to the crystal Alpine waters for centuries. The use of a code name ensured a measure of privacy, but by then Churchill was no longer Britain's prime minister, having been unceremoniously defeated at the polls.

His first stop was the cemetery in Milan where Mussolini had been hastily buried. He'd stood at the grave, hat in hand, for several minutes. Strange considering the deceased had been a brutal dictator and a war enemy. He'd then traveled north to Como, taking up residence at a lakeside villa. Over the next few weeks the locals spotted him out gardening, fishing, and painting. No one at the time gave it much thought, but decades later historians began to look hard at the journey. Of course, British intelligence had long known what Churchill was after.

Letters.

Between him and Mussolini.

They'd been lost at the time of Mussolini's capture, part of a cache of documents in two satchels that were never seen after April 27, 1945. Rumors were that the local partisans had confiscated them. Some say they were turned over to the communists. Others pointed to the Germans. One line of thought proclaimed that they had been buried in the garden of the villa Churchill had rented.

Nobody knew anything for sure.

But something in August 1945 had warranted the intervention of Winston Churchill himself.

Cotton climbed back into the Alfa Romeo and continued his drive up the steep road. The villa where Mussolini and his mistress had spent their last night still stood somewhere nearby. He'd read the many conflicting accounts of what had happened on that fateful Saturday. Details still eluded historians. In particular, the name of the executioner had been clouded by time. Several ultimately claimed the honor, but no one knew for sure who'd pulled the trigger. Even more mysterious was what had happened to the gold, jewels, currency, and documents Mussolini had intended to take to Switzerland. Most agree that a portion of the wealth had been dumped into the lake, as local fishermen later found gold there after the war. But as with the documents, no meaningful cache had ever come to light. Until two weeks ago, when an email arrived at the British embassy in Rome with an image of a scanned letter.

From Churchill to Mussolini.

More communications followed, along with four more images. No sale price had been arrived at for the five. Instead, Cotton was being paid 50,000 euros for the trip to Como, his negotiating abilities, and the safe return of all five letters.

The villa he was after sat high on a ridge, just off the road that continued on to the Swiss border about six miles away. All around him rose forests where partisans had hidden during the war, waging a relentless guerrilla campaign on both the fascists and the Germans. Their exploits were legendary, capped by the unexpected triumph in capturing Mussolini himself.

For Italy, World War II ended right here.

He found the villa, a modest three-story rectangle, its stone stained with mold and topped by a pitched slate roof set among tall trees. Its many windows caught the full glare of the early-morning sun, the yellow limestone seeming to drain of color as it basked in the bright light. Two white porcelain greyhounds flanked the main entrance. Cypress trees dotted a well-kept yard along with topiary, both of which seemed mandatory for houses around Lake Como.

He parked in front and climbed out to a deep quiet.

The foothills kept rising behind the villa where the road continued its twisted ascent. To the east, through more trees sprouting spring flecks of green, he caught the dark-blue stain of the lake, perhaps half a mile away and a quarter of that below. Boats moved silently back and forth across its mirrored surface. The air was noticeably cooler and, from the nearby garden, he caught a waft of wisteria.

He turned to the front door and came alert.

The thick wooden panel hung partially open.

White gravel crunched beneath his feet as he crossed the drive and stopped short of entering. He gave the door a little push and swung it open, staying on his side of the threshold. No electronic alarms went off inside. Nobody appeared. But he immediately spotted a body sprawled across the terrazzo, facedown, a crimson stain oozing from one side.

He carried no weapon. His intel had said that the house should be empty, its owner away until the late afternoon. MI6 had not only traced the emails it had received but also managed to compose a quick dossier on the potential seller. Nothing about him signaled a threat.

He entered and checked the body for a pulse.

None.

He looked around.

The rooms were pleasant and spacious, the papered walls ornamented with huge oil paintings, dark with age. Smells of musty flowers, candle wax, and tobacco floated in the air. He noticed a large walnut desk, rosewood melodeon, silk brocade sofas and chairs. Intricate inlaid armoires with glass fronts pressed the walls, one after the other, each loaded with objects on display like a museum.

But the place was in a shambles.

Drawers were half opened, tilted at crazy angles, shelves in disarray, a few of the armoires shattered, chairs flung upside down to the floor, some slashed and torn. Even some of the drapes had been pulled from their hangings and lay in crumpled heaps.

Somebody had been looking for something.

Nothing broke the silence save a parrot in a gilded cage that had once stood on a marble pedestal. Now the cage lay on the floor, battered and smashed, the pedestal overturned, the bird uttering loud, excited screeches.

He rolled the body over and noticed two bullet wounds. The victim was in his mid- to late forties, with dark hair and a clean-shaven face. The villa's owner was about the same age, but this corpse did not match the description he'd been given.

Something clattered.

Hard and loud.

From above.

Then heavy footsteps.

Somebody was still here.

The hiding place he sought was located on the third floor, so he headed for the staircase and climbed, passing the second-floor landing. A carpet runner lined the stone risers and cushioned his leather soles, allowing no sound to betray his movement. At the third floor he heard more commotion, like a heavy piece of furniture slamming the floor. Whoever was searching seemed oblivious to any interruption.

He decided on a quick peek to assess things.

He crept ahead.

A narrow green runner ran down the center of the corridor's wood floor. At the far end a half-opened window allowed in the morning sun and a breeze. He came to the room where the noise originated, the same room he'd been directed to find. Whoever had beaten him here was well informed. He stopped at the open doorway and risked a quick glance.

And saw a stout bear.

Several hundred pounds, at least.

The source of the crash was evident from an armoire that lay overturned. The animal was exploring, swiping odds and ends off the tables, smelling everything as it clattered down. It stood facing away, toward one of the two half-open windows.

He needed to leave.

The bear stopped its foraging and raised its head, sniffing.

Not good.

The animal caught his scent, turned, and faced him, snorting a growl.

He had a split second to make a decision.

Normally you dealt with bears by standing your ground, facing them down. But that advice had clearly been offered by people who'd never been this close to one. Should he head back toward the stairs? Or dart into the room across the hall? One mistake on the way down to the ground floor and the bear would overtake him. He opted for the room across the hall and darted left, entering just as the animal rushed forward in a burst of speed surprising for its size. He slammed the door shut and stood inside a small bedroom, a huge porcelain stove filling one corner. Two more windows, half open, lined the outer wall, which faced the back of the villa.

He needed a second to think.

But the bear had other ideas.

The door crashed inward.

He rushed to one of the windows and glanced out. The drop was a good thirty feet. That was at least a sprained ankle, maybe a broken bone or worse. The bear hesitated in the doorway, then roared.

Which sealed the deal.

He noticed a ledge just below the window, about eight inches wide. Enough to stand on. Out he went, flattening his hands against the warm stone, his spine pressed to the house. The bear charged the window, poking its head out, swiping a paw armed with sharp claws. He edged his way to the left and maneuvered himself out of range.

He doubted the animal was going to climb out.

But that didn't solve his problem.

What to do next.

CHAPTER TWO

THE KNIGHT LOWERED HIS BINOCULARS.

What a strange sight.

A man standing on a narrow cornice on the third story of a villa, with a bear roaring out a window, clawing at him.

He stood on a promontory about a quarter mile north of the villa, looking down through spring trees. He'd seen the Alfa Romeo driving up the road, a steady, precipitous, corkscrew climb, and took notice when it turned into the villa's drive. When he'd focused the binoculars on the driver who'd emerged he'd immediately noticed that it was the same man from Menaggio, the one asking questions around town yesterday evening. He'd managed, outside a café, a quick snap of a picture from his cell phone, and had been able to learn an identity.

Harold Earl "Cotton" Malone.

Formerly of the United States Justice Department, once attached to a special intelligence unit called the Magellan Billet. A naval commander, pilot, fighter-jet-qualified, with a law degree from Georgetown University. Malone worked at the Judge Advocate General's corps before being reassigned to the Justice Department, where he remained for a dozen years. Not yet fifty years old, he'd retired early and now owned a business. Cotton Malone, Bookseller, Højbro Plads, Copenhagen.

An intriguing change of careers.

Malone possessed a distinguished reputation as a competent intelligence operative, one who still occasionally offered his services out for hire. What he'd not been able to learn was exactly why this American of obvious skills and talent was here, in Italy, asking questions about things that only a few people in the world would know.

He turned from the chaotic scene below and stared at the villa's owner, hunched on the ground, wrists tied behind his back, ankles likewise restrained. A gag prevented the portly Italian from uttering a sound. An associate stood off to one side, keeping a watchful guard.

"You've proven to be quite a problem," he told his prisoner, who watched him with petrified eyes.

He'd arrived at the villa two hours ago. The groundskeeper had appeared without warning and his associate had shot him. He would have preferred no bloodshed, but it had been unavoidable. The villa's owner was already up for the day, dressed, about to leave. The idea had been to catch him before that happened. He'd asked the owner a few obligatory questions, hoping for cooperation, but no answers were forthcoming. Several more attempts at reason also failed, so he and his associate had brought the fat Italian up here, into the woods, still on the villa's grounds, where a measure of privacy among the trees offered an opportunity to make his point clear. As if two bullets into the groundskeeper had not been enough to impress the point.

He stepped over and crouched down, the musk of the cool morning filling his nostrils. "I imagine you now regret making that call to the British embassy in Rome."

A nod of the head.

"You just need to tell me where the letters are that you wanted to sell."

Supposedly, in 1945, after Mussolini was captured, the contents of two satchels found with him had been inventoried by Italian partisans. But no one seriously believed that any list created by them was accurate. He'd read their entries, which documented little to nothing of interest. Most likely that perfunctory effort had all been for show and the valuable stuff had never made it on the list in the first place. Nor had anything on the actual list ever surfaced in the years since.

And this Italian might hold the answer as to why.

"You're going to tell me all about those documents from Mussolini."

Of course the villa owner could not answer and he had no intention of removing the gag.

Not yet, at least.

He motioned and his associate grabbed a coil of rope lying in the leaves. High above stretched several stout limbs. He studied them, finally deciding on one about ten meters off the ground. It took his associate two attempts to toss one end of the coil over the limb. Then he dragged the villa's owner to the rope. He resisted, but with both hands and feet bound the effort proved futile. The Italian wiggled on the ground as his associate tied one end of the rope to the wrist bindings. With both hands his man then grabbed the end of the rope draping down from the limb and tightened the slack enough to tug on the Italian's arms.

Which telegraphed the whole idea.

Once hauled off the ground the man's arms would be extended upward from behind, at an angle that human joints were not meant to experience. The pain would be excruciating, the body's weight eventually dislocating the shoulders.

"You understand what I can do to you?" he asked.

The villa's owner gave a vigorous nod.

He reached beneath his jacket and found his revolver. "I'm going to remove the gag. If you call out, or even raise your voice, I'll shoot you in the face. Is that clear?"

The man nodded.

He freed the gag.

The man sucked in a series of deep, long breaths. He allowed him a moment, then gazed down and said, "The contents of Mussolini's two satchels have long been in dispute. So tell me, how did you come to acquire anything from them?"

The Italian hesitated, so he gestured and his associate tugged on the rope, which began to lift the man's arms up, his body rising from a squat and becoming more deadweight. So the Italian scrambled up to his feet.

"No. No. Stop. Please."

"Answer my question."

"My grandfather was there. In Dongo, when they found Il Duce. He helped sort out the papers from the satchels, and he kept some of them."

"Why?"

"He thought one day they could be sold."

"What did he do with them?"

"Nothing. He just kept them. My father had them next, then they came to me."

"How many documents do you have?"

"Fifty-five pages. All inside one of the original satchels, which he kept, too."

He fished his left hand into his pant pocket and removed the ring. "And did your grandfather find this, too?"

The Italian nodded.

It had galled him to see it in the villa, displayed inside one of the armoires as some curiosity.

He'd promptly liberated the sacred object.

"Do you have any idea what this is?" he asked, holding the ring's pewter face up for the man to see.

SATOR
AREPO
TENET
OPERA
ROTAS

No reply.

"Do these five words mean anything to you? Does the ring mean anything to you?"

He motioned for the rope to be tugged a couple of times.

"I have no idea," the man cried out, getting the message. "Only that it bears the Maltese cross inside. My grandfather told me it came from one of the satchels. That's why I have it. A memento."

Only a few people in the world knew the ring's true significance, and clearly this greedy soul was one of them.

A background check had revealed that this man had lived above Lake Como all of his life in a villa that his family had owned since the 17th century. It wasn't anything extravagant, similar to hundreds of others surrounding the lake. His prisoner dealt in antiques, usually buying from cash-strapped estates, but was not above stealing. No surprise that he was in possession of missing World War II documents.

He gestured and his associate tightened the rope more. The arms were about at their natural limit before the onslaught of excruciating pain, the man's feet still planted on the ground.

"A memento of what?" he asked, motioning with the ring.

"Il Duce. He had it with him. It bears the cross inside, but I don't know what it means."

"You never tried to find out."

A shake of the head. "Never."

He wondered whether to believe him.

"There are so many who still worship Mussolini," the owner said. "I know people who think he was a great man. My hope was that, one day, people like that would pay for mementos."

The Italian's breath was short, his voice fast and weak.

"And what do *you* think of the former great leader?"

"I care nothing for politics. None of that matters to me."

He pointed a finger. "I suppose only money is your god."

No reply.

"The British have no intention of buying your documents," he said. "It was foolish of you to contact them. They have a man, right now, inside your villa, surely there to steal them."

Fortunately, at the moment that operative was detained by some of the local wildlife.

"Where have you hidden the satchel containing those fifty-five pages of documents, including the letters you wanted to sell?"

"In the villa. On the third floor."

Finally, some cooperation.

He listened as the Italian described the hiding place.

"Ingenious," he said, when the explanation ended. "Is everything there?"

The man nodded. "All I have."

He wondered if Malone knew that information, too.

He gestured and his man relaxed the pressure on the rope, which allowed the arms to drop down.

The villa's owner sighed from relief.

"Why did you not display the letters?" he asked. "As you did the ring."

"My father told me that it might be risky. He said we should hold on to them quietly, until others were willing to pay."

"So why sell now?"

"I need money. I read an article in a magazine about Churchill and Mussolini that speculated about the letters. I decided, why speculate. I have them. So I called the British."

"What was to be your price?"

"Five million euros."

For the love of money is a root of all kinds of evils. It is through this craving that some have wandered away from the faith and pierced themselves with many pangs.

The Bible was right.

He hated greed.

Enough.

This endeavor had run its course.

He raised his arm and shot the owner in the head.

A sound suppressor at the end of the barrel made sure the round drew no attention. Just a pop that could not be heard beyond a few meters. This fool should have realized that the only bargaining chip he had was the hiding place. But fear stymied reason, and people always thought they could talk their way out of things.

"Do it," he said to his associate.

The body was hauled up, the dead man's arms wrenched hard backward. He heard a crack as the shoulders separated. Then the rope was tied around the trunk, the corpse dangling awkwardly in the air, as a reminder, just as had been done centuries ago.

Deuteronomy was right.

Vengeance is mine, and retribution. In due time their foot will slip. For the day of their calamity is near, and the impending things are hastening upon them.

He grabbed the binoculars and stepped back to where he could again see the villa below. The only disturbance came from the morning breeze hissing through the conifers, tugging at his clothes. His second problem was still perched on the third-floor ledge.

The bear was not in sight.

He lowered the binoculars.

That animal was about to be the least of Harold Earl "Cotton" Malone's concerns.

CHAPTER THREE

COTTON STOOD ROCK-STILL ON THE LEDGE. THE BEAR HAD disappeared back inside the villa, but he could hear the animal rustling around. There was a second open window, beyond the one from which he'd escaped, that offered an opportunity to flee his perch and go back inside. But that would mean passing by the bear's window, which did not seem like a good idea.

He strained his weight back on the balls of his feet, hands pressed tight to the wall, trying not to lose his balance. To his left, the tip of a gabled roof from a first-floor offshoot rose to a pitch. The jump down was about eight feet. He could make that. Since it seemed the only course available he sidestepped his way across the cornice, reaching a clawing hand around the corner and making the turn, keeping his body flat against the exterior wall.

He sucked in a few deep breaths.

Good thing Cassiopeia wasn't here. She hated heights as much as he hated enclosed spaces. He used thoughts of her to take his mind off his current predicament. He missed her. Their relationship was in a good place. They'd finally made peace with all of their demons. She was in France, working on her 13th-century castle reconstruction. They were scheduled to get together next week for a few days of fun in Nice. In the meantime he'd agreed to this supposed cakewalk of a job—an easy 50,000 euros—that had turned into anything but.

He stopped his creep along the edge above the gable.

The one thing he could not do was land directly on the ridge.

That would be life changing.

He jumped, angling for one of the sides, and his feet found hard slate. He had only a moment to secure a grip before he rebounded and slid off. His fingernails tore against the warm stone, then his hands caught on the ridge where he held on tight.

Releasing his grip, he scuttled down the slope of the slate toward guttering, his legs extended, using the soles of his shoes as brakes until he found the copper. The gutters squeaked in protest and shifted from his weight, but held. He lowered himself over the edge, clinging to it, wincing at every groan of protest the metal supports uttered. From there he dropped to the ground, landing in the grass near a copse of shrubbery.

Unfortunately, he had to go back inside the villa.

He could wait until the bear moved on, but that could take a while. The owner might return and find the body. The police would then be called and this would become a crime scene, preventing any attempt at finding those letters.

Now was the time, bear or no bear.

But he wasn't going to be foolish.

He hustled around to the front door. Earlier, he'd noticed a gun case in the ground-floor salon. He reentered the villa and heard the bear foraging upstairs. He found the case, which was locked. Eight rifles stood at attention inside. He grabbed a nearby chair and shattered the glass, removing one of the single-barreled shotguns. In a cabinet beneath he located shells. He slid five inside, then pumped the weapon, chambering a round, readying himself for the climb to the third floor. He didn't want to kill the animal but would if necessary.

He climbed the stairs again to the third-floor landing.

The bear remained in the bedroom from which he'd escaped out to the ledge. Judging by the noise, the animal was continuing to wreak havoc on the décor. He approached the open door. The bear's attention was elsewhere, which allowed him to scoot past to the other side, near the open window at the end of the hall. He was cornered, but it seemed the only way to herd the animal toward the stairway and down to the front door, which he'd left wide open.

A quick count to three and he stepped back into the doorway, firing a blast of the shotgun into the far wall. The bear jumped with a start, then roared in fright. Cotton fled back toward the open window in the hall, pumping another round into the chamber. The bear rushed from the bedroom, tossed a quick glance his way, then turned and loped down the third-floor hall in the opposite direction. To make sure the animal kept going, he fired again into the ceiling. Wood splinters and plaster dust showered down.

The bear disappeared onto the stairs.

He followed to the second-floor landing and watched as the animal rushed out the front door.

That worked.

But at a cost of noise that somebody might have noticed.

THE KNIGHT HEARD TWO GUN BLASTS.

The villa's owner had told him that what he sought waited inside a small study on the third floor. He'd watched as Malone had worked his way off the ledge, found solid ground, then reentered the house. The two gunshots were surely Malone's, so he had to assume his adversary was now armed.

At least the bear was gone.

The animal had fled the villa, running as fast as its bulk would allow into the trees beyond.

He was pleased. This might be the place.

Everything pointed in the right direction.

In his escape attempt Mussolini had taken many documents north with him, presumably those of the greatest importance, papers that could be used for political advantage. He'd been seeking refuge in a neutral country, one that had worked hard to stay out of the war. Hitler had wanted to invade Switzerland, but Mussolini had taken the credit for stopping him. Il Duce had been betting that Swiss authorities would be grateful enough to grant him political sanctuary. Historians all agreed that he probably brought with him written proof of his efforts to save the Swiss from the Germans. But apparently he'd also brought his legendary correspondence with Churchill, which had drawn the current interest of the British.

His hope?

Maybe, just maybe, there might also be something else within the villa owner's cache. Something special. What he'd sought for a long time. The appearance of the ring had encouraged him. This could, indeed, be the right place.

Was it there?

Only one way to find out.

COTTON SET THE SHOTGUN DOWN AND LIFTED ONE CORNER OF THE Turkish rug that covered the third-floor study. He examined the wooden floor planks, each pitted and weathered, and at first glance nothing seemed unusual.

Everything nailed in place.

He dropped to his knees and began to softly tap the surface, searching for the hiding place that he'd been told was there. Finally he detected a hollowness. He kept tapping, defining the outline of a square-shaped cavity. To get it open he'd brought along a hefty pocketknife he'd bought yesterday on his way north from the airport.

He opened the blade.

It took a few minutes but he managed to free a panel composed of fused planks. From the lack of dirt and grit in the joints it seemed that it had recently been removed, then replaced. Below the floor he discovered a small cavity that contained a tattered satchel, made of elephant skin, he'd been told, with a broken clasp bound by a sash cord.

He lifted it out.

Etched into the side was a perched eagle, wings extended, clutching a bundle of sticks with an ax.

It was an ancient symbol from imperial Rome, reflecting power over life and death. Nineteenth- and early-20th-century Italian political organizations had routinely adopted it as their emblem. Eventually it appeared on the flag of the National Fascist Party, which took its name from the *fasces* symbol.

He opened the satchel.

Inside was a well-preserved treasure trove of documents sealed within a thick fold of oilskin. He was fluent in Italian, and several other languages, one of the benefits of having an eidetic memory, so he took a quick inventory, flicking through the brittle sheets. Most dealt with the war, partisan activities, and military reports. There were a few typed letters from Hitler, originals, with Italian translations pinned to them, and some carbons sent to Germany. A few had postscripts and marginal notations in longhand. At the bottom of the stack lay a sheaf of prewar letters between Mussolini and Churchill.

More than five, though.

Eleven total.

Seemed the seller was holding a few in reserve.

Jackpot.

He replaced the documents and closed the satchel. All had remained quiet inside the villa. The bear was long gone. He should follow suit. He left the study, turning toward the staircase, passing several of the open third-floor doors. His orders called for him to drive to Milan and promptly turn over whatever he obtained.

Suddenly he was struck hard from behind.

His body jerked forward, as though hit by an explosion at his right ear. Trails of light arced before him. His legs caved. He quickly realized there'd been no explosion, only a blow to the back of his head. He tried to rebound, but collapsed, consciousness drifting in and out.

He hit the floor hard against his right shoulder.

Then all daylight vanished.

CHAPTER FOUR

Malta
9:50 A.M.

Luke Daniels loved the sea, which was strange for an ex–Army Ranger. Most of his service to the country had occurred on dry land. But ever since leaving the military and joining the Magellan Billet, he'd found himself on water more often than not. He'd first met Cotton Malone in the cold chop of the Øresund off Denmark, and only recently he'd completed risky assignments in the Indian Ocean and Java Sea. Now he was bobbing along off the north coast of Malta, sitting in the bow of a twenty-five-foot, deep V-hull, his short hair and open shirt damp with salt spray. He'd found an advertisement yesterday for a local water sports business, one of a zillion vendors that ran out of the many seaside resorts, each catering to the thousands of tourists who came here year-round.

Up, up in the air. Imagine a parachute glide using our special parasailing boat. Our guests take off from the boat and soar to 250 feet over the sea with breathtaking views of the island. At the end of this unforgettable experience, they land back safely on the boat. You can live this flying adventure alone or with a friend. You can glide either in the morning, or take off in the afternoon, to enjoy the famous sunsets of Malta. An unforgettable experience not to be missed. Try it with your friends. Flying duration is ten minutes.

He'd opted to omit anyone else and booked the entire boat for the morning, paying a premium since he wanted to be airborne longer than ten minutes and at a specific spot above the island at a specific time.

"Get ready," the helmsman called out. "We're almost there."

He was hunting for a big fish, but not the kind that occupied the blue waters around him. Instead he was tailing His Eminence, Kastor Cardinal Gallo, one of the current 231 princes of the Roman Catholic Church.

He'd been given the pertinent vitals.

Gallo had been born and raised on Malta, his father a commercial fisherman, his mother a schoolteacher. He left the island before the age of twenty and attended seminary in Ireland, but completed his studies at the Pontifical Gregorian University in Rome. John Paul II ordained him to the priesthood inside St. Peter's Basilica. He then served various parishes around the world, but ended up back in Rome studying canon law and earning a doctorate. Benedict XVI elevated him to the cardinalate, appointing him prefect of the Apostolic Signatura, the court of last appeal to any ecclesiastical judgment. There he'd stayed through the last two pontificates until his outspokenness got him into trouble and he was demoted. Now he carried only the title of patron of the Sovereign Military Order of Malta, a largely ceremonial post usually given to a cardinal near death or out of favor. At the relatively vibrant age of fifty-six, Gallo seemed firmly implanted into the latter category.

The boat slowed to a cruise.

Luke climbed from the bow, past the tanned driver, and hopped up on the stern platform, sitting on a low bench. A second crewman handed him a skimpy nylon harness, which he stepped into. As a Ranger he'd leaped from airplanes at all altitudes, several times into combat situations, twice into open ocean. Heights were not a problem, but the thought of dangling from a parachute at the end of three hundred feet of tow rope, held aloft only by narrow webs of nylon, bothered him. Like he always said, if flying was so safe, why'd they call the airport a terminal?

He slipped on the contraption.

The attendant checked the harness, tugging at places to make sure all was secure and tightening the straps around his chest. Stainless-steel D-clips were snapped onto metal rings, mating him to the chute.

"Sit back. Try not to hang," the guy yelled. "Don't hold on to anything and enjoy the ride."

He gave a thumbs-up.

The boat's engine revved.

The bow rose to a throbbing pulse, dividing the water with a milky-white wake. The brightly colored canopy above him, flapping in the stiff wind, caught air. Suspension lines drew taut. The tips of his tennis shoes swung freely as he rose from the stern. A thick nylon line unraveled from a hydraulic spool as he kept climbing.

Slow and steady.

He grabbed his bearings, about a quarter mile off the north shore.

Malta sat in the center of a narrow channel, 60 miles from Sicily, less than 200 miles north of Africa, an island in the Mediterranean of a mere 120 square miles, rising no more than eight hundred feet at its highest point. The Romans called it Melita, meaning "honey," after the rich local variety. Location had forged its history. The Phoenicians, Carthaginians, Greeks, Romans, Byzantines, Arabs, Normans, Swabians, Angevins, Aragonese, Hospitallers, French, and British all had claimed it at one time or another. Now it was an independent democratic republic, a member of the United Nations, the European Union, and the British Commonwealth. A barren rock devoid of water, arid in summer, drenched in winter, constantly raided through the centuries by one invader after another. The south shore loomed impregnable, mainly towering serrated cliffs, streaky hills, and jagged ridges, impossible to breach. But here, on the north shore, long bays jutted inland like fjords, creating marvelous harbors.

At the hotel last night he'd read a short history from one of the tourist books in the room. Since ancient times the native Maltese had always lived away from the coast to avoid weather, pirates, and slavers. The Sovereign Knights of Rhodes, though, had been a sea power. Once they arrived in the 16th century and became the Knights of Malta, to combat the threat of invasion and secure their hold on the island, they ringed the coast with watchtowers, built of local orange-brown limestone, positioned apart at strategic distances so they could signal one another in succession. Some were small, others mini fortresses. The one he was staring at now from three hundred feet above the towboat had been erected in 1658, still solid and serviceable.

Madliena Tower.

He'd learned about it yesterday during a quick on-site visit, including that it had served as an artillery battery during World War II. He'd climbed its spiral staircase to a parapet and stared out at the sea to exactly where he was now. Like its siblings, Madliena occupied a bare rocky promontory. Zero cover. Wide open. Making any type of meaningful surveillance from land impossible.

So he'd improvised.

He checked his watch.

10:00 A.M.

Shortly Cardinal Gallo should be standing on the parapet of the Madliena Tower.

Which in and of itself raised questions.

The pope had died thirteen days ago. The Apostolic Constitution mandated that the body must be buried within four to six days. Then a nine-day mourning period, the *novemdiales,* occurred. A conclave was required to be convened fifteen days after the date of death. But with less than a day left until it began, Cardinal Gallo had suddenly fled Rome for Malta. That act had caught the attention of Washington and Luke had been dispatched to monitor Gallo's activities. Why? That was above his pay grade.

He'd just been told to get there and watch.

He was now high enough that all sound had vanished. A warm, stiff wind played across his face. Foamed breakers smashed against the rocky shoreline. He was no longer a Magellan Billet rookie, or a Frat Boy as Cotton Malone liked to call him. More an experienced operative. His boss, Stephanie Nelle, seemed to have developed confidence in him. Even his relationship with his uncle, former president and now U.S. senator Danny Daniels, had evolved into a good place. He'd found a home at the Justice Department and intended on hanging around.

Time to earn his keep, though.

He reached back and freed the Velcro on the pocket to his shorts, removing the high-tech receiver. It had been waiting for him at his hotel yesterday when he'd arrived on the island. He took the advice of the guy below and sat back in the harness, stuffing fobs into both ears. He switched on the device and aimed its laser at the tower, about a quarter mile away. He stared down at the shoreline and was pleased to see that his target had arrived.

And he could hear every word.

CHAPTER FIVE

KASTOR CARDINAL GALLO STOOD ATOP THE MADLIENA TOWER AND soaked in the sun. The chilly northeast winds common to January and February were gone, replaced by a southern sirocco that had blown in from Africa, the dry, hot air ridding the island of its spring humidity. Today's weather was what his mother liked to label *healthy*, and he recalled as a child looking forward to the sirocco's periodic arrival.

He savored the earthy, decadent smell of the steamy land, accented by a hint of salt blowing in from the sea. He was annoyed to be out of Rome, the intrigue prior to a conclave a necessary evil that had to be endured. What one of his professors once said? *Suspicion can rot the mind.* True. But there was no better way to ease the anxiety of paranoia than to be present and alert. This time there seemed more of a pre-scramble than usual.

Canon law expressly forbid campaigning for the papacy, but no one paid that prohibition much attention. Kastor had participated in two conclaves since his elevation to cardinal. At neither had he been a serious contender. The first one because of his relative youth and inexperience, the next thanks to his outspokenness. His only vote at either had come from himself, made on the first ballot when it seemed a tradition to recognize those who would never be pope.

Four hundred years ago a knight adorned in a red cape with a white cross would have manned this tower, on the lookout for both friends and foes. He'd not chosen this spot for the meeting, somebody else had made the selection. But he appreciated the symbolism.

Friends and foes.

He had his share of both.

The upcoming conclave could be his last. Cardinals over the age of eighty were forbidden to vote. And though he was two dozen years away from that prohibition, depending on who was selected, the next papacy could be a long one. So if anything was going to happen his way, the coming few days could be his best shot.

A man clambered up from the stairway to the sunny parapet. He was swarthy, beak-nosed, with an unreadable expression. His face, neck, and hands cast the texture of desert sand, burned brown from the sun. Definitely Indian, but whether Hindu, Muslim, or Christian remained to be seen. He wore dark-green fatigues, a black pullover shirt, and boots. His hair, black, wild, and unruly, sprang from a high skull in uneven tufts that tousled in the wind. A piratical gold earring glinted in the sunlight.

"I'm honored to make your acquaintance," the man said in perfect Malti, which he'd not heard in a while.

A callused hand was offered to shake, which he accepted.

Kastor had come dressed not as a cardinal, resplendent in a black simar with scarlet piping, his chest wrapped in a scarlet sash, as he was accustomed to wearing in public. Today he wore street clothes, an ordinary man out to enjoy the sights. Thankfully, the parapet was empty, save for the two of them.

"What's your name?" he asked the man, keeping to Malti.

"How about *kardinali?*"

The reply rubbed him wrong. But since he knew nothing about this envoy he decided to keep the irritation to himself. Still, he felt compelled to point out, "I was under the impression I was the only bearer of a red hat here."

The man grinned, smug and self-contained. A finger was pointed his way. Long, with a slight upturn past the middle joint. "Quite right, Eminence. It's only that you're not dressed like a cardinal. Not even a ring to kiss. But I understand the need for discretion. You are, after all, a person of, shall we say, infamous notoriety."

Like he needed reminding.

Four years ago the now dead pope had decided the job of prefect of the Apostolic Signatura demanded a more moderate personality, somebody less outspoken, more complacent, a man who could *inspire trust not controversy*. True, he'd been warned about his public comments. And equally true, he'd ignored the advice. So his firing had not been a shock. But what happened afterward had given him pause. He'd been publicly chastised by colleagues and privately commanded to obey the Holy Father, ordered by the curia to keep his opinions to himself. He hated that bunch of bishops and bureaucrats, ingrates who administered the church as eunuchs had once run the Chinese court, attenuated to every subtlety, immune to all decency and emotion. They were supposedly concerned with the essence of Catholicism, practicing an obedience to superiors and a reverence for tradition.

Sadly for them, they were anything but.

Something he'd heard once had been driven home during the ordeal.

War doesn't determine who's right, only who's left.

And that had not been him.

For the first time in his professional life he'd felt like a pawn, powerless to either stop or change what was happening. Just a muted observer. What had the Vatican secretary of state told him?

If a man knows to do right and doeth it not, to him it is sin.

Jesus to the Pharisees.

But they'd seriously underestimated the indignation that their petty rationalizations could not extinguish. Thank heaven his reputation as a man who breathed the Catholic past had remained intact.

His beliefs had never been in doubt.

He strongly opposed the radical feminism of the church, which was why he'd publicly criticized a recent papal decision to allow altar girls. Marriage, to him, was only between a man and a woman, and homosexuality should never be tolerated. Abortion was nothing more than murder, no matter the circumstances. Embryonic stem-cell research seemed a heretical abomination. Euthanasia and assisted suicide repulsed him. Never should divorced and remarried Catholics be allowed to receive communion.

And Islam.

Nothing good would ever come from placating that plague on faith.

Thankfully, he was not alone in his orthodoxy. For him, and many others within the church, there was only black and white, the pope's job to steer toward the white. Of late, though, popes liked to proclaim nothing but gray. They avoided the extremes, craving the middle, wanting more to be loved and admired than feared.

Big mistake.

But he'd made his share of bad moves, too.

And paid a heavy price.

He'd been stripped of his office. Ostracized. Proclaimed *a threat to all the faithful in every parish of every country.* He became radioactive, the other cardinals withdrawing—even the damn hired help had avoided him. He'd gone into free fall, relegated to doing little to nothing these past four years, except wait.

The injustice only fueled his indignation.

But watching the church prostrate itself before the masses had sickened him most of all.

Then fate finally shone down.

Thirteen days ago a blood vessel in the pope's brain burst, bringing instant death. The pontificate had been meant to be one of average length, five to ten years at best. The pope had just started his fifth year. His plan had been to use the remaining time to quietly compel the support needed for the next conclave. Cardinals were, by nature, pliable. Negotiable. They also gathered in flocks. But it took a careful mixture of persuasion and intimidation to coalesce them into doing anything meaningful. Thankfully, he'd already amassed an impressive collection of damning information on many of the so-called princes of the church. Lots of juicy secrets.

But he needed more.

"What is your given name," he asked the man facing him, keeping his voice low.

"Arani Chatterjee."

He nodded, then stared out at the great sparkling plain of the Mediterranean, admiring the arc of a flawless azure sky. A tempest of swells rolled and tumbled, as they had all his life. He counted four parasailers enjoying the day.

"Men have searched a long time for what I seek," he said to Chatterjee.

"The *Nostra Trinità* has proven elusive, as it was meant to be."

This man was informed. "What do you know of it?"

"A great deal. The Turks tried to find it. Holy Roman emperors tried and failed. Napoleon came with an army, occupied the island, stripped the churches bare, but didn't find it, either."

"And Mussolini?"

Chatterjee inclined his head. "Now that is the question we are here to answer."

Kastor had no choice but to tolerate this man's brashness. But who was he to judge. He, too, had exhibited that quality on more than one occasion to more than one superior.

Pope Francis had been the worst.

They'd never seen eye-to-eye. How could they? The crazed Argentine was far more concerned with people worshiping him than protecting the faith. *It is not necessary to believe in God to be a good person.* What a ludicrous statement to be made by the Vicar of Christ. *The traditional notion of God is outdated.* How did Francis think a billion faithful would react to such nonsense? *It is not necessary to go to church and give money.* Really? Talk about naïveté. *For many, nature can be a church.* Pure garbage. *Some of the best people in history did not believe in God, while some of the worst deeds were done in his name.*

On that alone Francis had been right.

"Thankfully," Chatterjee said, "you have me to aid your quest. I've been working on this for some time."

News to him. "What have you learned?"

His visitor stepped close to the parapets. "Before we discuss that, there's a matter we have to deal with." Chatterjee pointed out to the water. "You see the black-and-red boat."

He watched as the designated towboat pitched through the water, keeping a single parasailer aloft in the hot sirocco, which continued to sough, rising in strength and hissing across the tower.

Chatterjee waved his arms in the air.

"What are you doing?" he asked.

"Solving that problem."

CHAPTER SIX

LUKE HEARD THE WORDS *SOLVING THAT PROBLEM* AND SAW ONE OF the men on the Madliena Tower waving his arms.

Crap.

He'd been made.

He glanced down three hundred feet at the towboat and saw the attendant who'd helped him into the harness wielding a machete.

Ah, come on.

"To the man out there hanging in the air," a voice in English said in his ear. "If you can hear me, raise your arm."

He decided to not be any more predictable than he'd apparently already been and did nothing.

"Really?" the voice said in his ear. "I know you can hear me."

What the hell. He raised his arm.

"Much better. Technology is such a marvel. Of course, I doubt you speak Malti, which is why I chose it up to now. I don't appreciate you listening in on my private conversation."

The voice carried—a British accent.

How had he been found out? Good question. He'd been abruptly rerouted from another assignment and told to fly directly to Malta, with intel on a meeting at the Madliena Tower at 1:00 P.M. today. He'd arrived yesterday, checked into a hotel, then immediately reconnoitered the locale and, while there, noticed parasailers offshore. So he'd quietly hired the boat for the next afternoon, but somewhere along the way there'd been a leak.

Big time.

"You'll not be making any reports back to your superiors," the voice said in his ear. "I'm told you're with American intelligence. This really doesn't concern the United States in any way."

I'm told? By who?

But this wasn't a two-way conversation.

"Here's an interesting piece of local folklore," the voice said. "The Maltese paint their boats in bright colors to ward off bad spirits and coax good luck. Sadly for you, the one headed your way will offer neither."

He stared out over the water and spotted a boat, striped in bright bands of blue and yellow, racing straight for his position. He saw two men, one piloting, the other shouldering a rifle, their attention directly ahead.

At the Madliena Tower he caught another wave of arms.

The man below on the towboat stepped onto the stern platform and started hacking at the braided nylon hoist rope. Each thrust was accompanied by a troublesome vibration that reached all the way up the line. The man then stopped chopping and started sawing.

The towrope snapped.

His forward acceleration stopped and for an instant he was suspended high in the air, floating, at the mercy of the strong southern winds. The new boat with the two men swept in closer as the towboat sped away. Other boats had moved off with their parasailers.

He started to descend.

Faster than normal. No surprise. These chutes were super lightweight, loaded with venting meant for staying up, not landing soft.

The Med was approaching fast.

He wasn't wearing boots, nor were his ankles taped for a hard landing. He wore only shorts and a shirt with tennis shoes, all bought this morning at a Valletta store. He'd brought along only a few euros, the laser ear, and keys to his rental car.

The water was less than fifty feet away.

Time to be a Ranger again.

He worked the harness, releasing the buckles, one hand over his head gripped to the steel riser that supported his weight on the chute. Once in the water he'd have to free himself fast, then deal with the newcomers.

He hit hard and submerged, shaking off the cold water, wiggling from the harness, then clawing upward. He broke the surface and saw that the boat with the two men had drawn close. He was a quarter mile offshore and the currents were working against him. No way he could swim to land. He saw the man with the rifle level the weapon, aiming his way. He sucked a deep breath, tucked and rolled, then powered himself deep.

Bullets swished downward, slowed by the dense water.

He stopped sinking and settled, maintaining depth, staring back up to the surface. He could not hold his breath forever. And what was the old saying? *A good offense is the best defense.*

He kicked hard and made a free ascent, swimming beneath the dark outline of the boat. The angle of the bullets still trying to find their way through the water indicated on which side the men thought he would surface. He kept his eyes on the keel, staying close to the swaying hulk. The outboard rested in idle, the boat drifting along with the current. If they decided to power up and speed off he could be in real trouble from a spinning prop.

He surfaced and sucked a quiet breath, waiting until his side of the boat rocked down, then he planted his palms and used the sway back up from the swells to flip out of the water.

His body felt primed, coiled, his brain calm and controlled. He had only an instant of surprise, which he used to his advantage, pivoting off the gunnel and kicking the pilot in the chest, sending the man over the side.

The guy with the rifle swung around.

Luke lunged forward and, with a solid right, caught the guy hard in the jaw, then pounced and wrenched the weapon away, slamming the rifle butt up under the shooter's chin.

Something cracked and the man slumped to the gunnel.

He shoved the body into the water.

That was easy.

Now he had the high ground.

He stared across at the Madliena Tower. Gallo and the other man were still there, watching. He laid the rifle down and pushed the throttle forward. The engine roared to life. He swung the boat around toward shore and heard a shot.

Behind him.

He turned.

Another boat was racing his way.

Single occupant wearing a ball cap, steering the craft and firing a handgun. He had the rifle, but he could not pilot the boat and fire too. He started to zigzag across the water, making himself a more difficult target.

Two more shots came his way.

He veered south toward Valletta. The other boat turned, too, angling toward him in a wide arc, closing the gap.

In a few seconds they were parallel.

He released his grip on the wheel and grabbed the rifle with both hands.

His pursuer drew closer.

He turned, ready to plant his feet and fire quick enough that his unmanned rudder would stay on course.

But the driver held no gun.

Instead the other boat suddenly slowed to a stop and the driver's hands were raised in the air, as if surrendering. He regripped the wheel and worked the throttle, swinging around toward the other craft. He eased up close and lifted the rifle with one hand, finger on the trigger, while he worked the wheel and throttle with the other.

His pursuer removed the cap and long blond hair draped out.

"Who are you?" he called out.

"Laura Price."

"And the reason you're shooting at me?"

"Just trying to get your attention."

Both of their boats bobbed in the choppy water.

"It worked."

"If I'd wanted to take you down, I would have."

He smiled. "You always so confident?"

"I'm here to help."

"You're going to have to do better than that."

"Mind if I get my cell phone?"

He shrugged. "Go ahead."

He trained the rifle on her as she searched for something in a pocket. Her hand came back into view holding a flip phone. He hadn't seen one of those in a while. She tossed the unit across the water at him, which he caught.

"Push 2," she called out.

He kept the rifle trained on her. With his other hand he pressed the button and lifted the unit to his ear, his eyes never leaving Laura Price.

Two rings.

The call was answered.

"This is Stephanie Nelle."

CHAPTER SEVEN

Lake Como

PAIN CLEAVED COTTON'S HEAD IN HALF, STARTING AT THE NAPE OF his neck and lancing forward to the back of his eyes. But he fought through the fog, grabbed hold of his senses, and saw a man running down the third-floor corridor, turning for the staircase.

He rose to his feet and rushed after him.

The guy had a head start and was already turning for the second floor. He decided to make up some ground and pivoted off the heavy stone railing, launching himself over the side and across the open space between the risers, catching his attacker in a flying tackle. Thankfully the other guy took the brunt of the impact and they rolled down to the next landing. The satchel flew from the man's grasp, over the railing, careening to the foyer below. Cotton broke free, came to his feet, and threw a punch to the face. His assailant lunged and they fell onto the balustrade with its thick array of stone spindles. The landing itself was more a narrow corridor leading from one side of the house to the other, its exterior wall broken by two windows, both closed.

He pushed away and made a quick appraisal of his problem.

Stocky, fair-haired, dressed in jeans and a pullover knit shirt.

The guy rushed forward, avoiding another punch, wrapping his arms across Cotton's chest in a tight embrace. Together they staggered back and crashed into one of the windows. The glass shattered from the impact and he tried to rebound, but the man kept pushing him closer to the shattered window. He kicked backward and caught the man just above the ankle with the heel of his shoe. A grunt of pain and the pressure around his chest slackened. He drove an elbow into the midsection and managed to reverse positions, thrusting one of his attacker's hands through the shattered window, raking the arm from side to side across ridges of broken glass. The man bellowed in agony and tried to withdraw, but Cotton shoved all of his weight forward, slashing the arm from elbow to wrist.

Another scream of pain and his adversary held up the torn arm, gaping at the ripped flesh that hung loosely like red ribbons.

Blood poured out.

The man retreated toward the stairs and the outer railing, trying to get away.

A bang startled him.

The man jerked from an impact, as if in a spasm. Blood spewed from an exit wound as a bullet ripped through the chest.

Another bang.

More spasms.

He realized what was happening. Somebody was shooting from below. A third bullet pitched the guy forward, then he fell, straight as a falling tree, smacking the floor face-first, fighting for breath, groaning in pain. Cotton dropped down below the railing and risked a peek through the spindles. No one was below. The rifle he had used with the bear still lay upstairs in the third-floor hall.

He heard another shot from beyond the front door.

His attacker was no longer moving or moaning. He rose and hustled down the stairs and out the front door. Black spots still danced before his eyes from the blow to his neck. Thankfully, adrenaline surged through him and helped with the vertigo. Outside he continued to see no one. The grounds rose steadily in three directions up toward the forested highlands. He heard the distant, muted churn of an engine coughing to life, the sound magnified by the silence.

But from where?

Echoes made it difficult to pinpoint.

He stared up toward the trees but saw no vehicle. Luckily there was only one road leading up from the lake. He might be able to cut off whoever had been here.

He turned for the Alfa Romeo.

And stopped.

The right front tire was flat.

Now he knew what the fourth shot had been for.

He wasn't going anywhere. Not quickly, at least. Somebody had come here ahead of him, prepared, obviously in the know.

Another buyer?

Possibly.

He headed back inside the villa and climbed to the second floor. He checked the body for a pulse and found none. He riffled through the dead man's pockets and discovered no ID or wallet. Perhaps MI6 could provide an identification.

He noticed something on one finger.

A ring.

Pewter.

Old looking.

With letters etched onto its face.

SATOR
AREPO
TENET
OPERA
ROTAS

He slipped it off and examined it closer. Nothing else appeared on its exterior, but inside he saw a tiny image.

The four distinctive arrow points, joined at the center, a dead giveaway.

An eight-pointed Maltese cross.

He pocketed the ring.

Then he recalled the satchel that had gone over the railing. He descended to the ground floor and searched for where it should be lying.

Nothing.

Apparently the shooter had retrieved it.

Wonderful.

The Brits were going to love this.

CHAPTER EIGHT

Malta

Luke's attention alternated between the phone and the woman in the boat across the water, one arm keeping the rifle trained. He was having trouble hearing over the hum of the outboard, so he cut the engine.

"Who is she?" he asked Stephanie.

"She wanted me to bring her on, noting you might need help. I asked how she knew anything about anything, but she offered nothing. I told her you could handle it without her help."

"Any reason you didn't pass that intel on to me?"

"Her call just came about an hour ago. I tried to reach you, but you didn't answer."

He'd left his phone in the rental car.

"I answered this call because it's the same number from earlier," she said.

He was drifting away from the other boat and watched as Laura Price maneuvered herself back near him. He lowered the rifle, deciding she was no longer a direct threat. But that didn't mean she wasn't trouble.

"Tell me about her," he said.

"What makes you think I know anything?"

"We wouldn't still be talking if you didn't."

He'd worked with Stephanie long enough to know that she never left anything to chance. She ran the Magellan Billet with military efficiency, accepting nothing less than perfection from her agents. Thanks to her personal relationship with his uncle, former president Danny Daniels, Luke liked to think that he enjoyed a closer connection with his boss, though he knew she would never show favoritism. Stephanie expected her people to do their jobs. Period. Who you were mattered not. Mistakes were barely tolerated. Results. That's what she wanted. And she'd diverted him here to get results.

But he'd messed up.

Bad.

"She works for the Malta Security Service," Stephanie said.

"This little island has an intelligence agency?"

"Part of the Armed Forces of Malta. It's not big, but it does exist. She worked at the CIA for a few years. They remember her at Langley. Seems she doesn't follow orders well. An adrenaline junkie. A loose cannon, but generally one that fires in the right direction."

"That sounds like me."

"My thoughts exactly."

"Any idea why the Maltese are involved in this?"

"Not a clue. But she's apparently been on you the whole time."

Which he'd missed.

Another mistake.

He stared across the water at his stalker. She was blond and striking with high cheekbones and a pretty mouth. Straight, squared-off bangs highlighted a narrow brow. She wore jeans, belted at the waist, with an open-collared shirt that revealed deeply tanned arms. A looker. No question. And she seemed in terrific shape, muscle-hardened in a way he liked. Obviously, she knew how to drive a boat, shoot a gun, and try to make herself useful. Combined with the balls of an alley cat he could see how she might be regarded as a loose cannon.

"What do you want me to do?" he asked.

"I don't like pushy people or liars. Get rid of her."

He smiled to himself. "It'd be my pleasure."

"Tell me what happened with Gallo."

"A slight problem. But I'll fix it."

"Do that."

And the call ended.

He continued to speak into the phone, pretending the conversation was ongoing, but assessing the situation. He still held the rifle. Laura Price lingered about twenty feet off his port side. He simulated ending the call and motioned with the phone that he needed to return it to her. If he kept it cool he may just be able to catch her off guard. Things were bad with the cardinal, but he'd find that trail again. Crap happened. The trick was not to let it stink everything up.

The rifle was pointed down toward the deck.

He motioned with the phone and she worked the boat closer. He tossed it over. She caught the unit and he used that moment to level the weapon and fire three rounds into her engine.

She lunged to the deck.

The outboard erupted in sparks and smoke.

He chuckled.

Those three hundred horses were now useless.

He turned the key and brought his own boat to life, spinning the wheel, engaging the throttle, throwing out a wake as he motored away that soaked the other boat. A glance back and he saw Price rebound to her feet, but he was already too far away for any meaningful shot from her on a pitching deck.

He threw her a wave, hoping never to see her again.

Time to find Gallo and get back on track.

He glanced toward shore and the Madliena Tower. The cardinal and the other man were gone. He worked the wheel and avoided some of the larger chops, paralleling the coast, cruising east toward Valletta where his rental car awaited. Vibrations from the engine rattled up through the deck and energized him.

No one was following.

Clearly, Laura Price would have to find a lift back to shore.

But those were the breaks.

He tried to fool himself into thinking that he understood women. But truth be told, he didn't. He liked to toss out a devil-may-care attitude and make the ladies think he was some kind of bad boy they could tame. That worked in his favor more times than not, but there was always the occasional disaster.

Actually he was a mama's boy, calling that saint of a woman every Sunday, no matter where he might be in the world. She knew that he was an intelligence agent. Stephanie had allowed him to reveal that to her and she'd loved it. Of her four children—whom they named Matthew, Mark, Luke, and John—he was the wild child. The others had respectable jobs, families, homes, mortgages. He alone remained single, traveling the world, doing what the Magellan Billet needed done.

He'd yet to find that perfect combination of lover, companion, confidante, and partner. Maybe one day. Women seemed to marry a man expecting him to change, but he doesn't. Men marry a woman expecting that she won't change, but she does. That was a problem. What had one potential bride told him? *Husbands are like cars. They're all good the first year.*

Lots of truth to that one.

Career, achievement, independence, and travel were tops on his list at the moment. Marriage and children not so much. Danny Daniels being his uncle may have cracked open a few doors that might have otherwise been closed, but those doors stayed open thanks to him being damn good at what he did. Of course, the past half hour had not been his finest moment.

He kept the boat headed south, recalling more of what he'd read last night.

After the Great Siege of 1565, when the Turks tried to forcibly take Malta, Grand Master Jean Parisot de Valette decided to build a fortified town on a barren limestone peninsula on the north coast. It would be Europe's first planned city since Roman times, laid out on a grid, with a moat on its southern side and bastion walls all around. Harbors shielded to the east and west, providing ideal anchorages. For a seafaring power like the Knights of Malta, the location proved a perfect headquarters, and they eventually adapted the island into an impregnable naval base.

Two miles long and a mile wide, Valletta's cluster of tightly packed buildings had long housed the knights and everything needed to support them. The city remained the sole witness to four centuries of hard work and magnificence. Its churches, shops, residences, palazzi, storehouses, forts, and the grand master's palace had somehow survived, even after Hitler relentlessly bombed every square inch during World War II.

Its buildings stood in straight lines, purposefully packed close to shade the streets from the intense Mediterranean sun and to allow a sea breeze to pass through unimpeded. All told, about two thousand structures of noble elegance had been built within five years. But it took another twenty-five years after to perfect it. Little had changed since the 17th century. Luke particularly liked what de Valette had said about his creation.

Built by gentlemen for gentlemen.

The white battlements of Fort St. Elmo came into view, standing point guard at the end of the towering peninsula, commanding a stunning view of the open sea. He imagined its cannon blasting out into the harbor, repelling the advancing Turks. The whole Great Siege seemed the stuff of Hollywood. Suleiman the Magnificent—what a name—sent 40,000 warriors and over 200 ships to take Malta for Islam. De Valette commanded 500 knights, 1,100 soldiers, and 6,000 local militia. Despite pleas, no Christian king lifted a finger to help, as they were too busy killing one another.

So de Valette stood alone.

The invasion came furious and bloody, all happening during a miserably hot summer. Fort St. Elmo held out a month before finally yielding. But a lack of supplies, little fresh water, and dysentery ravaged the Turks. Terror ran rampant on both sides. Dead knights were mutilated, their headless bodies floated across the harbor on crosses to the occupied forts on the other side. Grand Master de Valette's reply was to decapitate Turkish prisoners and fire their heads back as cannonballs.

Talk about tit-for-tat.

Finally, in September 1565, reinforcements arrived from Sicily and the Turks retreated. If things had turned out differently, Muslim shipping would have ruled the Mediterranean from a Maltese base and all of Europe would have been at risk.

But the knights saved Christendom.

He angled the boat past Fort St. Elmo and headed into the Grand Harbor, still girdled by forts and watchtowers. Waving flags cast a colorful welcome along the bastions and across the harbor in the Three Cities. A cruise ship nestled close to one of the long wharves, its passengers flooding onto the docks. Another was anchored offshore. He angled toward the marina. The towboat from earlier was nowhere to be seen. The boat's

engine lost its steady thumping beat and slowed, ready to reenter the protected haven crowded with yachts swinging peacefully at anchor.

His car waited in a small lot a few blocks away.

He eased the boat close to the dock, killing the engine and tying it off
to a couple of empty cleats.

He hopped off, leaving the rifle in the boat, and trotted ashore.

Two men cut him off.

CHAPTER NINE

Lake Como

THE KNIGHT LEFT THE VILLA AND FOUND THE HIGHWAY THAT LED back down toward the lake. The elephant-skin satchel lay on the passenger seat next to him. He'd retrieved it while the fight had ensued on the second floor. Malone had apparently found what the villa's owner had confessed was there. Even its contents were exactly as reported.

Thank goodness he'd moved fast.

He'd instructed his associate only to incapacitate Malone, then retrieve the satchel. A simple task. He needed the American alive. Apparently, though, something had gone wrong. What he could not allow was for his associate to be taken prisoner. So he'd handled that problem, retrieved the satchel, and made sure Malone had no way to give chase. The idea had been only to turn the trail ice-cold and send the ex-agent back to the Brits empty-handed. That had now been accomplished, but at a higher cost than expected.

He found the highway that snaked around the jagged shoreline and turned north. Four kilometers later he cruised into Menaggio. Façades of colorful stucco buildings lined its quaint streets. The morning sun bore down, painting the building exteriors in contrasting shades of golden tan. Craggy mountains and wisps of fog swept across a semi-circle of spring foliage that rose up sharply behind the steeply pitched roofs. He parked just beyond the Piazza Garibaldi, taking the satchel and walking slow, head down, casual, drawing no attention, using his ears rather than his eyes to keep watch around him.

He entered the hotel and climbed the wooden stairs to his room. Inside, he spread out the satchel's contents on a table. Amazing how it had stayed secreted since 1945. A quick perusal of the pages revealed carbon copies, originals, and handwritten notes. Mainly reports and assessments, some orders to the military. But the correspondence between Churchill and Mussolini was the jackpot. He scanned the eleven letters, easy for him as he was fluent in both German and Italian. One in particular, an original in English from Churchill to Il Duce, made him smile.

I write to implore you that we should thus discard the feelings of irritation that might arise by our turpitude, the persistently perfidious opportunism with which successive governments of ours have tried to falsify our relationship. Of late, circumstances in this world have obliged us to conduct business together, and we can scarcely conduct business in a spirit of moral indignation. Instead, we must be wary and precise and somewhat trusting in each other. I fear that in spite of the insistent temptation it will profit us little to be disagreeable. So let us properly address what might be enough to prevent you from entering into any long term military relationship with the abhorrent German Chancellor.

How long have you wanted to bring Malta within the Italian sphere? You have repeatedly proclaimed that the Maltese are part of the Italian race, that even their speech is a derivative of the Italian dialect. Your rhetoric has been clear that Malta historically was, and should be now, part of a greater Italy. What if such a thing were possible? What if you alone could achieve what countless Italian leaders before you failed to accomplish?

Having thus acquired this card in your hand as a mark of friendship, a possible surrender of this certain and valuable island, we would accept as a *quid pro quo* that Italy remain neutral in the coming conflict. No political or military agreement would be made with the Germans. No assistance would be offered to the German cause. We recognize that this course might cause difficulties between Italy and Germany. Hitler would never tolerate an open Italian alliance with Great Britain. So, in order to allow your neutrality to manifest itself in a way that cannot be denied, we would not publicly acknowledge Italy as an ally in the current struggle. Nor, though, would we treat you as an enemy. Instead, for us, you would become a nation with a 'belligerent status' toward the United Kingdom. Not friend, nor foe, just one to be wary about. This would provide you with credible deniability towards the Germans that you have agreed to no terms with us, as that is not the case. But such status would ensure Italy a place at the peace table after the Germans are defeated, and defeated they shall be. There, the Italian territorial claims to Malta can be discussed and finally arranged.

The letter went on to extol other virtues in defying Hitler and secretly climbing into bed with England.

It was signed in heavy black ink.

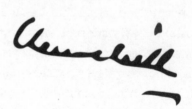

Churchill.

He noted the date.

May 18, 1940.

Churchill had just become prime minister. Apparently, the British Bulldog had wasted no time trying to make a deal, desperately wanting to keep Italy from formally entering the war on Hitler's side. The letter had been sent in response to one from Mussolini that had come a few days prior, a carbon of which was in the satchel.

I have been proclaiming for several years that Italy should have uncontested access to the world's oceans and shipping lanes. That is vital for our national sovereignty. The freedom of a country is proportional to the strength of its navy. We are now, and have been for a long time, a prisoner in the Mediterranean. Hitler is convinced that, to break British control, your bases on Cyprus, Gibraltar, Malta, and Egypt must be neutralized. Italy will never be an independent nation so long as she has Corsica and Malta as the bars of her Mediterranean prison and Gibraltar and Suez as the walls. Hitler's foreign policy takes for granted that Britain and France would someday need to be faced down. He has pointed out to me that, through armed conquest, Italian North Africa and Italian East Africa, now separated by the Anglo-Egyptian Sudan, could be linked. Even better, the Mediterranean prison would be destroyed. As you surely realize, at that point Italy would be able to march either to the Indian Ocean through the Sudan and Abyssinia, or to the Atlantic by way of French North Africa. That is meaningful to me. What Hitler offers is an alliance to make that possible. What do you offer, Prime Minister?

Churchill dangled Malta.

But cleverly, only after the war had been won, where it would be quietly ceded away. Which obviously had not been enough to entice Mussolini.

The knight knew his military history.

The British had been concerned about whether Malta could be properly defended. It was not the 16th century. Modern weapons were nothing like those the Turks had utilized in trying to breach the island's defenses. Bombers and ships with high-caliber cannons could wreak havoc. It would take a lot of men and weapons to hold the island.

Perhaps it was not worth it.

It had been the French, in May 1940, while their country was being invaded, who suggested that Mussolini might be appeased by handing over Malta. That way Italy would stay out of the war, allowing the Allies to focus on France. But Churchill convinced the War Cabinet that no such territorial concessions should be made, though others had favored a deal.

Now he knew why.

Churchill knew the offer would have been in vain.

On June 10, 1940, Italy declared war on Britain, then promptly the next day attacked Malta, laying siege. Rommel warned that *without Malta the Axis will end by losing control of North Africa.*

So their attacks were relentless.

Ultimately, Hitler dropped more bombs on Malta than on London. For five years most Maltese lived underground, utilizing the tunnels left over from the knights as air raid shelters, storerooms, and water reservoirs.

They took a pounding.

Over thirty thousand buildings were destroyed.

People nearly starved as food convoy after convoy fell to U-boats. A battleship, two aircraft carriers, thirty-eight submarines, and five Allied cruisers were sunk in its defense. Over a thousand Maltese died. Many more were injured. Churchill told the world that *the eyes of the whole British Empire are watching Malta in her struggle day by day.*

And they held the island.

After the war, the king granted the entire population the George's Cross. No wonder Churchill had wanted to make sure those letters never saw the light of day. Imagine what the British people would have thought of their revered leader had they known he'd been willing to cede that precious ground away.

Excitement surged through him.

He'd found most of what he'd been looking for.

But the one thing he'd been hoping to locate was not here. Had Malone removed it? Possible. But not likely.

No matter.

The Brits would be in contact. Of that he was sure.

He stared out the window and watched people move along the broad sweep of the piazza. He caressed the pewter ring that adorned his right hand, silently reading its five words.

Sator. Arepo. Tenet. Opera. Rotas.

Time for them to once again lead the way.

CHAPTER TEN

Malta

KASTOR HAD LISTENED AS CHATTERJEE SPOKE TO THE PARASAILER. He then watched as the unidentified man hit the water and eventually overpowered two men in a boat. Then another boat had given chase, firing shots as the parasailer sped away, confronting him farther down the coast. The last thing he saw was the parasailer heading off toward Valletta.

Alone.

"What was that about?" he asked Arani.

"People are interested in what you're doing, Eminence."

News to him. "What people?"

No reply.

So he asked, "Who was that parasailer?"

"An American agent, sent here to spy on you. We learned of his involvement yesterday. Thankfully I was able to get ahead of him and paid off that parasailing crew. Those other two men should have dealt with him but, as you saw, he escaped."

"Who was the woman in the other boat?"

"A good question. I have to make a call."

Chatterjee retreated to the far side of the parapet and used a cell phone.

He'd not liked any of what he'd just heard and resented being treated like an inferior. And who was the *we*, as in *we learned*.

He stared back out to the sea.

The north shore had always been different to him. He and his brother had been born on the south side of the island, on a plot of land overlooking another swath of the Mediterranean. The old farmhouse had been built of the local coralline limestone, an interesting compound that emerged from the ground soft and damp but eventually, after age and sun, turned hard and white.

Like himself. Pliable as a child.

Unbending in adulthood.

His father had fished the Med all of his life, back when it was still possible to make a living. Both of his parents had been good people, neither one of them going out of their way ever to make an enemy. Sadly, they died in a car crash when he was twelve. It happened in April, just after the alfalfa had bloomed, blanketing the ground in color and the air with an aromatic scent.

To this day he hated spring.

With no family willing to take them, he and his brother had been sent to St. Augustus orphanage, on the east side of the island, a dreary, unimpressive place run by the Ursuline Sisters. There he grew to know the church. Its stability. Rules. History. Along with the many opportunities it presented. And where some at the orphanage rebelled, he'd come to appreciate the nuns' insistence on discipline. Those cold, bland women were, if nothing else, consistent. They made their point only once and you were expected to obey. Three years ago he'd forgotten a few of the lessons those unbending women had taught him and overplayed his hand, allowing the pope to cut his legs out from under him.

A stupid, stupid error.

He'd held a position of great power and influence. Prefect of the Apostolic Signatura. In charge of the highest judicial authority of the Catholic Church. When it came to ecclesiastical matters only the pope's word ranked higher. That position had also made him privy to a wealth of confidential information on laymen, priests, bishops, and cardinals. He'd amassed a treasure trove of confidential files. The plan had been to eventually use that knowledge to privately elevate his stature within the College of Cardinals. And if played right, he might be able to adapt his colleagues' gratitude into a serious run at the papacy.

Any Catholic male who reached the age of reason, not a heretic, not in schism, and not notorious thanks to simony, could be elected pope. But in reality, only cardinals had a chance. The last non-cardinal elected was in 1379. Without question, certain cardinals were more likely than others to be chosen. The fancy word was *papabile*. Able to be pope. That used to mean Italian. Not anymore, thanks to a succession of foreign popes. Still, there was no way ever to know who would emerge as a favorite. What was the saying? *He who enters the conclave as pope, comes out a cardinal.* History had proven that nine times out of ten a non-favorite won. Which made sense. Every so-called favorite had his own carefully crafted support group. Many of those formed shortly before or during a conclave, and rarely did one group ever sway another to accept *their* candidate. Which meant the man finally elected was never everyone's favorite. Instead, he was just a compromise that two-thirds of the cardinals could agree upon.

Which was fine.

He wasn't interested in being anyone's favorite.

Contra mundum.

Against the world.

His motto.

Chatterjee returned after ending his call. "I'll deal with our American spy in the boat."

"In what way?"

The man chuckled. "Do you really want to know? Just accept that I'm here, at your service, Eminence."

He felt another rush of anger at the patronizing tone. But the past few years, if nothing else, had taught him some measure of patience.

"And the woman?" he asked.

"I'm working on that, too."

"Are you Hindu?"

"I'm an atheist."

He needed to calm himself and expunge the growing rancor simmering inside him. This conversation was going nowhere. But he needed to know, "What are your qualifications to deal with my current needs?"

Chatterjee stared him down. "I can fight, shoot, and don't mind killing someone if the need arises."

"Are we going to war?"

"You tell me, Eminence. As you pointed out, people have been searching for the *Nostra Trinità* a long time."

"And what do you know about it?"

"Quite a bit. I hold a doctorate in medieval history from the University of York. My dissertation was on Jerusalem between the times of the Jews, Muslims, and Christians, from the 1st to 5th centuries, with an emphasis on European brotherhoods and their effect on intersect occupation. The Sovereign Military Hospitallers Order of St. John of Jerusalem, of Rhodes, and of Malta being one of those. I'm also quite good at scouring and stealing from archives, libraries, and newspaper morgues. I have few to no morals, and will do whatever is necessary to get the job done. I wrote a book on the Hospitallers. Didn't sell all that well, but it did draw the attention of certain people likewise interested in the knights."

"Can you name a few names?"

Chatterjee chuckled. "Never kiss and tell. First rule of my business."

He could see that this man masked a tough and sinewy intelligence beneath an overabundance of carefully cultivated rudeness. Ordinarily, he would not waste time with such arrogance. But nothing about this situation was ordinary.

He bought a few moments to think by watching the swift passage of a gull, its wings set, as it rode the thermals and glided out to sea. What it must feel like to be that unencumbered. Finally he turned toward Chatterjee and said, "You realize that the conclave begins in a little over twenty-four hours. There is no time for nonsense."

"How about I whet your appetite with something I'm sure you don't know. A good-faith offering, if you will."

He'd been told to come here and *all would be explained.*

So he had to trust that this was not a waste of time.

"I'm listening."

CHAPTER ELEVEN

JUNE 1798

NAPOLEON BONAPARTE IGNORED THE SCREAMS THAT ECHOED THROUGH THE LONG corridors and admired the palace. For the past 225 years grand masters had dwelled within these walls, roaming the broad marble passageways, admiring the picture galleries, feasting in the great banqueting hall. There was even an observatory in the tower above. The building stretched long, like the Louvre, spanning two floors, its walls double-layered and filled with rubble like a fortress, a full one hundred meters of its elegant façade facing the Piazza dei Cavalieri, the Square of the Knights.

Sacred ground, he'd been told.

No Maltese had ever been allowed in the square, or the palace, without a permit. He'd already decided to curry favor with the locals by abolishing that law and renaming the plaza the Square of Liberty.

A good move.

The conqueror's prerogative.

He was thrilled. Everything had gone perfectly.

He'd sailed from France a month ago with hundreds of ships and 7,000 troops, all headed for the taking of Egypt. On the way he'd decided to seize Malta, arriving at Valletta three days ago. Standing on the deck of his flagship in the harbor he'd been impressed with the embattlements, the town itself sweeping down by terraces from the summit, the honey-colored buildings stacked one above the other, appearing as if chiseled from a single stone. He'd been informed that the numerous domes and towers would cast an exotic effect, and he'd seen for himself the truth of that observation.

What had the knights called it?

Civitates Humillima.

Most humble city.

Not since the Turks in 1565 had so many sails appeared off the Maltese coast. Back then the knights had been ready to defend to the death what they considered to be their island. This time the invader had caught them unprepared. Thankfully, his spies had proven their worth, identifying only 332 knights, 50 of whom were too old to fight, all undersupplied and poorly led. The fortress cannon had not been fired in a century, the powder rotten, the shot defective. Then, when the French knights, numbering nearly 200 of the 332, refused to fight, it all ended after two days with a total surrender, the grand master signing away the island and every vestige of sovereignty.

He stared again at the palace walls.

Little remained of its great heritage. It was more a melancholy air of desertion that emanated from its echoing walls and empty vestibules. What had happened to all those grand masters? Those select few who'd once teetered on the verge of absolutism. They lived as kings, wearing crowns, receiving ambassadors, and sending envoys to foreign courts. They kept a covey of chaplains and physicians, scores of servants, gamekeepers, falconers, drummers, trumpeters, valets, grooms, pages, wigmakers, clock winders, even rat catchers. Unlimited funds had been at their disposal. Popes and emperors catered to their wishes.

But no more.

Once the threat from Eastern infidels waned, the knights lost their purpose. They resorted to drinking and dueling among themselves, their former discipline disintegrating into chaos. The German and Italian langues *were gone. Most of the others were near collapse. A once grand institution had become little more than a place to support, in idleness, the younger men of certain privileged families. Even worse, revolutions across Europe, especially the one in France, led to their lands being seized, enough that, by one count he'd seen, the knights' revenues had been depleted by nearly two-thirds.*

Now all they had belonged to France.

He heard footsteps and turned. One of his aides-de-camp marched down the wide corridor, the click of his boots resonating off the marble walls. Napoleon knew what the man wanted.

They were ready for him in the Hall of the Supreme Council.

He nodded and led the way through the maze, the towering walls bare, all of the tapestries and paintings commandeered by his soldiers now stored on his flagship along with the other booty. His men had ravaged both Valletta and the rest of the island collecting armor, silver surgical instruments, ivory chess sets, furniture, chests of coin, and bars of gold. Even the treasured Sword and Dagger of de Valette, presented to that long-dead grand master by the king of Spain for his valor during the Great Siege, had been taken.

He had it all.

The L' Orient *packed with spoils.*

But he'd not found what he'd really come for.

The one thing that might prove more valuable than all of that gold and silver.

He entered the grand hall. At its far end, nearly thirty meters away, on a raised dais, surmounted by a crimson velvet canopy ringed with gold fringe, stood the throne of the grand master. This was where the supreme council and chapter general had gathered for centuries, the center of the knights' power. On the surrounding walls were twelve magnificent friezes that depicted the Great Siege. A memorial to a noble and hallowed time. A way to ensure the memory of that greatest moment never faded.

He could appreciate such propaganda.

The hall was empty save for a single trestle table at its center. One man sat before it, tied to a wooden chair, hands flat out in front of him, palms down, a nail piercing the center of each keeping them in place. The pitiful soul wore bedclothes, obviously seized by his soldiers while sleeping. The prisoner moaned, his head flopping down on the table, spittle dripping off his chin, blood oozing from the wounds. Napoleon stepped close and found it hard to take a satisfying breath thanks to the stench from bowels and bladder having relieved themselves.

"You are causing yourself so much pain, and for nothing," he said. "Your leader has abandoned you."

All true.

Ferdinand von Hompesch, the grand master, had handed over Malta without a fight, freely opening Valletta's gates. It helped that the knights swore an obligation not to take up arms against fellow Christians.

"Your grand master took the Arm and Hand of St. John and the icon of Our Lady of Philermo and sailed away."

He saw terror grow in the man's eyes as he realized his dire predicament.

"Before Hompesch left, though, I removed the ring from the hand of St. John." He displayed it on his finger. "A lovely jewel, which I will keep." He shrugged. "What good is it to a dead saint?"

No reply. But he didn't expect one.

"Your grand master left you here to face me. Alone."

"I . . . have told you . . . nothing. I will tell . . . you . . . nothing."

He motioned and his aide brought over a ceramic bowl, setting it on the table. The tortured Hospitaller looked up and seemed to recognize the bunches of plants that lay within.

"From the Rock of the General," he said. "I was told about its healing properties, so I had some of it retrieved for you."

Just off the coast of Gozo, north of Malta, rose a small limestone islet. Breakers had for eons chafed foam onto its gray, barren sides. Atop that rock grew a scrubby plant, unknown anywhere else in the world. He'd heard the tales of its styptic qualities, how it could stanch bleeding when packed on a wound. Fifty years ago a grand master had declared the islet off limits, posting guards, keeping the plant solely for the knights. Three years' confinement as an oarsman on a galley was the penalty for any violation. He planned to end that self-serving prohibition, after hoarding an ample amount.

"Can you smell it?" he asked.

The odor was sharp, pungent, mixing unpleasantly with the putrid waft of the tortured man's waste. He wanted to remove a handkerchief and shield his nose, but knew better. Generals in chief never flinched.

"Tell me what I want to know and the plant can soothe your wounds," he said.

No reply.

"You have kept your oath and not revealed a thing. I must admit, that is most admirable. But your life as a Knight of Malta is over. The order itself is over. There is no need to keep your promise any longer. Ease your suffering and tell me where I can find the Nostra Trinità."

The man's eyes grew wide with the mention.

"How . . . do you know . . . of that?"

"Its existence is no secret within the church, to certain cardinals. They told me about it, or at least what they knew. I'm intrigued and curious, so forget your promise and tell me where it is hidden."

The knight shook his head. "Promises are all . . . we have left."

The man's head collapsed back to the table.

He could only imagine the agony the nails were inflicting. He stepped closer and noticed the pewter ring on the right hand.

And the letters.

SATOR
AREPO
TENET
OPERA
ROTAS

He reached down and slid the trinket off.

The man raised his head at the violation. "That is . . . not . . . yours."

He stared deep into the man's pained eyes. "I was told of this ring, too. The sign of Constantine. The symbol of your Secreti. *A long-honored brotherhood." He allowed his praise to hang in the air, then made his point. "I have come for Constantine's Gift. Make no mistake, dear knight, your life depends on whether I obtain it."*

Kastor stared at Chatterjee. "How do you know all that?"

"As I said, Eminence, I have been working on this for some time."

So had he, scouring the Vatican Library. As prefect of the Apostolic Signatura he'd had access to even the closed portions, the so-called secret archives, labeled that only because they required papal permission to utilize. He'd used his time wisely among those stacks, learning all he could about the *Nostra Trinità.*

Our Trinity.

"Napoleon came to Malta searching for the Hospitallers' precious possession," Chatterjee said. "That knight with his hands nailed to the table never revealed a thing. I read about his heroism in old records. The ones that lie in attics, or in basements, forgotten by time, nobody really know-ing if they are truth or fiction. In the end Napoleon skewered the man through the chest, covering the floor in the Hall of the Supreme Council with as much blood as the heart could pump before he died."

"Which means he didn't learn a thing."

"Did I say that?"

Now he was intrigued.

"Are you saying we can find it?"

Chatterjee grinned. "We need to leave."

"Where are we going?"

"Someone wants to speak with you."

"I thought *you* were the person I was supposed to see."

"I never said that, Eminence. You simply assumed."

Yes, he had.

"A piece of advice," Chatterjee said. "Assume nothing. That course will serve you well in the hours ahead."

CHAPTER
TWELVE

Cotton entered the Four Seasons in Milan. He'd driven the thirty miles south from Como in a little over an hour.

The time was approaching 1:00 P.M.

His mind still reeled at the loss of the documents.

Failure was not his style.

Before flying from Denmark yesterday he'd engaged in a little research. The general consensus seemed to be that any letters between Churchill and Mussolini would have involved an attempt by Churchill to either prevent or sever Italy's alliance with Germany. Once he'd conquered Ethiopia in 1936, Mussolini had openly wanted to rekindle a friendship with Britain. He personally disliked Hitler and did not want to see Europe fall under Germany's influence. But the British thought appeasing Hitler, and opposing Mussolini, was the better course, so they'd rebuffed his advances. Not until 1938 had Britain finally capitulated. But by then it was too late. Italy had already shifted toward Hitler.

Historical speculation on what might have been written between Churchill and Mussolini ran rampant. Unfortunately he hadn't been able to read any of the letters inside the satchel. He'd planned on doing that once he returned to his hotel in Menaggio, even though the Brits had emphatically told him not to be so curious.

But what did they say about the best-laid plans?

He'd been able to change the tire, using the small spare the rental came equipped with, and he'd made it south without incident. The man who'd hired him waited in a sunny, elegant dining room that overlooked an inner courtyard. His name was Sir James Grant, presently of MI6, Great Britain's famed foreign intelligence service. He hadn't met or heard of Grant before yesterday, an urbane and elegant gentleman in his mid-fifties, with dark eyes that cast an expressionless quality typical of professional spies. He noticed that Grant wore the same three-button dark-blue suit with a vest from yesterday. Cotton had called ahead to say that he was on the way with an interesting story, specifically alerting his employer to the two bodies in the villa.

The hotel was impressive, a former convent located in the heart of Milan's fashionable shopping district. Apparently British intelligence's per diem for fieldwork was much more generous than the Justice Department's. He stepped into the dining room, sat at the table, and explained more of what had happened.

Grant laughed at the bear. "That's a new one. I've been at this for twenty years and never had an agent encounter that before."

"Was the satchel real elephant skin?" he asked.

"It's said Mussolini shot the animal himself. How many pages would you estimate were inside?"

"Fifty or so. But only eleven letters. I'm sorry about losing them. Whoever was there wanted that satchel."

"After you called earlier, I sent a man north to investigate. He found the body inside, as you described, and it seems to be the villa's groundskeeper. We also found the dead man upstairs. Shot twice with one arm shredded. Quite horrible, my man said. Then he located the owner, hanging from a tree in the woods north of the villa." Grant paused. "His arms had been pulled up behind his back, his shoulders separated, a bullet to the head."

Cotton sat back in the chair. "Have you identified the dead guy who attacked me?"

"Not yet. His fingerprints are not in any database. Which is unusual, to say the least. But we'll learn who he is." Grant motioned at a plate of pastries on the table. "Please. Help yourself. I ordered those in case you were hungry."

He caught the diversion, a way to move things off to another subject. Stephanie Nelle was known to use the same tactic. But since he was hungry, he helped himself to a couple of croissants. A waiter sauntered over and he ordered a glass of orange juice.

"Fresh-squeezed?" he asked the waiter.

"But of course."

He smiled. Perfect. Thanks to his mother, who'd discouraged him from both, he'd never acquired a taste for alcohol or coffee. But fresh-squeezed juice? Especially from those tart and tangy Spanish oranges?

That was the best.

The ring rested in his pocket. He decided to do a little hedging of his own and keep that tidbit to himself while he determined what this cagey Brit knew that he didn't. But he did decide to share a little. "There were eleven letters between Churchill and Mussolini. Five were being sold to you. Maybe the other six had been offered to another buyer. He wanted five million euros from you. More, probably, from the other guy. So you both decided it was cheaper to steal them."

"I agree, we were being played. I should not be surprised. The seller's reputation does precede him."

He enjoyed another of the pastries and pointed at the plate. "Those are good."

"Do you know the story of the croissant?"

More hedging.

He played along and shook his head.

"In 1686 a baker was supposedly working through the night while the Turks lay siege to Budapest. He heard rumblings underground, beneath his store, and alerted officials. They discovered a Turkish attempt to tunnel under the city walls. Of course, the tunnel was promptly destroyed. As a reward, the baker asked only that he been given the sole right to bake crescent-shaped rolls commemorating the incident, the crescent being the symbol of Islam. Bread the masses could eat, devouring their enemy. And the *croissant,* which is French for 'crescent,' was born."

Cotton buttered a fourth pastry.

"During the recent Syrian civil war," Grant said, "Islamic fundamentalists banned Muslims from eating croissants. They cited the tale I just told you to support their action. They wanted no part of anything that celebrated a Muslim defeat."

"You know that story from Budapest is bullshit."

Grant chuckled. "No doubt. A total fiction. But it sounds delightful. Just like the story that Winston Churchill wanted to sell out Great Britain during World War II. Sounds good. Plays good. But it's not real, either."

"Then why were you willing to pay a fortune for those letters?"

"The Churchill family is tired of hearing lies. Our hope was that this would put the matter to rest."

He pondered on that one a moment, considering what Matthew said in the Bible about naïveté. *Behold, I am sending you out as sheep in the midst of wolves, so be wise as serpents and innocent as doves.* Proverbs seemed instructive, too. *The simple inherit folly, but the prudent are crowned with knowledge.*

Damn straight.

"Those lies about Churchill are over seventy years old," he noted.

The waiter returned with his juice and he enjoyed a few sips.

Smooth and sweet.

"Definitely fresh-squeezed."

"It's the Four Seasons," Grant said. "What did you expect?"

The waiter left.

"I expect the gentleman who hired me to be honest. Three men are dead. Your letters are gone. Yet you haven't shown the slightest concern. Which means either, one, the letters are irrelevant. Two, there was something else you were after. Or three, both. I choose three. What's your vote?"

No reply.

Time to play his hold card.

He found the ring in his pocket and laid it on the table. Grant stared a moment, before lifting it and closely examining the letters.

SATOR
AREPO
TENET
OPERA
ROTAS

Cotton leaned in. "That came off the dead guy in the villa who attacked me."

"Which you failed to mention, until this moment."

He reached for a fifth croissant. "Yeah, I noticed that, too."

"You took it off the corpse?" Grant asked.

"It's my nature to be curious."

Grant smiled. "I'm sure you've seen that the words can be read the same in every direction. Up. Down. Left. Right. It's a palindrome. *Sator. Arepo. Tenet. Opera. Rotas.*"

"You know what it means? My Latin is a little rusty."

"In its purest form, *sator* is 'farmer, planter, originator.' *Arepo?* Unknown. There is no such Latin word. *Tenet* means 'hold, keep, preserve.' *Opera* is 'work, effort, deed.' *Rotas?* 'Wheels.'"

He assembled the meaning.

The farmer Arepo works wheels.

"It makes no sense," he said.

"The full meaning of these words has been a matter of debate for centuries. No one has ever ascertained an accurate meaning. What we do know is that this palindrome once served as the personal mark of Constantine the Great."

He'd recalled something similar from a few years ago.

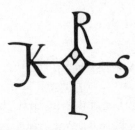

The monogram of Charlemagne. A sign of royal identity, usually formed around combining initials. When Charlemagne was crowned Holy Roman Emperor, the pope bestowed on him a one-word name.

Carolus.

Charles the Great.

So a monogram had been designed around that label.

The one on the ring seemed far more complex, and came four hundred years before Charlemagne.

"What do you know of Constantine?" Grant asked.

His eidetic memory recalled some details. Constantine ruled the Roman Empire in the 4th century, defeating all challengers, uniting the throne under one ruler. He founded a new capital on the Bosphorus, where Europe met Asia, which became Constantinople, a city set apart from Rome, ushering in the Byzantine culture. He was also the only Roman ruler to ever have *the Great* attached after his name.

He pointed at the ring. "There's etching inside."

Grant looked. "The eight-pointed Maltese cross."

"Can we get some bacon?" He was more hungry than he thought.

"Anything you like," Grant said.

He needed time to think, so more food might do the trick. "Bacon and eggs would be terrific. The eggs over hard. I hate runny."

"I couldn't agree more. Though, being an Englishman, that's probably an odd preference."

Grant motioned for the waiter and placed the order, then turned back and stared at him across the table. "Have we both hedged enough?"

He agreed, time to drop the act. "You paid me an obscene fee, then sent me in there blind just to see what would happen."

"And if that were true?"

"If I were still a Justice Department agent, I'd probably beat the living crap out of you."

"And in your retirement?"

"It's still up in the air."

He allowed his words to settle in, staring out through the wall of glass to the hotel's cloisterlike courtyard. Then he faced the Brit. "I'm going to eat my free breakfast, take my fifty thousand euros, and head home. As we like to say where I come from, I don't have a dog in this fight."

"What do you know of the Knights Hospitallers? Or, as they are called today, the Knights of Malta?"

"Not a whole lot."

"Thankfully, I do."

* * *

Sometime around 1070 a small group of merchants from Amalfi founded the Hospice of St. John the Almoner near the Church of the Holy Sepulcher in Jerusalem. They were Good Samaritans, stretcher bearers for pilgrims who'd survived the arduous journey to the Holy Land. Eventually they constructed hospitals across all of the land conquered by the Crusaders. In 1113 Pope Paschall II bestowed upon them papal legitimacy, their trademark habit a black surcoat with a cowl, an eight-pointed cross in white linen affixed to the left breast. By 1150 they had grown into soldier-monks, knights errant of the cross, becoming the Order of the Hospital of St. John of Jerusalem.

Their first duty always remained caring for the sick, but their second was tuition fifei. *Defense of the faith. Interested parents would place their son's name forward at birth and pay a large fee. Acceptance came at age eighteen. To be eligible then the young man had to be strong, well built, and fit enough to endure the life of a soldier.*

And the pedigree had to be perfect.

In the beginning, an applicant had only to be legitimately born into a noble family. By the 14th century that evolved into both parents having to be of noble, land-owning gentry. A hundred years later applicants had to prove nobility in the male line back four generations. Eventually, by the 16th century, all four grandparents were required to be of noble stock. Passage money, what it took to support a knight for a year in the Holy Land, became the final initiation fee. Once anointed, each knight endured a year's training, then swore to have faith, repent his sins, and live in humility, being merciful, sincere, wholehearted, and brave enough to endure persecution.

With the fall of the Holy Land in 1291, the age of the warrior-monk ended. The Knights Templar never grasped that change and faded in 1307. The Hospitallers adapted, keeping their primary mission charity but evolving from a land-based cavalry force to a sea power, conquering and taking Rhodes in 1310. They then became the Order of the Knights of Rhodes and acquired a new purpose.

Keeping both the Ottomans and the corsairs at bay.

After Constantinople fell in 1453, Rhodes became the last outpost of Christianity in the East. The knights acted as a buffer between the Latin-Christian Western world and the Eastern infidels. Their fighting ships and galleys dominated the Mediterranean, their white cross on a red matte striking fear into their enemies.

Members organized themselves into eight langues, *one for Provence, Auvergne, France, Italy, Castile, England, Germany, and Aragon, which represented the major political divisions of the time. Those were further subdivided into bailiwicks and commanderies. The* langues *headquartered in* auberges, *where members lived and ate communally. Traditional national rivalries never faded, though, and led to regimental conflicts between the* langues, *but enforced discipline and a strong hand eventually forged the* langues *into a tight, cohesive fighting force.*

In 1522 the Turks finally succeeded in retaking Rhodes.

The knights loaded their ships and left, drifting for seven years. In 1530 Charles V of Spain granted them Malta, and its twelve thousand inhabitants, in exchange for a single falcon, payable yearly to the viceroy of Sicily on All Saints' Day.

The island had not been much of a prize. Just a chunk of limestone seven leagues long and four wide. Its stony soil was unfit for growing much other than cotton, figs, melons, and other fruits. Honey was its major export and main claim to fame. Just a few springs near the center was all the running water. Rain was the main supply. Wood was so scarce the locals used sundried cow dung for cooking. The south coast claimed no harbors, coves, or bays, the shore tall and rocky. The north coast was the opposite, with plenty of anchorage, including two fine harbors suitable for any fleet. Which was perfect, since the knights were a seafaring power. But the gift of an island was not merely gratuitous. Charles intended for them to employ their forces and arms against the perfidious enemies of the Holy Faith.

Which they did.

Becoming the Sovereign and Military Order of the Knights of Malta, exempt from civil duties and taxes, bowing to no authority save the pope.

There they stayed until 1798.

"Now they are Sovereign Military Hospitallers Order of St. John of Jerusalem, of Rhodes, and of Malta," Grant said. "The world's oldest surviving chivalric order. Headquartered in Rome. The eight-pointed cross of St. John remains their emblem. Four barbed arrowheads, joined at the center, each point representing the eight beatitudes, the four arms symbolizing prudence, temperance, fortitude, and justice. Its whiteness is a reminder of purity."

The waiter brought Cotton's bacon and eggs. He pointed at the ring, which Grant still held. "Is that connected to the Hospitallers?"

"I believe it is."

He ate his late breakfast, noticing the eggs had been fried perfectly. "So the dead guy could be a knight?"

"That's my assumption." Grant sipped his coffee. "You may not believe this, but I was genuinely hoping this was only about the letters. A part of me wanted it to be that simple. But in this business nothing is ever simple." Grant paused. "The Hospitallers possess the largest, most extensive collection of Mussolini's writings and personal belongings in the world. They've been secretly acquiring it for decades. A bit of an odd obsession, wouldn't you say? But they refuse to confirm or deny anything. As they like to say, what they may or may not own is a private matter."

"Like that stops MI6." But he did connect the dots. "You think the Hospitallers were the ones after the Churchill letters?"

Grant reached into his inside jacket pocket and removed a cell phone. He punched the screen, then handed it over. On it, Cotton saw a man hanging from a rope, arms yanked up from behind, his neck angled over in death.

He handed the phone back. "The villa owner?"

Grant nodded. "When the Crusaders invaded the Holy Land, they became a brutal lot. They were fighting an enemy like none they had ever seen. The Arabs were tough, relentless, and unmerciful. To show their adversary that they could be equal to the task, they devised new means of torture and punishment." Grant gestured with the phone. "One of those involved hanging their prisoners in this particular way. It became a trademark. So yes, I think the Knights of Malta are involved."

Cotton kept enjoying his breakfast, waiting for the pitch.

"We need someone, other than us, to look into this," Grant said. "That's why I hired one of the best intelligence operatives in the world."

He grinned. "Now you're blowing smoke up my ass."

"Just being honest. You do realize that there are people at MI6 who still hold a grudge your way."

He knew what Grant was referring to. An incident that involved his son, Gary, and a former head of British intelligence. "I did what I had to do."

"Which is exactly why I want you on this. I have a situation here, Cotton. One that may be wider than I first thought. I need your help. I'll double your fee."

Music to his ears and, luckily, he had a few days free. But he wanted to know more. "What do you want me to do?"

"Make contact with the Knights of Malta." Grant laid the ring on the table. "Start with inquiring about why the dead man in that villa was wearing this. Then find out anything you can on their Mussolini collection. And I'm not particular on how you accomplish that objective."

Which meant the local criminal codes did not have to be observed. But he had to ask, "Is that all I get from you? Pretty damn vague."

"I would ask that you allow me the luxury of withholding further facts until I'm sure of a few matters. There is a possibility this might be nothing at all. That we are on the wrong trail."

"Looking for what?"

Grant did not reply.

He shrugged. "Okay. For a hundred thousand euros, I can be a good bird dog. I'll sniff around and see where it leads."

"Excellent. Hopefully, I'll have some clarity shortly that I can share."

"Can I at least know what you're waiting for?"

"A situation on Malta to resolve itself."

CHAPTER THIRTEEN

KASTOR EMERGED FROM THE CAR.

He'd ridden from the Madliena Tower with Chatterjee, following the north coast highway to the town of St. Paul's Bay. It began as a sleepy fishing village, the adjacent shoreline one of the easier points on the island from which to gain land. Now it was a popular tourist spot, its unstylish concrete buildings overflowing with an overpriced array of restaurants, cafés, and boutiques, the mass-market hotels and nondescript apartments packed with people year-round.

He caught sight of one of the coastal towers, high above, standing guard from its lofty perch. Another grand master creation, this one in 1610 by Wigancourt, who built six facing the sea. He knew about the famed Frenchman. A knight his entire adult life, including during the Great Siege, he was popular with the Maltese, which was rare for grand masters. The viaduct he completed delivered water to Valletta until the 20th century.

Out in the calm bay boats lay at anchor, so many that their bulk formed a carpet on the water. Beyond them, he spotted the small island where the faithful believed that Paul himself first came ashore. What a tale. In A.D. 60 275 prisoners were being ferried toward Rome to be tried, Paul included. Their ship was ruined in a dreadful storm, drifting two weeks before breaking up just off the coast. Despite not knowing how to swim, miraculously all of the prisoners made it to shore. The Bible itself recounted the event, noting that *later we learned that the island was named Malta. The people who lived there showed us great kindness and they made a fire and called us all to warm ourselves.* As the story went, while Paul was ashore a poisonous snake bit him but he survived, which the locals took as a sign that he was no ordinary man.

No. That he was not.

More a brilliant rebel.

Like himself.

Kastor stood before a formidable church, one of 360 that dotted the island, this one a high building of burnt ocher, with a graceful spire and a beautiful cupola, vivid against the drabness of the shady street. Not much had changed in thirty years. As a young priest, serving his first parish, he'd said mass here many times. He noticed that the same two clocks remained in the tower. One real, the other a trompe l'oeil, installed by overly superstitious locals to supposedly confuse the devil when he came to collect souls.

He and Chatterjee entered through the front doors. Inside was the same low roof supported by arches, with little pomp or circumstance, shadows still the only adornment. A solitary figure stood beside the front pew.

"Come in, my friend. Please. We have much to discuss."

A tall, stout, older man, with a noticeable midsection, paraded down the center aisle. He was robust, with a thick patch of pale-white hair and features framed by a pair of wispy white sideburns. Few angles defined the round face, the skin streaked by veins of yellow and purple, perhaps the lasting effects from years of smoking.

Danjel Spagna.

The few times Kastor had seen him at the Vatican, Spagna had worn the black cassock, purple skullcap, and silver pectoral cross of an archbishop. Today he was dressed casually, nothing reflecting any ecclesiastical status.

He'd never actually met Spagna, only heard the tales.

The press called it all the Vatican, but the Holy See was not the Vatican City State. The latter came into existence as sovereign territory only in 1929 because of the Lateran Treaty. It consisted of chapels, halls, galleries, gardens, offices, apartments, and museums. The Holy See, the episcopal seat of Rome and the pope, dated back to Christ, and was an independent sovereign entity that did not end at the death of a pontiff. The Holy See acted and spoke for the whole church, currently maintaining diplomatic relations with 180 nations. Ambassadors were officially accredited not to the Vatican City State, but to the Holy See. The pope was its unchallenged head, but it was administered by the curia, with the secretary of state acting like a prime minister, a buffer between the over two thousand employees and the pope. The old joke came from John XXIII. When asked how many people worked at the Vatican, he quipped *about half of them.*

As in any other nation, security had always been a concern.

The most secret agency within the Holy See had existed since the 16th century, created specifically by Pius V to end the life of the Protestant Elizabeth I and support her cousin, the Catholic Mary, Queen of Scots, for the English throne. Though it failed in that mission, ever since it had served popes through schisms, revolutions, dictators, persecutions, attacks, world wars, even assassination attempts. First called the Supreme Congregation for the Holy Inquisition of Heretical Error, then the much shorter Holy Alliance. In the 20th century it was changed to the Entity.

Its motto?

With the Cross and the Sword.

Never once had the Holy See acknowledged the Entity's existence, but those in the know regarded it as the oldest and one of the best intelligence agencies in the world. A model of secrecy and efficiency. Respected. Feared. Overseen for the past thirty-six years by Archbishop Danjel Spagna.

The pope's spymaster.

A Belgian, Spagna first came to the attention of John Paul II when, as a young priest, he learned that the Vatican might be bugged. Eight listening devices were found inside the Apostolic Palace, all of Soviet origin. The world was never told, but a grateful pope elevated Spagna to monsignor and assigned him to the Entity. There he became the Pole's personal envoy, a conduit between Rome and Warsaw, making many clandestine visits to Eastern Europe. Some said he was the one who secretly worked with the Americans to help bring down the Soviet Union, ferrying information to and from Washington. But again, nothing was ever confirmed or denied. After the Soviet Union fell, Spagna was elevated to archbishop and given full operational control of the Entity. A cardinal served as its titular head, but Spagna ran things on a daily basis. No publicity had ever surrounded him. No scandal. No controversy. Only the strongest had run with John Paul II, and Spagna may have been the toughest of them all. He'd even acquired a label.

Domíno Suo.

Lord's Own.

"What do you want with me?" Kastor asked. "I worked in the Vatican a long time, and never once did we speak."

"Don't be offended," Spagna said, his aging eyes the color of lead. "I only speak to a red vulture when absolutely necessary. They don't care for me, and I don't care for them. You, though, I have studied in detail." Spagna's lips twitched into an ironic smile. "You were born and raised on this barren rock of an island. A true Maltese. There aren't many of those left in this world. You said mass right in this church, as a young priest, back when you were fresh and new—and silent."

Kastor caught the jab.

"You have superb academic credentials from the finest institutions. A credit to a superior intelligence. You're handsome, photogenic, and articulate. Together those are rare qualities among the red vultures. In many ways you are almost too good to be true. That raised warning flags with me. So I took the time to look deeper." Spagna pointed. "That's where you really learn about someone."

He agreed.

"I spoke with one of the nuns who raised you. She's an old woman now, living out her retirement in Portugal, but she remembers you from the orphanage. Amazing how some things can stick in the mind." Spagna pointed again. "You stuck in hers. She told me a story about the festival of Our Lady of the Lily. Every town on this island holds at least one big festival each year. Quite the celebrations, I'm told. Seems like a lovely tradition. You were thirteen at the time, I believe. That nun watched as you stole three *pastí* from one of the street vendors. The owner never saw what you did. But she did. *Halliel ftit,* she called you. Little thief."

He said nothing.

"She told me how you took those pastries, went off, and devoured them like a rat. Amazingly, all of the nuns at the orphanage knew you liked to steal. Did you know that?"

No, he didn't.

"Some of them wanted to punish you. But the mother superior forbid it."

He was surprised at the show of generosity. He remembered that cranky old woman as a cold bitch.

"The old nun told me the mother superior wanted to see how far you'd go," Spagna said. "And you showed her. You stole trinkets, clothes, books, money, and never once did you show an ounce of remorse. The old nun said that the mother superior wanted you to destroy yourself. To be caught, chastised, shamed, ridiculed. She wanted you to mete out your own punishment. Yet that never happened. Instead, you left the orphanage and went off to become a priest. The mother superior thought perhaps God himself had decided to intervene, so she let you go and never said a word. Now here you are, poised to steal the papacy."

This man's interest in him was frightening. So for once he decided to keep his mouth shut and see where this led.

"That mother superior was right," Spagna noted. "You are, indeed, your own worst enemy. As an adult you managed to do what you failed to achieve as a child. You meted out your own punishment. To your credit, you achieved a position only a few of the red vultures have ever attained. Prefect of the Apostolic Signatura. That's a lofty post. Enabling, in so many ways. But your mouth. That foul, vile mouth of yours got you fired. For some odd reason you thought people cared what you had to say."

"Maybe I cared."

Spagna laughed. "That was never in doubt. I'm sure you cared a great deal. Which, dear Kastor Gallo, is another of your problems."

"Eminence. That is my title, *Archbishop*."

The older man flicked a hand, as if swiping the rebuff away. "You are a fool. Nothing more. Nothing less. Just a plain, ordinary fool."

He'd not risked this journey from Rome to be chastised by a subordinate. But he was damn curious as to what was going on. He'd been told to come to Malta immediately and meet with someone at the Madliena Tower. Since the person who'd sent the message was trustworthy and understood what was at stake, he'd not questioned the request. But never had he thought the Lord's Own would be the person he'd be seeing.

"Say what you have to say," he said.

"I want to find the *Nostra Trinità*. You've searched a long time. Now I want to join with you. I know things you don't."

He did not doubt that observation and was surprised by the request. This man had kept the Vatican's secrets for decades. Too long, if the murmurs he'd heard within the curia were to be believed.

"Why do you want it?" he asked.

"It's the church's ultimate secret. The one that has eluded us. Every organization has secrets. Ours is seventeen hundred years old. Before I die, or am fired like you, I want this secret secured."

He decided to be clear. "I want to use it to become pope."

Spagna nodded. "I know. You want to be pope. I want you to be pope."

Had he heard correctly? "Why?"

"Is that important? Just be grateful that I do."

Not good enough. "Why help me?"

"Because you actually have a chance at winning."

Really? "How? As you've just noted, I'm a thief and a fool."

"Both attributes are common to the red vultures, so neither is a liability. I also know for a fact that your ultra-orthodox views are shared by a great many. I'm assuming that, as prefect of the Apostolic Signatura, you amassed the necessary damning information on your colleagues."

He had, so he nodded.

"I thought as much. I'm privy to some of the same information."

That didn't surprise him.

"John Paul II wanted the world to think him a reformer, but he was a real hard-liner. There was nothing progressive about that Pole," Spagna said. "The Soviets tried to kill him, but he survived and stayed the course, held the line, and brought Moscow to its knees. I liked him. He loved to say one thing publicly, then privately do another. He was really good at that, and I learned from him. The church was stronger then. We were feared. We were also much more effective on the world stage. We destroyed the Iron Curtain and crushed the Soviet Union. We were a power. Not anymore. We've waned to nothing. And though I do consider you a fool, you'll be my fool, Kastor."

He didn't like the sound of that. "I doubt it."

"Don't be so hasty. I have something you don't."

He was listening.

"The leverage to bring the undecided cardinals over to your side. Enough to garner the magic two-thirds vote."

"The *Nostra Trinità* can do that."

"Maybe. But it's a bit of an unknown. And that's all contingent on you finding it. I can provide something more tangible. More recent. Something you can use either in addition to, or in lieu of, what you're after."

He liked what he was hearing.

Still—

"What do *you* want?"

"That blood vessel bursting in the pope's brain offers us both an opportunity," Spagna said.

Not an answer.

He needed to make a phone call. He'd apparently been kept in the dark about a great many things. Why? He wasn't sure. Having Spagna as an ally could indeed change everything. In some ways they were alike. Both pariahs. Everyone avoided the Entity, except the pope and the Secretariat of State, which had no choice but to work with it.

"What does it feel like to be alone?" he asked Spagna.

"You tell me."

"I'm not. I have friends. Supporters. As you said, there are many who agree with me. You have no one."

"He has me," Chatterjee said.

"And what is your job?" Kastor asked.

"I assist the archbishop, from time to time, on matters with which I have some expertise."

He recalled their talk at the tower. "Like scouring and stealing from archives, libraries, and newspaper morgues, doing whatever is necessary to get the job done?"

"Absolutely."

"Then we're lucky to have you. What about that parasailer? The Americans knew what you were doing."

"No, Kastor," Spagna said. "They knew what *you* were doing. Which is why I'm here."

Troubling to hear for a second time.

"The Entity itself is somewhat in crisis," Spagna said. "Many of my own people think it's time I step aside. I have subordinates who want my job.

The red vulture who's in charge despises me. But the dead pope liked me, so there was nothing anyone could do. That may not be the case after the coming conclave, depending on who becomes pope. I don't want to step aside. I don't want to be *forced* to step aside."

He stared at the bearlike man, a bit shambled in street clothes but definitely comfortable with his power.

"Your problem," Spagna said, "is that you've always wanted things too fast. Since childhood the concept of patience has been foreign to you. That's why you find yourself with the dubious title of patron of the Sovereign Military Order of Malta and not prefect of the Apostolic Signatura. Seven cardinals have held that patron post over the past sixty years. Seven losers. Now you're the eighth. I was surprised, after your firing, when you requested such an innocuous job, which the pope gladly granted. But that was precisely where you wanted to be. That's when I first became interested in what you were doing. But as always, you were impatient. You wreaked havoc inside the Hospitallers. They're now in a state of civil war, fighting among themselves, unsure what's happening to them. All thanks to you."

"Which gives me a great freedom of movement. I started that chaos. I control it. So I also know how to avoid it."

Spagna chuckled. "And there it is. The liar and the thief showing himself in all his glory. That's why you'll make a great pope. At least for me, you will. I can work with you, Kastor, like I did with the Pole. We'll understand each other. I saved your hide a little while ago with that American parasailer, as a show of my good faith."

"And what if I don't want your help?"

"Then I'll take my chances with another candidate. One who will appreciate the kind of assistance I can offer."

He got the message. "I'm listening."

Spagna retreated to the front pew and reached down, lifting up a thin sheaf of papers, bound together in a binder. The older man approached and offered them. The top sheet, visible through the clear plastic, was blank.

"I gave it no title. Perhaps you could offer one. After you've read it."

He accepted the binder and started to open to the next page.

"Wait," Spagna said.

He looked up, unaccustomed to being ordered.

"I offer this as a second show of my good faith," the spymaster said. "By reading it, though, you agree to work with me, on my terms. If you're not inclined to do that, hand it back and we will not speak again."

Choice time.

He had few allies in the world. As a kid he'd been closer to his brother than any other person. And for good reason. They'd shared a womb, born identical twins, Pollux the older by a little over a minute. As kids it had been difficult for anyone to tell them apart. That similarity had carried over into adulthood, though they both now tried hard to distinguish themselves. His brown hair was short and tight to the scalp, while Pollux's hung below the ears. He stayed clean-shaven. His brother had always sported the remnants of a monk's beard. Though their height, size, shape, and facial features remained mirror images, he wore glasses for nearsightedness and the scarlet of a cardinal, while Pollux retained perfect vision and had never favored the priesthood. Their father had named them for the constellation Gemini, Latin for "twins," and its two brightest stars, Castor and Pollux. As a fisherman, the stars had been important to their father. But that man was gone, and this was his decision alone. What was the old cliché?

Never look a gift horse in the mouth?

"I'll keep it."

Spagna smiled. "We'll be in touch before nightfall."

"How will you know where to find me?"

Spagna smirked.

"Please, Kastor. Asking ridiculous questions only shows your ignorance."

CHAPTER
FOURTEEN

LUKE SAT IN THE DARK, HIS BACK AGAINST A ROCK WALL, AND CURSED.
Good thing his mother wasn't around. His shorts and shirt remained
damp from the swim, shoes sodden and clammy. His luminous watch
noted the time at 2:20 P.M. He felt neither nerves nor fear. Only irritation. He was three for three on mistakes for the day.

He'd tried to avoid the two men who'd confronted him at the dock,
dodging and weaving through Valletta's unbroken cordon of waterfront
streets. But they eventually cornered him. An arm had snapped closed
across his throat, another hand clamped on his mouth, and then the arm
across his windpipe tightened until his vision had flashed with lights.

What happened after that was sketchy.

He vaguely recalled being carried into a building, down a flight of stairs,
into coolness, then lowered into the ground and dropped onto soft earth.
When he came around absolute blackness had enveloped him, so thick that
he couldn't see his hand in front of his face. He'd used his fingers to examine the rough-hewn walls of his prison, which was circular and measured about five paces across. Reaching up, he'd determined the hole was
wider at the bottom, the sides tapering inward as they rose. A clever way
to prevent any attempt to climb out since you'd fall long before making it
even halfway up.

The air hung humid and stale, as if it had been breathed to exhaustion.

Sweat coursed down the small of his back. His mouth felt pasty. What he'd give for a bottled water. As screwups went, this day ranked high on the list.

What would Malone say?

Good going, Frat Boy.

Hard to live up to a legend. And that perfectly described Cotton Malone. But if you were going to strive to be the best, then you had to know the best. Pappy might be retired and selling books in Denmark, but he remained if not at, then certainly near, the top of his game. Of course, he'd never tell Malone that. He'd worked with him twice and both times he'd learned things. The goal? Work hard another decade and new agents might talk about him the way the current ones spoke of Malone. That was possible. Why not? Everybody needed goals. And time was indeed the best teacher.

Trouble was, eventually it killed all of its students.

He wondered where Pappy was now. Probably at his shop in Copenhagen, doing whatever booksellers do.

What a day.

He reached down and played with a handful of the parched sand that formed the pit's floor. How long had this hole been in the ground? How many others had rotted away here? He figured he was somewhere beneath Valletta, as he vaguely recalled not being carried all that far. But where? Who the hell knew?

A sound disturbed the silence.

Like a door opening above.

Shafts of light appeared across the top of the pit.

He was now able to see that he'd been right. The hole was bell-shaped. About ten feet deep. Tapering upward to an opening about four feet wide.

He looked up and saw Laura Price.

Which caught him off guard. He'd been wondering who the two guys worked for. His best guess had been the guy on the tower with the cardinal.

A rope fell from above, which she used to climb down. The moment her feet hit the earthen floor, he clipped her legs out from under her and she dropped to the soft sandy floor.

He came to his feet and stood over her.

She shook her head. "Feel better after that cheap shot?"

"Where am I?"

"Inside a piece of history. You should feel honored. The Knights of Malta once dug these prisons all over the island. They're called *guvas*. Means 'birdcage.' Bad little knights were thrown in and left for days, or weeks, at a time. A few even forever. The only *guva* most people think still exists is beneath Fort St. Angelo, not far from here. But there's another, right here. As you can see, there's no way out except by ladder or rope."

She stood, wearing a look of unpredictability, her blond hair loosely gathered by a leather thong. Everything about her breathed freedom. He watched as she brushed the dirt from her clothes and examined the walls.

"Did you notice this?" she asked, pointing at the rock.

He stepped over and, in the dim light, spotted carved letters.

AD MELIORES.

"Toward better things," she said, translating. "Obviously, a plea from a former occupant."

He noticed more carvings. Names. Dates. Coats of arms.

"All they could do," she said, "was carve away and hope someone above showed mercy. This place is really old. Probably late 16th or early 17th century."

He couldn't care less about the history lesson. "Why am I here?"

"You stuck your nose where it didn't belong."

"I was doing my job."

Since this pain in the ass knew who he worked for there was no need to be coy. And besides, his main source of exercise was pushing his luck.

"Do you have any idea what you're into?" she asked.

"Why don't you enlighten me?"

Her right arm whirled through the blackness, her fist heading up for his jaw. But his guard was up and he was ready. His left hand stopped the potential blow with a quick grab of her wrist.

"Not bad," she said.

"I try."

"After you shot my engine up, to get here I had to steal a boat from a guy who came by."

He grinned. What was it about the badass girls that attracted him?

"Do you have any idea what's happening tomorrow?" she asked.

Because he talked with a Tennessee mountain accent, had never attended college, and showed little to no interest in current affairs, people always thought him uninformed. Truth be told he read several newspapers each day, online of course, and devoured the daily security updates all Magellan Billet agents received. Once assigned to Malta, he'd read everything he could on Kastor Cardinal Gallo and what was about to happen at the Vatican.

"A conclave," he told her.

"And this is going to be one for the record books. Mind letting go of my arm?"

He did.

"I bet that jaw of yours has had quite a few fists pounded into it."

She was working him and he knew it. But what the hell? He liked it. "It takes a beating but keeps on ticking."

"I bet it does. Like I said, this conclave will be a mess. There's no front-runner. No solid contender. No favorite. One hundred and fifteen cardinals will be inside the Sistine voting. Who will they select as pope?" She shrugged. "I have no idea. Neither do they, by the way. That's what happens when a pope dies suddenly. But I do know who some people don't want. Kastor Cardinal Gallo."

Interesting. "What people?"

"That's only for me to know."

"Have you been following me since yesterday?"

She nodded. "I assume that when Stephanie Nelle was telling you to get rid of me, she also told you who I work for."

"Why does an island this small need an intelligence agency?"

"We sit on the southernmost border of the EU. We're the front line between Europe and Africa. Get something onto this rock and you can easily get into the EU. That's why we need an intelligence agency."

"Why didn't you just identify yourself to Stephanie to start with?"

"We were hoping to keep this contained."

"Who is *we*?"

"My boss. He gave me an order. I do what he tells me."

"How did you know I was headed into trouble?"

"Same answer. My boss told me. The man on the Madliena Tower, with Gallo, sometimes works with Vatican intelligence. We've seen him before. He piqued our interest and led me to you."

He'd caught the magic words. *Vatican intelligence.* "The Entity is working with Cardinal Gallo?"

"It's a possibility."

Not a complete answer, and he could see that she was acquiring a case of lockjaw, a familiar malady with field operatives since the idea was to always get far more than you ever gave. "Any reason why you didn't help me out *before* that idiot cut the towline?"

"And miss all the fun of watching you at work? That was worth the price of admission. But I did tell your boss you were in trouble."

He shrugged. "What else could a guy ask for?"

"And so we're clear, if you hadn't shot up my engine, I would have saved you the trouble of being down here. As it was, all I had to work with was my phone."

"Which I so conveniently returned."

"Yes, you did. We need to leave."

"We?"

"I prefer to work alone, but I've been told you're now on the team whether I like it or not."

"What are we going to do?"

"Deal with Cardinal Gallo."

CHAPTER
FIFTEEN

3:00 P.M.

KASTOR WALKED PAST THE RECTORY OUTSIDE THE CATHEDRAL. AS the legend went, the Apostle Paul had been a guest of the local governor, a man named Publius. After curing the governor's father of fever and flux, Paul converted Publius to Christianity. He then designated the governor's house as Malta's first church and the Roman its bishop. Ever since, a church had occupied the same spot within Mdina's fortified walls, eventually becoming a cathedral in the 12th century and still serving as the seat for the Archdiocese of Malta.

Mdina sat nearly in the center of the island, surrounded by thick bastions, one of the world's few remaining walled cities. It served as the island's capital until the 16th century, when the knights arrived and built Valletta. Chatterjee had returned him to the Madliena Tower, where he'd found his rental car then driven alone to Mdina. The fact that Danjel Spagna was here, watching his every move, bothered him. As did the fact that the Americans were also watching.

Chatterjee had assured him they were dealing with the parasailer. He'd noticed there'd been no mention of the woman in the boat, but he assumed that problem was being handled, too. If it was anyone else besides the Entity he'd be concerned, but Spagna was renowned for his ability to get things done. The man had served five popes, surviving each successive purge when the old was swept away and the new welcomed. While that was thought somewhat therapeutic for the curia, it could be a bad idea for the intelligence business. Continuity was the name of that game. The Entity worked thanks to Spagna's institutional memory and his steady hand. The fact that the spymaster wanted to make him pope was both gratifying and frightening.

He needed all the help he could get.

He carried with him the thin plastic binder Spagna had offered. He'd resisted the urge to read the pages quickly, intent on finding a quiet place for a thorough review, practicing some of that patience Spagna had so unceremoniously advised.

He avoided the cathedral's rectory and kept walking through the walled town, savoring the waft of Mdina's sun-warmed stone. He could hear the voices of history, all the way back to antiquity, demanding to be remembered. Occasionally he caught sight of the soft-footed cats, most tawny orange and sullen black, that still prowled every nook and cranny, as they had during his childhood.

Malta's oldest families still lived among Mdina's aristocratic aloofness. For centuries the locals called it the Silent City, since the only sounds within the walls were footsteps. But it was here that the revolt against the French invaders began in 1800. Napoleon had looted every church, defiled every sanctuary, cleaned out every *auberge*. The little general then sailed off to Egypt, leaving a garrison of a thousand regulars to maintain order. The Maltese, though at first glad the knights were gone, quickly grew to hate the French even more. The final insult came here, when the invaders held an auction to sell off the contents of Mdina's Carmelite church. A riot erupted and the French commander was murdered. Church bells rang coast-to-coast, calling the people to arms. Within ninety days the entire garrison fled the island.

The lesson?

Never underestimate the Maltese.

He followed the labyrinth of angled streets, so narrow that you could reach out from the upper floors of one house and touch the one opposite. Wrought-iron grilles protected many of the windows, remnants from a time when those dwellings had to fend for themselves. He passed a flock of tourists, enjoying the sites, taking refuge from the sun within the cool cavern of passageways. He also caught the cross-currents of voices.

The Maltese were a proud lot. Always had been. They worked hard, longing mainly to get married, have children, and enjoy life. The church had once dominated everything, but not so much anymore. Malta had gone international, joining the EU, breaking further from Great Britain and its older generations. Divorce had even been legalized by a national referendum. Four hundred and fifty thousand people now lived on the island. And true, the locals could be petty toward one another, prone to jealousy, even quick to pick a fight—what was the saying? *A crossed Maltese stays cross*—but even with all its faults, Malta, and its people, were his home.

He found his favorite restaurant, tucked away in a quiet corner against the bastion walls. Two vaulted stone chambers from the 17th century served as the dining room, but his chosen spot was outside in an enclosed courtyard adorned with greenery and a tinkling fountain. It had been a few years since he'd last visited.

He ordered his favorite dish, rabbit stew, then laid the plastic binder on the table. There were maybe twenty typewritten pages inside. He glanced around. The courtyard was empty, no one enjoying a late lunch, or early supper, depending on your point of view. The waiter brought him a glass of red wine, Italian, as he'd never cared for Maltese grapes. He waited until the young man stepped back inside before opening the binder and reading.

> Two years ago the Holy Father directed that I conduct a confidential assessment and, if possible, an audit of certain departments within the Holy See. Prior to becoming pope, while he was a cardinal, the Holy Father had served within a variety of departments and was concerned about what he termed "systematic waste, fraud, and abuse." I was requested to conduct a thorough but wholly secret investigation, drawing no attention to my efforts. After twenty months of clandestine study I can now provide the following summary:
>
> (1) There is little to no transparency in any of the bookkeeping maintained within the Holy See. In fact, it is common practice for departments to maintain two sets of records. One that could be shown to anyone who might request information, the other detailing the actual income, costs, and expenditures. This practice is well

known to the cardinals currently overseeing those departments, as it is done under their direct supervision and many of them personally retain the more accurate, second set of books;

(2) Contracts for services by the Holy See to outside third-party providers (which total in the tens of millions of euros annually) are routinely secured without competitive bidding and without regard to cost. Corruption is rampant relative to the awarding of these contracts. Bribery and kickbacks are common. Many times as much as 200 percent over the current market value is paid by the Holy See for these goods and services, all linked to corruption;

(3) There is an ongoing and systematic theft of tax-free souvenirs from the Vatican's retail shops. This merchandise is being stolen by the pallet load, then secretly sold to outside vendors at vastly reduced prices. The moneys generated from these thefts are currently secretly being shared by at least three cardinals;

(4) One particular outside, third-party transaction is noteworthy. It involves a deal made with an American corporation allowing that company's cigarettes to be sold in Vatican stores, but only thanks to a secret fee paid to at least two cardinals. Part of that deal also allows several other cardinals to benefit from extreme discounts on at least two hundred packs of cigarettes, collectively, purchased by them each month, for their own use;

(5) An Italian charitable foundation for a local pediatric hospital recently (and secretly) paid €200,000 to renovate a cardinal's Rome apartment;

(6) The Vatican pension fund currently has a nearly €800 million deficit and is teetering on bankruptcy, though current public financial records show a balance sheet far to the contrary;

(7) There is no detailed inventory of the nearly 5000 buildings owned within Rome by the Holy See. Current balance sheets list the

total worth of the Holy See's real estate holdings within France, England, Switzerland, and Italy at €400 million. The best guess of the actual worth for these properties is over €3 billion. The best explanation for this odd discrepancy downward is that the curia sees public relations advantages in downplaying the actual net worth of the church;

(8) Retirement packages to at least three dozen cardinals are highly exorbitant, far beyond anything considered reasonable;

(9) The granting of free or low-rent apartments to cardinals currently serving within the curia is common. Rents in prime Rome locations are at times as much as 100 percent below market value. One example: a one-hundred-square-meter apartment near St. Peter's Basilica is currently being rented to one cardinal for €20.67 a month. If market rates were applied to all of the Holy See's rental apartments, somewhere around €20 million would be generated in revenue each year, as opposed to the less than €6 million currently being realized. The same discrepancy is present regarding the Holy See's commercial real estate, where many of the current leases are far below market value and could generate somewhere near €30 million more per year.

He could hardly believe his eyes.

It was incredible, made even more so since the information came from within the Vatican itself. Gathered by the Entity.

Straight from the curia.

The word *curia* meant "court," but in the sense of a royal court, not a court of law. Its principal departments consisted of the Secretariat of State, nine congregations, three tribunals, five councils, and eleven offices and commissions. Together they were the administrative apparatus of the Holy See, its civil service, acting in the pope's name, with his authority, providing a central, governing organization. Without it, the church could not function. Popes loved to both complain about, and tinker with, the curia.

But rarely had it changed.

It was presently controlled by the Apostolic Constitution *Pastor bonus,* issued by John Paul II in 1988, later revised by Francis I.

The waiter arrived with his rabbit stew in a thick-sided crockery bowl, leaving it, along with a basket of warm bread and another glass of wine. He took a moment and enjoyed the stew's aroma, remembering the way his mother would make the same dish. She'd spend Friday evenings searching for the best rabbit, killing it herself, then dressing and chopping the carcass, marinating the meat with red wine. He and his brother would watch the preparations with fascination, standing on their tiptoes, peering over the counter.

And the sounds.

They'd stayed in his psyche.

The basso tick of a clock hanging on the kitchen wall. The deep bongs of distant church bells. The water boiling. The snap of bone.

Saturday morning the house would wake to the smell of garlic as the stew simmered. He knew all of her ingredients by heart. Tomato passata, olive oil, sugar, bay leaves, carrots, potatoes, peas.

A wondrous mix.

He enjoyed a spoonful of what sat before him.

Not bad.

The restaurant prepared an admirable stew, but it was nothing like what his mother had created.

He missed those weekends.

Before the orphanage. Where there'd been no stew.

No mother.

Spagna was right. He had become a thief and a liar. Why didn't the mother superior do something? Why had she allowed it to happen? He didn't for a moment believe God had intervened, sending him off to the seminary and a new life. Faith was not something he'd ever totally embraced. Odd for a cardinal. But he could not help it. Fate was more his style. His life had been a series of fateful events, each one sending him along a seemingly predetermined path to this moment. Had he messed up with the last pope? Absolutely. But what did he have to feel bad about? According to what he'd just read, the Holy See seemed riddled with thieves and liars, too.

He kept eating.

The Roman Catholic Church carried the distinction of being the oldest continuous human institution in the world. It could deal with just about anything except the unexpected—and a pope dying in an instant certainly fit into that category.

Popes came in cycles of young and old.

A young Pius XII, then an old John XXIII. A vibrant Paul VI, followed by the frail John Paul I. The lion John Paul II, succeeded by the elder placeholder Benedict XVI. The pattern stretched back centuries, rarely varying. The last Vicar of Christ, now lying in the crypt beneath St. Peter's, had been older. His reign had been intended to be short, about a decade, giving other challengers the time to amass support. The longest-serving pope remained the first. Peter. Some said thirty-four, others thirty-seven years. Nobody really knew. So if history were to be trusted, the next pope would be younger, lingering longer, potentially having a greater impact.

He liked that he would not have to disrupt the natural cycle.

He finished the stew and the waiter returned to carry away the dishes. He asked for more wine, which was poured. The young man had no idea who he was serving. He liked how he could move about the world with anonymity. Few outside of the Vatican knew or cared that he existed. And who was he anyway? Just a priest from a rock in the Mediterranean who'd risen to great stature, only to have it all stripped away. Thankfully, they could not take his red hat. Nor the friends he'd made. Men who remained in positions of power and influence and who would shortly be looking for a leader.

There'd been Greek, Syrian, African, Spanish, French, German, and Dutch popes. One Englishman, a single Pole, two laymen, and a ton of Italians. All were either nobles, former slaves, peasants, or aristocracy. Never, though, had there been a Portuguese, Irish, Scandinavian, Slovak, Slovenian, Bohemian, Hungarian, or American pope.

Nor a Maltese.

Thankfully, that blood vessel suddenly rupturing would limit the cardinals' time for scheming. And make no mistake, cardinals schemed. The whole idea of sealing them away had been to limit the opportunities for bribery and shorten the time for deal making. The Latin root of the word *conclave* meant "a room that can be locked up."

That meant few cardinals would be prepared for the coming battle. Thankfully, it appeared he would not be one of those.

He glanced down at the plastic binder.

Thank God one truth remained inviolate.

Powerful men wanted only one thing.

To keep their power.

CHAPTER SIXTEEN

Cotton took a suite at Rome's Hotel d'Inghilterra, on the top floor with a balcony that ran the length of the building, spring geraniums bursting from its planters. He was being paid top dollar, so, as with the Alfa Romeo, he decided to splurge. He sat on the bed and stared out the terrace doors. Golden blocks of sunshine washed in through the clear glass. Beyond the railing stretched the city's trademarked irregularly shaped roofs, with their gnarled pipe vents and ceramic-crowned chimneys, satellite dishes the only nod to the 21st century.

He'd flown south with Sir James Grant in a private jet, the trip a quick seventy minutes, during which he'd learned little more about what was happening. Their talks had been about books and world affairs. Along the way he'd confirmed a transfer of one hundred thousand euros into his Danish account. Not that the Brits didn't have credit with him. It was just always better to be paid in advance.

He needed a shower and a change of clothes, so he took advantage of the hotel's amenities, the spacious bathroom an amalgam of shiny marble and mirrors. He'd chosen the Inghilterra not only for its reputation but also for its location. It sat only a short distance away from the Via Condotti, the most popular shopping street in Rome, an endless panorama of high-end clothes, leather, silver, glass, jewelry, and stationery. Also on the Via Condotti, at number 68, sat the Palazzo di Malta.

In 1798, when the Hospitallers were tossed from Malta by Napoleon, they wandered the world searching for a home. Finally in 1834 they found one in Rome. Two villas, one here, the other—Villa del Priorato di Malta—a few miles away atop Aventine Hill. About an acre and a half of territory between the two, both independent, holding allegiance to no one, a Roman Catholic country unto itself, making up the smallest sovereign nation in the world.

On the flight south he'd also made use of the onboard WiFi, learning as much as possible about the Hospitallers. Incredibly, they still existed, over nine hundred years after their founding. They were governed by a chapter general of the membership that met once every five years to choose a sovereign council of six members and six high officers who administered things on an everyday basis. The grand master supervised it all, elected for life, holding the rank of cardinal but with no conclave vote for pope. No longer warrior-monks, today they were a quiet, pious, humanitarian organization supporting international health care, operating war zone refugee camps, caring for South American slum children, treating leprosy in Africa and Asia, managing first-aid clinics in the Middle East, running blood banks, ambulance services, soup kitchens, and field hospitals worldwide. Their help was extended to all, regardless of race, creed, or religion. Membership, though, came by invitation only, with a current roster of over thirteen thousand men and women divided into two classes of knights and dames. Protestants, Jews, Muslims, and divorced people were not allowed. More than 40 percent of the members were connected in some way with Europe's oldest Catholic families. Over one hundred thousand people worked for the organization, 80 percent of those volunteers.

Fifty-five members, though, were special.

Knights of Justice.

Professed men who took religious vows of poverty, chastity, and obedience, they were the last remnants of the former Hospitallers. They were also its ruling class, holding all of the important positions of power.

The order itself was impressive.

One hundred and four countries maintained formal diplomatic relations, including an exchange of embassies. It possessed its own constitution and actively operated within fifty-four nations, having the ability to transport medicine and supplies around the world without customs inspections or political interference. It even possessed observer status in the United Nations, issuing its own passports, license plates, stamps, and coins. Not a country, as there were no citizens or borders to defend, more a sovereign entity, all of its efforts focused on helping the sick and protecting its name and heritage, which members defended zealously.

But the knights were troubled.

Big time.

He'd read several news accounts from *L'Osservatore Romano* about recent internal strife. Major stuff. The now deceased pope had even been drawn into a civil war within the knights' hierarchy that involved a cardinal, Kastor Gallo, and the grand master, a Frenchman. Gallo served as the Vatican envoy to the knights, a largely ceremonial post with supposedly little to no influence, there *to promote the spiritual interests of the Order, its members, and its relations with the Holy See.* But Gallo had interjected himself into the order's internal affairs. The dispute centered on an obscure Hospitaller program that had distributed condoms in certain parts of the world to help with the combat of sexually transmitted diseases and AIDS. Problem was, that conflicted with clear Vatican policy forbidding the use of contraception. Gallo used that error to drive a wedge between the grand master and the pope, forcing the former's resignation. That led to conflict among the professed knights, compelling the fifty-six to choose sides. They'd split almost fifty–fifty over the issue. Half supporting their grand master, the other half disagreeing. The pope had tried to counter the chaos, ordering a reversal of the grand master's resignation, but that effort failed. And though fighting among themselves, the knights had collectively resented both the pope's and Gallo's interference. One article from a few months back made the point crystal clear.

The Holy See has a unique relationship with the knights in that the pope appoints a cardinal patron to promote amicable relations between the Order and the Vatican. Cardinal Gallo was chosen for that position, after the pope removed him as head of the Vatican's supreme court. But Gallo and the pope have never been friends. In fact, Gallo has emerged as one of the pope's top critics and the Knights of Malta have now found themselves in the middle of that dispute. In an extraordinary rebuke of both Gallo and the pontiff, the Hospitallers said that the replacement of its grand master was an "act of internal governmental administration of the Sovereign Order of Malta and consequently falls solely within its competence. The Holy See, or any representative thereof, has no say in such matters."

The whole thing seemed a nasty business.

But he assumed that boys would be boys, politics the same everywhere.

According to other newspaper reports, there'd recently been a wholesale purge within the knights, with many of the highest-ranking officers replaced and the entire organization still reeling from the turmoil. Everyone seemed to be awaiting the next pope for guidance, as the current Vicar of Christ had died before the dust had fully settled. What remained unclear, at least to Cotton, was how a squabble within a modern-day charitable organization, albeit one nine hundred years old, had become a security concern of the United Kingdom.

Cotton entered the Palazzo di Malta, a tall archway opening from the street and draining into an enclosed courtyard lined with parked cars, mainly black Mercedes coupes, each with a similar license plate.

SMOM, followed by a single number.

Sovereign Military Order of Malta.

A giant eight-pointed, white Maltese cross adorned the dark cobbles. The buildings around him rose three stories, all of the windows shuttered and closed. James Grant had told him that this was the Hospitallers' main administrative headquarters—its magisterial palace, the seat of the grand master and where the sovereign council convened.

Waiting for him was a man, looking prim in a three-buttoned, dark suit. Cotton had worn only a pale-blue button-down with the sleeves rolled up, khaki trousers, and loafers. Seriously underdressed. But at least he was showered and shaved. Grant had called ahead and secured the necessary clearances to allow him into the courtyard. He was right on time and a little surprised at the lack of security, but the whole place was the definition of low-key. Only a small plaque on the wooden gates at the archway denoted who occupied the building.

He approached the man in the suit. "I'm Cotton Malone. I have an appointment."

The man bowed his head in a timid indication of welcome. "I was sent to meet you."

He wondered about the courtesy. "Is that customary?"

"Only for visitors that MI6 asks us to accommodate, on short notice."

He caught the unshielded wave of irritation that floated across the words. "Are you aware of why I'm here?"

"Definitely. May I see it?"

He fished the ring from his pocket and displayed it.

"Quite a special piece of jewelry," the man said.

"Care to offer more?"

Both arms were withdrawn from behind the man's back to display his right hand. On one finger he saw an identical ring with the same palindrome of five words.

"It's a badge," the man said. "From another time. A responsibility that is no longer relevant."

"And yet I retrieved this one and you're still wearing one. Two in a single day—from something, as you say, that is no longer relevant."

No reply.

"Are you a knight?" he asked.

"I am."

"Professed?"

The guy nodded. "You're familiar with us?"

"Actually, I knew little to nothing about you until a couple of hours ago. And I still know zero about this ring."

He displayed it again for the man to see.

"Where exactly did you get it?" the man asked.

He'd come here for answers, and to receive, sometimes you gotta give. "Off a dead man."

"Did he have a name?"

"MI6 is working on supplying one. He carried no identification." He found his cell phone and showed a head shot of the corpse that Grant had sent. "One of yours?"

"I'll find out. Can you provide me with this photo?"

"Absolutely. Do I get to speak with the grand master?"

"We don't have one at present. Only a lieutenant ad interim. A temporary replacement. We're awaiting the conclave and a new pope before choosing a permanent leader."

He'd read earlier that grand masters were elected by the professed knights, in secret. But before they assumed office, the election had to be communicated in writing to the pope. That, of course, presupposed that a pope existed.

"Do I get to speak with the lieutenant ad interim?" he asked.

The man nodded. "He's waiting for you." Then he motioned at the stone stairway to their right. "Follow me, please."

Twelve years he worked for the Magellan Billet. Stephanie Nelle had recruited him straight out of the navy and he'd come with little to no training, learning everything on the job. Along the way he'd acquired a set of instincts that kept him alive and allowed him to quit on his own terms, retiring early, able to buy a bookshop in Denmark, fulfilling a lifelong dream. One of those instincts had flared earlier in Milan when James Grant so easily agreed to double his fee. Another arose when the money was promptly paid. Now a third festered with the bad vibes he was receiving from this emissary. Luckily, this was not his first briar patch, and he knew how to walk among thorns.

He approached the stairs, his host two steps beyond.

"By the way," he said, "what's your position with the knights?"

"I have several titles, one of which involves providing security for the organization. I help make sure everyone and everything stays safe."

The words were delivered with a confidence that came from being dressed in a shirt and tie. But they made sense. He assumed an outfit as large as the Hospitallers had a need for security.

They climbed the stairs.

He heard the distinctive thump of rotors beating through air.

A helicopter. Close by and coming closer.

"What's that?" he asked.

"Your transportation."

CHAPTER SEVENTEEN

LUKE CLIMBED OUT OF THE *GUVA*.

Laura followed him, also using the rope. He caught her ease of technique and the fact that she barely needed a second breath from the effort. His original assessment seemed correct. She was in terrific shape.

He saw he was standing in an underground chamber, the walls more rough stone, the floor dank earth. Bright bulbs enclosed within metal cages lined the low ceiling and hurt his eyes. A door led out to a lit passageway beyond.

"These tunnels are from the knights," she said. "They burrowed like groundhogs under the city. They were mainly for water delivery and sanitation. But they also served as a way to move men and weapons around unnoticed. Miles of them still exist. During World War II the Maltese hid from the German bombers down here. Some are cleared and easy to get to. Others, not so much. This complex, and the *guva,* are known only to the government."

She started for the exit. The tunnel beyond seemed to go on forever. He didn't move. She stopped and turned back toward him, noticing his hesitation.

"You know what I want," he said to her.

She stood her ground. "I wouldn't press things. I'm not happy about having a partner. This does not involve the Americans in any way."

"Except for the fact that I'm now in on this."

"Only because Stephanie Nelle sent you here. Now my boss says you're to stay in."

"From what I hear, you don't take orders all that well."

"I do my job."

Something wasn't making sense. "Why did you call Stephanie in the first place?"

"To tell her that you were an idiot. Vatican intelligence made you the minute you hit this island."

"Why didn't you just say that to her?"

She shrugged. "I can take a hint. She clearly did not want my help. So I didn't offer anything."

"Did the Entity know I was coming here?"

"If it'll make you feel better, yes, they did."

She had an intensity in her eyes, a shade of brown that came close to blackness. She also had a wonderful square jaw that suggested tenacity.

Which he liked.

"Look," she said. "Contrary to what the faithful think, a conclave is not run by the Holy Spirit. Nothing from heaven comes down and inspires those old men on how to vote. The church was created by men and is run by men. It's men who will elect the pope. That means things can go wrong. Our focus is Kastor Gallo, the *kappillan* from Malta."

He smirked. "I don't speak Maltese spy language."

"A priest, who went on to become a bishop, a cardinal, then a total pain in the ass. He's caused a lot of problems, made a lot of enemies. Now he's making a play for the papacy."

"Who wants to stop him?"

"Hell if I know. It only matters to me because my boss says it does. Our problem is that Kastor Gallo is a lot of things, but he's not stupid. Unfortunately, you are. And thanks to you, he now knows he's being watched."

She was right. He'd definitely screwed things up by being made, and she was obviously pissed. He would be, too, if the roles were reversed. So he decided to lighten things up. "It's not all that bad. Who knows, you might learn something from this joint operation."

She shook her head. "Like how to be caught listening in on a conversation?"

"You don't back off, do you?"

"No, I don't. I have a job to do, and the clock is ticking. Right now we have to get ahead of Gallo." She shook her head. "I was supposed to observe and report. Simple and easy. But now, thanks to your interference, we have to change things up. I have less than one day left to deliver. And unlike you, I always deliver."

Her voice came low and throaty and strangely erotic. But it also held an odd quality, like she was trying to earn the trust of a small dog only to strangle it once she held it in her arms.

No matter.

He decided to quit pushing.

"For the record," he said, "there are a zillion people out there on the streets of Valletta. I had no way of knowing the Entity was on me."

"Your problem is you don't know the players. A little local knowledge goes a long way. I'm assuming that's why they now want us together."

"All you had to do was say that to Stephanie in the first place."

She tossed him a grin. "Okay. I'll give you that one. But I was hoping to leave you out there on the water."

Finally. The truth.

Which made sense.

He glanced around. "How do we get out of here?"

"Down that tunnel is a staircase up."

"Then what?"

"We have an appointment to keep."

CHAPTER EIGHTEEN

KASTOR CONTINUED TO READ.

Spagna had apparently been thorough with his investigation, especially with regard to the tradition known as Peter's Pence.

The alms of St. Peter were donations made directly to Rome, rather than to local parishes. It started back in the 9th century when the English king Alfred collected a pence from landowners as financial support for the pope. The practice eventually spread across Europe before fading with the Reformation. Pius IX, in 1871, brought it back but changed its purpose. No longer was the money solely for the pope's exclusive use—now it was spent to help the poor worldwide. The collection was taken each year, in all churches, on the feast of Saints Peter and Paul. Nobody outside the curia really knew exactly how much was acquired annually.

Except Spagna.

There is a serious and continual problem with the Peter's Pence collections. Currently, the annual total is between €200 and €250 million. Last year, the Holy Father called on each Catholic to be a witness of charity. He encouraged them to "open your eyes and see the misery of the world, the wounds of our brothers and sisters who are denied their dignity, and let us recognize that we are compelled to heed their cry for help." According to the Vatican's own website, the Peter's Pence collection "unites us in solidarity to the Holy See and its works of charity to those in need. Your generosity allows the pope to respond to our suffering brothers and sisters." Nothing could be further from the truth. Over the course of the past five years, 78% of what was collected through Peter's Pence has been used to fund budgetary deficits within the Holy See. These deficits were the direct result of the waste, fraud, and abuse, as is detailed in this summary report. A select group of cardinals are privy to both the false advertising and the misappropriation of Peter's Pence. No less than four cardinals are involved in the deception.

He could barely contain himself.

So many of the pompous, arrogant red vultures, as Spagna called the cardinals, had reveled in his demise. Yet apparently some of them were guilty of the most heinous of crimes. What many had suspected for decades, himself included, now seemed confirmed.

Corruption ran rampant in the curia.

In fact, it appeared to be institutionalized.

Worse yet, the ones in charge seemed intent on both covering it up and keeping it going.

Contrary to what people thought, the pope's word was not absolute when it came to running the church. The curia had existed for over a thousand years, and during that time it had perfected the art of survival. The system was so entrenched, so convoluted, that no one had ever successfully mounted any meaningful reform. Popes of late had tried, John Paul I and Francis I the most notable. Both failed. And one, Benedict XVI, resigned in frustration over making changes, as they would have entailed firing many of his longtime friends. Tales of internal investigations and secret audits had long run rampant. Francis had even empowered two so-called independent commissions to both investigate the abuses and recommend changes, but nothing ever materialized.

Which, again, was no surprise.

The curia were experts in procrastination and misdirection. Magicians extraordinaire. As Spagna had just confirmed, two sets of records and fanciful accounting were commonplace. So adept were they, even pressure from the pope himself could be deflected. Why? Because in the end, a pope needed the curia. It took people to run a multibillion-euro enter-prise and, as wasteful as it may be, the curia kept the Holy See going. Sim-ilar to the Allies after World War II who held their noses and made use of ex-Nazis all across Germany. Not the best choice, just the only choice.

He needed to finish the final few pages.

So he turned his attention back to the summary.

There is an incident that illustrates precisely the level and ex-tent of the current abuses. One cardinal, the beneficiary of a free apartment located close to Vatican City, wanted to expand his liv-ing space. When his neighbor, an elderly priest granted a rent sub-sidy for health reasons, was hospitalized, the cardinal commissioned renovations and broke through a wall between the two apart-ments, appropriating additional living space, even to the extent of retaining the elderly priest's furniture. Once discharged from the hospital, the priest discovered the intrusion. But there was nothing he could do. No one within the Holy See would challenge the cardinal. The priest died a short time later (which is why the inci-dent remained quiet) and that cardinal still has possession of his enlarged, rent-free apartment.

He rattled through his brain trying to put a name to the anonymous cardinal. He knew of several who lived in and around the Vatican. No matter who it might be, he was going to enjoy destroying that man.

Another curious anomaly has been discovered. John Paul I died in September 1978, after only thirty-three days as pope. But there exists within the Vatican bank an account bearing his name that cur-rently has €110,000 on deposit. Even more curious, there has been continuous activity within that account to this day. One cardinal's name is associated with that activity. There are at least eight other accounts associated with deceased persons where unexplained fi-nancial activity is occurring. The best explanation points to insti-tutionalized theft and embezzlement.

Then there is the process of sainthood where corruption appears to have risen to its greatest heights. The process of sainthood has been steeped in secrecy for centuries. To open a case for beatification a fee of €50,000 is currently charged. On top of that another €15,000 is required to offset "operating costs." These moneys go not only to the Holy See, but to pay the unreasonably high fees charged by expert theologians, doctors, and bishops who examine the proposed saint's cause. To that are added the costs for researchers, the drafting of the candidate's résumé, and the work of the postulator who champions the candidate's nomination. The average cost per sainthood candidate is nearly €500,000. But that is not all. At each point along the process there are festivities where prelates are invited to speak of the future saint's acts and miracles. Gifts are routinely provided to those prelates, which is in addition to the above-detailed expenses. In the end, the total cost to become a saint ranges somewhere between €600,000 and €750,000.

To illustrate the extent of this massive revenue stream, under John Paul II, 1,338 anointed blessed and 482 saints were named. The amount of moneys generated from these 1,820 accounts topped €1 billion. Incredibly, in 1983, John Paul II ordered that all of those moneys were to be managed, not by the Church but by the individual postulators, who were instructed to keep "regularly updated ledgers" on every single potential saint, detailing where all moneys collected were spent. But no oversight on these outsiders was ordered. No audits were ever performed. The postulators operated outside the Holy See with a free hand, one that still exists today. Needless to say, their misuse of over a billion euros exceeds the scope of this summary. But I am privy to their corruption and embezzlement, which is massive, all occurring under the watchful eye of at least six current cardinals, who have also secretly shared in those proceeds.

He stopped reading, astonished by the hypocrisy. What arrogant, pompous, lying thieves. Never once had he stolen from the church. No gratuities. No free trips. No special gifts, as he knew some of the cardinals called that patronage. Nothing. Odd, since Spagna was right. In his youth he'd been vastly different. Stealing had been common. But the older he became, the less physical things mattered. He was after something far more alluring. More satisfying.

Absolute power.

The café's courtyard remained empty. The time was approaching 4:00 P.M. He nursed a third glass of wine, his thoughts a whirlwind of confusion. He had no doubt that every allegation Spagna had made could be proven. The Entity would know how to follow money trails, how to sniff out dummy accounts and fraud, how to break through walls of secrecy and learn who was controlling what and how much.

Everything he'd read was true.

That was the whole point of passing it on. As was the lack of names. Not a single offender had been identified. This had been designed to merely whet his appetite.

And it succeeded.

Movement to his right caught his attention.

From the shadows he saw Arani Chatterjee, who entered the courtyard and calmly walked over and sat at the table uninvited.

"I see I was easy to find."

"Your love of this place is noted in our files." Chatterjee pointed. "Did you read it?"

He nodded. "Does he have the proof?"

"Oh, yes." Chatterjee reached into his pocket and produced a flash drive. "It's all on here. Audio recordings, documents, records scans, bank statements, surveillance reports. Every detail on every allegation, along with the name of every offender. Quite a list of bishops, monsignors, and cardinals, I'm told, most of whom should go to jail. Thankfully for them, the Holy See has no prisons."

He could only imagine that list of names. It had to include the heads of the Institute of Religious Works, a fancy label for the Vatican Bank, which controlled all of the church's financial assets. Also the *Amministrazione del Patrimonio della sede Apostolica,* which maintained the real estate holdings. The Governorate, which managed the museums and all of the for-profit commercial activities like the retail shops and stores. Along with the Prefecture for the Economic Affairs of the Holy See that oversaw every Vatican office. Those were the big four, and the cardinals currently managing them came from around the world. Chile, Honduras, the United States, India, Germany, the Congo, Australia. Not a one of them had ever lifted a finger to help him.

They would all go down.

But only after they voted for his papacy.

Every damn one of them would write his name on their ballot.

"What does Revelation warn?" Chatterjee asked. "That a corrupt church sits on the city of seven hills?"

Which is what Rome had long been called.

"And its corruption will grow and finally be destroyed," Chatterjee added, repocketing the flash drive.

All well and good, but, "I need to know what Spagna wants in return for this—invaluable—help."

"Right now? Simply that you find the *Nostra Trinità*. As he told you, he wants that secured. He understands that you want to use it to make you pope. If the legends are to be believed, it might have a certain value. But seventeen hundred years have passed since its creation. What you just read, though, is more immediate and has a far greater value. So he wants a trade. Let him have the Trinity, and you get all that,"—Chatterjee pointed at the pages—"plus the flash drive."

"Will he destroy the *Nostra Trinità*?"

"Absolutely."

He didn't necessarily disagree with that course. That had been his intention, too. Once he achieved the papacy, the last thing he'd want was for anything to cast doubt.

"Also," Chatterjee said, "after an appropriate time, no more than ninety days beyond your coronation, you will make the archbishop a cardinal. He wants to die with a red hat on his head."

"He doesn't seem to like the 'red vultures.'"

"He despises them. But he still wants to be one."

"He's a bit old."

"You will likewise appoint him head of the Entity, dismissing the current cardinal who oversees that department. He's no friend of the archbishop's and, by the way, no friend of yours, either."

"Making Spagna a cardinal will raise a lot of questions."

"So? Only a pope chooses a cardinal and that is not subject to question or review. It's solely your decision. And no secret appointments. This one is all public."

It was almost like this demon was reading his mind. Popes had the power to name cardinals *in pectore,* in the breast, with only the pope knowing of the appointment, *in his heart.* But *in pectore* cardinals could only function after the appointment became public. In modern times it had been used to protect an appointee from hostile political situations in places like China, Ukraine, Latvia, and Russia. Once the pope made the appointment public, the secret cardinal would then assume his duties and be ranked within the cardinalate back to the time of his selection. However, if a pope died before revealing the *in pectore* cardinal, the appointment died, too.

"John Paul II gave Archbishop Spagna an *in pectore* appointment, but died before revealing it," Chatterjee said. "Not this time. He wants the red hat and the investiture ceremony. He wants all of the red vultures to be there and watch as he joins their ranks. The one thing you and he agree on is a mutual hatred of the curia."

For so long the taste of failure had lingered in his mouth. Becoming pope would, in one stroke, regain everything he'd lost. He'd once said that the church's greatest sin of modern times was an unwillingness to become involved.

The sin of omission.

Popes had grown soft, their voices devoid of thunder.

He would change that.

He'd originally thought that what he sought might be the best weapon to use in the coming conclave to sway votes. Now it seemed only a means to a better end. And he had no problem with any of Spagna's demands.

But there were two things.

First—

"As head of the Entity, Spagna will do whatever I need done. No questions. No debate. Just do it."

"Of course, that goes without saying."

And second—

"What happened with the woman in the boat and the American parasailer?"

Chatterjee nodded. *"Alea jacta est."*

He grinned at the irony.

The die is cast.

CHAPTER
NINETEEN

COTTON FELT THE SWOOP AS THE HELICOPTER BEGAN TO DESCEND toward the Italian countryside. His greeter had led him to the top of the Palazzo di Malta, where a black-and-white AgustaWestland AW139 bearing civilian markings had landed on a small pad. He'd been under the mistaken impression that the interim grand master would be at the palazzo. Instead he'd been informed that the lieutenant ad interim waited at Villa Pagana, a seaside residence in Rapallo, about 250 miles to the north.

Evening was approaching, the late-afternoon sun hanging solemn in the western sky. Being transported a long way from Rome only raised more red flags in his already suspicious mind. True, the pessimist might be right in the long run, but he'd come to know that the optimist had a better time along the way. So he decided to keep an open mind.

He stared down at Rapallo, which looked like a typical seaside Italian town. An amphitheater of hills faced the sea supporting a jumble of white-washed houses with red-tile roofs that funneled downward to a stark stretch of sandy beach. A promenade lined the shore, flanked by a small castle. Boats and yachts rolled at anchor in the blue waters of the Ligurian Sea.

The chopper came in low over the shoreline and flew inland, angling toward one of the villas, an impressive three-story battlement of ocher

stone, set among a thick stand of maritime pines dominating a rocky promontory. A red flag with a white Maltese cross flew above its parapets.

"The villa was built in the 1600s," his escort told him. "But it has only
been the summer residence of the grand masters since the 1950s."

They sat in a comfortable rear compartment, free of vibration, with
black leather seats and enough insulation that their voices could be heard
over the rotors.

He glanced out the window and noticed the manicured grounds,
dotted with cacti, palm trees, and a carpet of flowers. At the promontory's
tip he spotted a ruined fortification. A small grassy clearing not far from
the house seemed to serve as a landing pad, and the pilot eased the helicopter down to a gentle stop.

A black Mercedes coupe waited beyond the wash of the blades, and he
followed his host to the car. In the backseat, across from him, sat a broad-
shouldered man with neatly combed dark hair. He was clean-featured with
a hard, lanky build. He sat straight with a military bearing, his jaw stretched
forward, the face as bland as milk. As with his escort from Rome, this one
wore a three-buttoned dark suit and striped tie, a pale-blue handkerchief
providing a discreet contrast of color at the top of the breast pocket.

"I'm Pollux Gallo, the lieutenant ad interim."

No hand was extended to shake, but his host did offer a slight smile of
welcome.

"Cotton Malone. Sir James Grant sent me."

The car drove across the grass and found a paved drive, heading away
from the villa.

"Where are we going?"

"To obtain the answers you seek."

He'd immediately noticed the ring on Gallo's right hand. He found
the one he'd taken from the dead man in his pocket.

"I was briefed by the British on what happened to you earlier today,"
Gallo said. "They told me about that ring. I believe I can shed some light
on the matter."

"Were you shown a photo of the dead man?"

Gallo nodded. "He's not one of us. But we've seen these copied rings
before. There are jewelry stores across France and Italy that sell them. The

palindrome is called a Sator Square, after the first word in the line of five. It has existed for a long time, with Roman origins."

"Why is a Maltese cross inside?"

Gallo shrugged. "A good question."

"I bet the one on your finger has a cross inside it, too. My guess is those copycats don't have that addition."

Finally a slight rise of the eyebrows signaling irritation. Good. This guy needed to know that he wasn't dealing with an amateur.

He'd always hated funerals and only attended them when absolutely necessary. His first had been as a teenager, when his grandfather died. His own father disappeared when he was ten, lost at sea in a navy submarine. As a teenager, he and his mother moved back to Georgia and lived on the family's onion farm. He and his grandfather grew close, and eventually seeing the old man in that coffin had hurt more than he'd ever imagined. He also remembered the funeral director. A dour man, not much different in looks and bearing from the statue sitting across from him, uttering predictable words.

So he told himself to stay alert.

"In 1957," Gallo said, his voice lowered, "a trial occurred in Padua, Italy, where some of the partisans involved in the 1945 disappearance of Mussolini's gold were prosecuted. Rumors had been rampant for years of how the gold might have been kept by the locals. Twelve years of investigation led to thirty-five defendants being charged with theft. Three hundred witnesses were subpoenaed. The trial was expected to last eight months, but was abruptly halted by the presiding judge after only twenty-six witnesses testified. It never reconvened and no further official inquiry was ever made into the gold's disappearance. The presiding judge at that trial resigned his post in 1958. Interestingly, afterward he lived a posh life in a villa. That judge's grandson was the man killed this morning. The owner of the villa by Lake Como."

"Obviously, the judge was paid off."

"I have no idea. I can only tell you what happened. We know that, on April 25, 1945, Allied forces were less than fifty miles from Milan. Mussolini called an emergency meeting of his cabinet and told them he was fleeing north to Switzerland. He then ordered what was left of the Italian treasury brought to the cabinet meeting. It consisted of gold ingots, currency, and the Italian crown jewels. He distributed the cash and jewels among his ministers and ordered them to leave the city with their caches. He kept the gold, some of the currency, and a few of the jewels. The best estimate is that about a hundred million U.S. dollars' worth, in 1945 values, came north with him. Most of the currency would be worthless today. But the gold and jewels are another matter. Surely worth over a billion euros in today's value."

That was indeed an impressive treasure.

"Which answers your question," Gallo said. "The Italian justice system leaves a lot to be desired. Corruption is common. There is little doubt that judge was bribed. But again, we'll never know the truth, as the matter was not investigated. But part of that 1957 trial record consists of depositions detailing the inventory of two elephant-skin satchels, which were taken from Mussolini when he was captured. Both had the party's symbol etched on the outside. An eagle clutching a fasces."

One of which he'd held in his hands earlier.

"Both of those satchels disappeared," Gallo said. "They have not been seen since 1945. By 1960 nearly everyone associated with what had been found with Mussolini had either died or disappeared. Ever since, men have searched. Now, today, you apparently found one of the satchels."

They were following a two-lane switchback road that descended from the promontory. The man who'd brought him from Rome sat in the front passenger seat, a third man in another dark suit driving. Neither had spoken, or even acknowledged that there was someone else in the car.

"What do you know about the letters between Mussolini and Churchill?" he asked Gallo.

"I'm familiar with the speculation. The British have long believed Mussolini brought some, or all, of his correspondence with Churchill north during his escape attempt. That is a possibility. There was an emissary of ours present both in Dongo and at the villa where Mussolini and his mistress were kept the night before they died. Mussolini spoke of documents he had that the British might find embarrassing. He even offered them in return for safe passage out of Italy. But he did not elaborate on what those were and, by the time he spoke of them, they were no longer in his possession. The partisans had them in Dongo."

"Why was an emissary of the Hospitallers talking to Mussolini?"

"We wanted something he stole from us returned. We hoped he'd brought it north, too."

Cotton motioned with the ring. "Something like this?"

Gallo nodded. "One of these rings was involved. Taken from a professed knight whom Mussolini had ordered killed. We definitely wanted it returned."

He waited for more, but nothing was offered. So he tried something easier. "I need to know more about this ring."

"It represents a sect that once existed within our ranks called the *Secreti*. They date back to the Crusades and our time in Jerusalem, and they were a part of us in Rhodes and Malta. Only the highest-ranking knights were invited to join, their numbers small. For a long time not even the grand masters were privy to their activities. That was because grand masters only lived a few years, or even a few months. Many of them inept and corrupt. The *Secreti* lasted longer and kept true to their vows. They became a law unto themselves, trusting no one, using their own methods, their own rules, their own justice to keep the order's secrets safe. The only thing those men trusted was God. For all intents and purposes, though, they ended when Napoleon claimed Malta. The knights dispersed across the globe, our secrets going with them. They were formally disbanded just after World War II."

"Yet you, the guy in the front seat, and the dead man back at Como are all still wearing the ring."

Gallo smiled. The effort seemed almost painful. "Merely ceremonial, Mr. Malone. A hark back to another time. We Hospitallers are appreciative of the past. We like to recall it. And to answer your question from earlier, there is a Maltese cross etched inside my ring. But the *Secreti* no longer exist. Our rings are mere copies, made by a Roman jeweler. I can provide his name and address, if you like."

It all sounded so innocent, so correct, but nothing about this man rang right. Particularly annoying was the lowered voice, which seemed a means of ascendancy, a way to shrink others down and control the conversation.

"You're in temporary charge of the Hospitallers?" he asked.

Gallo nodded. "I was selected to fill the position after the grand master was forced to resign. We planned on making a permanent choice two weeks ago, but the pope's death changed that. We will convene after the conclave and select a new leader."

He was curious, "Your last name. Gallo. Any relation to Cardinal Gallo?"

"He is my brother."

Now that was convenient. From the media accounts he'd read the cardinal had wreaked havoc within the Hospitallers, essentially masterminding the grand master's ouster. Then his brother emerged as the temporary man in charge? What were the odds on that one? He also recalled what James Grant had wanted him to explore.

"I'm told that the knights have a fascination with Mussolini?"

Gallo gave a slight shake of his head. "Not a fascination. More a historical interest. But that is a private matter, one we don't discuss outside our ranks."

Exactly what James Grant had warned they would say.

His host shifted slightly in the leather seat. Enough that Cotton caught a glimpse of what he thought might be a shoulder holster beneath the suit jacket.

Intriguing.

Why did a professed man of God carry a weapon? True, Hospitallers were once warrior-monks, defending the honor of Christ and the church.

But not anymore.

They were now climbing a ridge on a second switchback road. The Ligurian Sea stretched toward the western horizon, looking pale and weary in the faint red glow of the setting sun. The lights of Portofino could be seen in the distance. Ahead, he spotted an irregular group of buildings, perched on a precipitous neck of stone, facing the water. They had a fortresslike character from the crenellated walls to the distinctive towers, and seemed more hacked by the wind and rain from the rock than human-made.

"We're headed for that monastery?" he asked Gallo.

"It was once a holy place. But we acquired the site about sixty years ago."

The car kept climbing.

"When we were forced from Malta by Napoleon," Gallo said, "we took some of our archives with us. They were stored in various places around Europe, sometimes not all that carefully. Finally we obtained this site, refurbished the old buildings, and consolidated everything. There is a small repository still on Malta, but the majority of our records and artifacts are kept here."

The car turned onto a short drive, then passed through an open gate into an enclosed courtyard. Floodlights lit the cobbles to reveal another huge white Maltese cross etched into their surface.

The Mercedes stopped.

"You should feel privileged," Gallo said.

"How so?"

"Few outside the knights are ever allowed here."

But he was not comforted by the honor.

THE KNIGHT LOWERED THE BINOCULARS.

His view of the old monastery, now an archival repository for the Knights of Malta, was unobstructed from his dark perch. He'd watched from the trees as the car entered the lit courtyard and Cotton Malone emerged.

He'd traveled south from Como at a leisurely pace with the elephant-skin satchel and its contents safe within his car. Before leaving Menaggio, he'd read all eleven letters between Churchill and Mussolini, learning enough of the details that he could now speak intelligently about them.

And he had.

Talking to the British by phone, informing them as to what he possessed, what he wanted, and learning what they desired in return.

Which had surprised him.

But it had been doable.

He glanced at his watch.

Time to go.

He had a meeting.

CHAPTER TWENTY

5:40 P.M.

LUKE STEPPED OUT OF THE BUILDING ONTO ONE OF VALLETTA'S QUIeter side streets. Actually, more an alley between two walls of stone. He saw traffic moving along perpendicular at either end. He'd followed Laura Price up from the tunnels into a basement full of wooden crates. Mostly wine. From the looks of things, it was some sort of storage room. She seemed to know her way around the nooks and crannies.

The evening was still warm from the sweltering day. They headed to one end of the alley. When he caught sight of the harbor he realized he was not far from his car. He'd always been blessed with a keen sense of direction. Numbers and names were tough to recall. Faces not much better. But where he'd been? That stuck with him.

"I need my phone," he told her. "It's in my car."

"Can't it wait?"

"No. It can't."

He led the way.

"Cardinal Gallo is currently in Mdina," she told him. "That's about twelve kilometers from here. The man who was on the Madliena Tower, Arani Chatterjee, is there in Mdina with him."

Good. He owed that SOB.

"Chatterjee likes to call himself an archaeologist, and he has credentials, but he's really just a grave robber, a dealer in stolen antiquities."

They kept walking.

People filled the sidewalks, most dressed in T-shirts, shorts, and sandals. A brisk breeze swept in from the sea like an invisible river.

One question bothered him. "Why is everyone in such a panic over this conclave?"

"Picking a pope is a big deal."

"Really? I hadn't realized."

She caught his sarcasm.

"That's not the only thing in play," she said. "Gallo came here to meet with an archbishop named Danjel Spagna."

That name he knew. "He manages the Entity. I assume that's unusual."

"To say the least."

He loved a good book and spent much of his mandatory downtime reading. History was a favorite subject. He especially enjoyed books that dealt with the intelligence business. The exploits of the Entity were legendary, dating back centuries. It had been involved in one way or another with Britain's Elizabeth I, France's St. Bartholomew's Eve Massacre, the Spanish Armada, the assassinations of a Dutch prince and a French king, the attempted assassination of a Portuguese ruler, the War of Spanish Succession, the French Revolution, Napoleon's rise and fall, Cuba's war against Spain, several South American secessions, the fall of Kaiser Wilhelm during World War I, Hitler in World War II, and communism in the 1980s.

An amazing résumé.

He recalled what Simon Wiesenthal, the famed Nazi hunter, once said. *The best and most effective espionage service in the world belongs to the Vatican.*

Now here he was, at odds with it.

Ahead, he spotted the small parking lot where he'd started this morning. He hurried over and found his phone inside the rental, along with his Beretta, which he tucked at the base of his spine beneath his shirt.

"You do know that it's illegal to carry a weapon on this island without a special permit, which they rarely grant," she said.

"It's also illegal to assault and kidnap somebody. But that didn't stop you."

"I had no choice."

Maybe. But he was still pissed about it.

"Don't let the local police see that gun. Agent or no agent, they'll arrest you, and I don't have time to get you out."

"Not a problem."

"We need to head toward central downtown."

He wondered if Stephanie Nelle had really approved this joint operation. His last instructions had been to get rid of Laura Price. He should call in, but he decided to give this little venture a bit more time and see where things led before bothering the boss.

A few minutes' walk and they found themselves on busy Republic Street, which ran from the southern city gate, past Freedom Square, to bastions at the water's edge. An impenetrable mass of people had taken possession of it, many surely from the cruise ships he'd seen earlier. Cars were obviously not allowed. The steady breeze sponged away what would surely be the cloying, musty smell of crowded humanity. The shops and eateries, lined one after the other like rabbit hutches, were all doing a brisk business. The co-cathedral and grand master's palace were closed, but the cobbled squares radiating from both were choked with visitors. Valletta seemed to be living up to its reputation as a popular tourist destination.

"Where are we going?" he asked.

But she did not answer him.

Instead they plunged into the chaos.

Among the crowd he spotted three uniformed police on Segways, one of whose gazes lingered a bit longer in their direction than it should. He might have dismissed it as paranoia, but that same officer found a handheld radio and started speaking into it. His gaze raked more of the faces around him and he spied another uniformed officer, on foot, who also stared their way just long enough to grab his attention.

"You catching this?" he said to her.

"I count four. They're definitely watching."

He liked that she was alert, aware of what was around her.

He surveyed the crowd again, his professional curiosity at its max. The nearest threat was fifty feet away, but the cops were situated in every direction, blocking the alleys radiating off Republic Street.

"I'll identify myself and deal with them," she said.

Seemed like the right course. One good guy to another. Surely she was known to the locals. There might be some animosity between law enforcement agencies, like back home, but in the end everyone tried to get along. What bothered him was that none of the police had approached. Instead they'd assumed a perimeter, held their positions, and used their radios.

Calling who?

"Stay here," she said.

Thirty yards away a blue-and-white police car turned out of one of the alleys, lights flashing, and inched its way through the pedestrian-only crowd toward the square that fronted the co-cathedral. From its front passenger side a man emerged. Tall, older, heavily built, with a mat of silver-white hair and white sideburns, dressed casually. He paused to look around and sniff the air, as if he knew someone was watching. He then found a cigar from his back pocket, snipped the end with a gold-colored guillotine, and lit the tip as he continued to survey the scene.

"Get out of here," she said, under her breath.

"You know that guy."

"That's Danjel Spagna. Get out of here."

Not his style to cut and run.

The officers were converging, all four closing the circle, coming straight for them.

Spagna blew a cloud of bluish smoke to the sky, then pointed with the cigar and called out, "Ms. Price. I need you and Mr. Daniels to come with me."

"I vote no," Luke said.

"Ditto."

"Two each?" he whispered.

"Absolutely."

He whirled and pounced on the officer closest, kicking him off the Segway. A second cop rushed forward, but Luke was a step ahead, planting his shoulder into the man's chest with a quick charge that lifted the guy off his feet, flinging him backward and down hard to the cobbles. Turning, he saw that Laura was not having the same success. One of her two targets had tackled her to the ground and the other, whom initially she'd managed to take down, had rebounded. Now they were subduing her. He could intervene, but it would only be another few moments before all four cops were up and in the mix and who knew how many more would arrive.

She'd been right.

One of them had to get out of here.

And he was elected.

He dissolved into the sea of people that had parted when the confrontation started, tucking his head and elbowing his way forward, layering bodies between him and trouble. He heard shouts behind him and managed a quick peek over his shoulder, seeing Laura being yanked to her feet and led toward the man she'd identified as Spagna. He escaped the crowd at its outer fringes and made his way down one of the alleys. No one was in pursuit. He ducked into a recessed doorway and found his cell phone, connecting to Stephanie's direct line. She answered and he filled her in on all that had happened, including the latest dilemma.

"Things have changed, Luke. I need you to work with Ms. Price."

"So you okayed this partnership?"

"I went along with it. Temporarily."

"Ordinarily I'd be a good little soldier and do exactly as you say. But I need to know what the hell is going on. I'm flying blind here."

"All I can say is that Danjel Spagna being there, in Valletta, is proof enough that something big is brewing. Earlier I thought Ms. Price just an irritant. Now we need her help. She has institutional knowledge that can speed things up for us."

Stephanie's tone was slow and even, just like in every crisis. That's what made her so good. She never lost her cool.

But he was beginning to lose his. "Spagna has her."

"You're a smart guy. Change that."

He started to toss her a wisecrack but he knew what she wanted to hear. "I'll make it happen."

"Good. I have a two-front war at the moment, and the other end is in big trouble."

The last thing he ever wanted was to add to her problems.

His job was to solve things.

"It's Cotton, Luke. He's walked into a hornet's nest."

CHAPTER TWENTY-ONE

COTTON CROSSED THE PAVED COURTYARD, FOLLOWING POLLUX Gallo into the monastery's refectory, a spacious room of plastered limestone blocks and a tile floor littered with workstations.

"We spent a lot of money refurbishing this complex," Gallo said. "It was nearly falling in on itself. Now it is the Conservatory of Library and Archives. A state-of-the-art facility."

And unknown to the world, Cotton silently added. But he assumed a lot about the Knights of Malta would fit into that category.

His original greeter from Rome had accompanied them inside, the driver remaining with the car. Waiting in the refectory were two brown-robed monks. Both were young and short-haired, with a no-nonsense glint in their eyes. Not exactly the religious type. They stood quiet and attentive.

"I thought this was no longer a monastery," he said.

"It's not, but these brothers are part of a contingent that maintains the archive."

Gallo motioned ahead and they left through a plank door in the far side, entering a lit cloister that led past former monk cells on one side and a garden on the other. Each of the cells was identified by a number and letter, the old wooden doors replaced with metal panels and keypad locks.

"Each room contains a different segment of our archives," Gallo said.

"We have everything cataloged and electronically indexed for easy reference. The rooms are also climate-controlled."

They rounded a corner and, on the far side of the cloister, entered a room through another metal door, this one open, taller and wider than the others. The space beyond was more like a hall, what had surely once been the chapter house. Wooden benches, where the monks had congregated, still lined the now painted stone walls. He noticed the irregular shape and the two central columns that supported arched ribs for the vaults, dividing the floor and ceiling into three bays. He also felt the change in temperature and humidity, both lower, which signaled sophisticated climate control. Wisely, a fire-suppression sprinkler system dotted the ceiling, exposed metal pipes connecting each faucet. Lighting spilled out from hanging opaque, glass balls that tossed off a warm glow. Stout oak tables stood in rows across the tile floor. On them sat manuscripts, ecclesiastical plates, pectorals, reliquaries, and crosses. His trained bibliophile eye focused on the manuscripts, where he spied chrysobulls, sigillia, and documents bearing holy seals. Glass domes protected each from any casual touch.

"We have around fifteen thousand manuscripts stored in the facility," Gallo said. "Most are originals and first editions. There are rare Bibles, the classics, scientific texts, dictionaries. We have a little of everything, but we've been collecting for nine centuries. This room houses a few of the items we occasionally allow visitors to see."

"Potential contributors?"

Gallo nodded. "It takes over two hundred million euros to keep the order solvent each year. Most comes from governments, the United Nations, and the EU. But we also depend on the generosity of private donors. So yes, this collection can sometimes be helpful in spurring their interest."

The two robed brothers at first waited outside but eventually followed them into the chapter house. His escort from Rome had lingered back in the refectory. He knew Gallo was probably armed, and on the walk over he'd noticed the distinctive bulge of a weapon holstered at the base of the spine beneath each of the two robes as well.

Nothing but trouble surrounded him.

Which seemed the story of his life.

"Why don't we dispense with coy," Gallo said. His host stood with the straight back of self-discipline. "The British have long wanted to see inside this archive. They've covertly tried several times. Now they've finally succeeded."

"With your permission, of course. You know full well I'm here on their behalf. And we didn't ask for this tour."

"They called and demanded to speak to me. They insinuated that my fellow knights were somehow involved with what happened to you earlier today at Lake Como. Murder. Theft. Burglary. I told Sir James Grant that he was mistaken."

But that was a lie. Too much here just didn't add up. Or more correctly, it added up to something that wasn't good. Here he was again among that great, swirling maelstrom of possibilities where his life hung in the balance. Parts of him detested and parts of him craved the conflict. For a dozen years he'd lived with that threat every day. Move. Countermove. All part of the game. But he'd retired out early in order to quit playing.

Yeah, right.

He stepped close to one of the tables and examined through a glass dome what was noted as a 13th-century gospel with an exquisite wooden cover and Moroccan leather binding. He guessed it had to be worth several hundred thousand dollars. He kept his eyes down on the artifact but began to ready himself. As a Magellan Billet agent, most of his mistakes had come when there was too much time to think. Act. React. Counteract. Doesn't matter. Just do something.

"Where are they?" he asked, continuing to focus on the old gospel, its cover darkened with age and infested with a fine spiderweb of cracks like an unrestored Rembrandt.

Gallo seemed to know exactly what he meant and motioned. One of the robes walked to the far side of the next row of tables and lifted the elephant-skin satchel from the floor. He gave it a quick glance, then returned to perusing the objects on the table before him, inching ever closer to the second robed monk.

"Who shot the guy in the villa?" he asked Gallo.

"Why does it matter? That man failed to do his job."

He faced his adversary. "Which wasn't to kill me or be captured. No. You wanted the British to know you were there."

"I did, but thankfully the ring led you straight here."

"Along with you hanging a guy by his arms pulled up behind his back."

"Which once sent fear down the spines of Saracens in the Holy Land."

That was a bold admission, which meant Gallo thought himself in control of the situation.

He returned to perusing the objects on the table. "These manuscripts are impressive."

"As a bookseller, I thought you might appreciate our collection."

"I do. Why are the Churchill–Mussolini letters so important to you?"

"They are a means to an end."

Only two things made sense. Either James Grant had no idea what was going on and he'd sent someone to find out. Or he had every idea and he'd sent that same someone so they would not come back.

He chose option two.

Which made his next course clear.

His target was now about four feet away, and the blankness of the young, robed man's gaze seemed almost like a warning. He stopped and admired another of the exquisite manuscripts under glass. He almost hated what he was about to do.

But what choice did he have.

Gallo's gun beneath his suit jacket was in easier reach than the ones the brown robes toted. He'd need a few seconds so, on the pretense of admiring the manuscript before him, he suddenly grabbed the heavy glass cover and hurled it toward Gallo. His left hand flew up in a back fist to the face of the brother standing beside him, followed by an elbow to the kidneys.

The guy went reeling.

He used that moment to part the robe and grab the man's weapon. He then kneed the guy in the face, sending him downward. The glass cover had hit Gallo, but he managed to deflect it away where it shattered across the hard floor. The other brother was reaching back for his gun.

So was Gallo.

He sent two bullets their way.

Both men disappeared beneath the tables.

He readjusted his aim and fired into the lighted glass fixtures hanging above him, exploding two of them in a burst of sparks and smoke. Gallo was rising back up, so he fired that way again, the round ricocheting off the top of the table. He exploded another fixture, which added more sparks and smoke.

Would it be enough?

An alarm sounded and the sprinklers erupted, called to action by the possibility of a fire. He upended the table before him, depositing the artifacts it displayed onto the wet floor, their glass domes bursting to shards. He left the thick oak top lying perpendicular to the floor, using it as a shield to block Gallo and the other robe from firing beneath the tables. He could now use that protected route to make his way toward the exit. Dropping down, he rolled across the tile, alternating between patches of dry and wet as he passed more tables and the aisles in between. Gallo would surely figure it out and change positions, but it would take a few seconds.

He had to make the most of the time he'd bought.

Three shots came his way, but the downed table continued to run interference. He scrambled up on all fours and hurried past the last row. Before coming to his feet he carefully peered over the top and saw Gallo and the other robe standing, guns ready, waiting for him to emerge.

Water continued to rain down.

The klaxon still sounded.

Shots came his way.

He decided to keep doing the unexpected and fired twice, once each into the clear domes on the tables where the two men stood. Glass exploded, shards spreading outward like seeds cast from a hand. Gallo and his acolyte reared back to avoid the projectiles. He used that moment to flee the chapter house, back into the cloister. He could retrace the route toward the refectory, but that was a long, open run and he wouldn't make it far without drawing fire. Neither could he escape left or right—the cloister would only become a shooting gallery. But a set of double plank doors about twenty feet away might offer refuge.

He raced toward them and the iron lock clicked open on the first try. He shoved the leaden oak door inward, then closed it gently, hoping his pursuers wouldn't notice.

There was no lock on the inside.

More incandescent fixtures lantern-lit a chapel, the interior spacious, an impressive gilded altar and sculpted statues casting ghostly images through the dim light. No one was in sight.

The fire alarm stopped.

He searched the darkness toward the altar and spotted stairs to the right. A pallid glow strained from below. He headed for them and descended into a crypt, a cold cloud of worry filling him. Was he simply heading down into a dead end? An iron gate opened into an ample, three-naved wide space. The ceiling was low-vaulted, a small rectangular altar niche to his right. Three medieval stone sarcophagi topped with immense slabs of carved granite lined the center. The only break in the darkness came from a tiny yellow light near the altar that illuminated a few square feet. The rest of the space remained in shadows, the air stale and fetid and noticeably chilly.

He heard the oak door opening above.

His eyes, alert and watchful, shot to the top of the low vault not two feet from the crown of his head.

Footsteps bounded across the marble floor.

He crept across the crypt into a far nave. His mind filled with anticipation, which he tried to suppress with a wave of self-control. He'd fired a lot of rounds in the chapter house, so he checked the gun's magazine.

Empty.

Great.

He needed something to defend himself with, so he searched the darkness. In a small apse about twenty feet away he spotted an iron candelabrum. He hustled over. The ornament stood about five feet tall, a solitary wax candle, about four inches thick, rising from the center. He grabbed the stem and noticed its weight. Solid. He brought both the candelabrum and candle with him as he assumed a position behind another of the pillars.

Someone started down the steps to the crypt.

He peered around the edge, past the tombs, through the blackness. The tiny altar light offered little assistance. His emotions alternated between fear and excitement, his body alive with a strange kind of energy, an unexplained power that had always clarified his thoughts. In the archway, at the base of the stairs, stood the outline of one of the robed brothers.

The silhouette crept in, gun leading the way.

He tightened his grip on the iron stem and cocked his arms back. He knew he had to draw the guy closer, so he ground the sole of his right shoe into the grit on the floor. A quick glance around the pillar confirmed that the man was now moving toward him. Shadows bobbed, swelled, then lessened on the ceiling. His muscles tensed. He silently counted to five, clenched his teeth, then lunged, swinging the candelabrum. He caught the guy square in the chest, sending the shadow back onto one of the Romanesque tombs. He tossed the iron aside and swung his fist hard to the face. The gun left the man's grip and rattled across the mosaics.

His pursuer shot up and pounced.

But he was ready.

A second facial punch and another to the midsection sent the man teetering. He then tripped the guy's feet out from under him, which allowed the head to pop the flagstones hard.

The man's body went still.

He searched the floor for the gun, finding it and curving his fingers around the butt just as another set of footsteps bounded down and into the crypt.

Two shots came in his direction.

Dust snowed down from the vault as bullets found stone. He sought cover behind the pillar, peered around the edge, and fired once. The bullet ricocheted off the far wall, a signal that he was armed and ready.

It seemed to get attention.

"There's no way out."

Gallo's voice, lashing across the chamber with an icy menace, from a position behind the farthest tomb.

Between him and the only exit was an armed man bent on killing him. But Gallo was pinned, too. No way for him to get back to the stairs without being shot, either. He needed to draw Gallo out, cause a mistake.

He glanced around and spotted the thick candle on the floor.

He reached down and took hold of it, then focused across the dim nave, determining that there was enough darkness for the candle to be mistaken for something else. So he arced the wax cylinder across the open space between the pillars, flipping it end over end, hoping the diversion would draw fire.

And it did.

As the candle passed midway, Gallo stepped out and fired.

Cotton leveled the pistol and pulled the trigger twice, both rounds finding Gallo's chest.

The man staggered back but did not fall. Gallo swung his weapon around, leveling the aim, and started firing. Cotton dove behind the pillar as bullets pinged off stone in all directions. He stayed close to the gritty floor, as there was a real danger of being hit by a ricochet.

The firing stopped.

He gave it a few more seconds, then came to his feet.

A quick glance toward the other side of the crypt and he saw no Gallo.

He heard the door above open.

Clearly he'd caught the guy solid with both rounds, which meant body armor beneath that tailored suit.

These knights came prepared.

He raced for the stairs and headed back to ground level. The chapel was empty. The oak door at the far end hung three-quarters closed. He approached and stared out into the cloister, catching a fleeting glance of Pollux Gallo on the opposite side, reentering the refectory. He headed after him but, by the time he arrived, Gallo was ninety seconds ahead and the refectory was empty.

A car cranked outside.

He bolted for the exterior door and opened it to see the Mercedes fleeing the courtyard through the main gate.

Gallo was gone.

CHAPTER TWENTY-TWO

THE KNIGHT ABANDONED HIS PERCH OVER THE MONASTERY AS Malone entered the refectory. He climbed into his car and drove away, heading inland along the Italian coast.

The pope dying so suddenly had changed everything. He'd always thought there'd be more time to prepare. But that was not the case. Everything was happening fast. Luckily, Danjel Spagna had entered the picture. Usually, the archbishop lurked only in the shadows, never surfacing, working through minions. But not here. Obviously, the Lord's Own wanted something, too. His presence both simplified and complicated things. But it was just one more challenge that would have to be met.

He kept driving, heading away from the archive.

The die was now cast. There was no turning back. Only going forward remained a viable option. The next forty-eight hours would determine everyone's future. As much planning as possible had been imparted.

Now he just needed a little luck.

He checked his watch.

7:40 P.M.

He'd spent the past few years preparing for this moment. So much reading. Studying. Analyzing. And it all came down to the one man who'd stared down the Roman Catholic Church and won.

Benito Amilcare Andrea Mussolini.

To his good fortune, Mussolini rose to power as the church's influence within Italy had begun to wane. No longer was it a political powerhouse. Pius XI wanted a reinvigoration and Mussolini wanted his rule legitimized by what had always been the most influential institution in Italy. To appease the pope and show the people his supposed graciousness, Il Duce negotiated the 1929 Lateran Treaty that finally recognized the full sovereignty of the Holy See over Vatican City.

Italians were thrilled with the concession.

So was Mussolini.

For the next nine years he enjoyed almost no interference from the Vatican, killing and torturing whomever he wanted. Even Catholics were harassed. Churches vandalized. Violence against clerics became commonplace.

He had free rein.

Finally, in 1939, Pius XI decided to make a public denunciation. A virulent speech was written, printed, ready to be delivered and distributed to the world.

Then Pius died.

All printed copies of the speech were seized and ordered destroyed by the Vatican secretary of state. No one ever heard or read a word of that papal repudiation. As was noted at the time, *not a comma* remained.

Three weeks later the man who accomplished that suppression became Pius XII. The new pope was suave, emollient, and devious. He immediately returned to the previously charted course of political appeasement, one that never directly confronted either Italy or Germany.

And the knight knew why.

The *Nostra Trinità*.

Which, by then, Mussolini either had in his possession, or knew where to find.

A fact that Pius XII well knew.

He was now beyond Rapallo along the coast.

Everything had led to this moment. He would now either succeed or die in the process. No third option existed. Not with the evils he was contemplating.

He stared out the windshield. A car waited ahead, its headlights off, a man standing outside in the blackness. He stopped his own vehicle, climbed out, and walked the ten meters over to where Sir James Grant waited alone. Somewhere, not far off, he heard the pound of surf on rock.

"Is Malone dead?" Grant asked.

"It's being handled right now. I saw its beginning myself."

"All this goes for naught if Malone leaves that archive unscathed."

He actually didn't give a damn about any threat Cotton Malone represented to Grant. He'd told his people to deal with it but, if problems arose, to withdraw and not take foolish risks. Malone was not his problem.

To this point he'd led what could only be described as a sedentary life, his battles nearly all intellectual and emotional. He'd patiently watched as others rose and fell in stature. He'd learned how desire could sometimes water down determination and that realization, more than anything else, explained his current irrevocable course. It had started this morning and continued when he spoke, by phone, with James Grant a few hours later. He'd made a bold move to secure the Churchill letters from that villa, then left three calling cards. The owner hanging by his arms. The ring on the dead knight's hand. And Cotton Malone still breathing. All three messages had been received, and Grant had made contact.

Now it was time to make a deal.

"I want those letters," Grant said. "Now."

"And you know what I want."

He'd never realized until recently that the British held the key. It had been Danjel Spagna who'd passed that piece of vital information along a few weeks ago, when he'd first approached the Lord's Own for help.

"I know what you want," Grant said. "You've been searching for it since Napoleon took Malta. I know the story of the knight captured in Valletta during Napoleon's invasion. They took him to the grand master's palace and nailed his hands to a table."

"And the little general in chief skewered him. That man was *Secreti*. He wore the ring. He also kept the secret."

That knight's bravery had long been revered. With French troops bearing down on Valletta and the island doomed, he had been the one who oversaw the protection of the knights' most precious objects. Books, records, and artifacts were trekked to the south shore and hastily shipped away. Some made it to Europe, some didn't. A decision, though, was made to leave the most precious possession on the island.

The *Nostra Trinità*.

That doomed knight, foreseeing his own demise, had supposedly made sure the French would never locate the Trinity. But if the stories were to be believed, he'd also left a way for the right people to refind it.

"MI6 has long known about what Mussolini may have found," Grant said. "He was intent on your *Nostra Trinità*."

"I want what he found."

"And you'll have it," Grant said, "when I get those letters."

He pointed the remote toward his car and clicked the button. The interior lit up and the elephant-skin satchel could be seen propped on the passenger seat. "That's everything Malone acquired. Everything the villa owner was trying to sell. There are eleven letters inside."

"Did you read them?"

"Of course. They definitely change history."

"I wish you hadn't done that."

He shrugged. "I could not care less about British pride or the reputation of Winston Churchill. Now tell me what I want to know."

He listened as Grant explained all of what British intelligence had discovered in the 1930s. What had been hinted at in the phone call earlier.

He was amazed. "Are you certain of this?"

Grant shrugged. "As certain as decades-old information can be."

He got the message. A risk existed. Nothing new about that. A fact Grant should have realized, too.

"Is that all?" he asked.

Grant nodded.

"Then the letters are yours."

The Brit started to walk toward the car for the satchel. The knight reached beneath his jacket and found the gun. With it in hand, he stepped close and fired one round into the back of James Grant's skull.

The shot cracked across the night.

The Brit collapsed to the ground.

One reason he'd chosen this spot for their meeting was the privacy it offered. Few people frequented this area after dark. He replaced the gun in its holster and hoisted Grant's body over his shoulder. The man was surprisingly stout for an old codger. The other reason was its proximity to the sea. He walked through the dark toward the cliff and tossed Grant over the side. The car would be found tomorrow, but the body would take longer, if it ever was found. The tides here were swift and notorious.

He stared out at the black water.

What did Ecclesiastes say?

Cast the bread upon the waters, for thou shalt find it after many days.

He hoped not.

CHAPTER
TWENTY-THREE

LUKE WONDERED WHY COTTON MALONE WAS INVOLVED WITH ANY of this, but knew better than to ask Stephanie questions. None of that mattered to his situation. He was apparently one segment of a larger mission. Nothing unusual there. The job was to get his part right. To that end Stephanie had given him a directive relative to Laura Price and she expected it to be done. So that's exactly what was going to happen.

He made his way back toward Republic Street, which remained congested, the crowd still focused on the commotion. Dusk had passed toward darkness, the streets and squares all amber-lit. He kept to the alley and was able to see Laura, her arms being held by policemen, talking to the big man she'd identified as Spagna. The conversation did not seem amicable. Spagna continued to puff on the cigar. The local cops seemed to be taking their orders from him. Only two of the four were still there, while a fifth, the driver of the car that had brought Spagna, stood off to the side.

He liked the odds.

The head of Vatican intelligence had apparently come in search of both him and Laura. The big guy had specifically called out *Mr. Daniels.* So Spagna was privy to solid information. And what had spooked Stephanie? Her attitude had shifted 180 degrees. A lot was happening fast. But he was accustomed to the speed lane. In fact, he preferred it.

He watched as Laura was stuffed into the rear seat of the blue-and-white police car, its lights still flashing. Spagna hesitated outside the vehicle, speaking to one of the uniformed officers. The other uniform, the driver, climbed in behind the wheel. Finally, Spagna opened the passenger-side door and pointed with the cigar, barking something out to another policeman before folding himself inside.

They were apparently leaving.

But the going would be slow, considering the snaking current of pedestrians that choked the streets in both directions. They'd have to inch their way for a bit, until finding one of the alleys. He had his gun and could shoot his way in and out. But that could turn messy in an infinite number of ways.

Better to innovate.

He'd already noticed that the piazza near the cathedral and the grand master's palace was dotted with vendor carts. Some selling food and drink, others arts and crafts. He counted ten. The police car had begun its departure, keeping the lights flashing and tossing out short bursts of its siren to clear a path through the crowd.

He fled the alley and sprinted into the melee, maneuvering his way toward one of the carts, this one hawking color prints of Valletta and Malta. It was wooden, its heft supported by four large, spoked wheels. He noticed that two bricks were wedged under a couple of those wheels, one front, the other back, to keep it in place. He kept a sharp eye out for any more police, but saw none in uniform. Of course, that didn't mean they weren't around.

Not to mention cameras.

Surely this hot spot was under constant video surveillance.

He told himself to hurry. Get it done. Indecision was what usually got you. He'd learned that early on from Malone. Be right. Be wrong. Doesn't matter. Just don't hesitate.

He crossed Republic and entered the piazza, hurrying toward its far end where the police car had stopped, the siren still bursting off and on. He came to the cart with the artwork, its owner talking with potential customers. Other folks admired the prints hanging from its display. He kicked one of the bricks aside, then swung around to the rear and grabbed the stout, wooden handles. The owner and the customers were momentarily caught off guard and he used that instant to shove the heavy bulk forward.

He kept pushing, increasing speed and momentum, the wheels rattling across the old rutted cobbles, crashing the cart into the side of the police car, making sure he kept it nestled tight to the front passenger-side door.

The collision grabbed everyone's attention.

He realized there'd be a moment of confusion inside the car, but the driver would emerge quickly.

And sure enough, he did, opening his door.

Luke leaped onto the hood and pivoted across, planting both feet in the guy's face, driving the cop backward then down. He landed on the hood and dropped to his feet ready to deal with the driver, but the cop was out cold. He reached back and found his Beretta, aiming it inside the vehicle.

"Let's go," he said to Laura.

He opened the rear door from the outside, keeping his gun trained on the Vatican spymaster.

"You live up to your advance billing," Spagna said. "I was told you were one of Stephanie's tough young bucks."

"I get the job done."

"Only because I let you."

Laura stood beside him.

He couldn't resist. "What does that mean?"

"We don't have time for you two to spar," she said. "Come on."

And she motioned to Spagna, who climbed across the front seat and out the driver's side, minus the cigar.

That was a shocker.

"I assume you know what you're doing," Luke asked her.

"I always do."

The three of them pushed through the gawkers and headed for another of the alleys. No other police were in sight. A low, muted rumble of thunder shook the evening air.

"Mr. Daniels, I saw you watching and assumed you'd make a move," Spagna said, as they hustled. "Tell him, Laura."

He glanced her way.

"Before they put me in the back of that car, Spagna told me to be ready to go. He said you'd come."

"I was the one who alerted the Maltese to both of you," Spagna said.

"I used the attack on the water from earlier as the pretense. I wanted local resources to find you, but now we need to be alone."

"That conversation I witnessed between the two of you didn't look all that friendly," he said.

"I tell my people," Spagna said, "that sometimes an actor has to play, in a single room, what the script describes as forty rooms. He must make the audience believe all forty exist. To do that, he must change reality. That's what a good spy does, too. Change reality. Ms. Price is a good spy."

"Whose side are you on?" Luke asked Spagna.

"Always, my church. My job is to protect it."

"And what about you?" he said to Laura.

He didn't like being played. Not ever.

She stared him down. "The only side that matters. My own."

They kept moving.

He tried to calm down and be the eyes and ears Stephanie needed on the ground. They were now sufficiently far from Republic Street that they could slow their pace. They stopped at the end of an alley, where it intersected with another busy thoroughfare littered with cars. The shops here were all closed for the night. Fewer people on the sidewalks, too.

"It's nice to make your acquaintance, Mr. Daniels," Spagna said, offering a hand.

Play the part. Be the gentleman.

He offered his hand in return.

"You both should be honored. I don't usually work the field."

"Why are you now?" Luke asked.

Spagna extended his arms in a mock embrace. "Because everything is happening here, on this ancient island. And being at the center of the storm is always the best place to be."

This guy had style, he'd give him that.

"By the way, Mr. Daniels, do you have a cell phone?"

He nodded and found the unit. Spagna took it from him and tossed it into the street, where an oncoming car crushed the case.

Malone's voice rushed through his head.

Dumb-ass mistake, Frat Boy.

You think?

"We don't need to be tracked. I know the Magellan Billet's standard issue contains constant GPS."

"Aren't you a wealth of inside information," Luke noted. "I bet you'd be hell playing Spy Jeopardy."

"You can keep your Beretta," Spagna said, pointing to his exposed shirttail. "Call it a show of my good faith."

Comforting. But not enough to alleviate his suspicions.

"Tell him what you told me," Laura said to Spagna.

"I know what Cardinal Gallo is after."

"That's all great. But I need to check in with Stephanie Nelle," Luke pointed out. "She gives me my orders."

More thunder growled in the distance, signaling storms were coming.

"You can contact her," Spagna said. "Later. I'll make sure that happens. Right now she has her hands full trying to save a former agent named Cotton Malone."

CHAPTER TWENTY-FOUR

COTTON WALKED BACK THROUGH THE REFECTORY, PAST THE EMPTY workstations, and reentered the cloister. Pollux Gallo was gone, but it remained unclear if he'd fled alone. The two brown-robed brothers from the chapter house might still be somewhere on the premises.

He headed back their way with the gun ready.

His clothes were wet from the dousing of the sprinklers, and at the chapter house door he heard the faucets still spewing. He'd regretted the destruction to the manuscripts. All no doubt irreplaceable. But Gallo had brought him here to die. He'd had no choice.

The sprinklers shut off.

He came alert, wondering if that was automatic or by human hand. He peered inside. The tables with their glass domes dripped with water, the floor soaked and puddled. He slipped inside and made a quick run down the end aisle, looking for the guy he'd first taken down, but nobody was there. He fled the chapter house and headed back to the crypt and found the same thing. The robed brother he'd taken down there was also gone. Where were they? And why had Gallo not kept up the attack?

He needed to check the rest of the monastery. Grant had specifically wanted to know about anything on Mussolini. He decided that, so long as he was here, he'd see if there was anything to find.

He left the crypt and returned to the cloister, checking the metal doors, one after another, that lined its inner wall. All of them were closed and protected by electronic locks that required a code from a keypad. At a point diagonally opposite to the chapter house he stopped and stared out through the arches into the darkened courtyard. Lights lit the cloistered corridors on both the ground and second floors. Across, on the far side, he noticed a half-open door on the second level. He was still cautious about the two brothers who had vanished, so he made his way to the nearest staircase and hustled up, keeping a watch in all directions.

The second floor seemed as quiet as the one below.

He approached the half-open door, the room beyond lit with bright fluorescent bulbs. The space was small, maybe thirty feet square, with dark-stained timbers overhead. The stone walls were lined with shelves and cabinets, the center containing another of the stout oak tables, this one devoid of any displays.

He stepped inside and surveyed the shelves.

Many were filled with books, all on Mussolini, in various languages. His trained eye noticed the bindings. Some were cloth, others leather, most wrapped with paper covers protected by Mylar. Several hundred at least. He noticed no overhead sprinklers here. Which made sense. Green metal cabinets, lined in rows, flanked the walls. He opened one to find folios of documents bearing dates starting in 1928 and continuing to 1943. Many of the brittle and fragile typewritten pages inside reminded him of what he'd seen in the elephant-skin satchel. He scanned a few and realized this was the Mussolini archive.

To his right he saw another of the metal cabinets, its doors not fully closed. He stepped across and opened them, revealing four shelves of identical thin, leather-bound volumes. He noticed dates on the spines. All mid- to late 1942. Here and there a book was missing, perhaps nine gone. He slid one of the volumes free. The pages were filled with a heavy, masculine script in black ink. He read some of the Italian, each entry headlined with a specific date, as in a diary.

His gaze raked the room at the shelves and he began to notice gaps where more books had once stood. He wondered if this room had been picked over, the important stuff removed.

He heard a noise beyond the exit doors, out in the cloister.

A scuttle of footsteps.

Perhaps his two problems had finally materialized.

He hustled across and assumed a position to the left of the door, between two of the metal cabinets, his spine flat to the stone wall. He kept the gun at his side, finger on the trigger, ready, raising it as the noise drew closer. Maybe they intended on charging in with a frontal assault.

He waited.

Someone entered the archive.

He aimed his gun.

"I was looking for you," Stephanie Nelle said calmly.

He lowered the weapon. "What in the hell are you doing here?"

"That was actually going to be my question to you."

"I'm here because I got greedy and thought I could make an easy hundred thousand euros. I've been playing 'the bait' all day, and I almost got eaten. Why are you here? And heads up, there are still a couple of threats hanging around."

She waved off his concern. "I doubt they're still here."

"What brings you into the field?"

"There's a problem developing in Rome with the conclave set to start tomorrow. It's a big mess, Cotton, and the Entity is involved."

Those folks he knew all too well, including their head, Danjel Spagna.

"The Lord's Own?" he asked, adding a smile.

She nodded. "He's on Malta. He and I go way back, to my time years ago at the State Department."

He knew what she was referring to.

"Luke is on Malta, too," she said.

"How is Frat Boy doing? Last time I saw him, he was in a hospital bed."

"He recovered. But he has his hands full at the moment. And what's happening there relates directly to what's happening here. I came to enlist your help."

He'd heard that tone before and knew what it meant.

Shut up and listen.

"Grant sent you here for Gallo to kill you."

"I already figured that out."

"Grant is also going to trade for the Churchill letters, the ones that were taken from you this morning. I'm not sure where or how, but that's his plan."

He'd known at the breakfast table in Milan that Grant was holding back. He should have said no thanks and headed back to Copenhagen. But he'd kept going. Why? For the money. What else? And that wasn't like him. But a hundred thousand euros would go a long way to handle the overhead at his bookshop. And the bills had to be paid.

"Who's Grant going to trade with for the letters?" he asked. "And what does he have to offer?"

Behind Stephanie, in the doorway, a man appeared. A new face. Tall, broad-shouldered, thick brown hair falling to his ears, a monk's beard dusting his chin and jaw.

"Cotton," Stephanie said. "This is Pollux Gallo. The lieutenant ad interim of the Knights of Malta. I think he can answer both of your questions."

CHAPTER TWENTY-FIVE

KASTOR RODE WITH CHATTERJEE.

A torrent of rain glistened beyond the car windows with each stab and flash of blue-white lightning. The steady slapping of the wipers worked to dull his senses.

They'd left Mdina in Chatterjee's vehicle, heading toward Marsaskala, an ancient town nestled close to a sheltered bay on the eastern shore. A familiar place, with buildings that stretched on both sides of the water with a promenade that offered views of low shelving rocks, colorful fishing boats, and the old saltpans. He knew its name derived partly from *marsa,* Arabic for "bay," and *skala,* Italian for *sqalli,* meaning "Sicilian." In years past, Sicilian fishermen often sought harbor there, as it was less than a hundred kilometers south of their home. Summer was its busy time. Many Maltese families owned vacation homes there, its array of bars and restaurants catering to a seasonal crowd.

As a boy he'd come here often to swim, drying off on the warm rocks after a dousing in the cold Mediterranean. Back then the journey took a while, as the roadways were nothing like today. Few outside of Valletta were paved and none led anywhere except to dead ends, mostly at the water's edge. All that changed in the 1970s when tourism exploded. Despite the modernization, though, history still tugged at every glance around the island. The knights' presence remained strong, more, he knew, for the tourists than for any genuine love.

The Maltese and the Hospitallers never got along. They'd been resented from the start as foreigners who'd been given *their* land by another foreigner. The knights had not helped matters by bringing nearly continuous war to the island, their occupation deemed a constant threat to the Arab world. Even worse, they treated the local population more as tenement workers and soldiers in need than fellow citizens.

The knights never understood how to rule a place so small as Malta. People living so close to one another for so long had learned to appreciate the needs and desires of their neighbors. It was a kind, cooperative society, which the knights governed with heartless tyranny. By 1798 the Maltese were fed up and the French had been welcomed as liberators, with Napoleon lauded as their champion. Few on Malta had been sad to see the knights tossed out. But that joy had quickly been replaced with loathing, and the same mistake was not made twice. The French were vanquished within two years. Eventually, with the defeat of Napoleon in 1814, the British gained the island and maintained control until 1964.

September 21.

Independence Day.

That old nun from the orphanage had been wrong about the festival of Our Lady of the Lily and the three stolen *pasti*. All that had happened at an Independence Day celebration. He'd not corrected Spagna, but he remembered every detail. What had she called him?

Halliel ftit. Little thief?

His cell phone vibrated in his pocket. He removed the unit, noted the caller, and answered.

About time.

"I have good news," the voice said in his ear. "I now know where Mussolini hid what he found."

He closed his eyes in relief. "Tell me."

"The British have had the information all along. I was able to use the Churchill letters to obtain what we need from James Grant."

"Where is it hidden?"

"I can't say on an open cell line."

"Can you get it?"

"It might be a challenge, but it's obtainable."

"And the man you just mentioned?"

"No longer a factor."

He, too, was being careful with his words, but he was able to say, "I'm with a man named Chatterjee. He works with a friend from Rome. We have a problem. There's an American and a Maltese agent watching me."

"Has the friend you mentioned made contact with you?"

"A bit of a surprise. But yes. You could have warned me."

"It's better this way. He's the best in the world, and now he's on your side."

"Which came as news to me."

"But welcomed, I'm sure. I arranged it, so please take advantage of the situation. Only a few more hours remain. Stay anonymous and above the fray. Let your new friend handle the dirty work."

He did not need to be reminded. He'd begged for a fight with the last pope and had been given one. Unfortunately—though he foolishly thought otherwise at the time—that war had been over before it even started.

This one would be fought far differently.

He felt safe to say, "I've been supplied with some new information, the kind that will be powerful and persuasive. It involves a great deal of personal scandal. More than enough to get what we want."

"I'll be anxious to hear more about that."

"Is there a reason you withheld the identity of our new friend? He was never mentioned when you told me to come here."

"I apologize. It was a condition of his involvement. But take heart. In just a few days you will be his superior."

He loved the sound of that.

"Find whatever there is to be found," he said into the phone. "And quickly."

"I intend to do just that. One thing. Where is this new powerful and persuasive information you just mentioned?"

He glanced across the car. "Chatterjee has it."

A pause, then the voice said, "Take care."

He ended the call.

They motored out of Marsaskala and headed toward St. Thomas Bay, the snug anchorage protected by steep cliffs on three sides. A jumble of lit buildings lined the narrow lane on both sides.

"Where are we going?" he asked, glad that Chatterjee knew better than to inquire about the phone conversation.

"To speak with someone who knows things."

He was annoyed by the secretive reply. He should be in Rome. Cardinals were surely arriving by the hour, being assigned their rooms in the Domus Sanctae Marthae, readying themselves to be sealed away in conclave.

Yet he was here, in the rain.

"When do I get that flash drive in your pocket?"

Chatterjee chuckled. "The archbishop wants this hunt to play itself out first."

He was finding it hard to disguise his mounting frustrations. "Is finding the *Nostra Trinità* a condition for that to happen?"

"Not at all. If this effort fails, then it fails. But the archbishop doesn't see the need, at the moment, to hand over the details of the curia's corruption. You'll have the flash drive before you enter the conclave."

Then he saw the point, his thoughts borne along on a surge of revelation. "He thinks I'll use it beforehand. He wants all of the blackmail to happen inside the conclave, where no one can speak of it once things are over."

"A wise precaution, don't you think. Though he has full confidence in your ability to persuade the right cardinals to support your candidacy, if something goes wrong at least it will remain a private matter, the cardinals bound by their oath to secrecy."

"And I take all the blame."

"There's an element of risk in everything we do."

"Except for your boss."

"Quite the contrary. The archbishop has taken a huge risk backing you."

But he wondered about that observation. Spagna had not survived for as long as he had by taking *huge* risks.

He resented Spagna's invasion into his life. Sometimes, in the morning, while shaving, he caught the mirrored reflection of a man he might not ever have recognized but for the fact he'd created him. Crafted as carefully as a sculptor working a slab of stone. As with everyone, though, scars existed, the stigmata of a troubled past, and even he'd thought himself finished, his mistakes leading toward a lonely failure. But now it seemed he might have a second chance.

"Might I ask a question?" Chatterjee said.

Why not? "Go ahead."

"What name do you plan to take as pope?"

An odd question, but one he had definitely considered.

He actually admired the full title. His Holiness, Bishop of Rome, Vicar of Jesus Christ, Successor of the Prince of the Apostles, Supreme Pontiff of the Universal Church, Primate of Italy, Archbishop and Metropolitan of the Roman Province, Sovereign of the Vatican City State, Servant of the servants of God.

But that was a bit much, even to him.

The early bishops of Rome had all used their baptismal names after election. Then, in the mid-6th century, Mercurius wisely decided that a pope should not bear the name of a pagan Roman god. Mercury. So he adopted the label John II in honor of his predecessor who had been venerated as a martyr. Later on, when clerics from the north, beyond the Alps, rose to the papacy, they replaced their foreign names with more traditional ones. The last pope to use his baptismal name was Marcellus II in 1555.

Which he would emulate.

"I'll be Kastor I."

Chatterjee chuckled.

"What's so funny?"

"Spagna knows you all too well. The password for the flash drive is KASTOR I."

CHAPTER TWENTY-SIX

Cotton stared at the man who called himself Pollux Gallo. "The guy who just tried to kill me used that name, too."

"I know, and I apologize," Gallo said. "But I have a serious situation simmering within the ranks of the Hospitallers. The man you were dealing with was an imposter."

Obviously. "Who was he?"

"A knight, as were the others with him. Every organization has its share of fanatics. We are no exception."

That subject required more delving, but first he wanted to hear more from Stephanie.

"Cotton, I had no idea you were involved with any of this until a few hours ago," she said. "I've been working this situation for over a week, but I just learned about the Brits."

"What situation?"

"I'm not exactly sure. Things have been fluid, to say the least. I understand you've been dealing with James Grant, and Grant has been dealing with the Entity."

Back when he was active with the Magellan Billet he'd worked several times with Danjel Spagna's people. Most of the Western world's spy agencies did the same. The Vatican was an intelligence gold mine. Every day ecclesiastical, political, and economic information poured in from thousands of priests, bishops, laypeople, and nuncios. An amazing array of eyes and ears in nearly every country in the world. No one else possessed that kind of surveillance network.

"Of course," Stephanie said, "working with the Entity is not a one-way street. Information has to be traded. I've learned that a week ago, James Grant shared the fact that the Churchill letters had surfaced. He'd tracked the potential seller, then inquired if the Vatican had any information on that seller. Anything that might corroborate the letters' authenticity. Smartly, he didn't want to waste time dealing with a fraud. He spoke with Spagna personally."

He asked, "What did Grant learn?"

"Supposedly, Spagna was no help. Yet the Lord's Own is now on Malta, wreaking havoc, and Grant is here in Italy searching for those letters. Hopefully Luke has things under control there, though he's had some issues today."

He smiled at her performance assessment. "He'll get the job done."

"I'm sure he will. But like you, he's working blind."

Gallo said, "This is a difficult situation for me, Mr. Malone. My twin brother, Cardinal Gallo, is deeply involved with all of this. I'm afraid he's drawn himself into another difficult situation."

"I read about him and what's happening within your organization. You said twin. Identical?"

Gallo nodded.

Unfortunately, in the articles he'd read there'd been no photograph of Cardinal Gallo. Which would have been helpful in ferreting out the imposter he'd just encountered.

"Who just tried to kill me?" he asked.

"A group within our ranks known as the *Secreti*."

He noticed no ring on the man's fingers, and no evidence that he may have worn one in the past. "The imposter told me about them and said they no longer existed."

"And until a few hours ago I would have agreed with him. But that's not the case. They do exist, in some new form. It's my belief they're the ones who attacked you in the villa and killed three men, including one of their own."

"To keep me from taking him?"

Gallo said, "That seems logical. You have to understand, thanks to my brother, the Knights of Malta are currently in a state of fracture, polarized to the extreme. It's a civil war. One side is loyal to the order, the other is in open rebellion. You met some of the rebels tonight."

"Where were you when those rebels were trying to kill me?"

"In Rome. I only learned of the situation, and that you were at the Villa Malta, after you were airborne. I've been in contact with Ms. Nelle for the past few days, working with her. When I mentioned the situation and your name, we came north as fast as possible."

He had no reason to doubt this man, particularly with Stephanie involved.

"The *Secreti* want the Churchill letters," Gallo said, "so they can make a deal with the British. Supposedly, the British have information that the *Secreti* want."

"Like what?" he asked.

Gallo hesitated, but a nod from Stephanie seemed to answer his reluctance to speak.

"Tell him," she said.

"The Knights Hospitallers are unique among the warrior-monks," Gallo said. "The Templars are gone. The Teutonics barely exist. But the Hospitallers remain strong. We are a viable, worldwide charitable organization. Some of that survival is thanks to our adaptability, perpetually making ourselves useful. Some of it is due to perseverance, some to luck. But some is attributable to what we once knew. It involves something called the *Nostra Trinità*. Our Trinity."

"Sounds ancestral," Cotton noted.

"It is. In fact, it goes to our core. At first it was the *Nostra Due*. The Holy Duo. Two documents the knights had always held dear from our earliest existence. The *Pie Postulatio Voluntatis,* the Most Pious Request, from 1113, that recognized our existence and confirmed our independence and sovereignty. The second is the *Ad Providam,* from 1312, where Pope Clement V handed over all of the Templars' property to us in perpetuity. The Templars had been dissolved five years earlier and the *Ad Providam* gave us nearly everything they owned. There are signed originals of both of those documents in the Vatican, so there is little doubt of their existence. But we always kept our own originals."

"Why?" Stephanie asked.

"They are the sole evidence of our legitimacy, our independence. Both those principles have been called into question many times in the past, and it was always those two papal decrees that ended any debate."

"And the third part, which made it a trinity?" Cotton asked.

"It came to us later, in the Middle Ages, and is much more mysterious. No one alive today, to my knowledge, has ever seen it. It's called the *Constitutum Constantini.* Constantine's Gift. It's what Napoleon and Mussolini sought, and it's also what my brother is after. All three documents were kept together and guarded for centuries by the *Secreti,* whose members pledged an oath to protect them. And they did, until 1798, when all three documents disappeared and have not been seen since. To bind them together in solidarity, the *Secreti* wore a ring with a palindrome that dates back to Constantine the Great."

He explained to Stephanie about the ring and the five lines that could be read the same in every direction.

**SATOR
AREPO
TENET
OPERA
ROTAS**

"The Latin has been interpreted many different ways," Gallo said. "One variation is something like 'the sower, with his eye on the plow, holds its wheels with care.' Which is nonsense, as are all of the other interpretations."

Including Grant's from earlier.

"The real message is hidden." Gallo reached inside his jacket pocket and removed a pen and small notebook. He drew a cross of squares and inserted letters, adding four other boxes outside the cross.

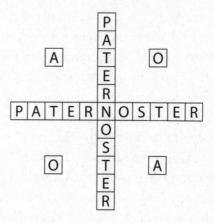

"Taken together, the letters of the five words are an anagram. The key is the N at the middle. All of the letters in the palindrome are paired except the central N, which stands alone. By repositioning the letters around the central N, a cross can be made that reads *Pater Noster,* in both directions. Latin for 'Our Father,' and the first two words of the Lord's Prayer. The remaining four letters, which are two A's and two O's, are a reference to Alpha and Omega. The beginning and end. Symbols of eternity, from the Book of Revelation. For Christians in the 4th century that meant the omnipresence of God."

"Who would have thought?" Cotton said. "That can't be a coincidence."

"It's not. Early Christians shared the five-worded palindrome as a way to identify themselves with one another. Constantine himself sanctioned its use. The *Secreti* eventually adopted it as their symbol."

"What does any of this have to do with the coming conclave?" Stephanie asked.

Cotton was wondering the same thing.

"Perhaps everything," Gallo said. "There's a relevance today to Constantine's Gift that my brother has somehow garnered. With Archbishop Spagna's help, I'm sure. As I've already told Ms. Nelle, Kastor wants to be pope."

That was new to the mix, and he filed further inquiry away for later. Right now he wanted more information about the third part of that trinity.

"Here's what I do know," Gallo said. "Constantine sanctioned Christianity over paganism. By then, it was no longer some small regional movement. A sizable percentage of the entire population was Christian. So he made it the official state religion, with himself in charge. The *Constitutum Constantini* has something to do with that move. What? I truly don't know."

"No one in the organization has a clue what the document says?" Stephanie asked.

Gallo shook his head. "My brother discovered in the Vatican archives that it has something to do with the early church. Its structure and organization. What that might be? I don't know. What I do know is that popes have long feared its surfacing, preferring that the document stay hidden. The Hospitallers accommodated that request and kept it hidden."

"Using that to their advantage," Cotton added.

"That's true. It's why we survived and the other orders perished."

He could tell Gallo was hedging. So he said, "Now's not the time to be coy."

The admonishment brought a curious stare, then a nod.

"You're correct. This is not the time. We did use what we knew to our advantage." Gallo paused. "Within five hundred years of Constantine's death, the church became the most powerful political force in Europe. Not until the 16th century and Martin Luther did anyone successfully challenge its authority. Then along came Napoleon. In his world there was room for only one omnipotent ruler with the ear of God. Himself. He wanted the church gone. He wanted his own *new docile religion,* to use his words. So he abolished both the Inquisition and the Index of Prohibited Books and established a new Catholic creed, even a new Christian calendar. Year One started in 1792, and he identified Paris as the *holy city,* with Rome as its subsidiary. He wanted a new world religion, like Constantine wanted with Christianity, and, like Constantine, he wanted himself as head. But first he had to destroy the Roman Catholic Church."

Cotton was familiar with some of what he was hearing, particularly the use of religion as a political tool. But other parts were new to him.

So he kept listening.

"Napoleon invaded Italy and defeated the papal army," Gallo said. "He then marched on Rome and entered unopposed, plundering the Vatican. In 1798 he proclaimed Rome a republic and demanded the pope renounce his temporal authority. Pius VI refused, so he took the pope prisoner, where he died in captivity seven months later. A new pope tried to make peace, but failed, and Napoleon invaded Italy again and took that pope prisoner, too. He was only released when the British ended Napoleon's rule in 1814. Then something extraordinary happened. After Napoleon was exiled to St. Helena, the pope wrote letters urging leniency. Can you imagine? After all Napoleon had done—held him prisoner, stripped him of everything—he still wanted mercy extended."

"Could simply have been the Christian thing to do," Cotton noted.

"Perhaps. But we'll never know. Napoleon died in 1821, still a prisoner. The pope in 1823. It has always been our belief that the Holy See thought Napoleon possessed Constantine's Gift and, for whatever reason, it was dangerous enough for them to placate him."

"Did Napoleon have it?" Stephanie asked.

Gallo shook his head. "But he ran a good bluff, using the two opportunities when he'd plundered the Vatican to his advantage. He likewise looted Malta."

Cotton was curious. "Did the church know that the Trinity had been lost when Napoleon invaded Malta?"

Gallo nodded. "Absolutely. But no one at the time had any idea where it had been hidden. We know now that the man who hid it away was executed, never revealing what he knew."

"And now your brother is after it," Stephanie asked. "Spagna too?"

"That's my assessment."

"You still have not explained why the *Secreti* just tried to kill me."

"That's simple," Gallo said. "The British asked for that to happen."

Stephanie nodded. "He's right. James Grant is running rogue."

No real surprise.

"And Mussolini?" he said. "How does he figure into all this?"

Gallo faced him. "That's precisely why my brother and Archbishop Spagna have teamed together."

CHAPTER
TWENTY-SEVEN

LUKE REFLECTED ON HOW FAST THINGS CHANGED.

He'd gone from hanging in the air to drenched in the Mediterranean, then thrown into a dungeon, attacked by the police, and now he was inside an apartment located in the heart of Valletta, led there by the head of Vatican intelligence and accompanied by an agent for Maltese security. He wasn't sure who, if anyone, he should listen to, much less trust. Laura Price had gone from telling him to get as far away as he could to seemingly now working with the enemy.

"We're near the old Inquisitor's Palace," Spagna said. "What a job that must have been. Appointed by the pope, sent here to eliminate heresy and all things contrary to the Catholic faith. His word was absolute. That's a position I would have relished."

Luke surveyed the tiny apartment. Only three rooms, brightened by cheerful curtains, the furniture all a bit too large. No photos, candy dishes, or knickknacks. Nothing personal. No one lived here, at least not on a long-term basis. He'd been in enough safe houses so far during his time with the Magellan Billet to know the look.

"This place one of yours?"

Spagna nodded. "Our people use it."

When they'd arrived he'd noticed an oddity out front, engraved into the eroding stone lintel above a set of shuttered windows. An eye sandwiched between two axes. Spagna had explained that it noted who'd lived in the building long ago.

The executioner.

No coincidence that the holder of that unenviable office lived near the Inquisitor's Palace.

Luke heard a vibration and watched as Spagna found a phone in his pocket, stepping outside to take the call.

"You want to tell me what's happening here," he asked Laura.

"Spagna told me that he was aware of Cardinal Gallo's presence on the island and that he had the situation under control."

"And you bought that?"

"He called my boss once we were in the car and I was ordered to cooperate. I'm betting your boss is going to tell you the same thing."

Except that his phone had been conveniently destroyed, making that difficult to determine. "You still have your phone?"

She shook her head. "Spagna took it."

No surprise.

"So we're isolated, with the pope's spy out there controlling the information flow. This is not good. On many levels."

He stepped over to the windows, parted the curtains, and glanced down at the deserted street two floors below.

Spagna returned and closed the door behind him. "First, let's be clear. Either of you can leave anytime you want."

"Then why corral us?" Luke asked.

"As you saw, the locals have a different opinion of you."

"Thanks to you."

Spagna nodded. "Sadly for you, that's true. I would prefer not to involve any of my assets. I have a chaotic situation at the moment that is extremely time-sensitive, and most of my people are readying the Vatican for a conclave."

Luke asked, "What's happening with Cotton Malone?"

"That was the subject of the call I just received. It seems Mr. Malone has extricated himself from danger. Your Ms. Nelle is with him now, as is the temporary head of the Hospitallers."

He was definitely being sucked into something bigger. That was obvious. And he had to keep going, no matter the risks. Some would call that foolish. He called it doing his job.

"My man Chatterjee has been with Cardinal Gallo for the past two hours," Spagna said. "I wanted the cardinal contained to give us time to deal with a more pressing problem."

Luke could hardly wait to hear.

"Listen up, this is your intel briefing. Books and movies love to show Christians being fed to lions. A little ridiculous, if you ask me. Yes, persecutions happened. No question. But seventeen hundred years ago Christians were finally in the right place, at the right time. Still, they had a problem. Their new religion had fractured into a hundred pieces, so many versions of Christianity, each fighting with the other. Constantine the Great saw the political potential of that new religion, but only if those factions could be united. So he called the Council of Nicaea and summoned bishops from all over the empire."

Luke had heard those words—*Council of Nicaea*—before, but knew little to nothing about their importance.

"The bishops came to Asia Minor," Spagna said. "Nobody really knows how many. Maybe three hundred. Some say more. It was the first great Christian council and they were deeply divided over Christ's divinity. One group said the Son had been begotten from the Father with no separate beginning. The other argued the Son had been created from nothing with his own beginning. Sounds silly to us. Who cares? He was Christ, for Christ's sake. But it was a big deal to them. And during the summer of 325, those bishops debated that point into the ground. Constantine himself presided over the sessions. In the end they came to a consensus, with the emperor's approval, that the Son came from the Father, equal to the Father. They created a creed that said that, and all but two bishops agreed. Those two were excommunicated and banished. They then decided the rest of what true Christians should believe. Things like when Easter would be celebrated, how priests would act, how the church would be organized. Everything contrary to that was deemed heretical, unworthy of belief. And so began the Catholic Church, as we know it today."

"And this has what to do with what's happening now?" Laura asked.

Luke was beginning to like her directness.

· "It has everything to do with now," Spagna said. "Once the council ended, Constantine invited all of the bishops to his palace for a grand banquet. Officially, the dinner was to celebrate his twentieth anniversary as emperor. But it became much more. From the precious few accounts that have survived, we know the bishops left that night with gifts for themselves and money for their churches. But they also executed a document. Signed by all, including the emperor himself. That document has a name. The *Constitutum Constantini.* Constantine's Gift. It stayed with the emperor until his death in 337. Eventually it came into the pope's possession, but he lost it. Then during the Middle Ages the Knights of Rhodes, who eventually became the Knights of Malta, obtained it. It became one of three documents they venerated and protected. Their *Nostra Trinità.* Our Trinity. Napoleon invaded Malta looking for it, but never found a thing. It all seemed forgotten, until the 1930s, when Mussolini searched again."

"Why would any of that matter now?" Luke asked. "It's so old."

"I assure you, the *Constitutum Constantini* still matters. Perhaps today more than ever. Cardinal Gallo understands its significance. I understand its significance. That's why we have to find it first."

"*We?*" Laura asked.

"I have assurances from both of your superiors that you're mine for the next few days."

"I think I'll wait on that one until I hear it from my boss," Luke said.

Spagna frowned. "Are you always so difficult?"

"Just to people I don't like."

"We just met, Mr. Daniels. How could you possibly know if you like me or not?"

"My mama used to say that she *didn't need to wallow with the pigs to know it stunk in the pen.*"

Spagna smiled. "Sounds like an intelligent woman."

"The smartest I've ever known. I'd say it stinks here, too."

"Regardless of your personal feelings," Spagna said, "we have a job to do. But first, some things have to play out in Italy."

Luke shook his head. More gobbledygook. "I'm assuming you don't plan to explain yourself."

Spagna smiled, pointed a finger, and said, "That's where you're wrong."

CHAPTER
TWENTY-EIGHT

COTTON WAITED FOR AN ANSWER TO HIS QUESTION OF HOW Mussolini factored into the situation.

"You must understand," Gallo said, "that my brother and I, though identical twins, are vastly different people. I chose a military career, then one of charitable service with the knights. He chose a purely religious path. And where ambition is not out of the question in my world, it can be fatal in his. I have no interest in the conclave, no interest in who is pope. But there are others who do. My brother sits at the top of that list, followed closely by Archbishop Spagna."

"The Entity is trying to influence the conclave?" Stephanie asked.

"They have on many occasions before. Why would this time be different?"

"Answer my question," Cotton said. "All this information here on Mussolini. Why do you have it? It can't just be historic curiosity."

"Far from that." Gallo motioned to the room. "This collection is a vast research project that has taken us decades. Let me tell you something only those within the ranks of the professed knights know. The order owns two properties inside Rome. The Palazzo di Malta, from where you departed, and the Villa del Priorato di Malta. There's a story about when Mussolini visited the Priorato."

* * *

Il Duce admired the grand priory, lit to the night in all its glory. The build-
ing sat on Aventine Hill, one of Rome's famous seven, overlooking the Tiber—
once a Benedictine monastery, then a Templar stronghold, now belonging
to the Hospitallers. Their jurisdictional claim was marked by a red flag with
a white, eight-pointed cross bristling in the warm night air.

The day had been glorious. He'd just returned from an operatic spec-
tacle staged in honor of a state visit by the German chancellor, Adolf Hitler.
Held at the Foro Mussolini, literally his forum, inside the Stadio del Cipressi,
where tens of thousands had heeded the call to attend. Everything had been
carefully rehearsed, including the triumphant conclusion of the program
where hundreds of torch-bearing youths had formed a huge swastika, yell-
ing Heil Hitler in the flickering flames. Hitler had been impressed. So much
that the chancellor had proclaimed the Roman state resurrected, from remote
tradition, to new life.

High praise.

With Hitler down for the night, he'd decided to head back into Rome and
handle another matter that required his personal attention. So he'd appeared
unannounced at the Villa del Priorato di Malta.

The grand master stood beside him.

Ludovico Chigi della Rovere-Albani.

The seventy-sixth man to hold the position. An Italian at least. Born to
a noble family with a lineage back to the 15th century. He'd been elected
head of the Knights of Malta in 1931 and, for the past seven years, he'd kept
a low profile.

But not quite low enough.

"I'm aware that you've been thwarting my efforts with the pope," he told
Chigi. "Going behind me, undermining negotiations."

"I only do as the Holy Father asks of me."

"Really? Would you kill, if the Holy Father asked that of you?"

"That would never happen."

"Don't be so sure. Your illustrious order slaughtered thousands of
people for centuries. All for popes. What makes you so different now?"

"Both we and the world have changed."

"And the Secreti? *Have they changed?"*

The older man's face remained stoic. He'd hoped to catch this man off guard, but the ruse had not worked. They stood in the parterre garden among sculpted shrubbery and tall cypress trees.

"I have the Nostra Trinità," *he proclaimed.*

"You have nothing."

"Don't be so sure. Your knights did not remain silent."

"Yet you killed them anyway."

"I killed no one."

"Which you say as though you truly believe."

He pointed beyond the garden, to the main gate. *"Is it true what they say?"*

"Have a look for yourself."

He paraded toward the tall stone screen. Beneath an arch-headed central portone *two iron doors stood closed. In one was the* Il Buco Della Serratura. *Such a long name for something so simple.*

The keyhole.

His spies had reported what could be seen through the opening. He approached the door, bent down, and peered through. In the distance, at the end of a garden allée, framed in clipped cypresses, he saw the lit copper-green dome of St. Peter's Basilica. He smiled at the intriguing symbolism and faced the grand master. "Is it an accident or by design that the Hospitallers have the center of Roman Catholicism directly in their keyhole?"

"That's not for me to say. But we have guarded the church for a long time."

"Extracting much in return for the service."

"We are good, loyal, and faithful. Unlike you."

"I am your leader."

"That's not true. Where we stand does not belong to Italy. This is a separate nation. I am leader here."

"It would take my Black Shirts only a few minutes to subdue all of you. Then I could burn this separate nation to the ground. I could then take the Palazzo di Malta and do the same. Don't tempt me."

Chigi shrugged, as if unconcerned. "Do what you must. We've been homeless before and survived."

Time to get to the point of the visit. "Tell Pius to leave me alone. Do that, *and the* Constitutum Constantini *stays with me. I've even done him a favor and sealed it away where no one can get to it. His precious faith will not be threatened. You see, O exalted one, king of your own country, I am now guardian of the church. Not you. Me. And the church will do as I say."*

"That encounter happened in May 1938, and the keyhole is still there," Gallo said. "People line up every day to peek through it at the dome of St. Peter's, over two miles away."

"How do you know about what Mussolini said that night?" Stephanie asked.

Good question. He, too, was skeptical.

"We worked with American and British intelligence during the war," Gallo said. "Our nation status gave us a diplomatic presence worldwide. We provided medical services in every combat theater, but we also passed on information about the Axis to the Allies. And we were a conduit to both of the Pius popes. In the course of that, we learned that Mussolini had blackmailed the Holy See into complacency, convincing the Vatican that he possessed Our Trinity. Both popes demanded proof from us that we still possessed the Trinity. Of course, we could not supply it. So they capitulated and stayed silent about all of the fascist atrocities. Pius XI had planned to break that silence, but died before that happened. Pius XII chose to maintain that silence. Historians have argued for decades why the Vatican did not do more to stop the evil in Italy and Germany. The answer was simple. The church was threatened by something important enough to command its attention."

"Did Mussolini have the *Nostra Trinità*?" Stephanie asked.

Gallo shook his head. "We have no idea. Il Duce killed three knights, one a *Secreti,* to obtain whatever he found. That we know for a fact. So we've spent the past seven decades gathering all we could." He motioned to the room. "This is the result of those efforts. Mr. Malone, you asked how Mussolini is important here. This is how."

"Is the church currently aware of any of this?" Stephanie asked.

"Archbishop Spagna certainly is. Perhaps a few cardinals know of the *Constitutum Constantini.* Within the order a handful know the history, I being one of those. But this certainly is not a subject of common knowledge. The pope dying so sudden has apparently aroused the ambitions of the archbishop, the *Secreti,* and my brother. All three want to take advantage of the situation."

"Aren't you the lieutenant ad interim, thanks to your brother," Cotton asked again.

"I agreed to serve as a way to try to heal the rifts within our ranks. But the petty infighting and ridiculous egos of the most senior of our officers has taxed my patience. Even so, my allegiance is to my brothers. And only to them."

"Over your own brother?"

"Even over my own brother." Gallo hesitated, then said, "I foolishly thought I was the only one who could keep Kastor in check. I know him. Perhaps even better than he knows himself. I apologize again for what's happened to you, Mr. Malone. I'm trying hard to rectify the situation."

He decided to cut the guy a little slack. "My apologies, too. I'm just trying to understand the lay of the land."

"I appreciate that. So what I'm about to tell you has remained within our ranks, as a cherished secret, for a long time. But I need your help, so I'm going to break protocol and tell you both a secret."

CHAPTER
TWENTY-NINE

LUKE LISTENED TO SPAGNA AS HE EXPLAINED.

"In the early 1930s Mussolini wanted to show the world that Rome had returned to all of its imperial glory. So he started a massive urban redevelopment project. Neighborhoods were razed, buildings leveled, grand boulevards cleared and paved. People come to Rome today from all over the world and marvel at the architecture. What they don't realize is that most of it bears the imprint not only of emperors and popes, but also of a cruel fascist."

He and Laura listened as Spagna told them how Mussolini had wanted to attract a World's Fair and even the Olympics. To do that he appropriated a tract of swampy land north of the city, adjacent to the Tiber, and constructed a grand complex.

The Foro Mussolini.

"Like the Forum Caesaris and the Forum Augusti. But in the ancient world those were places of commerce and religious worship. This one dealt only with sports, games, and politics. There were gyms, running tracks, swimming pools, and a garish twenty-thousand-seat travertine stadium, ringed by sixty marble statues of nude males wielding clubs, swords, and slings. It became a Black Shirt playground, home to the Fascist Academy of Physical Education, used for training and competitions. Mussolini himself worked out there regularly, and even more incredible, the place still stands."

That surprised Luke.

"The complex is used for international competitions," Spagna said. "The buildings house the Italian National Olympic Committee, a television station, a museum, a fencing academy, even a high-tech courthouse where terrorists and Mafioso were tried. The site has adapted, but there's one part that has remained exactly the same."

He waited.

"The obelisk."

COTTON HAD NEVER HEARD OF THE FORO MUSSOLINI AND THE obelisk that Pollux Gallo had just described.

But he was intrigued.

"The obelisk is fifty-five feet tall," Gallo said. "The largest single piece of marble ever quarried at Carrara. A perfect slab, free of cracks and imperfections, topped with a tip of gilded bronze. On it is inscribed MUS- SOLINI DUX."

He silently translated.

Mussolini leader.

"It was dedicated on November 4, 1932, to great pomp. Behind it stretches a huge piazza, paved with mosaics of muscled athletes, eagles, and odes to Il Duce. It's all so repulsive, so grandiose. Like the man himself. But the obelisk is one of the last remaining monuments that still bears Mussolini's name."

Cotton knew the significance of obelisks, symbols of imperial power for centuries. Egyptians, Romans, emperors, and popes all used them. A natural that the fascists would turn to one.

"But it's what lies inside the obelisk," Gallo said. "That's our real secret."

LUKE HAD TO ADMIT, THE WHOLE THING SOUNDED FASCINATING. But he had to keep telling himself to not get caught up with the story and pay close attention to Spagna. This man had an unknown agenda.

"By any standard, the forum and the obelisk were grand gestures,"

Spagna said. "But Mussolini went one better. He commissioned a codex to be written by an Italian classical scholar. A fanciful account on the rise of fascism, its supposed achievements, and its place in history. One thousand two hundred and twenty words of pure propaganda, which, on October 27, 1932, he sealed inside the base of the obelisk."

Spagna explained how objects were routinely placed inside monuments, first done as an offering, a superstition. Eventually the practice of foundation deposits was used to carry forward the memory of the builder or the people who produced the structure. Mussolini particularly enjoyed the custom, filming the ceremonies for the newsreels. He would sign a dedication document with great flourish, seal it within a metal tube, then cement it himself inside the *prima pietra,* the first stone.

"The story goes," Spagna said, "that in order to free the codex and read its grand fascist message, the obelisk would have to come down. For future generations to know the greatness of Mussolini, his monument would have to fall. Ironic, wouldn't you say?"

"Is that obelisk still standing?" Laura asked.

Spagna nodded. "In all its glory."

"And why is that important now?" Luke asked.

"The British learned that Mussolini sealed something else inside that obelisk, along with the codex, something that has become quite important of late."

Spagna reached into his pocket for an object.

And tossed it over.

COTTON FOCUSED ON WHAT POLLUX GALLO WAS SAYING.

"In the 1930s Mussolini managed to infiltrate our ranks," Gallo said. "He did that, at first, simply to know what we were doing, just as he did with the church. We watched him, too. From those efforts Mussolini came to learn some of our most precious secrets, and one in particular. How to find the *Nostra Trinità.* Supposedly a map was created. A way to locate the hiding place. We've searched since 1798 for that map, but it was Mussolini who may have succeeded in finding it."

LUKE EXAMINED WHAT SPAGNA HAD THROWN HIS WAY.

A coin.

No. More a medal.

Its obverse featured Mussolini in profile, his head sheathed in a lion skin. The reverse showed an obelisk and bore a legend.

FORO MVSSOLINI A.X.

"What does it mean?" he asked Spagna.

"By wearing the lion skin, he linked himself to Hercules and the first of his twelve labors, the killing of the Nemean lion. Mussolini was obsessed with mythology." Spagna pointed. "The obelisk on that medal is the same one at the foro, with the same inscription. Then there's one other piece of information. At the base of the obelisk is a stone that has ANNO X carved into it. That coin you're holding was found in Mussolini's pocket the day he was killed. One of the *Secreti* was there and retrieved it before they took the great leader and his mistress back to Milan and hung their corpses upside down for all to see."

Luke motioned. "Mussolini created this medal?"

Spagna nodded. "It was specially commissioned for the dedication of the Foro Mussolini. Several were placed inside the obelisk with the codex. Those were made of gold. The one you're holding is bronze. Made just for Il Duce, and it being in his pocket was significant. As was what Mussolini called out just before they shot him at Lake Como. *Magnus ab integro saeclorum nascitur ordo.* The great order of the ages is born afresh. Meaningless at the time. But not when you consider the text of the codex that Mussolini commissioned. The one inside the obelisk. It has an epigraph at its beginning. A quote from Virgil's Eclogues 4.5. *The great order of the ages is born afresh.*"

"That's too many coincidences to be a coincidence," Laura said.

"You're correct," Spagna said. "Which means what we need is waiting inside that obelisk, and it's up to Mr. Malone to find it."

COTTON WAITED FOR GALLO TO FINISH.

"We've suspected for some time that the obelisk served as Mussolini's hiding place for what he might have located. Probably behind a stone at the base, marked ANNO X. The time has come to see if that's true. And quickly."

He caught the urgent tone. "You think the men who just tried to kill me are headed that way?"

"I do."

Which might explain the fake Gallo's hasty retreat. He checked his watch. "They have less than an hour's head start. It's a long drive back to Rome."

"Three hours," Stephanie said.

"I can get us there faster," Gallo noted. "We have the helicopter, which is still at the villa."

Cotton glanced at Stephanie, who seemed to be reading his mind.

"I get it," she said. "This is the time for you to bow out. I wouldn't blame you. As you say, you don't have a dog in this fight."

That was right. He'd been hired for a job, which he'd extended, but it was over. He should find a hotel, go to sleep, then head for the nearest airport in the morning and fly back to Copenhagen. After all, he was retired from the intelligence business. But he wasn't dead. Not yet, anyway. And he was curious. What had the Knights of Malta guarded? The *Nostra Trinità*? The *Constitutum Constantini*? Which both Napoleon and Mussolini had been after? Perhaps waiting at the base of an obelisk in Rome? There since 1932? Which might affect the coming conclave and the election of a pope? That was a lot of fascinating questions. He wasn't due in Nice to meet Cassiopeia for a few days. So why not? He'd come this far.

"I'll stay in," he said.

She smiled. "The chopper will be here in fifteen minutes."

"Kind of sure of yourself, weren't you?"

"I was hoping. It'll get us to Rome a good hour before anyone else. I appreciate this, Cotton."

A man entered the archive and approached, whispering into Gallo's ear, who nodded as the messenger withdrew.

"I've learned some additional information that's disturbing," Gallo said. "I'm told men are on Malta, there to kill my brother."

CHAPTER THIRTY

Kastor entered the shop.

The door jingled as he and Chatterjee stepped inside, the dim space lit only by a couple of overhead bulbs. He took in the stale air with a hint of sea damp, along with the well-trundled floor, the cobwebbed corners, and the fascinating wares.

Clocks.

Most of their wooden cases were in various stages of construction. Some were being carved, others painted, a couple more half gilded. He tried to remember if he'd seen this shop as a child, but he could not remember ever visiting this side of St. Thomas Bay. He recalled that among the many summer homes ringing the bay there'd always been an array of eclectic shops and entrepreneurs. One, a potter who'd turned out dishes, bowls, and vases on a spinning wheel, came to mind.

But no one who crafted the famous *tal-lira* clocks.

He knew them well.

Dating back to the 17th century, they were unique to Malta and found all across the island. One had hung in the orphanage. His job one summer had been to wind its inner mechanism. Always two doors, one glassed on the outside, the other inside supporting the face and a small aperture revealing the pendulum. Traditionally, none had ever been produced on a mass level, each made individually.

Like here.

An old dog, worn and scraggy, appeared from behind the counter. It shuffled a few steps, then lay down. A wall shielded the front from the rear of the building, broken by an open doorway. A man emerged through a threadbare curtain. Aged, coarse-featured, silver beard, deep-set eyes peering out from behind thick spectacles.

"You don't look like a cardinal," the old man said.

He wanted to come back with a barbed comment but resisted the temptation. "Is this your shop?"

The man nodded. "My family has been making clocks for three hundred years. Sadly, though, I'll be the last. My two children have no interest in continuing the tradition."

"And you are?"

"Nick Tawil."

He faced Chatterjee. "Why are we here?"

"This man knows a lot about the *Nostra Trinità*. It has been his life's obsession."

"Is that true?" he asked Tawil.

"Guilty as charged."

A sharp flash lit the shop windows, followed by a clap of thunder. Rain continued to splatter the panes. He needed a moment to digest things. So he perused the clocks under construction. "How many do you make a year?"

"Seven, sometimes eight."

"What do you charge? Five, six thousand euros?"

"More like seven."

"That's a good living."

He recalled the clock that had hung in his parents' house. Not all that impressive, but it had kept impeccable time. He noticed gilding being applied to one of the frames. "Twenty-four-carat?"

"What else."

The finish looked a little dull, but he realized that the final product would eventually be buffed to a shine.

He turned back toward Tawil. "What is it you supposedly know?"

"I've been searching for the knights' Trinity a long time. My father searched. My grandfather searched."

"Are you a knight?"

Tawil shook his head. "I'm not Catholic."

His suspicious nature took hold and he glanced toward Chatterjee. "How do you know this clockmaker?"

"We've been friends a long time."

"That we have," Tawil added, walking over and crouching down near the dog, stroking the animal's dark coat. "There's a place not far away from here. An ancient graveyard beside the sea that has been there a long time. It's where the knight Napoleon killed in the grand master's palace, with his palms nailed to a table, is buried."

Now he knew where Chatterjee had learned the story.

"My grandfather told me that the map to the *Nostra Trinità* had been buried with him."

"How would he know that?"

"I have no idea. But my grandfather was no fool."

"Was the map buried there?"

Tawil shrugged. "We'll never know. In the early 1930s the grave was violated. My grandfather and several other men tried to stop the robbers. But they were killed, and the robbers got away. So no one knows what, if anything, was found."

He heard the pain in the man's voice.

"My grandfather spent much of his life trying to find the *Nostra Trinità*. He learned a great deal. I have all of his books and papers."

Which he'd like to examine. But first, "I want to see that grave."

"In the rain?" Tawil asked.

"Why not? I'm already wet."

The clockmaker chuckled. "Good point."

Headlights brushed through the store, sweeping inward from the street side windows. He came alert. Car doors slammed. He stepped to the window and spied out into the darkness. Chatterjee stood beside him. Two forms walked to the black shadow of the car he and Chatterjee had arrived in. A flash of light broke the darkness and the vehicle seemed to bulge from within, everything erupting outward, the roof flying off into the rain, followed by a blast of heat and light that tossed the hulk off the ground as it exploded.

His body froze in terror.

He'd never seen such a thing before.

The car smashed downward onto splayed wheels, a mass of gasoline-fed flames and smoke mushrooming upward. In the glow he saw the two men turn toward the shop and aim automatic rifles.

Chatterjee's sinewy arm yanked him toward the floor.

Tawil still stood near the dog.

"Get down," Chatterjee yelled.

A torrent of gunfire ripped into the shop.

Windows shattered from the onslaught.

Bullets found flesh with a sickening thud. Tawil groaned in pain and his body crumpled sideways to the floor, muscle spasms jerking from the wounds. The dog sprang up in fright and threw out a shrill bark before bolting toward the back of the shop. The storm outside could now be clearly heard. Rain and wind funneled through the destroyed windows and gave off a wet, eerie moan of longing. More rounds found their way inside, searching for targets.

"Crawl past the counter," Chatterjee said.

"What about the old man?"

"He's not my problem. You are."

Chatterjee reached back and found a gun he'd apparently been concealing. He gestured with the weapon. "Get going. I'm right behind you."

He stayed low and made his way to the other side of the counter and through the thin curtain. Chatterjee returned fire, sending two shots out into the dark, then belly-crawling his way through the curtain.

"That should at least slow them down, knowing we're armed. Let's go."

"And the clockmaker?"

"He's dead."

What was happening? Who was after him?

"How did these people know we were here?" he asked. "Where did they come from?"

"Eminence, this is not the time for analysis."

He caught no measure of respect with the use of his title.

Chatterjee stood. He did, too. They were in a dilapidated back room littered with mounds of debris. Darkness loomed, except for the weak light of a freestanding lamp in one corner. A stairway led up. Two windows opened to the outside, both covered in thin cheesecloth. No rear door.

Chatterjee stepped to one of the windows, stared out, then yanked the cloth coverings aside.

"Look out there."

He came close and saw it. A dock. With a small boat bobbing at one side.

"That's our ticket out of here," Chatterjee said.

The storm was still raging, more rain than wind, thank God. The Med could be unforgiving in rough weather. For centuries the sea itself had been the island's primary means of defense. The coastal currents were murderous, as was the rocky southern shoreline looming with deep gorges and bold headlands.

But all of that seemed far preferable to here.

The shop's front door banged open.

"We need to leave," he said.

But their path out was blocked by a filigreed iron grille. Chatterjee heaved at the inner wooden sash, which slid up with a protest, then he braced his feet against the wall and grabbed the iron with both hands. The grille gave a little from the tugs. He grabbed on, too, and together they forced the wet wood, crumbled with age, to release the screws, freeing the grille.

Chatterjee tossed the iron aside.

He clambered out over the sill. Chatterjee followed. The rain continued to fall with a monotonous determination out of a black sky. A path led from the shop to the dock. He was careful with his wild scramble across the wet rocks, his soles slipping with every step. He stole a few glances back over his shoulder at the threat behind. A sickening feeling of fear clawed at his stomach.

"Keep moving," Chatterjee said.

They reached the dock and he saw that the boat was a typical *dghajsa*. Small. Sturdy. High stem and stern. They were mainly used as water taxis around the Grand Harbor and the other bays. More like a gondola, not meant for the open sea. Usually propelled by oars, this one came equipped with an outboard engine. He could see Chatterjee was likewise concerned.

But they had no choice.

"Get in," Chatterjee said.

They hopped into the boat and he released the mooring lines. The choppy sea and wind pushed them quickly away from the dock. Chatterjee yanked on the outboard's starting cord and the engine revved to life.

They sped off into the night.

CHAPTER
THIRTY-ONE

COTTON SAT IN THE HELICOPTER, HEADING SOUTH TO ROME, Pollux Gallo and Stephanie flying with him. At first Stephanie had wanted to remain behind to coordinate what he was doing with Luke's activities on Malta. Gallo had offered her the Villa Pagana in Rapallo as her headquarters, and she'd nearly accepted his generosity, but in the end she opted to come along instead, wanting to be back in Rome.

"I know you must find this confusing," Gallo said to him. "Brother against brother. And twin brothers at that."

"Have you always been estranged?"

"Just the opposite, in fact. Our parents were killed when we were children, so we only had each other. We were raised in an orphanage, the nuns a poor substitute, but they did the best they could. Kastor and I clung to each other. But as we grew older, we drifted apart. Our personalities changed. Though we look alike, we don't think alike. By the time we were twenty, he was off to seminary and I was in the army."

"You said back at the archive that your brother wants to be pope. You know that for sure?"

"Without question. He told me so himself. He views this conclave as a gift from God, an unexpected opportunity that he must use to full advantage."

"You spoke on the subject?"

Gallo nodded. "We had a heated discussion. One of many of late."

"Is Archbishop Spagna his ally?" Stephanie asked.

"That's what I've learned. Kastor traveled to Malta yesterday specifically to meet with Spagna."

"And you know this how?" Cotton asked.

"Just like Spagna, we have spies, too."

He did not doubt that observation and he was still troubled by the comment made at the archive, which had yet to be explained. "Why do you think your brother's life is in danger?"

"We have people on Malta, inside Fort St. Angelo. Several knights are permanently stationed there. They've been watching my brother's activities and report he might be in danger."

"From who?" Stephanie asked.

"The *Secreti*. They're on the island. We know that for sure."

Cotton glanced across at Stephanie. "Nothing from Luke?"

She shook her head. "Silence. The GPS signal from his phone has also stopped. He's working with a Maltese security agent named Laura Price. They're both now with Spagna. The head of Maltese security tells me the situation is under control, so I have to trust Luke can handle himself."

"He can."

The chopper kept knifing through the night air. He glanced out the windows and spotted a dark rural landscape, broken occasionally by the lights of a village or a farmhouse. They were not yet to Rome, still north in Tuscany, he estimated.

"I see now," Gallo said, "that my brother's interest in the knights was totally self-serving, as is usual for him. He used his position to learn our secrets. To use them for his own advantage. Hopefully, we'll be able to prevent any further harm and end his bid for the papacy before he ever begins."

A canvas sack rested on the cabin floor. Gallo pointed toward it and said, "I brought what we'll need. I'm guessing the legend is not true and there's no need to destroy the whole obelisk to get to the codex, or whatever else Mussolini may have left inside. We've long thought a marked stone at the base could provide access to the repository."

"Planning on blowing it open?" Stephanie asked.

Gallo chuckled. "I'm hoping a sledgehammer will do the trick. But there are a great many in Italy who would not be sad to see that obelisk fall. The government has tried several times to raze it."

Yet it still stood. Like the flowers at the site where Mussolini had been shot.

"Why would the *Secreti* want your brother dead?" Cotton asked.

"He's antagonized half of the knights into enemies."

"But they're not the kind who normally kill people."

"The *Secreti* are fanatics, which makes them unpredictable and dangerous. They apparently view Kastor as a threat to the order. Their entire purpose is to eliminate threats. So the last thing they would want is for Kastor to become pope."

"And they'll kill to stop that?" Stephanie asked.

"I'm not sure what they'll do. All I know is that they are on Malta."

He felt the chopper start to descend and begin a wide turn. Outside the windows he saw they'd arrived on the outskirts of Rome. He caught sight of the forum, its two stadiums, running tracks, tennis courts, and other buildings, partially lit to the night, and the obelisk, rising at the entrance before an imposing avenue that stretched to a far piazza.

He checked his watch.

Nearly midnight.

It had been a long day.

THE KNIGHT STARED AT THE LIT OBELISK, ABLE TO SEE IN THE DIM wash of light the enormous inscription etched into its side.

MUSSOLINI DUX.

Finally. The truth may be told.

Was the map there? Or maybe the *Nostra Trinità* itself?

Waiting patiently?

Within the order a precious few were privy to the most confidential of information. Thankfully, he was one of those. He knew the story of Mussolini's visit to the Villa del Priorato di Malta and what he told Grand Master Rovere-Albani. *I've even done him a favor and sealed it away where no one can get to it.* If Mussolini truly found the Trinity, this could be his hiding place.

At least that's what James Grant had told him. Now it was time to determine if the information he'd risked everything to obtain was true.

Finally, the Brits were out of the way.

Only the Americans remained.

But he'd handle them.

CHAPTER
THIRTY-TWO

KASTOR HUNCHED IN THE LOW-RIDING *DGHAJSA* AS CHATTERJEE
headed them out of the bay and toward open sea. He didn't necessarily
agree with the wisdom of that move in the storm but decided not to argue. The idea was surely to get as far away from the men with guns as possible. To a place where they could come ashore in seclusion and safety.

The Mediterranean's great plain loomed dark. Giant thunderheads
banked overhead, bolts of lightning cracking inside the clouds, charging
them with a white glow. Waves clawed over the side as they rose and fell
into the troughs. On the distant horizon he saw more flickering of thun-
derclouds.

He knew the coastal geography.

South Malta was littered with towering cliffs, some dropping over 250
meters. They were now out of St. Thomas Bay heading toward Delimara
Point. He could see the lighthouse beacon through the storm. Though invisible in the night, he knew that Fort Delimara loomed ahead, built by
the British in the 19th century. Mostly underground, its armaments and
casements were set in the cliffs near the point. It had been a derelict during his childhood and, to his knowledge, remained so today. So no refuge
could be sought there.

The rain continued to squall.

Chatterjee angled the motor a quarter to starboard, on a path to cut across Marsaxlokk Bay. The bow heaved against the waves. High on emotion and lack of sleep, Kastor felt riddled with anxiety. He turned back toward Chatterjee and, in the distance, spotted the fast-approaching profile of a powerboat, running lights winking green and red.

"That could be trouble," he called out, pointing, his words thrown back in his face by the wind.

Chatterjee turned around and saw their pursuer, too. "These people came prepared."

Which made him wonder again who his enemy might be. "Why do they want me dead?"

"You think too highly of yourself, Eminence."

Then it hit him.

"They're after you?"

"I would say so."

They passed the southern tip of the bay. The famed cart ruts were nearby, at the Dingli Cliffs. Pairs of grooves cut into the rocky ground back in the Bronze Age that crisscrossed one another, a remnant of the past that he recalled from childhood. No one really knew how they originated. Sledges? Wheels? Slides? Hard to say. A mystery. One the nuns could never explain.

Like right now.

This was madness.

Out on the sea during a raging storm in a *dghajsa* propelled by a mere few horsepower, while a powerboat carrying who-knew-what bore down on them.

He grabbed his bearings.

Then he remembered the caves.

The south shore was littered with them, their names reflective of their history. Cat's. Reflection. Circle. Elephant. Honeymoon. The Ghar Hasan was perhaps the most famous. Supposedly the Saracen Hasan took refuge there with a young maiden he abducted. He recalled a footpath that led to stone steps heading down a limestone cliff. Inside were a series of passages, none of them hospitable, but Hasan had supposedly occupied one of them. That cave was too high from the water to be of any help. But the grottoes that existed below could provide a place to hide. The Blue Grotto was the most famous. He racked his brain and thought back. His gaze raked the darkened shoreline, periodically illuminated by lightning. The prop continued to bite the water. Their pursuer was coming ever closer, but still loomed a couple of kilometers away.

He pointed to the right. "Head toward shore."

"You're thinking the grottoes," Chatterjee asked.

"It's the only shelter we've got. If we hurry, we might be able to disappear into one without being seen. But you're going to have to get close for us to be able to see."

He checked his watch, the hands illuminated in the darkness.

12:20 A.M.

Another day had begun.

Which brought the conclave ever closer, now less than twelve hours away.

This was way beyond anything he'd ever experienced. Granted, he'd defied the Holy See with his outspoken dissension, but that was vastly different from men trying to kill him. Genuine fear surged through him, an unusual feeling. Never once had he feared the pope or the curia. Regret? Definitely, he'd felt that. Nobody liked to lose.

But this was nothing like that.

His eyes focused through the night, searching for an opening in the towering cliffs. Lightning continued to flash at regular intervals, offering a few precious seconds of clarity.

"There," he yelled, pointing ahead. "A grotto. I saw it."

"I did, too," Chatterjee said.

They rounded another point, the bow headed toward a small bay, homing in on the spot he'd seen in the last flash. Ill-tempered squalls kept scuffing the wavetops white. Another lightning bolt exploded overhead and he saw they were headed for an arch in the limestone wall, the entrance formed by a craggy arc of rain-sheered rock, a curtain of rivulets pouring down to the sea.

The powerboat was momentarily out of sight, which allowed them time to find the dark chasm in the cliff wall. Chatterjee navigated to the archway and they passed beneath the waterfall that spilled down across the opening. Kastor's clothes were soaked, the *dghajsa* puddled with water. Now, though, they were sheltered by a roof of stone, the grotto beyond calm to the night. During the day, combined with sunlight and the surrounding chain of rock, the water would reflect the phosphorescent colors of the submerged flora forming shades of blue and green. Tonight there was only black.

"There's a ledge," he called out, seeing its outline in the blackness.

Chatterjee eased to it. "Get out."

He stared back at the Indian.

"Get out," Chatterjee said again. "Stay out of sight. I'll divert them."

"Let's stay together."

For some reason he did not want to be alone.

"You're going to be pope. I'm hired help. Now get the hell out of this boat and let me do my job."

He hopped onto the limestone, the ledge perched just above the surface. He heard the *dghajsa*'s outboard rev and the craft sped away, deeper into the grotto, toward the exit on the far side. From beyond the entrance he heard the roar of the powerboat, drawing closer, its engine a steady drone above the wind and rain. Chatterjee slipped back out into the storm.

Then a new sound invaded the monotony.

Rat, tat, tat.

Gunfire.

More fear swept through him. He'd never felt more helpless. A need to withdraw came over him. He stared into the blackness and saw an even darker splotch. A cave? He carefully inched his way across the rough rock, slippery with seawater, and saw he was half right. Not a cave, more a tunnel. He knew most of them came to a dead end. He headed inside. This one drained into a small chamber hewn from the rock.

More gunfire could be heard.

He recalled the caves he'd explored as a child, most decorated with stalactites and splash deposits. Sometimes even crude paintings from antiquity. Hard to know if this one came with any of that. He sat on the wet limestone, breathing evenly, gathering his strength. He dared not give way to panic and forced his mind to behave.

What a predicament for a prince of the church.

He backed himself against the wall, his head pounding like a piston.

Once again he felt like Paul, who also supposedly found refuge in a Maltese cave. Paul was not one of the original twelve, but an apostle nonetheless. A servant of Christ who experienced a sudden, startling revelation that set him apart from others. He gained a reputation for bucking the law. His fate was sealed by writing letters to the Romans, Galatians, and Corinthians. He recalled the words from Acts about the viper on Malta. How the locals said, *No doubt this man is a murderer, whom, though he has escaped the sea, yet justice does not allow to live.* But Paul shook off the bite of the viper and *they were expecting that he would swell up or suddenly fall down dead. But after they had looked for a long time and saw no harm come to him, they changed their minds and said that he was a god.*

He'd planned to also shake off the viper, suffer no harm, and be regarded as a god. Like Paul, though, it seemed he might meet a horrible fate. No one really knew how or when Paul died. But every account that had survived described a violent demise in one form or another. Decapitation. Crucifixion. Stabbing. Strangulation.

Would his fate be similar?

There'd not been any more shots for a few minutes.

A good sign?

Had Chatterjee led them away?

From the tunnel's entrance, back into the grotto, he heard the hum of an engine. Low, steady. His gaze locked on the blackness.

A new surge of fear swept through him.

Footsteps approached. Coming his way across the hard stone through the tunnel. He dared not say a word. Then a form appeared in the chamber. No details. No face. Just a man.

"Eminence."

Chatterjee's voice.

Thank God.

"Are they gone?" he asked, hoping.

Chatterjee stepped farther inside. Another form appeared behind him, the outline of a gun in the man's right hand.

"No," Chatterjee said. "And I was caught."

He did not know what to say.

The form behind him stood still.

He wanted to stand but his muscles had frozen. Two bangs echoed off the stone walls, which hurt his ears. Chatterjee pitched forward and fell hard to the ground, not moving. He stared at the dark form in astonishment. Would it all end here? Alone? Inside a cliff. With no meaning or purpose? All that he'd endured would come to nothing?

He finally gave in to his calling and closed his eyes, saying a prayer, hoping God, if he existed, was indeed merciful.

Nothing happened.

He opened his eyes.

The sound of footsteps moved away.

CHAPTER THIRTY-THREE

LUKE FINISHED OFF ANOTHER OF THE RING-SHAPED LOAVES FILLED with cheese and meat. Laura called them *ftira,* something of a cross between a calzone and a sandwich. What he particularly liked was the thin slices of potato that adorned the outer crust. Unusual. But tasty. He washed the late supper down with a Kinnie, reminiscent of a Coke with less sugar. A beer would have been preferable, but none had been offered. He'd been grateful for the meal. He was hungry, and every growing boy needed three squares a day. Or at least that's what his mother always said.

Laura had eaten a little before an older, dark-haired man with a pouch around his waist appeared. She introduced him as Kevin Hahn, her boss, head of Maltese security. She then left with Spagna and Hahn. He'd wondered about all the chumminess that excluded him, but decided not to allow his feelings to be hurt, using the time to think.

A couple of newspapers were lying on the kitchen table. The *Malta Independent.* He noticed a front-page headline dated a few days ago—ALL IS READY FOR THE CONCLAVE—and scanned the article.

VATICAN CITY—Cardinals are filing into Rome for preliminary meetings to ponder who among them might be best to lead the church. Invitations to attend went out to all cardinal-electors under the age of 80 the day after the pope died. They arrive by private car, taxi, and mini bus at the gates of the Vatican for gatherings known as general congregations, closed-door meetings in which they will get to know each other and decide who will next lead 1.2 billion Catholics.

"We need a man of governance, by that I mean a man who is intimately connected with the people he chooses to help him govern the church," Cardinal Tim Hutchinson, the former archbishop of Westminster in London, said.

The voting-cardinals, numbering about 150, have been holding two meetings a day. One of their purposes is to select the conclave officers and review all of the rules. They also talk of the Holy See, the curia, and the expectations of a new pope. These preliminary sessions provide the cardinals a chance to size up potential candidates by watching them closely in the debates and checking discreetly with other cardinals about their qualifications or any skeletons in their closets. All necessary as these men come from all over the world and are rarely together.

"We've had meetings all this week to get to know each other better and consider the situations that we face," Hutchinson said.

He added that he could not say, at this stage, who the favorites might be. Cardinals never reveal publicly who they prefer but they do occasionally drop hints in interviews by discussing their view of the ideal candidate. The most frequently mentioned quality is an ability to communicate the Catholic faith convincingly. But the suddenness of the pope's death means that no front-runner currently stands out.

The Sistine Chapel itself is being prepared. The chimney is installed, leading down to the stove where the ballots will be burned after each vote. White smoke signals success. Black smoke failure. The color of each is ensured by a chemical pack added to the flames.

A further mix of high-tech gadgetry and Old World tradition will ensure secrecy, including a scrambling device that will block any attempt to phone or text the outside world. Bug sweepers will also guarantee the chapel is secure from unwanted eavesdroppers. Jamming will be used both inside the Sistine and at the nearby guest-house at Santa Marta where the cardinals will sleep during the conclave. Computers will also be banned, so email and Twitter are firmly out of bounds.

But it's not all down to high-tech gadgets.

A number of traditions will be strictly followed to ensure that the ballot is secret . . .

Luke recalled what Spagna had said about his people and conclave preparations. The Entity would possess all of the necessary expertise to ensure that secrecy was maintained. And who better than the Lord's Own to protect the faithful.

The door opened and Spagna returned.

Alone.

Now his feelings were hurt.

"Where's Laura?" he asked.

"She'll be back shortly."

"Is she in trouble with the boss?"

"I imagine that's a situation you are quite familiar with."

He grinned. "I've had my share of trouble."

"I bet you have. When she gets back, I'll need you both to take care of a situation that has arisen."

The rain had eased but was still drizzling down.

"I'm trying to find my man who has Cardinal Gallo contained," Spagna said. "But I'm having trouble making contact. He was headed toward St. Thomas Bay, to a local clockmaker's shop. I need you both to go there and see what's happening."

"You think there's a problem?"

"I have one of those bad feelings."

He'd heard that before from Stephanie, and though he'd learned to trust her instincts, this guy was a stranger.

"I have to check in with my boss," Luke made clear. "And that's not a request. If you have a problem with that, then I'm out of here."

"Your supervisor is on a helicopter headed toward Rome, unavailable at the moment. Cotton Malone and the temporary head of the Knights of Malta are with her. You should know that the temporary head is the twin brother of Cardinal Gallo."

"Aren't you a wealth of information," he noted.

"That's my job and, you're right, I lied earlier. I don't have Stephanie Nelle's okay to use your services. But I'll obtain it the moment it's possible. I do have permission to use Ms. Price, though. So for the moment, it's your call to stay or go. Make up your mind."

"Why aren't you working the conclave?"

"My people are preparing things as we speak."

"And here you are. On a treasure hunt. Makes a fellow wonder."

"Ever heard of multitasking?"

Luke rose from the table and tossed away the paper remnants from his supper into a trash can.

"There's a car downstairs, parked across the street. A green Toyota. Here are the keys." Spagna laid them on the table, along with a cell phone. "The directions to where you need to go are loaded on the map app. If you're in, head there when Ms. Price returns. If not, give both to her. She'll handle it. Either the both of you or her alone, find Gallo and my man and don't let them out of your sight. Call me when you have them. My number is also loaded in the phone as number 1 on speed dial."

Spagna left the apartment.

Bossy guy.

He had no choice. Which Spagna well knew. He had to stay. But now he had a cell phone. So he grabbed the unit and punched in the Magellan Billet emergency contact number. The phone did not connect. Instead, a message displayed that read INTERNATIONAL SERVICE NOT AVAILABLE.

He smiled.

Spagna was no fool.

He decided a trip to the head was in order. No telling when there'd be another chance. He laid his Beretta on the table, stepped into the bathroom, used the facilities, then washed his face and hands. Drying them with some paper towels, he walked back toward the trash bin in the outer room and tossed the paper away.

The door banged open, bursting from its jamb.

Which startled him.

Two men rushed inside.

Nothing in their look or manner signaled friend.

No way to reach the gun, so he spun on his right heel and jammed an elbow down then up into the nearest threat. His assailant crumpled from the blow, dazed. He lunged, gritted his teeth, and kicked again. The second man flew back against the wall, rattling the hanging pictures. He advanced to finish the second guy off and momentarily forgot about the first man. A blow to his spine came hard and unexpected.

Followed by another.

Electric pain resonated down his back. His legs went limp, the pain overtaking the adrenaline, compounding his uneasiness. But he was well trained, well conditioned, a combat veteran who'd fought hand-to-hand in close quarters. He knew how to block pain from his mind and fight while hurt.

He spun around.

A fist smashed into his face.

If not for the tingling in his spine he could have counteracted, but he was too dazed to respond. The image before him, a man standing firm and ready, twirled.

So did the room.

Another fist smashed into his jaw.

He staggered back.

A third fist slammed into his midsection and the wind left him. Breath strangled in his lungs. A final blow, an ax-handle combination of both arms with hands intertwined, came down across his neck.

He crumpled to the floor and vaguely heard one of the men standing over him, panting hard, say, "Grab him."

He tried to react, but couldn't.

The fog in his brain prevented his muscles from responding. His arms and legs were gripped hard. He tried to resist, but his muscles seemed paralyzed.

"Throw him through the window," one of the men said.

CHAPTER THIRTY-FOUR

COTTON HOPPED FROM THE HELICOPTER. THEY'D LANDED RIGHT IN the middle of the Stadio di Marmi, the Stadium of Marble, on a carpet of thin green grass. Benches for twenty thousand encircled them, just beyond a six-lane running track. The shadowy outline of colossal statues ringed the stadium's upper edge, like something out of ancient Greece or Rome.

The rotors wound down as they made their way for the exit. Gallo carried the heavy duffel bag, he and Stephanie following. The pilot waited with the chopper. This part of north Rome seemed wholly deserted at such an early-morning hour, the entire Foro Mussolini, or Foro Italico as it was now called, quiet.

They exited through a ramp up, the stadium itself sunk in the ancient way with the top row of seats at ground level. Gallo led them toward a fountain adorned with a massive marble ball that spun on a bed of pressurized water. To their left stretched a wide paved expanse.

"The Piazzale dell'Impero. The Empire Way," Gallo said. "A testament to fascist propaganda. One of the few left in the world. My brother would fully appreciate its audacity."

Amber lights lit the way, both sides lined with stout blocks of white marble. The avenue itself was all mosaic tiles forming maps, fasces, and sports images along with prophetic slogans. As they walked Cotton read a few. DVCE. Leader. DVCE A NOI. Leader with us. MOLTI NEMICI MOLTO

ONORE. Much enemy, much honor. DVCE LA NOSTRA GIOVINEZZA A VOI DEDICHIAMO. Duce, we give you our youth.

Audacity was right.

"This place was part training ground, part metaphor," Gallo said. "Mussolini hoped that sport and physical strength would secure Italy's place in the world. Entangling athletic and martial glory was central to fascism. My brother likes metaphors, too. He thinks reminding everyone of the Catholic past will somehow secure the future. As with the fascists, intertwining fear with ignorance is key to what my brother has in mind for the church."

"You two certainly disagree," Stephanie said.

"He's my identical twin, there's a bond between us, and I do love him. But thankfully, I've always been able to separate those emotions from how I feel about him as a cardinal of the church."

He knew little about Brother Gallo and nothing at all about Cardinal Gallo. But these two men definitely had issues.

"Anything from Luke?" he asked Stephanie.

She shook her head. "Nothing."

At the far end of the avenue stood the obelisk. No lights directly illuminated the white marble, which seemed fitting. It existed, but no effort was made to overly glorify its existence. Lights ringed a perimeter twenty feet away, angled up to the stars. Its style was likewise nontraditional, a series of irregular-shaped stepped stones rising upward to a tall, central pillar.

"They cut it from a single block," Gallo said. "Then encased it in wood and iron and floated all three hundred tons by the sea and the Tiber to here. It took three years to carve and stand upright. All thirty-six meters. Every step was documented and reported by the fascist press, extolled for the masses to worship and appreciate."

Interesting how dictators required shows of greatness as a way to prove they were entitled to power. Democratically elected leaders never had such a need since the people themselves vested them with power, and no one expected perfection. In fact, failure could be another stepping-stone to greatness. Dictators never accepted failure. They preferred to have their mistakes forgotten, overshadowed with spectacle.

They approached the obelisk.

Gallo pointed upward. "Notice the letters in the inscription."

He studied them in the dim wash of light. All uppercase, arranged vertically, MVSSOLINI on the spire, DVX beneath, each one over a yard high.

"They are incised rather than sculpted," Gallo said, "to prevent abrasion or removal. Il Duce thought ahead. He made them too large and too deep to ever be removed."

Ironic, Cotton thought. Similar to memories of fascism itself, which still seemed to linger in the 21st century.

They circled the monument.

Its marble was devoid of any other markings save the words OPERA BALILLA ANNO X carved into a tall panel at the base.

"The fascist youth organization Opera Nazionale Balilla immortalized itself, too," Gallo said. "Youth Organization Balilla. Tenth anniversary. The obelisk was dedicated on November 4, 1932, the tenth anniversary of the march on Rome and the start of the fascist regime."

"It's amazing the thing is still here," Stephanie said. "Every relic related to Hitler has been excised. Mussolini, though, seems different."

"Somebody tried to blow it up in 1941, but barely did any damage. People have suggested razing it for decades. But the Italians have never needed to delete their history." Gallo motioned at the obelisk. "Even if it's sometimes overdramatic. To them, destroying a monument like this is only a sign of weakness, of fear, not strength."

He continued to study the towering structure.

"We know Mussolini placed his codex inside," Gallo said. "Newspaper accounts from the time make no mistake of that fact. But no one knows where he placed the codex. It was done in a private ceremony, and no accounts have survived. As you can see, there's only one stone outside the central pillar with markings on it. The best guess is that the codex is behind it. What do you think? That marble has to be five centimeters thick."

"At least."

And the panel that bore the words OPERA BALILLA ANNO X measured about eight by four feet. A stout, solid stone rectangle built to last. And it had. For eighty years. He knew what Gallo wanted, so he climbed up on the four-foot-tall raised base and examined the large incised X—part of ANNO X—which had been intended as a reference to ten years of fascist rule. "How about X marks the spot?"

"Seems as good a place as any," Stephanie said.

Gallo unzipped the duffel bag and removed two sledgehammers and a flashlight. Cotton accepted one of the sledgehammers, and Gallo climbed up with the other.

Stephanie held the flashlight from below.

He nearly smiled at the irony. How many times had he damaged a World Heritage Site. Too many times to count, all just unfortunate occurrences. Now here he was about to intentionally deface a part of history.

He gripped the sledgehammer and swung.

The business end smacked the x hard. Gallo followed with a blow of his own. But the marble held firm.

They repeated the blows.

"Did you feel that," Gallo asked. "There's a little give. It could be hollow behind."

He agreed.

Stephanie aimed the flashlight at the x. Fissures had begun to spiderweb in all directions. Cotton glanced around and still saw no one. He wondered about security cameras. There had to be some. Yet no one had come to the obelisk's defense.

They resumed the assault.

A few blows later the marble gave way.

He and Gallo stepped back as chunks fell, creating a cloud of white dust. As they'd suspected, a small hollow niche loomed behind the outer wall. He laid the sledgehammer down and waited for the dust to settle. Stephanie handed him the flashlight.

He saw a metal tube, about two feet long and six inches wide, lying inside, a fasces etched into its dull exterior. Gallo reached in and removed the container, bringing it out to the base's edge.

"How do we open it?" Stephanie asked.

"They made them of lead and soldered the ends," Gallo said. "We should be able to break the joint. The idea was to be able to retrieve what they'd sealed away. I brought a rubber mallet, there in the bag."

"You know a lot about these things," Cotton noted.

"We've studied Mussolini and the fascists for a long time. We're hoping what we've been searching for is inside this repository."

She handed up the mallet. Gallo gently worked one end of the sealed tube, cracking his way around the soldered joint.

"They used a soft material and a light solder on purpose," Gallo said. "But keeping it airtight was essential."

The end cap gave way and Cotton shone the flashlight inside to see something rolled up.

Gallo slid it free.

Not paper. Stiff. Thicker.

Parchment.

Gallo unrolled the sheet, which measured about eighteen inches wide and two feet long. Black ink filled one side of the handwritten page. At the top were the words CODEX FORI MUSSOLINI. But what caught their collective attention was what had fallen free as Gallo unraveled the document.

Another sheet.

Thinner.

Browner.

More fragile.

Paper.

CHAPTER THIRTY-FIVE

LUKE HUNG IN THE AIR, HELD ALOFT AT HIS HANDS AND CALVES BY the two assailants. His head drooped down, still spinning. They were moving him toward one of the windows, intent on tossing him through the glass. In the open doorway behind him he saw the upside-down image of Laura rushing inside, pouncing on the man to his right, who released his hold and turned his attention toward her. He decided not to look a gift horse in the mouth and grabbed his wits, wiggling free from the other man's grasp, dropping to the floor and clipping the legs out from under his attacker. He rolled and wrapped his right arm around the man's throat and clamped hard, cutting off air and sending the guy into unconsciousness. Laura had already taken down her target, who lay still on the floor.

"Any idea who these idiots are?" he asked, breathing hard.

"Not a clue. But they came straight here, to an Entity safe house, which means they know Spagna's business."

"Where is the Lord's Own?"

"At another house, not far from here. He and my boss took me there when we left earlier."

That subject begged further investigation but, for the moment, he let it go and quickly searched both men. No ID. No weapons.

Forget them. Focus.

"Get a sheet off the bed," he said. "We'll rip it into strips and tie these bastards up for later."

He stepped to the table and grabbed the cell phone, car keys, and his gun.

They had to find Spagna.

He and Laura hustled west toward the piazza where everything had started, the sounds of cars fading as buildings began to soundproof the pedestrian-only zone. He kept a lookout behind them but noticed no one following. The only noise came from the occasional chatter of people and the whistle from a breeze.

Wispy high-level clouds veiled and unveiled a luminous moon, the storm having passed, the buildings and streets being strobed like a light turned on and off in a dark room. Floodlights encased the co-cathedral, bathing the ancient stone in a warm chalk-white glow. The building squatted like a massive four-legged creature, the bell towers ears, transepts paws, silently studying its territory. He followed Laura deeper into the old city. Past the cathedral zone the sidewalks became deserted. Streetlights periodically cast a lambent glow into a raisin-black night. Cars hunched close to the curb on both sides of every route, a few decorated with yellow summons, revealing the length of their illegal stay. Protective shutters were drawn tight on most of the apartment windows, only cracks of light indicating people inside. As he looked ahead, fifty yards, a new sound broke the silence.

One of the third-floor windows exploded.

A body flew out headfirst, flipped in midair, then slammed onto the hood of a parked car.

He raced forward.

Laura followed.

He instantly recognized the face.

Laura grabbed at the bloody shirt. "Spagna." Her voice carried a plea for a response. "Spagna."

He tried for a pulse. Faint. Blood poured from slashes across the face. The archbishop's nose bled profusely. But amazingly, he opened his eyes.

"Can you hear me?" Luke asked.

No response.

He saw panic in Laura's face. A first.

Spagna's bloody right hand jerked up and grabbed her arm. "Do . . . what I . . . told you. Both . . . of you."

A soft pop came from above and something whizzed close to Luke's right cheek. Spagna's chest exploded. Another swoosh and the skull ripped apart right before his eyes, blood and sinew splattering on him and Laura.

He whirled around and looked up.

In the shattered window three floors above, two men stood, guns pointed. Obviously, their first priority had been to finish what they'd started. In the instant it took them to re-aim their weapons at two unexpected intruders, he leaped at Laura, shoving her behind a car. They slammed onto the damp pavement, she on the bottom, he shielding her on top.

More soft pops echoed.

Bullets rained down.

One struck the hood next to Spagna's body, another shattered the windshield. Thankfully, the row of parked cars provided an ideal angle of protection, the third floor seemingly one story short of being high enough to shoot over them.

"We need to get out of here," she said.

"We can take these guys."

"Gallo is the priority now. That's what Spagna meant. We have to get to Gallo. Come on, and stay down."

She followed his lead, crouching low, using the cars as a shield while working down the street. More bullets tried to find a way through metal and glass. Fifty yards away he glanced back. The faces had disappeared from the window. Two forms suddenly popped out the building's front entrance. He and Laura took off running, turning at the first corner. He figured they had half a football field's lead. So he started making turns, trying to find a way out of the labyrinth of alleys.

They found a main boulevard.

He gulped in the humid air and looked around. The pavement was well lit and lined with more parked cars. Their pursuers were approaching, confirmed by the sound of running steps, coming closer.

Enough running. "Let's take these bastards out."

She didn't argue. He gripped his Beretta and they assumed a position on either side of the alley's end. But the footsteps could no longer be heard. They waited, but no one came.

What the hell?

Laura seemed surprised, too.

"In just a short time there are going to be a lot of police around here," she said.

He still had the car keys and phone with directions on it Spagna had supplied.

"Let's go find Cardinal Gallo."

CHAPTER THIRTY-SIX

COTTON REACHED DOWN AND LIFTED THE SINGLE SHEET THAT HAD fallen free. He was careful with his grip at the edges, mindful of how to handle something so rare, which was, after all, his main business.

He unrolled and studied the page.

Six lines. Typewritten.

He translated the German in his head and read it out for Stephanie, in English.

Deliver the contents personally into the hands of von Hompesch. This must be done at once and with all possible discretion. Where oil meets stone, death is the end of a dark prison. Pride crowned, another shielded. Three blushes bloomed to ranks and file. H Z P D R S Q X

"What does it mean?" she asked.

"Let's leave here, before we're found out," Gallo said. "I can explain some of it along the way."

Good advice.

They both hopped down and replaced the tools in the duffel bag. Gallo re-rolled the parchment and the single page, slipping them back into the metal tube. Cotton carried the tube as they retraced their steps down the avenue toward the stadium.

"The knight who wrote those words served Grand Master Ferdinand von Hompesch, on Malta, as the prior of *la nostra ronti maggiore della sacra religione*," Gallo said.

"Our major church of the sacred religion," Cotton translated for Stephanie.

"The conventional church of the knights," Gallo said. "The co-cathedral in Valletta. We've long thought the secret lay there, simply because of the connection of its prior to von Hompesch."

"There has to be more than that," Stephanie asked.

They kept walking.

"There is."

He listened as Gallo told them about a man tortured by Napoleon during his invasion of Malta. A man whose hands had been nailed to a table and still refused to tell the French invaders a thing.

"Legend says that the dead man left a way to find the *Nostra Trinità*. He was the prior of the cathedral and part of the *Secreti*. After Napoleon slaughtered him, he was buried along the east shore of Malta in a church cemetery. He lay there in quiet repose until his grave was violated in the 1930s."

"By Mussolini?" Cotton asked.

Gallo nodded. "And he clearly found something that commanded two popes' attention. Enough that he was able to compel them to stay out of his politics. We've always thought something significant came from that grave."

"Was it the message we just read?" Stephanie asked.

"It has to be. And there's one other thing." Gallo stopped, laying the heavy duffel bag down. "Mussolini killed three of our brothers to obtain what we just read. Those men, like that long-ago prior of the cathedral, died fulfilling their oaths. What we always believed, and now know to be true, is that Mussolini ultimately found nothing. He lied to the Vatican. A good one, for sure, but a lie nonetheless."

"How can you be so sure?" Stephanie asked.

"That's easy," Cotton said. "If he'd found the ultimate prize, it would have been inside that obelisk, instead of just clues as to where it might be."

Gallo nodded. "He also apparently altered the original message, since there were no typewriters on Malta in 1798. The original would have been handwritten. Let's hope he transcribed it correctly. It's now incumbent on us to find what he could not locate and return it to our custody."

He could hear the pain in Gallo's voice. Surely membership in any long-standing secret brotherhood involved a healthy dose of male bonding. But a society with overt religious overtones and ancient historical purposes added entirely different dimensions. Eighty-plus years had passed since those three brothers had died, yet the wound seemed fresh as yesterday to Pollux Gallo.

"We need to go to Malta," Gallo said.

"Why do you say that?" Cotton asked.

"It was in the words we just read. *Where oil meets stone.* What we seek is there."

THE KNIGHT HAD WATCHED WHAT WAS HAPPENING AT THE OBELISK with both fascination and worry. The *Codex Fori Mussolini* seemed to be exactly where the newspaper accounts from the 1930s had suggested.

An excellent turn of events.

It would be an easy matter to assume control of the situation and deal with the Americans here and now, as he'd done at the villa by Lake Como. He had the resources available. Just a simple gesture would call them to action. But that did not seem like the smart play.

Not yet, anyway.

Nothing had ever been gained through impetuousness. Rash thinking always resulted in unsatisfying results. He'd come this far thanks to smart choices and smart moves, timed perfectly. No sense stopping now. His grand plan contained many moving parts. So much had to go right, and at precisely the right time. The original path he'd mapped toward success now seemed obsolete. Too many new and unpredictable players had entered the field. Which seemed troublesome, but it also oozed with opportunity.

He'd been able to listen to the conversation at the obelisk. The information on the sheet that had fallen free of the codex had to be what

Mussolini stole, then hid away. The British were convinced of that fact, that's what James Grant had said, and now it seemed they may have been correct.

Better to let this play out.

And take advantage of his good fortune.

CHAPTER THIRTY-SEVEN

KASTOR HAD NOT MOVED.

Nor had Chatterjee, who lay a few meters away.

Once the black form had left the cavern, no one else had approached through the tunnel. After a motor revved, then faded, not a sound had betrayed the night beside the slosh of the sea from the grotto. He'd never seen anyone shot before. But tonight he'd borne witness to two lives ending that way.

Tiredness and a sense of hopelessness crept over him. He was shaking, fear seeping from every pore like a wounded animal. Probably shock setting in. Lying still, he tried to repair himself. But that self-awareness did little to alleviate a bleak despair. Which made him feel ashamed.

Thankfully, no one was here to see his weakness.

And he could not show even a trace of that in the days ahead.

The church was wounded and in turmoil. China and Russia were drifting from its orbit. Europeans were avoiding mass. In Central and South America its once strong moral hold had become frail. And America. The worst of all. Deviant priests and indifferent bishops had inflicted immeasurable damage. People were leaving the church in droves. Few studied for the priesthood anymore. Even fewer Catholics cared. Traditionalists had drawn many of the older faithful away, while the young were simply disenchanted with religion in general. An educated laity seemed no longer willing to blindly memorize catechism and ignore the dreaded question, why.

The time had come for a man of action. One who knew the church's laws and legacy, one who respected tradition and believed that the essence of truth lay within the Vatican, no reaching out required. The Roman Catholic Church was the greatest dynasty in human history. But malleable popes and a gluttony of poor thinking had led it astray.

That had to end.

He was about to challenge the College of Cardinals. Not all of them. Only a select few. The ones who could wield influence and bring the rest around where he could achieve the votes needed to win the papacy. He'd thought the *Constitutum Constantini* might be enough to accomplish that goal, but Spagna had unexpectedly offered something better.

And it was all on the flash drive Chatterjee had shown him.

He grabbed hold of his emotions and crawled across the rough stone, hoping it was still there. Chatterjee had fallen on his left side, so he rolled the body over and searched the pockets, finding the drive.

Thank God.

His salvation.

Provided it was real.

Too bad about Chatterjee. The man had tried to help, though he'd wondered what that help would ultimately cost from Spagna. It could not be as simple as Chatterjee had explained. Keep his job? A cardinal's hat? There had to be more at stake than that.

And there was.

Killers.

Men who shot other men in cold blood with no compulsion. Who were they? Why had they not shot him? If there was any semblance of faith left in his bones, he should come to his knees and pray to God for both thanks and guidance. But he'd long ago lost any belief that there actually existed a merciful omnipotent being who watched over the earth with the benevolence of a loving father. That was a myth, part of religion, which had been created by man, organized by man, and existed for over two thousand years thanks to man.

Spagna had been right about one thing. The pressure had to be applied once the cardinals were locked away inside the Sistine Chapel, where no one could seek help from the outside.

But first things first. Get out of here.

He came to his feet and felt his way through the black tunnel, back to the grotto. The *dghajsa* was tied to a rock, seemingly waiting for him. He wondered if it was a trap, a way to get him back out on the water. But he discounted that as justified paranoia. If they, whoever *they* were, had wanted him dead, they would have shot him with Chatterjee.

He hopped in the boat and untied the line.

Three pulls and the outboard cranked.

The last time he'd piloted a boat had been as a child, with his father. He maneuvered out of the grotto and into the bay beyond. The storm had abated, the rain slackened to sprinkles, the wind subsided. He swung the bow around and headed out toward the open Med. No other vessels were in sight. The question was where to go. He could turn and parallel the south coast, perhaps docking at the popular Blue Grotto, which wasn't all that far away. There he could make his way up to a road and find his way back to Valletta, leaving the island as fast as he could. Or he could retrace his route to the clockmaker's house. Surely the police were there by now, considering a car had exploded. He could seek their protection, invoking his status as a cardinal. Insist on being taken to Rome. But that could mean publicity, and he could ill afford anything negative at the moment.

Only a few more hours remain. Stay anonymous and above the fray. Let your new friend handle the dirty work.

The advice he'd been given just a short while ago on the phone.

Still, the clockmaker's house seemed the safest route.

He turned the tiller east.

LUKE DROVE THE VOLVO COUPE AND FOLLOWED THE DIRECTIONS provided on the cell phone. It helped that Laura knew the island and re-called a series of shops near St. Thomas Bay, just beyond the village of Marsaskala, one of them a longtime clockmaker. Neither of them had spoken of Spagna, their focus centered on getting out of Valletta.

"How deep is your boss involved in this?" he asked.

"He told me to work with Spagna. For once I decided not to argue and to do as I was told."

"Where did this conversation take place?"

"In the apartment Spagna was tossed from."

"You were gone awhile."

She was being stingy with the information and the tone of his question signaled irritation.

"Look," she said. "They didn't tell me their life story. Spagna said he needed us both to help him out. His more immediate concern was that he was having trouble making contact with Chatterjee. He wanted the two of us to check it out. He told me that he left a car, the keys, a cell phone, and directions with you. If you were there, then both of us should head out. If you were gone, then you'd decided to opt out and I was to do it on my own."

Exactly what the archbishop had told him, too.

"I headed back and found you were having a party without me."

"I appreciate you crashin' it. Any idea who those people were?"

She shook her head. "Probably with the same ones who found Spagna. They knew both locations."

"The Entity has a helluva leak."

"To say the least. But right now we need to find Cardinal Gallo."

The farther from Valletta they drove, the less it rained. She'd used the cell phone to confirm her own navigation, but she easily led them to the correct site. Ahead, he caught the strobe of blue lights off into the night before he saw the police and emergency vehicles.

"That's not good," he said. Then he spotted the burned-out hulk of a car illuminated by headlights and added, "Neither is that."

Apparently Spagna's fears were justified.

"Pull off somewhere," Laura said. "We don't need to be seen."

He veered from the road and into the first drive he saw.

They both exited the car.

KASTOR RETRACED THE PATH ACROSS THE WATER HE AND CHATTER-
jee had taken earlier. He was still shaken by everything that had hap-

pened. He felt out of control, in a spiral someone else had created and manipulated. People were dying around him with no explanation. Yet he was buoyed by the hope that the flash drive in his pocket might offer salvation. Even better, he would not have to deal with Danjel Spagna on terms of the other man's making.

He had leverage to use on the Lord's Own.

The sea had calmed, but the water remained stirred from the storm. The *dghajsa*'s outboard worked hard, and he struggled to keep the bow pointed toward shore. The feisty little boats could be finicky. They were built for durability, not ease or comfort. He rounded a dark point jutting from the shore and reentered the bay behind the clockmaker's shop.

He hoped his assessment would prove correct.

And that the trouble from earlier was long gone.

LUKE APPROACHED THE CLOCKMAKER'S SHOP.

He and Laura had crossed the road and made their way toward it from behind the scattered houses in the space between the buildings and the bay. They'd climbed a couple of fences, but nothing had impeded them except a few dogs who showed little interest. Back home in Tennessee he would have already been revealed by a pack of inquisitive, noisy hounds.

No police patrolled the rear of the clockmaker's shop. He examined the building and noticed the cracked stone, chipped paint on the windows, and vines creeping up one side. He spotted no back door, but one of the windows hung open with its iron grille gone. They rushed over and climbed into some sort of storage room. A doorway on the far side opened to what was surely the street side where all of the activity was still happening. Lights burned beyond a thin curtain. He signaled for quiet and they approached the barrier. Peering past the jamb he saw that the shop was empty, all of the windows shattered, fresh bloodstains on the wood floor. Outside, near the burned-out vehicle, stood four policemen.

"Somebody was shot," Laura whispered.

"Not to mention the extra-crispy car."

No body was evident. It must have been removed already.

Was it Gallo?

"I assume you know where the morgue is?" he asked.

She nodded.

Making contact with the locals could be problematic, especially after what had happened earlier when Spagna first appeared.

"You know what we have to do," he said.

She nodded her assent.

They retreated to the window and climbed out into the humid night. Before they could turn and head toward the car, an engine out on the water grew louder. He focused on a dock that jutted into the bay, lit by a small incandescent fixture. One of the colorful local boats appeared from the night and eased to a stop.

"You see that," he said to Laura, pointing.

Kastor Cardinal Gallo.

He shook his head. "Finally. A break."

CHAPTER
THIRTY-EIGHT

COTTON DOZED IN AND OUT, TRYING TO CATCH A QUICK NAP AS THE Department of Justice jet lifted off from Rome's Fiumicino–Leonardo da Vinci airport. He, Stephanie, and Gallo had used the helicopter for a short hop west from the obelisk and found the DOJ jet waiting, the same one that had brought Stephanie across the Atlantic. Only he and Gallo were making the ninety-minute flight south to Malta. Stephanie had been flown on to Rome in the chopper, deposited back at the Palazzo di Malta downtown, exactly where Cotton had started a few hours ago. She'd received a phone call on the trip to the airport and said that there were matters requiring her personal attention. She offered no details and, knowing better, he hadn't asked. Disturbingly, James Grant had dropped off the radar. London had no idea of his whereabouts, and the contact number Cotton possessed went to voice mail. Stephanie had told him she would monitor that situation from the U.S. embassy and asked to be kept informed as to what happened once they were on the ground.

Gallo himself had developed a case of lockjaw, sitting in his seat with his eyes closed, apparently trying to grab a little rest, too.

Actually, that was fine.

He needed time to think.

Where oil meets stone, death is the end of a dark prison. Pride crowned, another shielded. Three blushes bloomed to ranks and file.

What an odd assortment of phrases. Not random, for sure. But not coherent, either.

Then there were the letters.

H Z P D R S Q X

"What did you mean that the message points to Malta," he asked Gallo. "*Where oil meets stone.* You knew exactly what that meant."

Gallo roused from his rest, looking annoyed.

"The first part simply requests that it be delivered to von Hempesch. Clearly, the cathedral's prior created the message for his grand master. He also created it before being captured by Napoleon. Every piece of evidence indicates that only the prior was involved in the hiding. There is no record of him leaving the island in the forty-eight hours between the time Napoleon arrived and the prior died. It's doubtful he involved others, so whatever he hid away has to be on Malta. Then there is Mattia Preti. What do you know of him?"

"Never heard of him."

"He was like so many others who came to Malta in the 17th century. Men looking for a purpose, a place where they could live a full life and excel. He was an Italian artist who stayed the rest of his life, ultimately transforming the cathedral in Valletta into a wonder. The barrel vault of the church became his masterpiece. It took him six years to complete. When finished it depicted eighteen episodes from the life of St. John the Baptist. Normally murals like those were done with watercolors. But Preti broke with tradition and applied oil paint directly to stone."

He saw the connection. *Where oil meets stone.* "So everything points to the cathedral on Malta."

Gallo nodded. "It seems that way, and it makes sense. The French appeared in 1798 with no warning. The fight for the island took little more than a day before a full surrender. Sadly, only a small part of our treasures and records made it out of the city. Most were seized by the French during their plunder, lost forever when the ship where they had been stored on sank in Egypt."

Gallo went silent for a moment, then continued.

"It was a sad era in our existence. By the time Napoleon arrived the knights had lost all sense of purpose. The Protestant Reformation had reduced our ranks. Then, during the 16th and 17th centuries, revenues from European sponsors dwindled to nothing. Malta itself was a barren island with little to no export potential. To raise money we started policing the Mediterranean, protecting Christian ships from Ottoman corsairs. We became so good at it we evolved into privateers, capturing and looting Muslim ships, becoming corsairs ourselves. We made a lot of money from that but, as you might expect, such lawlessness leads to a moral decline, one that began to seep through the entire order. Eventually, we thought ourselves above kings and queens, exempt from the law, which made us even more enemies. So no one cared when the French took Malta and vanquished us." Gallo paused a moment. "By the mid-18th century we rediscovered our original purpose—aiding the sick. Thankfully, that tortured prior never faltered in his duty and denied Napoleon the *Nostra Trinità*. Our Trinity stayed hidden, and now we know that even Mussolini failed to find it."

Cotton pointed at the metal tube lying on another of the seats. "How can you be sure that the message is the same one from that prior? As you noted before, Mussolini prepared that typed sheet."

"We can't. But finding it is consistent with what I told you about Mussolini and his statements to our grand master in 1936 at their one and only meeting. He said he altered the memory to preserve it. Then he hid it where no one could get it. We have to believe that he changed nothing. Why would he? He might have had to really find it himself one day."

"It's interesting that Mussolini didn't go after it."

"He didn't have to. All he had to do was convince the pope that he could."

"But by hiding the message away, it's almost like he was placating the pope."

"He was. Definitely. For all his bravado, Mussolini was intimidated by popes. He pursued a policy of wooing both Piuses, and to a degree it worked."

"I wonder what it takes to blackmail a pope?"

Gallo stirred in his seat. "I've asked myself that for years. Of the three parts of the *Nostra Trinità*, only the *Constitutum Constantini* could pose a threat. The other two are known documents, with copies in the Vatican. But that Gift of Constantine has to be unique. We've always believed that Mussolini used the threat of its public release as private blackmail. But did he really? We'll never know. What we do know is that neither Pius XI nor Pius XII ever openly defied the fascist government."

"Still, the church has been around for two thousand years. There's not much that could strike a deep blow. It would have to be something that goes to its core. Cutting its legs right out from under it."

Gallo nodded. "Even more important, it has to be something that would have resonated in the 1930s and 1940s. Something that still carried a virulent punch, one the church thought it couldn't endure. That was a difficult time. The world was disintegrating into war. People were focused on merely surviving. Religion was not an important aspect of their lives. We've long speculated on what that document might have contained, but that's all it is, speculation."

"How long had you possessed it?"

"The best we can determine is it came to us sometime in the 13th century. How? We have no idea. That's been lost to time. But we know that it stayed with us until 1798."

"No one ever read it? No oral tradition is associated with it?"

"Not that has survived. It was closely held by the *Secreti.* Now, at least, we have clues as to where it might be."

"There's still the matter of the *Secreti,*" Cotton pointed out.

"I realize that, and we should stay alert. They'll be aware of the cathedral's importance, too. And I assume they'll know that I've come to Malta. We cannot underestimate their reach."

He agreed with that assessment. "What about your brother?"

Though Stephanie had said precious little before leaving for Rome, she had revealed that Archbishop Danjel Spagna had been killed, along with another Entity field operative. Cardinal Gallo, while initially missing, had been located by Luke, who had the situation on the ground under control.

"My brother and I will speak," Gallo said, the voice trailing off. "He's caused so much turmoil. It will take a long time to repair that damage."

Cotton was an only child. His father died when he was ten, lost in a navy submarine disaster, so he'd come to rely on his mother. A good woman. She still lived in middle Georgia, running the onion farm her family had owned for generations. She, too, had been an only child, so there were no more Malones. Not by blood, at least. His own son, Gary, an only child, was his in every way save for genes, the result of an affair his ex-wife had seventeen years ago. They'd all laid those demons to rest, part of the past, but he'd be a liar if he said that the prospect of the Malone bloodline ending didn't bother him.

"My brother and I shared a womb," Gallo said. "We're identical physically, though I've tried hard to alter my look so as not to be so readily identified with him. But mentally we are night and day. I've always strived to live a different life, to stay out of the spotlight, away from trouble. To make myself useful and not a nuisance. As I told you, I didn't ask for my current position. I took it out of necessity to try to minimize an already bad situation. Once there's a new pope, the brothers will meet and a new grand master will be chosen."

"You?"

Gallo shook his head. "That job will belong to someone else. I made that clear when I accepted this temporary post."

"I still don't see your brother's purpose in disrupting the Hospitallers. He seemed to go out of his way to create trouble."

"He thrives in conflict. He's after the *Nostra Trinità*, somehow thinking it will make him pope."

"Will it?"

"I can't see how, but he's convinced—as he always seems to be."

Gallo closed his eyes again and tilted his head back on the seat. The jet's windows were dark to the outside, the cabin lights dim. The drone of the engines cast a monotonous tone that seemed to only add weight to his own eyelids.

They'd be on the ground in a little over an hour.

Some rest would be good.

But answers would be better.

CHAPTER
THIRTY-NINE

LUKE STOOD ON THE TARMAC STARING UP INTO THE NIGHT SKY.
Laura was inside the small terminal building with Cardinal Gallo. They'd
driven the short distance from St. Thomas Bay to Malta's main airport.
Gallo had not resisted coming with them, and Luke could understand why
after listening to what had happened out on the water. He'd finally connected with Stephanie by phone and learned what had happened in Italy.
Laura had called in to her boss, and people had been dispatched to the
grotto Gallo had described in search of Chatterjee's body. Now Cotton
Malone and the cardinal's twin brother were on final approach, about to
land.

Thank goodness Stephanie had stayed behind. He didn't really want
to face her right now. He hadn't handled things like they'd needed to be
handled. A simple recon assignment had turned into anything but, and
now Pappy himself was on the way to save the day. He shouldn't feel that
way about Malone. He liked the man. More than that, he respected him.
But Malone was retired and this was *his* assignment. He'd been the one
to screw up and it was up to him to fix it, no help from an ex-agent-turned-
bookseller required.

But that wasn't his call.

Stephanie had already told him to follow Malone's lead and all would
be explained. Great. He could hardly wait.

The time was approaching 2:00 A.M. and the international airport's main terminal loomed quiet. No rumble of engines disturbed the night. He was standing near a building used by private planes, many of them parked off to his right. One multimillion-dollar jet after another. Flashing lights from the north grew brighter, and he watched as they dropped down for a landing and another pricey jet taxied his way. The words DEPARTMENT OF JUSTICE on the side identified its owner. The engines wound down and two men emerged from the open cabin door. Malone first, then another, whom he assumed was Pollux Gallo. Same height and shape as the cardinal, only different hair and a beard. He caught the facial resemblance as they drew close. Malone shook hands, then introduced him.

"Luke is active duty, Magellan Billet," Malone explained to Pollux Gallo. "He's the senior man on this job."

"That's not what I was told," Luke pointed out.

"And what did I tell you about working the field?"

He smiled, recalling the advice from their first encounter together. *You can do anything you want, as long as the job gets done.*

"Forget what Stephanie said. This is not my show," Malone said. "I'm backup. Where's the cardinal?"

That vote of confidence felt good. Another reason it was hard not to like Malone. He was a straight shooter, all the way. Luke pointed to the right and they headed inside the concrete-block building. He watched as the brothers greeted each other with the warmth of two alligators. No handshake. No hug. Not even a smile. Hard for him to understand that estrangement given how close he was to his three siblings.

"Are you pleased with yourself," Pollux Gallo asked, the tone not congenial.

"This is not the time," the cardinal said.

"It's never the time with you. People are dying, Kastor, because of your reckless actions."

"I require no lecture from you. I need to be back in Rome."

"Not until this is done," Luke said. "I've been fully briefed on everything from Italy, and my orders are to see this through before any of you leave this island."

COTTON LIKED THE NEW AND IMPROVED LUKE DANIELS.

Tough, confident, in charge.

Not the same cocky former Ranger who'd dropped out of the sky into the cold Øresund not all that long ago. Stephanie's report that things had not gone well here mattered little. Rarely did anything go as planned in the field. Getting knocked down was a constant occupational hazard. The trick was in knowing how to get back up and keep going. Some learned how, others not so much. Good to see Luke had fallen into the former category.

The two Gallos were a study in stark contrast. Pollux's face stayed as somber as a funeral director, while Kastor's flashed bright and alert. Their personalities seemed night and day. Interesting how identical twins could be so different. Apparently, environment really did affect genes.

Laura Price had stayed curiously quiet, watching the unfolding confrontation with clear interest. He knew nothing about her, which lumped her into the same category as both Gallos. Three unknowns usually added up to trouble, so he told himself to stay ready. He'd meant what he said. This was Luke's show, but he'd agreed to see it through as a favor to Stephanie. He'd always found it hard to tell her no. Besides, he'd been paid in full by the British and he owed them their money's worth.

"I just received a call from the people who went to find Arani Chatterjee's body," Laura finally said, "in the grotto the cardinal described. It wasn't there."

Cardinal Gallo seemed shocked. "He was dead. I checked myself. I saw him shot. Are you sure your people found the right spot? There are a lot of caves along the south shore."

"They were in the right place. But there was no body. And the two men Luke and I left tied up in the safe house are gone, too."

Cotton smiled. "Lots of stuff disappearing around here."

"We can't worry about any of that right now," Luke said.

He agreed and pointed at the metal tube they'd brought off the plane. "Show him."

Pollux slid the parchment and the typed page free and displayed both to his brother. The cardinal seemed uninterested in Mussolini's fascist manifesto. Instead he focused on the clues.

"I assume you read German," Cotton asked.

"I do, and this is gibberish."

"Which was surely the whole idea," Pollux said. "You would have to be privy to information that only a few people on earth would know to solve that riddle. Luckily, I'm one of those."

Cotton caught the unsaid words.

The cardinal was not.

"We have to go to the co-cathedral," Pollux said.

"I should return to Rome," the cardinal said. "This doesn't require me any longer."

"Except that you're the cause of it all," Pollux blurted out, in the first sign of any emotion. "You wanted the *Nostra Trinità*. Unfortunately, you're not going to get it. But we are going to finish this, brother. Finish what *you* started, so the Trinity can be restored to the knights, where it belongs." Gallo paused. "Then you and I are going to have a talk. In private."

Cardinal Gallo stayed silent.

"All this sibling rivalry is fascinating," Laura said. "But there are still threats on this island, and plenty of unknowns. Particularly with cars blowing up and bodies disappearing."

Cotton saw that Luke caught the wry grin on his face, which telegraphed exactly what needed to be made clear.

"Not a problem," Luke said. "We can handle it."

CHAPTER FORTY

KASTOR HAD ALWAYS ADMIRED THE CHURCH OF ST. JOHN THE BAP-tist. Solid, austere, its thick walls conveying an unmistakable message of power and strength. Two large towers with octagonal spires flanked either side of its main entrance, each housing bells. Nearly every church on the island mimicked its shape and style, which was not unintentional.

The knights had been smart with its location, choosing a high spot in the center of their new city and erecting a landmark that could be seen from nearly anywhere on, or off, the island. Its austere façade faced west, the altar east, as was traditional in the 16th century. Its sober and robust exterior shielded an amazing expression of baroque art inside, all dedicated to the knights' patron saint, John the Baptist. Everything about it was tied to the Order, but Napoleon had left a mark, too. As soon as the French stole the island, the bishop of Malta made a request. He wanted the church for his diocese and saw the invasion as an opportunity to wrest it away from the knights. So Napoleon handed it over and decreed that it would be forever called the Co-Cathedral of St. John the Baptist, available to all.

And the name had stuck.

He remained unsure what to make of the new additions to the team. But what choice did he have? Spagna and Chatterjee were both dead. Thankfully, the flash drive remained safe in his pocket. He'd not said a word about it and did not intend to. That prize was his alone. And what had happened to Chatterjee's body? Did the man who'd killed him return and ferry it away?

If so, why?

They rounded the cathedral's exterior and found a small square that spread out from a side entrance. The cobbles remained damp from the rain. A few people lingered in the square despite the late hour. On the ride from the airport Pollux had worked the phone, speaking with the cathedral's operating foundation, letting them know he was on the way. Though the Hospitallers no longer actually owned the church, they retained great influence over its use. It actually wasn't much of a church anymore. More a tourist attraction. Forty years ago things had been different. Fewer visitors to the island then. The world had yet to discover Malta. He recalled visiting with his parents several times, then many more once at the orphanage. Everything here was familiar territory. So why did he feel so out of place?

The wooden doors creaked opened and a middle-aged man in jeans introduced himself as the curator. He was pale-skinned, with an owlish face adorned by thick-rimmed glasses. His hair was tousled, his eyes tired, probably the effects of being woken from a sound sleep.

Pollux stepped up and assumed the lead. "I appreciate you being here at this late hour. It's important we be inside the church for a little while. Undisturbed."

The curator nodded.

It was odd to see his brother in a position of authority. Always it had been Pollux following *his* lead. But he told himself that Pollux was temporary head of the knights thanks to him. Whatever power his brother possessed came from him. He found it unsettling to take a backseat, though it seemed the wisest course. Nothing would be gained by a confrontation. Besides, he was curious about what they might find. Still, the clock was ticking down, the conclave set to begin in less than ten hours. Every cardinal who planned to be inside the Sistine Chapel voting had to be at the Domus Sanctae Marthae by 10:00 A.M. After that, there was no admittance.

He followed the entourage inside to a wide rectangular nave, flanked by two narrow aisles, topped by a ribbed barrel vault. The aisles were further divided into a series of impressive side chapels. The air was noticeably cooler. Lavish stone carvings, gilding, and marble ornamentation sheathed every square centimeter of wall, floor, and ceiling. Nothing had been omitted. Elaborate baroque motifs burst forth in profiles of foliage, flowers, angels, and triumphal symbols of all shapes and kinds. He knew that none of them had been added. Instead, everything had been carved straight from the limestone. Subtle amber lighting bounced off the marble walls, staining the dazzling blaze of color and decoration in a warm glow. Nearly five hundred years of constant pampering had resulted in a masterpiece. Some called it the most beautiful church in the world, and they might be right.

"I'll leave you alone," the curator said.

Pollux raised a halting hand.

"Please don't. We need your help."

COTTON HAD VISITED ST. PETER'S BASILICA IN ROME, THE CHURCH of the Savior on the Spilled Blood in St. Petersburg, and Westminster in London. None were even in this place's league. So much assaulted the eyes from every direction it was nearly overpowering—a combination of pomp, art, religion, and symbolism in a clash of period styles that somehow mixed seamlessly.

He asked about its origins.

"For the first hundred years, the interior was modest," the curator said. "Then, in the 1660s, the grand masters ordered a massive redecoration, one to rival the churches of Rome. Mattia Preti was placed in charge and spent half his life creating nearly all of what you now see."

That was the name Gallo had mentioned on the plane ride.

"This is perhaps the greatest expression of baroque in the world," the curator added. "Thankfully, it survived the bombing in World War II."

"We have something to show you," Pollux Gallo told the curator, and he handed over the typed sheet.

Where oil meets stone, death is the end of a dark prison. Pride crowned, another shielded. Three blushes bloomed to ranks and file. H Z P D R S Q X

"A puzzle for sure," the curator said. "One part is clear, though. The first four words."

And the man pointed upward.

Cotton stared up at Preti's masterpiece. Six defined ceiling bays, each divided into three sections, made for eighteen episodes. The painted figures looked more like three-dimensional statues than flat images, all forming a single, smooth narrative from the life of St. John the Baptist, transforming what was surely once a plain barrel vault into something extraordinary.

"It's all oil painted on stone."

As the curator continued to discuss the ceiling and the lines from the puzzle, Cotton turned his attention to the floor.

Another one-of-a-kind.

There were hundreds of tombs, each unique, composed of finely colored inlaid marble words and images, lined in perfect columns front-to-back, left-to-right, wall-to-wall. Every inch of the floor was covered, forming a stunning visual display. A few rows of wooden chairs stood toward the far end, near the altar, surely for people who came for prayer.

The rest was all exposed.

He noticed the lively iconography, the colorful mosaic arrangements depicting triumph, fame, and death. Skeletons and skulls seemed popular. He knew why. One represented the end of a physical being, the other the beginning of eternal life. There were also plenty of angels, either blowing trumpets or holding laurel wreaths, along with coats of arms, weapons, and battle scenes, surely a testament to the deceased's chivalry. A turbulent tone and character dominated, which he assumed was reflective of the times in which the men had lived. Most of the epitaphs seemed grandiose and wordy, mainly in Latin or the deceased's native tongue. He spotted French, Spanish, Italian, and German. Commonality abounded in style, but so did individuality. No two were exactly alike, yet they all seemed similar.

"There is also a connection," the curator said, "with the next words of your message. *Death is the end of a dark prison.* Let me show you."

The older man stepped across the floor, searching for one of the tombs.

"Here."

They all moved toward the center of the nave, where the curator stood before a particularly ornate memorial, centered with a shrouded skeleton before a wall of iron bars. Two columned pilasters supported an arch above the bars, the whole image flat, but animated in a three-dimensional trompe l'oeil effect. Cotton read the epitaph and learned it was the grave of a knight named Felice de Lando, who died March 3, 1726. Above the skeletal figure Italian words appeared in the arch.

LA MORTE E FIN D UNA PRIGIONE OSCURA.

Death is the end of a dark prison.

Coincidence?

Hardly.

KASTOR HAD ALWAYS LOVED THE CATHEDRAL FLOOR. NOTHING like it existed anywhere else in the world. And the tombs were not cenotaphs. Instead they were actual graves with bones beneath them—the more important the knight, the closer to the altar. All burials stopped, though, in 1798 when the French invaded. Important knights after that were buried beyond the city in far less elegant locations. Not until the British took the island in 1815 had they resumed, but then they ended forever in 1869. He knew all about them thanks to the nuns. The kids from the orphanage had routinely worked in the cathedral, himself and Pollux no exception. He'd explored every part of the building, finding the floor particularly intriguing. A mosaic of memory, ripe with words of consolation, instruction, and praise. Some exaggerations for sure, but memories needed "things" to prolong themselves, otherwise they never lasted.

The Roman Catholic Church was a perfect example.

As was his life.

His own parents died with nothing more than a simple funeral attended by a few friends. There was not even a stone marker over their graves. Nothing tangible remained of their existence, save for twin boys.

One of whom might soon be pope.

So far, two lines of the message had been deciphered.

One thing seemed clear.

They were in the right place.

COTTON TRIED TO THINK LIKE THAT CATHEDRAL PRIOR WHO, knowing the harbor was filled with French warships and an army was about to invade, still managed to get his job done.

Talk about pressure.

He said, "I'm assuming that since the *Secreti* existed in 1798, and all of the knights were housed here on Malta, any hiding places the *Secreti* may have used before the French came were on the island?"

Pollux nodded. "That is a reasonable assumption. The knights tried to confine things to this island. Their domain."

"So Malta falls," he said. "Knights start to flee, even the grand master leaves. To be safe, before the French take the island, the cathedral prior gathers up the *Nostra Trinità* from wherever it had been hidden and stashes it in a new place, one only he knows about. Then he creates a way to find it with clues the grand master can decipher, and instructs that the message be delivered to him. It never makes it that far, though, and ends up somewhere that Mussolini was able to locate it. Maybe the prior's grave? Who knows?"

He could see Pollux did not disagree with his logic.

He pointed down. "It has to be these mosaics. He specifically used an epitaph from this memorial, preceded by the words *where oil meets stone*." He motioned to the ceiling. "*Where oil meets stone, death is the end of a dark prison.* That's right here. There was no time for being ingenious. The prior was the caretaker of this building, so he adapted what he knew best."

"*Pride crowned, another shielded. Three blushes bloomed to ranks and file,*" Laura Price said. "Those words relate to this floor?"

He nodded, looking around at the many different images depicted on the memorials. "Yep. They're here. Somewhere."

"Any clues as to what *pride crowned* means?" Cardinal Gallo asked.

His mind was working on just that.

"Before we get too deep into this, I'm concerned about outside," Laura said. "We have no idea what's happening out there."

She was right.

Cotton faced Luke. "How about you two take a look. Make sure we don't have any unwanted visitors. We are a bit exposed here."

Luke nodded. "We'll take care of it."

He watched as they hustled back toward the entrance. He felt better knowing his flank was being guarded by Luke. He recalled Gallo's warning from the plane that the *Secreti* would know of the cathedral's possible importance and of the lieutenant ad interim's presence on the island. Solving this puzzle could take a little time, and whoever was out there might be waiting for that to happen before making their move.

Or the threat could already be here.

Inside the cathedral.

Watching right now.

THE KNIGHT WAS BACK ON MALTA.

It had been a while since his last visit.

Thanks to James Grant, he'd kept pace with the Americans. First at the obelisk, now here inside the co-cathedral. Right place, right time, and he was able to listen to everything Cotton Malone said.

He agreed.

The answer was in the floor.

And fitting, as each tomb told a story of men who gave their fortunes, lives, and reputations to God and Church. Men who fought at the Siege of Ascalon, the Battle of Arsuf, the Invasion of Gozo, the storming of Tripoli, and the Great Siege of Malta itself. Their graves stood side by side, linked together in a continuous smooth surface, a proper metaphor for the knights themselves. Too bad the remains of that brave prior who'd defied Napoleon never made it here. He would have earned a place of prominence near the altar. Instead his remains had been consigned to a run-down churchyard, his grave violated by a vile dictator. Sacrilege. Nothing less.

That wrong would have to be righted.

Mussolini had been shot like an animal, then his corpse hung upside down on a meat hook and pelted with vegetables, spat on, peed on, shot, and kicked. All fitting. Finally, he was buried in a Milan cemetery. Years later, to placate the conservative far right, his body was moved to the family crypt in Predappio, placed in a stone sarcophagus decorated with fascist symbols, and adorned by a marble bust. Flowers and wreaths remained a constant adornment. A hundred thousand people came each year on pilgrimage. April 28, the day he died, was still celebrated with neo-fascist rallies and a march through the town to the cemetery.

He'd even gone once himself.

To spit on the grave.

That abomination would end.

He'd personally see to that.

Nobody remembered the three knights Mussolini tortured and killed to get what he wanted. Nobody knew a thing about the cathedral prior who kept his oath and died at the hands of Napoleon.

Men with honor trying to protect—

What may now finally be revealed.

CHAPTER
FORTY-ONE

COTTON PLAYED THE PRIOR'S MESSAGE OVER AND OVER THROUGH HIS mind, focusing on the last two lines. *Pride crowned, another shielded. Three blushes bloomed to ranks and file.* He walked the floor, eyes down, taking in the collage of images.

"There are over four hundred tombs," the curator said. "Even I'm not familiar with aspects of them all."

He noticed something toward the front of the nave, just before the steps up to the main altar. "There are two here identical. One to the left of the steps, the other there, to the right."

"Two knights," the curator said, "both named Francesco Carafa, both from Naples. One died in 1632, the other in 1679. For some reason, which remains unknown, the latter Carafa chose to have his tomb identical to the former."

A curiosity, for sure, but not relevant to the present dilemma.

He ambled away from the twin tombs and continued to study the memorials. The others did the same. Each trying to find some connection between the words and the floor. Something caught his attention.

Three lion heads on a shield.

Crowned.

Then it hit him.

He'd been thinking in the wrong direction.

Pride crowned.

He'd thought *pride* an emotion or a reaction of some sort. Instead it was something much more tangible. A group of lions. Their social unit.

A pride.

He smiled.

That prior had been clever with words.

"It's here," he called out. "The grave of François de Mores Ventavon."

He read out loud more of the Latin on the tomb as the others headed his way. *"He was granted by his Religion the Commandery of Marseilles, the Priorship of the Venerable Tonge of Provence and, his last office, the Priory of Saint-Gilles. Three titles."* He pointed at the marble memorial. "Three lions crowned. Pride crowned."

"You could be right," Pollux Gallo said.

He thought of the next two words and said, "We need to find a lion on a shield."

KASTOR HAD NEVER BEEN FOND OF PUZZLES, MUCH LESS ONE OVER two hundred years old. But he knew the *Secreti*. They'd not kept the *Nostra Trinità* safe for centuries by acting stupid. The threat from Napoleon would have been the greatest danger they'd ever faced. That damn Frenchman changed everything.

The knights were never the same after 1798.

While serving as head of the ecclesiastical court, he'd first heard the stories of Constantine's Gift. The keeper of the Vatican archives had told him of how the 3rd century was a time of chaos. Plague ravaged towns, civil wars raged, corruption ran rampant, twenty-five different men sat on the Roman throne within fifty years. Finally, in 324, Constantine eliminated all contenders and assumed absolute control. Trying to change, or even influence, entrenched religious beliefs proved impossible, even for an emperor. So Constantine cultivated his own religion, one named for a Jew who'd supposedly died on a cross and left behind a group of disciples to spread a message of love and hope.

Christians.

He issued imperial decrees that allowed them to finally worship without oppression. He supported them financially, building basilicas, granting tax exemptions to clergy, and promoting Christians to high public office. He returned confiscated property, then built the Church of the Holy Sepulcher in Jerusalem and the first St. Peter's Basilica in Rome. To this day Constantine the Great held a special place within the Roman Catholic Church.

One he hoped to emulate as pope.

"Over here."

They all hustled to where Malone stood, his finger pointed down at another of the marble tombs.

"Another lion shielded," Malone said.

Kastor nearly smiled.

They were close.

CHAPTER
FORTY-TWO

LUKE STEPPED OUTSIDE, LAURA RIGHT BESIDE HIM, AND GLANCED AT his watch. 2:48 A.M. He should be somewhere in Eastern Europe, working his previous assignment. Instead he was on a rock in the Mediterranean doing God knows what. He still wore the shirt, shorts, and shoes from this morning, which didn't make him look out of place, though he'd felt a little odd being inside the cathedral dressed that way. They stood in what was noted on a placard as St. John's Square, maybe fifty people milling about beneath the glow of overhead lighting. The cathedral itself, lit to the night, was surrounded by streets on all sides. Plenty of opportunities for unfriendlies to make a move.

"Let's check the perimeter," he said. "All the way around."

His Beretta was tucked at his waist beneath his shirt. Laura was likewise armed, having acquired a weapon from her people while they'd waited for Malone to arrive. He was actually glad to be outside. Malone was onto something and that was Pappy's problem to solve. He had his own to deal with, and she was standing right beside him.

"I'll go this way," he said. "You take the opposite and we'll meet on the far side of the building."

She nodded and hustled off.

He walked through the cobbled square, but stopped beneath a stand of trees, using one of the trunks for cover. A quick glance back and he saw

Laura heading for the building's corner where she would shortly be out of sight, around to the other side.

His mind drifted back to when he was eleven years old. He, his father, and his three brothers were in the last few hours of the last day of his first hunting trip outside Tennessee. To Nebraska. In bone-chilling cold. They'd been at it for three days, chasing deer across the breaks just above the Republican River Valley. They'd sat in blinds for two mornings and an evening, and not a single deer had wandered by. His father and brothers had already taken their limit. Still nothing, though, for him. Frustrating since it was the first hunting trip where he could legally carry a gun and shoot on his own.

Just one chance, that's all he wanted.

So his father decided to do what any self-respecting Tennessee hunter would do.

He took them into the hills for some stalking.

They chased deer for two more days, pushing them from one draw to the next. But no matter how clever his father seemed to be, the deer always stayed one step ahead. Eventually, his father began to understand how, when, and where the deer were moving.

And he got ahead of them.

Two shots came from the far ridge.

His father checked the wind and noted that it was still blowing straight down the draw. Perfect.

"Other hunters just pushed 'em," his father had said. *"In just a minute or so, those deer are going to come right down this draw. It's your turn, son."*

He smiled recalling that first opportunity, bestowed upon him by the man he admired most in the world.

All five Daniels made their way toward the cedars at the edge of the draw. His father hiked uphill about twenty yards for a better view and gave them five fingers, representing the number of animals, and pointed from where they were coming. He could still feel his grip on the .30-30 Winchester 94 rifle. Tight. Almost a stranglehold. His brother Mark had shook his head and motioned for him to loosen up.

"Hold it like a baby."

Laura rounded the corner, out of sight. He fled the cover of the trees and headed off in the direction she'd gone, lingering long enough to give her a head start.

More memories of that hunt flooded his mind.

The deer approached through dried leaves and leftover snow.

Their breathing, puffs of clouds with each exhale, strong and steady. The lack of their awareness as to the danger that awaited them. How they stopped just above the narrow draw, twenty yards away. The cocking of the rifle. Slow. Quiet. The stock nestled to his shoulder. Him sliding out from behind the cedar, trying to get a clear shot through the trees, fighting the cold that ate away at his face.

Then pulling the trigger.

The bang and retort.

Stronger than he imagined, tossing him back on his heels.

Two does and a yearling scattered, but his shot found the buck's front shoulder, clipping the spine, dropping the big deer in its tracks.

Everything about that day had stuck in his mind.

His first kill.

Made even better by his father and brothers being with him.

And the lessons learned from that trip.

Lessons he never forgot.

Asking a dumb question is far better than doing something dumb. Watch and learn from other people. And never use everything offered to you. Instead, make that knowledge work for you, in your own way.

Good advice then, and now.

He found the corner of the cathedral and peeked around, seeing Laura about thirty yards ahead, halfway to the next corner. He watched, hoping he was wrong and she would turn right and continue her patrol of the perimeter, supposedly catching up to him. But she hooked left, doubling back toward him, just on the opposite side of the street.

He shook his head, both pleased and disappointed that his instincts had been right. He quickly retreated to the line of trees so he could use the shadows for cover, watching as she hustled down the sidewalk, past the church and the square, negotiating an intersection, then entering, through a side door off an alley, one of the many shops lining Republic Street, all closed for the night.

Interesting that she possessed a key to the door.

Like those deer, she'd been flushed back. But not by some other hunter's shots. This was done solely on her own. Thankfully, he was waiting, downwind. And like those deer, she had no idea what awaited her.

He reached back and palmed his Beretta.

Holding it gently.

Like a baby.

CHAPTER FORTY-THREE

C OTTON GLANCED UP FROM THE TOMB WITH THE SHIELDED LION, staring across the nave, back toward the altar where the other memorial, the one with the crowned pride, waited sixty feet away. The line between the two ran diagonally across the nave.

He turned his attention to the last few words of the puzzle.

Three blushes bloomed to ranks and file.

Another reference to something here on the floor.

In 1798 its obtuse wording may have been a deterrent, but in the 21st century it might not be much of a problem. He reached into his pocket and found his smartphone, noticing he had a solid connection to a local carrier. Technology was a great thing, so why not use it.

He accessed a search engine and typed in BLUSHES.

The expected came up first. Makeup. All sorts of blush for sale from various vendors.

"What are you doing?" Cardinal Gallo asked.

"My job."

He scrolled down and noticed an entry toward the bottom of the first page of hits. A definition site. The Free Dictionary. *To become red in the face. To feel embarrassed or ashamed. A red or rosy color. A glance, look, or view. Makeup used on the cheekbones to give a rosy tint. Middle English blushen, from Old English referring to roses.*

Flowers.

He'd seen a lot of those on the memorials.

He glanced up from the screen. "Search for roses."

The two Gallos and the curator fanned out.

He typed in RANKS AND FILE.

"Over here," the curator called out, from near the altar.

They all hurried that way and he saw three roses on a shield, above a Maltese cross. The first memorial, the one with the three crowned lions, was only twenty feet away, toward the other side of the nave.

"There are two markers at this end," he said. "The one with the shielded lion is at the other end. There has to be one more down there, in its vicinity."

He glanced at the smartphone's screen to see what came up for RANKS AND FILE. *A military term realting to horizontal "ranks" (rows) and "files" (columns). Enlisted troops, noncommissioned officers. People who form the major part of a group. A row on a chessboard (rank). A column on a chessboard (file).*

Several possibilities.

A lot of officers and knights lay beneath the cathedral's floor. Too many of each for any reference to the military being the correct answer.

It had to be the chessboard.

"Look for a checkerboard of some sort," he said. "Let's do it together."

They knew exactly what he had in mind, lining up in a row, each taking about a quarter of the floor, ten feet separating them. Slowly, they walked in unison from the altar at one end toward the huge set of double doors at the opposite side of the nave that served as the cathedral's main entrance. Eleven vertical columns of tombs stretched across, running the long side of the nave's rectangle. He'd counted six horizontal rows across the short side and they were just coming to the center. Another six or seven rows spanned ahead toward the main doors.

So far, no ranks and files.

They kept going, slow and steady, their heads down studying the myriad marble images.

At the thirteenth and final row, Pollux Gallo said, "Here it is."

Cotton stepped over and examined the tomb, a particularly macabre scene with a trumpeting angel, a pointing, accusatory skeleton, and a curious baby, all atop a checkerboard floor.

"This has to be it," Cotton said. "Ranks and files. What the rows and columns on a chessboard are called."

Four points on the floor.

Two toward the altar, the other two opposite.

Coordinates.

"We need to flag the four memorials."

The Gallo brothers walked back across the nave, Pollux heading left toward the lion pride, the cardinal finding the memorial with the shielded animal. The curator stood on the three roses. Cotton stayed with the checkerboard. Their positions formed a warped *X*, one line longer than the other, but an *X* nonetheless.

This had to be the solution.

"Keep your eyes on the man diagonally opposite and walk slowly in a straight line toward him. Try and meet at the center point of your line. We can adjust that once we're closer together."

They started walking, he toward Cardinal Gallo, the curator closing in on Pollux. He and the cardinal were on the longer line of the *X*, so Pollux and the curator met first. He and the cardinal kept approaching each other and met at a point a little off from where the other two had joined, which meant they hadn't found the center of their lines. So they adjusted to a spot where all four men stood together at the joining of the oblong *X*.

One tomb lay beneath their feet.

CHAPTER
FORTY-FOUR

THE KNIGHT WATCHED WHAT WAS UNFOLDING INSIDE THE cathedral, pleased that progress was being made. His patience finally was going to be rewarded.

The words of the *Pie Postulatio Voluntatis,* Most Pius Request, one third of the *Nostra Trinità,* written in 1113, had suddenly taken on a new meaning. Every member of the *Secreti* memorized that sacred document. When Pope Paschal II established the Knights Hospitallers he wrote in the *Voluntatis* that *it shall be unlawful for any man whatsoever rashly to disturb, or to carry off any of the order's property, or if carried off to retain possession of it, or to diminish anything from its revenues, or to harass it with audacious annoyances. But let all its property remain intact, for the sole use and enjoyment of those for whose maintenance and support it has been granted.*

That directive had been violated.

The Turks tried and failed, but Napoleon stole everything he could. Hitler bombed and wreaked havoc, but it was Mussolini who killed to find what he wanted. The *Voluntatis* dealt with the consequences of such actions.

If, therefore, at a future time, any person, whether ecclesiastical or secular, knowing this paragraph of our constitution, shall attempt to oppose its provisions, and he shall not make a suitable satisfaction and restitution, let him be deprived of all his dignities and honors, and let him know that he stands exposed to the judgment of God, for the iniquity he has perpetrated, and let him be deprived of the Sacraments of the Body and Blood of Christ, and of the benefits of the redemption of our Lord, and at the last judgment let him meet with the severest vengeance.

How much clearer did things have to be?

All was prepared outside. His men were ready to act.

The *severest vengeance* had arrived.

KASTOR STARED DOWN AT THE TOMB OF BARTOLOMEO TOMMASI DI Cortona and read its Latin epitaph. *Bailiff, son of Nicolao of the house of Cortona, a nobleman of his city is wasting away. Admitted to the Sacred Militia of the Jerusalemite Knights, from the year 1708 onward he was dedicated to its service, fulfilling, as long as he lived, his duties on land and sea with the utmost faith. He lived for 79 years, 6 months, 18 days.*

The inscription at its top seemed prophetic.

MORS ULTRA NON DOMINABITUR.

Death will not reign beyond.

Three symbols appeared above the epitaph.

$$\alpha \quad \maltese \quad \Omega$$

Alpha. Omega. The first and last. The Chi Rho in between, formed by superimposing the first two letters of the Greek word for "Christ." It was not used much today, but in Roman times things had been different.

He knew the connection.

On the eve of a decisive battle to decide the future of the Roman Empire, Constantine had a vision. A cross in the sky with the words *IN HOC SIGNO VINCES.* In this sign thou shalt conquer. Unsure of the meaning, that night he had a dream in which Christ himself explained that he should use the sign against his enemies. Of course, nobody had a clue if that tale of a vision was true. So many versions of it existed that it was impossible to know which one to believe. But it was a fact that Constantine directed the creation of a new labarum, superimposing the first two letters of the Greek word for Christ.

The Chi Rho sign.

He then ordered that symbol inscribed on his soldiers' shields, and with his new military standard leading the way he drove his rival into the Tiber River. Eventually, he defeated all challengers and unified the Roman Empire under his rule. He came to honor the sign of his salvation as a safeguard against every adverse and hostile power, and decreed that it be carried at the head of all his armies.

Kastor smiled.

That prior had chosen his clues with clarity.

COTTON TRANSLATED AS MUCH OF THE LATIN FROM THE TOMB AS he could understand, which was most of it.

"This is significant," Cardinal Gallo said. "That symbol there, in the center, is the cipher of Christ. The Chi Rho. Constantine the Great created it."

"I agree," Pollux noted. "This was intentional on the prior's part. He led us straight here."

Which was all fine and good, Cotton thought, but it didn't solve the riddle. He studied the imagery on the memorial. A skeleton, shield, crown, staff, skulls and crossbones, anchors, and a table with a broken clock, on a plinth, beneath an arch.

"It's the clock," the curator said. "It exists, here, in the cathedral."

Cardinal Gallo pointed downward. "He's telling us to open that clock."

"Where is it?" Cotton asked.

"In the oratory."

They followed the curator to one of the massive gilded arches that led into a side nave and a magnificent doorway adorned with four marble columns topped by a white marble dove and lamb. The room beyond spanned a long, tall rectangle encased by more gilded walls, the floor dotted by more marble tombs. At the far end, through another gilded arch, past an altar, hung a huge oil painting depicting St. John the Baptist's gruesome murder.

"Caravaggio's *Beheading of St. John*," the curator said, pointing to the painting. "Our greatest treasure."

Cotton gave the image only a passing glance, then focused on the room.

Maltese crosses were everywhere, the ceiling another grandiose baroque expression in gilt. A few pieces of furniture were pressed against the walls, one a paneled sideboard that supported a marble clock. About thirty inches tall, it was identical to the one depicted in the memorial back in the main nave. Except this one was intact.

He walked over and tried to lift it. Way too heavy.

"We've not moved it in years," the curator said.

He examined the exterior, gently running his fingers across the marble.

"That's a valuable piece of history," the curator said, in a tone that advised caution.

"I don't have a good track record with those." He'd already noticed that this clock had a glass front across the face that opened, exposing the hands—a way to wind it and surely to access the inner workings. The face was set to twenty minutes before two.

"Does this thing work?" he asked.

"Not to my knowledge. It's sat here since the 18th century."

Why was he not surprised. "You don't change a lot of things, do you?"

"It's important that the building remain as it was. History matters, Mr. Malone."

That it did.

Something occurred to him. "I thought Napoleon looted everything?"

"I doubt a heavy marble clock that doesn't work would have interested him. There's nothing special about it, beside the fact that it's old. It survived, as did a lot of other artifacts, because it carried no obvious value."

No way to determine if there was anything rattling around inside, but he assumed if that had been obvious somebody over the course of the past two hundred years would have noticed. Within his eidetic memory he visualized the targeted memorial.

"On the cracked-open clock out in the nave," he said, "if you close the hinge the time would read twenty minutes before two. Just like here. This one is also identical in size, shape, and color."

"It was not uncommon for items in the cathedral to become part of the tombs," the curator said. "Either the knight himself would fashion the memorial, or a relative or a friend would do it in honor of him. It all depended on the ego and resources of the knight."

The cardinal examined the clock. "What we want is inside this thing?"

"It certainly seems that way," Cotton said.

Though the sides and base were marble, the ornate, pointy top was fashioned of ceramic, cemented to the stone by a mortar joint.

Cotton examined the seam.

Solid and old.

"We're going to need a hammer and chisel," he said.

CHAPTER
FORTY-FIVE

LUKE STUDIED THE BUILDINGS FACING REPUBLIC STREET. ALL WERE dark and quiet, most of their windows shielded by metal accordion screens. Few people milled about on the sidewalks. Valletta had finally settled down for the night. But Laura Price had not. What was she doing in that shop? She'd clearly wanted to get there, as it had been her idea back inside the cathedral to check outside. He'd been suspicious of her ever since the safe house. He could not isolate one particular thing that had tripped his suspicion button, but something about her simply had not rung right.

He kept the gun at his side, close to his thigh, the barrel pointed down as he left the square, crossed the street, and approached the door she'd entered. It sat ten feet past Republic, in a darker narrow alley that ran on forever to another distant street. He tested the knob. It turned.

The door was open?

Nothing about that was good.

Why would she use a key to gain entrance, then leave it unlocked? Was she expecting someone else who didn't have a key? Or was this a trap laid just for him? Being the deer in the hunt was never fun. But like those cagey animals back in frigid Nebraska twenty years ago, he wasn't stupid. He pushed open the door, entered, then closed it, leaving it unlocked.

Why not?

Just in case there *were* others invited to the party.

He stood inside a small foyer. A doorway to the right opened into what appeared to be a souvenir shop. A stone stairway directly in front of him led up at a steep angle. Since all was quiet in the shop, Laura had to have gone up. He brought the gun out before him and climbed the narrow risers. Not a sound betrayed his presence. The stairway was nearly pitch-dark, only scant residual light leaking in from the shop windows below. He seemed vulnerable, as those deer should have felt when they were flushed back to the draw.

He came to the top.

A short hall led past two more open doorways.

He approached the first, pressed his right shoulder to the wall, and stole a quick glance inside. The minuscule room was filled with chairs, stacked one onto another, and collapsed folding tables propped to one wall, its single window faintly lit from the street below. At the next doorway the room was of similar size, but empty except for a small table set before another window, with a rifle lying on it. He noticed a nightscope and the caliber. Heavy duty. Meant for power and range. He stepped over and gazed out the window. The vantage point offered a perfect view of St. John's Square and the side entrance into the cathedral. In the dim light he saw a sound suppressor attached to barrel's end. Somebody was ready to do some serious hunting.

He heard the distinctive click of a gun hammer snapping into place.

"Nice and slow," Laura said. "Turn around. But first, let your gun hit the floor."

"You really want to go there?'

"I really do."

Okay. He released his grip and allowed the weapon to drop.

Then he turned.

"Kick the gun this way," she said. "Real slow."

He did as she requested.

"What gave me away?" she asked.

"Just a feeling."

"Not the dumb country boy you want people to think you are."

"I'll take that as a compliment. Let me guess. You've been working for Spagna from the beginning."

"Guilty as charged. When you showed up, he put me on you."

"I kind of got that impression when your boss appeared at the safe house and I wasn't part of the conversation. The cops on us, and Spagna taking you, that was all a dog-and-pony show?"

"Sort of. He needed to make contact, but not in a way that matched us together. He also needed you to stay in the dark. But you came to my rescue, as he predicted. So he decided to bring you on the team."

"That was the first moment I had my doubts. Those two local cops took you down way too easy. But when Spagna died, that cinched it for me. Everything was way too nicely wrapped with a pretty bow. Too many coincidences usually add up to a plan. The guys who tried to kill me. Entity people?"

She stepped into the room, gun still aimed, standing six feet away, just out of strike range. "That's the rub, Luke. They weren't Spagna's."

He was intrigued.

"There's so much more happening here," she said. "Things you know nothing about."

"Enlighten me."

She chuckled. "This is a solo job now."

He motioned to the rifle. "You planning on killing somebody? Is that what Spagna meant when he said to do what he told you?"

"That's exactly what he meant."

"I'm hurt. He only told me to find the cardinal."

"The archbishop always looked after the church and, right now, the church is being threatened."

"By Cardinal Gallo?"

"By what's happening inside that cathedral. I can't allow them to find the *Nostra Trinità*. It needs to stay gone."

"How can you be so sure they'll find it?"

"Spagna was aware of everything that happened in Italy with Malone and Pollux Gallo. He knew they were coming this way, to the cathedral, so he arranged for this perch. He, of course, had no way of knowing when the opportunity would present itself. But that's where I came in. I could see Malone was making progress. He's a smart fellow, or at least that's what Spagna said about him. It won't be long before Malone and the Gallos come out those doors."

"Is Malone on your hit list?"

"The *Nostra Trinità* must stay gone."

Not an answer, but close enough. "Who killed Spagna?"

"The same people who wanted you dead. The same ones who want Malone dead."

He waited.

"The *Secreti.*"

"You still haven't answered my question," he said. "Is Malone on your hit list?"

Movement behind her caught his attention.

A man stepped into the doorway.

Short, stocky, of indeterminate age.

"No, Mr. Daniels," a deep voice said. "We have no grievance with America."

CHAPTER
FORTY-SIX

COTTON ACCEPTED THE HAMMER AND CHISEL THAT THE CURATOR
had located. While they'd waited he'd examined every inch of the clock's
exterior and determined there were no other seams, except at the corners,
no visible way in, no hidden switches or levers. Whatever had been secreted
away must have been sealed inside from the top. With the hammer, he
gently tapped the exterior, the metal resonating off the stone with a dull
uniform sound.

"It doesn't appear to be hollow," he said.

The others watched him with clear curiosity, the curator with a concerned look on his face. There seemed little choice except to delicately bust
the mortared seam between the top and the rest of the clock.

"How old is this thing?" he asked.

"Four hundred years," the curator noted. "It dates to a grand master in
the early 17th century."

But before he used any force, he opened the circular glass door on the
front. The clock face was mounted by three screws that held it in place
and surely allowed access to the workings beyond.

"We need to be sure," he said.

The curator handed him a flat-head screwdriver, which he used to
loosen all three. Behind the face was nothing but the gears and springs

that would have powered the hands. He could see no access into the main part of the clock.

"Do it," Pollux Gallo said, seemingly reading his diminishing hesitation.

He pressed the chisel's metal tip to the mortar and started tapping. He took his time, careful that the lid would not be damaged and could be easily replaced. The mortar was hard and it took several blows at the same spot to produce results. Whether they were through-and-through fissures remained to be seen.

"Mr. Malone," Cardinal Gallo said.

He stopped chiseling.

"I think I've noticed something. May I hold the hammer a moment."

He was open to any better idea, so he handed over the tool. The cardinal studied the clock, then swung hard, slamming the metal end directly into the ceramic lid.

The curator gasped.

The lid shattered into several pieces, but those nearest the mortar joint remained in place.

He had to admit. *That'll work, too.*

"We don't have time for niceties," the cardinal said. "I have to be back in Rome in seven hours."

Pollux Gallo had remained silent, but nothing in his countenance or demeanor suggested he disagreed with the desecration.

"May I?" Cotton asked, wanting the hammer back.

Gallo handed it over, and he used it to tap away more of the ceramic, exposing enough of the lid so he could reach inside.

"Bring that chair over here," he told the curator.

One sat near the oratory's entrance, most likely for the docent to utilize during the day when visitors roamed. The curator retrieved the chair, which Cotton used to gain height on the exposed lid, allowing him to see down inside.

"It's filled with material," he said, carefully fingering the top layer, catching a glistening in the light. "You'd think it's sand. But it's broken glass, pounded to grains, packed tight."

"A defense and preservation mechanism," Pollux said. "Used by us in centuries past. I've seen other repositories with that packed inside."

He certainly could not stick his hand in and see what was there. The glass was packed tight, wall-to-wall, which explained the lack of any hollow sound when he'd probed earlier.

"You're going to have to be careful with any removal," Pollux said. "The glass could destroy whatever is inside. That's another security measure we've been known to use."

"The *Nostra Trinità*," the cardinal said, "would most likely be ancient parchments. They could sustain that kind of abuse."

Pollux shook his head. "It's not in there. The two papal bulls wouldn't fit inside that chamber. We've both seen the copies in the Vatican. They're much taller."

"And you're just now mentioning this," Cotton said.

"The *Constitutum Constantini* could be smaller," the cardinal said. "We don't know what form it took."

Pollux shook his head. "They would have never broken the Trinity. It's all or nothing. My guess is, what's inside this clock is a way to find the path to the *Nostra Trinità*."

Cotton had no idea who was right, but he did have a thought as to how to settle the debate.

He faced the curator. "Do you have a shop vac?"

KASTOR KEPT HIS FRUSTRATION IN CHECK. THIS WAS DRAGGING on forever and time was not on his side. It would take at least three hours to travel back to Rome, counting the time to and from both airports. He could slice that time in half if he could make a few calls. There were people in the private sector he knew, friends, who had access to jets. Perhaps one of those could be dispatched while the situation here played itself out.

"I need a phone," he said.

"In my office," the curator said. "You can make your call while I find the shop vac. We have several that we use to deal with water spills."

He followed the curator from the oratory, leaving Malone and Pollux with the clock. The office sat just beyond the cathedral's gift shop, on the back side of the building. The curator left him alone and he used the landline to make a call to Rome, waking up a longtime corporate ally, who agreed to send his corporate jet to Malta to wait for him, ready to go. Good to know that not everyone hated him. He'd actually amassed quite a roster of friends across a broad spectrum of government, banking, and industry. Men and women who believed, like him, that the Catholic Church had gone too far left. They were anxious for change, but smart enough to bide their time. What was the saying? *Good things come to those who wait.* Really? His experience had been that little to nothing came to those who wait.

Thankfully, his wait might soon be over.

He hung up the phone, his mind racing.

Normally, the power of a group soundly defeated that of an individual. And that, more than anything else, described a conclave. He'd planned to harness the power of that group through a select few individuals. The idea was both simple and time-honored. Infiltrate the adversary, learn everything possible, then turn that knowledge against them.

Which reminded him of the flash drive in his pocket.

He found it and studied the desktop computer that adorned the curator's desk. Why not? He was desperate to know if this was his salvation. He heard no footsteps or voices beyond the office door so he slid the drive into the USB portal. The display called for a password, so he typed KASTOR I.

A menu appeared that indicated only one file.

Titled PROOF.

A good sign.

He opened it and the screen displayed a copy of the summary he'd read earlier, laid out in the same order, with the same verbiage, only this time there was additional text, in red, listing the names of the offending cardinals along with links to an appendix. He clicked on a few and saw scans of financial records, contracts, investigatory notes, and other incriminating documents. Three held embedded recordings of phone calls between cardinals discussing incriminating details. He recognized all of the voices. More than enough proof to use as blackmail. He closed the disk, then ejected it and cradled it in his clenched fist.

Spagna was gone.

But thank heaven his work lived on.

COTTON FOUND HIS CELL PHONE AND CALLED STEPHANIE, SUR-
prised at the signal strength from inside the cathedral. He'd excused himself from the oratory, leaving Pollux Gallo alone with the clock, stepping
back into the main nave but maintaining a clear line of sight to make sure
everything remained inviolate. He watched through the open doorway as
Gallo found a cell phone and made a call himself, stepping toward the altar
and the Caravaggio painting at the far end. He explained to Stephanie
what they'd found.

"We should know more in about an hour," he said. "Emptying that
clock has to be done slowly."

"Where is Laura Price?"

"Outside with Luke."

"There's a problem with her. I was just told by Maltese security that
they no longer sanction what she's doing. She's supposedly working with
the Entity now. With Spagna dead, they decided to advise me of the situation."

"Mighty generous of them."

"I agree. I'm pissed, too. In the beginning, I thought she might be helpful. But Spagna played me. Maltese security played me. I have no idea
what the hell is going on there. I need to get this info to Luke, but he has
no cell phone. Spagna destroyed it."

"I'll deal with it, just as soon as I'm finished here."

"The Vatican is in an uproar over Spagna's death. There are a lot of
nervous cardinals concerned about what's going on. Thankfully it's the
Vatican, so they can keep a lid on things."

He kept watching Gallo, who stood a hundred feet away, at the far end
of the oratory. "I've got a set of identical twins who clearly don't like each
other. It's a little freaky at times. It's like the Roadrunner and Wile E.
Coyote. One's a fish on a hot dock, no telling what he'll do. The other is
semiconscious, on antidepressants, flat as Florida. Neither cares for the
other, so there's no telling where this will go if we find anything."

"The Vatican tells me that whatever you find is a private matter. They
want us to bow out at that point and let them resolve it among themselves.
I have no problem with that. I just need you to make sure that whatever
there is to find is found."

He knew the correct response. "Yes, ma'am."

"And get all that intel to Luke."

Across the nave he saw Cardinal Gallo returning with the curator, a shop vac with an extension cord in his hand.

"Gotta go," he told her.

CHAPTER FORTY-SEVEN

THE KNIGHT TRIED TO CONTAIN HIMSELF.

The story was one of long standing.

On October 13, 1307, the Knights Templar were rounded up en masse and arrested. They were tortured and many were killed, including their grand master, Jacques de Molay, who died a horrific death. Five years later the order was officially dissolved and most of its assets turned over to the Knights Hospitallers by the pope. No one ever questioned that move. No one ever challenged, or wondered, how that had been possible. Why would the pope do such a thing?

Simple.

Two hundred years earlier, sometime in the 12th century, during a raid in southern Turkey, a group of Hospitallers came across a cache of ancient documents. Mainly parchments. Religious texts. Most irrelevant and unimportant. One, though, seemed different.

The *Constitutum Constantini*.

Constantine's Gift.

A one-of-a-kind document that survived to the Middle Ages, staying with the Hospitallers during their time in the Holy Land, then with them on Cyprus, Rhodes, and Malta. Popes were eventually made aware of its existence. One in particular, Clement V, who sat on the throne of St. Peter in 1312 and knew of the document, proclaimed his *Ad Providam* granting all of the Templar assets to the Hospitallers. Proof positive of its apparent force. Occasionally, through the centuries, popes had required further persuasion and always Constantine's Gift would do its job.

Keeping the knights relevant.

But it ended in 1798.

Now, on this night, all that might change.

COTTON STOOD ON THE CHAIR AND MANEUVERED THE SHOP VAC'S nozzle across the layers of pulverized glass that filled the clock, slowly extracting them. The chamber measured about ten inches square and eighteen inches deep. He could not rush the removal as he had no idea what, if anything, had been left inside. He understood the advantage of glass as a packing material. It came with no mess, no dust. It also was dense, which made the clock extra heavy, further dissuading looters from carting it away. The shop vac was working perfectly, the granulations steadily rattling their way through the nozzle. He was concerned about Luke, but there was no way this task could be delegated to one of the men watching him intently.

He kept vacuuming. The top of something came into view. He maneuvered around the object and kept extracting. The outline of a bottle began to take shape. Wide mouth. Tall. Standing upright at about the halfway point. Sealed with wax. He kept going until over half of the container was visible.

"Shut it off," he said.

The curator killed the motor.

He laid down the nozzle.

"What's there?" the cardinal asked, impatient as ever.

He reached inside and gently wiggled the bottle free. Grains of glass rained off. He shook more away and held the container up for them to see. The opaque bottle carried a foggy, greenish hue. He saw the blurred image of something that filled the inside.

He stepped from the chair. "Any thoughts?"

Pollux examined the exterior. "Another message."

He agreed and grabbed the chisel from the table, working on the wax seal. The dark crimson scraped away in dry, bitter chunks. The wax filled the entire mouth, and he angled the bottle downward, careful not to allow anything to damage what was inside. A pile of two-hundred-plus-year-old wax, melted by a desperate prior trying to preserve the last bits of heritage to a dying organization, collected on the tabletop. He used the chisel to scrape away the remaining bits of the seal. He tipped the bottle and a piece of rolled parchment, stained the color of tea, slid out.

He set the bottle down.

"It can be unrolled," the curator said, seemingly reading his mind. "But carefully."

"Do it," the cardinal said.

Cotton laid the roll, about five inches tall, on the table. The curator used his index finger and thumb to hold down one edge. Cotton spread the roll out, slow and careful, the parchment's natural resilience still there after two centuries. He held his end flat and they all studied the image, the black ink bloated by time.

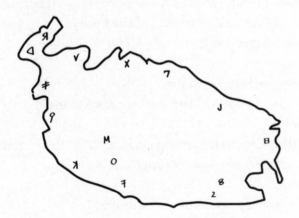

"It's Malta," the curator said.

Cotton agreed. A crude drawing of its shores, but the shape was unmistakable. Letters and symbols ringed the shoreline, a few more inland.

"That's the Latin alphabet," Pollux said. "The square with a line through it on the far right is the letter *H*. The two circles, joined, that looks like an *8* is the letter *F*."

"And their positions on the map could be watchtowers," the curator said. "There were thirteen encircling the island. There are thirteen letters close to the coast. The *M* could be Mdina, the backward *F* is roughly where the old Inquisitor's Palace lays. The *O* is near the Verdala palace."

It all made sense. The prior had made the clues difficult, yet not insurmountable, provided the person studying them knew the lay of the land. He'd wondered what the letters in the message found in the obelisk had referred to. H Z P D R S Q X. Now he knew.

"Do you know the whole Latin alphabet?" he asked.

Pollux nodded.

Perfect.

"We need to make a copy of this parchment. I need one I can write on."

LUKE TOOK IN BOTH THE DARK FORM OF THE MAN AND THE ANSWER he'd supplied about Malone not being in danger, then asked, "Who are you?"

"Monsignor John Roy. I was Archbishop Spagna's assistant. I'm now in temporary operational command of the Entity."

"You sound American."

"I am."

"The *Secreti* are here, on Malta?"

The black head nodded. "In a manner of speaking."

Odd answer.

"They killed Chatterjee and Spagna and tried to kill you," Roy said. "They're out there, right now. Waiting."

"For what?"

"To see what happens inside the cathedral."

Luke pointed at the rifle on the table before the window. "And who are you going to kill?"

"Don't tell me you haven't pulled the trigger before?" Roy asked.

"I'm not an assassin."

"Neither am I," Laura said. "But I do my job."

"I'm not going to allow either of you to kill anybody."

"This doesn't concern the United States," Roy said. "It's a Vatican problem, which the Vatican wants to handle itself."

"By killing people?"

"Washington interjected itself into this matter," Roy noted. "The Entity did not ask for your assistance. I'm asking you, as one professional to another, to walk away. I assure you, nothing will happen to Mr. Malone. At least not from us. The *Secreti*? That's another matter. You and Malone will have to deal with that problem. They're the enemy. Not me."

"They're after what Malone is locating right now? Inside the cathedral?"

"That's correct. And they're not going to stop until they get it. Archbishop Spagna was here to retrieve whatever might be found. He failed. Ms. Price and I will now finish that mission. You and Mr. Malone can go home."

Which actually sounded appealing.

As a boy he and his brothers had tended the cows his parents owned. Lazy animals. They loved nothing more than to loiter in the pasture all day, chewing cud. The horseflies were relentless. Nasty little creatures that left whelps with their bites. Some of the cows would run to get away from them. But most just stood there, chewing grass, using their tails to swat the flies away. Oblivious to any assault. Those cows that didn't run were bold suckers.

Like him.

"I can't leave, and you know it."

CHAPTER FORTY-EIGHT

COTTON HELD THE PARCHMENT FLAT AS THE BRIGHT LIGHT SCANNED
the image and produced a copy. They'd fled the oratory and returned to
the curator's office. The two Gallo brothers had stayed quiet, watching as
he studied the prior's puzzle. He rolled up the original and set it aside,
then laid the copy on the curator's desk, grabbed a pen, and wrote H Z P
D R S Q X on a pad.

"Give me the Latin alphabet letters for those."

Pollux took the pen and wrote the corresponding Latin letters. Cotton immediately saw that he was right. All eight appeared on the drawing, scattered at intervals around the island.

$$H - B \qquad R - O$$
$$Z - \ddagger \qquad S - Z$$
$$P - 7 \qquad Q - 9$$
$$D - Я \qquad X - X$$

He circled them on the map copy.

"They're markers. Reference points," he said.

But they were useless unless read together. So he studied them, arbi-

trarily deciding the ones closest together along the coast had to be connected by short lines.

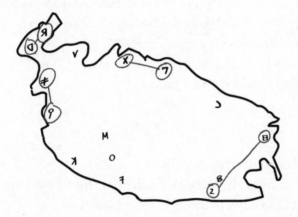

"You don't know that's right," the cardinal said.

"No. I don't. It's a guess, but it seems reasonable. We can try other
combinations if this doesn't work."

Common sense demanded that the map had to lead to a single point
on the island, and the only way that could be accomplished was by inter-
secting lines. In his mind he drew those lines, connecting differing points
of the eight circles. Only one combination seemed to provide what he
was after, the rest mere noise to confuse the searcher.

"It's like the X out there on the floor," he said. "You connect them
diagonally across the grid."

He took a ruler the curator supplied and drew the lines.

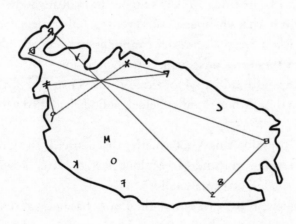

"It's a rough Maltese cross," the cardinal said. "A bit stretched, but one nonetheless."

"Which means where those lines intersect is where we have to go," he said. "Somewhere near the northwest coast, not far from St. Paul's Bay, if I'm not mistaken. Any idea what's there?"

"It can only be one place," the curator said.

Pollux Gallo nodded. "St. Magyar's."

LUKE GLANCED OUT THE WINDOW.

St. John's Square fronting the cathedral still loomed dim and quiet. Malone and the Gallos had not, as yet, emerged.

He still had time.

"Mr. Daniels, the church is facing a direct threat," Roy said, the voice resonant, controlled, logical. "This threat is made even more dangerous by the coming conclave. Once the cardinals are locked away inside the Sistine, we'll lose all control. It has to be dealt with right now. Archbishop Spagna discovered the threat and was working, in his own way, to eliminate it. He came here, personally, to deal with the situation. He planned to enlist both you and Ms. Price with his efforts. Unfortunately, the threat found him first."

"What threat?"

"I can't say. But I assure you, it's real."

"You have one of the best intelligence agencies in the world at your disposal. Deal with any threat. There's no need to kill anybody."

"Sadly, given what's happened this evening, only violence will end this now. Archbishop Spagna's murder cannot go unavenged. These people have to know there are consequences to their actions."

Something didn't add up. He said to Laura, "You said Spagna set this kill up for you. But when that happened, nobody had died yet. So what is this? A hit?"

"Again," Roy said, "this is not a matter that concerns the United States. Please, Mr. Daniels, you and Mr. Malone need to leave. Now."

"And let you kill Cardinal Gallo?"

"Mr. Daniels, as you just noted, the Entity has many resources. It has existed for centuries. We've survived by always doing what has to be done." Roy paused. "Killing is not unfamiliar to us. Never have we been afraid to do what was necessary. In centuries past, if the Holy Father ordered the elimination of someone in defense of the faith, we carried out that order. He is God's voice and we are his hand."

"This isn't the Middle Ages, and the pope is dead."

"Yet a threat remains." Roy shook his head. "But killing a prince of the Church is not part of our agenda here."

He'd assumed with the mention of the conclave that Cardinal Gallo was the target. That had been the entire reason for Stephanie Nelle involving him in the first place.

"His brother is our problem," Roy said. "Archbishop Spagna dealt extensively with Pollux Gallo. Too much, in my opinion. But the archbishop was not a man who accepted much in the way of . . . counseling. Sadly, my personal suspicions regarding Pollux Gallo have proven true."

Which Luke would love to know more about.

But that wasn't going to happen.

"Leave this to us," Laura said.

"I wish it were—"

Two pops broke the silence.

Like hands clapping.

Roy lurched forward, grabbing his chest, then collapsed to the floor, his face slamming the planks hard. Nothing had come through the window, so the attack had to be from outside in the hallway. Laura reacted by whirling around and aiming her weapon at the darkened doorway. Luke used the moment to drop to the floor and grab the rifle off the table on the way down, flattening himself out, becoming the smallest target possible. Before he could warn Laura to do the same, he heard another pop and her head snapped back as a bullet smashed through her face, up through the brain, and out the back of the skull.

Her body dropped to the floor beside the monsignor.

He sent three sound-suppressed rifle rounds into the blackness beyond the doorway.

Footsteps rushed away.

He sprang to his feet, pressing his body to the wall adjacent to the exit. Beyond, the corridor was much darker. But he neither saw nor sensed anyone. He switched the rifle for his pistol, which he grabbed from the floor. Then took a moment and checked for a pulse in Roy. None. Laura was clearly dead. Dammit. She hadn't deserved that.

He made his way to the stairs, then down. The door leading out to the alley was partially open.

Careful. Trouble could be outside.

He used the building's stone wall for protection and, with his right foot, kicked the door open. A few quick glances past the jamb and he still saw no one. He stepped outside. To his right, at the far end of the alley, a hundred feet away, where it merged with another street, he caught the image of a dark figure.

Running away.

He raced after it.

CHAPTER
FORTY-NINE

COTTON COULD SEE THAT BOTH GALLOS AND THE CURATOR SEEMED certain of the location.

"What is St. Magyar's?" he asked.

"It's one of the oldest chapels on the island," Pollux said. "It was built in the mid-16th century, not long after the knights arrived."

He listened as Pollux told him about the church. According to legend, in the 12th century a local maiden had been working the fields when she saw a number of Turks running her way. She fled, with the invaders in hot pursuit. Out of breath, she found refuge in a cave whose entrance was blocked by a mass of cobwebs. Inside, she dropped to her knees and prayed to the Madonna for help. The corsairs kept looking for her, even finding the cave and peering inside, but on seeing the veil of cobwebs they moved on.

"It was the cobwebs re-forming themselves after she passed through them that was considered a miracle," Pollux said. "So a chapel was built in front of the cave, dedicated to the maiden, who became St. Louise Magyar."

"Every church here has a story like that," the curator said. "This island is littered with churches. Three hundred and fifty-nine at last count, a little over one per every square kilometer. Sixty-three different parishes.

St. Magyar's is one of the wayside chapels, off to itself, not open to the public."

"It's owned by the order," Pollux said.

That was interesting.

"The original stone church was rebuilt by the knights in the 16th century," Pollux said. "It stays sealed, but we maintain the site. I can call our representatives here on the island and have it opened, waiting for us."

"Do it," the cardinal said.

Clearly, Pollux did not appreciate being given an order by his brother, but no argument was offered and Pollux left the office to make a call.

Something was bothering Cotton.

"What is it about this church you're holding back?" he asked the curator and the cardinal.

"When Napoleon ravaged the island," the curator said, "he didn't plunder St. Magyar's. It's always been a simple place, with no ornamentation. There was nothing there to steal. So it's intact. Just as it was in the 16th century."

"It was also the *Secreti*'s private chapel," the cardinal added.

Now we're talkin'.

Gallo explained that the *Secreti* had always maintained a certain distance from the rest of the knights. The whole idea of their select association was to be aloof. So after the order was gifted Malta, the *Secreti* constructed a chapel to be used only by members, the grounds declared off limits to all but those who wore the five-word palindrome that formed an anagram of *Pater Noster.* Our Father. The sign of Constantine.

"It was regularly used up to the time of Napoleon's invasion," the curator said. "Records show that French soldiers visited the site, but as I mentioned there was nothing there of value."

Apparently they were wrong. Cotton decided to shift tacks and faced Gallo. "You can go back to Rome now."

"I'll head there as soon as this is finished."

"Forgive me, Eminence, but what interest would a cardinal of the church have in all this? As I understand it, whatever there is to find belongs to the Knights of Malta."

"That's a matter of debate. And I'm the papal representative to that order. It's my duty to see this through."

"We can report our findings to you. Why does it require your *personal* involvement?"

He could see that scarlet feathers had been bristled by his directness. But he was pressing for a reason.

"I don't have to explain myself to you," Gallo said.

"No, you don't. But by your own statement there are men on this island trying to kill you. A conclave starts in just a few hours. Yet you insist on staying around. Some might call that reckless." He paused. "Or perhaps deliberate."

Like a cold mist, anger rose in Gallo's eyes.

"I'm a prince of the Roman Catholic Church, Mr. Malone, who customarily is shown respect. Even by those not of the church."

"Even when you lie?"

Before the cardinal could reply Pollux reentered the office, breaking the moment. "A representative will meet us at St. Magyar's with a key to the doors. The building has electricity. They will also bring some tools, as we have no idea what there is to find, or how to get to it." Pollux paused. "Mr. Malone, we can handle this ourselves from this point forward."

"I agree," the cardinal quickly added. "Go home."

Now a double team.

Interesting.

"My orders are to see this through to the end. We're not at the end."

"You've helped tremendously," Pollux said. "Your solving of the prior's message was masterful. But I have to concur with my brother, which is rare for me. This is an ecclesiastical matter, one we can now handle internally."

"The head of the Entity is dead. This is far more than a religious matter."

"I understand, and we'll address the *Secreti*," Pollux said. "All those responsible for any acts of violence will be dealt with. But the *Nostra Trinità* is a sensitive, internal issue, one we would prefer to keep to ourselves."

"How about this," he said. "Let's go have a look and see what's there. After that, I'm out of here. That would be the end, as far as I'm concerned."

"We don't need you," the cardinal said, with finality.

But Pollux nodded. "That seems reasonable."

CHAPTER FIFTY

LUKE RAN THROUGH THE DARKENED ALLEY.

The guy ahead of him had a huge head start. But so had Buddy Barnes back at Ranger school. A twelve-mile tactical march with full gear, the last test over two days of intense physical fitness training. Don't finish the march in under three hours and you're out. The failure rate hovered at a constant 60 percent. But he'd not only finished, he'd caught Buddy, making up a hundred yards over the last two miles to cross the end line first. The winner received the honor of buying the first round of drinks during the next leave. No matter it would cost a couple of hundred dollars, everyone wanted to win that march. Problem was, when the time came he didn't have a couple of hundred dollars. So Buddy had loaned it to him until the next payday. That was what Rangers did for one another. He missed Buddy. A roadside bomb in Afghanistan killed his friend, and he'd helped carry the flag-draped coffin to the grave at Arlington.

He kept running, stepping up the pace, careful with the damp cobblestones. This wasn't a flat dirt trail at Fort Benning. It was a rolling city by the sea full of hostiles and friendlies, and it was sometimes hard to know which was which.

He thought of Laura Price.

She'd been a little of both.

But she'd been careless and that sloppiness cost her big time.

His target disappeared around a corner about half a football field ahead. He felt a familiar pulse of adrenaline. He was in the prime of his life, ready for all challenges. But he told himself to be smart. Always be smart. He wasn't sure if the guy was even aware he had a pursuer, as the man's pace had not changed. He found the same corner and whirled around, not losing a step. He stared ahead and saw that his target was no longer running. Instead, the man was down in the middle of the street, in a firing stance, arms extended, gun aimed.

Damn.

He launched himself into the air, leaping to the right, catapulting his body onto the hood of a parked car and slamming into the windshield.

Two shots came his way.

He rolled to the sidewalk, gun still in his grasp, and lay on his stomach, his chin to the street, poking his head around a bumper.

Another round whined off the side panel.

He reeled back into a crouch and tightened his grip on the gun, then aimed and squeezed the trigger, sending a bullet of his own toward the target.

A quick peek and he saw the guy was gone.

He came to his feet and rushed ahead.

Another alley opened to the right of where the shooter had taken a stand. He stopped at the intersection and saw the man running near the bottom of a long, inclined path. Beyond he caught the glimmer of water. They were headed toward the harbor, which actually wasn't far away at any point within the city. He kept going, hustling down to the alley's end where he stopped and surveyed the scene. A marina dominated the concrete wharf. Boats bobbed on mooring lines inside a high-density basin. His gaze scanned the many finger docks. No one was around. But he caught the drone of an engine to his left.

He ran down the concrete walk that fronted the water and saw a Zodiac, out on the water, motoring away, heading into the Grand Harbor. Two figures stood inside the inflatable.

One of them tossed a taunting wave back at him.

Asshole.

He needed a boat.

Now.

He bolted back to the marina. Many of the boats he could see were sizable, twenty-plus-footers with all the bells and whistles. Impractical for this pursuit. Toward the end of one dock he spotted a small, fifteen-foot V-hull with a solitary outboard. Of course, he didn't have a key to trip the engine but that shouldn't be a problem. As a kid, he'd learned how to hot-wire an outboard. He and his brothers would just take a screwdriver and spark the leads beneath the ignition pad, which always did the trick. He didn't have any tools, but he shouldn't need any. He untied the mooring lines and, as the boat drifted from the dock, bent down beneath the key panel and yanked the two wires loose. He got lucky. They came free, leaving some of their copper exposed. He sparked them together and the engine coughed to life.

The revs steadied and he quickly twisted the wires together. He then hooked the wheel left and goosed the throttle. The prop bit water and lunged the hull forward toward the harbor. The Zodiac had a big lead, and his newly acquired pleasure craft did not have much more horsepower. The best he could do was keep up and see where they headed. What exactly he was going to do once he learned that information remained to be seen. But he was tired of being one step behind. Laura, Malone, the *Secreti,* Spagna. All of them had been ahead of him from the start.

He passed Fort St. Angelo and the harbor mole at the tip of Valletta's jutting peninsula. The Zodiac was about a quarter mile ahead, a black smudge skirting across black water.

Beyond it, out in open water, he spotted lights.

Another craft at anchor.

Which had to be their destination.

CHAPTER FIFTY-ONE

THE KNIGHT WAS PLEASED TO SEE HIS TARGETS LEAVE THE CO-cathedral and head for a car parked in a small lot across the street, toward the rear of the building. His men had already taken out Spagna and his minion, and they'd surely dealt with Laura Price by now. He'd severely underestimated the Lord's Own, not grasping the full extent of Spagna's passion and desires. But that problem was now solved.

The Americans, though, remained.

Killing both agents currently on the ground seemed the simplest solution, but that would only bring more inquiry. The Knights of Malta and the Roman Catholic Church were two huge, impersonal, monolithic objects, one unstoppable, the other unmovable. But the United States was something altogether different. He'd not expected their involvement and remained unsure exactly how to move them off the scent. Harold Earl "Cotton" Malone seemed highly capable, and the younger Luke Daniels had clearly held his own. But killing one or both of them seemed unwise, especially at this critical juncture. An ordered universe was always the goal. Everything to a certain arrangement according to set rules, all focused on a single goal. The route to that goal was fully prescribed within his mind. He'd been thinking about what was coming for a long time. Visualizing. Planning. Hoping.

Now he could see the end.

Not exactly how he'd envisioned it a few days ago.

But the end nonetheless.

Kastor rode in back of the car. Malone drove with Pollux occupying the front passenger seat. It was the same vehicle they'd used to drive from the airport to the cathedral. They were minus two others, though, as Luke Daniels and Laura Price had disappeared.

Good riddance.

The less involved the better.

They were headed out of Valletta along the north coast highway. Soon they would pass the Madliena Tower, where all of this had started yesterday. His right hand felt the flash drive through his trousers where it rested safely in his pocket. He'd been considering how best to use it. He probably would not make it back to Rome until just before the 10:00 A.M. reporting deadline. There would not be time to do much more than shower and change into his scarlet cassock before the cardinals assembled in St. Peter's for mass. No privacy or meaningful opportunity to speak to anyone would be available. Then they would all gather in the Pauline Chapel before walking in a televised procession to the Sistine while collectively singing the Litany of the Saints. All part of the required tradition adhered to at every modern conclave.

Then the hypocrisy would start.

Beginning after the doors to the Sistine were sealed, when they would each take an oath to observe the Apostolic Constitution, maintain secrecy, never allowing anything to influence their voting save the Holy Spirit, and, if elected, to defend the Holy See. Some of that was going to be a stretch for a few of them, though none of the guilty parties knew that as yet.

Then the cardinal dean would ask if any questions relating to the procedures remained. After the clarification of any doubts, the first scrutiny, the first vote, would commence. Ordinarily a few of the minor rules that rarely came into play would be unimportant. But not here. An ill cardinal was allowed to leave the conclave and could be readmitted later. A cardinal who left for any reason other than illness could not return. No attendants accompanied the cardinals, except a nurse for one in ill health. Priests were available to hear confessions. Two doctors were also there, along with a strictly limited number of staff for housekeeping and preparing meals. All potential problems once the pressure started to be applied.

Just three cardinals were permitted to communicate with the outside world, and only under the gravest of circumstances. The major penitentiary. The cardinal vicar for the Diocese of Rome. And the vicar general for the Vatican City State. None of whom were on his hit list.

Thank God.

But he had to make sure not a one of the dirty cardinals tried to seek help or feign illness. Everything had to stay contained within the conclave.

The first scrutiny always came quickly.

And was meaningless.

Few ever achieved election then. Most cardinals voted for either themselves or a close friend. A few would collate and cast their ballots for their favorite candidate, sending an early message. Generally, the votes were scattered across a wide spectrum and not until the second scrutiny would patterns begin to emerge.

The rules stated that if a scrutiny took place on the afternoon of the first day and no one was elected, a maximum of four ballots were held on each successive day. Two in the morning, two each afternoon. If no result came after three days of balloting—twelve votes—the process was suspended for one day of prayer. After seven further scrutinies, the process again would be suspended. If after another seven no result was achieved, a third suspension came for another day. After a final seven and no election, a day of prayer, reflection, and dialogue occurred. For any voting thereafter, only the two names who received the most votes in the last scrutiny were eligible in a runoff.

In modern times the voting had never even approached such lengths. But nothing about this conclave would be normal.

The critical moment?

After the first scrutiny, when the conclave recessed for the day and the cardinals headed back to their rooms, there would be a few hours between dinner and when everyone had settled down for the night when he could make the rounds and have a private talk with the ones who mattered. By then there would be a lot of chatter happening. That was the whole idea of the conclave. For the cardinals to be sequestered alone, where they could make up their minds among themselves. He was just going to provide some added incentive. Each offender would be told what he knew, what he could prove, and what would happen if he did not hear his name announced as having achieved a two-thirds majority.

He also didn't care how it was done.

Just that it happened.

And fast.

CHAPTER FIFTY-TWO

LUKE KEPT THE WHEEL STRAIGHT AND THE BOW POINTED OUT TO sea. The inflatable ahead continued to speed through the water with little noise, the engine barely audible thanks to the half-mile distance between them. Its destination seemed to be a glossy, light-colored hull with a clean, slick outline. A main cabin projected above the gunwale extending maybe fifty feet. Lights illuminated the hull, cabin area, and aft deck, where a shadow could be seen walking around.

The inflatable eased up to the stern and stopped. Two men hopped from the Zodiac and cinched the craft tight to an aft swim step. Luke glanced back and saw he was five hundred yards offshore, due north of Fort St. Angelo, which was lit in its full golden glory to the night. He had a tough decision to make, one with enormous ramifications if he was wrong. The men on that boat had killed four people, that he knew of, tonight. They'd even tried to make him the fifth. Laura had wanted them stopped, and though her methods were questionable she hadn't deserved to die. Shooting it out with these guys seemed nonsensical. This wasn't a Bond movie. There were far more of them than there was of him, and they certainly could see him coming as he was a mere quarter mile away and closing.

Three figures now stood on the aft deck.

He saw bursts of muzzle fire and realized they were shooting his way.

Volleys of automatic weapons rounds kicked up the water around him like giant raindrops. He ducked low enough for cover, but still high enough that he could see beyond the windscreen. The closer he got the easier a target he would make. The smart play was to take these guys out and find out who they were after they were in the water, either dead or rescued.

His best weapon roared beneath his feet.

The boat itself.

His target rested at anchor.

He aimed the bow straight for the yacht's midsection, the throttle full out. He knifed across the calm surface, cutting a path straight for the darkened hull. He'd have to time his move perfectly as he could not risk the rudder not staying straight.

New gunfire came his way.

Rounds thudded into the fiberglass hull.

One hundred yards.

He needed to be closer.

More *rat, tat, tat* from automatic fire.

One last look.

On course.

People liked to say he was sometimes two fries short of a Happy Meal, but what had his father liked to say? *Your strings have to all be in tune for folks to pick on you.*

Hell yeah.

He leaped from the boat, hitting the water with his right shoulder, his forward momentum skipping him across the surface before he sank. He stayed down, beneath the surface, but gazed upward as the pewter-black night transformed into a blinding light.

COTTON STEPPED FROM THE CAR AND STARED AT ST. MAGYAR'S. The squatty church seemed scooped out of the bow of the hill, tucked away under a rocky outcrop, hidden by both nature and the night. He didn't have to see to know that the ancient stone walls were likely twisted and discolored by centuries of bakery heat.

He was still concerned about Luke, who'd been nowhere to be found when they'd left the cathedral. He understood Stephanie's urgency at dealing with Laura Price, but he had problems of his own. Surely Luke would head back inside the cathedral, where the curator had been told to direct him this way. He'd commandeered the car they'd used to travel from the airport to the cathedral. The curator had said that he would make his personal vehicle available to Luke when he showed up.

Another set of headlights pierced the night, and a small SUV approached the church and parked. A younger man climbed out, whom Pollux identified as one of his colleagues from Fort St. Angelo. The newcomer opened the vehicle's hatch where there were two shovels, a pick, a sledgehammer, and some rope.

"I wasn't sure what to expect," Pollux said. "So I told him to bring what they had."

Cotton grabbed the shovels, Pollux the sledgehammer and pick. The cardinal brought the coil of rope.

"Wait outside," Pollux told his man. "I'll call you in if needed."

The younger man nodded and handed over a key to the front door.

The terrain around them was hilly, fading down into a valley that stretched farther south. Scattered lights indicated people. The church sat on the knob of one of the steeper hills with a graveled path serving as a driveway. There were two barred windows and a small bell cot. The main door was an arched oval, unusually low. Above it, an encircled eight-pointed Maltese cross was carved into the stone. The dial of Cotton's luminous watch read 4:40 A.M.

Another all-nighter.

Thankfully, he'd grabbed an hour's nap on the flight from Rome.

Pollux used the key and opened the oak door. He heard a click and lights came on inside. Not many, and not all that bright, which allowed his eyes to adjust easily. The interior was rectangular with a circular apse at the far end. Simple and bare, with stone benches lining the exterior walls, the floor a mixture of flagstones and beaten earth. Only faint remnants of wall frescoes remained. Empty niches accommodated no statues. Everything a bland, sandy gray.

"The main reason there are so many churches on Malta," Pollux said, "is isolation. Roads were few and terrible, so every town and village wanted its own church. Incredibly, the vast majority of those buildings have survived. This one, though, was built for a select few. The locals were forbidden to come anywhere near it, on pain of imprisonment."

Cotton noticed the plain stone altar at the apse end, another Maltese cross carved into its front. The lack of any pews seemed curious. "Did they stand to worship?"

"There was no worship here," Cardinal Gallo said.

He'd suspected as much. There had to be more to this place.

Pollux stepped beyond the altar into the apse. Three stone panels formed the curved walls, separated by moldings, with limestone benches wrapping the semicircle. Cotton watched as Pollux laid the pick down and knelt, reaching beneath one of the stone benches and pressing something.

The center panel released inward a few inches.

"Centuries ago there was a manual winch," Pollux said. "But today we're a bit more modern."

"Napoleon never found the door?" he asked.

Pollux shook his head. "The French were in a hurry and not all that smart. They came, saw nothing, and left. We installed the electric lock about five years ago. The stone is balanced at its center of gravity, on a lubricated center post. You can push it open with one hand."

The cardinal stepped forward and did just that, exposing two blackened rectangles, about two feet wide, centered by the short side of the stone wall.

They stepped through and Pollux activated another light switch.

A tunnel stretched ahead.

Tall. Wide. Spacious.

"Where does it lead?" he asked.

"To a wondrous place," Pollux whispered.

DURING THE CAR TRIP KASTOR HAD ADMIRED THE PWALES VALLEY, a picturesque region of timeless wetlands that dominated Malta's northern corner. The land undulated with hillocks of lichens and foul-smelling mushrooms. It stayed carpeted with cape sorrel, crow daisies, borage, and spurge. Unusual for Malta, which was not all that hospitable to plants.

Some of the most stunning views on the island could be seen here, though darkness prevented him from enjoying any of them now.

People had lived on the land for over five thousand years and there were cave paintings in the nearby ridges to prove it. Its many bays had long made it prone to outside attack. The knights had fortified the whole area against Muslim corsairs with coastal towers and garrison batteries. The British manned a fort nearby during, and after, World War II. As a kid he'd visited it several times. The nuns would buy them sweets and sodas. They'd also taken swimming lessons in the nearby harbor.

Those nuns.

They'd at least tried to make things bearable, which was hard to do given all of their children were orphans. Few ever left until they were old enough to walk out as adults. He'd always wondered how many ever ventured back for a visit. He never had.

He knew all about the Church of St. Magyar's, which was actually two chapels in one. The outer portion had served as an overt wayside chapel and gathering place for the *Secreti*. But it was the inner portion—the Church of St. John—that had held a special place.

But not John the Baptist.

John of Nepomuk, the patron saint of Bohemia, drowned in 1393 in the Vltava River at the behest of King Wenceslaus for refusing to divulge the secrets of the confessional. He was often depicted in statues with a finger to his lips, indicating silence, keeping a secret. The Jesuits spread the story of his martyrdom that eventually elevated him to sainthood. A cult devoted to his worship flourished on Malta in the 16th century, so it was easy to see why the *Secreti* would have named their chapel for him.

Kastor had never visited St. Magyar's, nor, he assumed, had 99 percent of the knights' membership. As with its patron saint, the secrets within this place had stayed secret. Why Pollux had chosen to reveal this sacred location to an outsider remained a mystery.

They carried the tools and walked down the lit tunnel.

"This is a man-made extension of the original natural cave," Pollux said. "The exterior sanctuary was built to conceal the true chapel of the *Secreti*."

The path was lit by a series of incandescent fixtures attached to the ceiling, connected by an exposed electrical cable. The floor was flat, hard-packed earth, dry as a desert. The air was noticeably cooler the far-ther inside they walked. The tunnel ended at a set of arched, oak double doors hung on heavy iron hinges. No locks, just two iron rings that Pol-lux used to push open both panels. Not a sound betrayed the hinges. Ob-viously, things around here were dutifully cared for.

Beyond was a towering space that stretched in three directions, two lateral vaults off a central core. Arches and pillars supported the rock overhead. Statues dominated every nook and cranny. Not separate addi-tions, either—as in the co-cathedral, each had been carved from the sur-rounding stone. He saw Madonnas, saints, Christ, animals. Most were freestanding. A few stood alone in niches, while others emerged from the walls in three-dimensional façades. Carefully placed floor and ceiling lights illuminated everything, casting the stone in varying hues of brown and gray, all combining for a hauntingly ominous atmosphere.

"All right," Kastor said to Malone. "What now?"

CHAPTER
FIFTY-THREE

COTTON HAD NEVER SEEN ANYTHING LIKE THE MACABRE UNDER-ground chapel, which, thanks to all of the life-sized images, made him feel like he was standing in a crowd. Thankfully, no disturbing feelings of claustrophobia had grabbed hold of him as the room, though cluttered, loomed airy and spacious.

"Is there climate control?" he asked, noticing the lack of humidity and the breeze.

"We have dehumidifiers," Pollux said. "We installed them when we changed out the door mechanism. The air-conditioning is natural. We've learned that you have to be careful with something like this. Touching with bare fingertips leaves oil that degrades the limestone. Artificial lights encourage bacterial growth. Lots of warm bodies exhaling carbon dioxide change the airflow, temperature, and humidity. It's important this place survives, so we took measures to ensure that it did."

"Is this where the *Secreti* worshiped?" Cotton asked.

Pollux nodded. "This is also where new members were inducted. The *Secreti* were quite peculiar about who they asked to join their ranks. They kept no written records, so it's impossible to know who was a member. Unless you wore the ring."

"I guess there were no jewelry stores copying them back then," he said with a touch of sarcasm.

Pollux seemed perplexed.

He told them what the fake Pollux Gallo had explained.

"There actually is truth to the statement," Pollux said. "I've seen a few of those copies over the years—"

"But since the *Secreti* are gone, what did it matter?"

He couldn't resist.

"Something like that," Pollux said.

Cotton had been thinking about the answer to the cardinal's question of *what now.* There'd been nothing in the outer chapel to draw his interest, which was surely the whole idea of keeping things simple there. Here, though, there were a multitude of potential hiding places represented by the numerous figures carved in stone. He turned to Pollux. "How far are you willing to go to find what you're looking for?"

"If you mean defacing any of this, that depends," Pollux said. "Let's see how certain you are of a result once when we reach that point."

His mind sorted through the possibilities. So far the dead prior's actions had been wholly practical. But nothing in any of the clues pointed to anything inside this statuary. Only to the chapel in general. Both Pollux and the curator had made it clear back at the cathedral that there were no other chapels or sacred sites near where the lines on the map had intersected.

So this had to be the place.

"No telling what godforsaken things happened here," the cardinal said.

"The *Secreti* were only a danger to those who threatened the knights."

"And today? Now? What's threatening the knights? Why are the *Secreti* killing people?"

Pollux faced his brother. "No one says they are."

"You did," Cotton said. "The urgency to get here was because the *Secreti* were on the move. Three men died at that villa. Two more here on Malta. You said the likely suspect in all five killings is the *Secreti.*"

"It seems logical," Pollux said. "But I will deal with that possibility after we locate the *Nostra Trinità.*"

Cotton's gaze had been raking the room and he'd settled on the only spot that made sense. At the far end, up three short steps, an altar had been carved from the wall. It jutted out and faced away from the worshipers, as would have been common five hundred years ago. Above it was a Madonna and child etched from the stone. Two winged angels flanked either side. But it was the altar's base that drew his attention. Five words that could be read the same from any direction. The palindrome from the ring.

The sign of Constantine.

SATOR
AREPO
TENET
OPERA
ROTAS

He pointed. "It has to be there."

They approached the altar.

"Constantine's sign was carved there when the church was built," Pollux said. "It's always been here."

Cotton set the shovels on the floor and knelt down to inspect the altar. The letters sprang from a recessed panel at the altar's center, right where a priest would have stood while saying mass. Four fluted columns carved from the limestone flanked left and right. With his finger he traced a mortar joint in the recessed panel—dry, brittle, and gray, like everything else.

"I say we bust this open."

He gave Pollux a moment to consider the ramifications. This wasn't a broken clock. It was a piece of something that had survived five hundred years. Something men had dedicated their lives to preserve. Thousands of knights and Maltese had died fighting to keep all of this inviolate.

And they'd succeeded.

Only to have it destroyed now by an outsider, with permission from one of their own.

Pollux handed over the sledgehammer, signaling his assent. Cotton gripped the wooden handle and decided there was no delicate way to do it, so he gave the center of the panel, right above the word TENET, a hard rap with the business end. The stone held, but there was a noticeable give, as at the obelisk.

"It's hollow behind it," he said.

He swung again.

Two more times and the stone broke into pieces, exposing a cavity beyond.

The two brothers watched as he cleared away the fragments, holding in his hand bits and pieces of the palindrome. He removed enough to see an object inside the chamber beyond. A horizontal glass cylinder resting on golden legs with animal paws as feet. About twenty-four inches long and eight inches high. Both ends were enclosed by gold mounts sealed with wax. Through the thick glass he could see the out-of-focus images of three scrolls, each loosely rolled.

Pollux made the sign of the cross and whispered, "Our Trinity."

Cotton reached in and lifted out the reliquary.

Heavy.

The three parchments appeared intact and in reasonably good shape. He laid the container on the altar where they could examine every aspect of it.

"This is where I must insist we part ways," Pollux said. "We've located the *Nostra Trinità*. It belongs to the Knights of Malta—"

"Or the Roman Catholic Church," the cardinal said.

"Precisely," Pollux finished. "This is a dispute we have to resolve among ourselves. It does not involve the American government in any way. We apologize for all that you've endured and appreciate your efforts. But the mystery is now solved and *we* have to deal with what happens next." Pollux paused. "Kastor and I. We have much to discuss."

Of that Cotton had no doubt.

"A lot of damage has occurred over the past day," Pollux said. "People have been hurt and killed. My brother and I have to deal with that. Patron of the Holy See to lieutenant ad interim. It's our problem. Not yours."

He was used to the rough-and-tumble of the intelligence business, willing to be banged up. God knows he'd had his share of injuries.

But the brush-off?

That kind of hurt.

But he'd done all Stephanie had asked of him. And though he would love to know what was inside the reliquary, Pollux Gallo was right. It really was none of his, or Washington's, business.

"All right," he said. "I'm out of here. But you feel this is a safe place for you to linger?"

"We're perfectly fine here," Pollux said, extending a hand to shake.

He accepted the offer.

"Thank you, Mr. Malone, for all your assistance. I never asked, but are you Catholic?"

"I was baptized that way, but religion is not my thing."

"A shame. You would have made a good knight."

Cardinal Gallo offered no hand to shake and his dour expression never changed. He shook his head and glanced back toward Pollux.

"Good luck."

And he left.

CHAPTER
FIFTY-FOUR

THE KNIGHT WATCHED AS COTTON MALONE LEFT THE CHURCH OF St. Magyar's. Finally, the last problem eliminated. The Americans were gone. Fitting that it would all end here at this sacred place, where the special ones formerly gathered. Their numbers had been small and closely held, each bound by a common purpose, their fate sealed by a secret French decree issued April 12, 1798. How ironic, he'd often thought. After centuries of fighting it wasn't the Turks, nor any corsair or Muslim enemy, but the French who defeated them. And not by violence nor invasion. Simply through the stroke of a pen. An edict issued to Napoleon, as the general in command of the army of the East, that he was to *take possession of the island of Malta for which purpose he will immediately proceed against it with all the naval and military forces under his command.*

And it had been easy.

Barely a fight.

Napoleon dispatched his orders and claimed the island for France. And though only a general at the time, he had his sights set on bigger things. Eighteen months after taking Malta he would be proclaimed first consul of France, in total command of the nation. Twelve years of nearly constant war followed. Napoleon wanted an empire. Like Alexander, Genghis Khan, Charlemagne, and Constantine before him. He also wanted control over that empire and knew that one tool could be used with absolute effectiveness.

Religion.

How better to keep the masses in line than through a fear for their immortal soul. It was self-working, self-regulating, and required little more than consistency to maintain itself. Occasionally, some displays of force were required—the Crusades and Inquisition two notable examples— but, by and large, religion sustained itself. In fact, if dished out correctly, the people would crave its effects like a drug. Demanding more and more.

Napoleon came to Malta to find the *Nostra Trinità*, thinking it might supply him the means to either control or eliminate the Roman Catholic Church. At the time it was the largest, most organized, most entrenched religion in the world. He'd learned how the Knights of Malta had always been shown great deference and privilege. How they skillfully escaped per-secution and elimination, surviving for centuries.

They had to have had some help.

But ultimately Napoleon was defeated and banished to St. Helena. Mussolini tried the same bullying tactics, and died a violent death. Now, finally, after over two hundred years, the Trinity had been found.

He stared at the reliquary.

Then turned to his brother and said, "We did it."

KASTOR SMILED. "YES, WE DID."

And he embraced Pollux for the first time in a long while.

A feeling of triumph hovered between them.

They stood inside the inner chapel, safe within a thick layer of rock, protected by time and the ages. The knight who'd brought the tools stood guard outside, but he'd just informed them that Malone had driven away and that they were now alone.

"You're to be pope," Pollux said, smiling. "We now have everything to make that happen."

Kastor stared at the reliquary, still perched on the altar. They'd not opened it, as yet.

"And the *Secreti*?" he asked Pollux.

"I said nothing with Malone here, but we have them under control. I told you I could deal with them. I've been told that their leaders have been identified and are now in our custody back in Italy. We were fairly sure of the traitors within our ranks. They're being held at the palazzi in Rome, on the knights' sovereign territory, subject to our jurisdiction. I'll deal with them. They are no longer a concern for you."

He was glad to hear that.

Pollux always took care of things. He'd been so glad to hear his brother's voice on the call earlier in the car with Chatterjee, assuring him that all was going well in Italy. He'd been able to stay brave in that cavern when Chatterjee died knowing that Pollux had his back.

He reached into his pocket and found the flash drive. "This is a gold mine. I've looked it over. There's more than enough here to extort the key cardinals. I can make them do whatever I want. Spagna did a good job. It was almost like he knew what we had planned."

"Spagna was an opportunist. I realized that from the first moment he and I spoke. But he told me nothing of any secret investigation. I suspect he was planning on shutting me out and making a deal only with you, thinking us enemies."

He motioned with the drive. "It's protected. The bastard used KASTOR I as the password."

"Nobody ever said Spagna was stupid. He had good instincts."

But not good enough. They'd done an excellent job faking a sibling rivalry. The entire internal attack on the knights and the forcing of the grand master from office had simply been part of that ruse.

"Was it the *Secreti* who killed Chatterjee and Spagna?" he asked.

Pollux nodded. "No doubt. But there's nothing to indicate that they knew anything about that flash drive. The ones we have in custody have been questioned but, so far, they've admitted nothing."

Which made sense. No attempt to retrieve the drive had happened in that grotto. They'd simply shot Chatterjee and left.

"Why didn't they shoot me?"

"You're their patron. A cardinal of the church. They abided by their oath to not harm a Christian. Chatterjee was a different matter. I'm not entirely sure of their plan at this point, but I'll find out while the conclave happens." Pollux stepped closer to the reliquary. "It's time."

"Open it."

Pollux found a knife in his pocket and worked the wax at one end of the glass cylinder, freeing the end cap and allowing the first exposure of fresh air to rush across the parchments. He then reached inside and slowly extracted the three rolls, laying them gently on the altar.

Kastor reached for one and slowly unrolled it. The parchment crackled, but the fibers held strong. The *Pie Postulatio Voluntatis*. The Most Pious Request. The papal bull from 1113 that recognized the Hospitallers' independence and sovereignty. He'd seen the other original housed in the Vatican archives.

Pollux unraveled a second parchment.

The *Ad Providam*. From 1312, when Pope Clement V handed over all of the Templars' property to the Hospitallers. He'd seen that other original, too.

They both stared at the final parchment, which was a little longer than the others, and thicker.

"It has to be," he said.

"It's two sheets rolled together," Pollux said, lifting the parchment and unrolling.

Faded black ink in tight lines, with narrow margins, filled the top sheet, which measured about forty-five centimeters long and a little less than that wide.

"It's Latin," Pollux said.

He'd already noticed. Latin had been Constantine's main language, so much that he'd required Greek translators in order to communicate with many parts of his empire. This document being drafted in Latin was a good sign toward authenticity, as were the parchment and ink, which would surely survive scientific scrutiny and be dated to the 4th century. But it was the signatures at the bottom of the second sheet that would prove the point. He counted the names, signed one after the other.

Seventy-three.

Some he recognized from historical reading.

Eustathius of Antioch. Paphnutius of Thebes. Potamon of Heraclea.

Paul of Neocaesarea. Nicholas of Myra. Macarius of Jerusalem. Aristaces of Armenia. Leontius of Caesarea. Jacob of Nisibis. Hypatius of Gangra. Protogenes of Sardica. Melitius of Sebastopolis. Achillius of Larissa. Spyridon of Trimythous. John, bishop of Persia and India. Marcus of Calabria. Caecilian of Carthage. Hosius of Córdoba. Nicasius from Gaul. Domnus from the province of the Danube.

Then there was Eusebius of Caesarea, the purported first church historian, who provided the only written account of what happened at Nicaea.

But the mark at the bottom cinched the deal.

Five rows. Five words.

The letters in the Latin alphabet.

A palindrome.

SATOR
AREPO
TENET
OPERA
ROTAS

The sign of Constantine.

"The emperor and the bishops all signed it," he said. "It's exactly as it should be."

"Yes, it is, brother."

And at the top of the first sheet were the two most important words.

Constitutum Constantini.

CHAPTER
FIFTY-FIVE

POLLUX STARED AT THE PARCHMENTS.

Everything pointed to their authenticity. Including where they'd been found. Here, inside the sacred chapel, at the end of a trail created by the *Secreti*.

"There's no time right now to study this," he said. "We can deal with that between now and this afternoon. I'll photograph and translate it myself and have an English and Italian version provided to you before you head into the Sistine Chapel." He allowed the parchment to recede back into a roll. "You'll take the original in with you."

"It'll be good to have it," Kastor said. "Cardinals have a natural affinity for the past. But the flash drive. That's what will win the day."

"It is that good?"

Kastor nodded. "Even better."

They'd planned so carefully. Years in the making, it all started when the pope fired Kastor from his post as prefect of the Apostolic Signatura. Where Kastor had seen that as a rebuke, a setback, possibly even the end, Pollux had realized the possibilities and insisted that Kastor seek out the position of patron of the Sovereign Military Order of Malta. Kastor, being Kastor, had thought the idea insane.

Until he explained.

Kastor never had been able to see the grand picture. Time had been a friend Pollux had willingly embraced, but never surrendered to, always being able to restrain his impatience. Kastor was a different story.

The elimination of the grand master had been a necessity. No way they could have enjoyed any freedom of movement with that man in charge. Too many of the order's officers were loyal to him.

Better to just eliminate the problem.

In any other situation a bullet would have solved things with haste. But killing the leader of 13,000 knights, 25,000 employees, and 80,000 volunteers would have drawn far too much attention. Shame had seemed a better weapon. Especially once the careless distribution of condoms had been discovered. It happened in Myanmar. Thousands were handed out by one of the knights' charitable arms. How it happened no one knew, since the church banned the use of contraception in any form. The program was stopped but Kastor, as patron, the pope's emissary to the Hospitallers, conducted an investigation and laid the blame at the top, forcing the grand master to resign.

Then out of nowhere the pope died.

Like a godsend.

In the chaos it had been easy to secure Pollux's temporary appointment as lieutenant ad interim. Many of the order's officers had been wanting to appease Kastor, fearing his growing influence. It helped that the late pope had stayed out of the fight and allowed Kastor to handle things, perhaps hoping for another misstep, but things had played out perfectly. Added to the charade was their supposed sibling rivalry and personal dislike, which comforted those knights who had supported the disgraced grand master. After that, Pollux's unassuming mask had misled everyone, Cotton Malone and Stephanie Nelle the latest to fall for his performance. "He was there only temporarily." "Until a new pope was chosen." "He had no interest in being grand master."

All true.

Only the Entity had seen through things.

"Spagna never told me about having that level of incriminating information," Pollux said.

"You sent me here," Kastor said. "I came and met that man Chatterjee at the Madliena Tower, exactly as you told me to do. He took me straight to Spagna, who was anxious to make a deal. You knew nothing of that?"

He shook his head. "Spagna was only supposed to make a deal with you to find the Trinity. That was what he and I agreed upon. I told him you knew things that no one else did."

Which was true.

But when he'd spoken to Kastor earlier by phone and told him about what had happened at Como and in Rome, he learned for the first time about the flash drive. Something Spagna had held close. His men were already on the way to that clockmaker's shop, so he'd told them to flush the targets out on the water where Chatterjee could be eliminated. But he'd specifically told them not to take the drive. He knew Kastor, being the thief that he was, would do that for them and bring it straight to him.

Which was exactly what had happened.

"It's time for you to head to Rome," he said.

"And the Americans?"

He shrugged. "Malone seemed perfectly satisfied. I dealt directly with him and his superior. They were of great assistance, and now they're done. Nothing draws them back our way. It's just you and me now."

Exactly the way he wanted it. Ending up here, alone and underground, in a controlled environment was another fortuitous occurrence. This was the perfect place to end one part and begin another.

But first—

"Did you bring an overnight bag?"

Kastor nodded. "It's at the rectory in Mdina. I'll pick it up on the way to the airport. I have a private plane waiting to take me back to Rome. A favor from a friend."

Good to know.

He glanced at his watch. 5:40 A.M.

Less than five hours left to get back to Italy.

"My aide has prepared my belongings," Kastor said. "Clothes, toiletries, papers, everything needed for the conclave. He texted me earlier to say it's all at the Domus Sanctae Marthae, in my room. I'll go straight there from the airport."

"I'll head to the Palazzo di Malta and deal with the *Secreti*. They've caused enough trouble. I'll also translate the parchments."

"We need the *Secreti* gone."

"They will be. You just concentrate on the conclave and achieving the ultimate goal. Nothing matters unless you become pope."

Pollux slipped the parchments back into the reliquary and replaced the end cap. That seemed the safest place for them. Earlier, when the knight arrived with the keys and tools, he'd also had the man bring one other item.

A short length of thin rope.

About a meter long.

Which he'd slipped into his pocket.

"Let's get the tools and go," he said.

Kastor headed for the shovels. Pollux used the moment to find the rope and secure both ends within his clenched fists.

"I'm still puzzled why the *Secreti* did not kill me in that cavern," Kastor said.

He advanced and, as his brother crouched to retrieve the shovels, he draped the taut rope over Kastor's head, looping it tight, stretching his arms outward and cutting off the windpipe. Kastor reached up with both hands and tried to free the stranglehold, but he tightened it even more. Kastor's legs began to flail. Arms came up behind his head, trying to grab his attacker. Pollux angled back, out of reach, but he kept the rope firmly in place, pulling it ever tighter. Kastor gagged, struggling to breathe. His hands groped for the garrote, the grip weakening, the choking becoming more intense.

Pollux had long wondered what this moment would feel like.

For so many years he'd languished in the shadow of his arrogant twin. Many knew the name Kastor Gallo, but almost no one, outside of the Hospitallers, knew of Pollux Gallo. His brother had chosen the priesthood and risen to a level of respect and authority. Then he'd thrown it all away with reckless nonsense. All that he could have accomplished tossed to the wind so he could simply run his mouth. He'd tried to tell him to keep quiet but Kastor, being Kastor, chose his own path.

Now Pollux had finally done the same thing.

Chosen.

All movement stopped.

He kept the rope in place a few more seconds to be sure, then relaxed his grip. Kastor's body went limp, the arms draped at the side, the legs rolled outward, the neck no longer supporting the head. He unwrapped the rope and allowed his brother to fold to the floor.

"They didn't kill you," he whispered, "because I wanted to."

Interesting that for all his smarts, his brother never even imagined that he was being manipulated. Probably because he thought himself superior, the dominant one in their sibling relationship. Their entire life it had always been Kastor and Pollux. Never the other way around.

But no more.

Pollux Gallo just died.

Kastor Gallo would be reborn.

CHAPTER
FIFTY-SIX

COTTON DROVE MINDLESSLY, HIS WORLD SHRUNK TO A RIBBON OF AS-
phalt and the occasional headlight of an approaching car. Dawn was not
far away, but some sleep would be welcome. Given the late hour, he'd decided to find a hotel room and head home in the afternoon. The past
couple of days had been interesting, to say the least, and he was a hundred
thousand euros richer, but, contrary to what he might have led James Grant
to think, it had never been about money.

Not that he had anything against money.

Federal agents weren't the best-compensated of public servants. About
sixty-five thousand a year at the end of his time with the Justice Department. But no one worked that job for the pay. You worked it because it had
to be done. Because you chose to do it. Because you were good at it. No
glory, as few ever knew what you did. Which came in handy at screwup
time. Nope. The satisfaction came from simply getting the job done.

He rounded a sharp curve in the highway and kept heading south, a
swath of black landscape on one side and the Med on the other. Thoughts
rummaged through his orderly mind, trying to seek a permanent residence.
During his career at Justice he'd learned that the worst picture was always what the brain fabricated. Never mind reality. A fiction could seem
far more immediate. So he'd come to rely on his subconscious to know if
something was out of order, didn't belong.

And something was out of place here.

But it wasn't his problem.

He'd done what Stephanie wanted and everything to be found was back in the hands of the Knights of Malta and the Catholic Church. The brothers Gallo and the Vatican powers that be would now sort it out. The cardinal would head for the conclave and do what cardinals did, and Pollux Gallo would dissolve back into his cloistered world. And the *Secreti*? Who knew? Did they even exist? If so, were they still a threat? Regardless, they were the problem of the authorities in Italy and Malta, where all of the crimes had occurred.

So he told himself to let it go.

He kept driving, paralleling the north shore. He'd visited Malta a few times and loved the island. Always he'd stayed outside of Valletta in the suburb of St. Julian's, at the Dragonara. Spacious rooms, good food, balconies that overlooked the Med. A lovely upscale seaside resort with all of the amenities, which he'd never had a chance to enjoy. But maybe he'd remedy that before he left later today, depending on the flight schedules. A few minutes by the pool. That'd be different.

He slowed and navigated through the narrow streets of St. Julian's, arriving at the hotel a little before 6:00 A.M. He valet-parked the car and headed for the front desk, where he was pleased to learn a room was available.

"Did you see the explosion?" the clerk asked. "Quite the excitement tonight."

That was true, but he was sure this guy had no idea how exciting his past few hours had been. So he asked, "What do you mean?"

"Big explosion out on the water a couple of hours ago. The boat burned for half an hour before sinking. We don't see that here often."

"Any idea what happened?"

The clerk shook his head. "I'm sure the morning *Independent* will let us know."

He accepted the room key and drifted from the front desk. Before going to bed he needed to make a report. He found his phone, connected to Stephanie, and explained what had happened at the cathedral and the chapel.

She told him, "Luke took down a yacht outside the Valletta harbor. He

306 | STEVE BERRY

drove his boat right into it. Four men are dead. Luke's in custody. The harbor police are holding him. Unfortunately, none of the bodies carried any identification, but we're working on that now through fingerprints. And there's more."

He was listening.

"Luke says Laura Price switched teams and was working with the Entity. She was ready to take a rifle shot when you and the Gallo brothers exited the cathedral, a shot that Spagna himself arranged. The *Secreti* interrupted, killing her and the temporary head of the Entity, who'd come to Malta to oversee the hit."

"Who was the target? Me or the cardinal?"

"Neither one."

And there it was.

One of those wandering thoughts just found a home. "The Entity was taking out Pollux Gallo?"

"That's right. Which raises a whole host of questions."

More thoughts dropped into place. The subterfuge and organized attack at the Hospitaller archive by the so-called *Secreti*. The sudden appearance of the real Pollux Gallo. His gracious cooperation. The lack of any outside interference at the obelisk, though the *Secreti* had been on the move at Lake Como and in that villa. Then the curious lack of concern at St. Magyar's chapel. Isolated and out in the middle of nowhere, with plenty of vulnerabilities, Pollux Gallo had seemed totally at ease.

Why would a mere lieutenant ad interim of a benign charitable organization be a greater threat than a cardinal who had, at least on paper, a chance to be pope?

"Where is Luke now?" he asked.

"In Valletta. I'm dealing with it."

"Get him out." He told her the chapel's name and where St. Magyar's was located, indicating that the curator at the co-cathedral could provide exact directions. "When he's free, send Luke my way."

"What are you going to do?"

"Head back there. I may have misjudged the wrong Gallo."

CHAPTER
FIFTY-SEVEN

POLLUX WAITED FOR HIS MEN FROM OUTSIDE TO MAKE THEIR WAY through the outer chapel and into the inner sanctuary, their movements calculated but quick. He'd delayed a few minutes before telling them to enter.

A little time alone with his departed brother seemed in order.

Their relationship had always been an illusion. Kastor had thought himself the better of the two, superior, a touch above. It had been that way their entire lives, even more so after their parents died and they moved to the orphanage. Kastor the talker, thinker, scholar—while he was the athlete and soldier. He doubted anyone at that orphanage even remembered he existed. But Kastor? No one would forget him. They couldn't. He made a lasting impression, sucking every drop of oxygen from every room he ever entered.

But none of that would have been possible without his help.

When Kastor had first come and said he wanted to be pope, Pollux had thought the idea ridiculous. Especially considering the mess made of his ecclesiastical career. Sure, there were people who agreed with him in their heart, but none were going to openly challenge the pope. He'd reviewed the dirt Kastor had amassed on some of the cardinals. Not bad. There was some clearly incriminating material. But not near enough to change a conclave. And with Kastor's loss of position and access, the prospects of acquiring more information seemed remote. That's when Kastor focused on the *Nostra Trinità*.

Thinking it might be enough.

He, too, had been intrigued by the Trinity, especially the *Constitutum Constantini,* which had certainly proved useful in centuries past. Kastor had discovered quite a bit of useful information from the Vatican archives. He'd supplemented that with annals the knights had long kept under lock and key. Together they'd made progress. The call from the greedy Italian at Lake Como had been one of those fortuitous events that sometimes made one think that there actually might be a God directing things in some sort of divine plan. He'd known for some time the British had information on Mussolini and the Trinity. There'd just not been anything to bargain with. So he'd headed to Como. Which had been fruitful since it led to Sir James Grant, which had sent him to the obelisk, then on to the cathedral in Valletta, and finally to here.

All had dropped right into place.

And while the pope's body had lain on view inside St Peter's Basilica and hundreds of thousands filed by, Spagna had appeared at the Palazzo di Malta with an intriguing offer.

A way to make Kastor pope.

The Lord's Own had become aware of Kastor's private investigations and his interest in the Trinity. But Spagna was several steps ahead, though he'd refused to share the details. Cardinals had long been bribed and coerced. Nothing new there. Before the 20th century the college had been small enough that it was easy to alter its course with just a few moves. Modern conclaves were different. 100 to 150 cardinals participated, which added mathematical challenges. But cardinals were men and men were flawed. So while the pope was buried beneath St. Peter's, he and Spagna had schemed. It had been Spagna who insisted Kastor be sent to Malta. He wanted to make a deal face-to-face, and he wanted Kastor out of Rome so he could not do anything stupid to ruin things.

And he'd made that happen.

Then, once the greedy Italian at Como had contacted the knights and wanted to sell the letters, a path opened to the Trinity. So he'd improvised and used the opportunity to finally bring the Brits to the table by acquiring the Churchill letters. James Grant had been easy to manipulate.

The Americans, too. But Kastor the easiest of them all. *Whoever exalts himself will be humbled, and whoever humbles himself will be exalted.*

The Bible was right.

Kastor never learned humility.

Neither had Spagna, which was why he had to die, along with his minion Chatterjee and Roy, his second in command. Spagna wanted the *Constitutum Constantini* destroyed. The Entity considered it a direct threat to the church, one that should be eliminated. Whether it was destroyed or not mattered little to him. But that flash drive.

It mattered the most.

So he'd allowed Spagna to play his hand. The fool had apparently wanted to be the pope-maker. And what better way than by providing a cardinal, with little to no moral structure, the ammunition needed to blackmail his way to the papacy. One who'd owe him big time.

What better way, indeed.

The only unexpected occurrence had been the Americans. But Spagna had assured him he had them under control.

He smiled at the dead spy's naïveté.

Sadly, the Lord's Own had never realized that the greatest danger he faced would come from within. Pollux's men had taken out Spagna, Chatterjee, Laura Price, and John Roy with each death blamed on the *Secreti*.

Which, of course, no longer existed.

It had all been a ruse. His creation.

"What a fool you were," he whispered to his brother.

Then he pocketed the flash drive, lifting it off the hard earth where it had fallen from Kastor's grip. He supposed he should feel some regret, but he harbored not a speck of remorse. Unlike the knight at the villa by Como. That death he'd regretted. Killing a fellow Christian had always been forbidden for the Hospitallers. It was part of their oath to protect Christians. But the murder had been unavoidable. He could not allow Malone to take that man into custody. Everything would have been placed in peril.

And killing Kastor?

He was a lot of things, but a Christian his brother was not. Just an opportunist who used the church to further his own ambitions.

Two men entered the inner chapel. One was the man who'd escorted

Malone from Rome to Rapallo, the other the man who'd impersonated him once Malone arrived and tried to eliminate the ex-agent at the archives. That had not turned out according to plan. He'd only made the attempt because James Grant had insisted. But once the effort failed, he'd adapted and decided to personally intervene, working the Americans himself. It had also allowed him to be on the inside and learn what Spagna and Stephanie Nelle were doing.

Just another of the many differences between him and Kastor. He possessed an ability to disregard what was not working and immediately change to something that would. It had been easy to ingratiate himself with both the British and the Americans. Easy to enlist their help to solve the obelisk and the puzzle at the cathedral.

The problems had come from Spagna.

A true maverick.

Impossible to control.

But not anymore.

He slipped the flash drive into his pocket.

"Grab him," he told his two men.

They grasped Kastor's ankles and wrists, lifting the body and following him deeper into the inner chapel. Another oak door waited at the end of a short apse. He opened its iron latch and switched on another series of lights. A spiral staircase led down, and he followed the corkscrewed path deeper into the earth. His two men, with Kastor, followed him down. His brother's bulk made the going slow.

At the bottom he navigated another corridor hewn from the rock to a small chamber. A doorway led out on the far side. The entire underground network of alcoves and corridors had been fashioned sometime in the 17th century. Most had served as gunpowder and ammunition depots. The hole in the ground before him had been dug long ago, too. About three meters wide, five meters deep, its walls bell-shaped, tapering outward the farther down they stretched.

A *guva.*

He motioned and they laid Kastor down on the parched ground. His men knew exactly what to do. All six of his trusted associates were now on Malta, three here for the past few days on the boat offshore, the other three standing ready at Fort St. Angelo, waiting for his call, which he'd

made from the cathedral once Malone had solved the riddle. There was no way he could accomplish anything alone. That was why the *Secreti* had been reactivated. Of course it was all mainly for appearance's sake, but he'd bound them all together with the ring and a promise of good things to come.

His two men undressed Kastor.

One reason strangulation had been chosen was the preservation of the clothing. He needed it all intact.

"I'll help finish this," he said, then motioned to one of his acolytes. "Get the shovels and rope."

The man left while he and the other finished removing Kastor's clothes. His brother's body was not nearly as fit as his own, but the size and shape were reasonably similar. He carefully folded the clothes and set them to the side, along with the shoes.

The other man returned.

To the right of the *guva* an oak post protruded from the ground. To it, one of his men tied the end of the thick hemp rope they'd brought in earlier. There had to be a way in and out of the pit, and a rope was the most practical choice, the post having been there for centuries. The coil was thrown into the black yawn. He nodded and his men tossed the shovels down then used the rope to descend into the *guva*. Burying his brother at the bottom of the pit seemed the perfect place as no one was allowed inside St. Magyar's without express permission of the grand master. Since there wasn't one at the moment, control of this locale fell to him as temporary head of command. But even after a new leader was chosen, no one would venture into this *guva*.

There'd be no reason.

And by then all traces of this night would be gone.

"Bury him deep," he called out.

He listened as they dug.

This was not just the closing of a chapter in his life. More like an entire part. Nothing would be the same after tonight. But he was ready. The Hospitallers had provided him the perfect refuge. He'd managed to learn things, build relationships, establish loyalties, all in anticipation of what was about to happen. Two days ago he'd been unsure if any of this was possible, but now he was much more confident.

His men stopped digging.

They both climbed back up using the rope. They were about to toss Kastor into the *guva* when he recalled something. He found his phone and snapped a picture of his brother's face and hair.

Then he removed the ring from the right hand.

Each newly elected cardinal was presented with a gold ring by the pope. Kissing that ring was a sign of respect.

He slipped it onto his own finger.

Then nodded.

And they dropped Kastor's naked body over the edge, the corpse finding the bottom with a thud.

His men climbed back down to finish the burial.

Not the end his brother imagined. Surely Kastor had thought his mortal remains would rest forever beneath St. Peter's along with so many other popes.

Not going to happen, he mouthed.

Or at least, not exactly.

CHAPTER FIFTY-EIGHT

LUKE SAT IN THE HOLDING CELL.

Familiar territory.

How many had he graced over the years?

His clothes were still wet from his second dip in the Med. His boat had sunk the yacht, killing all the men aboard. The harbor patrol had responded to the explosion and fished the bodies and him from the water, though he'd tried to avoid them in the dark.

Damn night-vision goggles.

It would have been so much easier to just swim back to shore unnoticed. The locals were rarely helpful. Most times they were a giant pain in the ass. And this time was no exception. He'd deflected all of their questions, practicing the ol' Sergeant Schultz of *I see nothing, hear nothing, know nothing.* He'd loved *Hogan's Heroes.* The only thing he had said was United States Justice Department and Stephanie Nelle, coupled with a request to make a call.

Which they'd allowed.

He'd explained his current dilemma to Stephanie, keeping his story short, and she'd told him to sit tight.

No problem there.

But over an hour had passed since then in silence.

Which had given him time to think.

The steel door beyond the cell clattered open and a man entered the holding area. He recognized the face from the safe house. Kevin Hahn, head of Maltese security, and he did not look happy.

"I've spoken with Ms. Nelle," Hahn said. "She told me about what happened with Laura. We found her body, and that of the Entity's second in command, just where you said." He pointed. "You killed four men, Mr. Daniels. This isn't the United States. Murders are rare here. Yet we've had seven in the past twelve hours."

He stood and faced the idiot through the bars. He wasn't in the mood for lectures. Like Malone taught him. *Never take crap from the locals.* "I'm an agent for the United States government, on assignment, doing my job. Now get me out of here."

"You're a pain in the ass."

"I've been called worse."

Over the past hour a lot had raced through his mind. Especially what Laura had told him when they first talked outside the *guva.* When he'd asked who'd told her he was on the island.

"My boss. He gave me an order. I do what he tells me."

"How did you know I was headed into trouble?"

"Same answer. My boss told me."

"How did you know that I'd been sent here?" he asked Hahn.

"Who says I did?"

"Your dead agent. What were you doing with Spagna at that safe house?"

"You don't really expect me to answer either question."

"Actually, I do."

"We need to go."

"That's not an answer."

"It's all you're going to get."

But he didn't need one. He'd already concluded that there was one constant across his entire encounter with Laura Price and that was this man, her boss. He was actually planning on looking this roly-poly up just as soon as he was sprung. Stephanie had just saved him the trouble.

"You were working with Spagna," he said.

And he suddenly saw regret in the man's eyes.

"I made a mistake. There's more going on here than I realized." Hahn paused. "Much more. Spagna asked for help. He made a good case, so I went along."

"Apparently Spagna and you underestimated the opposition. Whoever the opposition is."

"We're still working to identify the men from the boat."

"Laura and the guy from the Vatican said they were *Secreti*."

"That would be amazing, if true. That group was disbanded two centuries ago."

"They both seemed real sure that it was still around. And some of them tried to toss me through a window."

"Your Ms. Nelle was sparse on information when she called to tell me about you. Care to tell me what's going on?"

"I know about as much as you do."

Which wasn't far from the truth. But if Stephanie had stayed silent, so would he.

"She asked me to secure your release," Hahn said. "I've done that."

"I appreciate it. I also need a car."

"That can be arranged. Where are you headed?"

This guy was a bit of a Nosy Nellie, as his mother liked to say. So he gave him the standard reply.

"To do my job."

POLLUX STEPPED OUTSIDE INTO THE NIGHT. HE AND HIS MEN HAD come back to ground level to retrieve what they needed to finish. The clock was now ticking and there was a lot to be done.

Thankfully, he was ready.

He heard the buzz of a phone and one of his men drifted away and answered the call. He watched as the conversation ensued, then ended.

"We've just learned there's a problem. Our boat offshore was attacked and sunk. All of the brothers are dead."

He kept the shock to himself and calmly asked, "How?"

"The American, Daniels. He escaped during the kill on Laura Price and Bishop Roy and found his way to our boat."

Disturbing news, no doubt. But not game changing. And there it was again. That ability to shift directions at a moment's notice. To turn a problem into an opportunity. "Where is Daniels now?"

"In custody."

Perfect.

His personal motto came from the Book of James. *And let steadfastness have its full effect, that you may be perfect and complete, lacking in nothing.*

His life had been a series of hurdles. He'd dutifully served in the military, then was hired by the Hospitallers to work abroad in their medical missions. He eventually professed his allegiance and took the oaths of poverty, chastity, and obedience. Then he'd languished in unimportant jobs. Playing second to one knight after another. He eventually rose to grand commander, charged with spreading the faith, supervising priories, and compiling reports to the Holy See, becoming one of the order's top four officers.

Then came Kastor's chaos.

And he was made temporary head.

Time for another promotion.

"We keep going. As planned."

He headed back inside, then down to the *guva* chamber. His men followed, one carrying a folding chair and a duffel bag. He passed the hole in the ground and exited from the second door into another corridor that led to the next chamber. He'd chosen this spot for not only its privacy but also its lighting, which was much brighter.

"Set the chair up there," he said pointing. Then he pointed at the other brother. "Keep a watch outside. Though I doubt we'll be disturbed."

The man left.

He faced the remaining brother.

"Shall we start?"

COTTON ROUNDED A CURVE AND REALIZED THAT THE CHAPEL WAS not far ahead. His senses were on full alert. The situation had shifted from curious to serious. One or both Gallos could be in trouble.

He doused the headlights and stopped on the side of the road.

In the distance he saw the chapel on the ridge. A car remained parked out front. Were the two brothers still there?

How many times had he been in this exact situation?

Too many to count.

He thought of Cassiopeia. Where was she? Surely asleep, at home in France. He hadn't heard from her in a few days. Good thing, too. If she knew he was deep into a mess, she'd be on a plane headed his way. He didn't like placing her in danger, though she was more than capable of handling herself. She was an extraordinary woman who'd dropped into his life out of nowhere. Initially, neither of them had cared for the other, but time and circumstances had changed everything. What would she say now? *Figure it out. Finish it.* He smiled. Good advice.

He spotted a splash of light in the dark. The chapel's door had opened and a man stepped out into the night.

Alone.

He watched as the solitary figure stood for a moment, then eased away from the door, leaving it partially open. He waited to see if the figure was leaving. No. The car remained dark and still.

A guard?

Maybe.

He switched off the car's interior light, then eased open the door and slipped out, pocketing the key remote. The chapel was about three hundred yards away. He hustled in that direction, using the dark and a mass of low scrub and the few trees as cover. He approached from the western side and kept low, not catching sight of the man he knew was outside. It wasn't until he came close to the building that he spotted the figure about fifty yards away, back to him, surveying the valley that stretched to the south. A dull glow had begun to rise on the eastern horizon. Dawn was coming. He needed the guard distracted and had decided on the hike over that the car might prove the best mechanism. He pressed his body against the chapel wall and aimed the remote control back toward where he'd come from, hoping its range was sufficient.

Then he hesitated.

Pressing the button would set off the horn, accompanied by the head-lights flashing, and the element of surprise would be gone. He decided instead to be patient and glanced back again around the corner at the solitary figure. Darkness remained thick across the valley. The man casually turned to his right and moved farther away from the chapel, finding a cell phone and making a call. He crouched and used the shadows for cover, darting toward the open front door. He slipped in, keeping his eyes on the guard, who'd noticed nothing.

Inside was empty and quiet, the same lights from earlier still burning. He hustled toward the far apse and through the concealed panel, which also remained opened.

The inner chapel was likewise empty. This was as far as he'd gone earlier. The reliquary remained on the altar. He noticed chucks of red wax lying beside it and realized one end had been opened, but the parchments were still safe inside. He scanned the interior and noticed that the chapel extended farther into the limestone ridge. He followed its path and spotted another oak door, half open. Beyond, a spiral staircase wound down. He descended to a narrow, lit corridor. Immediately he was uncomfortable with the tight, enclosed space.

Not his favorite.

He sucked a deep breath and walked ahead to where he found a more spacious chamber with a black hole in the earthen floor. Everything was illuminated by honey-colored light, as thick and sickly sweet as the confined air around him. He glanced down into the hole and saw only blackness. A rope snaked a path from a wooden pillar embedded into the ground down into the void. He wondered how deep the thing was and its purpose.

He heard voices.

Coming from beyond a half-open door at the other end, about fifty feet away.

He crept toward the sound.

CHAPTER FIFTY-NINE

POLLUX SAT IN THE METAL CHAIR.

His man found a pair of shears in the duffel bag and began to trim his hair. To help, he held up the image of Kastor, taken a few minutes ago on his cell phone, and they took care to make sure his new cut mimicked that look. He'd not worn his hair so short since his teenage years.

His man finished the trim and he admired the work on his phone screen, the camera switched to selfie mode. He nodded and a bowl was removed from the bag, which he filled with water from a jug. He handed over the cell phone, then lathered his chin with shaving cream. He found a razor and carefully began to shear the monk's beard away, again using the phone as a mirror. No nicks. No cuts. It had to be a clean shave. He focused on the sound of blade to whisker, keeping the strokes short and light. He also constantly rinsed the blade in the water so the metal remained moist. When he was finished, he grabbed a towel from the bag and swiped away the last remaining bits of lather.

His man nodded.

He agreed.

Not since they were teenagers had he looked so much like Kastor. They were born identical and remained identical until they left the orphanage. Nearly forty years had passed. Now they were identical again.

He stood, undressed, and donned his brother's clothes, shoes and underwear included. He found the flash drive in his old clothes, then cleaned out Kastor's pockets, retrieving a wallet and cell phone, but no passport. It must be with the overnight bag in Mdina. Then he slipped on a pair of eyeglasses, identical to what his brother had worn, only with the lenses clear.

Kastor Cardinal Gallo lived again.

He felt free, untethered, in rhythm, doing what God and nature had surely intended. He was also rested, healthy, and finally worry-free. Danger lurked, for sure. But he was fully immersed in the moment, each second precious, fulfilling, and ordained.

His time had come.

He motioned and his man emptied the bowl to the floor, replaced all of the supplies inside the bag, along with his clothes, then refolded the chair.

"We can go," he said.

COTTON HEARD THE WORDS.

We can go.

Pollux Gallo's voice.

No question.

He hadn't been able to get close enough to see what was happening, and precious little had been said. He retreated to the room with the open pit, intent on leaving through the other exit and heading back up to ground level. But as he approached the door he caught sight of another man in the narrow tunnel beyond, headed his way.

He was trapped.

Danger on both sides.

He could simply reveal himself, but something told him that was not the smart play. Not yet. There seemed only one choice. He stepped to the pit, grabbed hold of the rope, and eased himself over the edge. Hand over hand he descended and found the bottom, about fifteen feet down.

POLLUX REENTERED THE *GUVA* CHAMBER WITH HIS MINION.

His second acolyte joined them.

"All is quiet outside," the man reported. "I also loaded the reliquary and one of the shovels into the car."

The other rested against the wall where he'd asked it to be placed.

"What of our brothers who died on the boat?"

"I checked. Their bodies are with the authorities. They'll surely be identified soon."

He'd already considered that possibility. But any trail would lead to the Knights of Malta. Which was no longer a problem for him, since Pollux Gallo would not exist after tonight.

"We'll deal with that once it happens," he said. "There's little that can be done about the situation now."

"The jet the cardinal mentioned is waiting at the airport," one of his men told him.

Excellent. He'd head there and fly on to Rome. Kastor had already told him that an aide had delivered what would be needed in the way of personal belongings to the Domus Sanctae Marthae. His room was ready, simply waiting on an occupant. His first test would come with convincing that aide as to his authenticity, but he'd practiced being Kastor for a long time.

"Did you bring the laptop?" he asked.

The brother nodded and found the device in the duffel bag. He'd need it on the trip to Rome. He wanted to study, firsthand, the flash drive.

"And the other item?" he asked.

His man produced a Glock from the bag.

He accepted the weapon.

Everything had come down to this moment. Initially he'd intended on keeping his faux *Secreti* intact as a personal police force. Those men would come in handy, working outside the Entity, providing him with an immediate way to deal with problems.

And the concept was not without precedent.

In the 16th century Julian II maneuvered his way into the papacy, then safeguarded his hold against rival cardinals by raising his own armed regiment of 150 Swiss mercenaries. The best fighters in the world at that time, they'd served popes ever since as the Swiss Guard. But five of his eight men were dead. Recruiting more could prove problematic, and on reflection he'd decided they might not be necessary.

"Let us kneel," he said. "We should give thanks."

He laid the laptop and gun on the ground and dropped to his knees, as did his two brothers.

"Centuries ago the founding bishops of our faith proclaimed what we should believe. The great Council of Nicaea settled all debate as to what was holy and sacred, and the Emperor Constantine, in thanks, bestowed upon us a great gift. Tonight, through the grace of God, we have retrieved that sacred gift. It finally, once again, is safe in our hands. Let us give thanks by reaffirming that great Nicaean Creed.

"*We believe in one God the Father Almighty, Maker of heaven and earth, and of all things visible and invisible. And in one Lord Jesus Christ, the only-begotten Son of God, begotten of the Father before all worlds, God of God, Light of Light, Very God of Very God, begotten, not made, being of one substance with the Father by whom all things were made.*

"*Who for us men, and for our salvation, came down from heaven, and was incarnate by the Holy Spirit of the Virgin Mary, and was made man, and was crucified also for us under Pontius Pilate. He suffered and was buried, and the third day he rose again according to the Scriptures, and ascended into heaven, and sitteth at the right hand of the Father. And he shall come again with glory to judge both the quick and the dead, whose kingdom shall have no end.*

"*And we believe in the Holy Spirit, the Lord and Giver of Life, who proceedeth from the Father and the Son, who with the Father and the Son together is worshiped and glorified, who spoke by the prophets. And we believe one holy catholic and apostolic Church. We acknowledge one baptism for the remission of sins. And we look for the resurrection of the dead, and the life of the world to come.*

"Amen."

His men had repeated every word. He nodded and stood, the lust inside him breaking free of the decorum he'd always felt obliged to show.

He bent down and regripped the Glock.

Then fired twice.

One bullet pierced the forehead of each of the brothers, collapsing them instantly in death.

The trail had to be painted cold.

True, the cathedral curator remained, but the new Kastor Cardinal

Gallo would deal with him, nothing there to arouse any suspicion. Eventually, a letter would come, in his hand, writing as Pollux, explaining his resignation from the knights and his retreat from the world. He doubted anyone would miss either his men or Pollux Gallo.

Sad.

But true.

He laid the Glock down and dragged both bodies to the pit.

He crouched down and cleaned out their pockets, finding the key for the chapel's front door and the car outside.

Then he rolled each over the edge.

They would need to be buried, eliminating any trace of foul play. This place itself might prove problematic but, to his knowledge, only a handful of people within the knights knew of the secret panel, and the inner chapel was almost never visited. Kastor was buried deep in the ground, gone for the ages. These two corpses required a similar fate.

Which was why he'd had a shovel left behind.

He stepped over, grabbed it, then tossed it into the pit.

He had to return to Rome.

Thank goodness there was one final knight still around to clean up the mess.

Cotton heard Gallo's voice as he gave thanks, then said the Nicaean Creed. Two sharp barks signaled gunfire, followed by what sounded like dragging across parched ground. He'd already determined that the pit was bell-shaped, its walls flaring out the farther down they went, with the lower circumference much wider than the top. He'd also noticed that the pit's floor was not hard, like the ground above. Instead, it had the consistency of freshly turned earth.

He looked up.

An arm hung over the top edge.

He eased himself to one side using the pit's flanged shape to his advantage. A body fell down from above and smacked the ground.

Followed by another.

He recalled that the bottom had not been visible from above. Too much darkness. So he ventured a glance upward and saw not Pollux, but Kastor Gallo staring down, a gun in his right hand.

Revealing himself seemed like suicide. He'd just wait for the man to leave then use the rope and climb out.

Gallo vanished above.

He stared at the two corpses. Too much darkness existed to see their faces.

Something fell from above and embedded in the soft floor.

A shovel.

The rope began to head upward.

And disappeared.

The lights extinguished.

He stood in total blackness.

CHAPTER SIXTY

LUKE DROVE DOWN THE COASTAL HIGHWAY, SPEEDING NORTH toward a place called the Church of St. Magyar's. Once he was out of jail, he'd contacted Stephanie, who told him where Malone had gone. She'd contacted the cathedral curator, who'd provided directions. He'd declined Hahn's offer of assistance, deciding to keep the locals out of the loop. Better to hold everything close from this point forward, as there were too many unknowns in this free-for-all.

How many times had he sped down a black highway in the middle of the night? After dates. High school football games. Nights out with the guys. The terrain around him was nothing like the mountains of east Tennessee. Not much in the world compared to that sacred ground. He'd spent the first eighteen years of his life there and tried to go back whenever he could. Which wasn't all that often. Those hills were rampant with high tales. Lots of myths, legends, and ghosts. His father had loved to tell the stories.

Like Old Skinned Tom.

A charming, handsome man who won over nearly every girl he came across, one day he set his sights on a beautiful married gal named Eleanor. They began seeing each other in secret, frequenting the local lovers' lane. Of course, Eleanor's husband found out and skinned Tom alive. Everyone believed that Tom's bloody skeleton still roamed lovers' lane, clutching a hunting knife, waiting to catch a cheating couple so he could teach them a lesson. Which seemed incredibly unfair of him, given the circumstances of his own death.

The apparition even had a song.

Have you see the ghost of Skinned Tom?
Bloody red bones with the skin all gone.
Wouldn't it be chilly with no skin on.

That it would. He felt a little bare-skinned and exposed at the moment, too. Running on empty, but at full throttle.

He turned off the coastal highway and headed inland, following the directions Stephanie had provided into a darkened valley. Ridges rose in the distance on both sides with few lights. He kept going on the straight stretch of blacktop. Ahead, off the shoulder, among a scattered stand of short trees, he spotted a parked car.

One he recognized.

He brought his vehicle to a stop and saw that he was right. Same car he'd used earlier. The same one Malone had apparently taken from the cathedral. He doused the headlights, shut off the engine, and stepped out into the night.

Malone was here and seemed to have decided on a stealth approach. He decided to take the same option. He started off on foot down the road, keeping a watch out for vehicles in both directions. Cicadas chirped their earsplitting trill into the darkness. He was tired and could use some sleep, but he'd learned how to run on autopilot. He was actually good in that mode. Being barely thirty, a bit anxious, ambitious, and well trained certainly helped, too.

A couple of hundred yards away he saw the outline of a building up on a ridge and another car parked out front.

Had to be the chapel.

Its main door suddenly opened, revealing a splash of light and a person. The dark form walked to the car toting a bag and what looked like a folding chair, which was deposited inside. The form returned to the building's door and the lights extinguished, as if a switch had been thrown.

The car then drove off and did not head his way. Instead it turned in the opposite direction and disappeared down the highway, deeper into the valley, to the west.

His instincts smelled trouble.

He trotted to the building and approached the door. He tested the latch and discovered it was locked.

And no conventional lock.

Big. Heavy. Iron. Taking a friggin' skeleton key.

He tested the oak panels.

Thick and solid.

No way he could force it open, and there were no windows. He had only one choice. So he ran back to the car and fired up the engine. He sped up the incline to the ridge and focused the headlights on the front door. He came close and stopped, nestling the front bumper to the oak.

Stephanie had told them that this building had been around for centuries. Malone was noted for his effect on historic spots, especially World Heritage Sites. It looked like he was about to join the club. He pumped the accelerator and drove the front end into the door, splintering it inward.

That was easier than he'd thought it would be.

He backed the car away, then shut off the engine and climbed out. Beyond the doorway he saw more black. With his hand he examined the wall just inside and spotted a switch, which he flipped activating a few scattered lights that threw off long streams of radiance illuminating a bare chapel with a gritty stone floor.

His eyes began a brisk, energetic scan of the interior.

Not a sound broke the silence.

The floor stretched maybe fifty feet ahead. He noticed a clear path in the grit leading from the doorway to an altar, then beyond. He stepped in and followed the path, which led to the opposite side and a circular apse.

Where it stopped.

Abruptly.

At the wall.

Before him rose a stone half circle. Three panels, separated by moldings, limestone benches wrapping the semicircle along with a cornice at the top and a line of chiseled molding breaking the center. Had someone walked to here and sat on the bench? Possible. But not likely. The floor was relatively undisturbed except for the footpath to the main door.

He faced the curved wall and tapped it at places with his fist.

Solid.

Whatever there was to find had to be at the center panel. He traced the groove on either side with his fingertips.

Nothing unusual.

The cornice at the top was out of reach, the center molding possessed of no indentations. It was all one piece, carved from the stone. He sat on the bench and stared at the floor. Why not? He dropped to his knees and looked underneath. Nothing there, the stone bench supported by two corbels at either end.

Come on. This can't be that hard.

He studied the corbels and noticed that they were curvy, extending from the wall to the end of the bench, supporting its weight. A notch existed from the corbel's end to the stone wall. Maybe an inch. Not much more. He stuck his finger into the space on the right. Nothing. Then the left. And felt an indentation. Circular. With something in it. A button. He pushed. The entire panel shifted inward.

He stood, sucking in the whole Indiana Jones vibe.

He pushed the heavy panel, surprised at its balancing act. It took little effort to move a lot of rock. Blackness loomed beyond. He found another switch and activated more lights. A corridor led to another chapel, this one a bit creepy with a ton of statues and images. Like a visit to a stone Madame Tussauds. He noticed the altar, which had been desecrated with a hole in its lower center.

That seemed like Malone's signature.

So he kept going, finding another door that led to spiral steps, leading down. He descended to the bottom and saw another light switch, which he activated. More lights sprang to life. He followed a narrow corridor into a room with a hole in the floor.

Which he'd seen before.

In Valletta.

A *guva*.

What had Laura said?

They were once all over the island. Now only two remained.

Make that three.

He stepped over and gazed down into the blackness, the bottom not visible.

"About damn time," a voice said from below.

CHAPTER SIXTY-ONE

POLLUX LEFT THE PWALES VALLEY. HE'D JUST KILLED THREE MEN. Add in the villa owner and James Grant, that made five murders. All regrettable, but necessary.

He'd made a call as soon as he left the chapel, using one of the phones he'd removed from the dead knights, telling the person on the other end to meet him at the Lippija Tower. It sat about ten minutes away from the chapel, a short, squat building from the 17th century, with two floors and a parapet roof facing Gnejna Bay on the northwest coast. He assumed the tower would be deserted at this hour and saw he was right as he drove close and switched off the car.

He reached over to the passenger seat and grabbed the laptop. It had been bought for him a few weeks ago and had sat dormant ever since, waiting. He could not bring his own laptop, or anything else, from his former life. Pollux Gallo would have left all that behind when he retreated from the world. There could be nothing that linked him with his own past. The transformation had to be complete in every way.

He slid the flash drive in and typed the password KASTOR I.

He opened the one file and began to read, closer at some parts, scanning others, but amazed at the wealth of incredibly damaging information. More than he could have ever imagined. For years he'd studied the cardinals, learning all of their pertinent biographical information. He'd even been privy to Kastor's private investigations and the bits and pieces that stumbled their way. But the information Spagna had amassed was so much more.

Kastor had been right.

It was a gold mine.

A car approached from behind, its headlights filling the rearview mirror. He had little time, but this matter had to be resolved before he left the island. He set the laptop aside and exited.

From the other vehicle, Kevin Hahn emerged and said, "Daniels is out of custody."

He waved off the concern. "The Americans should no longer be a problem."

"Except that Daniels killed four of our men."

"Which is a terrible tragedy. But that'll only lead to the knights, so we'll let them have that problem."

He and Hahn had been friends a long time. They'd met just out of their teens and served in the military together, then both joined the order. Hahn was not professed, but he was a knight. Over the years, it had been Hahn who'd kept him informed about all that happened on Malta. He was his eyes and ears on the ground, rising steadily to the position of head of Malta's internal security. When he'd formed the team that would make up his temporarily reconstituted *Secreti,* Hahn had been there from the start. Thanks to Hahn he'd become aware of the Americans on the island and all of what Spagna had been doing. With Hahn's help he'd learned of Laura Price's duplicity, her alignment with Spagna, and the attempt that would have been made on his life. Proverbs was right. *A friend loves at all times, and a brother is born for adversity.*

Hahn was more like a brother than Kastor had ever been.

"You look just like him," Hahn said.

And sounded like him, too. He'd been practicing for months. Not all that hard, as Kastor's pitch and tone were nearly identical to his own. Just a few variations, which he was concentrating on adjusting. The diction and syntax seemed the most difficult part. Everyone had their pet words, their own way of saying things, himself included. But he was no longer himself.

"Do you have any idea what Daniels might do?"

Hahn shook his head. "He told me little. He just left."

Surely Daniels would reconnect with Malone, who would report that the Trinity had been found and returned to the knights and the church, who would sort things out. Of course the incident with the boat would need resolution. Men were dead. But again, nothing led to Rome.

"What do you want me to do?" Hahn asked. "The Americans have asked for my help in identifying the men from the boat."

"Help them. It doesn't matter. Be cooperative. Let them investigate the boat and the four men. That will lead to the Knights of Malta, not to Kastor Gallo or you."

He could see that his friend agreed.

"Are you ready?" Hahn asked.

"I am." He reached out and shook Hahn's hand. "You've been a great help. But there's a problem at the chapel. Two of our brothers became greedy. They wanted more. I had to deal with them."

"I hate to hear that."

"They left me no choice. I need you to return there and bury them with Kastor. He's at the bottom of the *guva*, as are they. There's a rope and shovel there, too. Use them to clean things up. We can't risk anything being found. So far everything has gone perfectly and nothing leads back to the chapel. So let's finish this."

He knew his old comrade would not protest. Hahn was coming with him to the Vatican, eventually becoming the operational head of the Entity. Another reason why Danjel Spagna'd had to be eliminated. Having his man in charge of the world's oldest intelligence agency would be nothing but a plus. Though he would have preferred to do this alone, Proverbs again was instructional. *Iron sharpens iron, and one man sharpens another.*

"I'll get it done," Hahn said. "You go become pope."

"I have all of Spagna's information. It should be more than enough to convince the right votes."

He walked back to his car.

Pleased.

All that remained was to read the third part of the trinity.

Constantine's Gift.

CHAPTER SIXTY-TWO

A new consciousness of personal human dignity has emerged across our empire. Men feel the infinite value and responsibility of a new life. But within their realm of imposed happiness a strange thing is happening. As naturally as they have rejected the former political structure, men have begun to seek a religion of a more personal and intimate nature.

It is admitted that when in recent times the appearance of our Savior Jesus Christ had become known to all men, there immediately made its appearance a new religion, not small, and not dwelling in some corner of the earth, but indestructible and unconquerable, because it has assistance directly from God. This religion, thus suddenly appearing at the time appointed by the inscrutable counsel of God, is the one that has been honored by all with the name of Christ.

It is true that religion and civilization advance together. But it is equally true that religious creeds and practices can often lag behind civilization. We find that situation at present with the lingering of the pagan gods and the emergence of a new Christian faith. We find a further example of this with the new Christian faith fighting within itself, so many varied views as to what should or should not be believed. So many different ideas as to who and what is God and who and what is our Savior.

Any religion must reflect the pure ideals of the society in which it exists. Its practices and sacrifices can only be as the general sentiment allows. No new religion can easily claim the soil where other gods have long been worshiped. To survive, a religion must have structure, rules, order, and, most important, consistency. The following mandates are offered as a means to protect that which we have created:

Always remember that an Angry vengeful God is preferable to a benign, loving entity. We must Proclaim that Obedience and compliance with God's directives is the only way to obtain eternal peace in heaven, while disobedience leads to everlasting suffering. The fear of that perpetual suffering should be used to keep the faithful under our control. The faithful can never forget that the only salvation from their fear comes from the Christian faith, its Doctrine and practices never open to question, their obedience absolute.

Sin is the mechanism whereby control will be enforced. For the Hebrew nation the Ten Commandments, which Moses first delivered, have long stood as their basic tenets. But we need more. A list of Sins should be created, a list that adapts with the times, each sin designed to instill fear. There must be a clear belief that a failure to obtain forgiveness of sin places the immortal soul in the gravest of danger, with forgiveness obtained only through the Christian faith. This concept should begin at birth with a belief that all men are born into the world with sin. Never will they dwell with God unless there is absolution for this original sin through the Christian faith.

Many of the prior religions fostered a belief that when one lifetime ends another begins, the cycle never ending. This spiritual immortality, this reincarnation, is surely comforting, but the Christian faith will offer only one physical life and One opportunity at eternal salvation. When that life ends the soul moves to either heaven or hell, both of which we must not only create but define.

Never can the failings of man be blamed on any lacking or deficiency in the Christian faith. Instead an adversary must be created. A diabolos, a spirit, a devil, who constantly poses challenges along the path to salvation. All of man's sins and shortcomings must be blamed on this devil, who is always present, always tempting, never relenting, with the only path to resistance coming from Christian doctrine.

No spiritual abilities can ever be tolerated. Those who profess visions or an ability to speak with God are a danger. As treason is punishable by death, heretical thinking and acts must likewise know the wrath of God. Heretics can never be tolerated, their deaths a righteous calling, a warning to others that actions and thoughts contrary to the Christian faith come with dire consequences. Killing in the name of God is not a sin. Defending the faith with the spilling of blood is a duty we must never abandon.

Religion expresses itself in terms of the knowledge of the world in which it exists. If that be defective then religion likewise is defective. Never be afraid to change. It is the only way to survive. But never be anxious to do so, either.

Sacred objects are those things that man must not use or touch because they belong only to God. Creating these, whether they be churches, places, people, words, or things, is essential to rooting our Christian faith. Keeping them sacred through rules and punishment is equally important.

Priests shall become a special class unto themselves. I am the natural choice to ultimately lead those priests, as religion is a vital part of politics. The first duty of the state is to stay right with God and keep God on good terms with the people. The priests' duty is to keep the people on good terms with me.

Above all, good bishops, the Essence of Christianity must be in loving God and following him in faith, but it must also include upholding the authority of the Priests and believing in Christian doctrine without question. On this objective we must unite as the conduct of public affairs will be considerably eased if we take this step. The state of your individual lives will likewise be altered. Each of you will become far more in many varied ways. That which once divided us seems now quite trifling and unworthy of such fierce contest. Let us rejoice in unity.

CHAPTER
SIXTY-THREE

POLLUX STOPPED READING THE PARCHMENTS.

The Latin appeared on both pages in thin straight lines with minimal margins. The black ink was heavy, but mostly faded to gray thanks to seventeen centuries. He sat in the plush cabin of a private jet, flying north toward Rome. After leaving Kevin Hahn at the tower, he'd made it to the airport on Malta without incident, tossing the contents of the duffel bag away in three different dumpsters he'd passed along the way. The Glock was thrown into the ocean from a cliff. All of the evidence was now gone. He'd also stopped in Mdina and retrieved Kastor's overnight bag, including his Vatican passport. His mind was tired from months of worrying, scheming, and dreaming. But in a few hours he'd be inside the Sistine Chapel. And not as an obscure knight in a nine-hundred-year-old brotherhood. But as a *sanctae Romanae Ecclesiae cardinalis,* a cardinal of the Holy Roman Church.

For years he'd studied Latin and Greek, reading one text after another on Christianity and the Catholic Church, especially the time between its founding with Christ and the end of the third century. The formative years. Like when puberty shaped a child.

Then A.D. 325 came and everything changed.

Constantine the Great summoned the Christian bishops to Nicaea, bringing all of the players to one place for the first time, his terms simple.

Agree on a universal—a catholic—church, and the Crown would drape the new religion with great political advantage. Fail to do so and the persecutions would continue. Nobody knew for sure how many clerics heeded the call, but enough that they were able to forge a statement of their beliefs, one that to this day defined what it meant to be Catholic. They transformed the philosophy of a man who'd preached poverty, forgiveness, and nonviolence into a government ideology of power, one Constantine used for cohesiveness. Earlier, before sending his two acolytes to meet their God, Pollux had thought it appropriate that those ancient words—the famed Nicaean Creed—be uttered.

The history books loved to tell of how Constantine saw a vision in the sky, then won a great battle, crediting Christ with his victory. In gratitude, he supposedly converted and proclaimed Christianity as the official religion of the empire. But that was merely half right. Constantine only converted on his deathbed, though even that is open to debate. He spent his life hedging his bets, worshiping the old gods but using the new. The whole conversion story was but a way to make the new faith more acceptable in the eyes of the people. If it was good enough for the emperor, it was good enough for them. He did not create Christianity, but he did mold it in his image. And wisely, he never tried to defeat Christ, but he certainly wanted to define him.

And what Pollux had just read confirmed that conclusion.

Constantine wanted his own religion.

And why not?

Faith was the death of reason. Faith relied on blind allegiance, without thought, only an unquestioned belief. Irrationality seemed the nature of faith, and to institutionalize faith man created religion, which remained one of the oldest and strongest conspiracies ever formed. Look at what they fought about at Nicaea.

The nature of Christ.

The Old Testament was simple. God was singular and indivisible. That's what the Jews believed. The new religion had a trinity. Father, Son, Holy Spirit. Of course, that had been created by man as part of the new religion. But exactly what was Christ? Different from the Father since he'd been human? Or merely the same, immortal and eternal, despite being human? It all sounded so trivial, but the debate threatened to tear

Christianity apart. Even Constantine had thought the argument silly, *worthy of inexperienced children, not of priests and prelates and reasonable men.* He ended the division, proclaiming that Christ was *begotten, not made, being of one substance with the Father by whom all things were made.*

Religion had always been a tool. Its power came from capturing something dear, then offering a spiritual reality, with benefits, to all those who chose to follow. Didn't matter whether that was Christianity, Islam, Judaism, Hinduism, or even paganism. All of them created their own peculiar truths, then constantly misconstrued them to their advantage.

But all good things come to an end.

For the Catholic Church the end came in 1522 when Martin Luther translated the New Testament from Latin to German. For the first time the people could read God's word and they saw no mention of the church, indulgences, sins, cardinals, or popes. They could read the Gospel of Luke where it clearly said that *the kingdom of God is within you,* or Romans, which said *the spirit of God dwells in you,* both with no mention of any other place where God supposedly resided. Before Luther the scriptures were only for priests to read and the church to interpret, both providing a clear measure of control.

Exactly what Constantine had advised.

Priests shall become a special class unto themselves. I am the natural choice to ultimately lead those priests, as religion is a vital part of politics. The first duty of the state is to stay right with God and keep God on good terms with the people. The priests' duty is to keep the people on good terms with me.

Constantine wanted the bishops unified. He wanted his new religion to become a constant. Fitting, as his own name meant "steadfast." He realized that consistency bred confidence, and once the people acquired confidence they would unquestionably believe.

He made that clear at the end of his gift.

And indeed unto Abraham, who was a justified man, there was given by God a prophecy in regard to those who, in coming ages, should be justified in the same way as he. The prophecy was in the following words: And in you shall all the tribes of the earth be blessed. And again, He shall become a nation great and numerous; and in him shall all the nations of the earth be blessed.

What then should prevent those who are of Christ to practice one and the same mode of life, and have one and the same religion, as those divinely favored men of old? It is evident that the perfect religion committed to us by the teaching of Christ is a gift. But if the truth must be spoken, it should be spoken in one voice as the true religion. It is my hope that these directives will guide us all to that result.

The deal had been simple. Stay unified, follow his commands, and Christianity would flourish. Divide and disobey and imperial protection would end. Christians would find themselves back where they'd been before Nicaea. Ostracized and persecuted.

Not much of a choice.

In the beginning churches were started by planters, apostolic workers who moved from town to town, creating congregations. Each one of those became a religion unto itself, isolated and closely held. Eventually, elders emerged within those congregations, not special or set above the flock, merely serving within, chosen by seniority with no special powers or permanancy. But Constantine seemed to realize the political opportunities those elders presented. He saw an opportunity to cultivate an army of local supporters, men who did not wield a sword but instead could affect the hearts and minds of the people.

Smart.

Pollux knew his church history.

Constantine elevated the clergy. He granted them a fixed annual salary and exempted them from taxation. They were not required to serve in the army or perform any mandatory civil service. They truly became a *special class,* not subject to secular law or imperial courts. They dressed differently and groomed differently. They became the supposed guardians of orthodoxy, more powerful than local governors. A spiritual elite of holy men, supposedly vested with gifts and graces others did not possess. No surprise that so many men experienced a sudden call to the ministry.

Yet despite all of those privileges, the church languished for nearly five hundred years. After Constantine died his heirs made a mess of the empire. It split, the eastern portion becoming Byzantine, the western remaining Roman. Christianity likewise split. And though bishops were scattered across Europe, Africa, and Asia, the one in Rome began to assert himself over the western portion, rising above the others, claiming a lineage back to St. Peter and taking a pagan title. *Pontifex maximus.* Supreme pontiff.

By Christmas Day A.D. 800 the church was ready to expand.

It happened in Rome while the Emperor Charlemagne knelt in prayer. Pope Leo III placed the imperial crown on the king's head, then anointed the feet of the new emperor. History liked to say that the entire event had been spontaneous. Not in the slightest. It had all been planned. A Christian ruler could not be a god. That smacked of paganism. But he could be *chosen* by God, becoming the nexus from heaven to earth. In one masterful stroke, the king of the Franks became the first Holy Roman Emperor and the church became the means through which any claim to that throne acquired legitimacy.

A classic win–win.

Which changed the world.

All but a tiny portion of Europe eventually came under Rome's thumb. The Catholic Church became the dominant force in the world for the next eight hundred years. It systematically erased and replaced all competing spiritual beliefs, destroying every competing religion. It deadened the search for knowledge, persecuting mystics and heretics, and forced the mass conversion of anyone and everyone. At the same time it deprived its members of beliefs in prophecy, dreams, apparitions, visions, reincarnation, meditation, and healing. It assumed control of everyday life by claiming a divine authority to rule, then dominated every moment of the faithful's life.

A virtual stranglehold.

To keep its army of clerics special the church conceived the sacrament of ordination, modeled after the Roman custom of appointing men to high civil office. No one ever questioned that the New Testament made no mention of selective preaching and that baptizing new souls was to be limited only to the ordained. The Bible's personal access to God was re-placed with the church's rigid rules.

And now Pollux knew where it all started.

Constantine's Gift.

No wonder the church never wanted the document public. What faster way to lose control than by exposing it all as an illusion. For the masses to learn that none of the so-called church doctrine was divine, that all of it instead had been created by man for the benefit of man, would have been a public relations disaster. All fear would have dissipated. All wonder quelled. Irrationality would have been replaced with reason.

He stared at the two parchments.

The past had come back to the present.

What would the modern world think of Constantine's Gift?

An excellent question.

In ancient times the church relied on ignorance and fear. Modernity demanded much more. Education was no longer a rarity. Television, ra-dio, and the internet all captured people's thoughts. What would the mod-ern world think once it knew that a Roman emperor, from seventeen hundred years ago, laid out a framework for a new religion that ultimately prelates in the Middle Ages implemented to ensure obedience of the faith-ful and promulgate its own importance. No divine intervention. No heavenly influences. No conduit to God. Just a bunch of men who liked living high and wielding power.

He imagined that revelation would not be welcomed.

But was it fatal?

Hard to say.

No doubt, in a world where religion was waning and faith in authority disappearing, where people were leaving the church far faster than com-ing toward it, proof that the whole thing had been concocted would not be good. Kastor had thought it enough to pressure key cardinals into sup-porting his candidacy. The threat worked in the Middle Ages with many different popes, most of them immoral and corrupt. It worked in the 1930s with two more named Pius, who faced an uncertain world that ultimately went to war. Would it work again today? Maybe. Maybe not.

It certainly would not help things.

Thank goodness he now had Spagna's flash drive loaded with incriminating information on important cardinals.

That would definitely work.

The jet began its descent.

He leaned back in the leather seat, made a steeple out of his fingers, and rested his chin on the point, trying to check the anxiety that threatened to swallow him. His eyes burned. His nerves screamed. There was always a possibility of failure. That element of chance. The threat of error. Which would be catastrophic considering the sins he'd committed. Thankfully, he was a man of precautions.

Always had been.

Outside, the sun had crested on the eastern horizon.

Daylight had arrived.

If all went according to plan—

By tomorrow evening, or the next day at the latest, he should be pope.

CHAPTER SIXTY-FOUR

COTTON STARED UP AT LUKE DANIELS.

Who smiled.

Which he knew was coming.

"Got yourself into a bit of a pickle?" Luke asked.

"You could say that. Self-inflicted, but a wound nonetheless."

He'd already surveyed the pit's bottom, using his cell phone for light. There was zero signal out. No surprise considering the amount of rock around him. The two corpses lay across each other, the shovel off to one side. As he'd suspected, an area of the floor had recently been disturbed, its color and texture different. But he'd yet to investigate further.

"How did you know I'd come?" Luke asked from above.

"I didn't. But I assumed at some point you'd talk with either Stephanie or the cathedral curator, and one or the other would tell you where I went. Stephanie told me about Laura Price and what you did."

"The Entity wanted Pollux Gallo dead. Any idea why?"

"Actually, I do have a few thoughts on that matter. Did you see anyone leave here?"

"One man," Luke said. "Carrying a bag and a folding chair. But I was too far away to see who."

"I imagine he's headed to the airport, then on to Rome."

"The cardinal, then?"

He stared around at the macabre scene before him, masked by the darkness. Then he reached for the shovel.

"There should be a rope up there," he said. "Use it to climb down."

LUKE DID AS MALONE ASKED AND ALLOWED THE ROPE TO SNAKE A path over the edge and down into the pit's blackness. He wasn't particularly anxious to be back in another hole in the ground, but figured Malone had his reasons. So he climbed down.

"A little crowded, wouldn't you say," he said at the bottom, seeing the two corpses.

"Let's move them to the side. We need to get beneath them."

They heaved the bodies to one side.

Malone found his cell phone and activated the flashlight. Luke could see that the ground had been disturbed recently.

"Somebody's been diggin'?" he asked.

"It seems that way."

Malone knelt down and worked the soil with the shovel.

"What do you think is there?"

"Not what. Who."

"What's going on, Pappy?"

Malone kept digging. "When I was a kid, one night a bunch of us camped out in the woods. I was the youngest, about nine or ten, it was actually my first time sleeping under the stars. After we set up camp and ate dinner, the others took me out to a dark field and gave me a pillowcase. They told me there were snipes out in the field. Dark, furry creatures who prowl around at night looking for food. They made a great meal, like chicken or turkey. They wanted to catch one and roast it, so they taught me the animal's call. A ridiculous sound. They told me to keep a lookout and make the call over and over. When a snipe came running, I was to nab it with the pillowcase. Then they left me alone, in the dark, saying they were going to drive the snipes my way to make it easier. I believed every word, so I stood there, making those ridiculous sounds, waiting for a snipe, while they all laughed their asses off watching me from the trees."

He chuckled. "Sounds like somethin' I'd get myself into. How many did you catch?"

"You know the answer. It was a fool's errand. That's what I've been on. A damn snipe hunt."

Malone stopped digging. "I hit something."

He came over close and together they started clearing away the soil.

"The man who left here was Pollux Gallo," Malone said. "He shot those men in cold blood, after praying with them. He had no idea I was down here. If he had, he would have shot me, too. But I wisely kept my mouth shut."

Their excavations revealed skin.

A chest.

They cleared more of the gray dirt away to see a face.

Kastor Gallo.

"The only thing that makes sense," Malone said, "is that Pollux is going to make a play for the papacy. As his brother, Kastor. I saw him. He physically changed himself. Cut his hair. Shaved the beard. He's now a cardinal."

"Pretty damn bold. You have to give him that."

"I heard you've had a bold night, too. Sinking a boat. Taking out everyone aboard." Malone paused.

He could see Malone was gnawing on something. "What is it?"

"Gallo has no idea we're onto him. You saw him leave. Did he seem in a hurry?"

"Not at all."

"That means we have the upper hand. He thinks he has an open-field run with no need for blockers. We're now invisible."

Malone began shoveling the dirt back into the hole. "We need this covered over, so no one will know we're onto them."

He pointed, remembering other times. "You like being a corpse."

"It does offer a great advantage."

POLLUX STARED OUT THE WINDOW.

The sun had risen over southern Italy as the jet descended toward the airport. After he'd read through the two parchments, converting the words to a rough translation in his mind, he'd perused the flash drive in more detail, committing to memory many of the cardinal's sordid details. He would start at the first moment possible to use the information. Unlike Kastor, he knew none of the men personally, though he would have to act as if he did.

In the distance, through the morning sun, amid the clutter of Rome, he caught sight of St. Peter's dome. Impressive even from miles away, rightly bearing the label as the most renowned work of Renaissance architecture. And while neither a mother church nor a cathedral, it carried the distinction as the greatest of all sanctuaries in Christendom.

The same might one day be said of Kastor Pollux.

An obscure cardinal who rose to be a great pope.

He found it ironic that even with his transformation he was still dependent on Kastor for success. But at least he was now in total control. What kind of pope would he be? Hard to say. He possessed no faith and cared nothing for religion except for how to use it to his advantage. Thankfully, he'd studied the church in detail and had listened carefully to Kastor's countless rants. He was ready to lead. And that he would. Being pragmatic and purposeful.

The *Constitutum Constantini* had proven eye opening.

A literal blueprint for religion.

First, establish a consistent doctrine called the New Testament with select gospels that speak to a universal belief, which was precisely what the bishops had done at Nicaea. Then decree that all other beliefs are heretical, unworthy of consideration, and all who don't believe will be excommunicated. To further enforce dogma, create the notion of sin, adding that if it's not forgiven, the soul will be sent to eternal damnation in flames. Never mind that the Old Testament mentioned nothing of any such place. Just create one in your New Testament, then use it to cement loyalty and obedience.

The fastest way to ensure a constant laity is to proclaim that every person is born with the sins inherited as punishment for Adam's fall from grace. To purge that *original sin* a person must submit to baptism, performed only by a priest ordained by the church. A failure to rid that sin damns the soul to hell. To keep people dependent on the church for their entire lifetime, create more sacraments. Holy communion for children. Confirmation at puberty. Marriage for adults. Last rites on the dead. A womb-to-grave influence over every aspect of a person's life, each milestone dependent solely on adherence to church doctrine. Along the way the sacrament of confession allows a chance to purge oneself of sin and temporarily avoid hell—that forgiveness, of course, coming only from one source.

The church.

If an individual, or a group, or a nation, or anyone rises in opposition, root that dissent out and deal with it in the harshest of ways, including torture, execution, and genocide.

If the times require a change, do it. Adapt all teachings, as necessary. Which the church had done. Many times. Starting with Nicaea and continuing through other ecumenical councils and countless papal decrees. Change was good—just not too quickly, as Constantine had warned.

To ensure the outcome of any debate, declare that in all things spiritual the pope is infallible, incapable of error.

He really liked that part.

And even if a mistake is made, blame it all on the devil. Another New Testament creation. A fictitious nemesis upon which all bad things can be laid. The faithful have to believe that listening to the devil was the surest way to get a ticket to hell.

What a perfect, self-perpetuating concept.

And not a soul, until Martin Luther in the 16th century, effectively questioned any of it.

Even the first words of the so-called Lord's Prayer were pure hypocrisy.

Our Father who art in heaven . . .

What heaven? The Old Testament made no mention of any such place. It existed only because the early church fathers wanted to distinguish themselves from the Jews. So their God dwelled in heaven. And besides, if they'd told people that the kingdom of God dwelled solely within them, as the Bible said, it would not have been long before even the illiterate understood that there was no need for a church.

What a terrific concept. Done so effectively that few today, centuries later, had any clue as to how it all started.

Which would make the *Constitutum Constantini* pure poison.

He'd seen the numbers. Roman Catholic membership was dropping by double-digit percentage points annually. Of the Catholics that re-mained, less than 20 percent worldwide attended church regularly. Even more shocking, of the 20 percent that did participate, a recent survey showed that nearly 80 percent of them believed that people should arrive at their own spiritual beliefs, outside of organized religion. Imagine if they knew that a Roman emperor had suggested most of what they believed to be divine.

Yes, imagine.

Thankfully, they'd never know.

Once the conclave was over, and he was pope, Constantine's Gift would be burned. Nothing, and no one, would exist to threaten his papacy.

But he'd hold on to it until then.

Just in case.

CHAPTER
SIXTY-FIVE

COTTON STOOD ON THE TARMAC AT MALTA'S INTERNATIONAL AIR-
port. He and Luke had driven their vehicles here from the chapel and determined that a private jet had left the island three hours earlier and had
already landed in Rome. On board had been Kastor Cardinal Gallo. He
used his phone to call Stephanie, whom he placed on speaker. They stood
outside in the morning light.

"Gallo is now inside the Vatican," Stephanie said.

"At least we know exactly where he is," Cotton noted.

"Any idea on the guys I took out?" Luke asked.

"We're still searching for names. Nothing pinged on their prints."

"Surely they were hired help Pollux Gallo convinced to go along with
him," Cotton said. "Men who thought they'd be working for the next pope.
Gallo has no money, so they had to be in it for other reasons. Unfortunately, their severance package is a bit permeant."

He checked his watch.

8:45 A.M.

"The DOJ jet is still there in Malta," Stephanie said. "I can have it fired
up, ready to go in less than an hour."

"Do it," he said.

"And the cardinal?" Luke asked.

"Give him a long leash. Do nothing to spook him. We have to be sure before we do a thing." Cotton paused. "Absolutely sure."

"Then we split you two up," she said. "Luke, go back and get Gallo's body, and the other two, from that pit. Cotton, head to Rome. By the time you get here, we'll be sure."

Pollux stepped from the car and stood outside the Domus Sanctae Marthae. The five-story pale-yellow building sat in the shadow of St. Peter's Basilica and normally served as a guesthouse for visiting clergy. Pope Francis had actually lived inside, preferring its bustle and austerity to the isolation and luxury of the papal apartments. During a conclave it served as the residence for the participating cardinals. A total of 128 rooms, run by the Daughters of Charity of St. Vincent, complete with a dining hall and two chapels. Nothing luxurious, by any means. Just a place to eat, sleep, and pray. Far preferable to stretching out on cots in spaces divided by hanging sheets, as previous conclaves had endured.

Its many rows of windows were all shuttered. He knew that internet and phone services would be switched off and blocked, all designed to keep the cardinals in isolation, as conclave rules required. Two Swiss Guards in colorful ruffs and capes and knee breeches stood guard on either side of the entrance. He was now inside the Vatican proper, beyond the gates and the crowds of St. Peter's Square. Thousands of people had already congregated for the beginning of the conclave. They would stay there day and night, waiting for the white smoke to escape from the chimney above the Sistine Chapel, signaling the election of a pope.

He steadied himself and marched toward the entrance.

Kastor's aide waited outside the glass doors.

His first test.

"Eminence," the priest said, offering a slight bow. "Welcome. Your room is ready. I'll show you the way."

He nodded in gratitude and followed the young man inside.

LUKE DROVE BACK TOWARD THE CHURCH OF ST. MAGYAR'S. HARD to get lost on this island, the whole place smaller than back home in Blount County, Tennessee.

He wondered what his mother was doing. She lived a solitary life, his father gone to his reward a long time ago. Two of his brothers lived nearby and kept an eye on her. She lived off Social Security and his father's retirement, but Luke made sure she never wanted for money. Not that such oversight was easy. She was one proud woman, who never wanted to be a burden to anyone. But he'd worked out an arrangement with her bank where he could transfer money into her account with a phone call. And she could not transfer it back out.

Not that she hadn't tried.

He slowed the car as he entered a town. Farmland and vineyards surrounded its shops and businesses, which all seemed gauged to agriculture.

Finally, he was focused.

On track.

He stopped at an intersection, then turned the car toward the Pwales Valley.

POLLUX ADMIRED THE VESTMENTS LAID OUT ON THE BED. A FULL-length cassock, mozzetta, zucchetto, and biretta, all in scarlet red to symbolize the blood a cardinal supposedly was willing to shed for his faith. The rochet was a traditional white, Kastor's a simple embroidered lace signifying his lack of jurisdiction over any post or diocese. Others wore more elaborate designs presented to them by their congregations. But always white. He already wore the cardinal ring, but a gold chain with a crucifix lay on the bed, ready to be donned. Kastor's aide, a priest he'd dealt with before as Pollux, had never hesitated, assuming that the cardinal himself had arrived.

"Is all in order?" the priest asked in Italian.

He looked away from the bed. "Yes. Perfect."

The bedroom was a reflection of simplicity. Just the bed and a nightstand with a plain crucifix on a cream-colored wall. A silent butler filled one corner, there for hanging his clothes, the floor a polished parquet with no rug. The sitting room beyond was equally austere with a table, three chairs, and a buffet against one wall. Nothing adorned its walls. Nothing covered the parquet on the floor, either. Both rooms emitted a musty, lived-in waft with a trace of masculine musk.

"You should change quickly," his aide said. "The schedule is tight. Mass inside St. Peter's begins in less than an hour. Then, contrary to usual, the cardinals will proceed directly to the Pauline Chapel, then start the procession to the Sistine Chapel."

He'd brought the four parchments, safely tucked inside the reliquary within the duffel bag, which had been delivered to the room. They would stay here. Constantine's Gift might be needed later, when they all returned here for the night. His laptop was also inside the bag, the flash drive safe within his pocket, where it would stay all day. That would definitely come into play later this evening.

"Leave me," he said.

The aide withdrew, closing the door behind him.

He stared at the scarlet robes.

A cardinal.

Once a title given to second sons and ministers of ambitious monarchs, most often now it went to those in the curia. The post was mentioned nowhere in the Bible or in the teachings of Christ. It had been totally created by the church. The name came from the Latin *cardo*. Hinge. Since the election of a pope hinged on their deliberations.

Like now.

He smiled.

Time to complete the transformation.

CHAPTER SIXTY-SIX

LUKE REENTERED THE *GUVA* CHAMBER. THE CHAPEL'S MAIN DOOR REmained splintered into pieces, offering easy access. Malone had told him the Knights of Malta owned the building and would be informed of the entire situation once he was in Rome. Hopefully, they wouldn't send him a bill for the damage.

It should bother him that Malone had assumed the lead, dispatched to the Vatican while he was sent back to this hole in the ground with dead bodies. But it didn't. He was a team player. Always had been. Stephanie had sent him here and he would do what she wanted. Pappy would handle things in Rome, and together they'd get the job done.

And that's what mattered.

He agreed with Harry Truman.

It's amazing what you can accomplish if you don't care who gets the credit.

He stood at the edge of the hole, gazing down at the black void. The rope remained tied to the post, snaking a path downward. He grabbed hold and planted his feet on the side wall, an easy matter to work his way down. His eyes began to adjust to the darkness and he glanced toward the bottom.

No bodies.

No shovel.

He stopped.

Where the hell had they gone?

He'd seen no one and no other vehicles outside. But where he and Malone had dug earlier seemed disturbed, the area larger, nearly taking up the entire floor. Somebody had been here digging. Above, he caught the momentary flicker of a shadow in the light. Alarm bells rang in his head. He began to pull himself back up the rope, working his feet on the rough walls, hurrying. He came to the top, his head cresting the edge, his eyes seeing a man with his back to him, slicing the rope with a knife.

Damn.

The hemp snapped.

The fingers of his left hand swung up and dug into the hard earth, barely supporting his weight. He heard footsteps scrapping his way. He pulled himself up and saw Kevin Hahn, his right arm sweeping downward toward him in an arc, the knife coming straight for his hand.

Crap.

Pivoting, he swung out, his right hand finding the edge, which allowed him to yank the other away and continue to support his weight.

The blade pierced the hard ground. The fingers on his right hand ached. Hahn moved to withdraw the blade for another blow. Luke planted both hands and pushed up, one knee finding hard ground, his left hand grabbing hold of Hahn's ankle and yanking a leg out from under him.

He rolled out of the *guva*.

Hahn sprang to his feet, brandishing the knife.

Luke rose, too. "Are we seriously going to do this?"

"Let's see what you've got."

He gave the five-inch blade the respect it deserved, but he'd faced many a knife before. And what self-respecting east Tennessee redneck didn't like a good fight every now and then. Besides, he had a ton of questions for this bastard.

Hahn jabbed a couple of times, which he allowed, trying to gauge his opponent's potential. Which wasn't all that much. Surprising, given this guy's job. Maybe too many *ftíra* and too long behind a desk.

"You bury those bodies?" he asked.

Hahn's answer was another swipe with the blade.

Enough. He dropped back a step and allowed Hahn to advance. He feigned left, then shifted in the opposite direction, swinging his right fist up hard, catching Hahn's jaw. The head whipped back and he followed with a left jab to the stomach. Hahn crumbled forward. He kicked the knife out of his grasp. Hahn tried to right himself, dazed from the two blows. But Luke grabbed two handfuls of shirt and wrenched him upright, swinging Hahn around and angling him out over the *guva*. Hahn's arms flailed as he tried to find some semblance of balance but the only thing keeping him from dropping below was Luke's two-fisted grip on his shirt.

"It's a long drop," he said.

He caught the fear in Hahn's eyes.

"I'm going to ask some questions. You're going to answer. If not, I let go. We have a deal?"

Hahn nodded.

"Let's start with the question you ignored. Did you bury those bodies?"

He nodded again.

"You're not going to make me ask, are you?"

"I was told to do it."

He shook his head and pushed Hahn farther out at a dangerous angle, which immediately got the guy's attention.

"Okay. Okay. Okay."

He pulled him back.

"Pollux Gallo. I did it for him."

"And the cardinal? What do you know?"

"He's dead."

Now they were getting somewhere. "Who killed him?"

"Gallo. Brother-to-brother. He's down there."

"I want to hear it all. And talk fast. My fingers are getting tired."

"Pollux and I go way back. He came to me with a plan and made me an offer. I went along with it."

"You sold out Spagna and the Entity to Gallo?"

Hahn nodded. "I hated Spagna. He deserved what he got."

This guy was a wealth of information. Stephanie and Malone both needed good intel, but to acquire it would take a little time.

He pulled Hahn back to solid ground.

The guy looked relieved.

But not for long.

Luke shoved him over the edge.

CHAPTER
SIXTY-SEVEN

COTTON STEPPED FROM THE DOJ JET ONTO THE TARMAC AT ROME'S da Vinci–Fiumicino airport. The time was a little after noon and he was hungry. Some lunch would be great, but a white Vatican helicopter was waiting, its rotors turning. He hurried straight over and climbed inside.

The flight from Malta had been quick. He'd received no reports from either Stephanie or Luke. Obviously something was up, as Stephanie had managed to obtain the services of a Vatican chopper. Good thing, too. The drive from the airport to downtown would have taken a solid two hours. Rome traffic was some of the worst in the world, a cacophony of blaring horns, squealing brakes, and roaring engines.

And he had to admit.

Flying over it all was lovely.

LUKE LISTENED AS KEVIN HAHN DUG IN THE *GUVA* BELOW.

The moron had survived the fall and Luke decided Hahn would do the digging, retrieving the three bodies. He didn't much care about the two. It was the cardinal's that he needed exposed and fast. Hahn had been work-ing for nearly ten minutes with steady swishes of blade to earth.

"You there yet?" he asked.

"Yeah. I have him," Hahn said.

About time.

He peered down into the dark hole. At the bottom he saw Hahn use his cell phone as a light, illuminating the grave in the pit's bottom. The light revealed pale-white flesh.

"It's a shoulder," Hahn said.

"I need a face."

The light extinguished and he heard work resuming. He sat down on the ground at the hole's edge, his feet dangling over the side.

"You ordered Laura killed, didn't you?" he said to the void.

"Gallo did that."

"You helped."

The digging stopped. "I went along."

It started again.

"She meant that little to you."

"She meant nothing."

Bastard. "What do you get out of this?"

"I was going to become head of the Entity."

"How does Pollux Gallo think he's going to be pope?"

"He has incriminating information on the cardinals. Stuff Spagna accumulated. We maneuvered Kastor Gallo to Malta to get that information from Spagna. What they didn't count on was you and Malone."

"We like to be underestimated."

"You leave a lot of bodies in your wake."

"Don't sell yourself short."

The digging stopped.

He peered down.

The light reappeared.

He saw a face in the ground.

"It's the cardinal," Hahn said.

"Did you know him?"

"Since we were kids. I never liked him."

He found his cell phone and opened it to the home screen. "Catch this."

He dropped it down.

"Take a picture of the face." He watched as Hahn did as he asked. "Toss it back up."

Hahn hesitated.

"You don't want to piss me off," he said.

The phone came up through the dark.

Everything about this guy ate at his stomach. He was a turncoat, a traitor, a guy who put himself before his duty. Even to the point of selling out one of his own. No question, Laura Price had been pushy and overeager, but she never stood a chance. She'd been a pawn in a game that she never understood. And the guy in the pit below caused all of her problems.

The rope that had dropped down earlier, when Hahn cut it, came up out of the void in a coil and landed on the hard ground.

"Get me out of here," Hahn said. "I did what you wanted."

He needed to report in, but that could not be done from here. He had to return to ground level and get outside. Kevin Hahn was going to be the main witness in the prosecution of Pollux Gallo. And what better place to keep him on ice.

"Daniels. Get me out of here."

He turned to leave.

Hahn kept calling out.

He left the chamber and walked down the tunnel to the steps up. For added measure, he flicked the light switch off, plunging everything into darkness.

"Daniels," Hahn called out. "Daniels."

He climbed the stairs.

COTTON STARED OUT THE HELICOPTER'S WINDOW.

The triangular-shaped, walled citadel that was the Vatican came into view.

A little over a hundred acres with a population of a thousand. At its center rose the pillared façade of St. Peter's Basilica, capped by its majestic dome, which gleamed in the bright midday sun. Jutting off to one side were the long H-shaped galleries of the Vatican museums and the Vatican Library. Part of that complex included the Sistine Chapel, a simple rectangle at the southwest corner of the palace, where the cardinals would gather. Both religious and defensive in nature, as was evident from its austere exterior with battlements. The remaining pile of buildings, irregular in plan and clearly built at differing times without regard to any particular harmony, were all part of the administrative complex of the Catholic Church. The center of Christendom.

From his lofty perch he saw that over half of the enclosed space within the walls was consumed by the Vatican Gardens. A spectacular combination of poplars, maples, acacias, and oaks where popes once hunted for birds, deer, roebuck, and gazelles. The chopper swept in directly over the trees and he noticed a variety of medieval fortifications and monuments set among flowers, topiary, and grass. A rectangular slab of concrete at the far western corner, near the Leonine Wall, served as a helipad.

The chopper settled down on it.

He hopped out.

A priest at the far edge came forward and introduced himself, adding that Stephanie Nelle was waiting. He followed the younger man through the gardens, past Vatican Radio, the Ethiopian College, and the railway station, eventually entering St. Martha's Square. He'd never been into the closed areas of the Vatican before, though he'd visited the public portions. On the flight in he saw that St. Peter's Square, lined with the famed Bernini colonnade, was filled with people. The priest turned left and walked straight for the basilica and a side door that was being watched by a uniformed security guard.

Armed too.

Which was curious for a religious state.

But he assumed that the times were a-changing.

They entered the basilica.

No matter what a person's faith, or if they had no faith at all, it was hard not to be overwhelmed by the majesty that was St. Peter's Basilica. It had three claims to fame. A memorial to St. Peter. Coronation hall for popes and emperors. The foremost house of God in the world. Monuments and tombs were everywhere, adorning both the cavernous nave and the impressive side aisles. Every nook and cranny was dedicated to a pope or a saint. Beautiful marble empaneled the walls, the roof ornamented with sunken coffers richly gilded and stuccoed. Its immensity seemed disguised by the clear symmetry of its proportions. With few exceptions all of the wall images were mosaics, executed with such accuracy to scale and tint as to be almost surreal. The roster of artists boggled the mind. Raphael, Michelangelo, Peruzzi, Vignola, Ligorio, Fontana, Maderno. A perfect example of what five hundred years and unlimited resources could accomplish. Everything was made even more noteworthy by the fact that the building was empty.

Not a soul inside.

Making it possible to hear their footsteps echoing off the sheets of colored marble that formed the floor.

They passed the papal altar and its gilt bronze baldachin that kept watch on the stairs leading down to the tomb of St. Peter. It sat in the center of the Latin cross formed by the building itself. He glanced up into the main cupola that rose to the top of Michelangelo's dome. Mosaics filled its ribs, fading away toward the top as if dissolving into heaven.

The priest seemed unimpressed and just kept walking.

Off to the right he caught the bronze of a life-sized St. Peter, sitting as he gave a blessing while holding the keys to the kingdom of heaven. He knew it to be sixteen hundred years old. Intact, except for one part. For centuries pilgrims had kissed the right foot. Today people simply rubbed it. Each touch made little to no difference. But combined they had eroded the bronze, polishing the defined toes to smoothness. Surely there was a lesson in there somewhere.

They crossed to the far side of the nave and headed for an exit door, which was manned by another security guard. Probably a private firm contracted to assist during all of the commotion that came from a papal death and election. The exit door opened and Stephanie Nelle appeared, along with another man, dressed in black.

He stepped toward them.

"We have a big problem," she said.

CHAPTER
SIXTY-EIGHT

POLLUX ENTERED THE SISTINE CHAPEL, FOLLOWING IN THE procession with the other cardinals, two by two, all in their scarlet splendor, their hands folded in prayer. The chapel was forty meters long, thirty wide, and twenty tall, divided into two unequal parts by an elaborate marble screen, a loose interpretation of a Byzantium iconostasis. From the screen to the altar a raised dais had been built on each side to accommodate two tiers of cardinals sitting side by side in long rows. Each had a chair and desk space. All he needed now was a little luck, and the information on the flash drive, which rested safely in his trouser pocket beneath his cassock.

He'd visited the Sistine several times, but there was a special majesty about the chapel for a conclave. It owed its celebrity to the frescoes, where the great masters of the 15th century had left their most magnificent works. His eyes focused on the far wall and Michelangelo's *Last Judgment*. The largest painting in the world. At first glance it appeared confused and chaotic, but careful study allowed one to appreciate its mystic inspiration.

The singing stopped. The line dissolved.

He glanced up, past the arched windows on either side, at the flattened barrel-vaulted ceiling. He agreed with the critics. It may well be the most powerful piece of art ever created. When the despotic Julius II ordered the chapel redecorated, Michelangelo had rebelled. He was a sculptor, not a painter. But once inspired he'd entered into his commission with great enthusiasm. Four years he'd labored, creating a stupendous undertaking.

He studied the panels.

The Intoxication of Noah. The Great Flood. God Creates Eve. God Hovering Over the Waters. God Separates Light from Darkness. His gaze focused on one in particular. *The Brazen Serpent. And the Lord sent fiery serpents, and much people of Israel died, and Moses made a serpent of brass and those who beheld the serpent of brass lived.* He took comfort from Numbers 21. Some of the cardinals around him were about to behold a brazen serpent.

The presiding cardinal called out from the altar. "Please take a seat so that we may begin, brothers."

He found his assigned spot along the left wall, beneath Rosselli's *Passage of the Red Sea.* He settled into the chair, made comfortable by a red cushion and a pillow for the spine. So far his charade had worked perfectly. A few of the cardinals had approached him and made small talk. Some clearly were Kastor's friends, others not so much. He'd kept his comments short and vague, citing the distraction of all that was happening around him. Thankfully, the vast majority had ignored him.

The presiding cardinal, an Italian, the most senior in attendance, stood before the altar and told the assembled that they would now swear the oath, pledging to observe the norms prescribed by the various apostolic constitutions and rules laid down by previous popes. The process would take some time to complete as each cardinal, in order of seniority, would be required to step forward, place his hands on the gospels, and publicly swear.

He was going to enjoy watching that spectacle.

COTTON STOOD WITH STEPHANIE AND CHARLES CARDINAL STAMM, an Irishman, the man in charge of the Entity. He was thin, pinched in the cheeks, with a pockmarked face and a hooked nose. Just a trace of a scarlet bib showed below the white clerical collar above the top button of a plain black cassock. No signet ring. A simple brass pectoral cross was the only sign of his high office. Though Danjel Spagna had operational control, this man was the chair of the board, appointed too many popes ago to count. He was an older man, clearly past the age of eighty, which disqualified him from actively participating in the conclave.

"Luke called in," Stephanie said.

She showed him an image on her phone of the top half of a dead body.

"That's Cardinal Gallo," Cotton said. "Doubtful somebody killed Pollux Gallo, then cut his hair and shaved off the beard before dumping him in the ground. The guy inside the Sistine Chapel is an imposter."

They were huddled together inside the basilica, not a soul in sight. Both the uniformed guard and the priest who'd escorted him had retreated to the other side of the exit door.

"The head of Maltese security has confirmed to Luke that the Gallo brothers switched places," Stephanie said. "That man was also in league with Pollux Gallo. Now Gallo is inside the Sistine, pretending to be his brother."

"He must have a plan," Cotton said.

"He does."

And she explained about a damaging flash drive that Gallo had obtained from Spagna.

"Luke has been most persuasive in getting his prisoner to talk," she said. "He has him at the bottom of what he called a *guva*. He mentioned that you were familiar with the locale."

He chuckled. "I'll never hear the end of that one. But yes, I've visited the place."

"I'm aware of Archbishop Spagna's internal investigation," Stamm said. "It was done at the pope's specific request. But I was never privy to the results. Spagna falsely told me the investigation was still ongoing. Thankfully, I concluded he was lying. I suspect his plan was to use what he'd learned and have himself elevated to cardinal and replace me, taking both jobs for himself."

"Sounds like you didn't care for the guy," Cotton said. "Why keep him around?"

"Because he was extremely good at what he did. And the late pope liked him." Stamm shrugged. "This is not a democracy. There was nothing I could do. Except tolerate . . . and watch him."

"Cardinal Stamm is why the Magellan Billet is involved," Stephanie said.

"You knew Spagna was going rogue?"

"I strongly suspected. When some of my subordinates confirmed that he was on Malta, I knew there was a problem. But once I found out Cardinal Gallo was headed there, too, I decided to recruit some outside help."

"He quietly asked me to send an agent to keep an eye on the cardinal," Stephanie said. "Of course, we had no idea of the full extent of what was going to happen."

"To say the least," Stamm added. "I've lost my operational head and second in command."

"I'm glad you're here," Stephanie said to Cotton. "This is going to require care, skill, and experience."

"We need to get Gallo. Now," he said.

Stamm shook his head. "The sanctity of the conclave cannot be broken."

"The sanctity is already broken," Stephanie said. "The whole thing is a sham. It needs to end."

"We can simply wait until they break for the day, then move on Gallo," Stamm said.

But Cotton knew something about conclaves. "And what do you do if they elect him pope this afternoon? They'll take a vote today, won't they?"

Stamm went silent for a moment, then said, "Yes. They will. Probably sometime in the next hour."

"We have no idea what Gallo has done," Cotton said. "If the information he has is as bad as you say, he may have already applied pressure. He's been in Rome for several hours. This conclave has to end. I'm sorry if that's going to be a PR disaster, but the man is a murderer. Are the doors to the Sistine closed yet?"

"They are about to be."

"We need to move."

POLLUX WATCHED AS, ONE BY ONE, THE MEN IN SCARLET LINED UP and approached the lectern to take the oath. At his turn, he stood, laid his hand on the gospels, and swore to obey the Apostolic Constitution. Again, no one gave him a second look or even seemed to care.

But by tomorrow evening they would.

After the last man swore allegiance, the papal master of ceremonies uttered the classic words.

"*Extra Omnes.*"

Everybody out.

The public portion of the conclave had concluded and the functionaries at the back, beyond the marble screen—photographers recording the oath swearing, officials from the Vatican offices, along with various archbishops, priests, and monsignors who had helped prepare the event—left. Then the tall wooden doors were eased shut for the cameras beyond and latched from the inside. In centuries past it had been the opposite. That was when there were fewer cardinals, and such a small electorate magnified each vote and amplified the amount of corruption. Conclaves sometimes lasted months, even years. The bargaining among the participants anything but subtle. Finally, in 1274, Gregory X ordered that electors be locked in seclusion, their food severely rationed, until they came to a consensus. Needless to say, things began to happen faster.

This would be a short conclave, too.

Two days at best.

His election had to be viewed as one of divine inspiration, since Kastor's reputation was hardly *papabile*. The selection would be shocking to the world. He wondered if any of the offending cardinals would resist him. Maybe. But he'd make clear that they would end their tenure as princes of the church in disgrace, perhaps even in jail, with the world media knowing exactly what they'd done and the new pope forced to deal with their indiscretions. So why not have a friend on the throne of St. Peter. Albeit one who owned them. But nonetheless a friend.

Surely every one of them had realized the risks they were taking when they decided to break not only God's law but the laws of every civilized nation. The last thing they would want was to be exposed, but if that was their desire, he'd accommodate them. Instead of pope he would become God's Whistleblower. That should do wonders for the tarnished image of Kastor Cardinal Pollux.

But he doubted that would be the route they'd take.

Just a simple vote, in secret, one they could actually disavow later if they so desired, and all would remain as it was now.

If nothing else, cardinals were practical.

The doors to the Sistine were closed and locked. The conclave had begun. There would be another sermon, then the first vote would be taken. Before him on the clothed table were a few pencils, a scrutiny sheet where a count of any voting could be recorded, a copy of *Ordo Rituum,* the Order for Rites in the conclave, and a stack of ballot cards with the words ELIGO IN SUMMUM PONTIFICEM printed at the top.

I elect as Supreme Pontiff.

He planned to write his name on the first ballot. No one else would. And no one would think a thing of it, as many would vote either for themselves or for a friend, too. Never in modern times had a pope been chosen by two-thirds on the first vote. Supposedly that was to avoid the sin of pride.

But at least his name would enter the fray.

And by nightfall several of the men around him would fully understand that significance.

CHAPTER
SIXTY-NINE

COTTON FOLLOWED CARDINAL STAMM AS THEY WALKED FROM THE basilica toward the Sistine Chapel. They entered a room labeled the Sala Regia, the Regal Room. A large audience hall where emperors and kings were once received, the walls were decorated with more massive frescoes. He caught some of the Latin captions beneath them. The return of Pope Gregory XI from Avignon. The Battle of Lepanto. The reconciliation of Pope Alexander III with Frederick Barbarossa. Each depicted an important point in the church's history.

Braggadocio, for sure.

These were glory walls.

Overhead, the ceiling was an elegant barrel vault that boasted ornate insignia of popes, together with biblical figures. Like everything else inside the Vatican, the color and style more attacked than soothed the senses. At the far side was the entrance to the famed Pauline Chapel. In the center of one of the long walls stood towering wooden doors, a Swiss Guard on either side, both in billowy costumes of blue, orange, and red stripes.

The entrance to the Sistine Chapel.

Closed.

The high vaulted roof above echoed the murmur of the fifty or so people who milled about on the marble floor. Some priests, some bishops, most men dressed in suits and ties. Several held cameras, with press credentials draped from their necks.

"We're too late," Stamm said. "Give me a moment."

The cardinal drifted away toward a knot of suits.

"We can't let this go on," he said to Stephanie.

"Unfortunately, it's a Vatican matter."

"Pollux Gallo tried to kill Luke. That's an American matter."

"That's a reach."

"But it could be enough."

She gestured across the hall. "Those two guards aren't going to be impressed by our jurisdiction, and I'm sure this whole palace is loaded with security, ready to deal with any intrusion."

He got the message. This was going to require diplomacy, rather than force.

Stamm walked back their way, his movements slow, his whole air casual, nothing to signify urgency. "The doors have been closed for less than ten minutes. They will be listening to a sermon for a short while. It's traditional before the first scrutiny is taken."

That meant they had time to think, and Cotton could see the cardinal was debating the next course. More conversations swept through the hall, amplified by the marble surrounding them.

"We need to clear this hall," Stamm said.

"You've decided?' Stephanie asked.

"I never cared for Cardinal Gallo. I considered him a blowhard who knew little to nothing about anything. I never cared much for Archbishop Spagna, either. But it was not my place to judge either man. And no one deserves to be murdered. It's my duty to keep the church protected, its priests and princes protected, and the process of selecting a new pope free of taint." Stamm paused. "You saw the knights' *Nostra Trinità*?"

Cotton nodded. "We found it."

"I checked," Stamm said. "Cardinal Gallo arrived at the Domus Sanctae Marthae with a large duffel bag. I had his room searched a few moments ago. There are four old parchments there, inside an ancient reliquary."

"With red wax seals on each end?" Cotton added. "One of which is broken?"

Stamm nodded.

"That's it," Cotton said. "Inside that reliquary is Constantine's Gift."

"I haven't had a chance to see if that's true. But if after seven hundred years it has found its way back to us, there could be a problem."

"It's that important?"

"If the rumors are to be believed."

Cotton smiled. This man knew how to play his cards close to his vest.

"Our imposter wants to be pope," Stamm said. "I would imagine that the last thing he desires is for the church to lose stature, in any way. Instead he plans to extort his way to the throne of St. Peter. Your point is a good one, Mr. Malone. We cannot allow that first scrutiny. We have no idea what Pollux Gallo has done. Whether we stop it now, or later, the public relations damage is the same. So I've decided to act."

POLLUX LISTENED TO THE SERMON, WHICH SEEMED ONLY TO BRING a sense of duty and long-windedness. As if any of the men in the room required a reminder of their responsibilities. This was his first experience at seeing how the cardinals functioned as a group and he'd watched the faces. Some were clearly interested, but most were trying to keep stoic, revealing nothing, holding their thoughts within. Surely some deals had already been made, preliminary alliances forged. Nobody here, other than fools, was waiting for the Holy Spirit to swoop down and inspire them.

Maybe *he* was the Holy Spirit?

Perhaps the flash drive had been meant to fall into his hands.

The German monsignor finally shut up and the presiding cardinal stood before the altar. The first scrutiny was about to begin. He listened as the prelate explained the procedure, grateful for the final instructions. He'd read all about the process, but any refresher was appreciated. On the card before them each cardinal would write a name. Then, in order of precedence, they would take their ballot to the altar and deposit it into a gold chalice. Before casting their ballot, each cardinal would swear another oath. In Latin. *I call as my witness Christ the Lord who will be my judge, that my vote is given to the one who before God I think should be elected.*

In former times a cardinal had to sign his name to each ballot, along with a small motif, a symbol unique to him. The ballot was then folded to cover the signature and motif, then sealed with wax to provide a measure of privacy. But the scrutineers, the ones who counted the ballots, all knew who voted for who. Pius XII ended that nonsense. This method was much better. Secret should be secret.

The presiding cardinal finished his explanations and invited the balloting to begin. Some of the men immediately reached for their pencils, while others bowed their heads in prayer. He decided to take a moment before scrolling his brother's name.

A banging broke the silence.

Which surprised everyone.

From the main doors.

More banging.

Incredible.

Someone was knocking.

He came alert and watched as the presiding cardinal stepped from the altar and paraded down the center aisle, his hands folded before him. All of the men focused on the massive double doors beyond the marble screen. A slight murmur of voices arose. A few of the cardinals stood and crept into the center aisle. He decided to do the same. More of the puzzled men joined him there.

The presiding cardinal approached the double doors, released the inner lock, and eased open one side enough that he could step outside. Suspicion brushed across his mind. Nothing about this seemed good. They'd already been told about the second way in and out of the chapel, through a small door behind the altar that led either up to Raphael's Stanze or down to Collection of Modern Religious Art in the Vatican Museums. The museums themselves were closed, their massive exhibit halls empty. Restrooms were provided on either floor for cardinals in need.

But the route could also prove a means of escape.

He drifted away from the cardinals, their combined attention fixated on the doors. He, too, kept his focus on the center opening in the marble screen, hoping this was a false alarm.

The double doors swung open.

Cotton Malone entered.

CHAPTER SEVENTY

Cotton had stood with Stamm and Stephanie as they spoke with the presiding cardinal.

He was not happy.

"Charles, do you have any idea what you have done?" the man whispered in English.

"Fully, my friend. But there's a problem with the conclave. One that requires it be halted."

They'd cleared the Sala Regia of the people who'd been milling about on the pretense of providing utter quiet to the men beyond the double doors. All of them had been ushered into an adjacent hall and the doors closed, leaving only the two Swiss Guards. Their boss had been informed of the situation and sworn to silence, he bowing to Stamm since, as the older man noted, no one inside the Vatican, save the pope, argued with the Entity. Cotton listened as Stamm explained the situation, the presiding cardinal's eyes alighting with each revelation.

"Are you certain?" the older man asked when Stamm finished.

"There's no doubt."

And Stephanie showed the cardinal the image of Kastor Gallo's dead face.

"We need to take the imposter into custody," Stamm said.

The other man, clearly flustered, nodded. "Of course. Absolutely."

Stamm motioned and Cotton pushed the doors open and stepped into the Sistine Chapel.

A sea of scarlet-and-white-clad men stood beyond an elaborate marble screen. He walked to an opening in the center, his eyes searching the faces. "Gentleman, I need Cardinal Gallo."

The men seemed puzzled at first, then a few pointed at the tables.

"That's his seat," one of them said.

Empty.

Stamm and Stephanie came up beside him.

"Slippery thing, isn't he," Stamm whispered.

"I assume there's another way out?"

"Behind the altar. Stairs up or down, both will lead you into the museums. They're entirely closed for the conclave, the exits are manned by armed security. I can alert them to move in."

"No. Let me go get him. Maybe we can contain this within the museums. Keep the guards on the exits so Gallo can't leave, but alert them. They have radios?"

Stamm nodded. "Cardinals are not supposed to leave the museums. They are under seal."

"I get it. So if he tries, have them detain him. How about the cameras in the museums?"

"Off during the conclave to preserve privacy. Which also helps keep this contained."

He got the message. Stamm would like to keep them off. "I'll find him."

"Do that. I would prefer not to issue an apprehend order for a cardinal of the church."

"He's not a cardinal."

"He's worse. I'm relying on your abilities and discretion here, Mr. Malone."

"Cotton can handle it," Stephanie said.

Stamm gestured and one of the uniformed Swiss Guards hurried over. Cotton watched as the guard removed a radio that had been attached inside the costume, along with a small mike and earpiece.

Stamm handed them over.

"Go get him."

POLLUX DESCENDED THE STAIRS TO A GALLERY FILLED WITH PAINT-ings, sculpture, and graphic art. All modern. Contemporary. Ugly. He kept moving, turning left and heading for an open doorway, entering the old Vatican library. He passed through three rooms then found the famed Sistine Hall, which stretched some sixty meters ahead. Seven pillars sheathed with frescoes divided the ancient space into two wide aisles. The walls and ceiling were all colorfully decorated and gilded, furnished more like a reliquary than a library. Mosaic tables filled the spaces between the pillars and supported an array of porcelain vases. More tables displayed other precious objects under glass, similar to the knights' archive at Rapallo.

He kept moving through the Sistine Hall, passing one pillar after another. He hated leaving the *Constitutum Constantini,* particularly after all he'd endured to find it. But there was no time to retrieve it from his room.

His freedom was now at stake.

He heard no one either behind or ahead of him. Malone would surely come in pursuit, but the American would have to decide if his quarry had gone up or down after leaving the Sistine.

He could only hope that Malone chose wrong.

COTTON FLED THE SISTINE AND HURRIED DOWN A LONG CORRIDOR that led into the Apostolic Palace and a staircase.

Two, actually.

One up. The other down.

Where to? Good question.

He chose up and hopped the stone risers two at a time, exiting into a room filled with biblical allegories on the ceiling and obligatory frescoes on the walls.

"I'm upstairs," he said into the mike clipped at his shoulder.

"Then you're in the Room of the Immaculate Conception," Stamm said in his ear.

A glass case stood in the center. He gave it a casual glance and noticed ornamented volumes dating to the 19th century dealing with, sure enough, the Immaculate Conception.

"Leaving there and entering a small room housing tapestries," he said.

"The Apartment of St. Pius V," Stamm added.

He passed through and entered the incredible Gallery of Maps. This place he knew about. Over 350 feet long, a straight, unobstructed line from one side of the palace to the other. The overhead vault was decorated with white and gold stuccos populated by people, coats of arms, allegories, and emblems. But the walls were its claim to fame. Enormous colorful panels alternated with the bright exterior windows. Forty maps all total, together depicting topographically the entire Italian peninsula of the 16th century. Eighty percent accurate. Remarkable given the state of cartography at the time.

"I'm in the map gallery," he said. "There's no one here."

He ran down the marble floor. Out the windows, to his left, he caught glimpses of the Vatican Gardens with fountains and trees rising toward the observatory. On the right was an inner courtyard, with an enormous splashing basin, empty of people. Cameras were everywhere. All off, according to Stamm. He was on the third floor, more galleries and halls beneath him and on the other side of the building, beyond the courtyard. Those electric eyes might be needed.

"The exits remain manned," Stamm said. "No one has reported anyone trying to leave."

"I'm at the end of the map gallery," he said into the radio. "There's no way to go from here across to the other loggia?"

"Not on the third floor. There is a way below on the second floor to cross," Stamm said. "Keep going. You can traverse over at the end, past the Room of Biga ahead. There's also a stairway down to ground level."

He entered the dome space of the Biga room. Four niches between pilasters and four arched bays formed the walls of a small rotunda. In the center stood a triumphal chariot. Definitely Roman. Complete with wheels, shaft, and horses. But no Gallo.

"I'm beginning to think I went the wrong way," he said.

POLLUX CAME TO AN INTERSECTION WHERE ANOTHER SHORTER loggia to his right led across to the other side of the palace. The library continued on there, as it did ahead, through a series of smaller collection rooms. His view through them was unobstructed. There had to be a way out at the end of those rooms, where the palace ended. Forward seemed the shorter and smarter play than heading for the other side. He could not afford to take any wrong turns. He needed to leave this building, and the Vatican, too.

Quickly and unnoticed.

The crowd out in St. Peter's Square would provide more than enough cover. Becoming lost within tens of thousands of people would be easy. But getting to them not so much. Every gate out would be manned. Surely soon the word would be passed by radio to be on the lookout for a wayward cardinal. He kept going, walking through a series of galleries with familiar names. Pauline. Alexandrine. Clementine. Beyond them he came to the entrance for the Vestibule of the Four Gates and a stairway that led down.

He started to descend.

On the landing he turned, but quickly halted.

At ground level he spotted a uniformed security guard manning the doors that led out. He assessed the situation and decided on his next move. Steeling himself, he continued down the wide marble staircase, his hands tucked into the roomy sleeves of his cassock. The guard had his back to him, staring out the glass doors, which made it easy to approach.

The man turned.

"Eminence—"

No hesitation. Move. Fast.

He removed his hands and grabbed the guard, wrapping his right arm around the man's neck. He clamped his left hand to his right wrist and tightened the vise into a choke hold, cutting off the man's breathing. The guard was younger but thirty pounds heavier and never anticipated a cardinal attacking him. Apparently, no arrest or detain order had yet been issued.

The man went limp.

He allowed the body to slump to the floor.

Immediately he removed his mozzetta and rochet, then unbuttoned the cassock. Beneath he wore an undershirt and trousers. They were dark, like the guard's. Blue, not black, but they would do. It was the shirt and cap he needed, along with the radio and gun. He slipped on the shirt, a little big, but a tuck of the tail into his pants handled the excess. He clipped the radio to his belt and popped in the ear fob. The microphone he stuffed into a pocket. He doubted he'd be making any transmissions. He buckled the holster to his waist. Grabbing hold of both arms he dragged the guard out of the vestibule and through an open doorway, leaving him stretched prone behind a statue that filled one corner of the nearest gallery. He rushed back and retrieved his robes, which he tossed over the guard's body.

He stepped back to the exit doors and smoothed his clothes.

Then he left the palace.

CHAPTER
SEVENTY-ONE

COTTON STOOD IN THE ROOM OF BIGA CONSIDERING HIS OPTIONS. The word meant "chariot" in Italian, pretty much the only name for this space considering the huge one that dominated it.

He took no comfort from the sacred, the prodigious, and the miraculous that engulfed him. He had a job to do.

And it wasn't going all that well.

He walked over to a large, twenty-paned window and gazed out at the sunny afternoon. Beyond was the dome of St. Peter's, the Vatican Gardens, and an assortment of other buildings set among the trees. Below stretched a street with little to no activity. Understandable given the conclave. A couple of vehicles moved about and a few people walked the concrete. The Vatican wasn't shut down. Far from it. Business went on. On the other side of the palace tens of thousands of people filled St. Peter's Square waiting for a new pope. Media outlets from around the world had also set up shop.

But here? No one was around.

It was odd standing in one of the largest, most visited museums in the world alone.

Something caught his eye below.

A man.

Moving away from the building.

One of the armed uniformed guards, like back in St. Peter's.

The guy stopped for a moment, looked around, then donned a cap.

He caught the face.

Gallo.

POLLUX PARALLELED THE BACK SIDE OF THE PALACE AND MARCHED toward the basilica. He wasn't sure where he was headed, but at least he was free of the building and his vestments. One was a prison, the other like a flashing sign. Until the body of the guard was found, the uniform he now wore should open a lot of doors.

But he had to move fast.

He passed beneath the Arch of Gregory and rounded an outbuilding that projected from the backside of the palace. He found himself in a piazza with another fountain—Santa Marta, if he recalled—and followed the street. The hulk of the basilica lay ahead. The day seemed wonderful, partly cloudy with lots of sunshine. Warm too. Malone suddenly appearing inside the Sistine signaled that things had not gone well in Malta. Kevin Hahn must have failed. He should have shot the idiot before leaving the island, but the bodies had to be buried. The last thing he needed was for those corpses to be found. So he'd had no choice but to keep Hahn alive. Also, having a friend as operational head of the Entity would have proven beneficial.

But none of that mattered now.

He'd been found out.

Which meant Malone knew about Kastor, too.

He had to disappear.

But first he had to flee the Vatican.

COTTON HUSTLED DOWN THE STAIRS AND STOPPED AT THE GLASS doors. Stamm had said all of the exits were manned. This one wasn't, and Gallo was wearing a uniform. He stepped over to the entrance of the first gallery and immediately saw a pile of red and white garments piled on a body lying in the corner. He rushed over and checked for a pulse on the shirtless man.

There. But weak.

Decision time.

Gallo was out of his robes and into a uniform that would provide a great freedom of movement. A definite problem. But Stamm had said the guards all carried radios, and there was no radio. That meant Gallo had ears, too. No gun was at the guard's waist. So Gallo was armed. The man lying before him needed medical attention but there was no time. He could not allow Gallo to dissolve into the woodwork, which was becoming easier by the second. Putting out an alert would require not only an explanation but a photo and description as well. He doubted any of the guards would recognize Kastor Gallo on sight. An open alert would also spook Gallo, who would hear.

That meant he was the only one who could get this done.

"I'm sorry," he whispered to the unconscious man.

He stood and headed for the exit doors. Beyond the glass, fifty yards away, he caught sight of Gallo as he rounded the end of a building and vanished from sight.

He ran out into the sun.

POLLUX WAS ON THE BACK SIDE OF THE BASILICA, THE GOVERNOR'S Palace off to his right. In order to get to St. Peter's Square he'd have to keep circling the basilica, but the closer he came to an exit gate the more people he'd encounter. No question that every inch of these surroundings was under video surveillance. But so far, there had been nothing to alert anyone. Only after the guard's body was found would things change.

But he'd be long gone by then.

COTTON RAN TOWARD WHERE HE'D LAST SEEN GALLO, THE PALACE on one side, grass and trees on the other.

His footsteps slapped the pavement.

Pigeons, shaken from their perch, squawked into the bright sky.

He made it to the building edge and stopped, glancing around and seeing his target past a piazza—

Just as Gallo vanished around the basilica's apse.

POLLUX KEPT WALKING.

Cool and calm.

A guard heading to his duty station.

Unfortunately, towering bastions surrounded the Vatican on all sides. No way out over those. He came to another square, this one more open than the others. Now he could see a whole array of 20th-century buildings. The Domus Sanctae Marthae and papal audience hall were both in view.

He stopped, hearing nothing but his own thoughts.

Be smart.

Use your advantage.

A hundred meters away he spotted salvation. A simple white marble building close to the outer wall.

The railway station.

To its immediate left was an opening in the Leonine Wall, wide enough to admit a train. The papal arms, carved in stone, hung above its center. Huge iron doors were retracted into the recesses of the bastion. The brown caterpillar of a train was parked on the other side of the station, most of it jutting out of the right side. The locomotive was running, steam billowing, its front end just short of the open gate. A worker busily unloaded large-wheeled plastic bins from the last railcar.

He studied the open gate.

Two guards dressed like him were on duty to make sure no one entered. Surely once the train left the big doors would be retracted, sealing off the portal.

But at the moment they offered a means of escape.

COTTON HAD PURSUED A LOT OF PEOPLE. SOME PROS, SOME NOT. Pollux Gallo seemed somewhere in between. Cunning, he'd give him that, and ballsy. He almost got away with the identity exchange. But like most psychopaths, he never thought that anyone might best him.

He came to the far end of the basilica and stopped, peering around and catching sight of Gallo headed for a white marble building with a train on the other side pointed toward an open gate in the wall.

Should he call it in?

No.

Somebody could get hurt.

Gallo was close to escape, desperate and armed.

He'd handle this himself.

CHAPTER
SEVENTY-TWO

POLLUX AVOIDED THE INTERIOR OF THE RAILWAY STATION, HEADING around its right side and approaching the tracks. Five railcars were attached to the locomotive, their doors slid open, the spaces inside each of them empty. Several freight wagons were loaded with crates and boxes. A man stood off to the side, waving toward the locomotive.

He heard the powerful engine rev louder.

Finally, a break.

He pointed toward the worker and said in Italian, "I need to go out with this train for security."

The man did not argue.

He rushed forward and hopped into the second car behind the locomotive. The train began to move, heading toward the gate in the bastion wall.

He just might make it out.

Once beyond the Vatican he'd hop from the train and disappear into Rome. Where to go after that? He'd find somewhere.

He had no intention of spending the rest of his life in jail.

COTTON CHOSE TO GO LEFT, AS GALLO HAD GONE RIGHT. THE LEFT side of the station also offered more cover with a patch of grass with trees and bushes. A paved walk separated the grass from the building and led back to the tracks. The path also offered a way to get to the rear of the station without Gallo knowing.

He heard the diesel rev and the hiss of brakes releasing. The locomotive was no more than twenty feet from the open gate and would be outside the wall in less than thirty seconds. He counted five open railcars and saw a guy near a white van toward the end of the train. One of the tall bushes offered excellent shielding and, as the train passed, he caught sight of Gallo inside the second car.

The train gathered pace.

The third car passed.

The fourth.

He had no choice.

He sprang from the path and ran toward the final car. Most of the train was now beyond the wall, the front third rounding a bend in the tracks.

He leaped up into the empty car.

Someone yelled.

Had to be one of the guards at the gate, who suddenly vaulted into the car, too. He never gave the man a chance, stepping forward and planting a fist in the guy's right side. The man doubled over and he used the moment to shove the guard out the open door. The train was creeping along, yet to gain a full head of steam. The guard hit the ground and rolled away. He watched out the door as the train kept going and saw that the guard was okay, having landed on grass. The other guard who'd been watching the gate with him ran to the man's aid and helped him up. Surely they'd call in all the excitement, and Stamm would learn where he'd headed.

He decided to maintain his own radio silence.

He swung himself out of the doorway and grabbed hold of a steel ladder, which he used to climb to the top. Two cars were between him and Gallo, so he jumped to the next. The tops were flat but loaded with bumps and indentations made more treacherous by the constant vibrations from the tracks. He spread his feet against the roll and felt like a sailor on a rolling deck.

He leaped to the next car.

Pollux began to feel a measure of relief.

He was away from the Vatican and only the one unsuspecting man at the train station had seen him. It was a shame that he'd not been able to complete the plan. He'd been devising it for many years and thought he'd anticipated all of the seemingly endless obstacles to a successful conclusion. His attempts to neutralize the Americans had apparently proven insufficient. But he still had the flash drive and it might be useful. Cardinals had resources that he could exploit, and taking the moral low road was nothing new for the Holy See.

The train kept moving, creating a constant groan from the warped wood and rusty metal. He'd wait a little longer before leaving.

Something thumped on the roof.

Footsteps moved from one side of the car to the other.

He reached for the gun at his waist.

Cotton swung his body out and onto the steel ladder attached to the side of the railcar. Down two rungs and he jumped into the open door, facing Gallo, who was reaching for a weapon. He lunged, pushing his weight against the other man and bracing his feet. He grabbed the gun and swung upward, wrenching the hand down, freeing the grip. The gun clattered away, then disappeared out the open doorway. Gallo rebounded, jerking away and jumping into the air, throwing a dive punch that crashed down on Cotton's shoulder, which he absorbed as he shifted away and whirled, coming back around with a heel kick to the sternum that lifted Gallo off the floor and sent him sliding. That had to have cracked some ribs but Gallo sprang to his feet, taking a swing that was easily sidestepped.

Cotton moved in and swung, his right fist connecting with the man's jaw.

Gallo blinked, then swung again, finding only air, the clenched knuckles swishing past without connecting.

Wheels racketed beneath his feet.

Gallo advanced.

Cotton swung again, crunching his fist into Gallo's face. He felt his nose give way. Gallo staggered back, dazed but showing no signs of surrendering. He could not allow him to leave the car.

Brakes hissed.

Wheels screeched on the tracks.

The train slowed.

Apparently Stamm had gotten the message.

Time to end this.

Gallo swung.

Cotton parried the blow and chopped at the neck, then pounded another fist into his solar plexus. He wrestled Gallo's arms behind his back and shoved the head and upper body into the wooden wall.

Once. Twice.

The body went limp.

He allowed Gallo to sink to the floor.

The train stopped.

He hadn't had a full fight like that in a while. Nice to know he still had it in him. Beyond the open doors he saw shadows approaching. Then he spotted Cardinal Stamm and Stephanie standing below. They stepped close to the open doors and saw Gallo lying still.

"Seems the rat finally found the trap," Stamm said.

Stephanie tossed him a grateful smile.

"Good job."

CHAPTER
SEVENTY-THREE

COTTON WAITED IN CARDINAL STAMM'S OFFICE, LOCATED IN ONE OF the many buildings that filled the Vatican, this one on the north side of the Apostolic Palace amid the post office, pharmacy, media outlets, grocery store, and barracks of the Swiss Guards. It was an odd location for the world's oldest intelligence agency. Reminiscent of the Magellan Billet, which was headquartered in a nondescript government building in Atlanta.

Stamm had ordered the train to reverse down the tracks, back to the Vatican station. The loading platform had been cleared of the white van and freight wagons, no one around except two men who, Stamm had explained, worked for him. Gallo was taken into custody, hustled to a waiting car, then driven away. The conclave had been halted with the story of a mechanical failure within the Sistine Chapel affecting the air-conditioning and electrical systems. It had been deemed a possible fire hazard so the extraordinary measure of interrupting the cardinals had been ordered. Luckily, nothing had, as yet, occurred relative to voting so it was decided that the conclave would reconvene tomorrow. The press was consumed with the story, but the cardinals were sequestered inside their rooms at the Domus Sanctae Marthae, unavailable for comment, including the presiding cardinal, whom Stamm had assured would never reveal a thing.

He and Stephanie had walked with Stamm back across the grounds. The injured guard had been located and taken to the hospital. He'd been partially asphyxiated but should be okay. Both he and his company had been sworn to secrecy. Cotton still felt bad that he hadn't been able to do something for the guy sooner, but if he'd delayed any longer he would have lost Gallo. Hopefully the guard would understand.

He was tired, his face deep in stubble and in need of a shave. Some sleep and a good meal would be great, too. Stamm's office seemed the picture of efficiency. Nothing fancy. Just what he needed to get the job done. Which seemed to fit the man. No nonsense, but fully capable. Cotton was glad this was over. Time to head to southern France and a few days with Cassiopeia. Strange that his thoughts now included another person. He'd been a loner a long time. But not anymore. A woman was again part of his life.

Which wasn't a bad thing.

Stephanie entered the office. "I really appreciate what you did."

"All part of the job, and I got paid."

"Speaking of that. James Grant's body was found in the Ligurian Sea, with a hole in his head."

"Gallo?"

"No doubt."

"Lot of dead people," he said.

"I agree. This one came with a cost."

"What about the Churchill letters?"

"Disappeared. But the Knights of Malta are cooperating and conducting searches of Gallo's rooms. He most likely has them hidden somewhere. They're appalled that all this has happened. But Gallo was working rogue. He recruited his *Secreti* on the promise of Vatican positions. Proof positive that you can hire anybody to do anything."

"I understand that concept fully," he said, adding a smile.

"I know you do."

Stamm reentered the office and walked behind his desk, sitting in a plain, high-backed wooden chair, which had to be uncomfortable. But the guy seemed right at home.

"The situation is control. The Vatican press office is dealing with the conclave interruption. The cardinals are tucked away. The two guards at the railway gate have been told that this was an internal matter and that you were working with us."

"The guy I tossed from the car okay?"

"He's fine." Stamm paused. "We were lucky today. An untenable situation has been resolved. Thanks to you, Mr. Malone."

"And a guy named Luke Daniels on Malta," Cotton added.

"I've already told him the same thing," Stephanie added. "Luke is on his way here with a prisoner. They landed a couple of hours ago."

He was perplexed. "Why here?"

"It was at my request," Stamm said.

Cotton realized the implications. He was sitting on sovereign soil. Stamm intended on treating both Gallo and Hahn as Vatican prisoners and dealing with them per canon law.

"For obvious reasons, we cannot allow the Italian, Maltese, British, or . . . Americans to deal with these crimes." Stamm stood. "Would you come with me?"

They left the office and walked to the elevator. Once inside the car, Stamm inserted a key into the control panel then pushed an unmarked button. The building had four floors and a basement. The button that lit up was below the one for the basement.

"This is an old building," Stamm said. "Built in the 1970s over a part of the grottoes."

They descended and came to a stop. The elevator doors opened. They were underground, a tall, well-lit corridor stretching ahead. All painted concrete with a tile floor.

"These subterranean chambers have proven useful," Stamm said.

The cardinal led the way and they followed him toward an iron door. Stamm approached and rapped twice. A lock was released from the other side and the panel swung inward. They stepped into a long room, one side lined with bars separated by stone pillars.

Cells.

Stamm dismissed the man who'd been stationed inside.

A table stood before one of the cells. The reliquary from the Church of St. Magyar's sat on it with parchments inside and another roll lying outside. Cotton walked over to see Pollux Gallo behind bars. The cardinal and Stephanie joined him.

"These cells have been used by us for a long time," Stamm s.
"Mehmet Ali Ağca was held here for a time after he tried to kill Jonn
Paul II."

Cotton couldn't help but think of the infamous Lubyanka prison in
Moscow beneath the old KGB headquarters building, where political dis-
sidents, artists, writers, and reporters had been tortured. He wondered
why the Roman Catholic Church would need underground cells with re-
stricted access.

"Is that the *Constitutum Constantini*?" he asked, pointing to the parchment.

"It is," Stamm said.

"I don't suppose you'd tell me why it's so important?"

"It proves that all of this is a fraud," Gallo said, approaching the bars.
"The Roman Catholic Church is fake. Tell him, Cardinal. Tell him the
truth."

He waited for more.

"There's an African proverb. *Until the lions have their historians, tales of the
hunt shall always glorify the hunters.* It's so true. In our case, the glory went to
those who took the lead." Stamm paused. "Constantine the Great changed
the world. He first united the Roman Empire, then divided it into two
parts. Emperors ruled the eastern half. Popes eventually dominated the
western. But not until they heeded his advice."

Stamm pointed at the parchments.

"It's a blueprint for a new religion," Gallo said. "Instructions on how
to make Christianity important. How to involve it in every aspect of
people's lives. How to use it to dominate followers. How even to kill them,
if necessary, to preserve its existence."

Stamm seemed unfazed. "I've read it and he's right. Constantine
wanted a religion of his own making, a mechanism whereby the people
were kept away from revolt. All without them, of course, ever realizing they
were being dominated. Unfortunately, that never happened during his
life, or in the centuries after his death. Only bits and pieces of his ideas
were implemented. No grand scheme. Not until his gift was rediscovered
in the 9th century. Popes had, by then, become intoxicated with ambition. They were more than religious leaders. They were military and political leaders. By the 11th century the Catholic Church became the richest

and most powerful institution in the world. All thanks to Constantine's Gift."

"Is this the only copy?" Stephanie asked.

"As far as we know. The Hospitallers obtained possession of it starting in the mid-13th century. Popes were terrified that it would be revealed, so they left the Hospitallers alone and the knights kept the secret."

"Is it authentic?" Stephanie asked.

"With only a preliminary look, my experts tell me the script is Constantine's. They compared it with verified originals we have in our archives. It's in the original Latin, which is rare for one of his surviving manuscripts. We can test the parchment by carbon dating, but I'm sure it will date to the 4th century. I'm also told the ink is consistent for that time. It appears to be absolutely authentic."

Cotton had no doubt.

"Napoleon tried to find it. Mussolini tried, too, and came the closest," Stamm said. "But it stayed with the knights until 1798, when it was hastily hidden away amid the French invasion of Malta."

"What do you think kings and emperors would have done after reading it?" Gallo asked, disgust in his voice. "Realizing that divine law was not God's law. It was all man-made for their own selfish purposes."

Stamm's face never flinched. Not a muscle quivered to reveal what he might be thinking.

"What would the faithful think of the church's original sin," Gallo said. "The price we all supposedly pay for the fall of Adam and Eve. The sin of disobedience for consuming the forbidden fruit. It had nothing to do with any of that. It was just a way to create recruits straight from the womb. No need to actually convince anyone to join your church. Just decree that you're born tainted, and forgiveness comes only from baptism, administered only by the church. Of course, if anyone declines that forgiveness they rot in hell, with the devil, for all eternity. But both of those were more of Constantine's creations. None of it's real. It's all there to create fear and ensure obedience. And what better way to control people than through irrational, unprovable fear."

Stamm stood quiet and still. Finally, the cardinal said, "My guess is that there would have been no church. Christians would have continued to fight among themselves, breaking into factions, accomplishing little to nothing. If left alone they never would have collated into anything meaningful. It all would have faded away, and kings and queens and emperors would have fought each other without reservation. Civilization, as we know it, would have been vastly different. The church, for all its failings, provided a measure of stability that kept the world from spiraling out of control. Without it, who knows how humanity would have fared."

"You keep telling yourself that," Gallo muttered.

"But the world is no longer composed of illiterates," Stamm said. "People now think of religion far more skeptically than did those of the 13th century. This revelation, made today, would have a huge impact."

"Which was precisely what my brother was counting on. Your fear allowing him to get what he wanted." Gallo glared at Cotton. "That parchment is eye opening. Don't let them suppress it."

Stamm reached into his cassock and withdrew something that he displayed. "Along with this?"

The flash drive.

"Archbishop Spagna was quite thorough," Stamm said. "He found the many failings that have long existed within these walls and identified the offenders. His problem was his own ego. And the underestimation of his supposed allies."

"Spagna was a fool," Gallo said.

"Perhaps," Stamm answered. "But he was my fool."

"What are you going to do with that flash drive?" Stephanie asked.

"All of the offenders will be dealt with. Contrary to what would have happened if Spagna, or our imposter here, had succeeded with their plans."

The iron door behind them clanged opened.

Luke entered with another man in tow. Fresh off a plane from Malta.

"Head of Maltese security," Stephanie whispered to him. "His name is Kevin Hahn."

Stamm led the newcomer to a cell and locked Hahn inside. Cotton took the opportunity to shake Luke's hand.

"The gang's all here. Good job," he told him. He noticed the same shirt, shorts, and tennis shoes from Malta. "Casual Fridays?"

"It's been a long day." Luke grinned. "I hear you're riding trains now like in some *Die Hard* movie. It's good to know that Pappy still has some life left in him."

"Thankfully, it wasn't moving all that fast."

Luke noticed Gallo in the cell. "Damn. He looks just like the cardinal. Nobody would have ever known."

"What are you going to do with the *Nostra Trinità?*" Gallo asked Stamm.

"The two parchments inside the reliquary will be returned to the knights as their property. But the *Constitutum Constantini* is church property."

"So it goes into the Vatican archives?" Stephanie asked.

Stamm stepped to the table and lifted the rolled parchment. His right hand slipped into his cassock and came out without the flash drive. Instead he held a lighter. He flicked the flame to life, then set it to the brittle scroll.

Which ignited.

Stamm dropped the burning scroll to the floor, which turned to charcoal in a matter seconds.

"The matter is now closed," Stamm said.

"We're still here," Gallo called out from his cell. "We know everything. This isn't over."

Charles Cardinal Stamm stood stoic as a statue. Burning the scroll was the most animation Cotton had seen from the man. But he also detected something else in the eyes as they'd watched the parchment destroy itself.

Relief.

"Archbishop Spagna, for all of his failings, always defended the church," Stamm said. "As do I."

Cotton imagined that men like Stamm had been making hard decisions for centuries. Each one thinking he was doing the right thing. Each one wrong. A piece of history had just been destroyed. A piece that could have shed a different light on things.

"What about the flash drive?" Stephanie asked.

"I'll deal with those offenders. In my own way."

He could only imagine what that would entail. Most likely lots of private meetings, then hasty resignations.

"I'll tell the world the truth," Gallo said. "You can't burn that away. This is not over, Cardinal. There'll be a trial. I'll see you, and all of the other hypocrites in scarlet, exposed for what you are. I'll make sure the world knows what was on that parchment."

Stamm said nothing.

But Cotton realized that without the document all Gallo had was talk.

Stamm stepped close to the bars. "You underestimate me. *Defending the faith with the spilling of blood is a duty we must never abandon.*"

He could see that Gallo caught the significance of the words.

"That's what Constantine wrote," Stamm said. "All part of his gift. The freedom to kill while *defending the faith.* The church truly took that one to heart. We've killed millions."

Gallo said nothing.

"What are you saying?" Hahn said from the other cell.

Stamm stepped back so both prisoners could see him. "Neither one of you will leave here alive. There will be atonement for your heinous crimes. Two more will die in defense of the faith."

"What did I do?" Hahn asked.

"You had Laura Price murdered," Luke said.

"Along with Monsignor Roy," Stamm added. "You are as complicit as your co-conspirator."

And Stamm pointed to Gallo.

Then he gestured that they all should walk away.

"Malone," Gallo hollered. "You can't let him do this."

Luke opened the iron door.

"Malone. For God's sake. You can't allow this. We're entitled to a trial. This is murder."

They all stepped out.

But not before he heard one last loud plea.

"Malone."

He kept walking, but something from the Bible flashed through his mind.

Romans 12:19.

Vengeance is mine.

I will repay, saith the Lord.

WRITER'S NOTE

The travel for this novel involved some of the best trips Elizabeth and I have ever taken. First, we visited Lake Como and all of the sites associated with Mussolini's failed escape attempt and ultimate execution. What a spectacular corner of the world. Next, we twice ventured to Malta, which is truly an amazing place. Rome and the Vatican were locales we've explored several times before.

Now it's time to separate fact from fiction.

Mussolini's escape from Milan, in an attempt to flee to Switzerland, as recounted in the prologue, happened. Claretta Petacci died with him, both of them executed by partisans (chapters 1 and 40). To this day no one knows for sure who pulled the trigger. Many have claimed the honor, though. Most of what Mussolini says in the prologue is taken from his actual words, uttered near the end of his life but not at the villa. The addition of a representative from the Knights of Malta was my invention. Mussolini brought with him gold, currency, and two satchels full of documents (chapter 3). Only a tiny amount of the gold was ever found in Lake Como by local fishermen. The vast majority of the cache (including the documents) has never been seen since. There was an Italian trial in the 1950s where several defendants were accused of theft, but it ended abruptly, without resolution, and no further investigation was ever undertaken (chapter 19). The connection of the judge in that trial with the villa owner in the prologue is fabricated.

This story spans a multitude of fascinating locales. Lake Como, the site of Mussolini's execution, and the Four Seasons in Milan are faithfully described. In Rome the Foro Mussolini (which became the Foro Italico), the Hotel d'Inghilterra, the Palazzo di Malta, and the Villa del Priorato di Malta are there as described. I wanted this novel to showcase Malta, so a special effort was made to include as many locations as possible. Valletta, the co-cathedral, the grand master's palace, the Grand Harbor, the Madliena and Lippija Towers, Marsaskala, St. Paul's Bay, Mdina, the Pwales Valley, the grottoes along the south shore, the tunnels beneath Valletta built by the knights (chapter 17), and the Westin Dragonara are all real. Parasailing is a popular activity off Malta (chapter 4), one I (like Luke) enjoyed. Only the Church of St. Louise Magyar's (chapter 49) is fictional, but the maiden's legend I associated with it is accurate (chapter 32). Its inner chapel is modeled after the Church of Piedigrotta in Pizzo, Italy.

The fasces (chapter 3) is an ancient Roman symbol, and the Italian National Fascists took their name from it.

Mussolini did indeed leave a mark on Rome. Many of his building projects and grand roadways still exist (chapter 29). Inside the Foro Italico (once the Foro Mussolini) stands the obelisk described in the story. It's true that the *Codex Fori Mussolini* was sealed inside it in the 1930s, a manifesto to the greatness of fascism and its leader (chapters 28, 29, 34, and 36). We know this because its text was printed in Italian newspapers at the time. Unlike in this novel, though, the codex remains sealed inside. The medal commemorating the obelisk Luke examines in chapter 29 is real.

The tale about the croissant's origins (chapter 12) is one of those delightful fables nobody really knows is true. Charlemagne's symbol, as depicted in chapter 12, was his signature. I dealt with this extensively in *The Charlemagne Pursuit*. It's a fact that anyone can be elected pope (chapter 10), but the last time that happened was 1379. *Tal-lira* clocks are all over Malta (chapter 30), as are the colorful *dghajsa* boats (chapter 32). And the legend of Skinned Tom that Luke recalls in chapter 60 is popular in east Tennessee.

The Hospitallers, now known as the Sovereign Military Hospitallers Order of St. John of Jerusalem, of Rhodes, and of Malta, or more simply the Knights of Malta, have existed for nine hundred years. The eight-pointed Maltese cross (chapter 7) has long been their symbol. All of the history attributed to the knights (chapters 4, 12, and 16), and the laws quoted in chapter 44, are accurate. Today the knights are a highly successful humanitarian organization. The *Secreti* once existed within them. Whether the group still does today is unknown, since the inner workings of the order are closely guarded. My reconstituted *Secreti* are purely imaginary.

The two villas in Rome—Palazzo di Malta and the Villa del Priorato di Malta—together form the smallest sovereign nation in the world (chapter 16). The Villa Pagana, at Rapallo, serves as the grand master's summer residence (chapter 19). A nearby archive (chapter 21) is my invention. *Guvas* once dotted Malta, the underground prisons unique to the knights (chapter 14). Now only one remains, at Fort St. Angelo in Valletta. I created two more. The keyhole on Aventine Hill, at the Villa del Priorato di Malta, does offer an amazing view of St. Peter's Basilica (chapter 28). Whether that was intentional, or merely fortuitous, is unknown.

The *Nostra Trinità* (chapter 26) is totally my creation, but two of its elements, the *Pie Postulatio Voluntatis* and the *Ad Providam,* are actual documents. The *Constitutum Constantini* is all mine, as is its backstory (chapter 48), though the concepts it explores—that religion is a creation of man, and the Catholic Church formulated its core doctrine for survival—are real (chapters 62, 63, and 64). Religious historians have long explored that subject in minute detail.

The co-cathedral in Valletta (chapter 40) is magnificent, especially the floor, which is consumed by over four hundred marble tombs. Each one is unique and magnificent. All of the ones used in the novel exist (chapters 41, 43, and 44), including the tomb of Bartolomeo Tommasi di Cortona (chapter 45) that contains three symbols, one of them the Chi Rho that is closely associated with Constantine. There's a clock depicted on that tomb, but a real manifestation of that clock inside the cathedral is my creation (chapter 46).

Malta was besieged in 1565 by the Turks (chapter 8), but the knights resisted the invasion. That victory did in fact halt a Turkish advance across the Mediterranean and save Europe. Afterward, the island was ringed by a series of thirteen watchtowers that still stand. All of the ones mentioned in the novel exist. It was fun to incorporate them into the treasure hunt, even more fortunate that eight of them, when joined, formed a cross (chapters 47 and 48). The Apostle Paul did in fact visit Malta, bringing Christianity to the island, his exploits expressly depicted in the Bible (chapter 13).

All of the Vatican locales are accurately portrayed, including the Sistine Chapel, Apostolic Palace, museums, the Domus Sanctae Marthae, Vatican Gardens, and train station (chapters 65, 67, 68, 69, 70, and 71). The position of prefect of the Apostolic Signatura (chapter 5), which Kastor Gallo holds, is one of long standing.

The legal and political distinction between the Vatican City State and the Holy See (chapter 13) came into existence thanks to the 1929 Lateran Treaty. The curia (chapter 15) manages both, with the pope in sole command. The problem of trying to contain the curia is one of long standing. Sadly, all of the corruption detailed from Spagna's flash drive (chapters 15 and 18) is taken from actual scandals that have rocked the Holy See for the past decade. A good discussion on this subject can be found in *Merchants in the Temple* and *Ratzinger Was Afraid,* both by Gianluigi Nuzzi. The Vatican continues to deny there are any scandals or internal problems, but Nuzzi makes a good case to the contrary.

The Entity is real. It dates back five hundred years and is the world's oldest intelligence agency. The Vatican has never acknowledged that the organization exists, but its history is long and storied (chapter 20). There is also a pope's spymaster whose identity is kept secret. My label of *Domino Suo* is fictional. A terrific history on this subject is *The Entity,* by Eric Frattini.

The Churchill–Mussolini letters described in the story are a matter of legend, rumored to exist, but never seen. Mussolini having them with him when he tried to flee Italy in 1945 is my addition to their story. The letters quoted in chapter 9 are my creations, but I drew heavily on Churchill and Mussolini's own words. Churchill's signature is real. Upon assuming the office of prime minister, Churchill wanted to use Malta as a bargaining chip to keep Italy from aligning with Germany. But the British War Cabinet rejected the notion. Ultimately, Malta became critical and held out a multiyear siege by Germany and Italy, the entire country earning the George's Cross (chapter 9).

Mussolini's supposed alliance with Popes Pius XI and XII (chapter 38) happened. Neither pope was progressive. In many ways they saw eye-to-eye with Mussolini's ultraconservatism. It's a fact that Il Duce managed to keep the Catholic Church at bay. Never once did the Vatican publicly strike out against fascism. By 1939 Pius XI was ready to shift gears and do just that, but he died before he could openly challenge the government. Pius XII never carried through on that move. The full extent of Pius XII's attitudes toward Germany, the Holocaust, Nazis, and Mussolini will probably never be known. For more on this subject, take a look at *The Pope and Mussolini,* by David Kertzer.

Napoleon invaded Malta in 1798 and took the island without much of a fight (chapters 11 and 15). The knights had, by then, deteriorated to nothing. At that point Napoleon had not achieved emperor status but he was definitely scheming. Part of his grandiose plan involved eliminating the influence of the Catholic Church and the establishment of his own religion, one with himself at its head (chapter 26). To further that end, he ultimately sacked and looted the Vatican, twice. He likewise pillaged Malta, taking all of his spoils with him to Egypt where they ended up at the bottom of the sea.

The Knights of Malta were immensely unpopular on the island (chapter 25). They ruled with cruelty and arrogance. But the French were hated even worse, forced to leave in 1800 after only two years of occupation, opening the way for the British to seize control in 1814. Malta remains under the British Commonwealth, but enjoys independent nation status.

The Sator Square has fascinated me for some time (chapter 12). It's been around since Roman times and does have a connection to Constantine, but not quite the one I invented. What the five-worded palindrome means is unclear, but there is a connection to early Christians, the anagram letters forming *Pater Noster,* Our Father, with four left over for alpha and omega (chapter 26). That cannot be a coincidence. The five words can be found carved in a variety of places across Europe, and rings with the words on it can be bought (chapter 19).

The main theme of this novel centers on the origins of Christianity.

The Council of Nicaea was the first great ecumenical gathering, called by Constantine the Great (chapters 27 and 63). Nothing but mystery surrounds its proceedings since there is only one account of what happened, which is minimal at best. Even the number of bishops who attended is in doubt, though the partial list of names in chapter 54 is accurate. What we do know is that several doctrinal disagreements were settled and a statement of belief was adopted, the Nicaean Creed, which is quoted exactly in chapter 59. That creed, with only slight modifications, remains today the Catholic Church's main statement of purpose.

Constantine is regarded with great affection by the Roman Catholic Church. By the 4th century Christianity firmly existed, though it was stalled in persecution and pandemonium. Once he'd taken it under his wing, the emperor made many contributions to the new religion. Those included official sanction, privileges, money, and buildings. Among the countless churches he constructed are the Church of the Holy Sepulcher in Jerusalem and the first St. Peter's Basilica in Rome.

It's a fact that a banquet was held at the end of the Council of Nicaea where the emperor bestowed gifts on the bishops for them to take back to their individual churches. As to a document he may have presented to them, which the bishops supposedly signed—my *Constitutum Constantini*, Constantine's Gift—that never happened. Religion is a concept created by humans and long used by humans for political advantage. That's historical fact. That the ideas of original sin, heaven, hell, and the devil were church creations is accurate. And before you reject that statement as fantasy, consider what Pope Francis said in March 2018. When asked about hell and what happens to a sinner's soul, the pope said, *They are not punished, those who repent obtain the forgiveness of God and enter the rank of souls who contemplate him, but those who do not repent and cannot therefore be forgiven disappear. There is no hell, there is the disappearance of sinful souls.*

Quite a statement from the head of over a billion Catholics. Shortly after those words were published in *La Repubblica,* a leading Italian newspaper, the Vatican issued a statement claiming the article was "not a faithful transcript" and that the meeting between Pope Francis and the writer was private and not a formal interview.

But there was no categorical denial that they were said.

What many consider sacred church dogma, with divine origins, has a much more concrete and practical basis. The problem is we know precious little about the early Catholic Church and what its founding fathers actually did. What we do know is primarily thanks to one man. Eusebius, who lived during Constantine's time. He wrote so many treatises that he's come to be called the father of church history. He was also a close adviser of the emperor, and many of Eusebius's works have survived. His *Ecclesiastical History* remains a vital source material on the early church. His *Life of Constantine* is regarded as an important work but is clearly skewed by his love for the emperor.

How much of his accounts are true?

Nobody knows.

Such doubts also apply to another quotation attributable to Pope Francis, as detailed in the book's epigraph and chapter 5. There are many different versions out there, understandable given their controversial nature. Some say the variations were created by the Vatican, after the original statement was uttered, in an attempt to defuse their obvious implications and add confusion to authenticity. Again, nobody knows. Still, the comments, in any form, are odd for a pope. In closing, consider them once again:

> *It is not necessary to believe in God to be a good person.*
> *In a way, the traditional notion of God is outdated.*
> *One can be spiritual, but not religious.*
> *It is not necessary to go to church and give money.*
> *For many, nature can be a church.*
> *Some of the best people in history did not believe in God,*
> *while some of the worst deeds were done in his name.*

UPGRADE
AND REPAIR
YOUR PC

OTHER BOOKS BY AUBREY PILGRIM

Build Your Own Pentium Pro Processor PC
Build Your Own Pentium Processor PC, 2/e
Build Your Own Multimedia PC, 2/e
Build Your Own 486/DX PC

ADVANCED PC REPAIR TITLES

Stephen Bigelow   *Troubleshooting and Repairing Computer Monitors, 2/e*
Stephen Bigelow   *Troubleshooting and Repairing Computer Printers, 2/e*
Stephen Bigelow   *Troubleshooting and Repairing PC Drives and Memory Systems, 2/e*

In order to receive additional information on these or any other McGraw-Hill titles, in the United States please call 1-800-722-4726. Or visit us at www.computing.mc-graw-hill.com. In other countries, contact your local McGraw-Hill representative.

Upgrade
and Repair
Your PC

Aubrey Pilgrim

McGraw-Hill

New York · San Francisco · Washington, D.C. · Auckland · Bogotá
Caracas · Lisbon · London · Madrid · Mexico City · Milan
Montreal · New Delhi · San Juan · Singapore
Sydney · Tokyo · Toronto

Library of Congress catalog card number: 97-76510

McGraw-Hill

A Division of The McGraw-Hill Companies

Previously published in 1995 under the title *Upgrade or Repair Your PC.*

2 3 4 5 6 7 8 9 0   DOC/DOC 9 0 2 1 0 9 8   (hc)
2 3 4 5 6 7 8 9 0   DOC/DOC 9 0 2 1 0 9 8   (sc)

P/N 050236-6   P/N 050237-4
PART OF   PART OF
ISBN 0-07-913667-2 (hc)   ISBN 0-07-913668-0 (sc)

The sponsoring editor for this book was Scott L. Grillo, the editing supervisor was Paul R. Sobel, and the production supervisor was Pamela A. Pelton. It was set in Vendome ICG by Jennifer Dougherty and Joanne Morbit of McGraw-Hill's Professional Book Group composition unit, Hightstown, N.J.

Printed and bound by R. R. Donnelley & Sons Company.

CONTENTS

v

Contents

Contents

Contents

Contents

Contents

INTRODUCTION

One of the reasons you are looking at this Upgrade book right now is because you want to save some money. How much you can save depends on a lot of things which will be discussed in later chapters.

There are over 150 million computers in existence throughout the world. Most of them are obsolete in some way or other. But they should not be scrapped because most of them can easily be upgraded to take advantage of the new technologies and software.

Software upgrades are as necessary as hardware upgrades. I can guarantee that you can save several hundred dollars on your software upgrades.

Hands On

If you are in a book store, if you look around you may see several books about computer Upgrade and Repair. Go ahead look at them. Most of them will have a lot of generalities and specifications, but they won't tell you how to take a specific computer and do a specific upgrade on it. This is a hands on book. There are lots of easy to understand instructions and lots of photos. Computers are really very simple. They are made up of modular components that just plug together. You will be able to perform all of the upgrades yourself. In doing so, you will learn first hand about your computer. There is no better teacher than experience.

If you have an older computer that needs to be upgraded, look in the index. You will probably find a reference to a page number that can tell you how to upgrade your computer. Try the same thing in the other Upgrade books.

Why Upgrade?

Why upgrade? One reason is to save money. If you had lots of money you probably wouldn't even think about upgrading an older computer.

You would probably give your old one to your butler, then you would go out and buy the very best PC and the latest software that money could buy. Or if you really had lots of money, you would probably hire someone to go buy it for you.

Unfortunately, there are not many people who have that kind of money. Most of us have to try to save money wherever we can. This book can help you. You can upgrade an older computer to be equivalent to the best on the market without having to spend a fortune. Computers are made up of modular units and components. The units and components are standardized so you can remove and replace any or all of them very easily.

So you don't have to junk your old PC and spend a lot of money on a new one. Even if you know nothing at all about computers, this book can show you how to upgrade them.

Another very big reason to upgrade is so that you can take advantage of all the newer software. Most of the software being developed today works with Windows, specifically, Windows 95. If your computer is less than a 486, you may not be able to run the newer programs. Even a 486 may be slow and sluggish running some programs. If you are going to upgrade, I would recommend a Pentium, or Pentium class Cyrix or AMD motherboard or system.

How Much Can You Save

Since the titles of all my books include the phrase **And Save A Bundle**, I am often asked just how much one can save. Of course the answer depends on many different things: where the person shops, how well they shop and whether they buy brand names or clone products and the type of upgrade or repairs that they want. Another variable that makes it difficult to determine how much one can save is the fact that the prices continue to go down.

One writer claimed that you would not be able to save much at all in building your own computer. He used the comparison of buying computer components to that of buying the components to assemble a Chevrolet. Of course if you were buying individual parts for a Chevy, it would cost five to ten times more than what a new car would cost. But there is only one company who manufactures the parts for a Chevy. There are hundreds of vendors who manufacture the components for computers, all competing against one another for your dollar. It is a very competitive business. If a vendor assembles a system like this, he has to charge more to cover his overhead and expenses.

We have to tell you though that there are some vendors who assemble computers in their bedrooms, or some other place where they have very little overhead. They are then able to offer these computers at very attractive prices. I would be hard pressed to assemble a computer for the price of some of the no-name computers.

You should be aware that some of the components in these low cost machines are not exactly high quality. They may work fine, or they may fail in just a few days. If one of these low cost units does fail, it may be difficult to get the small vendor to repair it.

The Benefits of Doing It Yourself

There are several advantages of doing your own upgrade. One is that you can put only the components that you want into your computer. In doing it yourself, you will know the quality of the parts that are in it. One other very big advantage is that you usually get some kind of documentation with a component that you buy. If you buy a fully assembled computer, you may get no documentation for the individual components in it.

New Life For an Old Chip

Intel usually introduces a new bigger and more powerful chip about every two or three years. When the new chip comes out, the older chips become obsolete almost overnight. The Intel Pentium with 3.1 million transistors was introduced in March, 1993. When the Pentium Pro with 5.5 million transistors was introduced in 1995, everybody clamored for this more powerful and faster CPU. Like the XT, the 286, the 386 and 486, the once most powerful Pentium began the inevitable slide down the slippery slope to obsolence. But then something happened in late 1996 to give new life to the Pentium. Intel added the MMX technology to the dying Pentium.

This was a set of 57 instructions added to the CPU. MMX was said to represent Multimedia Extensions. The 57 instructions are designed to increase the speed of processing certain multimedia tasks. MMX technology can also increase the processing speed of many software programs even those not designed for it. The MMX CPUs can be almost as fast as the Pentium Pros, but much less expensive. Intel breathed new life into the Pentium, but this new life was only a temporary reprieve. Soon after the Pentium MMX upgrade, Intel introduced their Pentium Pro upgrade with MMX and called it Pentium II.

The Pentium II will run at 233MHz, 266MHz and 300MHz. The Advanced Micro Devices (AMD) and Cyrix also introduced similar CPUs but priced them about 25 percent lower than the Intel Pentium II.

The Pentium class CPUs, including those from Cyrix and AMD are still very good tools and can do just about everything that most people want from a computer. But if you are an elitist, they are passe. If you just want to save a bit of money and still have a good computer, they may be all you need.

An Example of How You Can Save

So here is an example of how one could save. Say you have an old 486, but you would like to have a new 200MHz Pentium MMX. Something like this would cost as much as $2500 to $3500 or more depending on the goodies installed. If you tried to sell the old 486 computer, you might not get more than $200 or $300 for it. However, if you spent about $600 for a 200MHz MMX Pentium class CPU and motherboard, you could have a new Pentium that would be every bit as good as the $2500 new machine. If you bought one of the Cyrix or AMD equivalent CPUs and motherboard, it would cost even less.

You would probably want to install a larger hard drive. You can get a 2Gb hard drive for less than $200. I have seen 6Gb drives for about $300. You may also want to install a faster CD-ROM. Depending on the speed, it may cost from $50 to $150. No computer is complete today without a fast modem. You can buy a 33.6K for about $50. At the time of this writing, no standards have been approved for the newer 56K modems. There should be a standard by the time you read this. So for less than $1200 you could upgrade the old 486 into a $2500 machine.

It would take you less than an hour to replace the motherboard. In that one hour you could save about $1300. Which is pretty good for that much time.

Troubleshooting

This book will also show you how to troubleshoot and find the cause of most common computer problems. Once you know what the problem is, it is easy to repair the computer.

We have to be honest though and tell you that you will not find the answer or cause to all of the problems. There are thousands and thousands of little things that can go wrong with a computer. For instance, I installed a copy of Quicken on my computer. Later I tried to access the internet but was unable to do so. At first I had no idea what was causing the problem. But since Quicken was the last thing that I had installed, I figured it must be the culprit. After several hours of telephone calls, I was told that a copy of Netscape is automatically installed when Quicken is installed, unless you tell it not to. I already had Netscape on my computer that was used for my internet. When the second copy was loaded, it caused a conflict so that neither one would operate.

I worked in the electronic industry for over thirty years before I retired so I know that sometimes it is very difficult to find the trouble. A thousand and one things can go wrong. I hope that this doesn't discourage you. One of the reasons to do your own upgrading is to learn what is in the computer so that it will be easier to troubleshoot and repair.

If your PC breaks down, it would be nice if you could have a repairman come out to your office or home to fix it. But you would probably have about as much luck getting a repairman to make a housecall as getting a doctor to make a housecall. If you take it to a shop to be fixed, it may cost from $50 to $100 an hour just for labor. Parts will be extra. Just taking your computer to a repair shop can be a real chore if you live in a large city. When it comes to repair shops or any good sale, you will have to contend with Pilgrim's law. This law dictates that no matter where you live, the repair shop, sale or whatever you need, will be on the other side of town. If you live in an area such as Los Angeles, that can be quite a distance. When you get there, all of the parking spots near the shop will be occupied. The nearest parking spot will be about a half mile away. You park and lug your computer to the shop. Just as you get to the door you will find that several people have decided to vacate the parking spots in front of the shop.

The dealer will look your computer over, then give you an estimate for the cost. Of course the cost will always exceed the estimate. You will probably have to leave your computer in the shop. You will be given an estimate of when it will be done. Don't expect it to be done by the time given.

You may also decide to call the vendor and see if the problem can be solved over the telephone. Lots of luck. When you call you will probably spend five to ten minutes playing telephone roulette. You will be offered a recorded menu of four or five choices. Any choice that you choose will bring up another menu of four or five choices. You may spend hours on the phone making choices, but never get to speak to a live person. No matter how many choices you are given, the odds are that none of them will come close to solving your problem.

This book will show you how you can avoid many of these problems. It will show you how to find the cause of most common problems or find defective components. You don't have to be an engineer or skilled technician to add or replace components in a PC or to repair a PC. There are lots of clear instructions and photos in this book. You can do it yourself.

Types of Upgrades

There are two main types of upgrades, hardware and software. The first part of this book will deal primarily with hardware type upgrades. The second part will be mostly about newer and better software.

Compatible Components

One of the fantastic advantages of the PC is that the components are all interchangeable. The components, such as the disk drives, the keyboards, modems and others, used in an old 286 can also be used in the latest Pentium MMX or Pentium II. Since the components are all interchangeable, it is very easy to plug in a new board, or faster modem. You can easily upgrade an older computer in thousands of ways. But the cost of most components have gone down so much, it may be better to toss some of the older components and install new ones.

Upgrading Your Peripherals

Besides upgrading your computer, you will find information on how you can upgrade your peripherals. The peripherals are such components as your monitor, printer, keyboard, scanner, modem/fax, floppy drives, hard drives, CD-ROM, sound cards, and many other items. Upgrading these items can make your computer work better, faster and give you more versatility and utility.

Software Upgrades

You will also find information about upgrading to the latest software. You must have software to run your computer. By using the suggestions in Chapter Seventeen, you can save several hundred dollars. This chapter alone can save you several times over what this book costs. There are thousands and thousands of software packages, so I can't list them all. But there are some short reviews and recommendations for the more essential software.

Do You Need to Upgrade?

Some people are still driving around in ten year old cars. The old car gets them to where they want to go. And it is usually paid for. There are other people who wouldn't be caught dead in an old car. They must have a brand new car every year.

When it comes to computers there are many people who are the same. There are some who are still using computers that are ten years old. I have a friend who has a small business. He is still using an old XT and programs like dBASE II and WordStar 3.0. This computer and software programs does all that he needs to do. He is perfectly happy with his system. He could easily afford the newer systems. But most of them come with newer software and hardware. The newer systems are bigger and better, but the person may have to learn new ways of doing things. Just learning to use a new word processor may be as difficult as learning a new language. If the old system does everything you need, maybe you don't need to upgrade. Just don't tell your friends and neighbors that you are using an old system or they may laugh and make fun of you.

The B-B Gene

There are other people who must have the biggest, most powerful and fastest computer available, even if they have to hock the family jewels and take out a second mortgage on their home.

I am convinced that there is a gene, as yet undiscovered, that influences and controls those people who must have the biggest, the best and the most expensive of everything available. This includes cars, homes, fancy clothes and even computers.

When this gene is finally discovered and documented, I suggest that it be called the Biggest and Best gene or the B-B gene.

There is little doubt in my mind that this gene exists in all of us. But it exerts a far greater influence over some than others.

Many of the people who are influenced by the B-B gene are also quite willing to pay exorbitant prices for goods that they perceive to be better than others simply because of a brand name or because it is first on the market. I have never had much money, so I try to make sure that I get all of the value I can for my few dollars. That is why it is difficult for me to understand why a person would pay three or four times as much for such things as a purse or shoes or jeans simply because the products have a well advertised brand name. The same goes for computers. I don't understand why some people will buy a computer just because it has an IBM or Apple logo. For the price of an IBM or Apple, you may be able to buy two or three equivalent compatible, no-name computers.

One of the large computer magazines recently did a comparison test in their laboratory. They found that the no-name ISA compatible clones performed as well as or better than the high cost brand name computers.

Please don't misunderstand. I think the B-B gene is a good thing. I am influenced by it myself when it comes to computers. Without it, there would not be much progress and innovation. Without the B-B gene we might all still be living in caves and using stone tools. Without that B-B gene we probably wouldn't have all of the many computer goodies that are available to us.

Some Reasons You Need to Upgrade

That B-B gene may not be exerting much influence on you, and your old computer may be doing everything you want it to do. Still there are a few reasons why you should consider updating.

Time

One of the foremost reasons is time. The old XT lumbered along at a speed of only 4,770,000 cycles per second (4.77MHz). It could run most of the DOS programs, but it sometimes took hours to complete. The Pentium Pro and some of the other new CPUs can process data at a speed up to 300,000,000 cycles per second (300MHz). The Pentium II can process data several hundred times faster than the old XT.

Time is important to all of us. We have so little of it. If you are wasting time while your old computer is struggling to run a simple program, then you should consider upgrading.

Software Driven Upgrades

You will need to upgrade your hardware system to run some of the newer software programs. Some of them simply will not run on the older machines such as the XT, 286 and 386. Some will not even run very well on a 486. There are some excellent newer programs that can make computing much easier and faster. There are thousands of new applications being developed every day. An old computer may be causing you to miss out on a lot of goodies.

Many software programs may cost from $500 to $1000. But some of the programs are so difficult that you have to spend an additional $500 to $1000 for classes and instructions on how to learn and use them. Hundreds of companies make a good business holding seminars that teach people how to use these high cost programs. There will also be several books written for each of the popular programs that will teach you how to use them. All of these programs come with instruction manuals. The programs also usually have extensive on-disk help. If the manuals and help files were any good, there would be no need for the extra books and the seminars.

The software developers are trying to remedy this situation. They are trying very hard to make the software programs user friendly and easier to learn and use. But there is still a price to pay. To make them easier to use, the programs must be larger and they require more memory and disk space.

Of course, the software developers are adding much more functionality and more utility to the programs which makes them larger. To install and run some of the newer programs requires 80Mb to 100Mb of disk space. You will also need a minimum of 16Mbs of RAM, even better is 32Mb.

Used Computers

This book will show you how to upgrade or repair your older computer to bring it up to date with the newest technologies. If you don't have an older computer to upgrade, don't let that stop you. Buy a used one and upgrade it.

The only trouble with buying a used computer is that you might have trouble finding one. I live in the Los Angeles area, but when I check the classified ads for computers, I seldom see more than two or three IBM or compatibles listed.

Over 200 million computers have been sold in the last 15 years. Evidently everybody is holding on to the old ones. They may be upgrading them or they are passing their old ones on to the kids or relatives and buying new ones. Many large companies are buying newer, bigger, better, and faster systems for the engineers and personnel who need them. But they don't get rid of the older ones. The companies just pass the old computers down the line to the personnel and departments who were doing without computers. Of course, an old 386 or 486 is better than no computer at all. Besides, many of those people probably don't need the high power and speed of the new Intel Pentium II, the AMD K6 or the Cyrix M2.

Perhaps one reason that you don't see too many used computers for sale is that computers are built primarily from semiconductors. If a system is designed properly, a transistor should last for several lifetimes. Of course, the disk drives, keyboards, and other components with moving parts will eventually wear out. But most of them can be easily replaced. It is very easy to upgrade an older computer.

Beware of Used Mechanical Items

It is perfectly okay to buy anything electronic that is working. But I would strongly advise against buying a used printer, disk drives, or anything that is mechanical. As I said earlier, the semiconductors do not wear out, but the mechanical components have a finite lifetime and will eventually fail. According to Murphy's law, they will usually fail at the most inopportune time.

Of course, if you find a mechanical component that is almost new, and you get a good buy on it, then go ahead. There are several companies who buy older hard disk drives and printers and re-build them. They often sell them for a very reasonable price. If you can get a good warranty on these products, they should be all right.

Buying a Bare-Bones Unit

You might consider buying a bare-bones system and building it up yourself. A bare-bones unit usually consists of a case, motherboard, and power supply. In order to have a functioning computer, you would need disk drives, a keyboard, a monitor and several other goodies. But you could buy them from different sources at the best price you can find. You wouldn't have to buy them all at once. You could gradually build your system as you could affort it. You can still save money, and you will have put together your own computer. If it doesn't suit you, then you will have only one person to blame.

Sources and Resources

There are very few companies today who do not have a web site on the World Wide Web. The Companies will list their products, specifications, where you can find the products, and just about anything you need to know. For most companies, use Netscape or Microsoft Internet Explorer or any other browser, then type www.companyname.com. Most of them are also set up for e-mail. E-mail is almost instantaneous. Besides, you don't have to have stamps.

One of the best upgrades you can make is to get a good fast modem.

Compatibility

A few years ago, IBM compatibility was essential. Clones or IBM compatible computers are now called Industry Standard Architecture (ISA) computers. IBM compatibility is not a problem today. There are billions of dollars worth of ISA hardware and software today. All of these components and software will operate on any of the ISA machines. You will have a vast number of products to choose from for you upgrades.

Organization of the Book

One of the problems in writing a book is that you don't know how much your readers already know. If you make it too simple, it will discourage the old pros. If you make it too technical, it will be over the heads of the new-comers. I try to take the middle ground throughout the book.

Another difficulty in writing a book like this is that the industry has grown so much that it is almost impossible to cover everything. In the medical field, there are specialists who concentrate on one area of the body. The human body is so complex that no one person can know all there is to know about the whole body. The computer industry is almost to that point. Already there are people who specializie in communications, networking and desktop publishing to name just a few. There are also different areas of programming that call for specialists. My point is that I have tried to cover as much as I could, but it is impossible for me to put everything that you or someone else may want in this book. If I could do that, then there would be no need for all of those other books. I am sure the bookstores would not like that.

I have used plain English throughout this book and tried to avoid using computer jargon unless it is absolutely necessary. In some cases, there is no other way. I have included a comprehensive glossary in the back of the book. If you come across something that is unfamiliar, check for definition in the glossary.

In the first part of each chapter, I will try to explain a bit about that particular component. Then at the end of the chapter, I will have detailed instructions about how to install it. If you are an old pro, you may want to skip ahead to the end of the chapters.

We Have Come a Long Way

In the old days there were three major car companies. It was easy to identify almost any car by manufacturer and year and model. Now there are hundreds of models and they all look pretty much the same. It has gotten almost to that point with the CPUs.

The Intel, AMD and Cyrix companies manufacture several versions of each of their CPUs. The CPUs are usually rated by the frequency at which they operate. They may have versions that operate from 75MHz up to 266MHz. The original 8088 CPU was a single version with an operating frequency of 4.77MHz. What a vast difference in that and the newer 266MHz. The original 8088 had 29,000 transistors. Intel has said that they will have CPUs with over 100 million transistors by the year 2000.

The computer industry is one of the fastest changing of any technology. I discuss many of the new and improved products in this book, but I can't possibly even list them all. Such a book could never be complete because thousands of new products are introduced every day.

You can be sure that faster, more powerful, and more useful computers will be on the market by the time you read this, but that doesn't mean that you should wait for the newest development. Remember, there will always be newer ones out tomorrow. Besides, maybe you don't really need the newest, the fastest and the most powerful computer. Perhaps you can get by with one that is almost the fastest and most powerful.

There is one truth that no one can dispute: technology does not stand still. Since the discovery of the transistor just a little over 40 years ago, there have been more technological advances than in the previous 4000 years. And it shows no signs of slowing down. These are wonderful times that we are living in.

You Can Do It

Some of the hottest selling books on the market today are those written for Dummies. I belong to Mensa, but I have bought copies of most of these books. Some of them have some very good information, but they are usually overly simplistic and leave out a lot of important information. I love books and have hundreds in my office. One of the books that is directly opposite of the Dummies books is Upgrading and Repairing PCs by Scott Mueller. Scott's books usually have about 1400 pages and covers all the specifications of just about every computer ever built, even those that have been obsolete for several years. His books are highly technical and very good for reference. His books are excellent, but they are quite different from my book. My book is more of a hands on book for the average person. My book covers both hardware and software.

The main point made in most of those Dummies books is that you don't have to belong to Mensa to use, repair or upgrade a computer. But despite all my assurances, some of you may still have doubts or fears that you cannot do an upgrade or repair. Don't worry. It does not require a lot of expertise. Computer assemblies require no soldering or electronic test equipment or instruments. Computers are made up of modular components that just plug in or connect together by cables. Please believe me, you can do it. And save a bundle.

I talked earlier about the benefits of doing your own upgrade and how much you can save. There are other benefits that you can't put a price on. One of the biggest benefits of doing it yourself is that you will learn a bit about your computer. Another fantastic benefit that you will receive is the feeling of accomplishment that you will get because you did it yourself.

Another Reason to Upgrade

If you are trying to get by with an old computer, your so-called "friends" may snicker and laugh at you behind your back. They may brag about their bigger and better computer and do everything possible to make you feel like a computer illiterate novice.

By spending a little money, you can upgrade your older computer to match any of the bigger and better ones. Then you too can join the elite crowd and look down your nose at anyone who doesn't have the biggest and best.

Acknowledgments

I want to thank Scott Grillo and Paul Sobel, the editors at McGraw-Hill, for their suggestions and help in putting this edition together.

I also want to thank Danny Hsu of Micronics for pulling some strings and getting a new Stingray Pentium II motherboard to me for the Chapter on Building a Dream Machine.

AUBREY PILGRIM

UPGRADE
AND REPAIR
YOUR PC

What's Inside

Why You Need to Upgrade

In the introduction, I explained several reasons why you should upgrade. Some people don't bother to read introductions, so I'll briefly recap the reasons here.

The first and foremost reason is that, whether you like it or not, we are in a Windows World. There is very little software developed today for anything other than Windows, more specifically, Windows 95. If you have an older computer, you might not be able to take advantage of all the good stuff that is available. There are some fantastic Windows software programs.

You could just go out and buy a complete new system, but you might not have the money for that. Depending on what you want to do with your computer, you can easily upgrade it to do just about anything you want at a very reasonable price.

The absolute minimum for running Windows 95 is a 386DX with about 8Mb of RAM and a 250Mb hard disk. This minimum system would not be able to run everything available. But a 386 might be so slow that you might nod off and go to sleep just waiting for a program to be processed.

A better system would be a 486DX running at a minimum of 66MHz, with 16Mb of DRAM and a 1Gb hard disk. Still better would be a Pentium MMX system running at about 166MHz with 32Mb of DRAM and a 2Gb hard disk. The best would be a Pentium II running at 266MHz with 64Mb of DRAM and a couple of 6Gb hard drives.

The MMX Technology

One of the major reasons to upgrade is the MMX technology. The Pentium CPUs had become almost obsolete and as dead as Lazarus. But Intel did a remarkable job of reviving and resurrecting them with the MMX technology. Below are a couple of press releases from Intel:

> Multimedia and communications are driving today's and tomorrow's most exciting and computer-intensive applications. MMX technology is a new extension to the Intel Architecture, which will enhance the performance of these applications, and enable altogether new features and capabilities.

> Intel's MMX technology is designed to accelerate the key elements of demanding multimedia and communications applications, such as audio,

video, 2D- and 3D-graphics, animation, and recognition. The technology introduces new instructions and data types that exploit the parallelism inherent in many media processing algorithms, yet maintains full compatibility with existing applications and operating system software.

It features 57 new instructions, 8 new 64-bit wide registers, and 4 new data types. Integer data, either bytes, 16-bit words, dwords, or a quadword, are packed into the 64-bit registers upon which the MMX instructions operate. A single MMX instruction operates on all elements of the 64-bit register in parallel, providing throughput improvement of as much as 8x for byte operations.

MMX technology uses general-purpose instructions, most of which operate in a single clock cycle. Instruction types supported include the following: basic arithmetic operations (such as add, subtract, multiply, etc.), logical operations (such as AND, OR, AND NOT, etc.), compare operations, conversion instructions to pack and unpack data elements, shift operations, and data movement instructions.

Those who use notebook computers can benefit as well from the Pentium processor with MMX technology. Applications designed for MMX technology desktop computers are also available to the mobile user. Examples of such applications include video conferencing over standard telephone lines, software-based video and 3D graphics, and digital image editing and communications. Notebook manufacturers will continue to keep pace with desktop computers not only in performance, but in significant enhancements such as MMX technology.

MMX technology maintains complete compatibility with the Intel Architecture and is also fully compatible with widely used operating systems and application software. The technology will be included in future processors, including Pentium OverDrive processors for upgradable Pentium processor-based systems.

Intel was first with the MMX technology, but Cyrix and AMD have MMX systems that match the Intel systems at a much lower price. Chapters 4 and 5 detail more about MMX.

Most companies now have web sites on the World Wide Web. These sites offer a wealth of information about their products, where you can purchase them, along with the latest press releases and news. To find out more about the MMX technologies, if you have a modem, Intel has a web site at www.intel.com, tel. 408-765-8203. Cyrix has a site at www.cyrix.com, tel. 214-968-8388. AMD has a site at www.amd.com, tel. 408-749-3060.

Major Computer Components

There are only a few major components in a computer such as the motherboard, plug-in boards, memory, disk drives, and power supply. When you pull the cover off, most computers will look pretty much the same, whether it be an old 286 or a powerful Pentium II. This chapter briefly describes the basic components you'll find inside. Each component is discussed in detail in later chapters. This chapter talks about the few tools needed to upgrade, how to remove the cover, how to identify the major components, and how to remove and replace them.

The chapter ends with a brief explanation of how computers work. If you are fairly new to computers, this can help you. If you are an old pro, you might want to skip that section.

When you remove the cover of your old computer, you will see a lot of cables and plug-in boards. You will also see one or more hard drives, one or more floppy drives and perhaps a CD-ROM drive. In one corner of the case, you will see a power supply. On the bottom of the case is the large motherboard. It will have several slots and other boards will be plugged into it.

It might look rather complicated and forbidding and you might hesitate trying to upgrade your system. But it is actually very simple. You can easily replace and upgrade any component in the computer. It is especially easy with the newer motherboards and components because they are all plug and play. In the old days, it was plug and pray. If you didn't set the switches and jumpers on the boards just right, you would have a lot of trouble making the system work properly. Now most boards have built-in firmware that can check the system and automatically configure the board or component properly. For instance, when you installed a hard disk a short time ago, you had to go into the CMOS setup and input the characteristics of the disk, the number of cylinders, number of heads, number of sectors, and several other specifications. Most systems can now automatically recognize all that information and automatically configure your CMOS.

Tools Needed

For the majority of all upgrading, the only tools needed are a couple of small screwdrivers. You should have a couple of different sized flat-blade screw drivers and Phillips-head screw drivers. Most of the computer systems use Phillips-type screws. Some use a Phillips-type head with a slot so that you can use either Phillips or a flat blade. Figure 1-1 shows some of the tools you might need.

Some systems use Phillips screws that also have a hexagonal head. You can use a $\frac{1}{4}$-inch nut driver on these type screws which makes it very easy to install or remove them.

You might find a few systems, such as Compaq, that use TORX screws. TORX screws are similar to the Phillips screws except that they have six slots. You might be able to remove them with a Phillips, but it is much easier with a proper sized TORX screw driver. The two sizes most often used are the T-10 and T-15.

If the screwdrivers are magnetized, it will help you to get the screws started. (Caution! Be very careful not to let a magnetized screwdriver or any magnet near your floppy disks. A magnet can erase them or partially destroy the data.)

Pliers

They might not be absolutely necessary, but you might need a pair of standard pliers and a pair of long-nose pliers. The long-nose pliers are very handy for retrieving dropped screws. The flat portion of the long-nose blades are also excellent for straightening the pins on integrated circuit (IC) chips or pins on connectors.

Fig. 1-1
Tools that you might need to upgrade your computer.

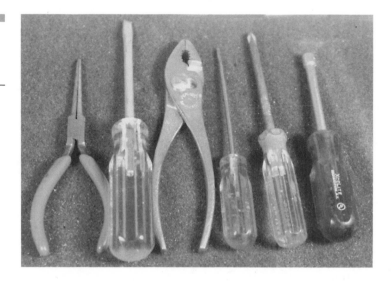

Flashlight

A flashlight or a good bench light is essential for trouble shooting and exploring your computer. A good magnifying glass also might come in handy for reading the types and part numbers on some of the chips.

Chip Pullers

Very seldom will you need to remove or replace a chip. Before removing any chip, make a diagram with the socket number found on the mother-board and the orientation of the chip. It is very easy to forget just where a chip belongs or how it should be oriented. To upgrade in the old days, you often had to remove and replace chips such as BIOS chips and mem-ory chips.

I once removed a couple of BIOS chips. There were four sockets on the motherboard, all exactly alike, but only two were used. When I got ready to replace the BIOS chips, I couldn't remember which sockets they came out of. Fortunately, I had documentation for the motherboard that showed the BIOS sockets. It would have saved me a lot of time if I had made a simple note before I removed the chips.

I haven't removed and changed a chip in a long time. Now most of the BIOS chips are made with flash memory. They can easily be upgraded by downloading a file with a modem or from a floppy disk.

Removing the Cover

The first thing to do before removing the cover, is to remove the power from the unit. Unplug the monitor, keyboard, and any other cables from the unit. But before unplugging any cable, make sure that the con-nectors and cables are plainly marked so that you can plug them back together properly. If the cables are not marked, take some masking tape or a felt marking pen and label each cable and connector. If there is a chance that any connector might be plugged in improperly, place a mark across both connectors so that the mark will line up when they are reconnected.

In the early days, we only had one or two different types of cases. Most of them were similar to the IBM-type XT or standard AT types. The covers of these cases are held in place by five screws on the back panel. There is one in each corner and one at the top center. When these screws are loosened, the cover can be slipped off toward the front.

There might be several other screws on the back panel. Some of them are for the power supply and various connectors. These screws should not be removed.

Many of the cases today are still similar to the old XT and AT types. But there are also many new styles available. Some are the low-profile and small footprint type. They all might use different methods of securing the cover.

The tower cases are about the same as the desktop cases, except that they stand on one side. There are usually six screws on the back that holds the cover in place. On most tower cases, the front bezel has a groove that accepts the front part of the cover so that no screws are needed in the front. It shouldn't be too difficult to determine which screws hold the covers on these various types of cases.

I often try out new boards and parts so I just leave the covers off my computers. Other than the messy look, it doesn't cause any problem. Actually, besides saving me time and trouble, leaving the covers off allows the system to run cooler.

Upgrading to a New Case and Power Supply

The desktop-type case is still quite popular. Most desktop types are limited to three or four bays for mounting disk drives. If you want to install two hard disk drives, a 1.44Mb floppy drive, and a CD-ROM drive, you will need one with at least four bays.

There are some low-profile type cases that are not even high enough to mount a vertical plug-in board. They usually have a single slot on the mother board and a daughterboard plugs into this slot. The daughterboard might have three to five slots for horizontally mounted plug-in boards. The low-profile cases limit the number of plug-in slots and also the number of drive bays available. Most of them will only have room for two drives, a single floppy and a hard drive.

I have no idea at all why they designed the low-profile cases. It doesn't save any desktop space, except for height. I don't mind height. I have several feet of empty space above my desktop. It is the space on my desktop that is at a premium. Despite the shortcomings of the low-profile case,

Compaq and some other companies are still offering computers crammed into them. The low-profile cases have little or no room to add any other boards or do any upgrading. If you are trying to upgrade a system with a low-profile case, I would recommend that you junk the case and make a new case a part of your upgrade. A new case might cost as little as $30; with the power supply, it might cost from $50 to $100.

The tower cases are very popular and handy. The tower case can sit on the floor and not use up any of your desktop space. The larger ones might have space for up to eight drive bays. This would provide room for up to four hard drives, a floppy drive, a tape backup, a couple of CD-ROM drives, and others.

The tower cases are a bit more expensive than the standard or the baby-size cases. There are three sizes of tower type cases: a mini tower for baby sizes, a medium size for baby and standard sizes, and a large standard size. The smaller sizes do not have as many bays for mounting drives. Most of the cases include a power supply with the cost. Make sure that any power supply is at least 200 watts, and 300 watts is even better. When you buy a new case, it will come with several small bags of screws, stand-offs, cables, and other necessary mounting hardware.

Static Electricity Warning

Caution! Once the cover is removed, before touching any of the components inside your computer, make sure that you discharge yourself of any static electricity. If you have ever walked across a carpeted room and got a shock when you touched a doorknob, you know what static electricity is. It is possible for a person's body to build up as much as 3000 volts or more of static electricity. If you touch any of the sensitive electronic components, that static electricity could be discharged through them. This static electricity could destroy or severely damage some circuits.

When you touch a metal door knob, you can discharge the static electricity. A much better discharge occurs if you touch something that goes directly to ground such as a water pipe. Because you probably don't have a water pipe near your computer, the next best thing is to touch a bare metal part of your computer.

The power switch on your computer should be unplugged from the wall. Even with the computer turned off, if it is plugged in, there could be a path through some of the very sensitive circuits.

Most boards and components will have a static electricity warning label on the packaging. In most cases you will have to break that warning label in order to open the package. It is a good idea to discharge yourself by touching something that is metal and grounded before handling any electronic component or board, especially if you have walked across a carpeted room.

Motherboard

Once the cover is removed, you will see several boards that are plugged into connectors on the large motherboard that sits on the floor of the chassis. There are usually eight slots on the motherboard for various types of plug-in boards. Here are some of the boards you might find in your computer: an adapter board for your monitor, a board for your printer (which might have connectors for a mouse, or other serial devices), a board for a modem and fax, one or more for your disk drive controllers, and perhaps several others.

Motherboard Slots

Most older motherboards will have eight plug-in Industry Standard Architecture (ISA) slots. (ISA is what was once known as the IBM-compatible standard.) Some later motherboards might have three or four ISA slots and three Video Electronics Standards Association (VESA) slots. You might also find some with Extended Industry Standard Architecture (EISA) slots. Many of the IBM machines had Micro Channel Architecture slots. (Chapter 5 details the motherboards and these different architectures and slots.) The motherboard slots, or connector receptacles, are for the various boards that you might want to use. Plug-in boards have an edge connector with copper-etched fingers that contact the spring-loaded contacts of the motherboard slot connectors.

The XT motherboard was 9 inches wide and 12 inches long. The original AT motherboard was 12 inches wide and 13 to 14 inches long. Later the Adaptec Company and some of the others began integrating several of the motherboard chips so that the size of the AT motherboard could be reduced to about the same size as the XT. They called these baby AT motherboards. Some of the early baby 286 and 386 motherboards had only seven slots. The early IBM PC had only five slots. Some high-end systems might have a motherboard with 12 slots.

The slots on these motherboards, whether the original AT size or the baby size, are placed so that they will line up with the openings in the back panel of the case, whether it be a large AT size, the XT size, or any of the tower cases.

If you have one of the older IBM PS/2 systems, there really isn't much available for upgrading them. You might be better off giving the system to your kids to play with or donate it to a charitable organization so that you can write it off on your taxes.

Motherboard Differences

The major difference between the XT, the 286, 386, 486, the Pentium, or the Pentium Pro is the motherboard and CPU. The 286 has six extra 36-pin slots above the standard eight 62-pin slots. The 386 motherboard often has four extra 36-pin slots and two extra 62-pin slots. The extra 36-pin slots are for 16-bit system boards. The two extra 62-pin slots on the 386 motherboard are for special proprietary 32-bit memory boards.

Having the 32-bit memory on a plug-in board had several disadvantages. It slowed the memory down a bit, it used up a precious slot, it was bulky, and there was little or no standardization. Later motherboard designs eliminated the extra 62-pin slots. Most motherboards now have sockets for single in-line memory modules (SIMMs). These memory sockets are tied directly to the CPU through a 32-bit bus.

The standard 62-pin slots on all of the motherboards are 8-bit slots. Boards developed to utilize the extra 36-pin slot are 16-bit boards. Notice that all of the 8-bit 62-pin slot connectors are separate from the extra 16-bit connector slots.

As you have probably deduced, an 8-bit plug-in board, even those designed for the antique XT, can also be used in any Industry Standard Architecture (ISA) or Extended ISA (EISA) computer. All 8-bit boards are compatible, even with the most powerful Pentium II. Of course a 16-bit board cannot be plugged into an XT.

If you have one of the older PCs, your motherboard might be mounted on nine standoffs. It might have nine screws or nuts on the bottom of the chassis and on top of the motherboard holding it in place.

Later systems had raised channels on the floor of the case. The channels had wide slots that became narrow to the right. Refer to Fig. 1-2.

Figure 1-3 shows a couple of brass white plastic standoff/retainers. These standoff/retainers are dropped into the wide portion of the slots on the raised channel. The motherboard is then pushed to the right and grooves on the plastic standoffs become engaged in the narrow portion of the channel slot. If you are upgrading an old XT, you might not be able to mount and install a new motherboard in that case. A new case might cost about $30.

A screw in the front center and one in the rear center are sufficient to hold the motherboard secure. To remove the motherboard, remove the two screws and pull the motherboard toward you until the standoffs are disengaged. Almost all cases now have a flat sheet metal panel on the bottom with slots that accept the plastic standoffs. Figure 1-4 shows the back side of a motherboard that is mounted in a newer case.

The Power Supply

If you have a desktop-type case, the power supply is located in the right-rear corner of the chassis. It has a chrome-plated cover around it. It has a cooling fan in it that generates the only noise that you hear, except for the disk drives, when your computer is running. The cooling fan sucks

Fig. 1-2
Floor of an older case showing the raised channels and slots of the standoffs.

Fig. 1-3
Brass and plastic
standoffs for
motherboard.

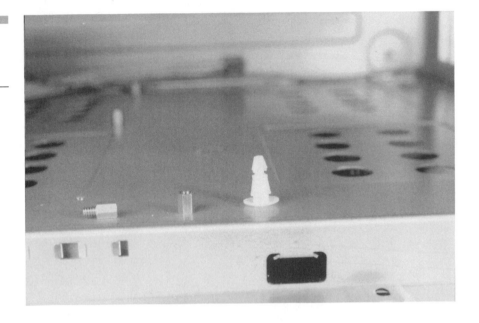

Fig. 1-4
The backside of
a motherboard
mounted in a case.
Notice the white
plastic standoffs in
the slots.

air in from the front of the computer and forces it out through the grill in the back of the power supply. All holes in the computer and blank slots in the back panel should be covered so that the air is drawn only from the front grill of the computer and drawn over the components. You should make sure that nothing in the front of the computer, or the back of it, will impede the air flow. The power supply usually has four screws on the back panel that holds it in place.

Transforming the Voltage

Computer systems use direct current (dc). The original systems used dc voltages of 12 Vdc and 5 Vdc. The CPUs used 5 volts. As more transistors were enclosed in the CPUs, the more current was used and the hotter the CPU became. Heat sinks and fans were used to keep the CPUs from burning up. The newer CPUs use a lower voltage, such as 3 volts, 2.5 volts, or 2.2 volts. By lowering the voltage, the current is lowered and they don't run quite as hot. But with the millions of transistors, they still need heat sinks and a special fan to keep them from burning up.

If you are upgrading an older system, you might have to buy a new power supply that can provide the required voltages. Some motherboards have special circuits built in for lowering the voltage and regulating it.

The voltage that is provided by the wall socket is usually 110 volts alternating current (ac). The computer power supply uses rectifiers and transformers to convert the ac voltage to the proper dc voltages.

The ac voltage that comes from the wall plug is alternating at 60 cycles per second, or 60 Hz. (Rudolph Heinrich Hertz (1857-1894) was a German physicist who was the first to produce artificial radio waves. In order to honor Hertz, a standards committee decreed that the frequency of cycles should be called *hertz*, abbreviated Hz. Many old timers still call it cycles per second.) To transform 110 volts at 60 Hz would require a large transformer. But a fairly small transformer can be used if the frequency is very high. Rectifiers are used to transform the ac to a 120 Hz chopped dc voltage. An oscillator circuit takes this 120 Hz chopped voltage and changes the frequency to a much higher frequency such as 50,000 Hz. The higher the frequency of the voltage, the smaller the transformer can be. This high-frequency voltage is input to a small transformer, which reduces the high frequency 110 volts to the required 12 volts, 5 volts, and lesser voltages.

Because the voltage that comes from the transformer is ac voltage, it is again rectified and made into dc voltage.

The 110 volts in the power supply is the only voltage in your computer that might harm you. That is one reason for the cover over it. Another reason for the cover is to reduce any stray radiation that might emanate from the high-frequency conversion process.

The early IBMs and most clones had a switch on the side of the power supply for turning on the computer. This switch turned the ac on and off. It was a bit inconvenient to reach around near the back of the computer to turn it on and off, so many of the newer systems have a switch on the front panel. There is usually a four-wire electrical cord that goes from the power supply to the switch. Often when you buy a new case, this switch is not connected to the power cord. The switch will have four terminals for the power connection. The four power cords connect to the switch terminals with slip-on connectors. Two of the four wires in the power cord brings 110 volts from the wall socket to the switch; the other two return the switched voltage back to the power supply. Care should be used in connecting the power to the switch. If it is not connected properly, it could cause a direct short across the power line. If you short the line out this way, you will see a lot of sparks, smoke, and maybe even a fire. You should get some documentation as to how the wires should be connected. The power supply might have a diagram showing how the switch should be connected.

Power Strip

You will have your computer, a monitor, a printer, and perhaps three or four more units to be plugged into the wall outlet. You should buy a power strip that has four or five outlets. They usually have a circuit breaker also in case of a power overload. Some have surge protection that can help protect your computer and the delicate electronics in it. Some low-cost strips might cost as little as $5, some might cost $25 or more.

The Disk Drive Bays

Depending on the type of case that you have, you might have bays for a two floppy disk drives and one or two hard drives. The bays for the floppy drives are accessible from the front. The hard drive bays might not be accessible once the cover is installed. If you have an older case, you might not have enough bays to hold all the drives that are now needed. The newer cases have four or more accessible bays from the front so that you can install one or two floppy drives, one or two CD-ROM drives, a hard disk drive with removable cartridges, perhaps a tape backup system, or some other type of drive. There would also be space for internally mounting four or more hard disks.

You might have an older case that only has two accessible bays that is occupied by a $5\frac{1}{4}$ inch and a $3\frac{1}{2}$ inch floppy drive. By all means, you need to install a CD-ROM drive. You might consider buying a combination floppy drive that has both $5\frac{1}{4}$ and $3\frac{1}{2}$ inch drives integrated into one system. But the $5\frac{1}{4}$ inch floppy systems are now obsolete. If you still have lots of stuff on these old floppies, it might be a good idea to copy it all to $3\frac{1}{2}$ inch floppies. You could then remove the $5\frac{1}{4}$ inch drive and use it for a door stop or a boat anchor.

The drive bays in the older cases might have slots and holes for mounting the drives. The drives will have several screw holes on their sides that will match up with the holes in the bays.

Some of the older cases have slots for using plastic or metal slides. The slides are attached to the drives. The drives are then inserted in the slots and pushed to the rear of the bay. A couple of screws or small flanges are then used to hold the drives in place.

The cases are not very expensive. If your old case doesn't allow for expansion to hold all the newer things needed, I would recommend that you buy a new case.

Cost of Components

Again, all of the PCs, even the Pentium and the Pentium Pro, use the same basic components except for the motherboard and the CPU. Because the common components are all interchangeable, you can shop around for the best buys. You can look at the ads in computer magazines, such as the *Computer Shopper, PC Magazine, PC World, PC Computing,* and others for an idea of what is available. These ads will also give you an idea of the cost of the various components and options. You can order the components through the mail, or if you live near a large city, go to a swap meet or to a local store.

It is almost impossible to put a real cost on components. The prices change daily, usually downward. A few approximate costs are listed for comparison purposes. There are hundreds of different manufacturers and many, many options, so the prices will vary. To get a better idea of the cost, look through computer magazines. Of course, brand names and the type of component will be a factor.

There will be a large variation in the cost of motherboards, depending on the brand name and CPU manufacturer. The cost will vary considerably depending on the operating frequency of the CPU; the higher the frequency, the higher the cost.

I paid $1850 for my first 386DX motherboard and CPU. It operated at only 16 MHz. My first 25-MHz 486 cost me $4450. You can buy a 200-MHz Pentium motherboard and CPU for less than $1000 today.

In Table 1-1 are some approximate prices of other common components. These prices are listed to give you an idea of what a basic system might cost at the time this book was written. The prices will change, usually downward, by the time you read this.

TABLE 1-1	Power supply and case	35-150
Component prices.	Motherboard, no CPU	75-300
	CPU, Intel, Cyrix, AMD	75-1000
	Monitor	200-1200
	Monitor adapter	40-400
	Memory, 16-32Mb	75-150
	Floppy drive, 1.4Mb	25-50
	Hard drive, 1Gb-2Gb	150-300
	CD-ROM drive	50-200
	Keyboard	20-150
	Mouse	10-100
	Modem	50-150
	Total	$805-4150

As you can see, there can be quite a large variation in the cost. The cost depends on several available options and whether the components have well-known brand names. There is also a large variation in cost from dealer to dealer. Some of the high-volume dealers might charge less than the smaller ones, so it pays to shop around a bit and compare prices. These figures are only rough approximations. The market is so volatile that the prices can change overnight. If you are buying through the mail, you might even call or check out the advertised prices before ordering. Often the advertisements have to be made up one or two months before the magazine is published, so the prices could have changed considerably.

At one time, Intel was the only manufacturer of the ISA-type CPUs. But Cyrix and AMD ISA CPU clones are now on the market. The Cyrix and AMD CPUs are equivalent to the Intel chips, but usually sell for about 25% less than the Intel chips. This added competition will force the CPU prices down even more. When the CPU prices go down, the motherboard prices usually go down.

Options

There are several common components that are not absolutely necessary for a system. If you don't need a lot of goodies at this time, you can buy the minimum components and add to your system later. You might not need two 1Gb hard disk drives to start out. You can always add one or more later.

Memory

When a computer runs a program, the program is temporarily loaded into memory and processed there. When the processing is completed, it is then loaded back on the hard disk, printed out, or sent to wherever you want it to go.

At one time we got by with as little as 64K of RAM memory. It is now difficult to run most programs with less than 16Mb of RAM. Better yet is 32Mb or 64Mb. You can start out with 16Mb and add more later. You cannot have too much money or memory.

On the older systems, the memory chips were usually located in the left-front quadrant of the motherboard. They used the dual in-line pins (DIP) type of chips. Chips to make 640K used about one-fourth of the entire motherboard real estate. Most systems today use the single in-line memory module (SIMM) or the dual in-line memory module (DIMM) type memory. These are small boards that have miniature chips on them. The board has an edge connector that plugs into special sockets on the motherboard. The SIMM and DIMM technologies allows up to 128Mb or more memory in a much smaller area than 640K required on the older motherboards that used the DIP chips.

A few of the older motherboards used a single in-line pin (SIP) type of memory. These are miniature chips mounted on a board and are very similar to the SIMM technology except that the boards have pins that plug into special sockets. The SIP type of memory is obsolete.

There are many different types of memory. Chapter 6 goes into detail about the many types.

Floppy Disk Drives

If you have a really old system, you might have one or two 360K floppy drives. At one time an IBM 360K floppy drive cost over $400. Today they are completely obsolete. You might still have some data on 360K floppies. If you insist on keeping these floppies, I would recommend that you buy a $5\frac{1}{4}$ inch 1.2Mb and a $3\frac{1}{2}$ inch 1.44Mb drive combination drive. The 1.2Mb drive will read and write to both the 360K and 1.2Mb floppies. You might even have some old $3\frac{1}{2}$ inch 720K floppies with data on them. The 1.44Mb drive will read and write to the 720K as well as the 1.44Mb drive.

If you have an old system, it probably had a floppy drive controller (FDC) board. Most all motherboards now have the disk controller built in. If so, there will be a double row of upright pins for connecting the disk drives. See chapter 7 for more details on floppy drives.

Hard Disk Drives

The original PC had a tape recorder for storing data. Later one or two single-sided floppy disk drives were added. It wasn't until the XT was introduced did we have a hard disk drive. After having to get by with the floppy disks, a 10Mb hard drive was almost like heaven. My first one cost over $500 and only lasted a short time before it burned out some of the onboard chips. I got it repaired, but I lost a lot of data. Because I had to contend with the early systems, I can really appreciate the magnitude of improvements that we have today.

Most of the older systems used the MFM, RLL, or ESDI type hard drives. They were physically large, clunky, and slow. They were also very limited in storage capacity. One of my early hard disk drives was 40Mb.

It was three inches high, six inches wide, and eight inches long. I paid almost $1000 for it. Because DOS 2.0 could only handle 32Mb, I had to buy special software in order to use the full 40Mb. A couple of years ago, I bought a 1.050 gigabyte (Gb) drive for $740. It is one inch high, four inches wide, and six inches long. I can buy the same drive today for about $150.

There are several hard disk manufacturers with hundreds of different models, sizes, and types of hard disks. The older hard drives needed a controller board that plugs into one of the slots. Often the controllers were made by companies other than the ones who manufactured the hard drives.

The integrated disk electronics (IDE) drives have all of the controller electronics on the drive itself. It still needs an interface to the system. The older systems used a low-cost interface that plugged into one of the slots. This interface is now built-in on most all motherboards as upright pins that accept the hard drive cable. In fact, most of them now have two sets of pins and can handle up to four IDE hard drives or a combination of hard drives and CD-ROM drives.

The *Small Computer System Interface* (SCSI, pronounced scuzzy) also has all of its controller functions on the disk. It also needs an interface card, but a SCSI card can handle up to seven different devices.

If you have one of the older hard disks, you should consider upgrading to one of the newer ones with a larger capacity. You just cannot have too much disk storage. You could keep your old hard disk drive and use it as a back up for a newer larger capacity hard drive.

It would be a good idea to install an IDE hard drive and a SCSI hard drive. One advantage of this type system is that you can use the two drives to back up each other. It is possible that one of the drives might crash or fail, but it is not very likely that both will fail.

If you are upgrading to a newer hard drive, I would recommend that you get at least 1Gb, or even larger if you can afford it. Some of the hard disk manufacturers are no longer manufacturing hard disk drives with a capacity less than 1Gb.

Backup

It is very important that you keep copies or backups of all of your software programs and important data. You never know when your hard disk might crash or have a failure. There are thousands of ways that you might lose some very important data. You should always have a current backup. There are many methods of backup, some using hardware and some that requires special software programs. See Chapter 9 for more details.

Monitors

There are a large variety of monitors that you can use. You can buy a fairly good color monitor for about $250. Or you can spend up to $1200 or more for a large screen, very-high-resolution monitor. The type of monitor you buy should match whatever you are using your computer for. If you are doing a lot of high-end graphics or computer-aided design (CAD), then you need a large screen with high resolution. If you are buying a system for the kids to play games, then a 14-inch system would be fine.

Monitor Adapter

You will need a plug-in adapter board to drive the monitor. (Some motherboards have a built-in adapter.) For standard VGA color, you should be able to buy one for about $40. For very-high-resolution color, it might cost up to $500. See Chapter 10 for more details on monitors and adapters.

Keyboards

The keyboard cable is plugged into a connector that is mounted on the back of the motherboard and is accessible on the back panel. The keyboard is a very important part of the computer. It is the main device for communicating with the computer. There are many manufacturers. Most of them have slight differences in the placement of the keys, the tactile feel, and special adjuncts such as trackballs, calculators, and keypads.

To run Windows and other graphical user interface (GUI) programs, it is essential to have a mouse, trackball, or other pointing device. Chapter 11 discusses keyboards and other input devices in some detail.

Modems, FAX, and Communications

You can use your computer to communicate with millions of other computers, with on-line services, and a host of other services. You can download software from bulletin boards. You can send a low-cost FAX to millions of other FAX sites.

You definitely need some communications hardware and software if you want to get the most from your computer. Chapter 12 discusses communications.

Printers

You have lots of options when it comes to buying your printer. There are several manufacturers and hundreds of different types and models. There are dot matrix, lasers, inkjets, daisy wheels, and many others. Some types are better for a particular application than others. So it depends on what you want to do with your computer and how much you want to spend. Chapter 13 discusses the various types of printers.

Software

You will need software for your computer. Before you even turn it on, you will need operating software, such as MS-DOS, DR DOS, IBM PC DOS, or OS/2. There are billions of dollars worth of off-the-shelf software that you can use. Some of the commercial programs might be a bit expensive. There are inexpensive public domain and shareware programs that can do just about everything the commercial programs do. See Chapter 19 for more about software.

Sources

You need to know where to buy all of the components that you will need to upgrade or repair your PC. If you live near a large city, there are probably local stores that sell the parts. The local vendors and computer stores will be most happy to help you. They might charge a bit more than a mail-order house, but if anything goes wrong, they will usually be very quick to help you or make it right.

There are also frequent computer swaps in most large cities. A computer swap is just a gathering of local vendors at a fair grounds, a stadium, or some other area. They usually set up booths and tables and present their wares. You can usually find all that you need at these meets.

You can go from booth to booth and compare the components and prices. The prices are usually very competitive and you might even be able to haggle a bit with the vendors.

The other good source for components is through mail order companies. Just look at the ads in any of the computer magazines. At one time mail order could be a bit risky. But it is very safe today.

If a price seems too good to be true, then the vendor has probably cut a few corners somewhere. There are some very good bargains out there. But you should be careful. Your best protection is to be fairly knowledgeable about the computer business. Computer magazines, and books like the one you are holding, are some of the better sources for this knowledge.

Another excellent source of knowledge and help are the local computer user groups. Most of the people in these groups are very friendly and anxious to help you with any problem.

If you are fairly new to computing, be sure to read the chapters on floppy disk drives, hard disk drives, monitors, keyboards, and the major components before you buy your parts. There are billions of dollars worth of products available. Many of them are very similar in functionality and quality. What you buy should depend primarily on what you want your computer to do, and how much you can afford to spend. If you are knowledgeable and you shop wisely, you can save a bundle.

Moore's Law

A few years ago, Gordon Moore, chairman of Intel Corporation, studied the microprocessor industry and noticed a very definite trend. He observed that the 286 had 125,000 transistors, more than three times the 29,000 in the XT. Very soon the 386 was introduced with 275,000 transistors, which more than doubled the 286, then the 486 with 1.2 million, then soon after the Pentium with 3.1 million, and then the Pentium Pro with 5.5 million. The new Pentium II will have over 10 million transistors. The trend is that every 18 months or so the number of transistors and computing power more than double. This trend has become so predictable that it is now known as Moore's Law. Intel said at one time they would eventually have microprocessors with 100 million transistors. According to Moore's Law, it will only take another three or four generations to reach that level, which should occur sometime within the next five or six years.

So go ahead and upgrade your computer to the very latest and enjoy the power and speed it can deliver. However, you should know that within a very short time your wonderful machine will be obsolete again. But not to worry. You now know how to deal with obsolescence.

How Computers Work

This section is very basic. If you are an old pro, you might want to skip ahead. If you are a beginner, this might answer a lot of your questions as to how a computer works.

A computer is made up of circuits and boards that have resistors, capacitors, inductors, transistors, motors, and many other components. These components perform a useful function when electricity passes through them. The circuits are designed so that the paths of the electric currents are divided, controlled, and shunted to do the work that we want done. The transistors and other components can force the electrons to go to the memory, a disk drive, the printer, or wherever the software and hardware directs them to go.

Computers are possible only because of our ability to control voltages. We control small voltages, usually direct current voltages (dc), by turning them on or off. So when the voltage is on, it can represent a 1; when it is off it is a 0. With these two digits we can digitize a world of things. We can digitize drawings, photos, movies, sound, speech, music, virtual reality, and many other things. Once these objects are digitized we can compress them, add to them, delete portions, or manipulate themin hundreds of ways. Sometimes it might be difficult to determine reality from virtual reality. A good example was Forrest Gump having a conversation with LBJ who has been dead for several years. Since that movie, several others have been made. Many commercials have been made using dead guys, might be because they don't have to pay them any fees and residuals.

A short time ago we couldn't do many of the things that we take for granted today because we just didn't have the computer power.

Computers and Electricity

Computers are possible because of electricity. Under the control of software and hardware, small electric on/off signal voltages are formed when we type from the keyboard. The absence or presence of magnetic bits on a hard or floppy disk can be detected and represented as on or off voltages. The small pits and islands on a CD-ROM disk can also be detected and represented as on or off voltages. The data sent or received over a telephone line from a fax or modem are just bits of on and off voltages. These on and off voltages are used to turn transistors on or off.

An electric charge is formed when there is an imbalance or an excess amount of electrons at one pole. The excess electrons will flow through whatever path they can find to get to the other pole. It is much like water flowing downhill to find its level.

Electricity is the life blood of a computer. Under the control of the software and hardware, small voltage signals are sent to different areas of the computer to accomplish the various tasks.

Electricity is something that we cannot see. We can only see the effects of it, and of course we can feel it. If it is a fairly high voltage it can knock you on your fanny, or even kill you.

All matter is made up of atoms. Atoms are made up of a nucleus that contains a given number of protons, neutrons, and several electrons in orbits around the nucleus. The number of protons, neutrons, and electrons in the atom will depend on what the substance is. Ordinarily, the number of electrons in orbit around a nucleus balances the protons and neutrons in the nucleus. But electrons can be displaced from the orbits of some substances. When this happens, there is an imbalance. Just as water will seek its own level, an atom that is imbalanced will try to regain its balance.

Italian Count Alessandro Volta (1745-1827) developed the first battery. We have improved batteries considerably since then, but they still use the same basic principle. We have also developed electric generators since then. We can use batteries and generators to create an imbalance of electrons.

Batteries and other electric sources have two electrodes, a positive and a negative, or ground. The negative pole will have an excess of electrons. If we provide a path with no resistance between the electrodes, the excess electrons will rush through the path at almost the speed of light to get to the positive pole.

Most electric or electronic paths have varying amounts of resistance so that work or heat is created when the electrons pass through them. For instance, if a flashlight is turned on, electrons will pass through the bulb, which has a resistive filament. The heat generated by the electrons passing through the bulb will cause the filament to glow red hot and create light. If the light is left on for a period of time, the excess electrons from the negative pole of the battery will pass through the bulb to the positive pole of the battery. Electrons will continue to flow until the amount of electrons at the negative and positive poles are equal. At this time there will be a perfect balance and the battery will be dead.

If we place a motor in the path between the electrodes, the flow of electrons through the coils of wire around the rotor will create a magnetic force which will cause the rotor to spin.

Soon after the battery was developed, George Simon Ohm (1789-1854) discovered that there was a direct relationship between the amount of voltage, the resistance of the path, and the number of electrons passing through the path. Resistance (R) is equal to the voltage (E) divided by the current (I). This is known as Ohm's Law. Using Ohm's Law, if you know any two values, you can determine the other one. Electrons moving through a circuit can be called *current* or *amperes*. The ampere is a very large number of electrons that pass a given point in a given amount of time. It was named for French mathematician Andre Marie Ampere (1775-1836).

When presented with two or more resistive paths, the electricity obeys Ohm's Law exactly. Using Ohm's Law, circuits can be designed in thousands of ways to make electricity work for us by controlling and directing it to where we want it to go. We can control voltage with switches, transistors, resistors, capacitors, inductive coils, transformers, and various other electronic components.

Transistors and Computers

The first and foremost reason that we have computers today is because we have transistors. The transistor effect was discovered by three scientists working in the Bell Labs in the late 1940s. The scientists, William Shockley, John Bardeen, and Walter Brattain, were awarded a Nobel prize in 1956. (I believe that the importance of the discovery and development of the transistor should rank right up there alongside the discovery of the wheel and fire.)

A very basic computer, the Electronic Numerical Integrator and Computer (ENIAC) was developed in the early 1940s. We had no transistors in those days so the computer used thousands of vacuum tubes and cost millions of dollars. It took several large rooms to house one of these computers. It was used during World War II to calculate cannon trajectories. It took 30 to 40 hours for hand calculations for each trajectory, but the new computer could do it in 30 seconds. It could perform fewer functions than a present day two dollar calculator. Computers now can do the same trajectory calculations in about 30 billionths of a second, or 30 nanoseconds.

Technology made a quantum leap forward when the transistor was invented. So how do we get those transistors to work for us? We use software that instructs the computer to turn the transistors on and off to perform the various tasks. Although most software is something that is written, when it is typed into the computer from a keyboard, each time a key is depressed, it generates electrical pulses which turn the transistors on and off. When the software is loaded in from a disk, the magnetic flux of the disk is converted to electrical pulses that are identical to those created by the keyboard. The end result of all software applications, no matter how it is input to the computer, is to cause the generation of on and off voltages that control the transistors.

Ordinarily, the more complex the software and the more transistors available, the more work that a computer can accomplish.

The transistor can act as a switch. It has three basic elements: the collector, the base, and the emitter. Suppose the collector of this transistor is connected to the positive pole of a 6 volt battery and the emitter is connected to the negative pole. No voltage or electrons will pass through the transistor. But if we connect a small voltage, as little as a millionth of a volt on the base of the transistor, it can act like a switch and allow a large number of electrons to flow through the transistor and anything that is connected between its collector and the battery. So a very small voltage on the base of a transistor can cause it to switch a much larger voltage on or off.

The transistor can also act as an amplifier. If the small voltage signal on the base of the transistor goes up gradually, then goes down, the transistor can cause a large voltage to go up and down in an exact replica of the input signal. When a radio or television station broadcasts its signal, it throws a high voltage out into the air. By the time it gets to your radio or television, it might only be a millionth of a volt. Using transistors, this voltage can be amplified in an exact replica of the original voltage signal so that it is strong enough to power a loudspeaker or to drive a 25,000-volt electron gun in a television set. The picture tube or cathode ray tube (CRT) of a television or computer monitor is similar to a vacuum tube. Figure 1-5 is a diagram of an old fashioned vacuum tube circuit and a transistor circuit. The transistor circuit can be thousands of times smaller and use only a fraction of the energy needed for the vacuum tube. The radio and television voltages vary up and down and are called analog voltages. Figure 1-6 is a diagram of square waves and analog sine waves.

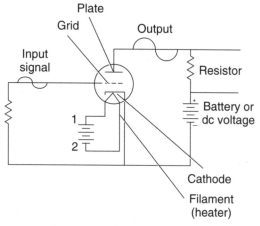

A vacuum tube and circuitry

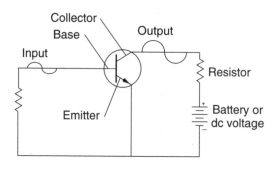

A transistor and circuitry

Computers use thousands of transistors. The main chip, or brains of a computer, is the central processing unit (CPU). The 486 CPU has 1.2 million transistors, the Pentium CPU has 3.1 million, and the Pentium Pro CPU has 5.5 million. In addition to the CPU, there are several other chips and components on the motherboard with many more thousands of transistors.

The transistors in the CPU, those on the motherboard, and those on the various plug-in boards and peripherals all respond to signals or voltages that are fed to them from sources such as the keyboard, floppy disk drives, hard disk drives, modems, scanners, or any of several other input devices. The voltages used by computers are digital voltages that have two states, either off or on. If we have two switches or two transistors, we can have four different states as follows: #1 off and #2 off, #1 on and #2 off, #1 off and #2 on, #1 on and #2 on. If we have four transistors, we can have 16 different

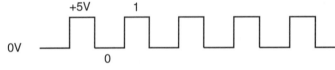

Fig. 1-6
Diagrams of square
waves and analog
voltage.

Square waves representing 0s and 1s

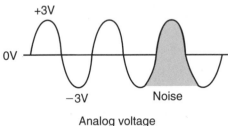

Analog voltage

states. If we double the amount of transistors to 8, which would be 2 to the power of 8 (2^8), we can have 256 different states. If we double the number to 16 (2^{16}) we can have 65536 different states. The different number of states goes up by the power of 2 with each additional transistor or switch. With 32 transistors, 4, 294,967,296 different signals can be produced.

Computers work with 1s and 0s, or bits. (*Bit* is a contraction of **b**inary dig**it**). It takes eight bits to make one byte. It takes eight bits, or one byte, to represent one letter of the alphabet or a single number.

For certain digital states, we can assign a number or a letter of the alphabet. In our decimal system, we assign values to wherever the numeral happens to be. For instance, in the number 321, the 3 is in the hundred place, the 2 is in the ten place and the 1 is in the 1 place. In the digital system, each place also has a value, but it works a bit differently than the decimal system. The right column is 1, the next is 2, the next is 4, then 8, then 16, 32, 64, 128, 256, etc. Note that each new column toward the left doubles. Here is what the output of four different switches or transistors would look like:

```
0000 = 0 = all off
0001 = 1 (the 1 place)
0010 = 2 (the 2 place)
0011 = 3 (the 2 place + 1)
0100 = 4 (the 4 place)
0101 = 5 (the 4 place + 1)
0110 = 6 (the 4 place + 2)
0111 = 7 (the 4 place + 2 +1)
```

1000 = 8 (the 8 place)
1001 = 9 (the 8 place + 1)
1010 = 10 (the 8 place + 2)
1011 = 11 (the 8 place + 2 + 1)
1100 = 12 (the 8 place + 4)
1101 = 13 (the 8 place + 4 + 1)
1110 = 14 (the 8 place + 4 + 2)
1111 = 15 (the 8 place + 4 + 2 + 1)

The ASCII Code

When the teletype was developed, they used the digital system to devise a code so that messages could be sent over telephone wires. This was called the *American Standard Code for Information Interchange*, or ASCII (pronounced asskee). The original code was 128 different characters, which included all of the characters found on a typewriter keyboard, including punctuation and spaces.

If the letter A was typed on a teletype keyboard it would cause a voltage to be turned on and off to produce 100001, equivalent to decimal 65, to be sent over the teletype wire. If a teletype machine in another city was connected to this teletype, the letter A would be typed out. If a B was typed, the signal 100020, or 66, would be produced. (The fourth place to the left is 16, the fifth is 32, and the sixth is 64, or 2^4, 25, and 2^6). This 128 character code worked very well for several years. Later the ASCII code was extended by an additional 128 characters and symbols for a total of 256 or 2^8. The extended ASCII code uses smiling faces, playing card symbols, Greek letters, and several other symbols. If you would like to see what some of these symbols look like, at the DOS prompt, use the command TYPE to type out any command that has an .EXE or .COM extension. For instance at the DOS prompt, type TYPE COMMAND.COM.

Software

If you type an A on a computer keyboard, like the teletype, it causes a digital voltage to be created equivalent to 1000001 or 65 decimal. This would cause certain transistors inside the computer to be turned on or off and the A character would be displayed, stored, printed, or whatever the software told it to do.

Inputs

The computer keyboard creates digital voltages for each key that is typed. But there are other ways to input data to a computer. The floppy and hard disks have a magnetic coating very similar to the tape in a tape recorder. A small voltage is created when the data is read by the head. This voltage is then amplified and routed to wherever the software tells it to go.

We can also have inputs from such things as a mouse, a modem, a scanner, or a network. They all produce a digital voltage that is used by the software and hardware to accomplish a task.

If an electronic circuit is designed properly, it should last several life times. There is nothing in a semiconductor or transistor to wear out. But occasionally, too many electrons might find their way through a weakened component and cause it to heat up and burn out. Or for some reason, the electrons might be shunted through a path or component where it shouldn't go. This might cause an intermittent, a partial, or a complete failure.

System Clock

The computer has a real time clock and calendar that keeps track of the date and the time. But the computer also has a system clock that is much more precise than the real time clock. Everything that a computer does is precisely timed. The timing is controlled by crystal oscillators. The computer carries out each instruction in a certain number of clock cycles. On the early XT system the clock operated at 4.77 million hertz (MHz), or cycles per second. Even so, it often took several clock cycles, moving 8 bits at a time, to perform a single instruction. The Pentium II can operate as fast as 266MHz and process several instructions per cycle. The foregoing is rather simplified, but it might help you understand what is happening inside your computer.

CHAPTER 7

Some Ideal Ways to Upgrade a PC

Even if you just bought it yesterday, in many ways your computer is obsolete. There is no way it could have all the things that could be installed in it. There are hundreds of ways that a computer can be configured and upgraded. Computers are made up of various components that just plug together. You can add hundreds of different boards, components, and peripherals to a computer. Only a very few of the ways to upgrade are discussed in this chapter. Each major component is discussed in more detail in later chapters.

When we speak of upgrading, we usually think about hardware, but software upgrades are every bit as important. Some of the essential software is discussed in later chapters.

Dream Machine versus Reality

If money were no object, here is what I would like in a perfect PC or dream machine: a Pentium II Motherboard with a 266MHz MMX CPU.

With this motherboard and CPU, it would be some time before it became obsolete. At the moment, there is little or no software that can take advantage of the speed and power. Software development always lags behind the hardware. Another big factor is that this CPU and motherboard will be very expensive when it is first released. You can probably buy two 200MHz MMX Pentium motherboards for what one Pentium II MMX will cost.

The original Pentium that was introduced in March 1993, had 3.1 million transistors and operated at either 60 or 66MHz. It was a fantastic advance at that time. The Pentium 75+ was introduced in March of 1994. It had 3.3 million transistors and originally operated at 75MHz, but was soon boosted to 100, 120, 150, and now 200MHz. The Pentium Pro with 5.5 million transistors was introduced in September, 1995. Originally, it operated at 150MHz, but was soon boosted to 200MHz.

Intel redesigned some of their 166MHz and 200MHz Pentiums and added a set of 57 multimedia extension (MMX) instructions to the chip. The MMX technology has given new life to the Pentium. It runs most normal software programs much faster. Those programs such as graphics, video and multimedia, written to take advantage of the MMX, can be processed very fast.

The Pentium II is the next generation of the Pentium Pro. Intel added the 57 MMX instructions to the CPU. The fastest Pentium Pro ran at 200MHz. The new Pentium II will run at 200MHz, 233MHz, and 266MHz. Eventually it will operate at 300MHz and maybe even as high as 400MHz.

Back to Reality

Realistically, for most applications, the 200MHz MMX Pentium CPU will do just about everything needed. This is especially so for home offices and small businesses. Owning a Pentium II is almost like owning an expensive automobile that can go 150 miles an hour, but there is no place where you could drive that fast except on a race track. At this time, unless you have some high-end applications, you would be much better off buying the 200MHz MMX Pentium CPU and investing the money saved on peripherals or other goodies.

Another alternative would be the 200MHz Pentium Pro. If you don't need to do a lot of multimedia, this CPU will still do just about anything that you need. I paid $2500 for my first 200MHz Pentium Pro motherboard when it first came out. You can get one now for less than $1000. At this time the Pentium Pro does not have the MMX instructions, but a new release will have them and should be on the market by the time you read this.

Dream: 128Mb of DRAM

When a program is being processed or operated on, it is loaded into dynamic random access memory (DRAM). Most programs today are very friendly, but the friendlier they are, the larger they are. So you will need a lot of DRAM.

Reality: 16Mb of DRAM

You can run most programs today with 16Mb of DRAM. At one time it was rather expensive, but the prices have dropped considerably in the last few months. If you are strapped for money at this time, you can start off with 16Mb, then add another 16Mb or more later. It is very easy to plug in more memory. You might never need all the memory you have available, but it is nice to have. It is something like having a car with a 427 horsepower engine. You might not ever need all the power, but it is sure nice to have when you do need it.

Dream: 512K of L1 Cache Memory

The CPU goes back and forth to the dynamic random access memory (DRAM) to get portions of the program for processing. Quite often a small portion of the program is processed over and over. If the most used portions of the program is stored in a very fast static random access memory (SRAM) cache, the system operates much faster. SRAM is much faster than DRAM, but of course, more expensive.

The Pentium Pro has a level 1 (L1) cache built into the same enclosure, very near the CPU. One model has 256K of SRAM and the other has 512K. Like all other systems, the Pentium Pro also has a level 2 (L2) cache on the motherboard. But it takes afinite amount of time for the electrons to travel the few inches to the L2 cache, so if they can make use of the nearby L1 cache, it is a bit faster.

The Pentium Pro with the 256K L1 cache has 15.5 million transistors. The one with the 512K L1 has twice as many, or 31 million, which makes it quite a bit more expensive than the 256K model.

Reality: 512K L2 Cache

Again, for most applications, if you can wait for a few nanoseconds, a 512K L2 cache on the motherboard will do just fine. You also have several lesser expensive CPUs to choose from also. The AMD K6 is about 25% less expensive than the equivalent Pentium Pro. The Cyrix 686 and M2 also offers equivalent, but less expensive alternatives.

Dream: A 6Gb IDE and a 6Gb SCSI Hard Drive

It doesn't happen too often, but it is possible for hard drives to fail. But even one failure can be disastrous. If you have both IDE and SCSI drives installed, you can quickly back up from one to the other. It is not likely that both of them would fail at the same time.

A gigabyte is 1000 million bytes. A 6Gb hard disk seems like a lot of memory, but you can never have too much. With a high-capacity disk like these, you could load on lots of graphics or even movies.

Reality: A 1.2Gb IDE and 1.2Gb SCSI Hard Drive

A couple of 1.2Gb hard drives would probably do all that one needed for a while, unless you have special needs. You can always add more later. Besides, the costs are coming down every day. At this rate, if you wait awhile, they will be practically giving them away.

Dream: A 24X Speed CD-ROM a CD-DVD

Some of the newer CD-ROM drives are 24 times faster than the original drives. That still does not make them as fast as a hard disk, but it is close. It was very difficult to view movies or some graphics on the original CD-ROM drives. The newer faster drives makes it very easy.

The standard CD-ROM disc can hold about 600Mb of data. (Note: CD-ROM discs are spelled with a *c* as differentiated from floppy and hard disks.) A single digitized frame from a movie might require as much as 25Mb. Compression techniques can reduce the amount of memory needed by as much as 200 percent or more. But that still doesn't allow more than a few minutes of motion and high-resolution graphics.

The CD-DVD discs hold as much as 17Gb. A 17Gb disc can store as much as 28 of the 600Mb CD-ROM discs. An entire two-hour movie can easily be stored on one disk. Of course, for business purposes, large databases and programs (and almost anything that might be needed) could be stored on one disk.

Reality: One or Two 10X CD-ROM Drives

The 10X CD-ROM drives are sufficient for most applications and are very inexpensive. When they first came out, I paid $400 for a 2X drive. You can buy a 10X drive now for about $100.

As dictated by Murphy's immutable laws, quite often the data that is needed is on another disc. The solution is to install two or more CD-ROM drives so that you can switch from one to the other. Several companies have developed low-cost drives that can hold four to six discs. Any of the discs can be quickly accessed. For large applications, jukebox type systems have been developed that can hold up to 100 or more CD-ROM discs, any of which can be quickly accessed.

Dream: A 4X CD-ROM Recordable System

The first system for recordable CD-ROMs was a 1X system and cost over $10,000. You can now buy a 2X recordable system for less than $400. These systems will usually read back at 4X.

It is difficult to record on a CD-ROM at much faster than 2X, but newer and faster systems will probably be available by the time you read this.

The recordable systems are great for backup, or for any kind of data that you want to archive and store for long periods of time. An entire 1.2Gb hard disk could be backed up on two CD-ROM discs. At the present time, many companies, doctor's offices, government facilities, and many others are still using mountains of printed paper to store data. It might take acres of floor space to house all of the over-stuffed file cabinets. Besides the cost of the floor space, paper, and file cabinets, these systems are very labor intensive. It takes lots of people to file and then to find the data. A couple of CD-ROM discs could hold all of that data. Another very distinct advantage is that the data can be searched by a computer and anything found instantly. This data can then be printed out, stored on another disk, sent through a modem or fax, or be easily manipulated in many ways.

They are also working on CD-DVD recordable systems that should be available by the time you read this.

Reality: 2X Recordable CD-ROM System

Every small business and home office should have a 2X recordable CD-ROM system. They are a bit slow, but quite inexpensive for what they can do. Of course, every doctor's office and any company, or anyone who generates a lot of data that must be saved, should be saving the data on a CD-ROM recordable system. A blank disc for a CD-ROM recordable costs about $5.

Dream: A 56K Modem

At the time of this writing, two different companies have introduced proprietary system 56K modems. Neither will talk to the other. Each company is promoting and trying very hard to get their system accepted as the standard. It is much like the confusion a few years ago with the Sony Betamax tape system versus the VHS system. A Betamax system could not play tapes recorded on a VHS system and vice versa.

Hopefully the International Telecommunications Union (ITU) will sort it out and adopt one or the other of the 56K systems as a standard.

Dream and Reality: Large Removable Hard Disk

Iomega, Syquest, and several other companies have developed hard disk drives that record on removable cartridges. With this system, you need never run out of disk space. When one is filled up, just shove in another blank cartridge. One big advantage is that sensitive data can be recorded on the disks, then removed and locked away. Large amounts of data can be recorded on the disks, then shipped across the country or next door to another computer.

The first Iomega Zip system used 100Mb cartridges; then Syquest introduced a 135Mb system for about the same price. Some systems now have cartridges that can store 2Gb or more. The removable systems are fairly inexpensive considering what they can do.

Dream: A 1.44Mb/120Mb Floppy Drive

OR Technology has developed the A:Drive, a floppy disk drive that can read and write to 1.44Mb floppies and to special 120Mb disks. The A:Drive is fairly reasonable. It can be a fantastic upgrade. You can reach OR Technology by phone, (408) 866-3000 or online, www.ortechnology.com.

Reality: 1.44Mb and 1.2Mb Combination Floppy Drive

The 1.2Mb floppy drive is obsolete, but I still have hundreds of both 360 K and 1.2Mb floppy disks. A combination $5\frac{1}{4}$ inch 1.2Mb and $3\frac{1}{2}$ inch 1.44Mb drive takes up no more space to install than a single 1.2Mb drive.

I would like to find time to load all my old $5\frac{1}{4}$ inch floppies onto my hard disk, but it is doubtful I will ever have that much time. Besides, most of the stuff on those old disks is so obsolete that I would never have any use for it. Still, I hate to throw it away.

PC-Card Slots

The PC Card is what was once the PCMCIA, an acronym for Personal Computer Memory Card International Association. A group formed this association to standardize the plug-in slot for memory cards for laptop and notebook computers. Besides memory, there are now dozens of different PC-Cards available, such as fax/modems, network cards, SCSI interface cards, and even small hard disks on cards. Having a slot on a desktop or tower-type computer makes it very easy to transfer data back and forth from a laptop.

Dream: A 64-Bit Sound Card and Hi-Fi Speakers

It is now possible to add sound and annotations to your files. It is also possible to play audio compact discs on a CD-ROM drive. Many CD-ROM discs have sound, text, graphics, and motion. The 64-bit card and good speakers might cost as much as $500 or more. A good system like this could satisfy most serious audiophiles.

Reality: 32-Bit Sound Card and Good Speakers

Actually, an 8-bit or 16-bit card would do fine for most business and office work. You probably don't need enough sound to fill a concert hall, so a 16-bit system would be adequate, and a 32-bit system is more than adequate for most applications.

Dream: A 31-Inch Multiscanning Monitor

Monitors go up in cost at an almost logarithmic fashion. A 14-inch monitor might cost a little over $200. A 31-inch monitor might cost as much as $2000. The bigger the monitor, the easier to see. For high-end work, you need a high-end monitor.

Reality: A 17-Inch High-Resolution Monitor

The 17-inch monitors are very reasonable at this time. Even the 19- and 21-inch monitors are coming down in price. For most general-purpose work, a 17-inch monitor is sufficient.

A 24-Bit Monitor Adapter

You will need a good monitor adapter to be able to display all of the possible colors. A good 24-bit monitor adapter with 2Mb of memory can give you true color. Good adapters have also come way down in price. Those with less memory are very reasonable.

Dream: Color Laser Printer

A good laser printer that could print both in color and black and white would be about all one should ask for. If your applications use color and you have lots of money, they are available.

Reality: A Good Laser and a Color Inkjet

You can buy a good color inkjet printer and a good black and white laser printer for a lot less than what it costs for a color laser. If your printing needs are rather modest, a color inkjet will do both color and black and white. I have a Canon color inkjet printer that is also a fax, a copier, and a scanner.

Dream: A Good Keyboard

The Key Tronics Corp., at (509) 928-8000, has a keyboard that can be elevated in the center and angled so that there is less chance of one getting carpal tunnel syndrome (CTS) or repetitive strain injury (RSI). It is rather expensive, at close to $300, but the cost of treating CTS or RSI can cost a lot more in hospital bills, lost work, and pain.

Key Tronics manufactures the keyboard that Microsoft sells. It is almost as good as the one that splits in the middle and can be elevated. The Microsoft keyboard is still a bit expensive at $70 to $80.

Reality: Low-Cost Keyboards

I don't know how they do it, but some companies are manufacturing and selling keyboards for as little as $12. If you are only using your keyboard occasionally, and not worried about CTS and RSI, they might be all you need. In fact you might buy a couple and keep one as a spare in case you ever need a replacement.

Dream: A Logitech Wireless Mouse

I often have trouble with the cord to my mouse getting tangled up. A wireless mouse would solve that problem. The big problem is that they cost about $90. Another good thing to have would be a good trackball, but they are still a bit expensive.

Reality: Low-Cost Mouse

You can buy a good mouse for as little as $10. For most Windows applications, they are fine if all you do is point and click. If you are doing high-end CAD type work, you would probably need to buy a better mouse with good resolution.

A Medium Tower Case

Most medium tower cases have about eight bays with four of them being accessible. This should take care of most needs.

A Network Interface Card (NIC)

I have several other computers in my office. It is very easy to connect them together in a simple network.

Bottom Line Cost

As long as I am dreaming, I would also like to have a Rolls Royce. But it is a whole lot easier to make your dream come true for the computer listed above than for a Rolls Royce. A system with all of the dream components listed above would cost between $5,000 to $10,000. Components for the reality machine might cost from $2,000 to $4,000.

If you have an older system, you can easily upgrade it with any of the components listed above.

The Ever-Changing Technology

Computer technology is advancing and changing faster than any other technology. The technology is changing so fast that if you walk out of a store with a brand new computer, by the time you get it home it is practically obsolete. If your computer is three or four years old, it belongs to the dinosaur age. But not to worry. Your computer, no matter how old, can be upgraded to take advantage of all the latest and greatest.

There are new software programs and hardware products being developed every day that cannot be used on some of the older systems. These new products can make life a lot easier and simpler. The answer is to upgrade the older systems so that you can take advantage of the newer goodies.

Except for the motherboard, the parts or components that make up a PC are all basically the same no matter whether it is a PC, XT, 286, 386, 486, Pentium MMX, or Pentium Pro. In-depth discussions of the major components are included in later chapters.

Power Distribution Panel

You will have several devices that need to plug into a power outlet. Most wall plates only have two outlets. There are adapters that can fit over the outlet to increase the number to four or even six. Or you might be tempted to run extension cords to other outlets. But it will make life a lot easier, and safer, if you buy a power strip that has about six outlets. Try to find one that is switchable and has a built-in fuse or circuit breaker.

Even more convenient is a power panel that is about one inch high and about the size of a desktop computer case. Your computer can sit on top of it. I use a power panel that is about 15 inches square and has six individual lighted switches, one for the master input power, a switch for the computer, one for a monitor, one for the printer, and two for auxiliary devices. I can plug in my computer, monitor, printer, and two auxiliary devices into these six outlets. I can then use the switches on the front of the panel to turn any of the devices on or off. It is very convenient and is rather inexpensive at about $15.

Surge Protection

When large heavy-duty electric motors and other electrical equipment are turned on, they sometimes create a very high-voltage spike in the nearby power lines. These surges can cause glitches and data corruption in your computer. A good surge protector can cause the spikes to be shunted to ground. Electrical storms can also cause surges in the power lines and telephone lines.

Some of the more expensive power distribution panels have surge protection. Some also have sockets with surge protection for connecting a telephone line to a modem. If you are in an area where there are large heavy-duty electric motors, they might send very high-voltage surges through the line. These surges could severely damage your system. There are different levels of quality surge protectors. Some are very inexpensive but might not offer much protection. Many of the UPS companies listed also sell good-quality surge protectors.

Need for Uninterruptible Power Supply

If you are working on data that is critical, and you live in an area where there are a lot of electrical storms, power outages, or brownouts, you should install an uninterruptible power supply (UPS). When you are working on a file, it is loaded into random access memory (RAM). This memory is volatile; that is, if the power is interrupted, even for a brief fraction of a second, the RAM loses all of its memory. The data that is being worked on will disappear and be gone forever. A UPS can take over when the power is interrupted and keeps the computer running until it can be safely shut down.

Basically, the UPS is a battery that is kept charged up by the voltage from the wall socket. If there is an interruption of power, the electronic circuits immediately switch so that the computer is supplied by the battery. Depending on the UPS model and the amount of wattage you are drawing from it, the UPS might be able to keep your system going for ten to fifteen minutes or more. This should give you plenty of time to close all your work and save it to disk.

If you live in an area where there are electrical storms, then by all means you should have a good lightning rod installed. If a severe electrical storm comes up, even with a good lightning rod, you should turn off your computer and unplug it. Just one good bolt can zap your system and fry it to a crisp.

Figure 2-1 shows an uniterruptible power supply from American Power Conversion. It is one of the better ones available. I live in the Los Angeles area. We seldom have lightning or thunderstorms here, but we do have electrical problems once in a while. With my computer plugged into this unit, I never have to worry about losing data due to loss of power.

There are several companies who manufacture UPS devices. Here are just a few companies who offer them:

American Power Conversion	(888) 289-APCC Ext.8129
	www.apcc.com
Best Power Technology	(800) 356-5794 http://bestpower.com
Deltec	(800) 854-2658 www.deltecpower.com
Minuteman UPS	(800) 238-7272
Tripp Lite	(312) 755-5400 http://tripplite.com

Call these companies for brochures and information.

Some of the UPS systems, such as the one from American Power Conversion might have several outlets so that you might not need a power strip. Each of the companies above have several models to choose from. Basically, the different models are designed for the amount of power or wattage that it will have to supply. The expense of a UPS will be more than offset if it saves you even once from a disaster.

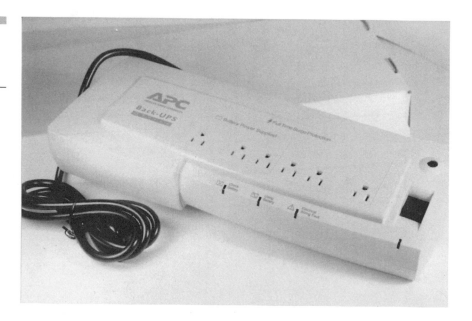

Fig. 2-1
An uninterruptible power supply (UPS) from APC.

Internal Upgrades

The computer is somewhat like an erector set or a set of building blocks. There are a very large number of components, modules, and devices that can be used to upgrade a computer by just connecting them together or plugging them in. Here are a few major upgrades that can make your computer faster, more powerful, and more effective. They are also quite cost effective.

New Plug-In Boards

Billions of dollars worth of hardware has been developed for the Industry Standard Architecture machines (ISA). The ISA machines are what used to be called the IBM compatibles. The ISA standard also included the older IBM machines such as the IBM PS/1 and several of the PS/2 models. The IBM PS/2 models 50 and up are Micro Channel Architecture (MCA). These computers use plug-in boards that have a different connector than the ISA type hardware. If you have one of these machines, you might not be able to do much in the way of upgrading it. The MCA plug-in boards and even the disk drives are different than most other ISA systems.

The ISA machines have a large motherboard with up to eight connectors or slots for plug-in boards. These connectors are also called *expansion slots*. Plugging a board into one of these slots allows you to expand the capability of your computer. Because of the open architecture, ISA computers can be configured to perform thousands of applications. It is not necessary to design or manufacture a computer to do a specific job. If you want to perform a task, such as being able to collect or measure data from a scientific process, you can use an ISA computer and plug in a special board for that task. If you need to tie several computers together in a network, there are special network interface cards (NICs) that allow you to do that. There are cards or boards that allow you to use your computer as a part-time fax machine or modem. Or you can plug in boards that allow you to use your computer to add sound and voice to your files, or to use the computer as a hi-fi system. There are hundreds of different boards that can be used to have the computer perform thousands of different tasks. The boards can be plugged into any one of the slots on the motherboard for a very easy upgrade.

Bus

The word *bus* is actually a shortening of the Latin word *Omnibus*, meaning all. A bus is usually a vehicle in which we can all travel from one place to another. In computers and electronic systems, a bus is a pathway over which electrical signals, in the form of power and data, can travel back and forth from one place to another.

The motherboard might have as many as eight slots or connectors for plug-in boards. Each pin on these slots is connected by a printed circuit to the same pin on all the other slots. So a board can be plugged into any slot. Eventually the printed circuit will connect with the RAM memory, with the hard disks, floppy disks, the keyboard, and the various other chips on the motherboard. Just like a city bus, data and signals can travel over the printed circuits to any desired location.

When IBM compatible clone makers began to outsell and outperform the true-blue IBM machines, IBM introduced their Micro Channel Architecture (MCA) bus. It was definitely an improvement over the old IBM-compatible standard, but it was incompatible with all earlier IBM machines and clones. Because the MCA was proprietary only to them, IBM hoped that they could recapture the market and that everyone would have to come to them.

The industry fought back and took control of the IBM-compatible standard that IBM had abandoned and renamed it Industry Standard Architecture (ISA). They also designed a new bus called the Extended Industry Standard Architecture (EISA). The EISA standard had all of the improvements that the MCA had, but in addition, it was compatible with all the billions of dollars of hardware that was available.

Later the Video Electronics Standards Association (VESA) designed a VESA local bus (VL). It added more improvements to the ISA and EISA bus systems. Just a short time later, Intel and a group of engineers designed still another bus, the Peripheral Component Interconnect (PCI) bus.

For some time, the EISA, the VL, and PCI competed for market share. It was difficult to decide which motherboard to buy. Manufacturers had trouble deciding whether to make EISA, VL, or PCI motherboards and plug-in boards. Some of them designed motherboards that incorporated either two or three of the options. The PCI bus has finally proven to be the choice of most manufacturers and users. The EISA and VL bus have all but disappeared with the demise of the 486. Almost all Pentium-class motherboards now have three or four PCI slots along with three or four ISA bus slots. Having a single standard has made it much easier for the manufacturers and for the buying public.

Depending on your needs, the old EISA and VL buses might be all you need. But there is not much that you can do to upgrade them to be equivalent to the newer Pentium-class standards. If you need more speed and power, you will have to buy a new motherboard.

Why You Might Need to Upgrade

Some of the reasons to upgrade is to get more versatility and utility from your computer. One of the foremost reasons to upgrade is to get more speed and power so that you can do the same job in less time. Computers operate by processing and manipulating bits of data in the form of 0s and 1s. The processing of some files might require the handling of millions of bits of data. Much of this data might have to be handled over and over again so that billions of iterations might have be performed on a relatively small file. The older computers might require several minutes to do a job that a fast Pentium Pro can do in a fraction of a second.

You might not care about how long you have to wait for a file to be processed. If so, you are a very unique person. Most people don't like to wait, even if it is only a few minutes or seconds. If they are using a computer, they hate to wait even microseconds.

Hertz and Cycles Per Second

When we speak of frequency or hertz, we are talking about how many times per second that an event ishappening. This is also the speed at which an event is occurring. In the old days, when I first became an electronic technician, frequency was called *cycles per second* or CPS. This was a very good description of the events. But someone decided to honor Heinrich Rudolf Hertz (1857-1894), who was the first to produce radio waves. So 1Hz is equal to 1CPS, and 1MHz is equal to one million cycles per second.

CPU Speed and I/O Speed

On the XT and early 286 systems, the I/O speed and the CPU was about the same. But in the newer CPUs the frequency was increased way beyond what some of the software and hardware I/O could support.

One thing that made the XTs so slow is that they were an 8 bit system, operating at 4.77MHz. This means that the CPU handled I/O data at a maximum of 8 bits at a time. The I/O is data that is input from the keyboard, from a disk drive, or any other type of input. Once the data is processed by the CPU, it is output to the disk drives, to a printer or other output device. It takes eight bits, or 0s and 1s, to make one byte. It takes one byte to represent a single character of the alphabet. Once the data to be processed is loaded into RAM, it is sent to the CPU over the eight-bit bus. The CPU processes portions of the data, then sends it back and forth to the RAM or hard disk or wherever it is meant to go.

The old XT communicated over the eight-bit bus between the CPU, the RAM and the I/O. Because it takes eight bits or one byte of on/off digital voltage to make an A or B or any other character, it could only send or receive one character at a time over the 8 bit bus. The XT bus had 20 lines between the CPU and RAM so it could only address 2^{20} (2 to the 20th power) or 1,048,576 or one megabyte.

The 286 was a vast improvement over the XT. It was a 16-bit system, so it could handle two bytes at a time. The 286 system also added four more lines to the bus for a total of 24. So we could now address 2^{24} or 16,777,216 or 16 million bytes of memory.

The 386DX was still another tremendous improvement over the 286 system. It was a 32-bit system, which means that it could transfer four bytes at a time back and forth to memory. Also 2^{32} bytes made it possible for the CPU to address 4,294,967,296 or four gigabytes (4Gb) in memory. Originally, the 386 operated at 16MHz. Later some systems were designed to operate as high as 40MHz.

The early 486DX operated at 25MHz. Like the 386DX, it had a 32-bit bus system between the CPU and the RAM. But it had an improved data handling capability and an 8K internal cache system that made it much faster than the fastest 386. Later the 486 CPU frequency was increased up to as 33Mhz, then 50MHz, then the 33MHz was doubled to 66MHz internally.

The 486DX has a built-in math coprocessor. Intel later introduced the 486SX, which did not have the math coprocessor. It was a bit slower for some operations but was much less expensive. Shortly after the 486SX introduction, Intel made available their OverDrive CPUs. The Over-Drive CPUs operate internally twice as fast as they do externally. For instance, an OverDrive CPU for a 25MHz system will double the clock frequency for an internal processing speed of 50MHz; a 33MHz system will operate at 66MHz internally. Because the OverDrive chips operate externally back and forth between the RAM at the original speeds of 25MHz or 33MHz, the actual overall speed increase was about 70%.

Intel then introduced the DX4 which tripled the 33Mhz to 99MHz. The original Pentium operated at 60Mhz and 66MHz. Later versions operate up to 200MHz. The Pentium II will operate as high as 266MHz.

This high-frequency operating CPU speed and overall computer speed is a bit misleading. The CPU can process the data at the stated speed, but getting the data to and from the CPU might be quite a bit slower. Some of the plug-in boards and some of the peripherals still operate at around 10MHz.

More Memory

My first computer, a little Morrow CP/M machine, had a whopping 64K of memory. That was plenty for the few applications that were then available. But programs were soon developed that required many times more than this. Most all major software programs today require a minimum of 16Mb. I have 32Mb of DRAM installed on my Pentium computer. Even that might not be enough in the future.

It is very easy and simple to install memory. The cost of memory has declined considerably in the last few months so that it is very reasonable at this time. For more about memory, see Chapter 6.

ROM BIOS

Your computer will have a basic input/output system (BIOS) on one or two plug-in chips on the motherboard. As the name suggests, it controls the input and output of data to the computer. In the early days, they were fairly simple because not too many applications were available. The original IBM PC didn't even support hard disk drives. BIOS chips have improved to meet the needs as applications have proliferated.

I have an ancient 286 machine that I put together in 1984. When the $3\frac{1}{2}$ inch floppy disks first came out, I immediately bought one for $325. But the BIOS had been designed before the $3\frac{1}{2}$ inch floppy was even dreamed of so I could not install it. I also had problems with several new programs and applications until I bought new BIOS chips.

The BIOS chips on newer motherboards are made with flash memory and can easily be upgraded with software.

CMOS Battery

Every time you booted up the old PC and XT, you had to input the date and time. It is helpful if the time and date is correct because every time a file is created, DOS stamps the file with the time and date. This makes it very easy to determine which of two files is the later one. Several companies made fortunes selling plug-in boards with a battery operated clock. When the 286 was introduced, it had a battery operated clock built onto the motherboard. The early systems used batteries that lasted about two or three years.

The batteries supply power for a complimentary metal oxide semiconductor (CMOS) transistor circuit. Besides keeping the date and time when the power was turned off, these low-power transistors kept the system configuration. It also keeps a record of what types and kinds of floppy hard drives, type of monitor, and keyboard that are used in the system. In some cases, it remembers what files or programs you were working on when the computer was turned off.

If your system does not keep accurate time, the battery might need to be replaced. The early IBM 286 ATs used a battery that cost over $30. Many of the clone builders designed a system that used the low-cost alkaline batteries. Most systems used a tubular lithium battery that was soldered to the motherboard. This made it very difficult to replace. Modern systems use batteries that are easily replaced. The battery is often a small blue cylinder. Several companies offer replacement batteries. Look in computer magazines such as Computer Shopper. These batteries might also only last two or three years. One factor in the battery life is how often you use your computer. While the computer is on, it draws its power from the wall socket. When it is off, the CMOS transistors must be kept alive by the lithium battery. If your system consistently loses time, it could be that you need to replace the battery. If your battery goes completely dead, it will lose all of your configuration data. You might not be able to use your computer. When this happens, some people might think they need to buy a new computer.

Before you replace the battery, make sure that you have a backup or written information of all of the information in your CMOS setup.

Once the battery is disconnected, or goes completely dead, the CMOS transistors lose all of their information. There are some utility programs that will make a backup of your CMOS setup. Usually it isn't that complicated. It will have the date and time, the type of monitor, keyboard, floppy and hard drives that you have. For older systems, the type of hard drives is critical. You must re-input to the system the exact data that was in the original CMOS setup. This data is the type of drive which tells the system how many cylinders the disk has, how many heads, how many sectors, the precomp and landing zone. If you don't replace the CMOS setup information exactly, you might not be able to access your hard drive. You shouldn't have that problem with most newer plug and play systems. The CMOS can automatically recognize the drive and all of its specifications.

Most systems will give you an opportunity to access your CMOS setup while it is going through the boot routine. Usually you have to press the Escape key, Delete key, or a combination of keys. You might have to check your documentation for which keys to press. I forgot the combination used on one of my systems, so I just hold down a key on the keyboard while it is booting up. The system will beep at me, then give me a keyboard error and tell me to press F1 to continue or F2 for setup. Most systems will react the same way.

If you replace the battery, make sure that you install it the same way. Make a diagram showing the positive and negative ends before you remove the battery.

It is very easy to forget how a battery or other chip was installed. Some of the batteries on the newer motherboards might be in a square chip-like device that can be plugged into a socket. I unplugged the battery on my Pentium Micronics motherboard to take a photo of it. When I got ready to plug it back in, I had forgotten how it was originally plugged in. There were no markings on the board to show how it should be installed. If I plugged it in backwards, it could ruin the CMOS chips. I was rather unhappy with myself until I remembered that I had taken some photos of the motherboard earlier. I was quite lucky in that one of the photos showed how the device was plugged in. Figure 2-2 shows the newer type battery on a Pentium motherboard. Figure 2-3 shows the early type of round cylinder type battery. It is seldom ever used now. Figure 2-4 shows a round, flat modern lithium battery at the right center edge. It is about the size of a quarter and is very easy to replace. It is used on many of the latest motherboards. The long slots at the bottom are for SIMM memory. It can accept four 30 contact SIMMs and two 72 contact modules.

Fig. 2-2
A plug-in battery.

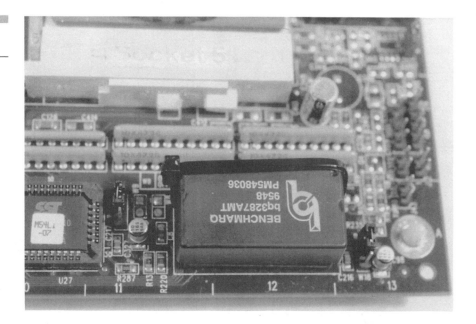

Fig. 2-3
An early cylindrical battery. This type is seldom used today. This photo also shows the correct way that the power supply should be plugged into the motherboard. It can be plugged in backwards. Notice that the four black wires are in the center when correctly plugged in.

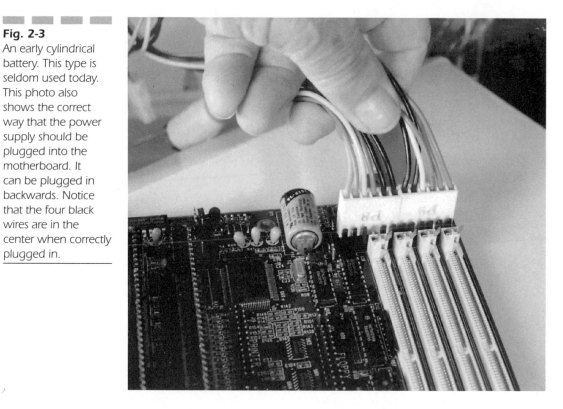

Fig. 2-4
A motherboard with a round, flat lithium battery in the right-center edge. The long sockets in the lower-right corner are for SIMM memory modules. This motherboard can accept 30 contact or 72 contact modules.

Backup Your Hard Disks

Before you do any upgrading, you should have a complete backup of your data. It is possible that some of your data can never be replaced. If your data is worth anything at all, it is worth backing it up. It is very easy to lose or erase files that might have taken many hours to create. It can disappear in a fraction of a second.

You will want to make sure that your hard disk is backed up at all times. You never know when it might fail, or you might accidentally erase a critical file. There are several good backup software programs available. One of them comes free with your copy of DOS, the BACKUP and RESTORE commands, but it is not very sophisticated. The commercial backup programs cost a bit of money, but their speed, versatility, and convenience make them worthwhile. Many hardware systems such as tape or a second hard disk can be very good backup methods.

By all means, you should have a boot disk with your autoexec.bat, config.sys, and the basic information from your CMOS setup.

Input Devices

One of the most used input devices is the keyboard. If you use your computer very much, then you know the importance of the keyboard.

It is the primary method of data input. If the keys are too soft, or they don't suit your typing style, then you should consider upgrading. Keyboards are now very inexpensive.

The PC and XT keyboards look exactly like the 286 and 386 keyboards, and even have the same connector, but if you plug one into a 286 or any later motherboard, it will not work. Some later model keyboards have a small switch underneath that allows them to work with both systems.

Add a Mouse or Trackball

One of the biggest selling points of the Apple Macintosh is the fact that it is so easy to learn and use. With a mouse you just point and click. The Windows programs makes using a PC as easy to learn and use as the Macintosh. There are thousands more programs and hardware available for the PC than for the Macintosh.

Trackballs operate much the same way as a mouse, but they might require much less desk space. Some companies have developed keyboards with a built-in trackball.

Scanners

A scanner is essential if you plan to do any kind of desktop publishing. There are many other times when you can save a lot of time by simply scanning a printed page or drawing into your computer.

There are now several different types of scanners and some very good software to go with them. Scanners are now fairly inexpensive, even the color ones. They are very easy to install. See Chapter 11 for more details about input devices.

Communications

With a modem your computer can communicate with thousands of bulletin boards, on-line services, and other computers. It uses the telephone line almost as easily as you do. Most bulletin boards are crammed full of public-domain and shareware programs. Many of these programs are as good as the high-cost commercial programs.

Downloading just one of these programs might pay for the cost of a modem.

At the present time we have two different companies with 56K modems competing to be recognized as a standard. One or the other should be adopted by the time you read this. The World Wide Web is absolutely essential to most business and general public today. A 56K modem will make it a lot easier to communicate on the Web.

Very few offices or businesses can exist today without a fax machine. Almost all modems now also have a built-in fax.

Printers

Printers are a very important part of your computer system. If you have an old dot matrix printer, you might be unhappy with the quality. New printers can deliver near-letter-quality type. Most of them are fast and comparatively inexpensive. Even the new laser printers are coming down in price to where they are quite affordable.

There are several types of color printers, from dot matrix with color ribbons, color ink jets, and laser-type color printers. The color printers are coming down in price.

Laser printers have many components in common with the copy and scanner machines. Some companies such as Canon and Okidata have now integrated several different functions such as a printer, copier, scanner, and fax into a single machine.

Gutenberg started developing movable print in about 1436. We have come a long way since then. Chapter 13 discusses the many types of printers that are available.

Plug 'n Play and Setup Advisor

There are some boards and components that are very difficult to install, especially if you do not have documentation for all of the boards and devices already installed in your computer. Many boards and components have to have jumpers or switches set so that they will operate on a unique interrupt request (IRQ) and memory address. If two devices are set to use the same IRQ, there will be a conflict, and it is possible that neither device will work. If you don't have the documentation that shows how the installed devices are set, you can only guess as to which IRQs might be free.

We now have Plug 'n Play system for most of our newer boards. The board or device will check your computer system and determine which IRQ and memory address is free. But there are still times when it is very difficult to install a unit.

The TouchStone Company at (800) 831-0450 has developed WINCheckIt. This software program will check your system for any IRQ conflicts and tell you which IRQs are available. You can then play "what if" by asking what would happen if you wanted to install something like a Sound Blaster board. The program would recommend which IRQ and memory address to use. The CheckIt Setup Advisor has a fairly large library of components and devices that can be installed in your PC. It knows how each one of them should be configured so when you ask "What if I installed a Novell network interface card (NIC)?", it would be able to tell you how to set it for whatever free IRQs that you had. WINCheckIt has several other essential utility programs for troubleshooting and maintenance of your computer.

If you ever intend to install a fax/modem board, a mouse, a network card, a printer, or any of dozens of other devices, you should have the WINCheckIt. It can possibly save you many hours of frustration.

Software

When we speak about upgrading a computer we usually think about hardware. But upgrading your software is just as important as upgrading the hardware. Without software, you could not run your computer. Software is as essential to a computer as gasoline is to an automobile.

There are thousands and thousands of different software programs that can be used with our computers. The software, along with the many different plug-in boards, makes the computer one of the most versatile tools ever developed.

You don't have to be a programmer to upgrade your computer's software. There are billions of dollars worth of software that has already been developed. There is ready made software for just about any application you can imagine. New programs and improvements are being introduced daily. This software can give you great versatility, utility, and capability.

Software to run your computer might cost even more than the computer. But there are ways to save hundreds of dollars and still buy first class brand name software. Read Chapter 19 about how you can trade in an older copy or a competitor's copy of a program to upgrade.

There are several public-domain and shareware programs that are either free or very inexpensive. Check the pages of most computer magazines for listings of shareware. Shareware is also available from most bulletin boards. You will find a listing of public-domain and shareware catalogs in Chapter 21.

Booting Up

Every time you turn on your computer it *boots* up. Boot is short for bootstrap, which is taken from an old saying of *pulling one's self up by their own boot straps.* When the computer is turned on, a small program in read only memory (ROM) causes the computer to search for a boot routine on track one of a floppy disk in drive A. If there is a non-bootable disk in drive A it will give you an error, and ask that you correct it. If there is no disk in drive A it looks for the routine on track one of drive C.

Ways to Benefit from Your Upgraded Computer

You can use your computer for thousands of things such as desktop publishing, for telecommuting, for bulletin board and Internet access, networks, and many other business uses. It can be a great educational tool. There are now thousands of educational programs for everyone from kindergarten up to and beyond graduate schools. It can also be a great recreation tool for playing games such as solitaire, chess, and hundreds of others.

Multi-Media

It is now possible to turn your computer into a full orchestra. You can add sound and MIDI interfaces. You can use it to play music with a CD-

ROM or sound boards. You can use a computer to create music, and you can do it even if you know very little about music. You can enter one note at a time, the software can then assemble it, add chords and other musical instruments, so that it might sound like a 100 piece orchestra.

CD-ROM

The cost of CD-ROM drives has come way down. I bought a CD-ROM drive in 1987 that cost over $1000. You can now buy a 24X that is 24 times faster for a little over $100.

The cost of CD-ROM disks has also come way down. There are now hundreds of programs that are quite reasonable. The programs include everything from games to very complex science and technology subjects. They can be an excellent educational tool.

There Is No End to Upgrade Possibilities

There are many other things that you can do to improve and enhance the performance and capabilities of your computer. It is impossible to list them all. One reason is that new devices, hardware, and software are being developed and introduced every day. We could never have a complete list.

Sources

One of the better sources for information about computers and components is computer magazines. There are hundreds of them being published today. Most are filled with ads because ad revenue is the thing that makes them possible. Several magazines are listed in Chapter 22.

Mail order is discussed in Chapter 22. It might be one of your better alternatives for purchasing your components and supplies.

Another good source is computer shows and swaps. If you live near a large city, there will probably be one going on every weekend. I enjoy going to them even if I don't need anything. It is almost like a circus atmosphere.

Of course, whenever possible you should patronize your local computer dealer. The prices might be slightly higher than the mail-order houses or the prices at computer swaps, but local dealers might be able to give you help and support and answer questions if you have problems.

You should also join a user group and attend meetings. You will find people at these meetings who can help you and exchange ideas with you. Most groups also are able to acquire public-domain software and other goodies at a discount.

Besides being able to download public-domain software, if you have a modem, you can access bulletin boards, the World Wide Web, and the Internet and usually get help for many of the problems that you might have.

Troubleshooting and Repairing

You have to know what is wrong in order to repair your computer. Chapter 23 tells you how to find most common problems and how to fix them.

In most cases you will want to replace, rather than repair. For instance, over the years, I have had several floppy disks become defective. In 1983, an IBM 360K floppy disk drive cost over $400. When one became defective, it was worth it to send it out and have it repaired.

You can buy a floppy drive today for about $25. Most repair shops charge from $50 to $100 an hour for labor plus parts. It is much better to throw the old drive away and replace it with a new one.

The same goes for most motherboards. It is possible that a circuit trace on a motherboard might become broken. Or one of the IC chips might become defective. It might take hours of time and some very sophisticated equipment to find the fault. Even when the fault is detected, it might require some highly technical skills to repair or to remove and resolder a component.

In most cases, it is more cost effective to scrap the motherboard and replace it with a new one. The same goes for most of the other components in your computer. In most cases, repairing means replacing the component.

Why You Should Do It Yourself

There are shops, and several mail-order stores, who will upgrade your computer for you. Of course, these stores cannot stay in business unless they make a profit, so it can be a bit expensive. It can also take a lot of time and cause a considerable amount of problems.

First, you have to find someone who will do it for you at a reasonable price. Then you have to lug the computer down to the shop during business hours. Or you can package it up and send it off to a mail-order store.

If you send it to a mail-order store for an upgrade, there can be a problem of communications. Just what do you want done to your computer? How much do you want to spend? How busy is the shop or mail-order store? How reliable is the shop? Can you get a firm price for the total cost and a date as to how soon they can get it back to you? How long can you wait for it? If the shop is very busy, it might take longer than promised to get it out.

What If It Is Too Old to Upgrade?

It is never too old to be enhanced or upgraded in some manner. You can add new monitors, large capacity hard drives, and many other peripherals to almost any of the older computers. I hate to say this, but, depending on what type of upgrade you want, or what you want to do with your computer, it might be better to buy a new computer. You can buy a less expensive one, then add to it to suit your needs.

If you decide that you don't want to upgrade your older computer, what do you do with it?

You might decide to try to sell it. But you probably won't be able to sell the computer for what you think it is worth. The computer that you paid $2500 for a few years ago might not be worth $100 today. Besides, you might not want to go through the bother and hassle of advertising and selling it, especially if you live in a city like Los Angeles. A news story reported that a gang would go to a person's house who had advertised a computer for sale. The gang would tie the person up, then take all of the computers and software that they could find. It would be bad enough losing a computer, but it would be disastrous if I lost all of my software.

If you live near a larger city, there might be computer swap meets every so often. Usually there will be a consignment table at these meets where you can sell your old hardware. But don't expect to make a lot of money off your old components.

Still another alternative is to pass it on to a relative or someone who is just getting started in computers. Or you can keep it and use it for word processing, for a dedicated printer server on a network, or for voice mail.

There are several DOS software packages that work very well on the 286 such as WordPerfect 6.0, WordStar 7.0, Microsoft Works, dBASE IV, and thousands of other perfectly good programs. Most of the standard DOS programs also run very well on an XT. The DOS programs might run a bit slower on an XT or 286 than they would on a 486 so you might have to wait a few seconds or a few minutes. If you are not exactly wealthy, perhaps you can afford to waste a bit of time rather than afford to spend money for an upgrade.

Another alternative might be to donate your old computer to a school, a church or to a charitable organization. Depending on your tax situation, you might come out ahead by donating it and deducting it as a gift on your income tax return.

Buying a Used Computer

You might find some very good bargains in buying a used computer. You can then upgrade it to suit your needs. You might look around your area and check the classified ads.

If you work for a large company, chances are that they are in the process of buying new more powerful systems to meet their added business needs. (A basic law, based on Parkinson's Laws, is that the need for more and larger computer systems grows in a logarithmic fashion each year that the company is in business whether or not the business increases.) Try to find out what the manager of the computer procurement department is doing with the old computers. Some companies pass them down to secretaries and other people who are low on the totem pole. Many companies will sell them to their employees for a good price. Talk to the manager and remind him how much goodwill that such a practice can buy for the company.

New Business Opportunity

After you finish this book, I think you will agree that it is very easy to upgrade a computer. Once you see how easy it is, you might even want to go into business. Worldwide there are several million computers in use at this time. About half of them are older computers that could be easily upgraded. Many of these older computers might be sitting in a corner and not being used because they might have a defective floppy disk drive or some other minor problem that could be easily fixed.

Many companies are buying new computers because they don't realize how easy and inexpensive it is to upgrade or repair their older ones. That is a terrible waste of money and good resources. After you have read this book you might want to go into business upgrading and repairing older computers.

A Few Minor Upgrades

About Upgrading

This chapter details a few minor upgrades intended to help you get your feet wet. By minor upgrades, I mean things like adding a sound board, a modem/fax board, a network card, an external modem, an external hard drive, a new printer, a new monitor, and other components. You can dive into the heavy-duty stuff, such as installing a new motherboard, hard disk drives, and CD-ROMs in later chapters.

If you have an IBM computer or a compatible clone, you have a machine that is quite versatile. There are over ten billion dollars worth of boards and peripheral hardware that can be used with your computer. With this hardware, an IBM or clone can be upgraded or configured to do almost anything that you can imagine.

There is also about ten billion dollars worth of software that can be used with the PC. There are still millions of old XTs and 286s in use today. Many of them still do everything that is needed, so there is no need to think about upgrading. But many of the software packages developed in the last few years, during the Windows era, will only run on machines such as the 486 and Pentiums.

You might not have to buy one of the newer and more powerful, and more expensive, machines to take advantage of the newer software and hardware. You can easily upgrade an older PC. Even if you have a fairly new PC, there are many ways that you can add to it to make it better.

One of the features that makes the PC so versatile and useful are the expansion slots on the motherboard. There are hundreds of different boards that you can plug into these slots to configure a PC to do almost anything that you want it to do.

If you have been putting off adding or replacing a board in your computer because you were afraid that you might mess something up, don't wait any longer. There is really not much that you can do to harm your computer or yourself. If you know which end of a screwdriver to use, you will have no trouble upgrading your computer. And you can save a bundle.

Installing a New Board

You might not have the money or the inclination to perform a major upgrade at this time. There are several minor upgrades that are very simple and very easy to do. If you have a fairly late-model computer with Windows 95, it is a snap because your computer will have plug and play. I don't want to discourage you, but it might be a bit more difficult to add some upgrades to older machines, especially if you do not have all the documentation. By documentation, I mean that you should have a manual or specification sheet for each board or device installed in your computer. Realistically, not many people have all the documentation, especially if the computer was bought some time ago.

Adding a new board is one of the most common upgrades. Maybe you need a modem so you can access the World Wide Web or a bulletin board system (BBS). Most of the bulletin boards are crammed full of public-domain software and other goodies. The download of a single public-domain program might be worth more than what a modem would cost.

Just a few years ago, I bought a combination 2400-baud modem and 9600-baud fax board for a little over $900. I recently bought a 33.6K modem/fax board for $79. One reason the boards are so inexpensive now is that an entire fax/modem can be integrated on one or two VLSI chips. Some of the new modems now can transmit at a speed of 56K. If you plan to do a lot of telecommunications, it will be well worth it to buy a new high-speed fax/modem.

Maybe you need to install something such as an adapter board for a new color monitor, or a sound card, or add any of several other boards and components. Here are some simple instructions to install a plug-in board:

Step 1: Remove case cover. First turn off the power and unplug the power cord. If you have an older desktop computer, it probably has five screws in the back that hold the cover on. There will be a screw in each corner and one at the top in the center. You might find four screws in the right-rear corner that holds the power supply. The air vent that you will see here is part of the power supply. You should not remove any screws except those that hold the case cover in place.

The inside of your computer is safe. Except for the power supply, which is completely enclosed, the highest voltage in your computer is only 12 volts. Of course if you are going to open your computer and add or change anything, there won't even be 12 volts in it. Because the very first thing that you did was to turn off the power. Right?

Caution! Once the cover is removed, make sure that you touch an unpainted metal part of the chassis so that you will discharge yourself of any static electricity. This is especially so if you are working in a carpeted area. You have probably walked across a room and touched a doorknob and got a shock. You can build up several thousand volts of electrostatic voltage on yourself. If you touch a fragile semiconductor, you could possibly damage it.

Another caution! Never plug in or unplug a board, cable, or any component while the power is on. The fragile transistors and semiconductors on these boards and components can be easily destroyed. It only takes a second to turn off the power.

Note: It is always a good idea to turn off the power when removing or replacing anything in your computer, but the PC-Card (PCMCIA) system does not require it. You can safely "hot swap" or unplug or plug in any PC-Card component while the power is on. A new Uniform Serial Bus (USB) will also allow hot swapping.

Step 2: Make a diagram. I mentioned this earlier, but it is worth repeating, if you are going to remove any boards or change any cables or switch settings, make a drawing or diagram of the original setup. It is very easy to forget how a chip or cable was plugged in. Many cables and connectors can be plugged in backwards or into the wrong receptacle. I am ashamed to admit it, but I once ruined an expensive BIOS chip because I plugged it into the wrong socket.

It only takes a minute to make a rough diagram. It might save you money and hours of agony and frustration in trying to solve a problem that was caused because something was plugged in backwards or into the wrong receptacle.

You might also use a felt tip marking pen or some fingernail polish and put a stripe on all the cable connectors and the board connectors before they are unplugged. Vary the location of the stripes on the connectors so that when they are plugged together the stripes will be lined up. You can tell immediately if it is the right connector and if it is plugged in properly.

Step 3: Set switches and jumpers. If you have a late-model computer with Windows 95, it will have a plug-and-play system. If the board or whatever you are installing was designed for the plug-and-play specifications, it should be recognized and automatically configured to the proper IRQ and memory address.

If you have an older "plug and pray" system, it might be rather frustrating trying to install a board that uses an IRQ and a unique memory address. This is especially a problem if you don't know which IRQs and addresses are used by other components in your system. If you are upgrading an older system, when you buy a board, or any component, always make sure that you get some kind of manual or documentation

with it. Check the manual or documentation for installation instructions. It might have some switches or shorting bars that must be set to
configure the board to your system, or to whatever it has to do. Your
computer has certain addresses and interrupt request (IRQ) assignments.
If two devices are set for the same IRQ it will cause a conflict. One very
good reason to build your own computer is that when you buy a component, you will get some kind of documentation. You will have documentation for each component in your system. When you buy an
assembled system, you might not get any documentation at all for the
individual components.

If you have several boards in your computer, they might already be
configured and set for certain addresses and IRQs. It would be nice to
have a document or log near your computer that shows how each one is
configured. This way you can look at the log and determine which IRQs
and addresses are available. If you don't have such a record, perhaps you
should start one with whatever board you happen to be installing.

If you have MS-DOS 6.0 or later on your computer, the MSD command can show you just how your computer is configured. Just type
MSD at any DOS prompt and it will give you several diagnostic options.

Getting all of the IRQs and memory addresses set properly can be
very frustrating and time consuming. The WINCheckIt utility software
from the TouchStone Company at 1-800-531-0450 does a much better job
than the MSD command. It spots existing configuration problems and
helps you avoid upgrade conflicts. It can greatly simplify the installation
process.

After you have set any necessary switches on the new board, look for
an empty slot and plug your board in. It doesn't matter which slot. The
slots are all connected to the standard bus. If you look closely at the
motherboard, you might see etched lines that go across the board to
the same pin on each slot connector.

Multi-layered motherboards In most cases, it is physically impossible to
plug a board into a slot backwards, but you should make sure that it is
plugged in all the way. Be very careful when you plug the boards in. Some
slot connectors are very tight, and it might be difficult to get the board to
seat properly. If you press down too hard you could flex and damage the
motherboard. The copper circuit traces on the motherboard that carry
the signals to all of the various components are very complex. Some traces
might have to cross over other traces. So they usually place traces that
would cross over others on separate thin layers of plastic. The traces on
the separate layers are then connected. There might be as many as 10 or

more layers in a motherboard or other printed circuit boards. The layers of plastic are then fused together into a solid board. The traces in the various layers are connected to each other at various points and to the components without having to cross over or interfere with other circuit traces. Using several layers for the various traces is similar to a highway system with overpasses and clover leafs.

If a motherboard is excessively flexed, it is possible to break some of these traces in the various layers and ruin the motherboard. The motherboard sits on plastic standoffs so there are areas beneath it where there is very little support.

After you are satisfied that the board is seated properly, install a screw in the back bracket to hold it in place. It helps if you have a magnetized screwdriver to hold the screws while getting them started. If you don't have a magnetized screwdriver, you can magnetize one by rubbing it vigorously against any strong magnet. (If you have a stereo system, your large speaker will have a strong magnet around the voice coil.) You should be careful not to place the magnetized screwdriver, or any magnet, near any of your floppy disks because it could partially erase them.

Cooling system   As long as you have the cover off, check to make sure that the openings in the rear panel above any empty slots have blank covers installed. The little electrons that represent bits of data might get hot as they go racing around through the semiconductors in your computer. Heat is an enemy of all semiconductors. What you hear when you turn on your computer is not from those little electrons. Most of the sound you hear is the cooling fan located in the power supply.

The power supply fan draws air from the front of the computer, pulls it over the boards and components, and forces it out through the rear opening of the power supply. To make it work efficiently, all of the openings in the rear panel should have blank covers installed. There should be no obstruction in the back or the front of your computer that would interfere with the flow of air through the power supply.

Some of the 486 and Pentium CPUs run very hot, so small fans might be installed on top of the CPU. Figure 3-1 shows a VL bus Pentium motherboard, the two brown slots. Figure 3-2 shows a Pentium motherboard with a PCI bus, the three white slots. More about buses in the next chapter.

Step 4: A final check.   Caution! Install only one item at a time, then turn on the computer and make sure that it works. If you install two or three items, and your computer does not work, you might have trouble determining which one is at fault.

Fig. 3-1
An early Pentium
motherboard with
two brown VL bus
slots in the upper
center. The 60MHz
CPU is shown upside-
down alongside the
Type 3 socket.

Fig. 3-2
A later Pentium
motherboard with
three white PCI
sockets. The 120MHz
CPU is shown
upside-down near
the CPU Type 5
socket.

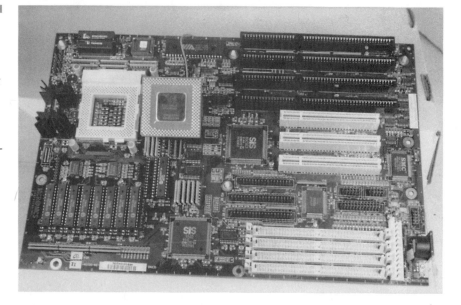

Once you have installed your new board, or whatever, check it again
to make sure that any switches and jumpers are set, cables are installed
properly, and everything is right. Then connect the keyboard, the monitor, and reinstall any boards or cables that were removed. If you are satisfied everything is proper, connect the power and try the system out

before you replace the cover. There have been times when I have installed new parts, then replaced the cover, turned on the power, and it didn't work. It was usually some small thing that I had not done, or had done improperly. So I would end up having to remove the cover again. It doesn't hurt at all to run your computer without a cover. I have several computers. I am constantly running tests, evaluations, and trying out new boards and products on my computers. Most of the time I don't even bother to replace the covers on them.

One reason to have a cover on your computer is to shield and prevent it from radiating television and radio interference. The FCC gets very concerned about this, but in most cases, the interference from a computer will not affect a television set unless it is within a few feet of it.

Some of the Functions of the BIOS

If you have just added a new component to your system, you might have to go into your BIOS system and configure it for the new component. If you have a late-model system and Windows 95, it might automatically recognize the component as a plug-and-play item.

During the boot-up, most systems will allow you to view the BIOS and make any changes necessary. On some systems, you have to hit the Delete key, on others it might require a combination of two or more keys.

Here is what the AWARD Software BIOS in one of my Pentium machines looks like:

STANDARD CMOS SETUP	SUPERVISOR PASSWORD
BIOS FEATURES SETUP	USER PASSWORD
CHIPSET FEATURES SETUP	IDE HDD AUTO Detection
POWER MANAGEMENT SETUP	SAVE & EXIT SETUP
PNP AND PCI SETUP	EXIT WITHOUT SAVING
LOAD BIOS DEFAULTS	
LOAD SETUP DEFAULTS	

Clicking on any of the items brings up another screen that offers several options. Clicking on the STANDARD CMOS SETUP brings up a screen that allows you to set the date and time, the type of hard disks you have, the type of A and B drive floppies, the type of video, the amount of memory, and several other options.

POST

One of the things the BIOS does every time you turn on your computer is a Power On Self Test (POST). If it finds that something is not present, it might stop and beep at you and display a code. Each manufacturer has their own code system, but there is a basic code listing in Chapter 23 under troubleshooting.

BIOS sounds a bit like BOSS. Actually the function of the BIOS is quite similar to that of a boss in a small factory. The boss gets there early, checks all the equipment to make sure it is in working order, then opens the doors for business. This is similar to the start-up procedures that happen when you first turn your computer on. It first does a Power On Self Test, or POST. It checks the RAM memory chips for any defects. (The early IBM memory check took a considerable amount of time to make a thorough memory check. Almost always the memory check was okay. The clone makers noted this, so they designed a BIOS that did a much faster check. Most of the newer BIOSs give you the option to bypass the RAM memory test if you want to.) The BIOS then checks the keyboard, the floppy and hard disk drives, the printer, and other peripherals. If it finds something wrong, it reports an error and displays a code number.

Hard Disk Drive Types

When IBM introduced the AT in 1984, their BIOS recognized only 15 types of hard drives. If your drive wasn't on the list, you were in trouble. IBM also had a diagnostic or setup diskette that was used to tell the computer such things as the type of floppy drives and hard drives, and the type of monitor that was installed. You also needed the floppy diskette to set the time and date.

The compatible BIOS developers soon came out with BIOS chips that allowed these functions to be set from the key board. You didn't need the floppy diskette. The types of hard disk soon grew from a list from 15 to 46 different types. But manufacturers kept developing more and more new hard disk drives. Rather than trying to have a standard type for each new hard disk, a 47th type was included that let the user input any characteristics or types not included in the 46 types listed.

Incidentally, many plug-in boards such as the hard disk controllers, monitor adapters, and peripheral devices have their own BIOS chips.

BIOS Utilities

Some of the older BIOS chips had some comprehensive diagnostics. They could be used to do a low-level format on a hard disk. They could test and determine the optimum interleave factor. They could do a surface analysis of the disk and mark the bad sectors. They could check the performance of the hard and floppy disk drives, measure their access speed, the data transfer rate, and measure the rotational speed of the drives. They could run tests on the keyboard, the monitor and adapter, serial and parallel ports, and do several other very useful diagnostic tests. Many of these tests and utilities such as the low-level format and the interleave factor are no longer necessary.

Boot Program

When the POST is run, if everything is okay, a signal is sent to the drive A: to run the boot program. If there is no disk in drive A:, it then tries to find a boot program on the hard disk. This boot program initializes the peripheral equipment, runs the config.sys and autoexec.bat programs, and allows you to start doing business.

Interrupt Control

During the day the boss, or BIOS, will receive several interruptions or requests for services. These interrupts might be minor or major. Depending on the type of request, the boss might shut down everything and put everybody to work to satisfy that one request. A minor request might have to wait until the present task is finished.

Depending on the software and type of computer, the boss might have the facilities to accomplish several tasks at the same time, or do multitasking. With the proper hardware and software, the BIOS might even be able to do multiusing functions and allow several computers to access it and utilize its software and hardware.

The boss must be savvy enough to work with many different types of requests and orders. There are thousands of different software programs and hardware. The boss must be able to take the orders, route them to the proper hardware device, such as the screen, keyboard, disks, printers, modems, or whatever. Sometimes the boss might be asked to do something that it doesn't have the equipment or the ability to do. Because the boss is very conscientious, it will keep trying to accomplish the impossible task. If you leave your computer on and come back a week later, it might still be trying to satisfy the request. It might ignore any requests from the keyboard to stop. Depending on the type of problem, you might have to do a "warm boot," CTRL-ALT-DEL, to restart the computer. You might even have to turn the power off and do a "cold boot," to completely clear the computer, in order to restart it.

The BIOS provides us with the date and time when we ask for it. It also appends the date and time to any file or program created. You can always reset the time and date. For older machines, you have to reset the time when going back and forth from standard time to daylight saving time. The Windows 95 automatically resets your system time. If the on-board battery becomes old and depleted, your computer might lose time. When this happens, you might need to replace the battery.

As you might imagine, the BIOS is quite an important part of our computers.

Compatibility

Many of the chips that are used to make a computer such as the CPU and the RAM chips might be made by many different companies such as Intel, AMD, and others. For their early PCs, IBM designed and developed their own ROM BIOS using EPROM chips. Because IBM was the biggest, the industry leader, and standard setter, a whole lot of software was written for the IBM PC and its BIOS system.

Just as it is possible to copy software from one disk to another, it is possible to copy the contents of one EPROM chip to another with the EPROM burner. Of course, you know that it is illegal to make and distribute copies of software that is copyrighted. But that has not stopped a lot of people from doing it. The same is true for illegal copying of ROM chips.

In order to be compatible with IBM, several of the early clone makers copied the IBM BIOS. Naturally IBM was not too happy about this and threatened to sue.

Phoenix Technologies and Award software were two of the several companies that began developing a compatible BIOS for the clone makers. Because they could not copy the IBM BIOS, their BIOSs could never be 100 percent compatible. But they did almost everything that the IBM did.

And in some cases, they did things better than IBM did, such as the reduced time for checking RAM memory.

It wasn't long before there were more compatible clones in existence than IBM PCs. It didn't take long for the software developers to take note of this fact, and they began writing programs that could be run on any machine, not just IBM. Today there are very few, if any, programs that have BIOS compatibility problems.

BIOS Size

The early BIOS programs were relatively simple. PCs and XTs used a single 64K chip for the BIOS. The early 286 needed a 128K chip. But the ever-changing technological advances forced changes. The later 286, 386, and 486 machines needed two 256K chips or a single 512K chip. To print out the entire contents of one 512K BIOS ROM would required about 250 pages. A whole lot of instructions and programs can be stored in 512K of ROM.

BIOS Upgrade

At one time, removing and installing a new BIOS was a very good thing to do to bring your computer up to date. Several companies were offering BIOS upgrades and they were fairly reasonable in cost. But it might not be worthwhile today to do a BIOS upgrade on an old XT, 286, or 386 computer. In the first place, you might not be able to find anyone offering an up-to-date BIOS for some of the older machines. If you did find one, it might probably cost more for a BIOS than for a complete new late-model motherboard with a new BIOS. It might be more cost effective to just scrap the motherboard from an old computer and buy a new one, rather than try to upgrade the BIOS.

But it might be well worthwhile to upgrade a machine such as a 486DX2-66 or any of the early Pentiums. When a computer is sold it will have a BIOS that is designed to handle any software or hardware that is presently available. But there are thousands of new products introduced every day. So if you have an older computer, there is a lot of software and hardware that you might not be able to use. You might not be able to use the IDE hard disk drives or IDE CD-ROM drives. You might not be able to run Windows, or some of the Novell and Netware software. You might also be wasting a lot of time while your BIOS tries to do its job.

The BIOS chip developers constantly introduce new versions of their chips to try to keep current. Many of the new motherboards now come with a BIOS in flash memory. This BIOS can be upgraded by download-ing the upgrade over a modem connection or by a floppy disk. In Fig. 3-2, the Pentium motherboard has a flash memory chip in the large square chip in the center. The Pentium motherboard in Fig. 3-1 has a 512K EPROM chip with a white covering, just below the VLB slots.

If you have a 486 or Pentium-class computer that is over two years old, chances are that they have developed a new BIOS that can give it new life. Replacing or upgrading the ROM BIOS is rather inexpensive, and so easy to do that anyone can do it. It is one of the better upgrades that you can do for your computer to bring it up to date.

One of the largest companies who provide BIOS upgrades is the Unicore Company at 800-800-2467. They also have a website at www.unicore.com. They claim to have the largest variety of BIOS upgrades of any company. They can provide upgrades, both flash and standard, for BIOSs from most all companies such as Award, Phoenix, AMI, MR BIOS, and others.

EPROMS

ROM is an acronym for Read Only Memory. *BIOS* is an acronym for Basic Input Output System. The ROM BIOS is a program that has been burned onto EPROM chips. *EPROM* is an acronym for Erasable Program-mable Read Only Memory, which is made up of special light-sensitive transistor circuits. The older BIOS chips were made using EPROMs. Almost all newer BIOS chips are now made using flash memory.

Some of the BIOS system resides in Complementary Metal Oxide Semiconductors (CMOS). These are very low-power transistor circuits that are kept alive with an on-board battery during the time that the computer is off. (Note: If your computer is more than four or five years old, you might need to replace the battery.)

The EPROM chips are made up of special transistors and are available in 64K, 128K, 256K, and 512K sizes. There is a clear glass window over the transistor circuits on the chip. These circuits are sensitive to ultraviolet light (UV). The transistor circuits can be electronically programmed in an EPROM programmer or burner. A program can be read from a floppy or a hard disk and fed to the burner. The individual transistors on the chip will be set to either on or off to reflect the 1s and 0s of the software program. So the program is copied to the chip, just as if it were being copied to another floppy or to a hard disk. Once it is programmed, the glass window of the chip is covered with opaque tape.

If something goes wrong and the program is not exactly right, or needs to be updated, it can be erased and reprogrammed. To erase the program, remove the tape from the glass window and expose the chip to ultraviolet light.

CPU Upgrades

At one time there were several companies who developed processor modules that could transform a 286 into a 386 or a 486, or a 386 into a 486. They also had modules that could double or triple the internal speed of processing. The chips could be installed in most ISA type machines including the PS/1 and PS/2.

There are still a few companies who put together upgrade kits with new and later model CPUs. They are discussed in the next chapter.

Installing a New CPU

This is a very easy upgrade. It takes less than 15 minutes to install a new CPU or module. Just pull off the cover, locate and remove the CPU, and plug in the new module. Before removing the old CPU, make a rough diagram of the orientation of the chips. There should be some indication of which is pin one on the chip or motherboard. Evergreen provides very good documentation, so you shouldn't have any problems.

Pentium Upgrade

The Pentium CPU has 3.1 million transistors, over twice as many as the 486. It is much more powerful and faster than the 486.

There are several Pentium motherboards available. The procedure for upgrading to a Pentium is the same as for any of the other upgrades mentioned earlier. Just remove your old motherboard and install a new Pentium. It is very easy to do.

AMD and Cyrix both offer Pentium-type CPUs that are equivalent to the Intel CPU, but they are much less expensive. More about these CPUs in the next chapter.

Pentium MMX Upgrades

The Pentium MMX and Pentium-class MMX clones are a very easy and excellent way to upgrade. They are discussed in Chapter 5.

Pentium Pro Upgrade

The Pentium Pro is a much more powerful and faster CPU than the Pentium. Cyrix and AMD have Pentium class clones that are much less expensive. It is very simple to replace an old motherboard with one of these units. This will be discussed in Chapter 5.

Pentium II Upgrade

The Pentium II is a version of the Pentium Pro revised to include the MMX technology. It is a very fast and powerful system. It is discussed in chapters 5 and 16.

The Obsolete XT

I would not advise anyone to spend any money upgrading an XT, a 286, or a 386. Because these systems are obsolete, parts for them are usually rather expensive. You could probably buy a new 486 or 586 motherboard for what it would cost to upgrade an old XT. Some might want to upgrade them anyway, either for sentimental reasons or for some other reason.

Though the XT is obsolete, there are still millions of them in existence. For some applications, they are still a good tool. For simple word processing, they can be as good as the most powerful Pentium. Of course, you would not be able to use any of the Windows software on an

XT. But the XT is a good tool for kids or for someone just starting out in computers. One of the best things about an XT computer is that you can buy a used one for peanuts. They are very inexpensive.

There are several things you can add to an old XT to make it better. You can add a color monitor, more memory, a new floppy drive, a hard drive, a coprocessor, a modem, a FAX, a scanner, a CD-ROM, and almost anything that can be added to the more powerful systems. If you need instructions to add any of these items, check the following chapters that discuss these items. Again, rather than make these upgrades, you would probably be better off buying and installing an AMD or Cyrix motherboard in the old XT case. I have seen AMD 586 motherboards, with CPU, for less than $100. More about motherboards and sources in the next chapter.

If you are upgrading an XT or PC, you might have to reset the dual-in-line (DIP) switches on the motherboard. The PC has two DIP switches, the XT has only one. The dip switches are set for various configurations. Here are the settings for the XT at various configurations:

1 is usually set to OFF.

2 is OFF without an 8087, ON with an 8087 coprocessor.

3 OFF, 4 ON if only 128K memory on motherboard.

3 OFF, 4 OFF if 256K or more on motherboard.

5 ON, 6 OFF for color monitor.

5 OFF, 6 OFF for monochrome monitor.

7 ON, 8 ON if only one floppy drive.

7 OFF, 8 ON for two floppy drives.

The motherboards of other systems will be considerably different than an XT. Most of them will also have dip switches or jumpers that need to be set. You should get some sort of documentation with your components. Be sure to check and follow directions.

Installing More Memory in an XT

If you have an XT you can have up to 640K of memory. The later models had DIP sockets for this much memory in the left-front quadrant of the motherboard. Some of the early models only had sockets for up to 256K. In order to add another 384K, you have to buy a memory board and plug it into one of the eight slots.

There will be four banks of memory, with nine chips in each bank. The systems that came with 256K of memory used 64K chips in each bank. For 640K, they used 64K chips in two banks and 256K chips in the other two.

If you need to add memory, check the type that you have installed and buy the same type. When you plug the memory chips in, make sure that they are properly oriented. Pin one usually has a small dot or some sort of marking. All of the chips should be oriented the same way.

Also make sure that all of the legs are plugged in properly. It is very easy to have a leg bend underneath the chip or go outside of the chip socket.

After you install the memory, check your documentation. You will have to set DIP switches 3 and 4 to match the amount of memory that you now have.

Power Precautions

If you have not done it already, a small upgrade that you should make is to install a power strip. This will allow you to plug all of your equipment into one source. You might have five or six power cords from your computer, your monitor, printer, lamps, and other devices plugged into various outlets and extensions. This can be messy and potentially dangerous.

Some older or less expensive equipment might have only two-wire cords. It is possible to plug these devices in so that there is a voltage potential between them. This could cause grounding problems. Check the prongs on the plug. One prong should be wider than the other. This is the ground side. The wider blade should be plugged into the wider slot in the receptacle. If at all possible, buy only those components that have a three-wire power cord and plug.

You should be able to buy a power strip with six outlets for $10 to $15. Each outlet should be able to accommodate the three wire plugs. Some companies advertise very expensive power outlets with filtering. In most cases, they only have a cheap capacitor and a varistor that filters some spikes from the voltage source. But ordinarily there is not that much need for filtering. If you do need a filter, make sure that the unit has a good electronic filter that should include coils and more electronics than just a capacitor and a varistor.

I have a power distribution center. See Fig. 3-3. It is metal enclosure that has a switch for the main power and for five different devices. I sit my monitor on it and can easily turn any of them on or off. The power center has surge and spike protection. It has a modem telephone line

Fig. 3-3
A power distribution
center with a main
power switch and
switches for five
devices. I sit my
monitor on top of it.

Fig. 3-3
A power distribution
center with a main
power switch and
switches for five
devices. I sit my
monitor on top of it.

input connector on the back so that the telephone line can be run through the power center so that electrical spikes can be suppressed before getting to the modem.

Uninterruptible Power Supply

While the San Francisco and Los Angeles areas have very few electrical storms, you might live in an area where there are frequent storms and power outages. If so, you might consider buying an uninterruptible power supply (UPS). This is essential if you do any critical work on your computer. Any time the power goes off, you can lose any data that you are working on. A UPS would take over and keep your computer going if the power is interrupted.

Most word processors and other software can be set to save your files to disk automatically every so often. That way if the power is accidentally switched off or interrupted, most of your file will still be on your hard disk.

The highest voltage that your computer uses is 12 volts. The power supply in the computer takes the 120-volts alternating current (ac) and converts it to direct current (dc) that the computer needs. Several UPS techniques provide uninterruptible power. Most use rechargeable batteries, some even use automobile batteries. The cost of the various systems will depend primarily on the amount of wattage that is needed.

There are a large number of UPS companies. Most advertise in computer magazines. Here are just a few:

Alpha Technologies	(206) 647-2360
American Power Conversion	(401) 789-5735
Best Power Technology	(800) 356-5794
Brooks Power Systems	(215) 244-0624
Clary Corporation	(818) 287-6111
Computer Power Products	(213) 323-1231
Sola Corporation	(312) 439-2800
Tripp Lite Corporation	(312) 329-1777
UPSystems	(213) 634-0621

Green PC

Green PCs help save energy, save you money, and help save the environment. In the past people didn't worry too much about how much energy their computer used. But there are about 150 million computers in use today. They are using a whole lot of energy.

A lot of computers are left on 24 hours a day, 7 days a week. Some believe that leaving the computer on might help make it last a bit longer. When an incandescent lamp is first turned on, a large surge of current passes through the lamp. Most lamps burn out as they are being turned on. A lamp that is never turned off will last longer than one that is frequently turned on and off. A similar thing happens in a computer. When first turned on, there is usually a high current that surges through the electronics. If it is left on, it stabilizes. The temperature also stabilizes. When first turned on, a hard disk might have difficulty operating properly until it has warmed up. For these reasons, some people and some companies never turn their computers off.

Another reason to leave the computer on is if it has a modem or fax board. Many faxes and communications are sent during the night for the cheaper rate.

There really isn't any scientific evidence that leaving the computer all the time will make it last longer. Besides, it will be obsolete before it wears out. However, the government has become concerned about the energy wasted by computers. Computers purchased by the government from now on will have to meet certain energy-saving requirements. Newer-designed computers will meet those requirements. If you are buying a new computer, look for the EPA Saver Star.

Besides directly saving wattage, when the computer and printer are off, less heat is generated. If your office uses air conditioning, it can help save a bit there also.

Even if the device doesn't pay for itself, it is your moral duty to try to save as much energy as possible. Any amount of energy saved helps that much to save the environment.

4

The CPU Upgrade

There are several highly integrated chips on the motherboard, but the most important one is the central processing unit (CPU). It is the brains of the computer. It is so important that the whole computer system will be called by whatever CPU is installed on the motherboard. Depending on what kind of computer you have and what you want to do with it, replacing the CPU might be a very good and cost-effective upgrade. It is also a fairly simple upgrade. In most cases, just remove the cover, remove the old CPU, and drop in a new one.

However, there are several different types of CPUs. The following is a description of a few of them so that you will know which one to choose.

One of the first CPUs was the 4004, introduced by Intel in 1971. It had 2,300 transistors, a fantastic amount at that time. It ran at a blazing 1 MHz. The next generation Pentium from Intel will have over 10 million transistors and can operate at frequencies above 300 MHz. Comparing the early 4004 to some of the CPUs today is about like comparing a World War I biplane to the Space Shuttle.

At one time, there were three major automobile makers in this country. I could look at almost any car and tell you the manufacturer, the year, and the model. Now there seems to be hundreds of auto makers and thousands of models. It is nearly impossible for the average person to look at a car and tell the year or even the manufacturer.

It is getting to be about the same with the CPUs. For several years, Intel was the sole manufacturer of the CPU for the IBM-compatible machines. Now there are several companies making them. Though Intel still has well over 80 percent of the CPU market, they have to constantly be on their toes to retain this share. The competition has helped keep the prices down and has spurred the companies to develop newer and better products.

At one time, the motherboard and CPU were sold as a single unit. In some cases, the CPU was actually soldered to the motherboard. But no more. Today, many of the motherboards are designed so that you can use a large number of different CPUs with them. So a good upgrade strategy might be to simply pull out the old CPU from the motherboard and replace it with a newer one.

Figure 4-1 shows the backside of three different CPUs, a 486 on the left, an early 60 MHz Pentium in the center, and a 120 MHz Pentium on the right. Figure 4-2 shows an Intel Pentium Pro with the cover removed. The CPU enclosure also has a built-in L2 cache. Figure 4-3 shows an AMD K6 CPU. Figure 4-4 shows the Pentium II installed in slot 1 with a heat sink and fan.

Fig. 4-1
The bottom side of three different CPUs, left to right, a 486, a 60MHz Pentium, and a 120MHz Pentium.

Fig. 4-2
An Intel Pentium Pro CPU.

Fig. 4-3
An AMD K6 CPU.

AMD-K6™ MMX Processor
The Superior Engine for Windows® Computing

Fig. 4-4
The Pentium II
installed in slot 1 with
a heatsink and fan.

How a CPU Is Made

Designing and creating a CPU or an integrated circuit is a very complex procedure. Basically, a large high-powered workstation and
computer-aided design (CAD) software can be used for the early
design. The transistors and circuit paths are actually drawn to scale.

The design then is printed out on a very large piece of paper. Once the design is checked for accuracy, it is reduced by several magnitudes, then photographed. The negative image is transferred to a silicon die. Then, using acids and photoengraving procedures and methods, portions of the die are etched away. Finally the photographic image becomes a CPU made up of transistors and circuits in the silicon die.

The CPUs are etched onto a thin slab of silicon about six to eight inches in diameter. Several CPUs can be etched onto a single slab. The chips go through several stages of processing. At the end of the processing, the individual CPUs are cut and separated. They are then tested and selected.

There is lots of money in manufacturing CPUs. But before you decide to go into the business, remember that the above description is very much simplified. The actual cost of setting up an advanced CPU manufacturing facility can be 2 billion dollars or more.

Built-In Coprocessors

The early CPUs were designed without a math coprocessor. If your computing involved a lot of number crunching, a math coprocessor was essential. All CPUs from the lowly PC up through the 486SX were designed without the coprocessor, but all the motherboards had a vacant socket for installing one. In the beginning they were fairly expensive, so unless they had a specific need many people never bothered to install a math coprocessor.

When the 486DX was introduced in April, 1989, it had a built-in coprocessor. Since then all CPUs have built-in coprocessors. This makes them very fast for applications such as spreadsheets and CAD programs that can utilize a coprocessor. But there are many software applications that do not require a coprocessor. The coprocessor is useless unless the software application is designed to use it.

If you have an older system, an XT, 286, 386, or 486SX, you can upgrade by adding a coprocessor. All of the coprocessors have an 87 designation in their number, for instance a coprocessor for an 8088 XT is 8087, for the 286 it is 80287. The 486DX CPU chip has 168 pins. Intel insisted that manufacturers of 486SX motherboards provide a 169-pin socket for a coprocessor. Intel developed a 487SX coprocessor for the 486SX. It was actually a genuine 486DX with an extra pin. When plugged in, it disables the 486SX and takes over all of the CPU and math coprocessor functions. The 487SX operates at the same frequencies that the 486SX does: 16 MHz, 20 MHz, or 25 MHz.

If you have an old 486SX, you could upgrade by buying a 487SX coprocessor. Or you could buy an OverDrive chip to replace the 486SX.

I would not recommend trying to upgrade any CPU with a coprocessor. They are rather difficult to find now. Even if you do find one, it would be rather expensive. It would probably cost less to pull the old motherboard out and replace it with a new one, which would have a new CPU and BIOS and lots of goodies not even dreamed of when some of the older motherboards and CPUs were designed.

What's in a Number?

At one time, there were only two types of CPUs and systems: the original IBM PC (for personal computer) and later, the XT (for extended technology). Soon after, IBM introduced the AT (for advanced technology). Most people eventually called it 286 because it used the 80286 CPU. Then came the 386, then the 486. Several companies began to make clones of the 286, 386, and 486. This did not make Intel very happy. They went to court and sued the companies for using their designations, but found that they could not copyright the CPU numbers. The next logical CPU number should have been 586, but because they couldn't copyright it, they called it the Pentium, which is copyrighted. This didn't bother the clone makers too much. AMD came out with a 586 and Cyrix with a 5X86. To match the Pentium Pro, Cyrix came out with a 6X86. Intel introduced the Pentium II with MMX technology; Cyrix introduced their M2, and AMD their K6. The clones are usually a few steps behind Intel, but are usually able to match anything that Intel produces. And at about 25% less in cost.

CPUs with MMX Technology

Here is an Intel description of its MMX technology:

> Multimedia and communications are driving today's and tomorrow's most exciting and computer-intensive applications. MMX technology is a new extension to the Intel Architecture, which will enhance the performance of these applications, and enable altogether new features and capabilities.

Intel's MMX technology is designed to accelerate the key elements of demanding multimedia and communications applications, such as audio, video, 2D-, and 3D-graphics, animation, and recognition. The technology introduces new instructions and data types that exploit the parallelism inherent in many media processing algorithms, yet maintains full compatibility with existing applications and operating system software.

It features 57 new instructions, eight new 64-bit-wide registers, and four new data types. Integer data, either bytes, 16-bit words, dwords, or a quadword, are packed into the 64-bit registers upon which the MMX instructions operate. A single MMX instruction operates on all elements of the 64-bit register in parallel, providing throughput improvement of as much as 8X for byte operations.

MMX technology uses general-purpose instructions, most of which operate in a single clock cycle. Instruction types supported include the following: basic arithmetic operations (such as add, subtract, multiply, etc.), logical operations (such as AND, OR, AND NOT, etc.), compare operations, conversion instructions to pack and unpack data elements, shift operations, and data movement instructions.

Those who use notebook computers benefit as well from the Pentium processor with MMX technology. By introducing this processor for desktop and mobile systems simultaneously, new applications designed for MMX technology are immediately available to the mobile user. Examples of such applications include videoconferencing over standard telephone lines, software-based video and 3D graphics, and digital image editing and communications. Notebook manufacturers will continue to keep pace with desktop computers not only in performance, but in significant enhancements, such as MMX technology.

MMX technology maintains complete compatibility with the Intel Architecture and is also fully compatible with widely used operating systems and application software. The technology will be included in future processors, including Pentium OverDrive processors for upgradable Pentium processor-based systems.

MMX is designed for the Pentium-class CPUs and later versions. Intel redesigned all of their Pentiums to include the MMX technology. A new Pentium that operates at 233MHz was also introduced. The Pentium Pro was redesigned for MMX and introduced as the Pentium II. AMD and Cyrix Corporations have also developed CPUs with MMX technology. At the present time, the only way to get MMX technology is to buy a motherboard designed for MMX or buy a complete system. The MMX technology is discussed in more detail in the next chapter on motherboards.

Basic Characteristics of CPUs

Table 4-1 shows some of the characteristics of some CPUs.

TABLE 4-1

CPU Characteristics

CPU	Freq.	Volt	Bus	Addr.	Mem.	Cache	Transistors	Date
8088	4.77	5v	8bit	20bit	1M	no	29K	6/79
286	6	5v	16bit	24bit	16M	no	134K	2/82
386	16	5v	32bit	32bit	4G	no	275K	10/85
486	25	5v	32bit	32bit	4G	8K	1.2M	4/89
486DX2	66	5v	32bit	32bit	4G	8K	1.2M	3/92
486DX4	99	5v	32bit	32bit	4G	16K	1.6M	2/94
Pent.	60	5v	32bit	32bit	4G	16K	3.1M	3/93
Pent.	75	3.3v	32bit	32bit	4G	16K	3.3M	3/94
Pent.Pro	150	2.9v	32bit	36bit	64G	16K	5.5M	9/95

Addressable Memory

The 386, 486, and Pentium can address up to four gigabytes (Gb), or 4,000,000,000 bytes of memory. The Pentium Pro can address 16 times more, or 64Gb.

At the present time, I don't know of any vendor who makes a motherboard that would accept even 1Gb of memory. Most Pentium Pro motherboards are designed to accept up to 128Mb of RAM. Eventually, motherboards that will accept several gigabytes of memory will be available.

Moore's Law

I mentioned Moore's Law in Chapter 1. A few years ago, Gordon Moore, chairman of Intel Corporation, noticed a very definite CPU trend. The previous chart basically shows what he observed. Note that the 286 had 125,000 transistors, more than three times the 29,000 in the XT. Very soon the 386 was introduced with 275,000 transistors, which more than doubled the 286, then the 486 with 1.2 million, then soon after the Pentium with 3.1 million, and then the Pentium Pro with 5.5 million. The next Pentium generation (P7) will have over 10 million transistors. The trend is that every 18 months or so the number of transistors and computing power more than doubles. Another trend is that as the power goes up, the price goes down, which is great news for us consumers.

In Table 4-1, the CPU operating frequency listed is the introductory value. Intel was usually rather conservative in the operating frequency recommended. In every case, soon after introduction, the frequency was revised upward. Even the old 8088 was eventually boosted up to as high as 10MHz. The 286 was introduced to run at 6MHz, but very soon many were running it at 8MHz, then as high as 12MHz. Near the end of its reign, some were running it as high as 25MHz.

The 386 was introduced to operate as 16MHz. Almost overnight, people were boosting it up to 20MHz. Eventually, it was revved up as high as 40MHz. When the 486 was introduced, it operated at 25MHz, so some of the 386 CPUs actually ran faster than some of the new 486s. But because of the internal design and number of transistors, the 486 could still outperform a 386 that was running faster.

The first Pentium operated at 60MHz, but before long it was revised so that it ran as high as 200MHz. The Pentium II can run as fast as 266MHz and will eventually run as high as 300Mhz. We have certainly come a long way since that first XT that ran at 4.77MHz.

CPU Frequency and Motherboard Speed

When a software program is run, the program is copied from a hard disk or some other source and loaded into random access memory (RAM). (Actually, it is dynamic RAM that is most often used, or DRAM.) To process the data, the CPU runs back and forth to the DRAM, brings parts of the data into the CPU, processes it and sends it back to DRAM. After the processing is completed, the data is sent back to the hard disk, the printer, or wherever it is needed. The speed at which the CPU operates internally and the external speed used on the motherboard to run back and forth to the DRAM might or might not be the same. The internal operating frequency might be 1X, 1.5X, 2X, 2.5X more than the external motherboard speed.

Memory Bus

As listed in Table 4-2, the 60MHz system processes the data internally at 60MHz and externally to RAM memory also at 60MHz. The Pentium 90MHz, 120MHz, 150MHz, and 180MHz operate internally at those frequencies, but externally at 60MHz. The Pentium 75MHz operates internally at 75 and externally at 50MHz. The Pentium 66MHz, 100MHz, 133MHz, 166MHz, and 200MHz operates internally at those frequencies but externally at 66MHz. Many of the motherboards have jumpers so that it can be configured for whatever speed of installed CPU.

One reason the systems don't operate faster going back and forth to RAM is that very high frequencies are difficult to control. The longer the distance and the length of the bus, the more problems. At very high frequencies, two circuit paths alongside of one another will have a capacitance and an inductance. It is possible that the contents or signals on one circuit would be picked up by the adjacent circuit. It takes extremely careful and costly engineering to design high-frequency circuits.

AMD and Cyrix are developing systems that will operate externally at 75MHz, which is faster than any of the Intel systems. It is expected that eventually systems will be developed to operate externally between the CPU and the RAM at 100MHz.

Remember that the memory bus is not the same as the bus for peripherals. Many of the peripherals, especially the Industry Standard Architecture (ISA) type boards and components still operate at 8 or

TABLE 4-2

Memory Bus Speed

CPU Type	Int. Freq.	Ext. Speed
Pentium 60	60MHz 1x	60MHz
Pentium 66	66MHz 1x	66MHz
Pentium 75	75MHz 1.5x	50MHz
Pentium 100	100MHz 1.5x	66MHz
Pentium 120	120MHz 2x	60MHz
Pentium 133	133MHz 2x	66MHz
Pentium 150	150MHz 2.5x	60MHz
Pentium 166	166MHz 2.5x	66MHz
Pentium 180	180MHz 3x	60MHz
Pentium 200	200MHz 3x	66MHz

10MHz. Because of this limitation, several new, faster bus systems were developed: the Micro Channel Architecture (MCA) by IBM, the Enhanced Industry Standard Architecture (EISA), the Video Electronics Standards Association (VESA), Local Bus (VLB), and the Peripheral Component Interconnect (PCI). There is more about these buses in the next chapter on motherboards. Despite the improved buses, few of them can feed data to the CPU fast enough to keep it busy.

Cache Systems

One solution to the high-frequency problem is to build a cache system as close to the CPU as possible. Often when a program is being processed, the CPU uses blocks of the same data over and over. If a cache is set up nearby to hold this data, then the processing speed can be improved.

Having the cache nearby is so important that, beginning with the 486, a small local 1 (L1) cache of 8K was built onto the same die as the CPU. Beginning with the 486DX4, the internal L1 cache was doubled to 16K. All of the Pentiums have the 16K L1 cache.

In addition to the L1 cache, all systems beginning with the 486 also have a L2 cache on the motherboard, as close to the CPU as possible. The L2 cache might be from 256K and up to 512K or more. With the Pentium Pro, Intel put the L2 cache about as close as it could possibly be to the CPU. They installed it in the same package very near the CPU.

The cache must be very fast, at least 15 nanoseconds (ns). The fastest standard DRAM is about 60ns. For the faster systems, static RAM (SRAM) is often used. The SRAM systems require six to seven times more transistors than DRAM. The Pentium Pro 256K cache uses 15.5 million transistors for 512K it requires 31 million.

Chip Sets

The CPU needs support for several functions such as for direct memory access (DMA), the Interrupts, the timer, and the clock generator. In the early systems, these were all separate chips installed on the motherboard. Now many of the support chips are integrated into a single set such as the Triton for the Pentium and Orion for the Pentium Pro. AMD has developed a chip set for their K6, called the 640 Chipset.

CPU Competition

It is rather interesting to note some of the dates for the introduction of the new CPUs. From the introduction of the 8088 in 1979 to the 286 in 1982 was three years. It was also about three years after this that the 386 was introduced in 1985, and a little over three years before the 486 was introduced in April of 1989.

It was at about this time that Advance Micro Devices (AMD) and Cyrix Corporation introduced clones of some of the Intel CPUs. Up until this time, Intel had no competition. They were selling every CPU that they could make. There was little incentive to spend a lot of money to build new fabrication factories. Such a factory might cost as much as two billion dollars or more.

Ordinarily, Intel would develop a product, then leave it on the market as long as it was still selling well. They would milk it as long as possible, even though they might have had more powerful and better products on hand. No one can dispute the fact that this was good business. But as soon as Intel was presented with a little competition in 1991, suddenly one or more new products have been introduced every year since. Quite often new products were introduced even though the old ones were still selling well. But as soon as a competitor showed any sign of taking a bit of the market, Intel would immediately switch to the new product. Then high-cost advertising campaigns were instituted to try to convince every one that the old product (that was also being sold by a competitor) was no longer a good buy, even though just a few months earlier, they were trying to convince everyone that this product was the best buy in the world.

We have no way of knowing for sure if it was the competition that forced Intel to introduce the new products, but in any case, the competition has been good for consumers. Besides having a greater choice of products, they are much less expensive. I paid $4,450 for my first 486 motherboard, which operated at 25MHz. A Pentium Pro operating at 266MHz costs less than half that much today.

Clone Equivalents

The clone makers have tagged along after Intel at almost every step. They have products that match Intel's CPUs, and at a much lower price.

Soon after Intel introduced the Pentium, Cyrix introduced their 5x86 and AMD their 586. When Intel introduced their Pentium Pro, Cyrix answered with the 6x86. When Intel introduced their Pentium II, Cyrix introduced their M2 and AMD introduced their K6.

There might be a new Pentium-class CPU available by the time you read this. The Centaur Company, a division of Integrated Device Technologies, has announced a new CPU that will operate up to 200MHz and have MMX-compatible instructions. It will be smaller than Intel, Cyrix, or AMD, and it will still be socket 7 compatible. The Company plans to market it at a price much less than Intel, Cyrix, or AMD. They expect to eventually develop a chip that will operate above 200MHz and match the speed of any other comparable chip. They also plan to develop a chip that will work in the Slot 1 socket that Intel developed for Pentium II.

Despite the equivalency, compatibility, and lower price of the clones, Intel still enjoys about 80% of the CPU market.

ICOMP: Why You Might Want to Upgrade

The CPU frequency or speed by itself might not tell you the whole story about a system. There are many things that determine the overall performance of a system. The overall design, the cache, amount of memory, programs being run, and many other variables. But people constantly want to know which system is the best.

Many of the computer magazines have a monthly test report of various systems. In some cases, these test reports might not be entirely fair. One system might be a few nanoseconds faster than another due to some small factor. This might cost the company lost sales if the magazine does not give it a good score. There are several benchmarks that have been developed to compare the various systems. Peter Norton's Utilities from the very beginning had a systems information utility that could measure a system performance against the performance of the XT standard of 1. This is a very basic type test and is not very comprehensive. Intel developed the Intel Comparative Microprocessor Performance (ICOMP) Index test, a series of several benchmark tests that gives you a fairly good idea of how much better the later-model CPUs are compared to early ones. Table 4-3 lists some of the ICOMP figures for some of the Intel CPUs.

TABLE 4-3

Intel ICOMP

CPU	ICOMP
386SX-16	22
386SX-20	32
386DX-25	49
386DX-33	68
486SX-20	78
486DX-25	122
486DX-33	166
486DX2-40	182
486DX2-50	231
486DX2-66	297
486DX4-75	319
486Pent.OD 63	380
486DX4-100	435
486Pent.OD 83	500
Pentium 60	510
Pentium 66	567
Pentium 75	610
Pentium 90	735
Pentium 100	815
Pentium 120	1000
Pentium 133	1110
Pentium 150	1176
Pentium 166	1308

Replacing the CPU

Several CPU upgrades have been developed that can upgrade older CPUs. Shortly after the XT was introduced, one company even made a CPU, the V30, that could upgrade the old XT 8088 CPU. There were several companies that offered kits to convert 286s into 386s. Later most of these same companies offered kits that could convert 286s and 386s into 486 systems by replacing the CPU.

At one time this was a simple and cost-effective method to upgrade a 286 or 386. Today, rather than try to upgrade a 286 or 386 CPU, you would be much better off replacing the motherboard. More about motherboards in the next chapter.

Not listed in the chart is the fact that Intel developed several CPUs to double or even triple the internal frequency of some of their CPUs. They called them *OverDrive CPUs.* Most of them were designed for the 486. Some of them are still available. They have also developed OverDrive CPUs for the original 60 and 66MHz Pentium CPUs. These CPUs used socket-type number 4 with 273 pins. (See the socket chart of Table 4-4.) These motherboards also used a 5-volt source. The later Pentiums used sockets number 5 or 7 with lower voltage and 320 or 321 pins. An OverDrive for the Pentium 75 is also available. This CPU would use the socket 7.

There are millions of 486 systems installed in homes and businesses throughout the world. They are still good machines, but they might be a bit slow. One of the easiest and least expensive upgrades is to remove the old 486 CPU and replace it with a Pentium-class CPU that can operate about four times as fast. Several companies have developed kits that will let you do that. Some of these companies and products are listed later.

One of the limiting factors in replacing the CPU is the type of socket that is installed on your motherboard. Intel created a socket with a Pin Grid Array (PGA) of 168 sockets for the 486, and one with 169 pins for the 487SX CPU. Intel insisted that motherboard makers include both the

TABLE 4-4

Standard CPU Sockets

Socket #	# Pins	Voltage	CPUs
Socket 1	169	5v	486SX, 486DX, 486DX2, 486DX4 OverDrive
Socket 2	238	5v	486SX, 486DX, 486DX2, 486DX4 OverDrive 486 to Pentium OverDrive
Socket 3	237	5v/3.3v	486SX, 486DX, 486DX2, 486DX4 OverDrive 486 to Pentium OverDrive
Socket 4	273	5v	Pentium 60/66, Pentium 60/66 OverDrive
Socket 5	320	3.3v	Pentium 75-133, Pentium 75+ OverDrive
Socket 6	Not used		
Socket 7	321	VRM	Pentium 75-200, Pentium 75+ OverDrive
Socket 8	387	VRM	Pentium Pro

168-pin and the 169-pin sockets. If the motherboard has both sockets and has a 486SX installed, it can be upgraded to a 486DX, a 486DX2, or 486DX4 OverDrive.

Later other PGA sockets were designed for 238 pins up to 387 pins. They are simply called socket 1 through 8. Table 4-4 is a chart for the various sockets.

Socket Standardization

Most of the sockets have the socket number on them, but in some cases it is very lightly molded onto the socket. For socket 7 and 8, the VRM means *voltage regulator module*. The VRM is a small circuit board that is plugged into a socket on the motherboard near the CPU. The Pentium CPUs operate at different voltages anywhere from 3.3 volts down to 2.5 or lower. The low voltage for the CPU must be well regulated, clean, and devoid of spikes.

The Pentium MMX, the AMD K6, and Cyrix M2 all use the standard socket 7. These CPUs can be used on any of the motherboards with the standard socket 7. Intel has created a new socket, the single-edge connector (SEC) for their Pentium II type CPU. AMD and Cyrix are not too happy because this will create a separate proprietary standard. Some have accused Intel of acting like IBM when they created their proprietary MCA system. (MCA is discussed in the next chapter.)

Why Lower Voltage

Heat is an enemy of transistors and other semiconductors. The more transistors, the higher the frequency, the more current is required, the more wattage used, and the more heat generated. Watts used is equal to the amount of current times the voltage. So the lower the voltage, the less wattage used, and the less heat to worry about.

Another reason to use less voltage is that the etched lines between the transistors are becoming thinner and thinner, some as thin as 0.25 microns, or 25 millionths of an inch. That would be several times smaller than a human hair. The connecting lines are made thinner in order to crowd more transistors into the limited space. But it wouldn't take much for a voltage to break through the thin lines and short out. So the voltage is carefully regulated and fans and heat sinks are used to dissipate the heat.

The early XT, 286, 386, and 486 did not need heat sinks or special cooling. Even though they all used five volts, the fewer transistors and lower frequency did not generate enough heat to cause a problem. The later 486 DX2 and DX4 did require extra heat sinks and fan cooling.

Steps to Upgrade a CPU

A CPU upgrade is a very simple thing to do. You might have a bit of difficulty removing the older 486 CPU from its 169-pin socket. It might take a special tool to remove the large square chip, or you might try a small screwdriver and pry up gently around the edges. These chips usually have one corner that has been cut off. This cut corner is sometimes the only indication of pin one. There might not be any markings on the motherboard. Before you remove the chip, use a felt marker or pen to show where the cut corner was located. (Don't ever use a pencil to mark on a board of any kind—pencil lead is conductive and could cause problems.) If you are buying an upgrade CPU, you should get some documentation with it telling you how to remove the old chip and install the newer one.

A Word of Caution in Handling CPUs I discussed static electricity and the cautions that should be taken earlier. Before handling a CPU or any electronic chip or board, be sure to discharge yourself by touching something that goes to ground.

Another caution is that the pins on the CPUs are very fragile. It is very easy to bend one or more. They can usually only be bent twice, down and up, before they break. If a pin breaks off, the CPU is then worthless. If the pins are just slightly out of line, they must be carefully straightened and lined up or you won't be able to plug them into the socket. If the pins are bent out of line, you might be able to use a knife blade to line them up.

ZIF Sockets

Almost all motherboards now use the zero insertion force (ZIF) sockets for the CPU. These sockets have a lever, that when raised, allows the chip to be easily removed and replaced. The ZIF socket has split contacts for the pins from the chip. A lever opens the socket contacts so that the chips just fall in. When the lever is closed, the contacts are forced together so that they make intimate connection with the pins.

In the early days, there were very few occasions or need to remove and replace a CPU. But today there are so many different CPUs and so many options that the ZIF socket is a necessity. No matter whether it is the old-style socket or the ZIF, you must note carefully where pin 1 is located.

Again, be aware that it might be more cost effective and less expensive to buy a new motherboard and CPU rather than install a CPU upgrade. Some of the clone motherboards are very inexpensive. Be sure to check all of your options.

Upgrading a 486 to a Pentium-Class

Here are some press releases and information about some of the CPU upgrade kits.

Kingston Technology

TurboChip 133 Processor Upgrade

Kingston Technology's TurboChip 133 is a 5x86 CPU upgrade that takes your 486 DX2, DX, SX2, or SX system to 5x86 clock-quadrupled processor technology.

Product Overview

Kingston Technology's TurboChip 133 is a 5x86 CPU upgrade that upgrades a 486 DX2, DX, SX2 or SX system to 5x86 clock-quadrupled processor technology. At 133MHz, TurboChip 133 is rated at Pentium 75-plus performance. TurboChip 133 features 16Kb internal cache, a built-in math coprocessor, and up to 33MHz external bus speed processing.

TurboChip is a high-performance and convenient solution to increase a computer's performance 250% over its current 486 processing speed to provide the power necessary to run today's popular multi-tasking computing environment.

TurboChip is a chip-for-chip replacement processor upgrade, which installs directly into the existing processor socket, or an Intel OverDrive socket. Many 486 computers use ZIF (zero-insertion-force) sockets with a lever or retaining screw to make removing the CPU chip quick and easy. Kingston provides a PGA (Pin Grid Array) socket extension to use with certain types of ZIF socket installations. TurboChip also uses a cooling fan to control TurboChip's operating temperature to ensure years of reliable performance.

Reasons for Introduction

- Rapidly advancing computing technology causing shorter system productive life cycles. 486-based systems are the largest installed-base of computers, over 75 million units installed worldwide, especially in the corporate computing environment.
- Standardization of personal computers and clone acceptance.
- Growing adoption of processor-demanding software applications including Microsoft Windows 95, NT, and OS/2 Warp.
- Increasing demands of added system functionality such as multi-tasking, multimedia, and Internet access.
- Ideal complimentary product to memory.
- Decreasing price of processors.
- Large installed base of 486 systems without OverDrive sockets such as Compaq Prolinea desktop computers.
- 486 systems becoming technologically outdated.

Target Market

Any 486-based system user looking for a 5x86 performance upgrade. 486 installed-base system users are found largely in:

- Corporate America (37.5 million units)
- Small to medium sized businesses (16.3 million units)
- Home market (21.5 million units)

Features and Benefits

- Increases performance over 250%.
- Users are more productive.

- Provides 5x86 clock-quadrupled processor power that's superior to Pentium-75 performance. The TurboChip 133 provides 486 systems with the power needed to run the processor-demanding software applications, such as Windows 95, NT, and OS/2 Warp.
- Designed with Advanced Micro Device's Am5x86-P75 microprocessor, AMD has proven to be a highly reliable, high-performance manufacturer of processors. AMD processors are currently being used by systems manufacturers including Compaq and AST, and these processors are Windows compatible certified.
- Upgrades most 486-based DX2, DX, SX2, and SX systems.
- IDC reports there are nearly 75 million units under this category, making it the largest installed-base of systems that will be seeking upgrades. TurboChip 133 is the most powerful and cost-effective solution available.
- Compatible with all existing software and hardware.
- User can still use all existing software applications, only now they will run faster. There is no need to reload software or reconfigure the system to achieve higher performance.
- Designed with 32-bit x86 microprocessor core running at 133 megahertz. Since 486 systems are not designed for Pentium command execution, TurboChip 133 is the upgrade of choice over the Intel OverDrive upgrades.

Includes 16Kb Internal Cache

TurboChip has 16Kb internal cache. Such large cache provides greater performance because it limits reads to the comparably slower motherboard memory and system hard drive.

Internal Math Coprocessor Included

486SX users who upgrade with TurboChip can obtain the valuable math coprocessor function, which increases overall system performance in high calculation situations, such as spreadsheets and CAD/CAM applications. 486DX users who upgrade to TurboChip will retain their math coprocessor function.

Simple Chip-for-Chip Replacement Upgrade Solution

Users do not need to worry about installation difficulties and physical restrictions when upgrading with TurboChip. TurboChip is the same physical footprint as the original 486; however, the cooling fan makes it $\frac{7}{8}$" higher. It's as easy as "plug and play."

168-Pin PGA Layout Design

The 168-pin layout allows TurboChip to upgrade systems with or without the OverDrive socket. This one part number for all solution eliminates the hassle to determine which processor upgrade for what system type.

Designed with a 5 to 3 volt voltage regulator and cooling fan. TurboChip 133 is designed to upgrade a large installed-base of 486 systems with 5-volt motherboards and the regulator allows the energy conserving 3-volt Am5x86-P75 processor chip to execute commands from the motherboard. The cooling fan keeps TurboChip 133 under operating temperature regardless of internal system box configuration.

Questions and Answers

Q: How do I know if TurboChip 133 is compatible with my system?

A: TurboChip 133 was tested to be compatible with most 486-based DX2, DX, SX2, and SX systems. During our field compatibility test, where we tested 50% name brand systems (IBM, Compaq, Gateway, AST, Hewlett-Packard, etc.,) and 50% clones, TurboChip achieved a 95% compatibility rate. Users might want to try out a TurboChip and we have resellers that will allow a 30 day money back guarantee to try TurboChip in their systems.

In addition, the Evaluation Group will also provide risk-free trials for corporate endusers, Kingston Evaluations Group toll-free number is (800) 435-0664.

Q: Will TurboChip 133 damage the system if it is not compatible?

A: No, TurboChip will not damage the system. If it's not compatible then replace it with the original CPU and the system should be back to the way it was. TurboChip does nothing more than speed up the execution cycles from the motherboard, it does not generate power current that's detrimental to the circuit board. The trial is absolutely risk free. However, many factors are involved when TurboChip does not run during the first installation. Refer to the user's manual when problems occur. In addition, our knowledgeable technical support team would help resolve the problem for free.

Q: How does TurboChip 133 stack up against Intel's OverDrive upgrades?

A: The following is a list of advantages TurboChip 133 offers over the OverDrive upgrades:

- The $129 retail price. Current OverDrive prices range from $199 for the DX2 upgrade and up to $299 for the P83 upgrade.
- Performance. The Wintach Score graph in features and benefits comparing TurboChip 133 versus OverDrive upgrades tells the whole story. TurboChip 133 outperforms the top two offerings from Intel at half the price.
- One part for all solutions. TurboChip will upgrade systems with or without OverDrive sockets, it also automatically clock-quadruples the different base clock-speeds such as 16, 20, 25, and 33 megahertz. Intel does not have a Pentium-class upgrade for systems not equipped with OverDrive sockets.
- Life-time warranty. Intel offers only a three year warranty on its OverDrive products.

Q: How does TurboChip 133 rate on the Pentium scale of performance?

A: TurboChip 133 is rated exactly between Pentium-75 and Pentium-90 processing performance.

Q: How much performance increase will my system gain from TurboChip 133?

A: On average, TurboChip 133 will provide over 250% of performance gain from a singled-clocked system, SX and DX. For SX2 and DX2 systems, the performance generally increase around 200%. TurboChip 133 will significantly increase the performance of systems running today's processor-demanding operating systems, such as Windows 95, Windows NT, OS/2 Warp, as well as communications and multi-tasking applications. The results from the Excel Recount experiment translates into almost 60% of the amount of time saved when upgrading with TurboChip 133. Hypothetically, any user who averages 20 hours a week working on Excel will now need only 8.2 hours to do the same amount of work.

Kingston Technology
17600 Newhope St.,
Fountain Valley, CA 92708
800-337-8410 www.kingston.com

Call Kingston for its large catalog that describes all of its products.

TurboChip 133 Processor Upgrade Incompatibility List

(Last Update: as of 1/17/97)

This list is provided as a guide for customers who do not wish to spend any down-time with trial and discovery. Many systems once thought to be incompatible have become compatible with the latest version BIOS. It is recommended customers give it a try whenever possible, because we cannot guarantee it will work in all computers due to the unlimited possible hardware combinations, motherboard manufacturer's designs, and BIOS revisions.

- ■ ACER

    - ■ Acer Acros 486 DX2/50
    - ■ Acer ENTRA (system/partnum: 91.AA840.006) (MM)
    - ■ Acer ENTRA (system/partnum: 91.AA840.006)
    - ■ Acer Power VT 486 DX2/66

- ■ ALR

    - ■ ALR Business VEISA 486/25 (requires BIOS chip v1.00.34b from AST $50.00)

- ■ ASI

    - ■ ASI 9000 computer 486 DX 33

- AST
  - AST Advantage Pro sx/25 (PR)
  - AST Premium II 486/33 (PR)
  - AST Advantage 486sx33 (with MB S/N=HMB1394583.202601-004x9)
  - AST Advantage Adventure (4050d) (if motherboard P/N: 501582.001)
  - AST Advantage Adventure (8066d)
  - AST Advantage Pro sx/25 AST 486/66D Bravo/66D
  - AST BRAVO 486/66 DX
  - AST Premium Server SE 4/33 (TC133 runs as DX2/66 so minimal performance gain)
  - AST Premium II 486/33

- AT&T
  - AT&T/NCR model 3350 486SX/25

- Compaq
  - Compaq Presario 724 CDS (LK) (PR)
  - Compaq Deskpro 433I
  - Compaq Deskpro XE 433S
  - Compaq Deskpro XL 466
  - Compaq Presario 500 series computers
  - Compaq Presario 510CDS
  - Compaq Presario 520 CDS
  - Compaq Presario 524 CDS
  - Compaq Presario 526 DX/2
  - Compaq Presario 528 CDTV
  - Compaq Presario 650 DX2/50 (note: sx2/66 is compatible)
  - Compaq Presario 744 CDS
  - Compaq Presario 720 CDS
  - Compaq Presario 724 CDS
  - Compaq Presario 920 CDS and CDTV
  - Compaq Presario 924 CDS
  - Compaq Presario 486 2/66
  - Compaq Prolinea 4/33s (SX/33 Assm#003651 mbd#164560-001), but is compatible if jumper p9 exists - Assm#003434-002, mbd#160420-001
  - Compaq Prolinea 4/50 (with DX250 MB#003759)
  - Compaq Prolinea 4/66 (with DX266: MB#003760, or MB#003652)
  - Compaq Prolinea Enhanced 4/50S
  - Compaq Prolinea 4/66 enhanced
  - Compaq SystemPro/XL 486/50 fileserver

- Compudyne
  - Compudyne 486 SX25

- Compudyne True DX/50
- Compudyne 486 SX25

- Dell
  - Dell 486 SX 33
  - Dell 486/66
  - Dell Optiplex 466/series

- Digital
  - Digital Celebris 466 DX2/SL66
  - Digital Venturis 433SX Digital Venturis 450 S2
  - Digital Venturis 466
  - Digital 433 DX
  - Digital DECpc CL 466d2 mini-tower (DX2/66)
  - Digital 486/20sx

- Gateway
  - Gateway 2000 P4D-66, (Enigma Systemboard DX2/66 486 (MBD:PCI003AAWW))
  - Gateway 2000 486/66 Mini PD4-66
  - Gateway 2000 486DX2/50 (desktop or tower models) Gateway 2000 DX2/66 486 (compatible if Micronics JX30 mbd and free BIOS upgrade)
  - Gateway 2000 4DX/33V (with Micronix MB#30208064)
  - Gateway 2000 4DX2/66V
  - Gateway Enigma Saturn II Systemboard
  - Gateway Micronics Systemboard MLB486-P24T

- Hewlett-Packard
  - HP XM2 4/66
  - HP Vectra 486/25N
  - HP Vectra 486/25M
  - HP Vectra 486/33M
  - HP Vectra 486/33N (compatible with BIOS ver T.04.05 11/22/95 from HP WEB site)
  - HP Vectra 486/33T
  - HP Vectra 486/33U
  - HP Vectra 486/66N
  - HP XM2 4/66

- IBM
  - IBM Aptiva Model 2144-67P
  - IBM PC300 330

- IBM Aptiva Model 2144-27P
- IBM Aptiva Model 2144-67P
- IBM Aptiva 510 Model 2168-62P
- IBM Aptiva 530
- IBM EduQuest
- IBM PS/1 2133-G46
- IBM PS/1 2133-S53
- IBM PS/1 2155-G52
- IBM PS/1 2155-P57
- IBM PS/1 2155-24M 486/33 SX
- IBM ValuePoint 6381-M50
- IBM ValuePoint 6381-M00 433DX SL.
- IBM ValuePoint 6381-F30 SX/25
- IBM ValuePoint 6381-937
- IBM ValuePoint 6387
- IBM ValuePoint 6482-L5F IBM Ambra T466DX (DX2/66) (this is Pentium upgradeable only)

- NEC

  - NEC PowerMate 466(DX2/66)

- Packard-Bell

  - Packard Bell Legend 10CD (max perf. only 100Mhz since no jumpers for 33Mhz)
  - Packard Bell 2555CD (DX2/66) (SN: 84094010056527)
  - Packard Bell Legend 125 (conflicts in Windows/Graphics) (PR)
  - Packard Bell Legend PB 25 SX
  - Packard Bell Legend 10CD (max performance only 100mhtz since no jumpers for 33Mhz)
  - Packard Bell Legend 34CD
  - Packard Bell Legend 125 (conflicts in Windows/Graphics)
  - Packard Bell. Legend 204CD DX2/66
  - Packard Bell Legend 234 (works but performance limited to a 100Mhz)
  - Packard Bell Legend 1910 Supreme
  - Packard Bell 186 DX2 66
  - Packard Bell 430A SX25 486
  - Packard Bell 2555CD (DX2/66) (SN: 84094010056527)
  - Packard Bell Canada Force 2010MM

- Clones/Motherboards

  - Clone Insight Clone VL/ISA486 Sv2
  - Clone Omega IBM clone I486DX 33

- ASUS 486VLB DX33 (not upgradeable, requires oscillator replacement)
- Micronics JX30 Systemboard (compatible if BIOS v4.05.07 by MicroFirmware)
- Zeos with Panteras motherboard #100-0052-00 (TC133 runs but no performance increase)
- CPU types:
  - SLC or SLC2—Physically too small, old 386 16-bit technology
  - Cyrix DLC—132-pin configuration (Is not Intel compatible 168 or 169 pin)

Note: Because the systems above are incompatible for Kingston, they are probably incompatible for the other companies that offer a similar upgrade. This might seem like a fairly long list of incompatibles, but remember that there are over 75 million 486s in existence. I hope your computer is not on that list.

CCT Company

CCT 486/586 Upgrade Kit

The CCT 486 and 586 upgrade kit is CCT manufactured specifically for the new AMD Am486 DX4-100 and Am5x86 133Mhz CPUs. The Upgrade Kit provides a very simple, drop-in method of installing these new super power AMD three-volt processors on older, slower five-volt 486 CPU motherboards. Tremendous power gains can be realized to easily handle Windows 95, NT OS/2 & reg, UNIX and other 32-bit operating systems, through the use of this easy, economical, and powerful product. The kit can replace almost any 486SX or 486DX CPU without additional hardware or software upgrades.

Easily upgrade your old, slow 486SX or 486DX motherboard to run the AMD Am486 DX4 100Mhz or Am5x86-133Mhz CPU. We are offering a complete drop-in upgrade kit, recommended by AMD, which consists of the CCT Programmable Adapter with 169-pin PGA socket, 5-volt to 3.45-volt voltage regulation, heatsink, ball-bearing fan, AMD 486 or 586 CPU, and complete installation instructions. The entire kit is about the size of the CPU, only standing approximately $1\frac{1}{4}$ inch high. This kit will function on any motherboard capable of running a 20Mhz or faster CPU, at up to a full 133Mhz in user-selectable clock-doubled, clock-tripled, or clock-quadrupled mode. Write-through and write-back caching is also user selectable. Only the CCT upgrade kit incorporates these CPU hardware-programming features! The kit can replace any 486DX or 486SX CPU, or drop into any Overdrive & reg; socket. Our toll-free CCT technical support is included for easy installation. There is a full three-year parts and labor warranty.

Independent benchmark testing shows the AMD 486 100Mhz outperforms a 60Mhz Pentium, and the 586-133Mhz outpaces the 75Mhz Pentium's! See the AMD Specifications for a complete technical overview.

The purchase of any CCT upgrade kit includes the Winstone 97/Winbench 97 Benchmark Suite CD. Upgrade memory, hard disk, and video—CCT Bundling Discount Program. Multiple purchase reseller, corporate, and government discounts are available.

For ordering or additional information:

EMail: Direct Sales at sales@cct.com
Resellers: Reseller.sales@cct.com
Corporate: corporate.sales@cct.com
Government: government.sales@cct.com
Technical support: support@cct.com
Customer service: customer.service@cct.com
Phone: (800) CCT-MENU (1-800-228-6368)
FAX: (520) 646-6587—Attention: Sales
Mail: CCT
PO Box 3350
W. Sedona, AZ 86340-3350

Review CCT On-Line Product Support for motherboard and BIOS information (required prior to installation).

Trinity Works Company

The Power Stacker

The Trinity PowerStacker 5x86 133MHz processor upgrade is a true system upgrade for 486-based systems. The existing 486 processor is replaced with a new 133MHz clock-quadrupled processor. The PowerStacker 5x86 is the convenient, economical way to increase your system's performance 250% over its current 486 processor without investing in a new system. This upgrade gives you the power and performance for today's most demanding software applications. And it's 100% compatible with your existing software and hardware. You will only notice the faster speed.

Easy-to-install, processor upgrades most 486-based SX, SX2, DX, and DX2 systems AMD Am5x86-P75 clock-quadrupled processor with built-in FPU and 16kb internal cache 5 V to 3.5 V. Smart Module converter automatically configures the processor's clock speed based on your existing bus speed and does not require an OverDrive socket.

Greater performance than the Pentium-83 OverDrive processor makes your games run smoother, move faster, and more fun to play. Designed for Windows95 and compatible with your existing hardware and all x86 software. No software drivers are needed and there is a lifetime warranty.

- Installation is as easy as 1-2-3.
- Speeds up to 133MHz 75 and Cx5x86.
- Compare before you buy.
- Package contents include:

  - Trinity PowerStacker 5x86 133MHz Processor Upgrade
  - Chip removal tool
  - 168-Pin Chip Extender
  - Trinity Utilities Disk
  - CD-ROM with free software
  - Installation guide video

PowerStacker Px86

The Trinity PowerStacker Px86 processor upgrade is a true system upgrade which replaces your existing Pentium processor with a new AMD K5 processor. Designed for Windows 95, the PowerStacker Px86 has the performance rating of a 133MHz Pentium and features a built-in math coprocessor, 16kb internal cache, 64-bit architecture, and Super-scalar design, all in a simple plug-in module.

The PowerStacker Px86 is the convenient, economical way to increase your system's performance without investing in a new system. The Power-Stacker upgrade gives you the power and performance for today's most demanding software applications. This upgrade is 100% compatible with your existing software and hardware. You will only notice the faster speed!

Package contents include:

- Px86 for P-60/66.
- Px86 for P-75.

- Trinity PowerStacker Px86 Processor Upgrade.
- Trinity Utilities Disk.
- Installation guide.
- CD-ROM with free software.
- Specifications are subject to change at any time.

Installing the 5x86

The PowerStacker 5x86 processor upgrade has been designed to work in a large variety of 486DX, SX, SX2, and DX2 computers. The upgrade installation might vary according to the type and location of your 486 processor socket. Also, the orientation when installing the PowerStacker 5x86 will depend on the location of pin 1 on the processor socket. Included is a PGA socket extender for 168-pin sockets and overhead-bar ZIF sockets that prevent the retaining bar from closing once the processor upgrade is in place. Follow the steps below to install the PowerStacker 5x86 into your computer.

Installing the PGA Socket Extender

Computers that have a 169-pin socket do not need the socket extender. If your computer has a 168-pin socket or the overhead bar-type ZIF socket you need to install the PGA socket extender before you install the PowerStacker.

Install the PGA socket extender as follows: Locate the beveled edge or white triangle on the socket extender. Align this edge, pin 1, to the pin 1 on the system board's processor socket. Position the socket extender's pins over the holes on the 486 CPU socket. When the alignment is correct, gently press the socket extender down until it is seated properly into the socket on the system board. If you have an overhead bar, lower the overhead bar down to lock the extender in place. You are now ready to install the PowerStacker 5x86 into the extender socket.

Warning: If the processor upgrade is not installed correctly (pin 1 to pin 1), it might result in damage to the computer, the processor upgrade, or both.

For Standard Sockets or Sockets with the PGA Socket Extender Installation Once the alignment is correct, grasp the sides of the

PowerStacker 5x86 with your thumb and forefinger. Apply an even pressure while gently, but firmly, pushing the PowerStacker 5x86 into the socket. Repeat on opposite corners of the upgrade.

Note: If the processor upgrade is resisting, stop and check the pin alignment. If the alignment is incorrect, remove the processor upgrade and begin the insertion again.

For Side Bar or Retaining Screw ZIF Sock   Make sure the side bar lever is fully rotated upward or the retaining screw is loose. With the socket in the unlocked or open position, align the pins on the PowerStacker 5x86 with the holes on the ZIF socket. You do not need to force the PowerStacker 5x86 into the socket. Apply gentle pressure, only if needed, to make sure the processor is completely inserted. Lower the sidebar lever or rotate the retaining screw to lock the socket.

Completing the Installation   Replace any cards or drives removed earlier. Replace the cover of your computer, and reconnect the cables. Check that your computer starts correctly. It should begin memory count and run its POST (power-on-self-test). If it does not boot-up, refer to the Technical Guide manual for help.

Congratulations! You have just increased the speed of your computer! If you experience any problems, refer to the Technical Guide. If your problem is not listed or if you have any questions regarding this product, call the Trinity Works, Inc. at:

Technical Support
12201 Technology Blvd.
Suite 145 Austin, Texas 78727
Email:tech@trinityworks.com
Phone: 800-278-4944
Fax: (512) 249-0570

Darrell H. Hughes
Vice President Sales & Marketing
12201 Technology Blvd.
Suite 145 Austin, Texas 78727
Email:dhhughes@trinityworks.com
Phone: (512) 249-1099
Fax: (512) 249-0570

Evergreen Technologies Company

Below are press releases and information from the Evergreen Website at www.evertech.com.

Evergreen 486 Upgrades

Based on AMD's 133 MHz 5x86 PFQP processor, this is a one-size-fits-all upgrade for 486SX, DX, SX2, DX2 desktop computers and boosts system performance to Pentium levels. Introducing the Evergreen 586 for 486SX, DX, SX2, and DX2 personal computers. The Evergreen 586 represents the cutting-edge in processor upgrades, linking 486 computers to the newest generation of power. The upgrade utilizes the highest rated 133 MHz AMD5x86 processor, a low-profile processor (PQFP) that does not require a fan. Evergreen's engineering experience in CPU architecture, cache coherency, bus management, and BIOS compatibility provides you with an industry-leading upgrade for your 486. The Evergreen 586 installs easily in your existing 486 or OverDrive processor socket. Please take a moment and review some of the features of the Evergreen 586.

Product Highlights

- Upgrades a 486 system to a 586/100, 120, or 133.
- Supports both 168 (169) and 237 (238)-pin CPU and OverDrive socket styles.
- Includes 16K of level one cache.
- Includes high-speed floating point math unit.
- Quadruples clock speed for 25, 33, DX2-50, and DX2-66 systems (DX2-50 and DX2-66 become 586/100 and 586/133 respectively).
- Triples clock speed for 40 MHz systems.
- Maintains PC investment and extends the life of 486 systems.
- Includes three-year warranty.

Evergreen Pentium Upgrades

Evergreen PR166 Processor for Pentiums

This upgrade delivers 166MHz Pentium performance to specific brand name Pentium systems running at 75 MHz and higher. To determine if the upgrade supports your system, qualify your system now!

Features

- Advanced next generation processor.
- 64-bit data bus.16K write-back cache.
- 80-bit floating point unit.
- PR166 performance rating.
- Socket-5 and socket-7 compatible.
- Upgrades specific systems and motherboards from 75 MHz and up. (See compatibility list.)
- System prequalification utility.
- Three-year warranty.

Benefits

- Upgrades Pentium systems to 166MHz performance.
- Protects PC investment, extends life of Pentium system.
- Increase Windows performance up to 150%.
- Fraction of the cost of a new 166 MHz Pentium system.
- Simple hardware and software installation.
- Faster speed options than Intel Pentium OverDrive:

Original Pentium	Intel OverDrive	Evergreen PR166
75MHz	125MHz	PR166
9/120MHz	150MHz	PR166
100/133MHz	166MHz	PR166

System Compatibility List 4/25/97

The following is a listing of known systems that support the Evergreen Processor for Pentium CPU upgrades. These and other models, Evergreen recommends that users run our PENNTINFO system qualification software. Bookmark this page for periodic updates.

- Packard Bell
- Packard Bell Axcel 453CD

- Packard Bell Axcel 461CDT
- Packard Bell Axcel 4630
- Packard Bell Axcel 467CD
- Packard Bell Axcel 853CDT
- Packard Bell Force 448CDT
- Packard Bell Force 480CD
- Packard Bell Legend 108CDT
- Packard Bell Legend 401CD
- Packard Bell Legend 406CD
- Packard Bell Legend 408CD
- Packard Bell Legend 415CD
- Packard Bell Legend 422CDT
- Packard Bell Legend 436CDT
- Packard Bell Legend 70CD
- Packard Bell Legend 74CDT
- Packard Bell Legend 812CD
- Packard Bell Multimedia D135
- Hewlett Packard
- Hewlett Packard Pavillion 5040
- Models with Intel /ZP, /MN, /AS, /EV, /ZE, /HL, /AS motherboards

Selected Models

- Gateway 2000 P5 selected models
- Midwest Micro selected models
- PC-Specialist selected models
- Proline/Schadt selected models
- Selected models

Press Release—April 2, 1997

Contact: Bill Blagdan
Vice President, Product Development
(541) 757-0934
ext. 245.
e-mail to: blagdan.b@evertech.com

Evergreen announces CPU upgrade using AMD-K6 MMX chip; replaces original Pentium CPU with speed grades up to 233 MHz. Corvallis, Oregon—Evergreen Technologies, Inc., an industry leader in processor upgrades for personal computers, announced the industry's first MMX processor upgrade for Pentium-based systems using the new AMD-K6 MMX CPU. The Evergreen MxPro Processor for Pentiums enables existing Pentium users to dramatically boost Windows and Multimedia performance by replacing the original Pentium CPU with the highest performance MMX processor.

Unique Technology Enables Upgrade

Evergreen's exclusive BIOS and voltage technology allows the AMD-K6 MMX processor to be used as a direct processor replacement for Pentiums. The Evergreen MxPro combines Evergreen's exclusive Flash Upgrade Technology with AMD's K6 processor, making it easy for users to upgrade their older systems regardless of the original BIOS, motherboard, and voltage, said Daniel McKenna, Evergreen's vice president of engineering. Delivers unprecedented performance boost to older systems. "The AMD-K6 MMX processor delivers industry leading performance on Windows NT, Windows 95, and MMX software while leveraging the cost-effective socket-7 infrastructure," said Rob Herb, AMD Vice President, Strategic Marketing, Computation Products Group. AMD benchmarks show that the AMD-K6 MMX processor meets or exceeds the performance of similarly clocked Intel processors including both the Pentium with/MMX and Pentium Pro.

Improves ROI of Installed PCs

By refreshing older Pentium PCs, Fortune 1000 corporations can improve return-on-investment (ROI) of their installed systems. Businesses get the processing power needed to transition to Windows NT 4.0, plus the functionality of MMX technology for new software such as video conferencing. "Businesses can increase the useful life of installed PCs by upgrading the CPU," said Mike Magee, President and founder of Evergreen Technologies, Inc. "With the MxPro, MIS managers can avoid the PC obsolescence treadmill and save money."

Leapfrogs Intel CPU Upgrades

The Evergreen MxPro leaps ahead of the Intel MMX OverDrive by delivering the first 6th-generation MMX processor upgrade. In addition to its advanced architecture which delivers superior 16-bit and 32-bit performance, the Evergreen MxPro allows higher clock speed settings than comparable Intel MMX OverDrive CPUs. "The MxPro runs at the full PR2-166, -200, and -233 speed grades of the AMD-K6 MMX CPU regardless of the original Pentium system speed," said Bill Blagdan, Evergreen Vice President of Product Development. "The Intel OverDrive MMX upgrade's fastest speed is 166 MHz currently, but is limited to 125 and 150 MHz speeds for Pentium-75 and Pentium-90 systems respectively."

Pricing and Availability

The Evergreen MxPro Processor for Pentiums is expected in June 1997, and will list for under $500 suggested retail price (SRP) for the PR2-166 version. The PR2-200 and -233 versions are planned for the second half of 1997. The MxPro will be available through major worldwide distribution channels and carry a three-year warranty. Additional product information is available from Evergreen Technologies Inc. at (541) 757-0934 and via the world wide web at www.evertech.com.

Contacting Evergreen Technologies, Inc.

Mailing address:
806 NW Buchanan Ave.
Corvallis, OR 97330-6218
Phone: (541)757-0934
Technical support: (541)757-7341
Fax: (541)752-9851
Sales: email to: sales@evertech.com

For presales and compatibility information:
Technical support email to: techsupport@evertech.com
For technical assistance marketing email to: marketing@evertech.com

Note: Evergreen also does upgrades on several models of portable computers.

Intel OverDrive CPUs

Intel manufactures OverDrive CPUs for some of the 486s and early Pentiums. There is lots of information at their website. Go to www.intel.com then search for OverDrive processors. The following was taken from their site:

> Complex software applications and operating environments are fueling a demand for more powerful systems. For consumers who are not in a position to purchase a new Pentium processor-based system, the best option for boosting overall system performance is to upgrade their Intel486 CPU-based system to a higher level with an Intel OverDrive processor. There are currently three types of products in the Over-Drive processor family to choose from: the Pentium(R) OverDrive processor, the IntelDX4(TM) OverDrive processor, and the IntelDX2(TM) OverDrive processor.

Which OverDrive Processor Fits Your System?

The Pentium(R) OverDrive Processor   The Pentium Over-Drive processor is the newest and fastest member of the Intel OverDrive processor family of CPU upgrades. The Pentium OverDrive processor provides most Intel486 PC users the ability to upgrade to Pentium processor technology. It is the recommended upgrade option for upgradable IntelSX2 and IntelDX2 CPU-based systems and is the superior upgrade option for upgradable Intel486 SX and DX CPU-based systems.

The Pentium OverDrive processor is based on the same 3.3 V, 0.6 micron Pentium processor technology as today's highest-volume Pentium processors. It features the Pentium processor's superscalar design, branch prediction, and faster floating point, as well as a larger 32K cache, a 32-bit bus interface, an on-package voltage regulator, and fan/heatsink. It also operates at two and a half times the speed of the system bus. All this adds up to the highest-performance OverDrive processor available.

The Intel DX4(TM) OverDrive Processor   The IntelDX4 OverDrive processor is the mainstream CPU upgrade for Intel486 SX and DX CPU-based systems. It features Intel's speed-tripling technology, along with an on-chip math coprocessor and enhanced 16K cache, thus providing users with increased performance across a wide variety of software applications.

The Intel DX2(TM)OverDrive Processor The IntelDX2 OverDrive processor is Intel's most affordable CPU upgrade for Intel486 SX and DX CPU-based systems. It features speed-doubling technology and an on-chip math coprocessor, providing users with increased software performance across a wide variety of software applications.

Socket Configurations

Your Intel486 CPU-based system might have a single- or a two-socket configuration. If you have a single-socket system, you must first remove the original Intel486 CPU and install the OverDrive processor in the CPU socket. If you have two-socket system, you will install the Over-Drive processor into the OverDrive processor socket.

Your Intel486 CPU-based system might have a socket that is larger than the original CPU. To upgrade with the Pentium OverDrive processor, your system must have this larger socket (237 or 238 pins rather than 168 or 169 pins). This socket can also be used for the IntelDX2 and IntelDX4 OverDrive processors; these OverDrive processors will have an extra row of holes surrounding them when installed in the larger socket.

Future OverDrive Processors

Intel plans to offer future Pentium OverDrive processors to upgrade most of today's Pentium processors. A future OverDrive processor upgrade for the Pentium Pro processor is also planned. Specifically, the following future Pentium OverDrive processors for upgradable Pentium processor-based systems are planned:

Original Pentium CPU Speed	Pentium OverDrive CPU Speed
60/66 MHz	133 MHz
75 MHz	125 MHz
90 MHz	150 MHz
100 MHz	166 MHz
120 MHz	180 MHz
133 MHz	200 MHz

To determine whether your system supports these future Pentium OverDrive processors, ask your system manufacturer.

Upgrading to Pentium Pro

To upgrade to a genuine Intel Pentium Pro would mean that you have to have a motherboard with a socket type 8. If you have a 150MHz or 180MHz Pentium Pro, you can easily upgrade it to a 200MHz Pentium Pro by simply replacing the CPU and resetting the jumpers on the motherboard.

If you have one of the Pentium-class motherboards with a socket type 7, you can easily upgrade to the Cyrix 6x86 CPUs.

Some motherboards might also let you install a Pentium class MMX CPU in a socket type 7. However, if your motherboard is a couple years old, it might be better to buy a motherboard and CPU for the MMX upgrade. Many of the newer models have added several new utilities.

Intel Pentium II

The following is an article from Intel about the Pentium II:

Intel's highest performance processor combines the power of the Pentium Pro processor with the capabilities of MMX technology. At 266MHz, the Pentium II processor delivers a 1.6x to over 2x performance boost compared to the 200MHz Pentium processor on industry-standard processor benchmarks, and over twice the performance on multimedia benchmarks. It takes advantage of the same high-performance Dual Independent Bus architecture used in the Pentium Pro processor for high bandwidth and performance.

Single edge contact (S.E.C.) cartridge packaging technology delivers high-performance processing and bus technology to mainstream systems. It is optimized for 32-bit applications running on advanced operating systems. 32KByte (16K/16K) non-blocking level one cache. 512KByte unified, non-blocking level two cache. Enables systems which are scalable up to two processors and 64GByte of physical memory.

Data integrity and reliability features include system bus ECC, fault analysis, recovery, and functional redundancy checking.

Highlights

The Pentium II processor integrates the best attributes of Intel's processors, the dynamic execution performance of the Pentium processor, plus the capabilities of MMX technology, bringing a new level of performance to PC buyers.

The Pentium II processor is easily scalable to two microprocessors in a multiprocessor system. The Pentium II processor extends the power of the Pentium Pro processor with performance headroom for business media, communication, and Internet capabilities. Software designed for Intel's MMX technology will unleash full-screen, full-motion video, enhanced color, realistic graphics, and other multimedia enhancements. Systems based on Pentium II processors also include the latest features to simplify system management and lower the total cost of ownership for large and small business environments.

Product Description

The Intel Pentium II processor family includes 233, 266MHz versions for desktops, workstations, and servers, and a 300MHz version especially for workstations. All are binary compatible with previous generation Intel Architecture processors. Pentium II processors provide the best performance available for applications running on advanced operating systems such as Windows 95, Windows NT, and UNIX.

The Pentium II processor core has 7.5M transistors and is based on Intel's enhanced 0.35 micron CMOS process. The processor core is provided in the single edge contact cartridge package enabling ease of design and a flexible motherboard architecture.

The Pentium II processor family's significant performance improvement over previous Intel Architecture processors is based on the seamless combination of Pentium Pro processor technology and Intel's MMX media enhancement technology.

The result is higher software performance plus headroom for applications that take advantage of Intel's MMX technology.

Pentium Pro Processor's Dynamic Execution Technology

Multiple branch prediction predicts the flow of the program through several branches, accelerating the flow of work to the processor. *Dataflow analysis* creates an optimized reordered schedule of instructions by ana-lyzing data dependencies between instructions. *Speculative execution* car-ries out instructions speculatively, based on this optimized schedule, keeping the processor's superscaler execution units busy and boosting overall performance.

Intel's MMX Media Enhancement Technology

Intel's MMX technology includes new instructions and data types that allow applications to achieve a new level of performance. Intel's MMX technology is designed as a set of basic, general-purpose integer instructions that can be easily applied to the needs of a wide diversity of multimedia and communications applications. The highlights of the technology are:

- Single instruction, multiple data (SIMD) technique.
- 57 new instructions.
- Eight 64-bit wide MMX technology registers.
- Four new data types.

Other Features

- High-performance dual independent bus architecture (system bus cache bus) for high bandwidth, performance, and scalability with future system technologies.
- The system bus supports multiple outstanding transactions to increase bandwidth availability. It also provides "glueless" support for up to two processors. This enables low-cost, 2-way symmetric multiprocessing, providing a significant performance boost for multi-tasking operating systems and multi-threaded applications.
- A 512KByte unified non-blocking level two cache, which improves performance by reducing the average memory access time and providing fast access to recently used instructions and data. The performance is enhanced through a dedicated 64-bit cache bus. The level two cache scales with the processor core frequency. With the core at 266MHz, the cache bus runs at 133MHz, twice the speed of a Pentium processor's cache access. Level two cache data bus ECC is

planned for a future version of the Pentium II processor family. It also incorporates separate 16K instruction and 16K data level one caches, each twice the size of the Pentium Pro processor's caches.

■ A pipelined floating-point unit (FPU) for supporting the 32-bit and 64-bit formats specified in IEEE standard 754, as well as an 80-bit format. It is capable of sustaining over 300 million floating Point Instructions per second (MFLOPS) at 300MHz.

■ Parity-protected address/request and response system bus signals with a retry mechanism for high data integrity and reliability.

■ ECC (Error Correction Code) allowing for correction of single bit data errors and detection of 2-bit errors on the system bus.

■ The Pentium II processor also includes several features used for testing and performance monitoring. These features include:

   ■ Built-in self test (BIST), providing single stuck-at fault coverage of the microcode and large logic arrays, as well as testing of the instruction cache, data cache, translation lookaside buffers (TLBs) and ROMs. IEEE 1149.1 Standard Test Access Port and Boundary Scan mechanism, allowing testing of the Pentium II processor and system connections through a standard interface.

   ■ Internal performance counters for performance monitoring and event counting.

Single Edge Connector

The Pentium Pro CPU was mounted in a pin grid array (PGA) that fit in socket type 8. The Pentium II CPU is installed on a circuit board with etched contacts. This board plugs into a special slot on the motherboard. Intel calls it slot 1. The Pentium Pro had the L2 cache nearby in the same enclosure. The Pentium II has the L2 cache mounted on the circuit board on each side of the CPU.

If you want to use a Pentium Pro on one of these motherboards, the CPU can be installed on a special riser board which plugs into the slot 1. When the Pentium II was first introduced, I called several Intel distributors and tried to buy a 266MHz CPU. There were lots of 233MHz units available but no one had a 266MHz unit. Every other week there is a large computer swap meet at the Los Angeles County Fairgrounds. There were over 300 booths at a recent meet. I tried all of the booths and found one vendor who had just sold his last 266MHz. There was another booth nearby that had one for sale at $860. I decided to look around a bit more, but no one else had the 266MHz units. About 20 minutes later I went back to the booth and the price had been raised from $860 to $870. I quickly bought it before they had a chance to raise the price even more. It was still a bargain even at that price. The Intel distributors had quoted me a price of $1130.

Resources

For more information on any of these CPUs, contact the following companies:

AMD Corp.
One AMD Place, P.O. Box 3453
Sunnyvale, CA 94088-9968
Tel. 408-749-5703
http://www.amd.com

Intel Corp.
2200 Mission College Blvd.
Santa Clara, CA 95052
Tel. 408-765-7525
http://www.intel.com

Cyrix Corp.
P.O. Box 853917
Richardson, TX 75086-3917
Tel. 214-968-8388
http://www.cyrix.com

For latest press releases from Intel, point your browser to: http://www.intel.com/pressroom/archive/releases/DP050797.HTM

Installing a New Motherboard

If you have an old computer you might tell your spouse that you need a new computer. If your spouse is in charge of the purse strings, you might be asked, "Why in the world do you need a new computer? You haven't worn out your old one yet."

The purse string holder has gotcha. Those little electrons racing around inside the computer do not cause any wear at all. Except for the mechanical devices, such as the disk drives, it is very difficult to wear out a computer. But the ever-changing technology causes computers to become obsolete sometimes before you can get it home from the store. The original PC, XT, and 286 were fantastic in their time. But compared to today's technology, they are as ancient as the first horseless carriage. The old 386 and 486 were excellent machines for their time. Today they are as obsolete as the old Model T Ford. Like the old Model T, these old machines might still get you to your destination, but slowly and without many of the modern conveniences. If your time is worth anything at all, it is worth upgrading.

You can say to the tight-fisted spouse, "Well how about if I just replace my motherboard?" Your spouse might go along with that.

This is a biggie. A new motherboard is the most important and most cost-effective upgrade that you can make. It is also one of the easiest upgrades to make. A new motherboard can give you most of the benefits of a new system at a fairly reasonable cost. Just pull out your old motherboard and install a new Pentium-class motherboard.

In early 1985, I spent $2,500 for a 286 motherboard. This was in the days when each dollar was worth about three times what it is today. I still have it. If I tried, I couldn't even give it away. If you try to sell one of these old machines, people would probably laugh at you.

The 286 motherboard was bigger than my XT motherboard. so I had to buy a bigger case. However I was able to use almost all of the components from my old XT. The 286 was so much faster and more powerful than the XT that it was well worth the money.

Besides the CPU, the motherboard will have several other chips, five to eight slot connectors for plug in boards, sockets or slots for memory chips, and upright pins for printer, mouse, and disk interface cable connections. I still have a 286 motherboard from my first 286 computer. It is the AT "standard" size or about a third larger than the "baby" AT size of almost all motherboards today. Figure 5-1 shows my old 6MHz 286 board on the left and a Micronics 150MHz Pentium Pro on the right. My old 286 motherboard has over 150 separate chips on it. Soon after the 286 came out, Adaptec and several other companies started integrating several chips into a single package. Most of the motherboards now have about 20 separate chips. With fewer chips, there is less chance

Fig. 5-1
My old 286 motherboard on the left and a Pentium Pro motherboard on the right. The top-right corner of the 286 has 36 DIP memory chips for a total of 1Mb. Up to 128Mb could be installed in the four white SIMM memory slots on the Pentium Pro.

of having solder problems, there is less chance of stray capacitance, there is less distance between the components, and there is much greater reliability. It also costs much less to manufacture a board with fewer chips.

Even with 150 separate chips on the old 286 motherboard, I still had to buy a separate board for the mouse and printer, a separate controller board for the floppy drives, and one for the hard drives. Motherboards now have sets of upright pins for most of those functions. All that is needed are cables from such peripheral components as the disk drives, mouse, printer, or CD-ROM.

To show the advances that have been made, Fig. 5-2 shows figures along the edge of a Micronics motherboard. (The pen points to crystal can.) There are a lot of components on this motherboard. The motherboard is 9 inches wide and 13 inches long. One of the little niceties that Micronics did was to put marks in inches from 1 to 13 along the sides of the board and from A to I in inches along the ends of the board. This is somewhat like a map and with the coordinates, you can easily find any jumper or component on the board.

Figure 5-3 is a diagram of the Micronics motherboard, which shows the various chips and slots. Notice that it has built-in connections for a parallel printer, floppy drives, connections for a primary and secondary Enhanced Integrated Drive Electronic disk drives, serial ports COM1 and COM2. The primary set of EIDE pins can be used for two IDE hard drives. The secondary set of EIDE pins can be used for IDE CD-ROM drives, tape backup drives, or other IDE devices.

The original IDE interface was usually on a plug-in board. This IDE interface wouldn't let you use a hard drive with more than 1024 cylinders and 63 sectors, or a maximum of 528Mb. It also had a rather slow transfer rate of 5.22Mb per second. The enhanced IDE supports a transfer rate of 15.5Mb per second. It can also support hard drives with up to several gigabytes capacity.

The set of pins for the floppy drives can control two floppy disk drives. They can be any two drives such as 360K, 1.2Mb, 720K, 1.44Mb, or 2.88Mb. The parallel port connector is for the printer or other parallel device. It has enhanced parallel port (EPP) and expanded capability Port (ECP). Parallel ports have eight lines and transmits one bit of data at a time on each line. Ordinarily a parallel port only transmits data out, but these ports can be used for output or input. The EPP and ECP ports can operate at the same speed as the ISA bus and can transfer data at up to 1Mb per second. These ports can be used not only for printers, but for tape backup drives, for external hard disks, for CD-ROMs, for small local area networks, and for several other new products.

The serial COM1 and COM2 ports has the 16550 universal asynchronous receiver transmitter (UART). This UART is much faster than the earlier 16450 chips. Computers handle data in 8-bit bytes, or one word. But mice, modems, and several other peripherals are serial devices. They use data one bit at a time. For output, the serial ports change the standard 8 bit bytes into single bits for transmission. When receiving data, it changes the single bits back into 8 bit bytes. In addition to the COM ports, many of the newer motherboards now have built-in small computer system interface (SCSI) and universal serial bus (USB).

In early 1986, I pulled the 286 motherboard out and replaced it with a 386 motherboard that cost $1,800. Again, I was able to use most of my old components, but I had a new computer that was worth about twice as much as the cost of the motherboard. In 1989, I bought a 486 motherboard

Fig. 5-3
A diagram of a Micronics motherboard showing the main components.

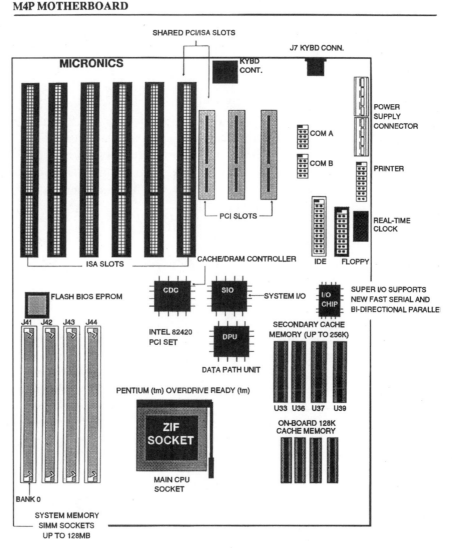

M4P MOTHERBOARD

M4P System Board

for $4450 and replaced my 386 motherboard. My new 486 CPU operated at a blazing 25MHz, the old 386 operated at only 16MHz. I had been getting by with a MFM 40Mb hard drive. After spending all that money, I bought a second 40Mb hard drive, which cost $379. (I have just bought a 3.5Gb hard drive for $215. That is 87.5 times more storage space for about half the price.) I got the Stacker software from Stac Electronics and was able to double the disk capacity on each to 80Mb for a total of 160Mb. That was fantastic. (Today, there are some single programs that takes more than 80Mb to load and run.) I had spent quite a lot of money, but I had a top-of-the-line system that I could really brag about.

I have assembled several other bigger and more powerful systems in the last few years. I kept the old 486 as a backup system. A couple of years ago, I upgraded the 486 25MHz CPU with a 50MHz Overdrive CPU and sold it to a friend for the cost of the Overdrive CPU. He and his kids are still using it.

Chapter 4 detailed replacing the CPU. Replacing the motherboard can be an even better upgrade and make an older computer every bit as good as a brand new computer. If you don't have the money all at once, set aside a small amount each week until you get enough to buy that new must-have motherboard. You definitely can save money by spending a little to upgrade.

Using Old Components

Even if you are moving up from the oldest PC or XT, you might still be able to use some of your old components, such as the case, plug-in boards, and disk drives in your new system. All of the components in PCs are basically the same except for the motherboard.

Of course if you decide to install a new Pentium-class motherboard, you might not want to use your old monochrome or CGA monitor. You will also want to move up to larger capacity hard drives and newer floppy drives. But if you are on a tight budget, you can always use your old components until you can afford the newer goodies.

Backward Compatibility

All newer systems are backward compatible so that they can run and use the older hardware and software. This backward compatibility has been a slight problem and bottleneck to developing new products. If the old systems were abandoned, new products could be made to run much faster and they could be less expensive. But if new incompatible products were introduced, it would be disastrous and extremely costly to millions of users. Intel, and other industry leaders, determined that it is much more important to protect the consumers who have invested so heavily in the earlier products.

Keyboard Differences

The early IBM keyboard was a fine piece of machinery, built like a Rolls Royce. But if you decide to use your old components when you upgrade, you might not be able to use your old keyboard. It might still be perfectly good and you might love the feel and action of the keys. Although the PC, XT, and AT type keyboards look exactly alike and have the same connector, the early keyboards will not work on AT type systems. The AT type systems includes the 286, 386, 486, and Pentium-class computers. These systems have a scanner frequency that is different from the original PC and XT.

Though the XT is obsolete, some of the keyboard manufacturers provide a small switch on the back side that allows them to be switched from one type to the other.

Many Motherboard Options

If you do decide to install a new motherboard, you will have a lot of options and choices. There are hundreds of different manufacturers. Of course, every one of them wants to differentiate their product, so they are all a bit different in some respect. Even though they might be a bit different, they are all still compatible and will accept all of the usual hardware and software.

At one time we only had a couple different CPUs and motherboards. Now we have hundreds of different types and variations of motherboards. One reason for the many different types and variations is that Intel, and several other clone companies, now manufacture a large number of different CPU versions. The motherboard and computer type depends on whatever CPU is installed such as the 386, 486, and the Pentium class. There are several different versions for each of the systems. Intel alone manufactures over 50 different CPU versions. Many of the different versions are based on the operating frequency of the CPU.

As you can see, you will have a lot of different options. What you choose should depend on what you want to do with your computer, and how much you want to spend.

What the Motherboard Is

The motherboard is the largest and most important board in your system. It has the central processing unit (CPU) and all of the chips and electronics that makes computing possible.

The original 286 computer case size was a bit larger than the XT. The XT was 5 inches high, $19\frac{1}{2}$ inches wide, and $16\frac{1}{2}$ inches deep. The 286 case was 6 inches high, $21\frac{1}{2}$ inches wide, and $16\frac{1}{2}$ inches deep. The XT motherboard was $8\frac{3}{4}$ inches wide and 12 inches long. The 286 motherboard was 12 inches wide and $13\frac{3}{4}$ inches long. By combining several chips into single very large-scale integrated (VLSI) chips, the clone builders soon developed a "baby" 286 motherboard that was the same width as the XT, except that it was one inch longer. The new baby 286 could still fit in the XT case. Since that time all new motherboards have been as small or smaller than the baby 286. The baby size is now the new standard, even for the Pentium and PowerPC.

There are a large number of different types and sizes of cases available today. The baby size motherboards can be installed in any size desktop case or any of the tower cases. The holes and slots usually line up with no problem.

Expansion Slots

The motherboard usually lies on the floor of the chassis. Most motherboards have eight slots or connectors for plug-in boards. Some motherboards, such as those used in the PS/2 and low-profile type systems, might only have a single slot for a daughterboard. The daughterboard can have two to five slots.

Some motherboards might have fewer slots if they have several built-in functions. Some of the motherboards with the peripheral component interconnect (PCI) boards bus might only have four or five slots for ISA type plug-in boards, but they might have three or four slots for PCI.

We never seem to have enough slots. There are so many different boards that we can use in them. Because of this problem, some special motherboards have up to 12 slots. Of course with this many slots, it has to be the large standard-size board. It would also require a special case to accommodate extra slots for rear panel connections.

Most all motherboards now have built-in functions for hard disk and CD-ROM IDE and printer and mouse ports and interfaces. Many companies are designing motherboards with more built-in functions, such as a sound board, a monitor adapter, a SCSI interface, and universal serial bus (USB).

Expansion Bus

The slot connectors have two rows of contacts that mate with both sides of the edge connector of the plug in boards. Each contact in each slot is connected to the same contact on all of the other slots. This is called a *bus*. Because all of the slots have the same bus connections, a plug-in board can be inserted into any one of the slots.

A bus is more or less a generic term. It can be just etched circuits on a board, some wires, or anything that provides a signal path. There are several different types of buses, the input/output (I/O) bus, a memory bus, ISA bus, the PCI bus, and the PC-Card bus (formerly known as the Personal Computer Memory Card International Association or PCM-CIA bus).

Buses are also differentiated by their width or number of lines. The XT has an 8-bit bus and the 286 has a 16-bit bus for accessing memory and for Input/Output (I/O). The 386 and 486 have a 32-bit memory bus, but any Industry Standard Architecture (ISA) board would still operate their I/O bus at 16 bits and be limited to a speed of 8MHz to 10MHz. This means that any board or peripheral that wanted to communicate with the CPU had to do so over the 16-bit I/O bus at a fairly low speed.

To help overcome this problem, newer boards were designed. But there was, and still is, billions of dollars worth of hardware available for the older ISA machines. Many businesses and individuals still had large investments in the ISA hardware. IBM ignored this large segment and developed their incompatible Micro Channel Architecture (MCA) system. A consortium of companies developed the Extended ISA (EISA) system that used special boards, but could also still use the older hardware. Then the Video Electronics Standards Association (VESA) developed the VESA local bus (VLB) system that used special boards, but it could still accept ISA cards. The PCI bus was then developed, primarily by Intel.

The VLB and the PCI bus allows certain peripherals, such as hard drives, video adapters, and network interface cards (NICs), to communicate over the special 32 bit bus. The PCI and version 2.0 of the VLB will allow the Pentium peripherals to communicate on a 64-bit bus.

Most PCs, even the 386, 486, Pentium, EISA, and MCA systems operate at an I/O speed of 8 to 10MHz. This is so that they will be downward compatible with early software and hardware. The fact that they are compatible allows us to use the early software and hardware, but it can be a real bottleneck for some operations and applications where speed is important.

The CPU

The motherboards are named and differentiated according to the CPU chip that is installed on them. The XT has an 8088, the 286 has an 80286 CPU, the 386 an 80386 CPU, the 486 an 80486 CPU, and what should have been the 586 is called the Pentium.

Within these designations, there are several other CPU variations, such as the 386SX and 486SX. There are also variations according to the speed and frequency of the CPU. For instance, there are 16MHz, 20MHz, 25MHz, 33MHz, and 40MHz variations of the 386. There are even more variations of the 486 CPU. There are several variations of the Pentium CPUs, the Pentium, the Pentium MMX, the Pentium Pro, and the Pentium II. The Pentium is the MMX version of the Pentium Pro. There are also several clones, such as the Cyrix 5x86, the 6x86, and their M2. Advanced Micro Devices (AMD) also has several clones, such as the 586 and the K6. There are variations for all of the Intel, Cyrix, and AMD CPU and motherboards often depending on the speed or frequency of the CPU.

The Cyrix 5x86 and AMD 586 are equivalent to the Intel Pentium. The Cyrix 6x86 is equivalent to the Pentium Pro. The Cyrix M2 and the AMD K6 are equivalent to the Intel Pentium II.

MMX Technical Details

Here is a press release from Intel's Website, www.Intel.com:

The new MMX processors are built on Intel's enhanced 0.35 micron CMOS process technology which allows it to deliver high performance with low power consumption. Packed with 4.5 million transistors, the Pentium processor with MMX technology includes several architectural enhancements, in addition to MMX instructions. They include a doubled on-chip cache size to 32KB and more efficient branch prediction, which provide increased performance of 10 to 20 percent on standard CPU benchmarks. The addition of MMX technology-enabled software will provide even more performance and quality improvements, depending on the type of application and the extent to which the software developer incorporates the new instructions.

On Intel's Media Benchmark the Pentium processor with MMX technology delivers more than 60 percent performance improvement when compared with an equivalent speed Pentium processor. This benchmark, which measures performance on media-rich applications, consists of audio, video, imaging and 3D geometry components.

SPEC CPU95 performance for the 200 MHz processor is 6.41 SPECint95 and 4.66 SPECfp95. Performance for the 166 MHz processor is 5.59 SPECint95 and 4.30 SPECfp95. The iCOMP(R) Index 2.0 ratings are 182 and 160, respectively.

Both the desktop and mobile versions of the processor utilize dual voltage levels. The processor's input and output pins operate at 3.3 volts for compatibility with today's components. The desktop processors inner core operates at 2.8 volts while the mobile processor operates at 2.45 volts. The lower core voltage enables desktop and mobile systems to operate within efficient thermal ranges. Maximum power dissipation for the desktop processor is 15.7 watts and thermal design power for the mobile version is 7.8 watts.

Boxed processors for desktop systems are packaged with a fan heatsink, CD sampler with software developed for MMX technology, installation manual, certificate of authenticity, and Intel Inside. program label. Pricing and availability of boxed processors can be obtained from authorized Intel distributors.

Motherboard Memory

A 386, 486, or Pentium motherboard should have sockets, or provisions, for the installation of at least 16Mb of RAM memory on board. Most of them will have provisions for 16Mb and up to 128Mb on board. The majority of the motherboards will use single in-line memory module (SIMM) type sockets. It allows for the most memory to be installed in the least amount of space. Today, except for SRAM chips for cache, motherboards don't use the older dual in-line package (DIP) type memory chips. They require too much board real estate. You can install about 128Mb of SIMM memory in the space that one megabyte of DIP memory would require. The old XT motherboard had 640K of DIP chips which took up about one fourth of the entire motherboard real estate. The Pentium motherboard has four white sockets for SIMMs. Up to 200 times more memory could be installed in those four Pentium SIMM sockets than in the 36 DIP sockets of the XT.

Before you order memory, make sure that you get the right type for your motherboard. Get the right speed, the right memory size, and the right physical size. There are two types of SIMM configurations and sockets: 30 contacts and 72 contacts. The 72-contact SIMMs are usually designated as 1 X 36 which is 4Mb, 2 X 36 which is 8Mb, 4 X 36 which is 16Mb, etc,. For most systems, you have to install memory in multiples of two. You would have to install two 1 X 36, or two 2 X 36, or whatever amount you wanted in multiples of two.

Your motherboard will probably be sold without memory. Make sure that you order the type and speed of memory that is required for your board. You can probably get by with 80 nanosecond (ns) for a 20MHz 486SX. For 25MHz you will want 60 ns to 70 ns, and at least 60 ns for 33MHz and faster systems.

DRAM

The primary memory used in PCs is Dynamic Random Access Memory (DRAM) chips. The older PCs reserved about one fourth of the motherboard area for memory chips. The early boards used 64K chips. (64K is 64,000 bytes). It took nine chips to make 64K and that is all that some of the motherboards had. Later they developed 256K chips and up to 640K was installed on some motherboards. Today we have 64Mb single in-line memory modules (SIMMs) that allow us to install up to 256Mb on a motherboard in less space than it took for the original 64K. If you refer back to Fig. 5-1, the four white slots below the fan on the Micronics motherboard are for SIMM chips. The SIMM sockets can be located anywhere on the different motherboards.

Cache SRAM

When processing data, quite often the same data is used over and over again. Having to traverse the bus to retrieve the data can slow the system down considerably.

The 486 has a small built-in 8K cache which contributes to its speed. Because 8K is not nearly large enough for some programs, many motherboards have sockets for adding a very fast cache. This cache is usually made from static random access memory (SRAM). Memory is discussed in more detail in the next chapter.

Other Motherboard Chips

Besides the CPU and memory chips, there are several other chips and systems on the motherboard. The early PCs and the AT had a very large number of chips. I have an early 286 motherboard with one megabyte of memory on it. It has over 150 separate chips on it.

The Chips and Technology Company, using very large scale integration (VLSI), combined several motherboard chips into just a few chips. Other companies followed them so that today we have only a small number of chips on the motherboard.

The smaller number of chips means fewer solder connections, more reliability, more speed, less board real estate required, and less cost. Some motherboards are now as small as one third the size of the original XT and might have only five or six large VLSI chips on them.

ROM BIOS

You won't have to worry about read only memory (ROM). ROM is memory that cannot ordinarily be altered or changed. ROM comes with the motherboard. The principal use of ROM in PCs today is for the basic input/output system (BIOS).

The BIOS chip is second in importance only to the CPU. Every time you turn your computer on, the BIOS does a power on self test (POST). The BIOS checks all of the major components to make sure that they are operating properly. It also facilitates the transfer of data among peripherals. Many BIOS chips also have diagnostics and several utilities built in. BIOS sounds a bit like BOSS, and that is its principal job.

The BIOS performs its important functions under the control of firmware programs. These programs are similar to software programs except that the ROM is actually made up of hundreds of transistors that are programmed to perform certain functions.

Most newer BIOS chips now use flash memory. But until recently, the ROM BIOS programs were usually burned into electrically programmable read only memory (EPROMs) chips. Special devices were used to input a software program into the ROM chip. As the program voltages pass through the chip, the transistors are turned on and off to match the input program. When a normal transistor has voltage applied to it, it will turn on or off as long as the voltage is present. The EPROM transistors are different from ordinary transistors. When the EPROM transistors are turned on or off, they remain in that condition.

Fairly large programs and text can be stored on a ROM chip. The ROM BIOS for an early XT could be programmed onto a 64K ROM chip. The 486 ROM BIOS uses a 512K. All of the text in the book you are holding in your hand can be stored in less than 512K.

Companies that manufacture the BIOS chips are constantly improving and adding new functionality to the BIOS. You can perform some useful upgrades to an older computer by just installing a new BIOS. Figure 5-4 shows a couple of 286 BIOS chips. This type of chip is still used in some systems.

In some cases, installing a new BIOS might not be cost effective. I had a 386 computer in my office that I put together in early 1988. It had a 16MHz CPU, which was very slow by today's standards. But it served me well for a couple of years. I decided to upgrade it by adding a 250Mb hard drive. But the largest hard drive the system would accept was 114Mb. The BIOS had been written in 1988 and a 250Mb hard drive was something few people could afford at that time.

A new BIOS for the 386 system would cost about $50. I decided that it wasn't worth it. The system would still run at 16MHz. For just a few dollars more than the cost of the new BIOS chips, I bought a 40MHz 386 motherboard complete with a new BIOS.

Fig. 5-4
Some BIOS chips
from an old 286.

Many motherboards now come with BIOS in a flash memory chip. The flash memory chips can be upgraded by software from a floppy disk or even downloaded by modem through the telephone line. You will soon see many other motherboards with flash memory BIOS. It will become the industry standard. Figure 5-5 shows a Pentium with a flash BIOS chip.

There are still a lot of older computers that could be easily upgraded this way. You might have an older computer with a lot of special boards, a loaded hard disk drive, and other components that you want to keep. You might want to add a larger hard drive, a CD-ROM drive, or any of several other upgrades. But an older BIOS might not let you do any of these things. An upgrade BIOS might well be worth the money.

There aren't too many companies who provide BIOS upgrades today. One that has upgrades for most computers is the Unicore Company at 800-800-2467. If you are on the Internet, send e-mail to: Jason@unicore.com.

Fig. 5-5
The pen points to a
flash memory BIOS.
It can be upgraded
electronically.

Fig. 5-5
The pen points to a flash memory BIOS. It can be upgraded electronically.

Keyboard BIOS

The keyboard is a small computer in itself and has its own special BIOS chip on the motherboard. It is usually a long 40-pin chip located near the keyboard connector. See Fig. 5-6. You might not see this chip on some of the newer motherboards because many of them now integrate it into a VLSI chip.

A scan code or signal is sent to the BIOS when a key is pressed and another signal is sent when the key is released. When two keys are pressed, it can detect which one was pressed first. It can also detect when a key is held down longer than normal and will start beeping at you. The last 20 keystrokes are stored in the keyboard memory and are continually flushed out and replaced by new keystrokes.

System Configuration and CMOS

The CMOS system and batteries were discussed in Chapter 2. When you install a hard drive, you have to tell the system configuration setup what kind it is, the number of heads, sectors, and other information. The configuration system also needs to be informed as to what kind of floppy drives you have. If you want to reset the time or date, you do it with the CMOS system setup.

The system configuration or setup is stored in complementary metal oxide semiconductors (CMOS). These CMOS transistors use very little power. So there is a small battery mounted on the motherboard that can keep the transistors turned on so that they retain the date and time and setup information even when the computer is turned off.

The battery was soldered onto the older motherboards which made it very difficult to replace them. If you didn't know how to use a soldering iron, you could ruin a motherboard. The older batteries usually lasted three or four years. Most newer motherboards have a square plug-in Dallas battery or a round lithium battery. The lithium battery is about the size of a quarter and is held in place by a clip. If the time and date are consistently off, or your computer asks you to enter the time and date when you boot up, your battery might be dead or very low.

The round lithium battery is available at most drugstores and even grocery stores. If you need one of the older batteries or the Dallas battery, call 1-800 batteries or 1-800-228-8374. This company also has batteries and peripheral components for notebooks. They have a website at www.800batteries.com.

Fig. 5-6
A keyboard BIOS on an old 286 motherboard.

■ ■ Timing

A computer depends on precise timing. Several of the chips on a motherboard control the frequency and timing circuits. The timing is so critical that there are usually one or more crystals on the motherboard that oscillate at a precise frequency to control the timing circuits. The crystals are usually in a small, oblong, shiny can. In Fig. 5-2, the pen points to a crystal oscillator can.

■ ■ DMA

The direct memory access (DMA) system allows some processing to take place without having to bother the CPU. For instance, the disk drives can exchange data directly with the RAM without having to go through the CPU.

■ ■ IRQ

The interrupt request (IRQ) system is a very important part of the computer. It can cause the system to interrupt whatever it is doing and take care of the request. Without the interrupts, nothing would get done. Even if the computer is doing nothing, it must be interrupted and told to perform a task.

There are 16 IRQs, numbered from 0 to 15. Each input/output (I/O) device on the bus is given a unique IRQ number. Software can also perform interrupt requests. There is a priority system and some interrupts take precedence over others.

Sixteen IRQs might seem like a large number, but it isn't nearly enough. Several of the interrupts are reserved or used by the system so that they are not available. It would have been wonderful if the Pentium had provided about twice as many, but no such luck.

If you want to see how your system is using IRQs, if you have DOS 6.0 or later, just type MSD (for Microsoft Diagnostics). This command will not only let you look at your IRQs, it will tell you about most of the other important elements in your computer.

See Table 5-1 for how the 16 IRQs might be used.

TABLE 5-1

IRQ Assignments

IRQ	Address	Description	Detected
0	OCO8:0103	Timer Click	Yes
1	OCO8:0113	Keyboard	Yes
2	OA7D:OO57	Second 8259A	Yes
3	E939:1FAD	COM2: COM4	COM2
4	OA7D:0087	COM1: COM3	COM1
5	OA7D:OO9F	LPT2:	No
6	OA7D:OOB7	Floppy Disk	Yes
7	OO7O:O6F4	LPT1:	Yes
8	OA7D:OO52	Real-Time Clock	Yes
9	FOOO:EED3	Redirected IRQ2	Yes
10	OA7D:OOCF	(Reserved)	
11	OA7D:OOE7	(Reserved)	
12	OA7D:OOFF	(Reserved)	
13	FOOO:EEDC	Math Coprocessor	Yes
14	OA7D:O117	Fixed Disk	Yes
15	FOOO:FF53	(Reserved)	

As you can see, out of the 16 IRQs, 10, 11, 12, and 15 are available. IRQ 5 is for LPT2, but because I don't have a second printer attached, it could be used for other devices such as a mouse, a sound board, or network card.

UARTs and Serial Ports

Mice, modems, Universal Power Supplies, game controllers, sound controllers, fax boards, some printers, plotters, and many other devices communicate with the computer through a serial port. They operate with serial data. The data must be furnished over a single line with one bit following another. The computer operates with parallel data. It takes eight bits to make a byte, so for eight bits it will have eight lines; for 16 bits, it will have 16 lines. Obviously, this data cannot be sent out over a modem or any of the other serial devices. The serial ports receive these 8-bit bytes, then convert them to single bits so that they can be transmitted over the phone lines or wherever. When receiving data from an outside source, it must be converted back to the 8-bit form. The conversion is done with a special universal asynchronous receiver transmitter (UART) chip.

In the older systems, you had to have a special board to provide the serial ports. Some manufacturers made multifunction boards to provide them. All modern motherboards have them built in. If your motherboard has built-in COM ports, you will have one or two Universal Asynchronous Transmitter-Receiver (UART) chips somewhere on the board, but you might not be able to find them. These chips are integrated into VLSI chips on most of the newer motherboards. If your motherboard does not have built-in serial ports, then you will have to have a plug-in board that has these chips. The early chips had the designation 8250, later chips were designated 16450 and 16550.

If the serial ports are not built in on the motherboard, they are usually integrated on a multi input/output (I/O) board. This board can have serial port COM1 and COM2, printer port LPT1, a game port, and often a floppy disk controller and IDE hard disk interface. Some of the inexpensive multi I/O boards are still using the old 8250 chips. For fast modem transfers, you should have the 16550 UART. You probably won't be able to see it because it will be integrated into a larger chip. You can determine what type is installed in your computer by invoking the Microsoft Diagnostics MSD command. Just type MSD at any prompt and use your mouse to click on COM Ports. You will see a vast amount of information about your computer.

Ordinarily, only two serial ports can be used, and each requires a dedicated IRQ. COM1 uses IRQ4; COM2 uses IRQ3. You might have four or more different serial devices that you would like to attach to your computer. It is possible to add two more virtual ports, COM3 and COM4; but, they must share the COM1 and COM2 IRQ lines (COM3 uses IRQ4 and COM4 uses IRQ3). There are some devices that are rather selfish and don't like to share. You need special software in order to use COM3 and COM4.

The COM ports also have specific addresses in memory. COM1 uses 3F8h, COM2 uses 2F8h, COM3 uses 3E8h, and COM4 uses 2E8h. Life would be a whole lot simpler if only we had four or more dedicated IRQ lines for the COM ports. Of course, you would also need two more UART chips for the additional ports.

A large number of the problems encountered in adding or upgrading a system is due to the serial ports and IRQs. If a device conflicts with another one as to the assigned IRQ or memory address, neither device will work. (Refer to Table 5-1 to see how IRQs are assigned.) I have spent hours and hours trying to figure out why a new board would not operate. There are several programs that can help you determine which ports are being used. One of the better ones is a low-cost shareware program called Port Finder. It is available from James McDaniel of mcTRONic Systems, (713) 462-7687.

Architecture

The *architecture* of the computer refers to the overall design and the components it uses. The architecture is also concerned with the type of bus that is used. The bus is the internal pathways over which data is sent from one part of the computer to another. The 8-bit systems use 8-bit parallel paths, 16 use 16, 32 use 32, and 64 use 64. The flow of data over a bus is often compared to the flow of traffic on a highway. If there are only two lanes, the flow of traffic might be limited. Adding more lanes can vastly improve the flow of traffic.

ISA

The Industry Standard Architecture (ISA) is what was once known as the IBM compatible standard. IBM more or less abandoned the standard when they introduced their micro channel architecture (MCA) in 1987. There were far more IBM-compatible clone computers in existence than computers manufactured by IBM. Because IBM was now directing most of its efforts toward the MCA, the clone makers took over the standard and changed the name.

An ISA computer can be anything from the oldest and slowest XT up to the newest and fastest Pentium. The old XT used an 8-bit bus, which means that 8 parallel lines connected to the same pins on all of the slot connectors for plug-in boards. When the 286 was being developed by IBM, it became apparent that an 8-bit bus was too slow and was clearly inadequate. So they devised a 16-bit slot connector by adding a second 36-contact connector in front of the original 62-contact connector. This was a

Fig. 5-7
An 8-bit board on
top, then a 16-bit
board and a VL bus
board on the
bottom.

brilliant innovation. Figure 5-7 shows an 8-bit ISA board on the bottom
and a 16-bit ISA board on the top.

Compatibility

There was about five billion dollars worth of 8-bit hardware in existence
at the time IBM introduced their 16-bit AT 286. But with the 16-bit connector, either an 8-bit or 16-bit board can be used in a 16-bit system. The
industry loved it because it did not obsolete their present investment in
plug-in boards.

This downward compatibility still exists even with the fastest and
most powerful 486 or Pentium. But there is a price to pay for the compatibility. The CPU operates over a special memory bus to communicate
with RAM at the CPU's rated frequency. The 386 and 486 are 32-bit systems; 64 bits for the Pentium. The 386 and 486 ISA systems communicate
with the system RAM over a 32-bit bus back and forth to memory. But
the system can only communicate with their plug-in boards and peripherals over a 16-bit bus. Even though the 486 might operate at 66MHz, to
be able to run all previous software and hardware, the ISA I/O bus is limited to a speed of about 8 MHz and an I/O bus width of 16 parallel lines.

MCA

IBM decided that the 16-bit ISA system was inadequate. They designed a new system they called the micro channel architecture (MCA). This architecture was a 32-bit bus system for plug-in cards and memory. This wider bus was a much faster and more powerful system. But IBM also wanted to be downward compatible with the available software, even if they weren't compatible with the hardware. So the I/O speed from the plug-in boards and peripherals was still limited to 8 to 10MHz.

Before they introduced their MCA systems, IBM had been losing a large share of their business to the low-cost clones. They had let the design of the original PC slip away from them. This time they very carefully patented every thing about the MCA and kept most of the critical specifications secret. They developed a machine that only they could manufacture and sell without any competition from the cloners.

The big problem was that the new MCA system could not use any of the billions of dollars worth of hardware that was available. The connector contacts of the MCA boards were much smaller than those on the ISA boards. There was no way they could be used in ISA systems. New boards had to be designed for the MCA slots. Figure 5-8 shows an 8-bit board on top and a MCA board on the bottom.

IBM was confident that the added speed and power of their new system would more than make up for the added expense. Besides, IBM had

Fig. 5-8

An 8-bit board on top and a MCA board on the bottom.

a very large and loyal following, especially among the large corporate buyers. Many of the large corporations have pretty deep pockets. But most of the ordinary buyers usually have to watch their budget. IBM computers have always been expensive. Their new MCA PS/2 systems were even more expensive than the original IBM PCs. The boards needed for the MCA systems were also very expensive. There were millions and millions of clones in existence. Because of the large number of systems, and the competition of the many vendors, the cost of a board for a clone was much less than that for a PS/2.

IBM is now a changed company. They have reduced the prices on most of their products. At one time you had to go through authorized dealers to buy any IBM product or to have any repairs done. They have now set up several companies for selling in the direct market. They will sell you any of their products through mail order.

IBM no longer makes the PS/1 and PS/2 MCA machines. They are obsolete, but many of them are still doing a good job. There are several ways that they can be upgraded.

EISA

A group of compatible or IBM clone makers realized that IBM was right about needing a wider bus and more room for expansion and improvement. They devised the extended industry standard architecture. This standard specified a new connector with almost double the number of contacts and added several new improvements to the ISA standard. Unlike the IBM MCA system, the EISA system was downwardly compatible with all previous hardware. The billions of dollars worth of present boards could still be used with the EISA system, even the old 8-bit plug-in boards.

The standard contact on an ISA connector is 0.06-inches wide. There is a 0.04-inch space between each contact. The EISA board was designed with a second set of contacts immediately below the ISA contacts. A connecting trace is placed between the ISA contacts for the lower set of EISA contacts. The EISA plug-in slot on the motherboard has two sets of contacts to match the contacts on the plug-in boards. The EISA boards have cutouts on the boards to match bars across the lower EISA section of the slot connector. When an ISA board is plugged in, the bars prevent it from being inserted deep enough to contact the EISA contacts. Figure 5-9 shows an EISA board.

Fig. 5-9
An EISA board.

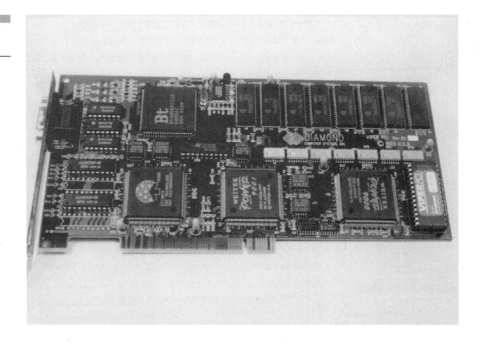

Like the MCA system, the EISA system provides a 32-bit bus. But also like the MCA, they wanted to remain downward compatible with earlier software and hardware. Therefore the communication between the plug-in boards was still limited to a speed of 8 MHz.

The 486 EISA system was much faster and more powerful than the ISA system. But it is now obsolete. If you have invested a lot of money in an EISA system, there might be several things you can do to upgrade it. You could replace the CPU with one of the upgrade options mentioned in the previous chapter. You could add more memory, a larger hard disk drive, a CD-ROM drive, and several other upgrade options.

The VESA Local Bus

The PC bus has long been a bottleneck. The 8-bit bus at 4.77MHz was okay for the XT. The 16-bit bus was a great leap forward when the 286 was introduced. The 286 CPU communicated with its RAM over a 16-bit memory bus at whatever speed the CPU operated. But in order to remain compatible with previous hardware and software, the input/output (I/O) bus speed was locked in at 8 to 10MHz.

When the 386 and 486 were introduced, they communicated with their RAM over a 32-bit memory bus at the speed of the CPU. But the I/O bus still operated on a 16-bit bus at 8 to 10MHz. Some peripherals, such as fast hard disks and monitors, were slowed down considerably.

The Video Electronics Standards Association (VESA) developed a set of specifications for a new bus that eliminated some of the bottlenecks.

The VESA local bus or VL bus (VLB) specification added a second slot connector in line with the 16-bit slot connector. This solution was similar to that which was used to migrate from the 8-bit slot to the 16-bit. That solution was to add a second connector to the 8-bit slot connector to turn it into a 16-bit system. This system allowed the use of both 8-bit and 16-bit cards. The VL bus is quite similar. It adds a second connector in line with the 16-bit connectors so that VL or 16-bit boards can be used in these slots. The VL connector uses 116 miniature contacts that are similar to the MCA connectors. The connector provides a 32-bit path from the plug-in boards and peripherals to the CPU. The VL bus is a direct extension of the CPU bus and runs at the same speed as the CPU. The VL bus increases the performance of a PC considerably, yet adds very little to the cost of the system. Figure 5-10 shows my combination ISA/EISA/VLB 486DX2-66. From the top, the fourth, fifth, and sixth slots are EISA connectors. Slots 6 and 7

Fig. 5-10
A combination ISA, VLB, and EISA 486 motherboard.

Fig. 5-11
A 16-bit I/O board on the bottom and two VLB I/O boards above. The board at the top has slots for up to 2Mb of hard disk buffer memory.

have the additional VESA local bus connectors. Figure 5-11 shows a 16-bit IDE hard disk interface and multi I/O board on the bottom and two VLB IDE hard disk interface and multi I/O boards above. The VLB board on the top has slots for adding buffer memory. The difference is that the VLB board is considerably bit faster than the standard 16-bit IDE board. Each of the boards can control two IDE hard drives, two floppy disks, has serial ports COM1 and COM2, a parallel port LPT1 connector for the printer, and a set of pins for a game port or joystick. One of the COM ports can be accessed through the top connector on the back panel, the other COM port is accessed through the 10 upright pins on the board.

Thousands of vendors adopted the VL bus configuration. There was lots of competition, so the cost of the VL bus plug-in boards was quite reasonable.

The VL bus was not a perfect solution. The system only allows three connectors. They are ordinarily used for fast IDE hard disks, for video adapters, and for network interface cards (NICs).

The VL bus allows I/O communication over the 32-bit lines at the same speed as the CPU. But the other input/output (I/O) components in the system are still relegated to the 16-bit bus at 8 to 10MHz. Even the Pentium will have this same standard ISA bus for I/O and peripherals in order to remain backward compatible.

The VL bus systems can be used on the ISA, EISA, MCA, and Pentium motherboards. Some of the early Pentium motherboards had both VL bus and the PCI bus.

The VL bus is now obsolete. There are still millions of VLB systems in use. If they do all that you need to do, just upgrade them. There are several ways that they can be upgraded—add more memory, CD-ROMs, larger hard drives, and many other cost- effective upgrades.

The Intel PCI Bus

The Intel Peripheral Component Interconnect (PCI) has become the standard on all new motherboards. The VL bus connected directly to the CPU. The PCI bus is a bit different in that it is a separate bus. Many of the PCI bus connectors and boards are stand-alone. Boards designed for the VL bus system were not stand-alone because the boards used both the 16-bit and the VL bus pins. Figure 5-12 shows a PCI monitor adapter on the bottom and a VLB adapter on the top.

It can sometimes be very frustrating when adding a plug-in board. Often you have to set several dip switches or jumpers so that it does not conflict with the assigned interrupt request (IRQs), serial and parallel ports, and DMA channels of other plug-in boards.

Fig. 5-12
A PCI monitor adapter on the bottom and a VLB monitor adapter on the top.

One of the advantages that the PCI bus had over the first version of the VL bus is that the PCI was a plug-and-play system. It had an auto-configuration capability that would automatically configure a PCI add-in board. The original version of the VL bus was a "plug-and-pray system." Version 2 of the VL bus was a plug-and-play system, but it was too late to save it from obsolescence.

Another advantage of the PCI is that it can allow up to ten connectors. But for most practical purposes, the same three used in the VLB system (the hard disk, video, and network) will be all that is needed at this time.

The PCI bus can be used with ISA, EISA, or MCA system type motherboards. But the EISA and MCA systems are obsolete. All of the modern motherboards still have three or four ISA connectors that can accept 8- or 16-bit boards.

ISA-EISA-VL-PCI Combos

Several manufacturers produced combination motherboards that had ISA, EISA, VLB, and PCI slots. They might have had two or three EISA slots, two or more VLB slots, two or three PCI slots, and two or more ISA slots. If you have one of these boards, there is several ways that you can upgrade it. You could upgrade to one of the CPUs discussed in Chapter 4. You can add more memory, new and larger hard disks, CD-ROM drives, new software, and many other upgrades.

PC CARD BUS

Many personal and desktop computers now have a PC Card slot. It was formerly known as PCMCIA which stands for *Personal Computer Memory Card International Association*. The PCMCIA specification was originally developed for adding memory to laptop and notebook computers, using memory cards the size of a credit card. You might ask, why would anyone want a desktop computer with a PC Card? The answer is because there are now many devices and components besides memory that can be plugged into this slot. Dozens more new devices and components are being developed every day. Adaptec has a SlimSCSI adapter that can be used with several SCSI devices. A PC Card slot can be more useful than an extra slot on the motherboard. In order to change a board on the motherboard, you have to shut everything down, remove the cover, then install the new board. On a PC Card slot, if you want to use a modem, just plug it in. You don't even have to shut off the power. After you have finished with the modem or fax, plug in an ethernet card, a hard disk, a sound card, a SCSI interface, or any of the other PC Card devices that are available. A PC Card slot can add a vast amount of utility and expansion capabilities to a computer.

Built-In Goodies

It is amazing how soon you can fill up all of the available slots on the motherboard. One way to get around having to use plug-in boards is to have many of the functions built in on the motherboard. At one time there were very few built-in functions. Most motherboards now have several built-in functions and utilities. One of the arguments against built-in functions is that the functions might become obsolete, or they might become defective. But, if necessary, the on-board functions can usually be disabled and replaced with a plug-in board. Here are some of the things that can be built in:

IDE Interface

Many motherboards now have the IDE interface for hard disks and a floppy disk controller built in on the motherboard. They have rows of pins protruding from the motherboard that will accept the ribbon cables from the drives.

SCSI Interface

Many of the Macintosh models have built-in SCSI interfaces. That is one of the reasons for their popularity. The PC industry has been lax in not following suit. SCSI is something that is essential, not only for multimedia, but for many PC applications. A few motherboard manufacturers are now including a built-in SCSI interface.

Universal Serial Bus

The universal serial bus (USB) is being integrated on most newer high-end motherboards. It is an excellent reason to upgrade. Here is some information about it from the Intel website at www.intel.com:

What It Is USB will allow users to connect up to 127 different peripherals all at once, using a single standard connector type. There will be no more guesswork about which serial or parallel port to choose, and nontechnical PC users will be able to say good-bye to DIP switches, jumpers, IRQ settings, DMA channels and I/O addresses. USB features hot insertion and removal, so users will be able to attach and detach peripherals anytime, without powering down their system.

In fact, USB hardware solutions from Intel are so flexible, they will make it easy to connect with the fast-growing world of new and existing digital peripherals, computer telephony integration (CTI) applications and popular multi-user games. In addition, USB enjoys widespread support from the industry's leading suppliers of PCs, peripherals and software. Intel supports USB with PCI chipsets and the industry's first single-chip USB peripheral USB Controller. For those developing and marketing products for PCs, it's time to make your own connection with USB now.

USB is an open and royalty-free specification with broad industry support. Developed by Compaq, Digital Equipment, IBM, Intel, Microsoft, NEC, and Northern Telecom.

The USB Implementers Forum consists of more than 250 semiconductor, computer, peripheral, and software companies, providing marketing and technical support to help accelerate USB product development.

Printer Port

There are very few computers that are not tied to a printer of some sort. There are still a few printers that use the serial port, but most printers today use one of the two parallel ports, LPT1 or LPT2. On older systems, you have to buy a multifunction board with a printer port on it. But most systems now integrate the parallel ports on the motherboard.

Game Ports

Many of the multifunction boards sold today have a game port for joysticks used with several of the games that are available. With the increased interest and popularity of multimedia, the game port has become almost mandatory.

Monitor Adapter

Every computer needs a board or adapter to drive the monitor. Some motherboards have had built-in monitor adapters for some time. They are great for many applications. The main problem is that the developers keep making the adapters faster, with better resolution, true colors, and more and more complex. If your adapter is built-in, then you are stuck with whatever resolution or functions it provides. Most of the motherboards with built-in functions have jumpers or switches that will allow you to disable those functions so that a board can be plugged in to take over from the built-in functions.

Benchmarks

Benchmarks are tests designed to give a standard measure of performance that can be used to predict how well and how fast a computer will run actual applications. There are many factors that will affect the outcome of a benchmark test. Some of the factors are the computer CPU, the architecture, the design, system software, hardware, and many other combined characteristics of a computer.

There are several different benchmarks. Some are designed to test only a specific portion of a system.

MIPS

In Table 4-1, MIPS is an acronym for millions of instructions per second. Notice that the XT could only do 0.75; the Pentium can do 112 MIPs, which is almost 150 times faster than the XT. We have truly come a long way since 1981.

The MIPS benchmark is good, but it does not measure all of the capabilities of a CPU while performing different tasks. A much better benchmark is one that measures the performance while running several actual applications. For instance, a 486SX can run number crunching programs, but a 486DX that has a built-in floating point math coprocessor would be much faster. A Pentium would be even faster because it can handle two instructions per cycle and it also has a 16K built-in cache.

SPEC92

A group of organizations got together in January of 1992 and formed the *Systems Performance Evaluation Cooperative (SPEC)*. They developed a suite of benchmark programs that effectively measures the performance of computing systems in actual application environments. The SPEC92 tests have become the industry standards. The tests for various applications are identified by including the acronym SPEC. For instance, SPECint92 is a very effective benchmark to measure integer application performance; SPECfp92 measures floating point performance.

Other Benchmarks

An early benchmark was the Norton System Information (SI) that came with Norton's utilities. It provided a measure for a system's throughput, including processing speed and the speed of some peripherals. The Norton SI reference 1.0 is based on the original IBM XT, which had a CPU frequency of 4.77MHz. Later systems are measured against this reference. My 486DX2-66 system measures 42.4, which means that it is over 42 times faster than the original XT. The 66MHz frequency of the 486 is just a little over 13 times faster than the XT at 4.77MHz, but the newer technologies and operation of the CPU system yields over 42 times better performance.

There are several other benchmarks. Whetstones measures arithmetic operations. Dhrystones measures MIPS. WinBench executes on top of Windows and gives WinMark measures. Other benchmarks have been developed by organizations such as the Ziff-Davis Labs. They do a lot of testing for the system reviews that are reported in their various magazines.

The Landmark Research at (800) 683-6696 has developed the Landmark benchmark which, among other things, measures CPU operations. The Landmark Company has also the developed several diagnostic software tools such as WinProbe and DOS for Windows.

iCOMP Index

The Intel Comparative Performance (iCOMP) index rating provides a simple relative measure of microprocessor performance. It is not a system benchmark, but a test intended to help nontechnical end users decide which Intel CPU best meets their needs. The iCOMP is based on both 16- and 32-bit CPU performance processing integer, floating point, graphics, and video performance. The higher the iCOMP index, the higher the relative performance.

Deciding What to Buy

One of the first things that you will have to decide is which motherboard you want. Or, if you are like me, decide which one you want at a price you can afford.

I subscribe to several computer magazines. Most of them have articles and reviews of software and hardware. And of course they have lots of ads from stores that sell by mail. The ads give me a fairly good idea of the prices so that I know what I can afford. Mail order might be one of the better ways to purchase your parts, especially if you don't live near a large city.

Usually, the larger cities have lots of computer stores. The San Francisco Bay area and the Los Angeles area have hundreds. There are also computer swap meets every weekend. If I need something, I will go to one of the swap meets and compare the prices at the various booths. I often take a pad along, write the prices down, then go back and make the best deal that I can. Sometimes you can haggle with the vendors for a better price, especially if it is near closing time.

Replacing a Motherboard

It is very easy to replace a motherboard. Basically, it is the same whether it is an XT, 286, 386, 486, or Pentium. There are some step-by-step instructions and photos at the end of this chapter to help you through it.

Upgrading a PC or XT

When it was first introduced in 1981, the XT was the hottest thing around. It was the best desktop computer that one could buy. The XT is now obsolete. But there are a lot of people who ignore this fact and still use them for good, productive work. For some applications, such as word processing, they might be as good as the fastest and most powerful 486 or Pentium. The XT systems can also be used as a low-cost terminal on a local area network (LAN).

The original PC and XT used the 8088 central processing unit (CPU). This CPU has about 29,000 transistors and operates at 4.77 MHz. Computers perform their operations by moving blocks of data in precise blocks of time. The PC and XT can cycle 8-bit blocks of data at 4.77 million times per second. That sounds fast, but it takes 8 bits to make a single byte. It also takes 8 bits to create a single character of the alphabet. And it takes a whole lot of bytes if you are using graphics. It can be painfully slow if you have to run a CAD program or a large spreadsheet.

Soon after IBM introduced the XT, compatible clone makers introduced the turbo XTs. They were souped up so that they could be shifted into "high gear," up to 8MHz or even up to 10 or 12MHz.

If you have an old 4.77MHz XT that you are in love with, there are many 8-bit boards still available that can be used with it. These boards can be used to drive a color monitor, as an interface with a hand scanner, a modem/fax board, a multifunction I/O board for COM ports, printer, and games, and many others.

The XT BIOS might not let you use 1.2Mb or 1.44Mb floppies. It might not recognize hard disks above 32Mbs or so. Higher density floppies and high-capacity hard disks are an absolute necessity nowadays. The XT would let you use them if you install a new BIOS, which would cost about $50. For just a bit more, you could replace the motherboard with a 486 or 586 motherboard. You can install a fairly large SCSI hard disk with an older 8-bit SCSI interface even with the old BIOS. You can even install a CD-ROM and a sound card, but it will have to be one that uses the 8-bit system.

You can attach a laser printer to an XT. In fact, in a large office network, it might be a good idea to dedicate an XT to drive a laser printer. This would free up the other computers from having to wait for the printer.

Replacing the XT Motherboard

The things that can be added to the XT are limited. Even after you have added the new components to an XT, it is still an old, obsolete, and slow machine. You would be much better off by replacing the motherboard.

It might cost a bit more than just replacing the BIOS. You will need at least 8Mb of memory which at this time costs about $30. You might also need a new keyboard, which might cost from $15 to $40.

If you have an original true-blue IBM PC, it will only have five slots, so the case or chassis has only five openings on the back panel. The XT has eight slots with eight openings in the back panel. Almost all motherboards now have eight slots. Your old PC case with the five openings in the rear panel will not accommodate the eight-slot motherboards. Some plug-in boards do not need to be accessed from the rear panel. But the spacing of the slot openings on the back panel would not match those that do need to be accessed, such as your printer, monitor adapter, mouse and other peripherals. Your best bet is to scrap the old case with the five-slot openings and buy a new case. It will cost about $35 to $45 for a new case with a power supply. If you are in love with the IBM logo, just rip it off and glue it to the new case.

If you are upgrading an original IBM PC, you will need a new power supply. The original PC had a puny 63-watt power supply. The XT and later models had 135- or 150-watt power supplies.

Replacing the motherboard is very simple whether it is an XT, 286, 386, 486, or even a Pentium. To replace a motherboard, just unplug the cables and plug-in boards, pull out the old motherboard, and slip in a new one. There are detailed instructions at the end of this chapter.

Upgrading a PC or XT to a 286

I would not recommend this type of upgrade. A short time ago, converting an XT to a 286 was a very good upgrade, but the 286 is now obsolete. The IBM AT (for Advanced Technology) uses the 80286 CPU, or more commonly called the 286. It has 125,000 transistors and is a 16-bit system. The original IBM AT operated at a very conservative speed of 6 MHz, but many of the 286 clones immediately boosted the speed up to 12 MHz, 16 MHz, and even up to 25 MHz.

A 286 CPU handles data in 16-bit chunks, just twice that of the 8088. A 286 operating at 10 MHz would be more than four times faster than an XT operating at 4.77 MHz. Because it handles twice as much data per cycle, the 286 will still be twice faster even if the XT is operating at the same 10 MHz.

The 286 was a great machine in its day. There are millions of them still in use and giving good service. For just a few dollars more you can move up to the 486 or Pentium world. For minor upgrades, there are hundreds of 16-bit boards and peripherals that can be added to a 286 to give you more utility. The trouble is that the 286 is still a 16-bit system. It is still very slow compared to most newer systems.

The 286 can run Windows, but only in the standard mode. It cannot take full advantage of Windows and many other newer software packages.

If you have an old 286, the best upgrade would be to replace the old motherboard. You can easily drop in a new 486DX or a Pentium. You can use all of your plug-in boards, keyboard, disk drives, and other peripherals. You will have to buy new memory chips. Depending on what you want to use your computer for, you should have a minimum of 8Mb, even better would be 16Mb.

Upgrading a PC, XT, 286, 386, or 486SX to a 486DX

If you want something inexpensive that offers many of the advantages of the larger systems, a 486 will run any of the new software and can use any of the 8- or 16-bit boards and hardware.

As in all of the other upgrades, just pull out the old motherboard and install a 486DX motherboard. Most of the motherboards have several built-in options such as serial and parallel ports on board, monitor adapters, floppy controller, and IDE hard-disk interface. In addition, the 486 motherboards have sockets for a static random access memory (SRAM) cache.

At one time the cost of the 486 CPU was more than $1,000. They are practically giving them away now. I suggest that you choose the fastest one you can afford, either a 486DX2-66 or an even faster 486DX4. I have seen some of these CPUs advertised for as little as $40.

Upgrading a PC, XT, 286, 386, or 486 to a Pentium

As I've mentioned, it is very easy to pull out a motherboard and install a Pentium. Some of the Cyrix 5x86 and AMD 586 motherboards are very reasonable. This would be one of the more cost-effective upgrades.

Internal Frequency versus External Frequency

Strange things happen when a circuit operates at high frequencies. In a low-frequency circuit, the effects of stray capacitance and inductance can usually be ignored. But it is a very big factor in high-frequency circuits, and the higher the frequency, the more of a problem it becomes. It might be such a problem that a circuit will not operate at all. It is very difficult and costly to devise high-frequency circuits. The distance between the components might also be a problem in high-frequency circuits. Even if the distance is only a half inch or so between components, at a high frequency, a large portion of the signal might be lost.

The distance between transistors inside the CPU is very small. The capacitive and inductive effects are also small, so the frequency inside the CPU can be much faster than that in the external circuits.

Upgrading a 486SX CPU with the Intel OverDrive

The Intel OverDrive CPUs can be used to upgrade a 486SX. Just remove the 486SX chip and drop in the OverDrive. There are several different versions and speeds of the OverDrive. You should get one that matches the external speed of your 486SX. The OverDrive uses the same technology as the 486DX2 and doubles the internal processing speed of the chip.

Upgrading to the 486DX4

Intel modified several of their CPU chips so that they would operate internally at two or three times their original frequencies.

The 486DX4 CPU is essentially a 33MHz 486 that operates internally at 99MHz. (They list it at 100MHz because it is so close.) But the 486DX4 has had several important differences from the 486DX2. The most important is that they now operate at 3.3 volts instead of the normal 5 volts. This means that you cannot just replace an older 486 CPU with the newer 486DX4 unless you have a special socket or motherboard designed for the 3.3-volt supply. Some companies are designing special adapter sockets with a regulator that reduces the 5 volts to 3.3. The CPU will be plugged into this socket, then the special socket will plug into the motherboard socket.

Another difference in the 486 and the 486DX4 is that they now have 1.6 million transistors instead of the original 1.2 million. Some of these extra 400,000 transistors are used to increase the built-in cache from 8K to 16K. This larger cache and higher frequency makes them almost as powerful as the Pentium 60MHz, but at a lower price. At one time this was a good upgrade, but the DX4 is now obsolete.

Upgrading a 486 to a Pentium OverDrive

Many of the later-model 486s had a large empty 238-pin socket on the motherboard. If you have one of these motherboards, this socket will let you install a 486DX4 or a Pentium OverDrive.

There are some disadvantages. The 486 motherboard was designed for a 486. The Pentium OverDrive cannot give you all of the advantages of a Pentium. It seems a shame to have paid $300 or $400 for the cost of the original 486 CPU, then have to pay another $200 or $300 for an upgrade. It would be nice if you could trade the old CPU in to Intel or be able to sell it. After all, there is nothing in the CPU to wear out. But it is obsolete. You probably couldn't even give it away.

Upgrading an IBM PS/1 or PS/2

If you have one of the old IBM PS/1 or PS/2 systems, there might not be much that you can do with it. These systems had a lot of built-in goodies on the motherboards. They had built-in floppy and hard disk controllers, monitor adapters, parallel and serial ports for printers, ports and connectors for mice, and other peripherals. They were designed to be much like the Macintosh. They had just about everything that a home user could want so that there was no need to add anything. It was great for those people who didn't want to bother about technology. All you had to do was find a wall outlet and plug it in.

The IBM PS/2s were similar to the Apple products in that they were a special proprietary design. There were millions of clones that were all the same design. The competition and a large number of clone users helped keep the costs down. Because of the much-smaller PS/2 market, not too many companies designed and developed components for the PS/2 systems.

The PS/2 systems had a lot of good advantages, but like Apple, they wanted to keep it all proprietary. IBM has seen the error of their ways and is now one of the top cloners. Apple has also had some second thoughts and have licensed a couple of companies to manufacture Macintosh clones. In some cases, the Mac clones are superior to the original. It is amazing what a little bit of competition can do.

Advantages of Built-In Utilities

It was great to have so many utilities built-in on the motherboard. All computers need these utilities. This integration reduces, or eliminates in some cases, the need for cables. Cables can be the source for many problems. Integration also reduces problems by reducing the number of solder joints and components. The more solder joints and components there are, the more chance for errors and failures.

Disadvantages of Built-Ins

The disadvantages are that if one of the utilities fail, the entire motherboard might have to be replaced. The motherboard is usually the most expensive component in the system. If the utilities are on plug-in boards and it fails, it is fairly inexpensive to replace the single board. Most all systems today that have built-in utilities have jumpers or switches that allow you to disable the built-in utility in case of failure, so that a board can be installed.

The biggest disadvantage of the proprietary systems is that technology does not stand still. The clone machines can be upgraded in thousands of ways with thousands of different components. But if you have one of the proprietary systems, you might not be able to do much to upgrade. You might be able to add a few things such as more memory or larger disk drives.

Installing a New CPU

Most of the upgrade CPUs discussed in chapter 4 can also be used to upgrade the PS/2 systems. Just remove the cover, unplug the old CPU, and replace it with the new CPU.

Ordering from IBM

It might be possible to order a new motherboard from IBM and replace your old one; however, the systems are obsolete. You can call IBM at 1-800-IBM-2YOU (1-800-426-2968) for Personal Systems, or call their Fax Back Service at 1-800-426-4329. Ask for New User Instructions, then ask for Personal Systems documents. You should be aware that even if they do have upgrade components, they will probably cost you more than it would to buy a complete new system.

You can order upgrade parts for any of the PS/1 or PS/2 models. But first, you have to know what the part number is. IBM sells reference manuals for all of their systems. These manuals are quite detailed and highly technical. They might give you more information than you need. The manuals are not free. For instance they sell a separate manual for each model that they manufacture called *Guide to Operations and Quick Reference Manual Part Numbers and Prices*. There are different prices for each manual. The Model 25, part number 75x1051, sells for $28.75. The manual for their Model 25 286, part number 15F2179, sells for $42.50. The manual for their Model 60, part number 68X2213, sells for $54.25 and for the Model 80, part number 15F2186, the manual sells for $63.75. They have manuals for the XT, the AT, and other systems. They even still have manuals for the PCjr, part number 1502292, for a price of $23.25.

They also have *Hardware Maintenance Manual Part Numbers and Prices* manuals. For some manuals, they offer a complete library of the manuals for the various systems. These libraries might cost from $150 up to $268. You can use a credit card when ordering by telephone.

Here are some IBM telephone numbers:

- Technical and Service Publications   (800) 426-7282
- Authorized Dealer Locator   (800) 447-4700
- IBM Part Number ID and Lookup   (303) 924-4015
- IBM General Information   (800) 426-3333

I probably don't have to tell you that IBM is a very large company, spread out all over the world. There are hundreds and hundreds of different phone numbers. They have a lot of 800 numbers. When you call, be prepared to listen to several recorded options, and any option that you choose might lead to several other options.

For PS/2 systems, probably the best number to call is (800) 426-2968. There is also a Help number at (800) 772-2272.

Upgrading to the Pentium

It is very easy to upgrade an older computer to a Pentium class. A new Pentium motherboard will give you all of the advantages of a new Pentium, but will be much less expensive than buying a complete new system.

The Pentium will allow graphics and CAD programs to run much faster. It will also allow full-screen motion pictures to run.

At one time the price of the Pentium CPU chip was $750 each for 1000 lot orders. The motherboard with CPU sold for a price of $1,100 to $2000. The 486 systems were about this expensive when they were first introduced. Today you can buy a Pentium-class motherboard with an AMD 586 or Cyrix 5x86 for less than $100. No one should be without a Pentium-class computer. That is less than what it would cost for a pair of modern tennis shoes.

Dual Pentium Pros

It is possible to install two and as many as eight Pentium Pro CPUs on a motherboard. Of course, having eight Pentium Pro CPUs on a motherboard is probably something that the ordinary user does not need. But having multiple CPUs is ideal for some high-end applications. Multiple CPUs, with Windows NT or other special software, can provide the power of a minicomputer or even a small size mainframe.

Several companies offer motherboards for dual Pentium Pros at a fairly reasonable price. For quad and eight CPU systems, the special motherboards are rather expensive.

Compaq Corp. produces a ProLiant 5000 with four Pentium Pro CPUs; the cost is around $85,000. The Axil Computer Co., (408) 286-5700, www.axil.com, has developed a system with eight Pentium Pro CPUs.

Their system will sell for about $100,000. These prices might be a bit less by the time you read this.

Pentium II Motherboards

Intel not only manufactures the CPU, they also design and manufacture motherboards for the CPU. Here is some information from the Intel website at www.intel.com about Pentium II motherboards:

Pentium II Processor-Based Motherboards

Easy to integrate Intel's boxed motherboards and boxed processors provide a comprehensive set of building blocks to integrators and OEMs assembling systems based on the Pentium II processor.

By ordering just two boxes from an Intel Authorized Distributor—the PD440FX motherboard and boxed Pentium II processor—an integrator needs to supply only tools and a suitable chassis and power supply complying with ATX specification 2.01. A processor installation video designed for the boxed motherboard is included on a CD-ROM in the box, along with the processor retention mechanism.

The DB440FX is a low-profile motherboard designed for the Pentium II processor. There are several custom configurations available to direct OEM customers.

Time to Market with a Proven Design

The PD440FX and DB440FX motherboards offer time to market for the Pentium II processor using a proven design. Both boards are based on the second generation of products built around the Pentium Pro processor, including the Intel 82440FX PCIset. The chip set optimizes system performance for 32-bit application software in 32-bit operating system environments.

Performance and Features

Motherboards manufactured by Intel for the Pentium II processor offer a high level of flexibility for today's multimedia applications and tomorrow's uses. The Pentium II processor combines the design/Pentium II performance of the Pentium Pro processor with the multimedia enhancement capabilities of MMX technology. The motherboard products also provide a high level of integration, including such advanced features as dual universal serial bus (USB) connectors.

A Lower Total Cost of Ownership

Manageability was designed into the PD440FX and DB440FX motherboards from the beginning. The Desktop Management Interface (DMI) compliant BIOS and on-board hardware management ASIC provide constant monitoring of voltage and temperature to ensure high up-time and allow for preventative maintenance. The boxed PD440FX motherboard also ships with Intel's LANDesk Client Manager application to enable remote monitoring and configuration of the system.

Available in the Most Popular Form Factors

Intel-manufactured motherboards for the Pentium II processor are available in form factors adopted by the industry's largest companies. The PD440FX board complies with ATX specification 2.01. And future motherboards for the Pentium II processor will use the emerging NLX low-profile form factor. Both layouts were designed with the latest processor technology in mind for ease of integration and maintenance.

The ATX Motherboard and Power Supply

Most of the cooling in a computer is from a small fan in the power supply. The original power supply drew air in from the front grill and pulled it over the components. The newer ATX power supply draws air in from the back and blows it over the components. The power supply has a socket that can only be connected to a motherboard with an ATX socket. If you buy a motherboard for the Pentium Pro, be sure to check the power supply connector. Some of them still use the original connector, but most of the later models use the ATX socket. Figure 5-13 shows a motherboard with both connectors. All of the Pentium II motherboards will use the ATX socket.

Fig. 5-13
A Micronics Pentium
II motherboard with
both standard and
ATX power supply
connectors.

The original power supply had two connectors with six wires each for the inline motherboard socket. The power connectors plugged in side by side into the motherboard socket. If one was not careful, it was possible to plug them in backwards or improperly. This could be disastrous and ruin the motherboard. When properly plugged in, the four black ground wires should be in the center of the socket. Figure 5-14 shows the connector plugged in so that the four black wires are in the center. The ATX power supply has a connector that can only be plugged in properly to the motherboard socket. See Fig. 5-15.

If your new motherboard has an ATX socket, you can buy an ATX power supply for about $30 to $40. It would be better to by a new case with the power supply already mounted for $60 to $70. Then you will need to buy an ATX power supply. The original systems power supply has an output of −5V, +5V, −12V, and +12V. The new ATX system has added 3.3V for the newer CPUs.

In the older systems, an on/off switch was provided either on the front panel or on the side of the case. This switched the incoming 110V to the power supply. The 110V goes directly to the power supply on the ATX systems. These power supply systems provide power-on and 5V-standby signals. Power-on is a signal that Windows 95 and NT can use to power the system on or off. An option allows the keyboard to use these signals to power up or down. The low-current 5V-standby signal is present at all times, even when the main system is powered down.

Fig. 5-14
A standard power supply connector. The connectors can be plugged in wrong. With the connectors plugged in properly, the four black wires are in the center.

Fig. 5-15
Plugging in an ATX-type power supply connector. It has more wires and can only be plugged in properly.

Motherboard Variations

Some of the motherboard manufacturers are building in several goodies, such as sound and video. This integration saves a precious slot and even a bit of money that it would cost for a plug-in board.

Unfortunately, many of the Pentium Pro and Pentium II motherboard manufacturers do not adhere to any standards. Some of these motherboards still use the old-style power supply connectors. Some of them cover all bases and install both the ATX and the old-style connectors side by side.

Another variation is that some of the motherboards have a PS/2-type keyboard and mouse connector. That means that you cannot use your standard keyboard and mouse. Several cable companies provide adapters that will let you use the old keyboard and mouse. The adapters cost about $5 each, which isn't bad, but it might cost more in finding a vendor and ordering the parts. It might especially be time consuming if you have ordered a motherboard through the mail, hoping to be able to use it right away, but then finding that you either had to buy a new mouse and keyboard or some adapters.

One reason for using the PS/2 connector for the mouse is that it saves having to use one of your two COM ports. The PS/2 keyboard and mouse connectors are stacked one on the other. The mouse or keyboard can be plugged into either connector.

Many of the Pentium II motherboards now have Universal Serial Bus (USB) connectors. This bus is faster than SCSI, is simpler to configure, and will handle up to 127 devices. It will be the new standard.

Many of the local computer stores will have the adapters and cables that you need. But it is often easier to order by mail rather than go downtown and look for something like this. Here are a few companies who can send you adapters for the PS/2 connectors and the USB cables and connectors:

- ASP   (800) 445-6190
- Belkin   (310) 898-1100
- Cables to Go   (800) 826-7904
- Monster Cable   (415) 871-6000
- Primax Cables to Go (800) 826-4000
- QVS   (313) 641-6700

Which Motherboard Should You Buy?

There are several motherboard vendors. All vendors try to differentiate their product from the others. So you will have several choices. Which system you should choose depends on what you want to use your computer for, and how much money you want to spend.

If you can afford it, buy a Pentium II motherboard, which is selling at this time for about $300. Of course, if you want a 266MHz Pentium II CPU, it will cost an additional $800 to $1,200. A 233MHz will only cost $700 to $1,100 at this time.

If you don't have that kind of money, you can buy a universal motherboard with a zero insertion force socket number 7. You can buy one of these motherboards for about $200 at this time. You can then buy an 233MHz AMD K6 for about $600. This would give you a motherboard and CPU for a total of $800 or less. An equivalent Intel 233MHz Pentium II CPU and motherboard would cost from $1,000 up to $1,400. The K6 system will do just about everything that the 233MHz Pentium II will do.

There are hundreds of other Pentium-class motherboard available. Most of them are now universal with a socket 7 and lots of jumpers. They can be configured to accept almost any Pentium-type CPU.

There are also lots of 486 motherboards still available. Because it is now obsolete, the vendors are practically giving them away. One of these motherboards might be all you need.

Sources for Pentium Motherboards

Because there are several Pentium motherboard manufacturers, the competition will keep the prices fairly reasonable. I do a lot of my buying and shopping by mail order. I look through computer magazines, such as the *Computer Shopper, Byte, PC World, PC Magazine,* and about 50 others to compare prices and products. Several of the computer magazines have a section near the back where they list the products advertised for that month. The items are categorized and grouped by product type. The page number for each ad is listed so it is easy to find what you are looking for. This is a great help when you consider that the *Computer Shopper* might have 1000 large tabloid-sized pages.

If you live near a large city, there will probably be several computer dealers around. You can ask them about components. The local dealers might be a bit more expensive than mail order.

Again, if you live in a large city, there will probably be computer swap meets every so often. Most of your local dealers will meet at a large auditorium, or fairground, and set up booths to sell their wares. Most dealers usually offer very good prices and discounts. You can go from booth to booth and compare prices and products.

I often go to swap meets even if I don't need anything. There is usually a large crowd and lots of excitement in the air. It's almost like a circus.

W/O CPUs

I have seen lots of ads for 486 and Pentium motherboards for very low prices. Then somewhere in small print it will say w/o CPU. You have to pay close attention to the ads. Some are rather misleading. In their defense, one reason some vendors don't list a price for the 486 and Pentium-type motherboards with a CPU is that there are so many different CPUs and options to choose from.

Instructions for Upgrading to a New Motherboard

If you are ordering a motherboard through the mail, find out what kind of CPU socket it has, what kind of power supply connector, ATX or standard, what kind of keyboard and mouse connector it has, and if it has a USB connector. You might also ask about other built-in goodies, such as sound.

Once you get your new motherboard, you can easily install it in a few simple steps. The following basic procedures can be used for installing any of the motherboards.

1. Know your CMOS setup. You must be able to tell the CMOS setup on your new system what type of hard disk drive you have. If you do not furnish all of the proper information as to the type, the number of cylinders, the number of heads, and the number of sectors you might not be able to access the data on your hard disk.

If you don't have your system configuration written down somewhere, run your system CMOS setup to determine the data. Many of the older machines used several different methods to access the CMOS setup. If you have documentation, it should tell you how to access the setup mode. On most systems, you are given the opportunity to press something, such as the Escape key and Del key while the system is booting up. On some systems, if you hold down a key of the keyboard while it is booting up, it will give you an error and tell you to press F1. This usually puts you into the setup mode. Run it and write down the type of drives, the number of cylinders, heads, sectors, landing zone, and any other information given. You might not be able to install your drives with your new motherboard unless you tell the new CMOS memory exactly what kind they are. If you cannot install your hard disk drives, you will not be able to access any of your data on them.

2. Backup up your hard disks. You might not need it, but you should stop and make a complete backup of your hard disk before you remove the old motherboard. You should have a current backup; if you don't, shame on you. Chapter 9 discusses the important reasons why you should have backups at all times.

3. Mark and disconnect cables on the back panel. The next thing to do is to shut off the power and disconnect the power cord and the keyboard cable. You will probably have several other cables on the back panel of the PC. It is very easy to forget how and where things were plugged in. It might be a good idea to use a felt marking pen to put a distinctive mark on the cable connector and the board connector. When you get ready to plug the cables back into the new system, all you have to do is line up the various marks on the cables and board connectors. This will ensure that every cable is plugged back into the same board. After you have marked all of the cables, then disconnect them.

4. Remove the case cover. Locate and remove the screws that hold the case or cover on. For most early systems, there were five screws on the back panel, one in each corner and one in the top center. The four screws that hold the power supply in place should not be removed. Once the cover screws are removed, you can slide the cover off toward the front.

Some of the newer cases might have different screws to hold them on. You shouldn't have any trouble determining which ones to remove.

5. Make a diagram before disassembly. Once the cover is removed, before doing anything else, take a piece of paper and make a rough drawing of where each board is plugged in and any cable that might be plugged into it. Then use a felt marking pen to mark each cable and connector in a way so that you can be sure to match the cable and connectors back up to the same board. For instance if you mark a slash on the cable connector and board near one end, it will be easy to match the two when you plug them back together. Some cables can be plugged in backwards or upside down. You can prevent this if the connectors are marked. Note in particular how the two connectors from the power supply are plugged into the motherboard. Notice that the four black wires are in the center. These two connectors must be connected to the new motherboard in the same way. If you bought one of the new motherboards, you might have an ATX-type connector for the power supply. This connector can only be plugged in properly.

Most of the cables will be ribbon cables from the floppy and hard drives to the controller. You might be able to leave the cables connected to the boards and just pull the boards out of the motherboard slot. You shouldn't have to remove any of the disk drives. Leave the cables plugged into the drives if possible.

6. Remove all of the plug-in boards and cables. There will be cables from the power supply plugged into the motherboard, usually near the right-rear corner of the motherboard. At the front there might also be several small wires for the front panel light emitting diodes (LEDs) and for the speaker. If these small wires and connectors are not marked, you might take some masking tape and put labels on them. Your new motherboard will have similar pins for the connectors, but they might be in a different location.

Once all of the boards are removed and all of the cables are disconnected, look for a screw near the front and in the center of the motherboard, and another in the rear of the motherboard.

When these screws are removed, pull the motherboard to the left then lift it out. You might have to jiggle it a bit. The motherboard has grooved, plastic standoffs that slide into raised slots.

7. Set switches and jumpers and install new motherboard. You should have received some documentation with your new

motherboard. Set any switches or jumpers that are needed to configure the system. Install any extra memory chips.

Make sure that you have installed all of the plastic standoffs in the proper holes, then drop the motherboard into the slots and push it to the right until it locks in place. Replace the screws in the front and back of motherboard.

Connect all the front panel LED wires and the speaker wires. The motherboard should have some markings to indicate where each small connector should be plugged in. You might have to refer to your documentation for some wires. Many of the newer cases come with these cables all bundled in a ribbon cable plainly marked.

Next, connect the power supply cables to the motherboard. Note! This connector can be plugged in wrong. When connected properly, the four black wires will be in the center adjacent to each other. The power supply connector is usually in two separate cables with six wires in each cable. They are sometimes marked P8 and P9. Again, if you have an ATX-type power supply and motherboard, you can only plug it in properly.

If you have built-in systems on the motherboard such as pins for IDE, floppy controller, and COM ports, connect the proper cables to these pins. There should be an indication on the motherboard as to which is pin 1. Your flat ribbon cables will have a different colored wire on one side (red, black, blue, or red stripes) that indicates pin one. Make sure that the cables are plugged in properly.

8. Reinstall boards. Reinstall all of your plug-in boards and reconnect any cables to the boards that were disconnected. Connect the monitor and keyboard. Plug in the power cord. Recheck all of your connections to make sure that everything is plugged in properly, then turn on the power. You should try the system before you put the cover back on. This way if it doesn't work, it will be fairly easy to check all of the boards and cables to make sure they are installed correctly.

9. Turn on and bootup. If you have reconnected everything right, the system should work. Depending on what type of BIOS you have, it will probably tell you that the time and date is not set and give you an error message about your drives. You might have to check your documentation for instructions on how to set the time, date, and how to tell the CMOS memory what type of floppy and hard drives you have installed.

If everything was done properly, then you should not have any problems. If you have problems, check your documentation, recheck all of the cables, switches, and boards. If the problem remains, you might turn to Chapter 23 for troubleshooting.

10. Reinstall cover. If everything works okay, put the cover back on.

11. Congratulate yourself for having saved a bundle.

Sources

The best place to look for any of the motherboards and components mentioned is computer magazines. They are full of ads for computers and components. You can get a good idea of what something should cost. If you live in a large city, there are probably computer stores nearby. The larger cities will probably have computer swaps once in a while also.

If you can't get to a store or a computer swap, then order through the mail from the ads in the computer magazines. You have to read the ads closely. The advertised price of many of the motherboards does not include a CPU. Almost all of the boards are advertised with 0K or without memory. See Chapter 23 for more about mail order.

Memory

Memory is one of the most critical elements of the computer. Computing as we know it would not be possible without memory. The PC uses two primary types of memory, ROM and RAM.

ROM

Read only memory (ROM) is memory that cannot be altered or changed. The principal use of ROM in PCs is for the basic input/output system (BIOS). The BIOS contains routines that set up the computer when it is first turned on. It facilitates the transfer of data among peripherals.

The ROM programs are usually burned into erasable programmable read only memory (EPROM) chips. The ROM BIOS for an early XT could be programmed onto a 128K chip. The 486 ROM BIOS needs 512K. It is possible to print out the programs stored in ROM. To give you some idea of how much 512K is, the entire text in some of my earlier books was less than 512K.

RAM

When you open a file from a hard disk or a floppy, the files and data are read from the disk and placed in random access memory (RAM). When you load in a program, be it word processing, a spreadsheet, database, or whatever, you will be working in the system RAM. If you are writing, programming, or creating another program, you will be working in RAM.

Actually it is dynamic RAM or DRAM. Random access means that you can find, address, change, or erase any single byte among several million bytes.

You can also randomly access any particular byte on a floppy or hard disk. You cannot randomly access data on a magnetic tape system. The data on the tape is stored sequentially. In order to find a particular byte, you would have to run the tape forward or backwards to the proper area.

Being able to randomly access the memory allows you to read and write to it immediately. It is somewhat like an electronic blackboard. Here you can manipulate the data, do calculations, enter more data, edit, search data bases, or do any of the thousands of things that software programs allow you to do. You can access and change the data in RAM very quickly.

RAM memory is an essential element of the computer. Of course, if you are working on a large file you will need a lot of RAM. If you are using Windows and you don't have enough RAM, some portions of the file might be loaded onto a special area of the hard disk and used as a swap file.

An Easy Cost-Effective Upgrade

One of the easiest upgrades you can make is a memory addition. If you don't have enough memory, your computer might run very slow. Just a couple years ago, 4Mb was a lot of memory. For many applications today, 8Mb or even 16Mb, is not enough. Adding memory is very easy, just open your computer and plug in the new memory. Before you rush out to buy more memory, open your computer and check to see what kind you have installed. If you have a manual, that might also tell you. You will need to buy the same type. If you have an older computer, it is possible that you have rather slow and out-dated memory. It will be perfectly okay to install faster memory. At one time there was a large differential between the slower memory and the faster. Today there is very little difference. There is step-by-step instructions for installing the memory later in the chapter.

RAM Volatility

An important difference in ROM and RAM is that RAM is volatile. That is, it disappears if the machine is rebooted or if you exit a program without saving it. If there is a power interruption to the computer, even for a brief instant, any data in RAM will be gone forever.

You should get in the habit of saving your files to disk frequently, especially if you live in an area where there are power failures due to storms or other reasons. Many of the software programs now will automatically save open files to disk at frequent intervals. Of course, if the file is saved to disk, a power failure will not affect it.

How RAM is Addressed

Each byte of memory has a separate address. The cells in the memory bank could be analogous to the "pigeon holes" for the room keys of a large hotel. They would be arranged in rows and columns so that the pigeon holes would correspond to each room on each floor. If the hotel had 100 rooms, you could have ten rows across and ten down. It would be very simple to find any one of the 100 keys by counting across and then down to the particular room number. Memory addressing is a bit more complicated than the hotel pigeon holes, but with just 20 address lines (2^{20}) any individual byte out of one million bytes can be quickly accessed.

One byte is also called a word so the old 8-bit XTs can only address one word at a time. The 16-bit 286 can address two words, the 32-bit 386 and 486 systems can address four words, and the 64-bit Pentium can address eight words at a time.

The CPU and the RAM Bus

The CPU is the brains of the computer. Almost everything that happens in a computer must travel over a bus path and go through the CPU.

Suppose you have a very fast and powerful Pentium. You will probably have several plug-in boards and peripheral components. These components will communicate with the CPU over a 16-bit bus at about 8MHz. But data that moves between the RAM and the CPU has its own special memory bus. Data moves back and forth on the bus between the RAM and CPU at the CPU speed or frequency.

You might also have several components installed on a VL bus or a PCI bus which will communicate with the CPU at the CPU frequency.

The amount of work that a computer accomplishes depends on how fast it can process data. There might be billions of bits in a software program. It might take a lot of shifting, adding, and moving around to process the program. The faster the computer can handle these billions of iterations, the better.

One of the critical factors that determines the speed of a computer is the time that is spent shifting the data back and forth from the CPU and RAM. The width of the path or bus between the CPU and the RAM is a critical factor in the operating speed of the computer.

The original PC had an eight bit memory bus connected to the CPU. The bus was doubled to 16 bits for the 286 CPU. It was doubled again to 32 bits for the 386 and 486 CPUs. For the Pentium the bus width will be whatever the motherboard was designed for. It could be 32 bit, 64 bit, or even 128 bits. For a 128-bit bus, some designers have developed a 64 bit bus going in one direction to the CPU and another 64 bit bus returning from the CPU. The computer technology has come a long way in just a few short years.

The bus has been likened to a highway. If there are only eight lanes, it might be rather slow. Twice as many cars can get through on a 16 lane highway, and four times as many if there are 32 lanes. If there are 64 lanes, the traffic can really whiz along.

A Brief Explanation of Memory

Computers operate on binary systems of 0s and 1s, or off and on. A transistor can be turned off or on to represent the 0s and 1s. Two transistors can represent four different combinations: both off; both on; #1 on, #2 off; or #1 off, #2 on. A bank of four transistors can represent 16 different combinations. With eight transistors, you can have 256 different combinations. It takes eight transistors to make one byte. With them you can represent each letter of the alphabet, each number and each symbol of the extended American Standard Code for Information Interchange (ASCII). With eight lines, plus a ground, the eight transistors can be turned on or off to represent any single one of the 256 characters of the ASCII code.

Each byte of memory has a separate address. It would be laid out similar to a large hotel's "pigeon holes" for the room keys. It would have a row of pigeon holes for the rooms on each floor. They would also be laid out so that the holes would be in columns. If the hotel had 100 rooms, you could have ten rows across and ten down. It would be very simple to find any one of the 100 keys by counting across and then down to the particular room number.

One megabyte of memory would require many more pigeon holes or cells, but with just 20 address lines and one ground line, any individual byte can be quickly accessed. Actually it would be 2^{20}, or 2 to the 20th power, which would equal 1,048,576 bytes.

Programs that Stay in RAM

In the DOS era, besides the application programs that were loaded into the 640K of RAM, there were certain DOS system programs that were kept in RAM at all times. These are programs such as Command.Com and the internal commands. There are over 20 internal commands such as COPY, CD, CLS, DATE, DEL, MD, PATH, TIME, TYPE, and others. These commands were always in RAM and were available immediately. The Config.Sys file and any drivers that you might have for your system were also loaded into RAM. There were several others such as SideKick that were loaded into RAM and stayed there. They were called Terminate and Stay Resident (TSR) programs.

All of these things contributed to the utility and functionality of the computer and made it easier to use. But unfortunately, they took big bites out of our precious 640K bytes of RAM. There might have been less than 400K left for running applications after loading all these memory resident programs. There were many programs that would not run if you had less than 600K of free RAM.

Windows 95 has now solved most of those problems. It can load several programs in extended memory above the 640K. These programs can then be available at any time. Windows 95 also allows us to have several programs open at the same time. You can be working on one in the foreground and have another running in the background. Of course, this requires lots of memory.

Motherboard Memory

The XT motherboard could only accept 640K of Dual In-line Pin (DIP) memory on the motherboard. The early 286 motherboard was also limited to 640K of DIP memory. Because the 286 could handle up to 16Mb, more memory could be added by using plug-in memory boards. The later model 286 and 386SX had sockets for 4Mb to 8Mb. On some of them you might be able to use the 4 megabyte chips, but on some of them if you want to add extra memory you have to use a plug-in memory board.

This is not usually a problem with most of the 386DX and 486 system motherboards. Some of them have SIMM connectors that will accept up to 128Mb of DRAM.

The PC, XT, and the AT Bus

The PCs and XTs use an 8-bit bus. The AT systems, which include the 286s, 386s, and 486s, use a 16- and 32-bit bus. The 8-bit 8088 communicates with its RAM over a 20-line bus. With the 20 lines, it is possible to address any individual byte in 1Mb, that is 2^{20} = 1,048,576 bytes of RAM.

The 16-bit 286 communicates with its RAM over a 24-line bus. The 24 lines allows them to address 16Mb or 2^{24} = 16,777,216 bytes.

The 32-bit 386 and 486 CPUs communicate with their RAM over a 32 line bus. They can address 4 gigabytes or 2^{32} = 4,294,967,296 bytes. A gigabyte is also the same as a billion bytes.

Cost of Memory

I don't like to talk about cost because it changes so quickly. Here is what I wrote a couple of years ago about the cost of RAM:

> Although the 386 and 486 can address 4 gigabytes of RAM, without special software DOS will not let you access more than 640K. (Incidentally, 4 gigabytes of DRAM, in 1Mb SIMM packages, would require 4096 modules. You would need a fairly large board to install that much memory. It would also be rather expensive. At $35 per megabyte, 4096 modules would cost $143,360).

Here are some figures from a recent advertisement for memory:

Capacity	Pins	Non-Parity	Parity	EDO
1Mb	30	6.00	7.50	
4Mb	30	19.00	25.00	
4Mb	72	16.00	21.00	17.50
8Mb	72	31.00	41.00	32.00
16Mb	72	57.00	79.50	58.00

A couple of years ago, memory was about $35 per megabyte. Today it is less than $3.50 per megabyte. So you could install 4Gb of DRAM for $14,000 or less. Quite a change from $143,360.

Memory prices are still coming down. By the time you read this the prices will be even lower. Note the difference above in the prices for the parity, non-parity, and EDO chips. Most newer systems today are being designed for non-parity or EDO type memory.

Virtual Memory

In its virtual memory mode, the 386, 486, and Pentium-class CPUs can address 64 terabytes, or 64 trillion bytes, that is 64,000,000,000,000 bytes. This is the amount of data that could be stored on 3,200,000 20Mb hard disks.

Virtual memory is a method of using part of a hard disk as RAM. Many large programs will not run unless the entire program resides in RAM. So the program can be partially loaded in the available RAM and the rest of it in a virtual RAM section of the hard disk. Of course, having to access the disk for data can slow the processing down considerably, but it is one solution. The virtual disk system must be implemented by the operating system.

Memory Boards

Some of the older systems had all of the sockets filled with chips. If you wanted to add more memory, you bought a plug-in board with memory installed on it. But memory on plug-in boards can slow a system down considerably. The XT ran at 4.77MHz and the original 286 CPU ran at 6MHz. But the CPUs communicated with RAM, the plug-in boards, and any other I/O devices over an 8- or 16-bit bus at about 8MHz.

Can you imagine a 100MHz 486 or a 200MHz Pentium having to communicate with its memory over a 16-bit bus at 8MHz? It would be a terrible waste of its speed. It would be like having a very fast car, but driving around in second gear all of the time. Most systems now have a special bus between the CPU and the memory that allows communication at a much faster speed. Memory on plug-in boards, at one time, was necessary but it has been obsolete for several years.

Dual Inline Package (DIP)

The early DRAM chips had two rows of 8 pins. They were bulky and used up a lot of motherboard real estate. The 16 pins also imposed limits on them. Later one megabyte DIPs were developed that had 18 pins.

You won't find DIPs on motherboards now except perhaps for SRAM L2 cache systems. DIP sockets might also be used for VGA adapters and special uses.

Single Inline Package (SIP)

Some older motherboards used SIP memory. It is similar to the SIMMs except that they have pins. Few if any motherboards use the SIP memory now. Figure 6-1 shows a 1Mb SIP module on the bottom. The two modules on the top are 16Mb SIMMs, with 72 contacts.

Single Inline Memory Module (SIMM)

Your computer motherboard will have sockets for SIMMs unless it is an old XT or 286. If it is a late model motherboard it might have sockets for dual inline memory modules (DIMMs).

Fig. 6-1
A 1Mb SIP memory chip on the bottom. The two above are 16Mb SIMM modules.

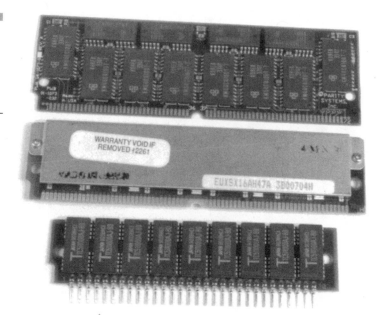

The early 30-contact SIMMs are assemblies of miniature DRAM chips. There are usually nine chips on a small board that is usually plugged slantwise into a special connector. Some SIMMS might have three of the nine chips integrated into one, so they might have only three chips. These chips require a very small amount of board real estate. The SIMM chips are usually mounted on a small board that is plugged slantwise into a special connector. Figure 6-2 shows a 30-contact 1Mb module.

The early PCs used dual in-line pin (DIP) chips with two rows of 8 pins, 16 pins total. The DIP chips used up a lot of motherboard real estate. It takes nine chips of whatever type memory designated. For instance, for 64K, it takes 8 64K × 1 bit chips plus 1 64K × 1 bit chip for parity checking. If they are 256K chips, it takes 8 256K × 1 bit chips, plus 1 256 × 1 bit chip for parity checking. Even with the high-capacity SIMMs, it still takes nine chips to make up the designated memory. For one megabyte it takes 8 1024 × 1 bit plus 1 1024 × 1 bit for parity. For a four-megabyte SIMM, it takes 8 4096 × 1 bit plus 1 4096 × 1 bit for parity. The same system is used even for the $n \times 36$ SIMM chips. Sometimes, instead of having nine individual chips, they might have three or more integrated into a single chip. So you might see some SIMMs with only three chips in the module.

Fig. 6-2
A 30-contact 1Mb
SIMM module.

I know this is a bit confusing so here is a brief chart:

64K =   64K × 1 bit +   64K × 1 bit for parity

256K =   256K × 1 bit +   256K × 1 bit for parity

1Mb =   1024K × 1 bit +   1024K × 1 bit for parity

4Mb =   4096K × 1 bit +   4096K × 1 bit for parity

Figure 6-1 shows two different 16Mb 4 × 36 SIMM modules in the upper part of the photo. The module on the top has eight large 16Mb × 1 bit chips, and four smaller 4Mb × 1 bit chips for the parity.

Figure 5-1 in the previous chapter shows two different motherboards, a large standard size 286 at the left and a Pentium at right. To illustrate how much space the DIP chips require, there are four rows of DIP chips in the top-right corner of the 286. There are a total of 36 of the 128K chips to make one megabyte. The four white SIMM 72-contact sockets on the left-center of the Pentium motherboard can accept up to 128Mb.

The DIP chips were rather difficult to install. It was very easy to install them backwards in the socket or to bend one of the pins so that it did not make contact. Over a period of time, some of the DIP chips could actually creep up out of the socket. The SIMM chip is very easy to install. It has a cutout on one end so that it can only be inserted one way. Just lay the assembly slantwise in the socket, then push it to an upright position. There is a small hole in each end of the SIMM board. There is a projection on the socket that fits in this hole when the SIMMs are inserted in the socket. Spring-loaded clamps on each end locks the assembly in place. To remove the assembly, press on the clamps on each end.

Memory must be configured in banks. Most motherboards are designed for four banks, bank 0, 1, 2, and 3. Check the documentation that came with your motherboard. You must fill the lowest numbered bank before filling other banks. You must also install the SIMMs in multiples of two. For instance, for 16Mb, you would have to install two 8Mb modules. The bank designations might be different on motherboards from different vendors. Some motherboards might designate bank 0 on one side of the socket assembly, others might designate the other side.

Caution: The SIMM chips are very easy to install. Just drop them in on a slant and lift them slightly until they lock in. But it is possible to have a module that is not seated properly. If this happens, the computer might not boot up. The screen might be completely blank with no error messages or any indication of the problem.

I wouldn't even consider installing 1Mb SIMMs. Memory is so inexpensive today that if I were upgrading an older system that has 1Mb SIMMs, I would throw them away and install either 4MB, 8Mb, or even 16Mb SIMMS. Before buying memory, check the type that you need. Most of the older 386 and 486 motherboards have the contact-type sockets for the n × 9 SIMMs or 30-pin sockets. Some of the later 486s and most Pentium motherboards now have longer 72-contact SIMM sockets for the n × 36 type SIMMS or 72-pin sockets.

Many of the motherboards only provide four slots for memory. If you install 1Mb SIMMs, you could only install 4Mb of memory. It is very difficult to get by today with only 4Mb of RAM. You would be much better off if you installed a minimum of 16Mb.

The 1 × 36 SIMM is made up of four 1Mb assemblies, each with nine chips, therefore the designation 1 × 36. A 1 × 36 SIMM gives 4Mb in one 72-contact slot. The 2 × 36 will give you 8Mb in each slot. There are also 4 × 36 for 16Mb and 8 × 36 for 32Mb. You can install 128Mb in just four slots by using 8 × 36 SIMMs.

The SIMMs will have speeds of 80, 70, and 60ns. You should buy the speed recommended by your documentation. The older 60MHz Pentium can use 70ns or 60ns. The 70ns is a bit less expensive than the 60ns. You can use 80ns chips in some of the slower 25MHz 486 systems, even those that are operating at 50MHz by using the OverDrive DX2 CPUs.

I would suggest that you buy as much memory as you can afford. Memory is somewhat like money in that you can never have too much of it. Usually, you must have two SIMMs of the same type and capacity because memory is interleaved. If you intend to install 16Mb of RAM, then you need to buy two 8Mb modules. If you install a single module instead of the required two, the computer might not boot up. The screen might be completely blank. Interleaved memory is discussed in more detail later.

Because the memory comes in modules and is socketed, you can add as much as your motherboard allows. Memory chips sometimes fail. The BIOS does a power on self-test (POST) every time the computer is booted. During this test, all of the memory chips are tested. If an assembly becomes defective, it is easy enough to replace it.

If you install extra memory, you might have to set some switches or install some jumpers to configure your motherboard to the amount of installed memory. Check the documentation that came with your motherboard.

Parity

The old DIP chips have two rows of eight pins, or 16 pins total. It requires nine chips of whatever type memory designated. For instance, for 64K, it takes 8 64K × 1 bit chips plus 1 64K × 1 bit chip for parity checking. If 256K chips are used, it takes 8 256K × 1 bit chips, plus 1 256 × 1 bit chip for parity checking. Even with the high-capacity SIMMs, it still takes nine chips to make up the designated memory. For a four-megabyte SIMM, it takes 8 4096 × 1 bit plus 1 4096 × 1 bit for parity checking. The nine chips would all be on the one small SIMM plug-in board. The same system is used even for the $n \times 36$ SIMM chips.

The Macintosh systems do not use the parity checking chip, so they have only the 8 × whatever the SIMM designation. Memory is one of the few areas where the components for Macintosh might be less expensive than those for ISA machines. A memory advertisement in a current computer magazine listed a price for an 8-chip Macintosh SIMM of 4 × 8, 70 ns at $120. For a 9-chip ISA SIMM of 4 × 9, 70 ns, the price was $137. Some have said that the 9th chip for parity checking is not necessary. Some of the Pentium Pro motherboards are now using non-parity 4 × 8 SIMMS.

Memory must be configured in banks. Most motherboards are designed for four banks, bank 0, 1, 2, and 3. Check the documentation that came with your motherboard. You must fill the lowest numbered bank before filling other banks.

Because memory is interleaved on most systems, you must install the SIMMs in multiples of two. You cannot intermix SIMMs of different values. For instance, for 16Mb, you would have to install two 8Mb modules. If you install a single module instead of the required two, the computer might not boot up. The screen might be completely blank. Interleaved memory is discussed in more detail below.

Caution: It is possible to have a module that is not seated properly. If this happens, the computer might not boot up. The screen might be completely blank with no error messages or any indication of the problem.

Memory Socket Expanders

Most motherboards come with only four sockets for SIMMs. If you have an older system, you might want to add more memory. A few companies, the Minden Group at 800-746-3973, SIMMSTACK at 800-209-7126, and SIMMSaver at 800-636-7281 have memory socket expansion boards that plug into the original sockets. Each plug-in expansion board has four additional sockets to allow you to add more SIMMs. Some of these boards will allow you to use the old 30-pin modules in the newer 72-pin sockets. If you are upgrading, the expansion sockets might let you use your old memory if it is fast enough.

If your old memory is not fast enough, you might be able to trade it in or sell it to some of the memory chip vendors. Several vendors are buying used memory. After all, it doesn't ever wear out. Just don't expect to get a whole lot of money for you old memory.

DIMMs

Dual inline memory modules (DIMMs) are very high-density, fast-memory chips. They look very much like the SIMMs, but they have two banks of chips soldered to a circuit board. Because they require less space for the same amount of memory, it is expected that DIMMs will become the chip of choice eventually. Most SIMMs now have 72 pins. DIMMs might have 72 pins or 168 pins. The motherboard has to be designed to accept the chips. Figure 6-3 shows two 168 dual contact DIMM modules. Each module is 32Mb.

Flash Memory

A few years ago, Intel developed flash memory, which is similar to erasable programmable read only memory (EPROM). AMD and several other companies now also manufacture it. Flash memory is fairly slow compared to DRAM and SRAM, so it can't replace them. But it can be equivalent to hard disk memory. The hard disk is a mechanical device that will eventually wear out or fail. The flash memory is strictly electronic and should last several lifetimes. A disadvantage is that flash memory is still rather expensive and limited in the amount of memory that can be installed on a card. Most Pentium Pros now use flash memory for the BIOS chip. In Fig. 5-5 of the last chapter, the pen points to a BIOS in flash memory. The BIOS can be

Fig. 6-3
Two 168 dual
contact DIMM
modules. Each
module is 32Mb.

updated electronically by floppy disk, by a modem from a BBS, or over the Internet.

Video RAM

Video RAM (VRAM) chips are a bit different than DRAM chips. They are special memory chips that are used on the better (and more expensive) monitor adapter cards. The VRAM chips are unusual in that they have double ports so that they can be accessed and refreshed at the same time.

A new memory standard, Unified Memory Architecture (UMA) is being used on many of the high-end graphics and video accelerator adapters.

Printer Memory

Your laser printer probably came with a minimum amount of memory, or about 512K. A laser printer determines where each dot on a printed page should be, then prints the whole page. Most printers require memory that is installed on special proprietary boards. You might need to add more memory for better printing speed. Most lasers will perform much better if they have a minimum of 2Mb.

Memory Chip Capacity

The size and speed of the chip is usually printed on the top of the chip. For instance, a 256K chip at 150 ns might have the manufacturer's logo or name and some other data. But somewhere among all this would be "25615." The 15 indicates 150 ns (the zero is always left off). A one megabyte 100 ns chip might have "102410."

The chips are usually arranged in banks or rows of nine. Almost all ISA computers use an extra ninth chip for parity checking. This chip checks and verifies the integrity of the memory at all times. It is usually the same type of chip as the eight that are used to make up the bank. The Macintosh systems don't use this chip and some experts say that it is a waste of memory to use it on the ISA systems.

The XT and early 286 motherboards had their RAM memory usually located in the front-right corner of the motherboards. They all used the DIP type of chips. To make 640K, most boards filled the first two banks, banks 0 and 1, with 256K chips which would equal 512K. The next two banks, 2 and 3, were then filled with 64K chips to make 128K for a maximum 640K.

Many of the early 286 and 386 systems filled all four banks with 256K DIP chips for a total of 1Mb. Although the 286 was capable of addressing 16Mb with special software, for most ordinary uses it was still limited to 640K. Boards that had the extra 384K could use it for a RAM disk, print spooling, or for other extended memory needs with the proper software.

Until Windows 95, the 386, 486, and Pentium was limited to 640K without special software that could take advantage of extended memory.

The Need for More Memory

One of the upgrades that you probably need is more memory. For some applications, you might need to buy several megabytes more. In the old days we got by fine with just 64K of memory. Many of the new software programs such as the spreadsheets, databases, and accounting programs require a lot of memory.

If you bought a new motherboard through mail order, you might have received it with 0K memory. You probably know that 0K does not mean OKAY, it means zero K memory. The price of memory fluctuates quite a lot. Advertisements are sometimes made up and placed two or three months before the magazine comes out. Because of the fluctuating prices, some vendors will not advertise a firm price for memory. Besides, if they included the price of the memory, it might frighten you away. They usually invite you to call them for the latest price. The good news for us consumers is that memory prices are dropping every day.

Things to Consider before You Buy Memory

There are several different types, sizes, speed, and other factors to consider before buying memory. You should buy the type that is best for your computer.

Dynamic RAM or DRAM

This is the most common type of memory used today. Each memory cell has a small etched transistor that is kept in its memory state, either on or off by an electrical charge on a very small capacitor. Capacitors are similar to small rechargeable batteries. Units can be charged up with a voltage to represent 1s or left uncharged to represent 0s. But those that are charged up immediately start to lose their charge. So they must be constantly "refreshed" with a new charge. Steve Gibson, the developer of SpinRite, compared the memory cell capacitors to a small bucket that had a hole in the bottom. Those buckets, or cells, that represented 1s were filled with water, but it immediately started leaking out through the hole in the bottom. So it had to be constantly refilled. You didn't have to worry about filling those buckets, or cells, that represent 0s. A computer might spend 7 percent or more of its time just refreshing the DRAM chips. Also each time a cell is accessed, that small voltage in the capacitor flows through a transistor to turn it on. This drains the charge from the capacitor, so it must be refreshed before it can be accessed again. In our bucket of water comparison, when the cell is accessed, the bucket is turned upside down and emptied. So if it represents a 1, it must be refilled immediately. Of course, it takes a finite amount of time to fill a bucket or to place a charge on a capacitor. If the memory cell has a speed of 70 nanosecond (ns), it might take 70ns, plus the time it takes to recycle, which might be 105ns or more, before that cell can again be accessed.

Refreshment and Wait States

The speed of the DRAM chips in your system should match your system CPU. You might be able to install slower chips, but your system would have to work with *wait states*. If the DRAM is too slow, a wait state will have to be inserted. A wait state causes the CPU and the rest of the system to sit and wait while the RAM is being accessed and then refreshed. Wait states could deprive your system of one of its greatest benefits, speed. A terrible waste of time.

If the CPU is operating at a very high frequency, it might have to sit and wait one cycle, or one wait state, for the refresh cycle. The wait state might be only a millionth of a second or less. That might not seem like much time. But if the computer is doing several million operations per second, it can add up.

It takes a finite amount of time to charge up the DRAM. Some DRAM chips can be charged up much faster than others. For instance, the DRAM chips needed for an XT at 4.77MHz might take as much as 200 nanoseconds (NS) or billionths of a second to be refreshed. A 486 running at 25MHz would need chips that could be refreshed in 70ns or less time. Of course, the faster chips cost more.

The 486DX2-66 and DX4 100MHz could both use the same speed memory of about 60ns. The CPU might be operating internally at 66MHz or 100MHz, but they both access the RAM at the 33MHz rate. The Pentuim-class CPUs might operate internally as high as 200MHz, but externally over the memory bus to RAM at a speed of 60MHz to 66MHz.

Interleaved Memory

Most of the newer faster systems use interleaved memory to prevent having to insert wait states. The memory is always installed in multiples of two. You might install two banks of 512K, 2Mb, 4Mb, 8Mb, 16Mb, 32Mb, 64Mb, or 128Mb of memory.

One half of the memory would be refreshed on one cycle, then the other half. If the CPU needed to access an address that was in the half already refreshed, it would be available immediately. This can reduce the amount of waiting by about half.

SRAM

Static RAM (SRAM) is made up of actual transistors. They can be turned on to represent 1s or left off to represent 0s and will stay in that condition until it receives a change signal. They do not need to be refreshed, but they revert back to 0 when the computer is turned off or if the power is interrupted. They are very fast and can operate at speeds of 15ns or less.

A DRAM memory cell needs only one transistor and a small capacitor. It takes a very small amount space for a DRAM cell. Each SRAM cell requires four to six transistors and other components. So SRAM is much more expensive than DRAM. The SRAM chips are assembled in the DIP type package so they are physically larger and require much more space than the DRAM chips. Because of the physical and electronic differences, SRAM and DRAM chips are not interchangeable.

Except for Pentium Pro and Pentium II, most motherboards will have sockets for SRAM chips for a L2 cache. The Pentium Pro and Pentium II have L2 cache built into the same enclosure as the CPU. Many of the 486 motherboards only had sockets for up to 256K. You might have sockets for up to 1Mb or more on your Pentium motherboard. My original 60MHz Pentium motherboard came with 512K of SRAM. See Fig. 6-4. The long chips on the left end of the motherboard are SRAM. The 32K SRAM chips have 28 pins, but newer 64K SRAM has 32 pins. Some motherboards have 32-pin SRAM sockets that can accept 28-pin or 32-pin SRAM. So you might have a choice of installing 256K, 512K, or 1Mb of SRAM. Using 32K SRAM chips, you would need 16 chips for 512K. You should check your motherboard documentation for instructions on how they should be installed. Be careful because it is possible to plug them in backwards. Look for some indication on the motherboard as to which is pin one. There should be a slight u-shaped indentation on the end of the chip that has pin one. You might also have to set some switches or install some jumpers to configure your motherboard for the amount of SRAM that you install. Check the documentation that came with your motherboard.

Cache Memory

A cache system can speed up computer operations quite a bit. When running an application program, the CPU often loops in and out of certain

Fig. 6-4
My old 60MHz
motherboard. The
long chips on
the end are SRAM.

areas and uses portions of the same memory over and over. A cache system is usually made up of very fast memory chips, such as SRAM, that can store the often-used data so that it is quickly accessible to the CPU.

The data that is moved back and forth between the CPU and RAM are electrical on and off voltages. The electrons move at almost the speed of light. Still it takes a finite amount of time to move a large amount of data. It takes even more time to access the RAM, find the data that is needed, then move it back to the CPU.

The computer can also be slowed down considerably if it has to search the entire memory each time it has to fetch some data. If this often-used memory is stored in the cache, it can be accessed by the CPU very quickly. A good cache can greatly increase the processing speed.

The Pentium CPU has a built-in 16K level 1 (L1) cache in among its 3.1 million transistors. This cache helps considerably, but a good fast external L2 cache can help speed things up even more. The speed and static characteristics of SRAM makes it an excellent device for memory cache systems.

The Pentium Pro CPU has a 16K L1 cache, but it also has a 256K or 512K cache nearby in the same enclosure.

Hit Rate

A well designed cache system might have a "hit rate" of over 90%. This means that each time the CPU needs a block of data, it will find it in the nearby, fast cache. A good cache system might increase the speed and performance considerably.

Level 1 and Level 2 Caches

A Level 1 (L1) cache is one that is built into the CPU. This makes the cache very close and fast. The 486 was the first CPU with an internal L1 cache. Intel built in an 8K cache among the 1.2 million transistors in the CPU. They increased the L1 cache to 16K in the 486DX4 and all of the Pentuim-class CPUs. The L1 cache allows the CPU to access memory that is often used without having to travel outside to the external RAM. Because of the short distance and the high-speed transistors, the L1 cache operates at the same internal speed as the CPU. Many of the CPUs operate externally two to three times slower than the internal speed.

The 486 and Pentium CPUs also use a level 2 (L2) or external cache made up of fast SRAM located on the motherboard. The speed and static characteristics of SRAM makes it an excellent device for memory cache systems.

But again, it takes a finite amount of time for the data to move from the CPU over the bus at an external frequency to the SRAM cache. The Pentium Pro lessened this problem by building a L2 cache in the same enclosure as the CPU. The L2 cache is closely coupled to the CPU and communicates with it over a very short 64-bit interface or special bus at the internal CPU frequency. The L2 cache will either be 256K or 512K. Cache made up of SRAM transistors are very fast, but they require lots of transistors. It takes six transistors for each bit of SRAM so a 256K cache requires 15.5 million transistors; 512K requires 31 million. It only takes one transistor for each bit of DRAM so 256K would require 2.6 million transistors and 512k would need 5.2 million.

The 486 has an 8K cache system built into the chip, the 486DX4 and the Pentium CPUs have two 8K caches. This built-in cache gives the CPUs about a 90% hit rate. The 486DX also has a math coprocessor in among the 1.2 million transistors in this chip, the 486SX does not have a math coprocessor.

It takes a large number of transistors for a cache, even one as small as 8K. The Cyrix Company built in a 1K cache on their 486 clone. They claim that this still gives them an 80% hit rate. Cyrix also left the coprocessor off their 486 clone, but they package an external coprocessor with each CPU. By reducing the number of transistors on their CPU, they made the chip to be the same size as the 386 CPU.

Write through and Write Back

After the data is processed it is returned to RAM. The write through systems simply sends the data back to RAM. System operations are delayed while the data is being written back to RAM. The delay might be only microseconds, but if you are processing a lot of data, it can add up.

The write back systems keeps the data in the cache until there is a break in operations, then writes the data to RAM.

Fast Page Mode

Fast page mode DRAM is faster than standard DRAM. It works on the principle that once an address has been accessed, it will access the following next. The fast page mode works well with a large cache.

Extended Data Out (EDO)

As the CPUs keep getting faster and faster, it is increasingly difficult to develop DRAM chips that can keep up. A type of DRAM being manufactured by Micron Technology, at (208) 368-4000, is called Extended Data Out (EDO). It operates about 10 percent faster than ordinary DRAM and is still fairly reasonable in cost. Conventional DRAM requires two wait states for accessing and refreshment times. Due to its architecture, EDO only needs one wait state. EDO also uses a wider bandwidth during the address select so that there are fewer cache misses. The motherboard must be designed to accept the EDO DRAM.

Burst EDO (BEDO)

An advanced type of EDO memory is burst EDO. Its design and architecture requires zero wait states to read or write. BEDO DRAM will increase system efficiency by as much as 13 percent or more.

Synchronous DRAM

Another type of memory is synchronous DRAM (SDRAM). SDRAM should not be confused with SRAM. The DIMM chips shown in Fig. 6-3 are SDRAM assemblies rated at 10ns. The fastest standard DRAM is 60ns. The SDRAM system couples the operation of the memory very tightly to the processor clock. At this time not all motherboards will accept SDRAM. The Pentium II motherboards made by Intel accepts it, but my Micronics Pentium II cannot use it. I tried it and my system will not boot up. Several companies are manufacturing it. It is very fast and comparatively inexpensive. Some believe that it will eventually displace standard DRAM chips and be the choice for the main memory.

CMOS

The complementary metal oxide semiconductors (CMOS) use very little power to keep them alive. They are actually SRAM transistors that stores your system setup. Several of the computer features that are configurable, such as the time, date, type of disk drives, and other features that can be changed by the user are stored in CMOS.

You should take a pad and write down all of the features stored in your CMOS setup. For instance, if you lose the data in your CMOS, and you don't know what type of hard drive is in the setup, you will not be able to access your data on the hard drive.

A lithium or a rechargeable battery keeps the data alive when the computer is turned off. If your computer is not used for a long period of time, you might have to reset the time. If you have to reset the time quite often, you might need a new battery. The early IBM AT used batteries that only lasted a couple of years. The batteries were soldered onto the motherboard and are very difficult to change. Most motherboards today have lithium batteries that last about ten years.

Why the 640K Limit Exists

When DOS was first introduced in 1981, one megabyte of memory was an enormous amount. It was believed that this amount would be more than satisfactory. After all, many of the CP/M machines were getting by fine with just 64K of memory. So DOS was designed to operate with a maximum of one megabyte. Of this one megabyte, 640K would be used for running programs and applications. The other 384K was reserved for purposes such as the BIOS, the video control, and other special hardware control. This 384K is called the upper memory area and is divided up into blocks called *upper memory blocks* or UMBs.

Sometimes when I try to load and run a program, I get an error message "Not enough memory," or "Insufficient memory." But I have 32Mb of DRAM in my computer. I know that the program that I am trying to run is less than 500K. So why shouldn't I be able to run it if I have 32Mb?

The reason is simple. The program that I am trying to run is a DOS type program that cannot handle extended memory. It is limited to the 640K of conventional memory. But if the program is only 500K, why can't it run in the 640K?

The reason is when I booted up my computer, the Command.Com and several other internal DOS commands were loaded into that 640K. In addition, any terminate and stay resident (TSR) programs were also loaded into the 640K. Any drivers for special devices such as a fax-modem, a CD-ROM, or other device drivers listed in my Config.sys and Autoexec.bat are also loaded into the conventional memory. After all of this stuff is loaded, there might be less than 400K left. So if the program is larger than 400K, it will not run. Many programs and applications today are so large that they might need 600K or more of RAM.

The DOS internal commands and many TSRs are loaded are in memory at all times. These commands can be invoked by just a few keystrokes from any directory. There are about 75 DOS commands. About 30 of them are internal commands such as copy, del, md, cd, and type. (In many of the early versions of DOS, these were all separate commands. But DOS now incorporates them all into COMMAND.COM.) They are always loaded and immediately available. If you want to run one of the external commands, such as find or diskcomp, you have to go to the DOS directory and load them.

Tremendous improvements have been made in computer technology since the original PC. But in spite of all of the improvements in the technology, we are still limited to the original 640K unless we have programs such as Windows that can take advantage of any extra extended memory that we might have. One reason for this limitation was to make sure that the computers remained compatible with, and could still run, the billions of dollars worth of software that was already created. I still occasionally hear someone complain about the 640K barrier, but this backward compatibility is one of the foremost factors that made the computer what it is today.

The 640K barrier is not really much of a problem today. Much of the reserved 384K upper memory space is never needed by the system.

MS-DOS and several other programs such as DESQview can load the internal commands, drivers, and TSRs into the unused 384 of upper memory. In most cases, you can have over 600K left for running programs. The MS-DOS version 5.0 and later, has a MEMMAKER command that can search the 384K of upper memory and find all of the unused cracks and crannies. After this, every time you boot your computer, it will automatically load most of the internal commands, drivers, and TSRs into these upper memory blocks (UMBs).

Windows 95, Windows NT, and IBM's OS/2 is not limited to the 640K barrier. When running programs designed for Windows, these systems will let you use all of the RAM that is available if it is needed.

Conventional Memory

Conventional memory is the one megabyte of memory that includes the 640K. DOS-type applications are loaded into this area and processed here. In early versions of DOS, several commands were loaded into this area which decreased the usable area available for user applications. Figure 6-5 is a diagram of how conventional memory is arranged.

Fig. 6-5
Installing a SIMM module. Insert at an angle, then pull forward until it locks in.

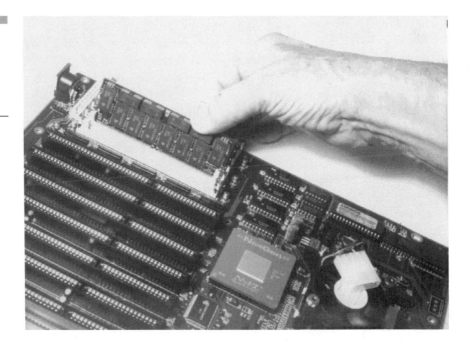

Extended Memory

Extended memory is memory that can be installed above one megabyte. The Pentium can address up to four gigabytes of extended memory. If it weren't for the DOS 640K limitation, it would be a seamless continuation of memory. Windows 95, Windows NT, and OS/2 2.1 can also use extended memory to run two or more programs at the same time, or do multitasking.

Flash Memory

You will probably want a laptop or notebook computer for the times when you are on the road. If you do buy one, it should have the PC Card (originally called PCMCIA) connectors for flash memory.

Intel developed flash memory, which is similar to erasable programmable read only memory (EPROM). Flash memory is fairly slow compared to DRAM and SRAM, so it can't replace them.

Flash memory is often installed on small plug-in cards about the size of a credit card. The cards are ideal for use on laptop and notebook computers. When first introduced, the cards were quite limited in the amount of memory that could be stored on a card. But cards are now available that can store several megabytes. They can be a good substitute for a hard disk on small notebook computers.

The Personal Computer Memory Card International Association (PCMCIA) adopted a standard and connectors so that several products can be used with laptop and notebook computers. Most laptop and notebook computers now include the PC Card connectors so that flash memory and other peripherals can be installed.

There are several advantages of the PC Cards over a hard disk in a laptop. The hard disk is a mechanical device, which will eventually wear out or fail. The PC Card flash memory is strictly electronic and should last several lifetimes. But the flash memory is still rather expensive and limited in the amount of memory that can be installed on a card.

Using flash memory and the PC Card standard companies have developed several other peripherals for the laptop and notebook computer. They have developed things such as high-speed modems and network adapters using the credit card sized PC Card standard. A flash floppy has been designed that can store from 2Mb up to 100Mb. Some desktop PCs are installing PC Card sockets so they can take advantage of the technology. It makes it easy to download or transfer data back and forth to a laptop.

VRAM

Video RAM chips are a bit different than DRAM chips. They are special memory chips that are used on monitor adapter cards. They are especially optimized for graphics.

Printer Memory

Your printer will probably come with a minimum amount of memory. Most printers require memory that is installed on special proprietary boards. You will need to add more memory for better printing speed.

Buying Chips

Buying chips that are faster than what your system can use only costs you extra money. It doesn't hurt to use faster chips, or even to intermix faster ones with slower ones.

If you plan to upgrade the memory in an older system, you might have trouble finding the older chips. The older systems used the dual-inline package (DIP) chips. Make sure that you buy only the type that will fit in your system. For instance, the 64K and 256K DIP chips have 16 pins, the 1Mb chips have 18. Some memory boards have both 256K and 1Mb sockets interlaced so that you can use either size chip.

The SIMM chips are the type of chip used most often today. But you cannot use a SIMM module unless your motherboard is designed for it.

How Much Memory Do You Need?

This will depend primarily on what you intend to use your computer for. For word processing or small applications, you can get by with **640K**.

If you have more time than money, you can get by with a minimum of 8Mb. But you will be much better off with at least 16Mb if you expect to use Windows, large databases, or spreadsheets. DRAM is fairly inexpensive today so most computer systems are being shipped today with at least 24Mb of DRAM. Two of the most important things that makes a computer powerful is the speed of the CPU and the amount of memory available.

Having lots of memory is like having a car with a large engine. You might not need that extra power very often, but it sure feels great being able to call on it when you do need it.

If you are upgrading an older PC, you might not have enough room to install more memory. It was mentioned earlier, but you can order one of the Memory Expanders. There are different styles, but one of them is a board that plugs into one of the existing sockets. This board then has four more sockets that can be used.

Installing the Chips

Caution: Electrostatic Voltage Before handling your memory chips, or any electronic components, the first thing that you should do is to discharge any electrostatic charge that might have been built up on you. If you have ever walked across a carpet and got a shock when you touched a door knob, then you know that you can build up static electricity. It is quite possible to build up 3000 to 5000 volts of static electricity in your body. So if you touch a fragile piece of electronics that normally operates at 5 to 12 volts, you can severely damage it. You can discharge this static electricity from your body by touching any metal that goes to ground. The metal case of the power supply in your computer is a good ground if it is still plugged into the wall socket. The power does not have to be on for it to connect to ground. You can also touch an unpainted metal part of any device or appliance that has three wires and is plugged into a socket. You should always discharge yourself before touching any plug-in board or other equipment where there are exposed electronic semiconductors.

Memory chips and most other critical electronic components come in a special packaging. Before unwrapping any component, one of the first things that you should do is to discharge any static electric charge that you might have on you. This is especially important if you are working in an area where there is carpet. Touch some metal object such as a lamp that is plugged into an outlet to discharge yourself of any static electricity.

You can mix chips of different speeds in the same bank, such as 60 ns and 70 ns, but you would be limited to the 70 ns speed. You should not use a chip slower than the speed of your CPU. You cannot mix chips of different capacities such as a 1×9 and a 4×9. To install SIMM modules, just lay the module in the socket at an angle, press down lightly, and pull forward until it locks in. See Fig. 6-5.

If you are using the old DIP chips, they might have a small notch at one end or a round dot in one corner. The notch or dot indicates the end that has pin one. The socket will have a matching notch or outline on the board to indicate how the chip should be plugged in. Ordinarily, all of the chips on a board are installed or oriented in the same direction.

To install a DIP chip, set the leads in one side of the socket, then with a bit of pressure against that side, line up the leads on the other side and press the chip in. Be careful that you do not bend the leads. Check to make sure that all of the leads are inserted in the sockets. It is very easy to have one slip out and not be noticed. If this happens you will have memory errors when you try to run the system.

If you are installing the memory on a PC or XT, you might have to reset the dip switch on the motherboard to reflect the amount of memory. Some of the older ATs have a jumper that has to be set.

To install SIPs, look for markings on the modules. Many of them will have pin one marked and there will usually be a mark on the motherboard sockets for pin one. The motherboard will also probably have markings for the individual banks, such as bank 0, bank 1, bank 2, etc.

The SIMM modules have a cutout on one end of the small board. It can only be plugged in one way.

If you plan to add extra memory, be sure that you get the kind and type for your machine. Make sure that it is fast enough for your system. Check your documentation. It should tell you what speed and type of chips to buy.

If you have just installed some chips for a memory upgrade, check the chips to make sure they are properly seated. Also check the motherboard for any switches or jumpers that should be set to recognize the new configuration. If any of the SIMM modules are not seated properly, the system will not boot up.

Then turn your computer on and make sure that it operates. If it works okay, replace the cover and congratulate yourself.

Floppy Drives and Disks

The Floppy Evolution

It is possible to run a PC with only floppy disk drives, but you would be severely limited in the programs that you could run, and it would take a whole lot of time. Floppy disks were all we had in the early days. Some PCs had a single floppy drive. Almost all of the early drives used single-sided floppy disks that were from 140Kb to 180Kb. It was a great leap forward when IBM introduced a PC with two floppy drives that could handle-double sided floppy disks. The floppy disks could be formatted to a whopping 180Kb on each side for a total of 320Kb. Even if you were fortunate enough to have a PC with two floppy drives, doing any kind of computing involved an endless amount of disk swapping and it took forever to get anything done.

My first computer had two single-sided 140Kb drives. It was slow and required a lot of disk swapping. Floppy systems have come a long way since those early days. The 140Kb systems were soon replaced with 320Kb double-sided systems, then 360Kb, then 1.2Mb, 1.44Mb, 2.88Mb, and now even 120Mb on a floppy disk.

Most software programs today are very user friendly. The more user friendly they are, the larger they are. Many of the programs require from 80Mb up to 120Mb or more to be installed and to be able to run. It would be impossible to run programs such as these with a floppy disk system. With the low prices of hard disk drives today, I can't imagine anyone running a PC without a good high-capacity hard drive. To do any kind of productive computing, this can be one of the better upgrades.

Floppy disks and floppy drives are a very important part of your computer. Until the last couple of years, the majority of all software programs came on floppy disks. Until recently, most programs were fairly small. In a compressed form, most of them didn't require more than four or five 1.44Mb floppies. But some programs today are over 100Mb. Even in a compressed format, this would take a large number of floppies. Many companies are now using CD-ROMs to distribute their software. Eventually all software will be distributed on the high-capacity CD-ROMs. No matter how you receive it, the software is usually copied to a hard disk.

Don't worry that the CD-ROM will replace the floppy disk. Floppy disks can do many things that a CD-ROM can't do, such as making archive copies of small programs, backing up small files from a hard disk, or moving a small program from one computer to another. The floppy system will be around for a long time. But a new floppy disk drive from

OR Technology, called A:Drive, might hasten the demise of the 1.44Mb floppy as we know it. The A:Drive can read and write to the 1.44Mb format, but it can also read and write to a special 120Mb floppy disk.

With the A:Drive, there might be no need to upgrade to a larger capacity hard disk. With several 120Mb floppies, you would never run out of space. A disadvantage of course is that the file that you need will always on the other floppy disk.

How Floppy Drives Operate

Computers rely to a very large extent on magnetism. Magnetic lines of force can be produced when voltage is passed through a coil of wire that is wrapped around a piece of iron. The amount of magnetism produced varies enormously depending on such factors as the voltage level, the number of turns of wire, the properties of the iron core, the frequency of the voltage, and many other factors.

Conversely, voltage can be produced when a coil of wire is passed through a magnetic field. So we can use voltage to make magnetism or use magnetism to make voltage.

The floppy drive spins a disk much like a record player. The floppy disk is made from a type of plastic material called *polyethylene terephthalate*. This is coated with a magnetic material made primarily of iron oxide. It is similar to the tape that is used in cassette tape recorders. The drive uses a head, which is basically a piece of iron with a coil of wire around it. The iron core for the head is shaped somewhat like a C. When voltage is passed through the coil of wire, a magnetic field is produced between the ends of the C. The space between the ends of the C might be very small and is called the *gap*. The head records (writes) and plays back (reads) the disk much like the record/playback head in a cassette tape recorder.

There is a considerable difference in the methods of recording on a tape recorder and digital recording. When audio is recorded, the sound waves cause a diaphragm to vibrate in a microphone. Attached to the diaphragm is a magnet that moves in and out of a coil of wire because of the sound vibrations. The movement of the magnet in the coil of wire generates a voltage that goes up and down to exactly match the up-and-down vibration of the sound. This sine wave analog voltage is then amplified and fed to the tape record head. The record head responds with a voltage or current output that is a replica of the original sound.

The varying current from the head magnetizes the tape with an exact replica of the original sound. When the tape is played back, as the magnetized image on the tape passes by the head, it causes a voltage to be produced that is a replica of the original sound. Of course the voltage produced by the magnetism on the tape is very small, so it must be amplified.

Placing a small voltage on the base of a transistor can cause it to turn on and amplify or create a much larger replica of the small original voltage.

The voltages in the tape recorder are alternating current, that is, they vary up and down. Most of the voltages used in computers is direct current, usually 3 to 5 volts dc. Transistors, which act like a switch, can be used to turn the direct current on and off. When the current is on, it can represent a 1; when it is off, it can represent a 0. A transistor can be switched on and off millions of times per second.

When the head on a disk drive writes or records on the iron oxide surface, a pulse of electricity causes the head to magnetize that portion of track beneath the head. A spot on the track that is magnetized can represent a 1; if the next spot of the same track is not magnetized, it can represent a 0. When the tracks are read, the head detects whether each portion of the track is magnetized or not. If the spot is magnetized, it creates a small voltage signal to represent a 1, or a 0 if it is not magnetized.

Computers operate with a very precise clock rate based on internal crystal oscillators. If a voltage remains high for a certain length of time, it can represent two or more 1s, or if it is off for a certain length of time, it can represent two or more 0s.

The floppy disks are divided into several concentric tracks. Each track is then divided into sectors. This system allows us to find any particular item on the track. It is amazing to me that the head can find any one byte on a floppy disk that might have over a million bytes. It is even more amazing that the same system can find any one byte on a hard disk that might have over 2 billion bytes or 2 gigabytes.

On a 1.2Mb floppy disk, 80 tracks are laid down at the rate of 96 tracks per inch. So each track occupies $\frac{1}{96}$ of an inch or about 0.0104 inches wide. The record current that passes through the heads might vary considerably. A stronger current might even magnetize adjacent tracks. To prevent this, the actual recording part of the head is only about $\frac{1}{3}$ as wide as the track width. There are two erase heads on each side and behind the record head that extend to the full width of the track. As the record head lays down the square waves that represent 1s and 0s, the erase heads trim any signal that might have exceeded the normal width of the track. These side erase heads form guard bands between each track. (More about tracks and disk formats later.)

360Kb Drives

At one time there were over 40 million 360Kb drives in use. At that time all software was distributed on 360Kb floppies. Later the 1.2Mb floppy was introduced, then the 1.44Mb. Software programs began to grow larger and larger so most vendors began distributing software on 1.2Mb or 1.44Mb disks in a compressed form. Most of the software is now distributed on CD-ROM disks, which can hold over 600MB. But even that might not be enough for very long. You can expect to eventually see software distributed on the 17Gb DVD discs.

There are still a few small shareware programs that are distributed on 360Kb floppies. Many were distributed on 1.2Mb disks, but now most of them are on 1.44Mb disks. The old 360Kb format served us well, but it is now as obsolete as the old city street gas lights.

The Virtual Drive

DOS reserves the letters A and B for floppy drives. If you only have one drive, you can call it both. For instance, you can say, "copy A: to B:". The drive will copy whatever is in the drive, then prompt you to insert a disk in drive B:. Of course, you could have said "copy A: to A:" and got the same results.

High-Density Drives and Disks

By just looking at a 360Kb and a 1.2Mb drive, you wouldn't be able to tell which was which. The main difference between the two is magnetic and electrical differences. The 1.2Mb drive has an oersted (Oe) of 600, the 360K has an Oe of 300. The higher Oe means that the material requires a higher head current for magnetization.

In order to store 1.2Mb on the floppy, 80 tracks on each side of the disk are laid down. Each of these tracks are divided into 15 sectors, and

512 bytes can be stored in each sector. These 80 tracks are just half as wide as the 40 tracks of a 360Kb disk. The 1.2Mb drives switch to a lower head current when writing to the 360Kb format.

The 3½ inch 1.44Mb and 720Kb drives also look very much alike. The main difference is that the 1.44Mb drive usually has a small microswitch that checks for the square hole in the right-rear corner of the 1.44Mb disks. The 1.44Mb drives will read and write to the 720Kb format as well as the high density. The 720Kb drive is as obsolete as the 360K.

The All-Media or Combination Floppy Drive

The 1.2Mb drive system is also obsolete. But you might have several 1.2Mb disks with small programs on them. I have about 500. I might never use them, but I just hate to throw them away. If you have several 1.2Mb disks, you might consider buying a combination drive. Most older systems never had enough bays. Many of the desktop cases only provided three or four bays to mount drives. You might not have had space to mount two floppies, two hard drives, a tape backup drive, and a CD-ROM.

The CMS Enhancements Company, (714) 222-6316, noted this problem. They created an all-media floppy drive by combining a 1.2Mb and a 1.44Mb floppy drive into a single unit. The 5¼ inch part of the drive can handle 5¼ inch 360Kb and 1.2Mb floppies; the 3½ part handles 720Kb and 1.44Mb floppy disks. The combination drive requires only a single drive bay. The two drives are never both used at the same time, so there is no problem. They can even share most of the drive electronics.

Teac, Canon, and several other companies also manufactured the combination drives, but they are practically obsolete now so you might have trouble finding one. Figure 7-1 shows an old 360K drive on the left, a 1.2Mb in the center, and a combination drive on the right.

Extended Density Drives

The 3½ inch extended density (ED) 2.8Mb floppy drives have been available for a while. The 2.8Mb disks have a barium ferrite media and use perpendicular recording to achieve the extended density. In standard recording, the particles are magnetized so that they lay horizontally in

Fig. 7-1
An old 360K drive on the left, a 1.2Mb drive in the center, and a combination 3½ inch 1.44Mb and 5¼ inch 1.2Mb drive on the right. Note the rubber "O" ring drive belt for the old 360K drive.

the media. In perpendicular recording, the particles are stood vertically on end for greater density.

The ED drives require a controller that operates at 1MHz. The other floppy controllers operate at 500KHz. Several companies are now integrating the ED controller with the other floppy controllers. Most of the Pentium Pro motherboards now have built-in floppy controllers for 2.88Mb and other floppy drives.

The ED drives are downward compatible and can read and write to the 720Kb and 1.44Mb disks. At the present time, the ED drives and disks are still rather expensive. Not many people are using them. They don't offer that much of an advantage over the 1.44Mb drives. I would not recommend them. With the introduction of the Iomega Zip 100Mb and the Compaq 120Mb drives, the 2.88Mb system will probably just fade away.

The Iomega 100Mb Zip Floppy Disk and Drive

The Iomega Zip drive uses a 3½ inch disk that is similar to a floppy, but this 3½ inch disk can store 100Mb. This system is much less expensive than the Bernoulli. At this time, the Zip drives cost less than $200 and the disks cost less than $20. With a few disks, you would never have to worry about running out of hard drive space. See Fig. 7-2.

The 1.44Mb/120Mb A:Drive

The 1.44Mb/120Mb floppy disk drive can be one of the best upgrades that you can make. See Fig. 7-3. The following information is from the OR Technology web site at www.ortechnology.com:

> The a:drive from OR Technology was designed to replace the floppy disk drive. While its outward appearance is almost indistinguishable from that of its floppy technology counterpart, the a:drive achieves 120MB of storage when used with LS-120 media. At the same time, the a:drive is downward compatible with current 3.5-inch floppy disk technology. It can read and write to both 720KB and 1.44MB diskettes, providing an upward migration path for millions of personal computer users and the billions of diskettes they own.As its name indicates, the a:drive can be used as a bootable drive in any system in which it is installed. From the start, OR Technology created the 1-inch high

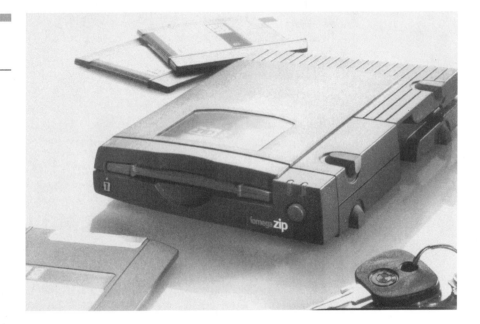

Fig. 7-2
An Iomega 100Mb ZIP drive.

Fig. 7-3
The A:Drive. It can
read and write to
1.44Mb disks and to
120Mb disks.

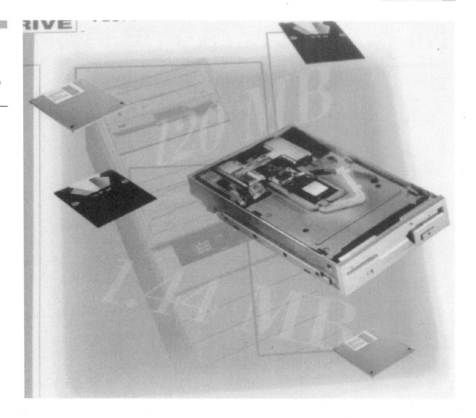

a:drive with this purpose in mind. Extensive development has opti-mized the device for internal use as an integral system component.

It was designed to be the ideal form, fit, and function replacement for the floppy disk drive. The a:drive is an advanced technology product, yet so familiar you already know how to use it.

OR Technology has worked closely with Microsoft Corp. and Compaq Computer Corp. developing standards to enable the operating system, the computer system, and the a:drive to work together. Both Windows 95 and Windows NT operating systems have now been updated to recog-nize the a:drive as a bootable drive in both 120MB and 1.44MB mode. To accomplish this, changes were required to the system BIOS.

In addition, OR Technology has been active in the ATAPI standards commit-tee developing the necessary protocol for devices that read and write. As a result the a:drive is ATAPI compatible and can be attached to the same internal IDE cable the hard disk drive uses. Unlike alternative technologies, the compact a:drive meets current industry standards established for floppy disk drive and floppy diskette form factors. It can be easily configured for use in standard notebook or desktop PC drive bays.

At the present time, the drives are selling for about $150. The preformatted special 120Mb floppy disks are selling for $19.95. I am sure that they will be less by the time you read this.

O.R. Technology
42 West Campbell Ave.
Campbell, CA 95008
Tel. 408-866-3000
Fax. 408-866-3008

For questions or comments, please send an e-mail to:
mktg@ortechnology.com

Disk Drive Motors

Disk drives have two motors. One motor drives the spindle that rotates the disk. Then a stepping motor, or actuator, moves the heads back and forth to the various tracks.

Spindle Motor

If you have an older computer, then no doubt you have a $5\frac{1}{4}$ inch 360Kb floppy drive, or maybe two such drives. If they are very old, they might be full height, or about $3\frac{1}{2}$ inches high. If they are original IBM drives, then they probably have a plastic or rubber O ring for a drive belt from the motor to the disk spindle. The O ring deteriorates and stretches with time. The speed of the disk is very critical. When the O ring stretches, the speed will slow down and the spindle might not even turn at all.

I replaced an IBM $5\frac{1}{4}$ inch 360Kb floppy drive in 1985 because it kept giving me errors in reading floppies. It cost $425 for a new IBM drive. A $5\frac{1}{4}$ drive today costs about $25. I didn't realize it at the time, but I could have just replaced the O ring. Most of the newer drives use direct drive motors. Modern floppy drives use a direct drive where the spindle is just an extension of the motor shaft. Figure 7-1 shows an old IBM 360K drive on the left, a 1.2Mb in the center, and a combination $3\frac{1}{2}$ inch and $5\frac{1}{4}$ inch drive on the right.

The motors are regulated so that the speed is usually fairly constant. The speed of the old $5\frac{1}{4}$ inch 360Kb floppy drive is 300 RPMs. The $5\frac{1}{4}$ inch 1.2Mb drive rotates 360 RPMs, even when reading and writing to a 360Kb disk. All of the $3\frac{1}{2}$ inch floppy drives rotate at 300 RPMs. Note that the old 360Kb had a rubber belt to drive the spindle. The belt was subject to stretching, deterioration and slippage. This was an IBM floppy that cost over $400. Later they changed to the much more reliable direct drive motor.

Head Actuator Motor

The head actuator motor is electronically linked to the file allocation table. If a request is received to read data from a particular track, say track 20, the actuator motor moves the head, or rather *heads*, to that track. Floppy drives have two heads, one on top and one on the bottom. They are connected together and move as a single unit.

Several large companies manufacture the floppy drives such as Sony, Toshiba, Fuji, Teac, and others. Each company's prices are within a few dollars of the others. Most of them are fairly close in quality but there might be minor differences.

On some of the older drives, a fairly large actuator stepping motor is used to position the heads. It is very quiet and works smoothly as it moves the heads from track to track. It has a steel band around the motor shaft that moves the heads in and out. In Fig. 7-1, the actuator motor is the large square object in the lower-left corner of the 1.2Mb drive. There is a steel band attached to the shaft of the stepper motor and to the heads that moves the heads in discrete steps across the disk. It can find and stop on any track.

The actuator stepping motors on the combination drives are small cylindrical motors with a worm screw. The motors groan and grunt as they move the heads from track to track. Other than being a bit noisy, they have worked perfectly. In Fig. 7-4, the cover has been removed from the $3\frac{1}{2}$ inch drive. You can see the small round worm screw motor in the center. The heads are mounted on the worm screw and as the motor turns, the heads move in and out to access the various tracks. If the software tells the motor to go track 15, it knows exactly how far to move the heads. If the worm screw becomes worn, or the steel band on the 1.2Mb drive that is attached to the actuator motor shaft becomes loose or out of adjustment, the drives might not be able to find the proper tracks. If the hub of

Fig. 7-4
A 3½ inch drive with the cover removed to show the worm drive. The heads are connected to the worm screw and as the monitor turns, the heads move back and forth over the disk.

the disk you are trying to read has become worn or is not centered exactly on the cone spindle, the heads might not be able to find a track that was previously written, or one that was written on another drive.

If your heads are out of alignment, you can write and read on your own machine, because you are using the same misalignment to write and read. But another drive might have trouble reading a disk recorded with misaligned heads.

Cost of 1.44Mb Drives

I recently went to a weekend computer swap here at the Los Angeles County Fairgrounds. I bought a 1.44Mb drive for $17.95. I didn't really need one, but at that price, it makes a good backup spare. I like to keep spare components so that if something goes bad I can easily replace it.

Floppy Controllers

A floppy drive must have a controller to tell it when to turn on, and to go to a certain track and sector. In the early days the controller was a large board full of chips. Later some manufacturers integrated the floppy disk controller (FDC) onto the same board as the hard disk controller (HDC). These were large full-length boards that were rather expensive at about $250. Now the floppy drive controllers (FDCs) are usually built into a single VLSI chip and integrated with a hard disk controller or IDE interface. Now the FDC and the IDE hard disk interface are often built-in on the motherboard. These motherboards usually have a set of upright pins for the flat ribbon cable connectors. See Fig. 7-5. There will usually be pins for the floppy drives, for IDE hard drives and CD-ROMs, for a short printer cable to a back panel connector, and pins for COM1 and COM2 for short cables to back panel connectors for the mouse.

The older controller boards had an edge connector for the cable. Later boards had two rows of pins for the connector. Be very careful when plugging in the cable connector. Look for pin one on the board and make sure that the different colored wire goes to that side. If the cable is plugged in backwards, the floppy disk will not work properly. If the cable is plugged in backwards, and you try to boot up, the floppy drive will erase portions of the boot section of the floppy disk. You will no longer be able to boot up with the disk. I know that this happens because I have made this mistake. Fortunately, I had a backup boot disk.

Fig. 7-5

The upright pins on a motherboard for the connection of floppy drives, hard drives, printer, and COM ports.

Drive Select Jumpers

It is possible to have four different floppy drives connected to one controller. The floppies will have a set of pins with a jumper so that each
drive can be set for a unique number. The pins will be labeled DS0,
DS1, DS2, and DS3. Some manufacturers label them DS1, DS2, DS3, DS4.
The vast majority of systems use only two drives. These jumpers will
also let you determine which drive is A: or B:. In most cases, you
will use them as they come from the factory and never have to worry
about these jumpers. Most drives are received with the second set of
pins jumpered, which means they are set for drive A:. If you install a
second floppy drive, it will also have the second set of pins jumpered
just like the A: drive. Don't change it. Because the floppy cable has some
twisted wires in it, the controller automatically recognizes it as drive B:.
This can be confusing and you might or might not get any documentation at all with your drive. Fortunately, they usually work fine as
received from the factory.

The combination drives usually have small jumper pins near the
miniature power cable connector. The combination drives have two
columns of pins, one for each drive. There are six pins in each column
and four pins in each column are jumpered. Again, you should never
have to reset or bother with these pins. The two drives share a single
controller cable connector. If you want to use the $5\frac{1}{4}$ inch drive as
drive A:, then plug the end of the cable with the twisted wires into the
cable connector. If you want the $3\frac{1}{2}$ inch 1.44Mb drive to be drive A:,
then plug in the middle connector that has no twists. Again, fortunately, there is usually no need to move the jumpers.

Data Compression

Data compression can double your disk capacity. One of the most popular compression programs is Stacker from Stac Electronics (800-522-
7822). Windows 95, MS-DOS versions 6.2, and IBM PC DOS 7.0 come
with the Stacker compression utility. It can be used on floppy disks as
well as hard disks. Compression can be the least expensive way to
increase disk capacity.

Differences between Floppy Disks

The $5\frac{1}{4}$ inch 360Kb and the $3\frac{1}{2}$ inch 720Kb disks are called *double-sided double-density* (DS/DD). The $5\frac{1}{4}$ inch 1.2Mb and the $3\frac{1}{2}$ inch 1.44Mb are called *high-density* (HD). The $3\frac{1}{2}$ inch double-density disks are usually marked DD, the high-density disks are usually marked HD. But the $5\frac{1}{4}$ inch 360Kb and the 1.2Mb disks usually have no markings. They look exactly alike, except that the 360Kb usually has a reenforcing ring or collar around the large center hole. The high-density 1.2Mb disks do not have the ring.

Figure 7-6 shows a 1.2Mb floppy in the upper-left, a 360K in the upper-right, a 1.44Mb in lower-left, and a 720K in the lower-right. The 360Kb disk shown in the upper-right has a white collar or ring; most of the new disks have a black ring.

One of the major differences between the 720Kb and the 1.44Mb is that the high-density 1.44Mb has two small square holes at the rear of the plastic shell, while the 720Kb has only one. The $3\frac{1}{2}$ inch drive has a small media sensor microswitch that protrudes upwards. If it finds a hole on that side of the disk, it knows that it is a 1.44Mb disk. If there is no hole, it is treated as a 720Kb.

Fig. 7-6
Floppy disks. Upper-left is 1.2Mb, upper-right is 360K, lower-left is 1.44Mb, lower-right is 720K. The only difference in the $5\frac{1}{4}$ inch disks is the white hub ring on the 360K. Some might have a black hub ring. The difference in the $3\frac{1}{2}$ inch disks is that the 1.44Mb has an extra square hole on the left.

When looking at the backside of the two disks, the square hole on the right-rear of the shell has a small black slide that can be moved to cover the hole. Another small microswitch on the drive protrudes upward and checks the hole when the disk is inserted. If the hole is covered, the switch is pressed downward, allowing the disk to be written on. If the hole is open, the switch protects the disk so that it cannot be written on or erased. The $3\frac{1}{2}$ inch write-protect system is just the opposite of the system used by the $5\frac{1}{4}$ inch disks. They have a square notch that must be covered with opaque tape to prevent writing or unintentionally erasing the disk. (Incidentally, you must use opaque tape. The $5\frac{1}{4}$ inch system uses a light to shine through the square notch. If the detector in the system can see the light through the notch, then it can write on the disk. Some people have used clear plastic tape to cover the notch with disastrous results.)

There might be a time when you would want to make a diskcopy of a 720Kb and all you have are 1.44Mb. Or for some reason you might want to use a 1.44Mb as a 720Kb. You can cover the hole with any kind of tape and it will format as a 720Kb.

360Kb and 1.2Mb Disks

Although the 360Kb and 1.2Mb disks look exactly alike except for the hub ring on the 360Kb, there is a large difference in their magnetic media formulation. Several materials such as cobalt or barium can be added to the iron oxide to alter the magnetic properties. Cobalt is added to increase the oersted (Oe) of high-density floppy disks. Barium is used for the 2.88Mb extra high-density (ED) disks. Oe is a measure of the resistance of a material to being magnetized. The lower the Oe, the easier it is to be magnetized. The 360Kb has an Oe of 300, the 1.2Mb is 600 Oe. The 360Kb disks are fairly easy to magnetize or write to, so they require a fairly low head current. The 1.2Mb is more difficult to magnetize so a much higher head current is required. The 1.2Mb system can switch the current to match whatever type of disk you tell the system you are using.

If you place a 360Kb floppy in a 1.2Mb drive and just type format, it will try to format it as a 1.2Mb. But it will find several bad sectors, especially near the center where the sectors are shorter. These sectors will be marked and locked out. The system might report that you have over a megabyte of space on a 360Kb disk. This disk could be used in an emergency, for instance, to move data from one machine to another. But I would not recommend that you use such a disk for any data that is important. The data is packed much closer together when it is recorded as 1.2Mb. Because the 300 Oe of the 360Kb disks are so easy to magnetize, it is possible that nearby data might be affected. The data might migrate and eventually deteriorate and become unusable.

720Kb and 1.44Mb Disks

The 3 $\frac{1}{2}$ inch disks have several benefits and characteristics that make them superior to the 5 $\frac{1}{4}$ inch disks. The 720Kb disk can store twice as much data as a 360Kb in a much smaller space. The 1.44Mb can store four times as much as a 360Kb disk in the same small space.

The 3 $\frac{1}{2}$ inch floppy disks have a hard plastic protective shell, so they are not easily damaged. They also have a spring-loaded shutter that automatically covers and protects the head opening when they are not in use.

The 3 $\frac{1}{2}$ inch systems are much more accurate than the 5 $\frac{1}{4}$ inch systems in reading and writing. The 5 $\frac{1}{4}$ inch drive systems have a cone-shaped hub for the large center hole in the disks. If the disks are used for any length of time, it is possible for the hole to become stretched or enlarged. If the disk is not centered exactly on the hub, the heads will not be able to find and read the data.

The 3 $\frac{1}{2}$ inch floppies have a metal hub on the backside. This gives them much greater accuracy in reading and writing, even though the tracks on the 3 $\frac{1}{2}$ inch systems are much closer together.

One-Way Insertion

It is possible to insert a 5 $\frac{1}{4}$ inch floppy upside down, backwards, or sideways. When I first started using computers, I inserted a floppy that had the original software on it into a drive. I waited for a while and nothing happened. Then I got an error message, "Not ready reading drive A. Abort, Retry, Fail?" I almost panicked. I thought for sure that I had destroyed the software. I finally discovered that I had inserted the floppy upside down. I was still scared that I had damaged the disk. So I did what I should have done when I first got the program. I made a diskcopy backup of the disk. I found that the software was still okay.

You can't actually damage a disk by inserting it upside down. You can't read it because the small hole that tells DOS where track one begins is on the wrong side when inserted upside down. And of course you can't write to it or format it because of the small hole and also because the write-protect notch is on the other side.

The 3 $^1/_2$ inch disks are designed so that they can only be inserted properly. They have arrows at the left-top portion of the disks that indicate how they should be inserted into the drive. They have notches on the backside that prevents them from being completely inserted upside down.

The 720Kb 3 $^1/_2$ inch disks might have an Oe of 600 to 700. The 1.44Mb might have an Oe of 700 to 720. The Oe of the extra high-density 2.88Mb disks might be about 750. The 360K and 720K disks are both obsolete.

Disk Format Structure

Tracks

A disk must be formatted before it can be used. This consists of laying out individual concentric tracks on each side of the disk. If it is a 360Kb disk, each side is marked or configured with 40 tracks, numbered from 0 to 39.

If it is a 1.2Mb, 720Kb, or 1.44Mb, each side is configured with 80 tracks, numbered from 0 to 79. The tracks have the same number on the top and bottom of the disk. The top is side 0 and the bottom is side 1. When the head is over track 1 on the top, it is also over track 1 on the bottom. The heads move as a single unit to the various tracks by a head actuator motor or positioner. When data is written to a track, as much as possible is written on the top track, then the head is electronically switched and it continues to write to the same track on the bottom side. It is much faster and easier to electronically switch between the heads than to move them to another track.

Cylinders

If you could strip away all of the other tracks on each side of track 1 on side 0 and track 1 on side 1, it would be very flat, but it might look like a cylinder. So if a disk has 40 tracks, such as the 360Kb, it has 40 cylinders; the 1.2Mb and 1.44Mb have 80 cylinders.

Sectors

Each of the tracks are divided up into sectors. Each track of the 360Kb is divided into nine sectors, each of the 1.2Mb tracks are divided into 15 sectors, each of the 720Kb tracks are divided into nine sectors, each of the 1.44Mb tracks into 18 sectors and the 2.88Mb tracks into 36 sectors. Each sector can contain 512 bytes. Multiplying the number of sectors times number of bytes per sector times the number of tracks times two sides gives the amount of data that can be stored on a disk. For instance, the 1.2Mb has 15 sectors times 512 bytes times 80 tracks times two sides which would be $15 \times 512 \times 80 \times 2 = 1,228,800$ bytes. The system uses 14,898 bytes to mark the tracks and sectors during formatting so there is actually 1,213,952 bytes available on a 1.2Mb floppy.

Figure 7-7 is a diagrammatic representation of how the tracks and sectors are laid out on a disk.

Fig. 7-7
A diagram of how the tracks and sectors are laid out on a disk.

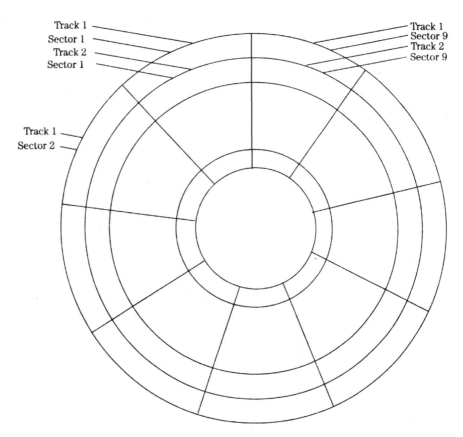

Track 1
Sector 1
Track 2
Sector 1

Track 1
Sector 9
Track 2
Sector 9

Track 1
Sector 2

Clusters or Allocation Units

DOS allocates one or more sectors on a disk and calls it a *cluster* or *allocation unit*. On the 360Kb and 720Kb disks, a cluster or allocation unit is two sectors. On the 1.2Mb and 1.44Mb each allocation unit is one sector. Only single files or parts of single files can be written into an allocation unit. If two different files were written into a single allocation unit, the data would become mixed and corrupted.

File Allocation Table (FAT)

During formatting, a file allocation table (FAT) is created on the first track of the disk. This FAT acts like a table of contents for a book. Whenever a file is recorded on a disk, the file is broken up into allocation units. The head looks in the FAT to find empty units, then records the parts of the file in any empty units it can find. Part of the file might be recorded in sector 5 of track 10, part in sector 8 of track 15, or any place it can find empty sectors. It records the location of all the various parts of the file in the FAT. With this method, parts of a file can be erased, changed, or added to without changing the entire disk.

TPI

The 40 tracks of a 360Kb is laid down at a rate of 48 tracks per inch (TPI), so each of the 40 tracks is $\frac{1}{48}$ of an inch wide. The 80 tracks of the high-density 1.2Mb is laid down at a rate of 96 TPI, so each track is $\frac{1}{96}$ of an inch. The 80 tracks of the $3\frac{1}{2}$ inch disks are laid down at a density of 135 per inch or 0.0074 inches per track.

Read Accuracy

The $5\frac{1}{4}$ inch disks have a $1\frac{1}{8}$ inch center hole. The drives have a spindle with a conical hub that comes up through the disk center hole when the drive latch is closed. This centers the disk so that the heads will be able to find each track. The plastic material that the disk is made from is subject to environmental changes, and wear and tear. The conical spindle might not center each disk exactly so head to track accuracy is difficult with more than 80 tracks. (If you have trouble reading a disk, it might be off center. It might help if you remove the disk and reinsert it.) Most of the 360Kb disks use a reinforcement hub ring, but it probably doesn't help much. The 1.2Mb floppies do not use a hub ring. Except for the hub ring, the 360Kb and 1.2Mb disk look exactly the same.

If your drive consistently has trouble reading your disks, or especially reading disks recorded on another machine, the heads might be out of alignment. The steel band or worm screw from the actuator motor that moves the heads might have slipped or become worn. So the actuator or head positioner might not be able to move the heads to the proper track. It is possible to have the heads realigned, but it is time consuming and expensive. Computer service time might cost from $50 or more per hour. It would probably be much less expensive to scrap the drive and buy a new one.

The 3 1/2 inch disks have a metal hub on the back which is used to center the disks. The tracks of the 3 1/2 inch floppies are narrower and greater in density per inch. Because of the metal hub, however, the head tracking accuracy is much better than that of the 5 1/4 inch systems.

Some Differences between Floppies and Hard Disks

Hard disks have very accurate and precise head tracking systems. Some hard disks have a density up to 3000 or more tracks per inch so much more data can be stored on a hard disk.

The floppy disks have a very a smooth lubricated surface. They rotate at a fairly slow 300 RPMs. Magnetic lines of force deteriorate very fast with distance. So the closer the heads, the better they can read and write. The floppy heads are in direct contact with the floppy disks.

Hard disks rotate at speeds from 3600 up to 7200 RPMs. The heads and surface would be severely damaged if they came in contact at this speed. So heads "fly" over the surface of each disk, just a few millionths of an inch above it.

Comparison of Floppy Disks

Table 7-1 shows some of the differences in the various types of floppy disks. Notice that the maximum number of root directories is the same for the 720Kb, the 1.2Mb, and the 1.44Mb. The 2.88Mb has four times the capacity of the 720Kb yet allows only 16 more root entries. This means that you can enter 224 different files on a 1.2Mb disk, but if you try to enter one more, it will not accept it, even though you might have hundreds of unused bytes.

The reason is that the DOS file allocation was designed for this limited number of files. There is an easy way around this problem. Just create subdirectories, like those created on a hard disk. Just type MD for make directory. If necessary, you can even make subdirectories of the subdirectories.

TABLE 7-1

Capacities of
Various Disk Types

Disk type	Tracks per side	Sectors/ track	Unformatted capacity	System use	Available to user	Max. dirs
360K	40	9	368640	6144	362496	112
1.2M	80	15	1228800	14898	1213952	224
720K	80	9	737280	12800	724480	224
1.44M	80	18	1474560	16896	1457664	224
2.88M	80	36	2949120	33792	2915328	240

Formatting

It is possible for you to use almost any version of MS-DOS, even the old 1.0. But unless you are using the latest versions, you are handicapping yourself and your computer. If you are using an older version of MS-DOS or any other DOS, one of the best upgrades you can make is to move up to Windows 95.

For those who might still be using an older version of DOS, but have a 1.2Mb for the A: drive, to format a 360Kb disk with the 1.2Mb drive, type FORMAT A /4. To format a 1.2Mb disk, you only have to type FORMAT A:. If you insert a 360Kb disk, it will try to format it to 1.2Mb. It will probably find several bad sectors.

To format a 720Kb disk on a 1.44Mb B: drive, type FORMAT B: /f:720. To format a 1.44Mb disk, just type FORMAT B:.

The format command in newer versions can take a very long time before it starts. It searches the floppy disk, then will save unformated information on the disk. If you decide later that you want to unformat the disk, just type unformat. But for most cases, I don't want to unformat a disk, especially if it is one that has never been formatted before. You can speed up the formatting process by typing format a:/u. This performs an unconditional format. If the disk has been formatted before, you can type format a:/q. This gives you a quick format by just erasing the first letter of the files in the file allocation table of the disk.

The MS-DOS manual is not too much help for many commands, including help for formatting. The on-disk help is much better for most commands. If you have trouble with the format command, just type help format. For any command that you need help with, just type help then the command.

I recently had the need to boot up my computer from a floppy disk with the minimum boot files. After I had booted up, I tried to make a new bootable floppy by typing format A:/S. I got the error message "General failure reading drive A. Abort, Retry or Fail?." I tried another floppy and got the same message. This is a message you often get when the disk is bad. But I couldn't believe that several disks were bad. I then tried the format command without the /S and it formatted immediately. After it was formatted, I had no trouble invoking the SYS command to transfer the operating system. I was a bit puzzled at first as to why it would give me a general failure reading drive A when I tried to format the disk with the /S. I finally figured out that when the system is normally booted up, it loads several files into memory. These files were not present on the minimum disk that I had booted up from. Because they were not present, they were not loaded into memory, therefore I couldn't make a bootable disk with all of the system files on it.

Formatting with Windows 95 is much easier. Just point your mouse to the My Computer icon and click. All of your drives will be shown. Point to whichever one you want to format and click. It will be highlighted. Point to File and click and you will be given several options one of which is to format a disk.

Cost of Disks

All floppy disks are now quite reasonable. The 1.44Mb are so inexpensive that many companies are sending out demo disks, press releases, and junk mail on 1.44Mb floppies. I usually erase them and reuse them. I feel it is my duty to recycle. One Internet company sent out several million copies of their sign-up software. I got so many copies of their software that I didn't have to buy any floppies for some time.

There are several discount mail-order floppy disk stores. Check the computer magazines for advertisements. Some companies are selling 1.44Mb preformatted disks for as little as 20 cents each. These are real bargains. At one time I paid as much as $2.50 each for 360Kb floppy disks.

How to Install Drives

To install your drives, you will need a Phillips and a flat-blade screwdriver. (It helps if they are magnetized. Be careful with magnetized tools around your floppy disks. They can partially erase or damage them.) You might also find it helpful to have a pair of long-nosed pliers.

Step 1: Set Any Switches or Jumpers   You should have received some sort of documentation with your drive. The drive might have jumpers that must be set depending on the type of system with which it will be used. Check the documentation and, if necessary, set the jumpers before you install the drive. In most cases you can use the drive as it comes with the factory default settings.

There are exceptions. I once overlooked the setting of a jumper on one of the $3\frac{1}{2}$ inch drives that I had installed. It seemed to work fine but if I typed DIR, it would display the directory of whatever disk that was in the drive. If I removed that disk, inserted another, and did another DIR, it would display the same directory from the first disk. The other drive on my system worked fine, so I knew something was wrong with the new drive. I finally found that one of the jumpers had not been set to the usual factory default setting.

The documentation that comes with most of the drives and other components is often very poorly written and organized, and you might have trouble understanding it. Your dealer might not be able to help you, especially if you bought it from a mail-order house. This is a good reason why you should belong to a good user group if possible. Such a group can be a tremendous help if you have problems.

Step 2: Install Expansion Frame if Necessary   All of the older cases had bays for the $5\frac{1}{4}$ inch drives. The $3\frac{1}{2}$ inch drives are much smaller than the old standard $5\frac{1}{4}$ inch. Many of the newer cases have small bays or provisions for mounting the $3\frac{1}{2}$ inch drives. If you have an older case, you might need to buy an expansion bracket that allows the drive to be mounted in any standard $5\frac{1}{4}$ inch drive bay. An expansion bracket might cost from $3.00 to $5.00. You should determine what type of case you have and order the expansion bracket at the same time you order the drive.

Usually, four screws mount the drive to the bracket. For some of the older cases, you might have to install plastic or metal slide rails on each side of the bracket assembly.

Step 3: Remove the Cover   You are now ready to install the drive in the system. The first thing to do, of course, is to unplug the power. If you have one of the older standard cases, remove the cover by removing each of the screws in the four corners of the back panel. There is usually one more screw in the top center of the back panel. Slip the cover off. If you have one of the tower-type cases, there are usually three screws on the back along each side. The edges of the front part of the cover fit under the panel. Remove the screws from the back, then pull the cover back slightly and lift it off.

Once the cover is off, make a rough diagram of the cables and how and where they are connected. Pay close attention to the position of the colored wire on each ribbon cable. Now you can remove your old drives. If you are going to use the same controller, leave the cable plugged into it.

Step 4: Mount the Drives   Mount the drives in the chassis. If the drives are not to be mounted with slide rails, there are several holes on the sides of the drives and the bay. Line the holes up and insert the screws. Make sure that you use only the proper screws. If they are too long, they could damage the drive.

Don't over tighten the screws. The metal is very soft and it is very easy to strip the threads.

Step 5: Reconnect Cables   The flat ribbon cable to the drives should have three connectors. The connector on one end will have a split and twist in some of the wires. This connector goes to drive A:. Figure 7-8 shows the ribbon connector with the split already connected to the A: drive. The connector in the middle will go to the B: drive, as shown in Fig. 7-9, if you have two floppy drives. The one that gets the connector on the end with the twist will be drive A:. The middle connector goes to the B: drive, and the connector on the other end plugs into the controller card or upright pins if the motherboard has a built-in controller.

Caution: The connectors can be plugged in backwards. Note that the edge connector on the drives will have a narrow slit between contacts

Fig. 7-8
The floppy disk ribbon cable will have a split and twist on the end connector. This connector will go to whatever drive is to be A:Drive. The photo shows the power connector being inserted.

Fig. 7-9
The ribbon cable will have a connector in the middle that will go to the B:Drive if you have one. This cable has connectors for the edge-type connection that is being used, or for the pin type.

2 and 3. That end of the board has contact number 1, the colored wire on the ribbon cable that goes to pin 1 of the connector. You might also see a number etched on the board. All of the even numbers of the contacts are on top of the board, and the odd numbers are on the back. You might see a small number 2 near the narrow slit and a 34 on the other end.

The drive shown in Fig. 7-10 is a combination of both $5\frac{1}{4}$ and $3\frac{1}{2}$ drives, so there is only one cable connection. With the configuration shown, this will make the $5\frac{1}{4}$ inch drive the boot drive. To make the $3\frac{1}{2}$ inch drive the boot drive, just connect the middle connector here. Or there are a set of small white jumpers that can be set to configure the drives almost any way that you want to. It is up to you to decide which one to make drive A: or drive B:. The $5\frac{1}{4}$ inch drive is practically obsolete, so you probably should attach the middle connector so that the $3\frac{1}{2}$ inch drive is the A:drive.

The power to the drives is a four-wire cable from the power supply. This cable can only be plugged in one way. Refer to Fig. 7-8.

The $3\frac{1}{2}$ inch and the combination drives use the miniature power connector. The miniature connector is shown in Fig. 7-10. The newer power supplies come with miniature connectors. If you have an older supply, you will have to use an adapter. You can always buy one at your local computer store for about $3.

After you have installed your drives, try them out before you replace the cover. Format a blank disk, write a file to it, then read it back. It should work fine.

Fig. 7-10

A combination drive. Plugging in the connector with the twist makes the $5\frac{1}{4}$ inch drive the A:Drive. To make the $3\frac{1}{2}$ drive the A:Drive, plug in the middle connector. I recommend making the $3\frac{1}{2}$ inch drive the A:Drive. The $5\frac{1}{4}$ inch drive is practically obsolete.

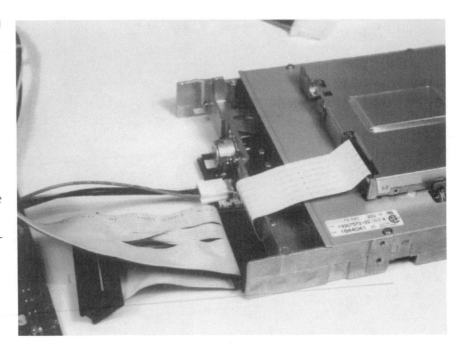

Choosing and Installing a Hard Disk

Large books have been written about hard disks, but even a whole book cannot cover all of the questions that you might have about hard disks. Because hard disk drives are such an important part of your system, this is one of the longest chapters in the book. This chapter covers some hard drive basics, some of the different types of hard drives, and how to install them in the computer. This chapter also explains how to format and configure hard disks once they are installed.

The IBM term for hard disk drives is *direct access storage devices* (DASD, pronounced Dazdee). The hard drives are also called *Winchester* drives. The IBM plant that developed the first hard drives is located near the Winchester House in San Jose, California. The house was built by the widow of the famous inventor of the Winchester 30-30 repeating rifle. The first IBM hard disk had 30 tracks and 30 sectors per track. Because the IBM system was a 30/30, someone hung the name Winchester on it. You don't hear it too often nowadays, but for several years all hard drives were called Winchester drives.

Floppy and Hard Drive Similarities

A hard disk drive is similar to a floppy disk drive in some ways. Floppy drives have a single disk, the hard drives have an assembly of one or more rigid disks. The hard disks platters are coated with a magnetic plating, similar to that of the floppy disks. Depending on the capacity, there can be several disks on a common spindle. A motor turns the floppy spindle at 300 RPMs; the hard disk spindle might turn from 3600 RPMS up to 10,000 RPMs.

There is a read/write head on the top and one on the bottom of each disk. On floppy disk systems, the head actually contacts the disk; on a hard disk system, the head "flies" just a few millionths of an inch from the disk on a cushion of purified air. If the head contacts the disk at the high speed that it turns, it would causes a "head crash." A crash can destroy the disk, the head, and all the data that might be on the disk.

Tracks and Sectors

Like the floppy disk, the hard disk is formatted into several individual concentric tracks. A 360K floppy has 40 tracks on each side; a high-capacity hard disk might have 3000 or more tracks. Also like the floppy, each hard disk track is divided into sectors, usually of 512 bytes. But the 360K floppy system divides each track into nine sectors; a hard disk system might divide each track into as many as 84 sectors.

Clusters and Allocation Units

A sector is only 512 bytes, but most files are much longer than that, so DOS lumps two or more sectors together and calls it a *cluster* or *allocation unit*. If an empty cluster is on track 5, the system will record as much of the file as it can there, then move to the next empty cluster, which could be on track 20. DOS combines sectors into allocation units depending on the capacity of the hard disk. For a 100Mb disk DOS combines four sectors, or 2048 bytes, into each allocation unit; for 200Mb, each allocation unit is composed of eight sectors or 4096 bytes.

File Allocation Table

The location of each part of the file and which cluster it is in is recorded in the file allocation table (FAT) so the computer has no trouble finding it. Usually the larger the hard disk partition, the more sectors are assigned to each cluster or allocation unit.

A 500Mb hard disk would actually have 524,288,000 bytes. Dividing this number by 512 bytes to find the number of actual sectors gives 1,024,000 sectors. If each allocation unit is made up of four sectors, there would only be 256,000 of them; if eight sectors are used, then DOS would only have to worry about the location of 128,000 allocation units. If DOS had to search through 1,024,000 entries in the FAT each time it accessed the hard disk, it would slow things down considerably. The FAT is updated and rewritten each time the disk is accessed. A large FAT would take a lot of time and disk space.

I have a 500Mb hard disk that is divided into three logical disks: a 100Mb and two 200Mb. The 100Mb uses four sectors per allocation unit, so it has 51,219 clusters or allocation units. The 200Mb uses eight sectors per allocation unit, so they each have 51,283 allocation units, about the same number as the 100Mb disk.

The FAT is very important. If it is damaged or erased, you cannot access any of the data on the disk. The heads wouldn't know where to look for the data. The FAT is usually written on track 0 of the hard disk. Because it is so important, a second copy is also made near the center of the disk so that if the original is damaged, it is possible to use the copy.

Cylinders

Just like the floppy, each same numbered track on the top and bottom of a disk is called a *cylinder*. Because a hard disk might have up to ten or more platters, the concept of cylinders is even more realistic. Incidentally some of the BIOS chips in some of the older computers might not allow you to install a hard disk that has more than 1024 cylinders and 63 sectors, which is about 504Mb. It is possible to install a disk larger than 500Mb by using special driver software.

Head Actuators or Positioners

Like the floppy, a head motor or head actuator, moves the heads from track to track. The head actuator must move the heads quickly and accurately to a specified track then detect the small variations in the magnetic fields in the specified sectors. Some of the less expensive and older hard disks use a stepper motor similar to those used on floppy disk drives to move the head from track to track. Most newer hard disks use a voice coil type of motor, which is much smoother, quieter, and faster than the stepper motors.

The voice coil of a loudspeaker is made up of a coil of wire wound on a hollow tube that is attached to the material of the speaker cone. Permanent magnets are then placed inside and around the outside of the coil. Whenever a voltage is passed through the coil of wire, it causes magnetic lines of force to build up around the coil. Depending on the polarity of the input voltage, these lines of magnetic flux will be either the same or opposite as the lines of force of the permanent magnets. If the polarity of the voltage, for instance a plus voltage, causes the lines of force to be the same as the permanent magnet, then they will repel each other and the voice coil might move forward. If they are opposite, they will attract each other and the coil will move backwards.

Most of the better and faster hard disks use voice coil technology with a closed loop servo control. They usually use one surface of one of the disks to store data and track locations. Most specification sheets give the number of heads on a drive. If you see one that has an odd number of heads such as 5, 7, or 9, it uses the other head and disk surface for servo information. Because all the heads are on the same spindle, they all move as one. When the servo head moves to a certain track and sector, the other heads follow. Feedback information from the closed servo loop positions the head to the exact track very accurately.

Figure 8-1 shows a Seagate hard drive with the cover removed to show the heads and disks. The voice coil actuator is the section in the top-left corner of the drive. It can quickly and accurately swing the arm and head to any track on the disk. Each platter has a head on the top and bottom just like the one on top.

Speed of Rotation and Density

As the disk spins beneath the head, a pulse of voltage through the head will cause the area of the track that is beneath the head at that time to become magnetized. If this pulse of voltage is turned on for a certain

Fig. 8-1
A Seagate hard drive with the cover removed. The head is on the end of the arm. The voice coil actuator in the left upper corner moves the head back and forth over the spinning disk platter. There is a head on the top and bottom of each platter. all of them move together.

amount of time, then turned off for some amount of time, it can represent the writing or recording of 1s and 0s. The hard disk spins much faster than a floppy, so the duration of the magnetizing pulses can be much shorter at a higher frequency.

The recording density depends to a great extent on the changes in magnetic flux. The faster the disk spins, the greater the number of changes. This allows much more data to be recorded in the same amount of space. Most hard disks spin at a rate between 3600 to 7200 RPMs. Seagate's Cheetah spins at 10,000 RPMs. They have two models, a 1-inch high model with four platters has a capacity of 4.55Gb. A 1.6-inch high model with eight platters has a capacity of 9.1Gb. The Quantum Atlas is also 1.6 inches high and has a capacity of 9Gb, but it has 10 platters. With the two extra platters, it should have more capacity than the Seagate, but the Quantum spins at 7200 RPM.

Areal density is the number of bits per inch times the number of tracks per inch. The areal density continues to be improved. At the present time, some manufacturers are achieving 1 billion bits per square inch. Within a couple of years it should reach 10 billion bits per square inch.

Timing

Everything that a computer does depends on precise timing. Crystals and oscillators are set up so that certain circuits perform a task at a specific time. These oscillating circuits are usually called *clock circuits*. The clock frequency for the old standard modified frequency modulation (MFM) method of reading and writing to a hard disk is 10 MHz per second. To write on the disk during one second, the voltage might turn on for a fraction of a second, then turn off for the next period of time, then back on for a certain length of time. The head sits over a track that is moving at a constant speed. Blocks of data are written or read during the precise timing of the system clock. Because the voltage must go plus or zero, that is two states, in order to write 1s and 0s, the maximum data transfer rate is only 5 megabits per second for MFM, just half of the clock frequency. The RLL systems transfer data at a rate of 7.5 megabits per second. Some of the ESDI drives have a transfer rate of 10 megabits per second or more. (Note that these figures are *bits*, remember that it takes eight bits to make one byte). The SCSI and IDE systems might have a transfer rate as high as 10 to 13 megabytes or more. So a SCSI or IDE system that can transfer 10 megabytes/second is eight times faster than a 10 megabit per second ESDI.

You have probably seen representations of magnetic lines of force around a magnet. The magnetized spot on a disk track has similar lines of force. To read the data on the disk, the head is positioned over the track and the lines of force from each magnetized area causes a pulse of voltage to be induced in the head. During a precise block of time, an induced pulse of voltage can represent a 1, the absence of an induced pulse can represent a 0.

Pulses of voltage through the head will cause a magnetic pulse to be formed which magnetizes the disk track. When reading the data from the track, the small magnetic changes on the recorded track causes voltage to be produced in the heads. It is a two-way system. Forcing voltage through the heads causes magnetism to be produced, bringing a magnetic field into the area of the head when reading can cause a voltage to be produced.

Head Spacing

The amount of magnetism that is placed on a disk when it is recorded is very small. It must be small so that it will not affect other recorded bits or tracks near it. Magnetic lines of force decrease as you move away from a magnet by the square of the distance. So it is desirable to have the heads as close to the disk as possible.

On a floppy disk drive, the heads actually contact the diskette. This causes some wear, but not very much because the rotation is fairly slow and the plastic disks have a special lubricant and are fairly slippery. However, heads of the hard disk systems never touch the disk. The fragile heads and the disk would be severely damaged if they made contact at a speed of 3,600 to 10,000 RPMs. The heads fly over the spinning disk just microinches above it. Hard disks are sealed and the air inside is purified. The air must be pure because the smallest speck of dust or dirt can cause the head to crash. You should never open a hard disk.

Disk Platters

The surface of the hard disk platters must be very smooth. Because the heads are only a few millionths of an inch, or microinches, away from the surface, any unevenness could cause a head crash. The hard disk platters are usually made from aluminum, which is nonmagnetic, and lapped to a mirror finish. They are then coated or plated with a magnetic material. Some companies are using tempered glass as a substrate for the platters.

The platters must also be very rigid so that the close distance between the head and the platter surface is maintained. The early $5\frac{1}{4}$ inch hard disks had to be fairly thick to achieve the necessary rigidity. Being thick, they were heavy and required a fairly large spindle motor and lots of wattage to move the large amount of mass.

If the platter is made smaller, it can be thinner and still have the necessary rigidity. If the disks are thinner, then more platters can be stacked in the same area. The smaller disks also need less power and smaller motors. With smaller diameter disks, the heads don't have to travel as far between the outer and inner tracks. This improves the access time tremendously.

You should avoid any sudden movement of the computer or any jarring while the disk is spinning, because it could cause the head to crash onto the disk and damage it. Most of the newer hard disk systems automatically move the heads away from the read/write surface to a parking area when the power is turned off.

Physical Sizes

One of the first hard drives I ever owned was a full-height 10Mb drive. Full height meant that it was over $3\frac{3}{4}$ inches high, 6 inches wide, and 8 inches deep. The original full-height floppies were the same size. Later, they developed half-height drives for both hard drives and floppies.

The drives were physically large and clunky and operated at a very slow 100ms. They were also expensive. A 20Mb hard disk cost as much as $2500. And that was back in the days when $2500 was worth about three times what it is today. You can buy a 2Gb hard disk today for less than $200. A modern 2Gb drive is only 1 inch high, 4 inches wide, and 6 inches deep, yet it has 100 times greater storage capacity, operates ten times faster at about 10ms, and is $2300 less expensive than a large 20Mb was ten years ago. If you weren't around in those early days, you can't begin to appreciate the advances in the technology. We have come a long way.

How They Can Make Smaller Drives

One of the reasons they can make the hard disks smaller now is because they have developed better plating materials, thinner disks, better motors, and better electronics.

Zone Bit Recording

There are several reasons why the old hard drives were physically so much larger than the newer drives. The old MFM drives divided each track into 17 sectors. A track on the outer edge of a $5\frac{1}{4}$ inch platter would be over 15 inches long if it were stretched out. You can determine this by using the simple math formula for pi times the diameter. So pi or 3.14159 × 5.25 is 16.493 inches in length. A track on the inner portion of the disk might only be 1.5 inches times pi, or 4.712 inches in length. The MFM system divided each track into 17 sectors, no matter whether it was 16 inches long or only four inches long.

It is obvious that you should be able to store more data in the outer, longer tracks than in the short, inner tracks. That is exactly what the newer drives do. One reason the newer drives can be made so much smaller with so much more capacity is that they use zone bit recording (ZBR). The platters are divided up into different zones depending on the area of the disk platter. The inner tracks which are shorter might have relatively few sectors. There is an increased number of sectors per track toward the outer and longer tracks.

Rotational Speed and Recording Density

The recording density or bits per inch (bpi) for each zone changes from the inner tracks to the outer tracks. The reason for this is that the speed at which the inner tracks pass beneath the heads is faster than that of the outer tracks.

The overall drive speed is still another way of increasing the amount of storage. The old MFM drives spun at 3600 RPMs. The newer drives have a rotational speed of 6,300 up to 10,000 RPMs or more. One big factor in the amount of data that can be recorded in a given area is the frequency of the changing zeros and ones and the speed of the disk. The higher the speed of the disk, the higher the recording frequency can be.

The rotational speed of the disk is also one of the factors that determines the seek, access, and transferal time. If you want to access data on a certain track, the faster the disk rotates, the sooner that sector will be available for reading. Hard disk technology has improved tremendously over the last ten years.

Choosing a Hard Drive

You have the option of a very large number of different types and capacities of disks to choose from. Of course what you choose will depend on what you need to do with your computer and how much you want to spend.

Capacity

When you consider capacity, buy the biggest you can afford. You might have heard of Mr. C. Northcote Parkinson. After observing business organizations for some time, he formulated several laws. One law says, "Work expands to fill up available employee time." A parallel law that paraphrases Mr. Parkinson's immutable law might say, "Data expands to fill up available hard disk space."

Just a short time ago, 200Mb was a large disk. But that was before Microsoft and other companies began developing bloatware programs that required 80Mb or more. Don't even think of buying anything less than 1Gb. Better yet would be 2Gb minimum. New software programs have become more and more friendly and offer more and more options. Most of the basic application programs that you will need, such as spreadsheets, databases, CAD programs, word processors, and many others, will each require 40 to 80 megabytes of disk storage space. Office 97 requires about 120 megabytes.

Most of the major hard disk drives are fairly close in quality and price. My recommendation is to buy the highest capacity drive that you can possibly afford. I have just bought a 3.5Gb hard disk drive for $215. That is about six cents per megabyte. That is absolutely fantastic. Just two years ago I paid $750 for a 1.05Gb hard drive. I would not have believed that it was possible for a precision piece of machinery like this to be sold for any less.

Speed or Access Time

Speed or *access time* is the time it takes a hard disk to locate and retrieve a sector of data. This includes the time that it takes to move the head to the track, settle down, and read the data. For a high-end, very fast disk, this might be as little as 9 milliseconds (Ms). Some of the older drives and systems required as much as 100 Ms. An 85-Ms hard drive might have been fine for an old slow XT. A 9-Ms drive might not be fast enough for a Pentium II. Some of the newer drives have an access time of less than 6 Ms.

Types of Drives

Here is a brief overview of some of the old, obsolete drives for those who might still own them. I do not expect many people to be installing the old MFM type drives. After all, that would be a downgrade, not an upgrade. Even if someone offers to give you an old MFM type drive, I would recommend that you install a newer IDE or SCSI type instead. Here are some of the factors that should influence your decision:

MFM

The modified frequency modulation (MFM) system is an early standard method for disk recording. In the early 1980s, Seagate Technology developed the ST506/412 interface for MFM, and it became the standard. This method formats several concentric tracks on a disk like those laid down on a floppy diskette. The MFM systems divide the tracks into 17 sectors per track, with 512 bytes in each sector. They usually have a transfer rate of five megabits per second. The MFM method can be used with drives from 5Mb up to several hundred megabytes.

The older MFM drives are rugged and reliable, but they are physically large, slow, and limited in capacity. Like the 360K and 720K drives, they are as obsolete as the Model T Ford. But like the Model T Ford, the old MFM drives will get you there if you have the time and don't need much capacity.

The head actuator used in most of the MFM drives is a stepper motor. It makes a loud clunking noise as it steps the heads in discrete movements from track to track. Some people like this feature, because they can hear that something is happening. Many of the newer hard drives have voice coil type head actuators, which make very little noise as they move smoothly from track to track. It might be difficult to determine if anything is happening unless you look at the disk activity LED on the front panel.

Because the MFM drives are obsolete, no major companies are manufacturing them now. About the only place to find one of the old drives is at a company that rebuilds and refurbishes hard drives. Even a refurbished MFM drive will cost almost as much as a new IDE drive with three or four times more capacity.

RLL

The run length limited (RLL) system is a modification of the MFM ST412 system. The RLL drives, when used with a RLL controller, formats the disk to 26 sectors per track. This allows the storage of 50% more data than the 17 sectors per track on an MFM drive. For instance, a 20Mb could store 30Mb; a 40Mb could store 60Mb. They have a transfer rate of 7.5 megabits, 50% faster than MFM. Not all drives are capable of running RLL. Seagate used an R after the model number to denote the RLL drives.

Except for being just a bit faster and being able to store 50% more data, the RLL drives were about the same as the MFM types. These drives are obsolete.

ESDI

The enhanced small device interface (ESDI, pronounced ezdy) is another modification of the MFM system. Most of the ESDI drives were usually over 100Mb, a very large capacity at that time. Today 100Mb is much too small.

ESDI drives could be formatted to 34 sectors or more per track, so they can store more than twice as much data as the 17 sectors of standard MFM. They had a fairly fast access speed, usually 15 to 18 ms, and a data transfer rate of 10 to 15 megabits or more per second.

Controllers

When the computer commands that data be read or written to the hard disk, the heads are quickly moved to the proper tracks and sectors. One reason the early MFM type drives were so slow is that the electronics in the controller board were not able to keep up with the disk. Many of them used a system of reading a sector into the controller electronics, then skipped the next several sectors while the electronics digested the data it had just received. The data was then passed on and the controller was free to accept more data. The systems would read one sector, then let two, three, or as many as six sectors pass before reading another sector. This was called *interleaving*. Of course an interleave of 2:1 was much faster than an interleave of 6:1. The interleave had to be set when the drive was low-level formatted. Controllers were usually made by companies other than the ones who manufactured the hard drives. Some controllers performed better than others; some hard drives performed better than others. If the interleave was set too high, it could cause errors; if too low, then you would have a performance penalty in wasted time. It was often difficult to find the optimum interleave. In the late 1980s, new controllers were developed that allowed interleaving of 1:1 on most MFM hard drives.

The hard disk controllers also act as interfaces to the computer. Whenever any device is attached to a computer, it must go through some sort of interface, port, or I/O device. The edge connector of the plug-in controller boards connect to specific contacts on the bus. These contacts provide voltage signals that control the disk head actuators. The controller also makes contact with the bus data signal lines which transfers the data to the proper area.

The newer IDE and SCSI hard drives have built-in controller electronics on board. You no longer have to worry about low-level formatting and interleave settings, but you still need an interface between the hard drive and the computer. The IDE interface and the SCSI host adapters are discussed later in this chapter.

Adding a Second MFM or RLL Type Hard Disk Drive

If you are using an older hard disk, you are probably running out of disk space. If you only have one hard disk, you can add another one. If you are considering adding another hard disk, you should get one that is the same type as what you already have. This might be a problem if it is an old MFM or RLL type because they are no longer manufactured.

I do not recommend this type of upgrade, but if you insist, here are some instructions. If you are able to find an older MFM or RLL hard disk, it is fairly simple to install it. You should have a 34-pin flat ribbon cable that is similar to the floppy disk cable. It should have a connector in the center such as the one on the floppy cable. Plug it in so that the red or colored wire on the edge of the cable goes to pin one on the drive. You will also have a 20-wire ribbon cable for the data lines. Make sure that it is plugged in so that the side of the cable with the colored wire goes to pin one. Plug the other end of this cable into the controller board. Again, make sure that pin one and the colored wire are in agreement.

You might have to install jumpers on a set of pins to tell the system that this is a second drive. The pins are often located near the rear of the drive close to the edge connectors for the ribbon cables. In Fig. 8-2, the pen points to the pins for drive number configuration. There might be designations on the board for the pins such as DS0 or DS1. The first hard drive is called drive 0; the second drive is drive 1. Some hard disk 34-wire ribbon cables have a twist near the end connector that is similar to the twist in the floppy drive cables. (Although the cables are similar to the floppy cables, they are not interchangeable because different wires are twisted.) If the cable has a twist, then both drive 0 and drive 1 are jumpered as drive 0. If the cable is straight through for both connectors, then one drive is jumpered as drive 0, the other as drive 1. Check your documentation.

Fig. 8-2
The pen points to pins that must be jumpered to config-ure the drive a master or slave. This is a Max-tor drive. Pin location on other drives may be different.

Terminating Resistors

The hard drives have small resistor plug-in packs that are used for termination. Terminating resistors help to balance the electronic circuits on the disk drives. You only need one terminating resistor pack. The resistor pack should be removed from the second hard disk, or the one on the middle connector. The terminating resistor pack should be left in place on the first drive or the one on the end connector. The terminator is actually a group of eight small resistors. Different companies used different configurations, but most commonly, the pack is a flat package with pins that plug into a socket. Check your documentation for the location of the resistor pack. Once the drive is installed, it might need to be low-level and high-level formatted.

A Better Upgrade

Rather than installing a second obsolete MFM or RLL drive, a much better upgrade would be to install a fairly high-capacity SCSI or EIDE drive.

IDE or AT Type Drives

The most popular drives today are those with integrated drive electronics (IDE). They are sometimes called ATA (for advanced technology attachment) drives because they were first developed for use on the 286 AT. The drives are similar to the SCSI drives in that all of their controller electronics are integrated on the drive. You do not need a controller card, such as those required by the older MFM, RLL, and ESDI drives, but you do need an interface. The interface might be a plug-in card or it might be a set of upright pins on the motherboard.

Enhanced IDE ATA-2

The BIOS in some systems cannot recognize a hard disk with more than 1024 cylinders, so most of the early IDE drives were no greater than 504Mb. An ANSI committee developed a new set of standards for both the IDE and SCSI devices. The new enhanced IDE ATA-2 standard is able to go beyond 1024 cylinder limitation up to 8Gb.

If you are trying to install a large IDE hard disk on an older machine, your system BIOS might not recognize the larger capacity IDE drive. Your vendor might be able to supply you with software drivers. You could install it as a 500Mb with 1024 cylinders, but if you are installing a 1Gb drive, you are wasting half of it. You could determine what company made your BIOS then contact them for an upgrade. But don't be surprised if the cost of the upgrade BIOS would be more than what you would pay for a complete new motherboard with a new BIOS. The major BIOS manufacturers are American Megatrends Inc. (AMI), Award, and Phoenix. A fairly new BIOS company is Microid Research or MR BIOS. Most of these companies will not sell you an upgrade. You will have to go back to vendor or to a distributor.

The *Computer Shopper* is one of the largest magazines in size and in circulation. It usually has about 1000 large tabloid size pages with thousands of ads. A recent issue had only one ad for BIOS upgrade chips. That one company was the Unicore Company at 800-800-2467. The Unicore Company also has a web site at www.unicore.com.

The new enhanced IDE ATA-2 is somewhat similar to SCSI. It can support up to four devices, including CD-ROM and tape drives. Of course these drives will have to be designed to operate off the EIDE interface. The new specification allows data transfer up to 13.3 megabytes per second. The older IDE specification had a transfer rate of 4.3 megabytes per second.

Installation Configuration

If you are only installing a single IDE drive, the installation might be very simple. The drive should have jumpers set at the factory that make it drive #1 or master drive. Check your documentation and the jumpers, then just plug the 40-pin cable into the drive connector and the other end into a board interface or into a set of pins on the motherboard. You must make sure that the colored side of the ribbon cable goes to pin one on the drive and on the interface.

If you are installing a second IDE drive you might have some problems. You will need to set some jumpers so that the system will know which drive to access. When two IDE drives are installed, the IDE system uses the term *master* to designate the C: or boot drive and the term *slave* to designate the second drive. You will have to set the small jumpers to configure the drives. The drives usually come from the factory configured as a single drive. If the drives are not configured properly, you will get an error message that might tell you that you have a hard disk or controller failure. You will not be able to access the drives.

There were no standards as to how the early IDE drives should be configured. Different manufacturers used different designations and sometimes different functions for the pins. So it might be difficult, or even impossible, to install and configure two of the early IDE drives in a system. If you have one of the early IDE drives and decide to install a second drive, try to get one that matches your first drive, or at least a drive that is made by the same company.

Later a group of IDE manufacturers got together and agreed on an IDE standard specification. They called the specification common access method AT attachment or CAM ATA. Almost all IDE drives now conform to this specification. You should have very little trouble connecting drives made by different companies, or drives of different capacities, if they conform to the CAM ATA specifications.

Most later models have three sets of pins for jumpers to configure the drive as a single drive, for a master and slave, or for a slave. The pins might have a marking such as DS, SS, or SP.

Some of the early Conner IDE drives, such as the 100Mb CP3104, used the designation ACT, C/D, and DSP for the pins. For a single drive, ACT and C/D must be jumpered. For a master and slave drive, jumper ACT, C/D, and DSP on the master and remove all jumpers from the slave.

Some early Conner IDE drives such as the CP3204 used pin designations E-1 and E-2. For a single drive, jumper pins E-2, for a master, jumper E-1 and E-2, and remove all jumpers from the slave.

Some of the older Seagate IDE drives such as the ST1057A, ST1102A, and ST1144A have numbered jumpers. Pins 3 and 4 are jumpered for the master and pins 5 and 6 are jumpered if a slave is present. You might have trouble with these drives, and some other drives, if you try to install them in a machine that has an older BIOS. An older BIOS might be one that was made before 1990.

Some drives have pins that can be jumpered so that they will be read only. This is a type of write protection that is similar to write protecting a floppy. This could be used on a hard disk that had data that should never be changed or written over.

You should have received some documentation with your drive. In Fig. 8-2 the pen points to the small configuration jumper pins on a Maxtor drive. Your drive might be different. If you don't have the configuration information, call the company or dealer. Most all companies now have websites. Most of the websites have e-mail addresses of the various departments within the company. Here are some addresses and websites:

Conner
URL: www.conner.com
Tech support phone: 408-438-8222
Tech support fax: 408-438-8137
Fax back support: 408-438-2620
Automated support: 800-732-4283
Conner Peripherals is now a subsidiary of Seagate.

Fujitsu
URL: www.fcpa.com
Tech support phone: 800-626-4686
Fax back support: 408-428-0456

Maxtor
URL: www.maxtor.com
Tech support phone: 800-2-Maxtor
or 800-262-9867
Tech support fax: 303-678-2260
E-mail: Technical
Assistance@Maxtor.com

Micropolis
URL: www.micropolis.com
Tech support phone: 818-709-3325
Tech support fax: 818-709-3408

Fax Back Support: 800-395-3748
E-mail Support: tom˜earthlink.net

Quantum
URL: www.quantum.com
Tech support phone: 800-826-8022
Tech support fax: 408-894-3282
Fax back support: 800-434-7532

Samsung Electronics America
URL: www.samsung.co.kr
Tech support phone: 800-726-7864
Fax back support: 800-229-2239

Seagate
URL: www.seagate.com
Tech support phone: 408-438-8222
Tech support fax: 408-438-8137
Fax back support: 408-438-2620
Automated support: 800-732-4283

Western Digital
URL: www.wdc.com
Tech support phone: 507-286-7900
Fax back support: 714-932-4300

I mentioned earlier that I had bought a 3.5Gb Maxtor drive at a swap meet. I paid $215 for model 83500A. Figure 8-3 is a photo of the drive beside an early, much larger 40Mb MFM drive. It is absolutely amazing that the much smaller drive can store 87.5 times more than the large one. It is also about ten times faster than the large one.

The vendor didn't give me any documentation so I went to the Maxtor URL, www.maxtor.com, and downloaded the information about this drive and several others in this model family.

Several other companies also provide information about their drives similar to that given by Maxtor. This information is listed as an example of what you might find.

Fig. 8-3
An early Seagate 40Mb MFM drive on the left. On the right is a Maxtor 3.5Gb IDE drive. The small drive can store 87.5 times more than the large drive and is ten times faster. The large drive cost $479 a few years ago when money was worth about twice what it is now. The small drive cost $215.

The Maxtor website has similar information about all of their drives, even those that were made a few years ago. Most of the other websites also have similar information and technical support for their drives.

IDE Interface Board

Almost all motherboards made today have the EIDE drive interface, floppy disk drive interface, COM ports, and printer ports built in. If you are trying to upgrade a system that has an older motherboard, you might have to buy an interface board.

The IDE drives need only a very inexpensive interface to connect with the bus. Figure 8-4 shows the drive connected to a VLB IDE interface card. It is also a multi input/out (I/O) card. It has an interface for the IDE drives, a floppy disk controller, parallel printer ports, and two serial ports. An IDE interface/multi I/O card can be plugged into any of the

Fig. 8-4
A hard drive connected to an IDE VLB interface board. It is also a multifunction input/output (I/O) board.

eight slots. I try to install the board as close to the drives as possible so that the cables won't be draped over other boards.

When plugging the connector into the pins for the floppy and hard drives, be very careful that you locate pin one on the board and plug the cable in so that the colored wire goes to the pin-one side. If you plug the cable in backwards, you could possibly damage some of the built-in electronics on the hard disk.

The IDE drives are a bit less expensive than the SCSI. One major difference is that the IDE interface might cost nothing because it is usually built-in on all new motherboards.

SCSI

Most companies who manufacture IDE drives also make identical SCSI drive models. The built-in electronics on the two drives are very similar, except one has an SCSI adapter. SCSI means small computer system interface. It is called small computer because when it was first proposed, the big iron mainframes ruled the computer world. However the desktop PCs were proliferating and there was a real need to be able to connect various peripherals to these PCs. It was a very ambitious undertaking.

There wasn't even a standard among the PCs at that time. You can imagine the problems in trying to devise a standard that would work with several nonstandard machines. In addition this standard would have to work with several different peripherals from different companies. Devices that conform to the SCSI standard have most of their controller functions built into the device.

A SCSI board can interface up to seven different intelligent devices to a computer. SCSI devices are called *logical units*. Each device is assigned a logical unit number (LUN). The devices have switches or jumpers that must be set to the proper LUN.

The different devices might be two or more hard SCSI type hard disk drives, one or more CD-ROM drives, a scanner, a tape backup up unit, or other scuzzy products.

Besides handling up to seven scuzzy products, many of the early interface boards also had a built-in controller for two floppy drives. This sometimes caused problems if you had another floppy controller board or a built-in floppy interface. If both of the controllers were configured to be on, then neither would work. Any time you have two utilities that are the same, you must disable one or the other. Usually there are jumpers that can be used to enable or disable a utility. Figure 8-5 shows a SCSI drive cable being connected to a SCSI interface. Note the elevation on the connector. It fits in a slot on the shell of the board connector so that it can only be plugged in properly. Not all cable connectors have this feature. Most hard drive manufacturers do not manufacture controllers. In many cases, you buy a drive from one manufacturer, then buy a controller from another manufacturer. The IDE and SCSI drives have most of the disk controlling functions integrated onto the drive. This makes a lot of sense because the control electronics can be optimally matched to the drive. The electronics still require an interface card to transmit the data in 8-bit parallel back and forth to the disk, much like a parallel printer port. Because it can handle eight bits of data at a time, it can have very fast transfer rates. The MFM, RLL, and ESDI drives are serial systems and transfer data one bit at a time over the lines.

The equivalent SCSI and IDE hard drives made by most companies are physically the same size. They both use the same type of zone bit recording and rotational speed. The only difference in the two is the on-board electronics.

The SCSI systems need a host adapter, or interface card, to drive them. The SCSI interfaces are rather complex. Some of the older systems were very difficult to set up. Some of the newer systems are the plug 'n play (PNP) variety and are very easy to install.

Fig. 8-5
Connecting a SCSI cable to an interface board. Note the raised elevation on the connector. It fits in a slot on the connector shell so that it can only be plugged in properly. Not all connectors have this feature.

SCSI Drivers

Most hard drives require that you enter the drive type into the CMOS setup. The setup lists several drive types that describes the hard disk characteristics. The setup allows only two drives and they must be the same particular type such as two IDE, two ESDI, two RLL, or two MFM drives. But you can add up to 28 SCSI drives or devices along with the other two drives in your CMOS setup. The SCSI interface has its own drivers so it does not have to be entered into the CMOS setup. The SCSI interface is more properly a bus. An interface card can support up to seven different devices in a daisy chain. Up to four SCSI interface cards can be installed in a PC. Each interface, which is actually a SCSI device, can support up to seven other SCSI devices so that as many as 28 different devices could be attached. However, DOS would only let you install as many as 24 of these devices. You couldn't have more because that would use up all the letters in the alphabet. DOS reserves the letters A and B for floppies and C for the first hard disk. DOS can then assign the other 23 letters for additional hard drives, CD-ROMS, backup tape machines, scanners, and other SCSI devices.

A few years ago, SCSI did not seem to be very important to the ISA type world. The open ISA type PCs usually had enough slots to accomodate most needs. Besides, the SCSI devices were usually more expensive and there weren't that many products available. And most importantly, the SCSI standard was not well established or observed. It was often very difficult to install a SCSI device.

Times change. Now there are several good reasons to adopt the SCSI Standard. There have been several revisions to the SCSI standard. It is now quite easy to use. There are even plug-n-play systems available. There are now several good SCSI products available at a cost that is very close to IDE or other proprietary devices.

It was sometimes difficult to set up some of the early SCSI devices, especially if you were trying to daisy chain two different devices to a single interface. SCSI devices must have a special driver. Each of the manufacturers provided different drivers for their devices. Often the drivers from one company would not work with an interface from another company. You sometimes had to buy a separate SCSI interface to match the SCSI device. This served to defeat one of the better features of SCSI.

Advanced SCSI Programming Interface

Advanced SCSI programming interface (ASPI) is a set of standards that was first developed by the Adaptec Company. Adaptec has been one of the foremost companies in the design of SCSI products. The ASPI standard has been widely accepted by most other manufacturers. You still need a separate driver from each manufacturer for individual devices. These drivers are set up in your Config.Sys file, then the ASPI driver is installed in the Config.Sys. If the device drivers are software compatible to the ASPI specification, the ASPI driver then controls the other drivers. It is much easier to install SCSI devices that comply with the ASPI standard.

The Corel Company has one of the best drawing and graphics software programs available. Corel, at 800-836-7274, www.corel.com, has also developed one of the best programs for installing SCSI devices. CorelSCSI is ASPI software that supports hundreds of SCSI devices. It makes it very easy to daisy chain up to seven devices and install the device software drivers. CorelSCSI supports hard drives, removable hard drives, CD-ROM drives, CD-ROM Juke Boxes, DAT tape drives, QIC tape drives, WORM and magneto-optical hard drives, and other SCSI devices.

An industry committee designed another SCSI specification they called common access method (CAM). It was designed primarily for OS/2 applications.

Host Adapter Sources

You should be able to find several sources for SCSI host adapters or interfaces in computer magazine ads and in computer stores. One of the first companies to develop SCSI adapters was Adaptec at (408) 945-8600, www.adaptec.com. Future Domain at (714) 253-0400, was also in the forefront in developing SCSI adapters. Future Domain has now merged with Adaptec. They can supply needed driver software for almost all SCSI products along with their adapters.

There are many different manufacturers of SCSI host adapters and many different models. There are SCSI adapters for ISA, EISA, VLB, PCI, and MCA systems. Some adapters might have one or more megabytes of cache memory. Some adapters might have a built-in floppy controller on the board. There are also 8-bit, 16-bit, and 32-bit SCSI adapters. Many of the newer adapters are plug-n-play, which are very easy to install.

The price of the adapters can vary considerably. The price depends on factors such as brand name, amount of cache, built-in goodies, and if it is an 8-, 16-, or 32-bit bus.

Fast SCSI-2 and Wide SCSI-2

SCSI-1 as defined in 1986 is an 8-bit bus with a transfer rate of 5 MHz. In 1992, ANSI added the SCSI-2, which can allow data transfer rates up to 10MHz. It is backward compatible so that it can also support SCSI-1 devices.

Wide SCSI-2 is a 16-bit bus that allows twice as much data to be transferred. The transfer can be as high as 20 MHz, but few if any devices have been developed at this time that can achieve this high rate. This specification will also allow as many as 16 devices, counting the host adapter. The wide SCSI-2 will have a 68-pin connector.

SCSI ID

Because there might be up to seven devices attached to a host adapter, each device is given its own unique number. There is usually a set of jumpers or switches that can be set to assign a number to the unit. The lowest numbered units have priority. Ordinarily, the hard disk is given number 0, although you can assign any number to it that is not being used by another device. Figure 8-6 shows a SCSI CD-ROM drive being connected to a cable. To the left of the connector are several pins that can be used to configure the drive for whatever logical unit number (LUN) that you assign to it.

Cables and connectors

The standard SCSI cable is a 50-wire flat ribbon cable. The standard connectors are Centronics types, but some devices might have a small miniature connector. Most devices have two connectors in parallel for attaching and daisy chaining other devices. I have a Future Domain host adapter that has a miniature connector for external devices. In order to

Fig. 8-6
Connecting a cable to a SCSI CD-ROM drive. At the left of the connector are pins that can be shorted out to assign a logical unit number (LUN) to the drive.

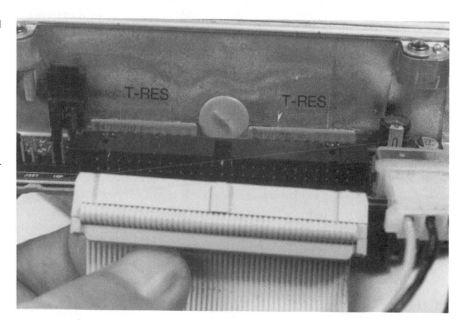

attach my Epson 800 Pro scanner, I had to buy a cable with the miniature connector on one end. It cost almost $40. I found out later that
there are adapters for this purpose that cost about $5.00. Try some of the
cable companies that advertise in the *Computer Shopper* and other computer magazines.

Not all of the 50 wires in a flat-ribbon cable are needed for data.
Many of the wires are ground wires placed between the data wires to
help keep the data from being corrupted. The better, and more expensive, cables are round cables with twisted and shielded wires. This type
of cable might be necessary for distances greater than six feet.

You should be aware that the advertised price of a SCSI device usually does not include an interface or cables. It might not even include
any software drivers. Be sure to ask about these items when you order a
SCSI device.

Frame Adapters

If you are upgrading an older computer and installing newer hard drives or $3\frac{1}{2}$ inch floppy drives, you might need to buy an expansion
frame adapter. The bays in the older computer cases were made for full-
height and half-height drives. There are inexpensive frames that you can
buy that allow installation of the smaller drives in a larger bay.

What to Buy: IDE or SCSI

If you can afford it, buy one or more of each. You can have up to four
IDE drives mounted internally all on one interface. Theoretically, you
could have up to 49 SCSI drives in a daisy chain, but DOS only allows
24. The letters A and B are reserved for floppies, but you might have
one hard disk for each of the other letters of the alphabet. This would
probably be a little more disk space than the average home office or
small business would need. But some large businesses need this much
and more.

At one time the IDE drives were limited to about 500Mb, but now it
seems that the sky is the limit. As much as 10Gb or more are now common capacities in both IDE and SCSI drives. One IDE and one SCSI

drive like this should be able to satisfy the needs of most home users and even small businesses.

One reason to have two or more drives is that one can be used to quickly back up critical data onto the other. It is not likely that both drives would fail at the same time. This can be a simple way to implement a RAID system. RAID is an acronym for Redundant Array of Inexpensive Disks. Most businesses that handle critical data use a RAID system of some sort.

IDE devices are mounted internally. SCSI drives can be mounted internally or externally. There are other SCSI devices that can be attached externally such as scanners.

Removable Disk Drives

There are several companies who manufacture removable disk drives. There are several different models and types. There are some advantages and disadvantages in removable drives.

SyQuest Drives   SyQuest, at 800-245-2278, www.syquest.com, has several models of hard disk drives with removable cartridges. Each cartridge is actually a single hard disk platter. Their Syjet has 1.5Gb cartridges. Their EZ230, as the name implies, uses 230Mb cartridges. I have one of their earlier models, EZ135, which uses 135Mb cartridges. It is great for back up, to transfer large files from one machine to another, and just general storage. The cartridges sold for about $20. The EZ135 has now been discontinued. They have different models of each unit so that they can be mounted internally, on SCSI, or externally through parallel ports. Figure 8-7 shows my EZ135.

Olympus MOS330E   The Olympus MOS330E, at 800-347-4027, www.olympus america.com, has a 3.5 inch magneto-optical drive system. It uses 230Mb cartridges. The cost of the drive is about the same as the Syquest, but the cartridges are very reasonable, at about $10 each.

Fujitsu DynaMO 230   The Fujitsu DynaMO 230, at 800-626-4686, www.fcpa.com, is a 230Mb magneto-optical drive. It is designed to be used in a PC Card type II slot. (The PC Card is the new name for the PCMCIA system.) This drive can be used with most laptops or any desktop that is equipped with the PC Card slots.

Fig. 8-7
My EZ135 drive that can be attached to the parallel printer port. It uses 135Mb cartridges. This model has been replaced by Syquest with a EZ230 that uses 230Mb cartridges.

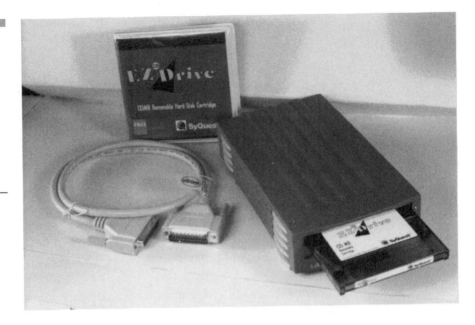

The Iomega Jaz Drive   The Iomega Jaz Drive from the Iomega Company, at 800-697-8833, www.iomega.com, is a drive that uses 1.07Gb magneto-optical cartridges. It is a SCSI device. If you have a laptop with SCSI, it can be plugged in externally. Cartridges are less than $100 each. The drive is very fast and great for backing up data.

The Iomega 100Mb Zip Floppy Disk and Drive   The Iomega Zip drive uses a 3 1/2 inch disk that is similar to a floppy. But this $3\frac{1}{2}$ inch disk can store 100Mb. This system is fairly inexpensive, but it is practically obsolete now.

Avatar Shark 250   The Avatar Shark 250, from the Avatar Peripherals, at 408-321-0110, www.goavatar.com, is as its name implies, a 250Mb drive. The main difference in the Shark 250 and other removable drives is its size. They advertise it as the world's smallest drive. The drive is $5\frac{1}{1}$ inches long and $3\frac{1}{2}$ inches wide. It weighs less than a half pound and the 250Mb $2\frac{1}{2}$ inch cartridge is about the size of a matchbook. It plugs into the parallel port. Unlike other paralell port drives, the Shark gets all the power that it needs from the parallel port, and does not need a separate power supply. It is great for desktops as well as laptops. Figure 8-8 shows the small Avatar Shark.

Parallel Port Hard Drives

Many of the drives just listed are available as parallel port models. As such, they can be used with laptops, PS/2s, or any computer with a parallel port. These drives are great for backup, for removal and security, and for data transport.

They come in several capacities from 100Mb up to 1Gb or more. They are great for backup or for adding a second hard drive. Because these drives plug into the computer's only parallel port, the hard drives usually provide a parallel port connector for the printer. Most of them come with a small transformer power supply.

Magneto-Optical Drives

The magneto-optical (M-O) drives are a combination of the magnetic and optical technologies. Magnetic disks, especially floppies, can be easily erased. Over a period of time, the data on a magnetic disk, hard or floppy, will gradually deteriorate. Some critical data must be renewed about every two years.

If a magnetic material has a high coercivity, or a high resistance to being magnetized, it will also resist being demagnetized. Coercivity is measured in oersteds (Oe). But the higher the Oe, the more current that

Fig. 8-8
The Avatar Shark 250. It can store 250Mb on a cartridge that is about the size of matchbook. It can be used with laptops or any other computer.

is needed to magnetize the area. A large amount of current might magnetize a large area of the disk. In order to pack more density, the magnetized area must be very small.

The Oe of a material decreases as it is heated. Most materials have a Curie temperature whereby the Oe might become zero. By heating the magnetic medium with a laser beam, a very small current can be used to write data to a disk. The heated spots cool very quickly and regain their high coercivity. The disks can be easily written over or changed by heating up the area again with the laser beam.

The most popular M-O drives at this time have a capacity of 128Mb and 256Mb. The M-O disks will have a minimum lifetime of more than ten years without degradation of data.

Recordable CD-ROMs

There are several companies who now offer drives that can record CD-ROM discs. When first introduced, the recordable drives cost up to $10,000. There are some that are available today for less than $3500. The CD-ROM blank disc can hold up to 600Mb of data. This is a great way to back up or archive data and records that should never change. However, the blank CD-ROM discs cost less than $20 each, so if you wanted to change some of the data, just change the data and record it onto another disc.

Unlike magnetic media that deteriorates or can be erased, data on a CD-ROM should last for many, many years. CD-ROMs are discussed in more detail in a later chapter.

WORMs

The write-once, read-many (WORM) type of drive is a laser system similar to the recordable CD-ROM. One difference is that it uses a larger disk and can store much more data. Another is that there are no standards for the system. Several companies manufacture proprietary systems that are incompatible with other systems. The WORM systems are also much more expensive than the CD-ROM systems.

Advantages of Removable Disk Drives

Here are some of the advantages of removable disks or cartridges:

Security   There might be data on a hard disk that is accessible to other people. If the data is sensitive data such as company design secrets or personal employee data the removable disks can be removed and locked up for security. After all, you wouldn't want anyone seeing just what salary the boss was getting or what his golf score might be.

Unlimited Capacity   With enough cartridges you will never have to worry about running out of disk space. If you fill one cartridge, just pop in another and continue.

Fast Backup   One reason people don't like to backup their data is that it is usually a lot of trouble and takes a lot of time, especially if you are using tape backup. It might take several hours to back up a large hard drive onto tape; it might take only seconds or minutes to backup the same data onto a removable drive. A big advantage of the removable cartridge backup is that the data can be randomly accessed; a tape backup can only be accessed sequentially. If you want a file that is in the middle of the tape, you must run through the tape to find it.

Moving Data to Another Computer   If you have two or more computer systems with the same type removable drives, you can easily transfer large amounts of data from one machine to another. It is possible to send the data on a cartridge through the mails to other locations that have the same type of system.

Multiple Users of One Software Copy   Most people don't bother to read the license agreements that come with software. Who can blame them. The agreements might be one or more pages long, in small type, and filled with lawyer-type jargon. Essentially, most of them simply say: You are granted the right to use one copy of the enclosed software on a single computer.

Suppose you have several computers in an office. Some of the people might be doing nothing but word processing most of the time. Others might be running databases or spreadsheets. Occasionally, these users might need to use one of the other programs for a short time. If these users all have standard hard disks, then legally, you need a separate copy of all of the software used on the computers. Some software programs cost $1000 or more. If you have several computers in an office, providing individual packages for each machine can be quite expensive.

If these computers had removable disks, then a copy of a software program could be installed on the cartridge and the cartridge could be used on the different machines.

Some Disadvantages of Removable Drives

Here are some of the disadvantages of removable disks or cartridges:

Limited Cartridge Capacity   Many of the removable cartridges have a capacity of only 100 to 250Mb. At one time that was a whole lot of storage space. But that might not be enough to store all of the data that you need to operate some of today's large programs. And according to Murphy's law, there will always be times when you need to access a file that is on another cartridge. If you only have one removable drive, it could be a problem. If that is a problem, because these are SCSI drives, you could install up to seven of them. Of course data compression can be used with all of the removable disks as easily as on hard disks.

Cost of Cartridges   Another disadvantage is that the removable drives cost a bit more than a standard hard drive. A cartridge might cost from $35 to over $100. But if you consider that, with enough cartridges, the capacity is unlimited, the cost might be quite reasonable. The M-O disks are about the least expensive of all the cartridges, but the initial cost of the drive itself is much higher than other drives.

Need for Accessible Bays   If you intend to buy an internal system with removable cartridges, you will need to access it from the front panel. If you have a system that has a limited number of bays that are accessible from the outside, it might be a problem. Some desktop cases only have four bays, two accessible bays for floppy disk drives and two internal bays for hard disks. If your system does not have enough bays, you might consider buying a larger case, perhaps a tower case. A case and power supply will cost from about $35 to over $100 for the large tower case with a 325-watt power supply. Many of the tower systems have from five to eight bays. It is very easy to transfer a system from one case to another. The main component to be transferred is the mother-board. Refer to Chapter 5 for motherboard installation.

The external drives with removable disks usually cost a bit more than the internally mounted drives. The extra cost is because of the need for the power supply and drive case.

Access Speed   Still another disadvantage is that some of the removable drives are a bit slower than most standard hard drives. The M-O drives are especially slow because it takes time to heat the area with the laser. But if you don't mind waiting a few milliseconds, it shouldn't be too much of a problem.

Data Compression   The capacity of all of the hard drives mentioned can be doubled by using data compression with them. Windows 95 comes with a utility called DriveSpace that can compress data on hard drives and on floppies. Before Windows 95, MS-DOS, IBM PC DOS, and DR DOS all had a disk compression utility. Stacker, from Stac Electronics, was one of the most popular stand-alone compression utilities. Microsoft and Stac Electronics are now partners. The DriveSpace utility is the result of that partnership. Using data compression is certainly inexpensive and easier than installing a second, or larger, hard disk. But as the cost of hard disk drives are now very reasonable. Rather than compress your data, you might sleep better at night if you install a larger hard disk.

Mean Time between Failures (MTBF)

Disk drives are mechanical devices. If used long enough, every disk drive will fail sooner or later. Manufacturers test their drives and assign them an average lifetime that ranges from 40,000 up to 150,000 hours. Of course, the larger the figure, the longer they should last (and the more they cost). These are average figures, much like the figures quoted for a human lifespan. The average man should live to be about 73 years old. But some babies die very young, and some men live to be over 100. Likewise, some hard disks die very young, some older ones become obsolete before they wear out.

I have difficulty in accepting some of the manufacturer's MTBF figures. For instance, to put 150,000 hours on a drive, it would have to be used 8 hours a day, every day, for over 51 years. If they operated a drive for 24 hours a day, 365 days a year, it would take over 17 years to put 150,000 hours on it. Because hard drives have only been around about ten years, I am pretty sure that no one has ever done a 150,000 hour test on a drive.

Near Field Technology

The TeraStor Company of San Jose is working on a new technology called near field recording. It combines facets of the magneto-optical technology and standard hard disk technology. It will be able to store over 20Gb on a plastic disk about the size of a CD-ROM. TeraStor is at 408-324-2110. They have a website at www.terastor.com.

Hardware Installation of Hard Disk Drives

The following are steps to install a hard disk. If you are installing a hard disk in one of the older cases, you might have to buy an expansion frame. The bays in the older cases were made for $5\frac{1}{4}$ inch drives. Most of the drives sold today are the $3\frac{1}{2}$ inch size. Most of the newer cases have bays for the $3\frac{1}{2}$ size drives. If you have one of the older cases, you should order the expansion frame at the same time you order your drive.

Step 1: Remove the cover. Find and remove the screws that hold the cover on. Unplug the power cable. The older cases had five screws on the back panel, one in each corner and one in the top center. There are other screws on the back panel that hold the power supply in place and for connectors. Do not remove these screws. When the screws are removed, the cover can be slid forward and off.

The newer tower-type cases also have screws in the back panel along each side that hold the cover on. When these screws are removed, the cover can be pulled toward the rear, then lifted off.

Step 2: Check the instructions and set jumpers and switches. Check the documentation that came with the disk. Unless you are installing a second hard disk, you might not have to set any jumpers or switches.

Step 3: Install in a bay. Place the drive in a bay and use screws to secure it. If it is one of the small $3\frac{1}{2}$ inch drive form factors, you might have to use an expansion frame to mount the drive in a standard 5¼ inch bay. Most newer cases have both 3½ inch and 5¼ inch bays.

If you are installing the drive in one of the older cases, you might have to install slide rails on the drives. There are several holes in the side of the disk. The easiest way to determine which ones to use is to try them. The tapered end of the rail should go toward the rear. Insert the disk in the bay, and check for the proper fit. If you are lucky and have started them in the right holes, then install the rest of the screws in the rails.

Installing Controller and Cables

Now that you have the drives installed, you need to check any instructions that might have come with your controller or interface card. Set any switches and jumpers as necessary. Plug the board into an empty slot, preferably one near the disk drives so that the cables will not have to be draped over other boards.

For IDE or SCSI Connections

If you are installing an IDE drive, you will have a single 40-wire cable; for SCSI it will be a 50 wire cable. In most drives, the cable can only be plugged in one way. If the IDE interface is built-in on the motherboard, you might only have a set of upright pins. There will usually be a set of pins nearby for the floppy disk drives and printer. These connections can be plugged in backwards. You will have to determine which is pin one and orient the cable connector so that the colored wire goes to that side.

Check your documentation. SCSI drives need to have a switch or jumper set for their ID number. IDE drives must also have jumpers set to configure the drive as master or slave.

Install Drive Power Cables

The power cables for the drives are four-wire cables from the power supply. They can only be plugged in one way.

Installing a Second Hard Disk

You never know when a hard disk might fail. You should always have them backed up. A hard drive can be backed up to another hard drive in just seconds. The probability that both drives would fail at the same time is quite small.

I mentioned the fact that the need for storage is seldom satisfied. Even if you have a disk with five gigabytes of storage, you will soon be trying to store ten gigabytes of data on it. A second hard drive can help this problem.

You should have some sort of documentation for your drive that tells you what switches or jumpers to set. Follow any instructions that came with the drive.

You might be very limited in the size of the drive you install on an XT, 286, 386, or 486. Some of the older BIOS chips never heard of some of the drives that are available today. That's just one more reason to throw out the old XT motherboard and install a late-model, Pentium-class motherboard.

Fill All Blank Panels

All of the back panel slots should be covered with blank panels. The fan in the power supply should draw air only through the vents in the front of the computer. It then passes this air over the components to cool them. If there are additional openings in the case, it cuts down on the efficiency of the cooling system.

The newer ATX-type systems developed for the Pentium Pro and Pentium II are just the opposite. The fans in these power supplies draw the air in from the back grill and blows it over the components and out the front grill.

Software Installation and Formatting

Once the drives are installed and connected, you can turn on the power, boot up the computer, and enter the drive type into your CMOS setup table. Boot up the computer from your floppy A: disk drive. Besides the system files for booting up, the floppy should have the FDISK and Format command on it.

Windows 95 and most BIOS systems can automatically recognize newer hard disks that are installed and formatted. For older systems, you won't be able to access or do anything with your hard drives until you tell your system what type of drive you have. What type of drive you have is determined by the number of cylinders, heads, sectors, and all of the other information necessary for that drive. In the early 1980s, IBM determined that there were only 15 different types of hard drives available. It was made into a standard table which was included in the BIOS of the IBM and all compatible clones. Soon more and more different type drives were developed. The first 15 types remained standard, but as new types were introduced, each BIOS manufacturer produced different tables. It soon reached the number 46 when it became apparent that there was no end in sight. There are now hundreds of different types. Most setup routines now will allow you to enter type 46 or 47 and then type in data for any drive that does not fit any of the listed types.

Setup Routine

When you install a hard disk, your BIOS must be told what type it is. (If you are installing a new drive, you must use the Fdisk utility to partition and format the drive before you do anything else. The format procedure is explained later in this chapter.) The BIOS also must know the number and type of floppies you have, the time, the date, type of monitor, and other information. The setup routine asks several questions, then configures the BIOS for that configuration. This part of the BIOS configuration is in low power CMOS semiconductors and is on all the time. Even when the computer is turned off a small battery on the motherboard supplies power for the CMOS semiconductors.

The setup usually only allows you to enter two drives, C and D. But you might have two very large drives that are divided into several smaller partitions. So your D drive might be a part of the hard disk that has your C drive. So ignore the designation for drive D. You should enter the information for your first drive, the C drive, then enter the information under the D drive for your second drive. The CMOS setup would be less confusing if it asked for information about hard drive number 1, then number 2, instead of C and D.

Booting from a Floppy

Caution: Never boot up with a floppy disk version that is different from the DOS version used to format the hard disk. There is a short boot record on the hard disk. If a different version is used to boot up, you might lose all of your data on the disk.

Entering Drive Data into CMOS

If you have Windows 95 and a plug-n-play BIOS, it will automatically recognize the hard disk. If you have an older system, you will have to enter the information. To enter the drive type information into the CMOS setup, turn on your system and press the necessary key or keys to enter the setup. Vendors use different keys to access the setup. The AMI setup is accessed during the bootup by pressing the Delete key. Some systems require you to press the ESC and Delete keys or some other combination during bootup. Your motherboard documentation should tell you which keys to press. If you don't have your documentation, you might be able to access the setup by holding down one of the keys on the keyboard during bootup. The system will beep at you and say that you have a keyboard error. It will then usually give you the option of pressing F1 to enter the setup.

Once you access the setup, enter the type data for your drive. You might not be able to find your drive type in the BIOS table. In that case, choose one that is close to your type. Try to find a type with the same number of heads. You can format the drive with a lesser number of heads and cylinders, but not more than the drive type supports. This would mean that you were not using the entire capacity of the drive. It is possible to format a hard disk for a smaller capacity, but not as a larger one than what it is. If the BIOS will allow it, use the type 46 or 47 User Defined option.

The Purpose of Formatting

Formatting organizes the disk so that data can be stored and accessed easily and quickly. If the data was not organized, it would be very difficult to find an item on a large hard disk. I have about 3,000 files on my two hard disks. Those files are on tracks and sectors that are numbered. A file allocation table (FAT) is set up to record the location of each track and sector on the disk.

A brief analogy of disk organization would be similar to that of a developer of a piece of land. The developyer would lay out the streets and create blocks, then partition each block into lots and build a house on each lot. Each house would have a unique address. A map of these streets and house addresses would be filed with the city. A track is analogous to a street, and a sector number is similar to a house number.

The FAT is similar to an index in a street atlas or a book. When a request is sent to the heads to read or write to a file, it goes to the file allocation table, looks for the location of that file, and goes directly to it. The heads can find any file, or parts of any file, quickly and easily. Formatting is not something that is done every day, and can be rather difficult in some cases. One reason the disks do not come from the manufacturer preformatted is that there are so many options. If you have a 540Mb hard disk, you will probably want to divide or partition it into two or three different logical disks.

For the old MFM-type drives, one reason they did not preformat the drive is that there were so many different controller cards. The controller cards are usually designed so that they will operate with several different types of hard disks, so most have DIP switches that must be set to configure your particular hard disk. Usually some documentation comes with the hard disk controller. Like most other manuals and documentation, the instructions are sometimes difficult to understand, especially if you are a beginner.

FDISK Options

FDISK means *fixed disk* or it could also mean *format disk*. It is a DOS command on the boot disk that comes with your system when you buy a copy of Windows. You will not be able to use a hard disk until it has been partitioned with FDISK, then high-level formatted.

If your computer and BIOS was made before 1994, it might not support the EIDE standard. You will not be able to format a disk over 504Mb. Most vendors can supply a DiskManager utility from OnTrack that will allow you to work around this limitation.

DOS 3.3 and earlier versions could only handle hard disks up to 32Mb. If you bought a 40Mb hard disk, you could only use 32Mb of it unless you used special software such as DiskManager. DOS 4.0 and later versions allows very large size partitions, up to 2 gigabytes.

I would recommend not making a partition of more than 500Mb. If there are several partitions on a disk and one of them fails, you might be able to recover the data in the other partitions. If your disk is one large partition and it fails, you might not be able to recover any of the data, especially if the FAT is destroyed. Norton Utilities can be set up to make a mirror image of the FAT. If the primary FAT is destroyed, you can still use the mirror image.

DOS uses all of the alphabet letters for disk drives. It reserves A and B for floppy drives and C for the boot drive. So if you have a very large disk, you can make up to 23 other logical partitions or drive D: through Z:.

Using FDISK can be a bit confusing. The manual that comes with MS-DOS 6.2 and Windows 95 is no help at all. MS-DOS has on-disk help for all of its commands, just type help and command name. But the Help FDISK help is not much help. The Microsoft Press is a division of Microsoft that primarily prints books about how to use Microsoft software. Some people have asserted if their manuals were well written, you would not need to buy an extra book to learn how to use the software.

The older MFM, RLL, and ESDI hard disks had to have a low-level and a high-level format. Newer drives have the low-level format done at the factory. Many of the newer BIOS systems have a utility for doing a low-level format, but do not use it on an IDE or SCSI drive that has already been low-level formatted.

If the low-level format has been done, you can do the high-level format. Boot up from your floppy disk drive with a copy of DOS and type DIR C:. If the message comes up, invalid drive specification, put a copy of DOS that has the FDISK command on it in drive A:.

When you type FDISK, if you are using MS-DOS 6.2 or a later version, this message will be displayed:

FDISK Options

Current Fixed Disk Drive: 1

Choose one of the following:

1. Create DOS Partition or Logical DOS Drive

2. Set active partition

3. Delete Partition or Logical DOS Drive

4. Display partition information

5. Change current fixed disk drive

Option 5 is only displayed if you have more than one drive. Enter the first choice, create DOS partition or logical DOS drive. Press ESC to exit FDISK.

If you choose 1, and the disk has not been prepared, a screen like this comes up:

Create DOS Partition or Logical DOS Drive

Current Fixed Drive: 1

Choose one of the following:

1. Create Primary DOS partition

2. Create Extended DOS partition

3. Create logical DOS drive(s) in the Extended DOS partition

If you want to boot from your hard drive (I can't think of any reason why you would not want to), then enter the first choice, create primary DOS partition. Press ESC to return to FDISK Options. If you choose 1, a prompt will come up and ask:

Do you wish to use the maximum size for a Primary DOS Partition and make the partition active (Y/N)....? [Y]

If you type Y for yes, the entire drive will be made into one large C: drive. If you answer N, it will display the maximum disk size and ask what percentage or number of megabytes to assign as the primary drive. You can type in 50% or any number of megabytes. You can make the whole drive a single partition, but it is better to have two or more partitions. After you create the primary partition, press ESC and this same screen will be displayed again:

Create DOS Partition or Logical DOS Drive

Current Fixed Drive: 1

Choose one of the following:

1. Create Primary DOS partition

2. Create Extended DOS partition

3. Create logical DOS drive(s) in the Extended DOS partition

Because you have already created the primary partition, choose option 2 to create an extended DOS partition. This will show the amount of space that is left over from the primary drive assignment. Press ESC to return to FDISK Options.

You cannot partition the drive at this point. Accept the figure given. If you try to partition the drive at this point, whatever you choose will be all that you can use. For instance with option number 2, if you have 1500Mb left and you try to divide it into two 750Mb partitions, it will figure that the entire extended drive is to be only 750Mb. You will not be able to use the other 750Mb. You must tell it to use the 1500Mb that is available. Then press ESC to return to the options, then choose option number 3, Create Logical DOS Drives in the Extended DOS partition. You can now divide this partition into as many drives as you want.

It will tell you how much space is available for the extended partition. The default is the maximum amount of space shown. If you want to accept it and have a single primary drive and a single extended drive, just press Enter. Otherwise, type the number of megabytes or percentage desired. Type a number followed with the percentage symbol, for instance 25%. Continue creating logical drives until the entire disk is assigned. You can press ESC and delete and revise any of the partitions that you have created.

Installing a Second Hard Disk

If you are installing a second hard disk, then you will see this display:
FDISK Options
Current Fixed Disk Drive: 1
1. Create DOS partition or Logical DOS Drive
2. Set active partition
3. Delete Partition or Logical DOS Drive
4. Display partition information
5. Change current fixed disk drive

Option 5 is only displayed if you have more than one drive. Choose option 5 to change drives. The Primary partition is only on the C: drive and it contains the boot utility. Use the options to create more logical drives just as you did on the first drive. Press ESC to exit FDISK.

High-Level Format

After the FDISK options have been completed, return to drive A: and high-level format drive C:. Because you want to boot off this drive, you must also transfer the system and hidden files to the disk as it is being formatted, so you must use a /S to transfer the files. Type FORMAT C: /S. DOS will display a message that says:
WARNING! ALL DATA ON NON-REMOVABLE DISK DRIVE C: WILL BE LOST!
Proceed with Format (Y/N)

If you press Y, the disk light should come on, and you might hear the drive stepping through each track. After a few minutes, it will display:

Format complete System transferred

Volume label (11 characters, ENTER for none)?

You can give each partition a unique name, or volume label if you wish to. You can test your drive by doing a warm boot by pressing Ctrl, Alt, and Delete at the same time. The computer should reboot. Now that drive C: is completed, if you have other partitions or a second disk, format each of them.

Drive Copy

You might have just bought a new hard drive to add to your system. One reason you might have bought it is because your C: drive might have been bursting at the seams. It seems that every program wants to be loaded on C:, so a hundred megabytes can be used up in a hurry. It would be nice to be able to just copy all of the files on drive C: onto a new much larger drive, but Windows 95 has all kinds of hidden files that must be copied along with the parent files. Besides that, you need to create new directories before you can copy files into it. It can be quite time consuming.

Drive Copy from PowerQuest will do all of the work for you in a very short time. The program is rather inexpensive and is well worth the money. PowerQuest has a home page at www.powerquest.com. Send e-mail to drivecopy@powerquest.com. The telephone number is 801-226-8977.

PartitionMagic

In addition to DriveCopy, PowerQuest Corporation also makes PartitionMagic. PartitionMagic 3.0 is the revolutionary utility that lets you resize your drives and reclaim wasted disk space. It will also let you safely boot and run multiple operating systems and organize and protect your data.

Everyone wants to get the most they can out of their hard drive. But, up to 40 percent of your hard drive might be totally wasted due to inefficient storage methods. PartitionMagic 3.0 increases your usable disk space by shrinking large FAT partitions and restructuring cluster sizes to reclaim up to hundreds of megabytes of lost disk space.

Check the PowerQuest home page at www.powerquest.com, and send e-mail to magic@powerquest.com. The telephone number is 801-226-8941.

Partition-It

Partition-It is another relatively inexpensive utility that will let you partition large hard drives into smaller, more manageable drives. Partition-It can do this without having to backup. It is all automatic. It scans the drive and calculates what the optimum cluster size should be for maximum storage.

Partition-It is made by Quarterdeck Corp. www.quarterdeck.com; send e-mail to info@quarterdeck.com. The telephone number is 800-683-2391.

Sources

Local computer stores and computer swap meets are good places to find a disk drive. You can at least look them over and get some idea of the prices and what you want. Mail order is a very good way to buy a hard disk. There are hundreds of advertisements in the many computer magazines. Check the list of magazines in Chapter 22.

Backup and Disaster Prevention

"I was told to backup my hard disk. How do I put it in reverse?" This might sound funny to an old pro, but to a beginner, it might be a serious question.

Making backups is a chore that most people dislike, but if your data is worth anything at all, you should be making backups of it. You might be lucky and never need it, but there are thousands of ways to lose data. Data can be lost due to a power failure or a component failure in the computer system. In a fraction of a second data that might be worth thousands of dollars could be lost forever. It might have taken hundreds of hours to accumulate and it might be impossible to duplicate it. Yet many of these unfortunate people have not backed up their precious data. Most of these people are those who have been fortunate enough not to have had a major catastrophe. Just as sure as earthquakes in California, if you use a computer long enough, you can look forward to at least one unfortunate disaster. But if your data is backed up, it doesn't have to be a catastrophe.

By far, most losses are the result of just plain dumb mistakes. I have made lots of mistakes in the past. And no matter how careful I am, I will make mistakes in the future. As the poet said, "To err is human."

Write Protect Your Software

When you buy a software program, you should make a diskcopy of the program and store the original away. If you should ruin the copy, you can always make a new copy from the original. But the very first thing you should do before you make a diskcopy is write protect the original floppies. It is very easy to become distracted and write on a program diskette in error. This would ruin the program. The vendor might give you a new copy, but it would probably entail weeks of waiting and much paperwork.

If you are using 5¼ inch floppies, you should cover the square write protect notch with a piece of opaque tape. Don't use Scotch or clear tape. The drive focuses a light through the square notch. If the light detector can sense the light, it will allow the diskette to be written on, read, or erased. If the notch is covered with opaque tape, the diskette can be read, but it cannot be written on or erased. Some vendors now distribute their programs on diskettes without the square notch.

If you are using 3½ diskettes, you should move the small slide on the left-rear side so that the square hole is open. The 3½ inch write-protect system is just the opposite of the 5¼ inch system. The 3½ inch system uses a small microswitch. If the square hole is open, the switch will allow the diskette to be read, but not written on or erased. If the slide is moved to cover the square hole, the diskette can be written on, read, or erased.

It takes less than a minute to write protect a diskette. It might save months of valuable time. If a program diskette is ruined because it was not protected, it might take weeks to get a replacement for the original. You might even have to buy a complete new program.

Protect Your Original Floppies

At one time most software was distributed on 5¼ floppies. But they are obsolete now. You still might have some with valuable data on them. You disks can be protected from dirt and dust, especially the 5¼ inch floppies, by sealing them in plastic sandwich bags.

Floppy disks also should not be exposed to heat. I ruined a half dozen disks one day by leaving them in a closed car where the sun hit them. The heat melted the plastic sleeves on the disks.

You should also be very careful not to let a magnet come near your diskettes. There are magnets in several devices, such as loudspeakers, telephones, and even magnetized tools.

There is not much chance of harming the data on a CD-ROM disc unless you scratch it or mishandle it.

.BAK files

There are functions in many of the word processors and some other programs that creates a .BAK file each time you alter or change a file. The .BAK file is usually just a copy of the original file before you changed it. You can call up a .BAK file, but you might not be able edit it or use it unless you rename it. Usually, just changing the .BAK extension is all that is necessary. Most word processors and other programs, such as spreadsheets and databases, can be set up to automatically save any file that you are working on at certain times when there is no activity from the keyboard. If there is a power outage, or you shut the machine off without saving a file, chances are that there is a backup of it saved to disk.

Unerase Software

One of the best protections against errors is to have a backup. The second best protection is to have a good utility program such as Norton's Utilities from Symantec. DOS and Windows 95 also have undelete utilities. These programs can unerase a file or even unformat a disk. When a file is erased, DOS goes to the FAT table and deletes the first letter of each file name. All of the data remains on the disk unless a new file is written over it. If you have erased a file in error, or formatted a disk in error, do not do anything to it until you have tried using a recover utility. To restore the files, most of the utilities ask you to supply the missing first letter of the file name.

Delete Protection

I assume that you are using Windows 95 now. If you delete a file, it is sent to the recycle bin. If you decide later that you still need that file, you can search through the bin and recover it. The recycle bin might take up a lot of disk space. If you have don't have a lot of spare disk space, you might have to go to the recycle bin every so often and dump certain files that you know you won't need or dump the entire bin.

If you delete just portions of a file, while revising it, the original might still be saved in the recycle bin. If you decide that the revision is not what you wanted, you might be able to recover the original and start over. I have Norton Utilities installed. Norton also has a recycle bin that has a few more utilities than the one that comes with Windows 95.

Every few minutes, my word processor automatically saves copies of the file I am working on. Of course, every time it saves a file, it is the same as deleting it. I just checked the Norton recycle bin for this file that I am working on. There are several versions of this file in the bin. The bin gives the exact time that the file was updated and saved. I could go back and recover any of those earlier versions.

I am sure that many people are still using DOS. After all, it did just about everything we wanted for several years. Erasing or deleting files by mistake was so common in DOS that Microsoft licensed the undelete technology from one of the major utility companies. They included an undelete command in all late versions of MS-DOS. There are three levels of protection with Delete Sentry, Delete Tracker, and the standard Undelete. PC DOS 7.0 from IBM also has similar undelete utilities.

The undelete command is available immediately from any DOS prompt and any directory. To find out more about the undelete command, type help undelete at any DOS prompt and any directory.

The early versions of MS-DOS made it very easy to format your hard disk in error. If you happened to be on your hard disk and typed format, it would immediately begin to format your hard disk and wipe out everything. Later versions will not format unless you specify a drive letter.

The early versions of DOS would also let you copy over another file. If two files were different, but you told DOS to copy one to a directory that had the file with the same name, the original file would be gone forever. MS-DOS 6.2, IBM PC DOS 7.0, and Windows 95 now ask if you want to overwrite the file.

Jumbled FAT

The all-important file allocation table (FAT) was discussed in the previous chapter about disks. The FAT keeps a record of the location of all the files on the disk. Parts of a file can be located in several sectors, but the FAT knows exactly where they are. If for some reason track 0, where the FAT is located, is damaged, erased, or becomes defective, then you will not be able to read or write to any of the files on the disk.

Because the FAT is so important, a program such as Norton Utilities can make a copy of the FAT and store it in another location on the disk. Every time you add a file or edit one, the FAT changes. So these programs make a new copy every time the FAT is altered. If the original FAT is damaged, you can still get your data by using the alternate FAT.

Norton Utilities from Symantec, at (408) 253-9600, is an excellent utility software package. If you accept the defaults when installing Norton Utilities it causes Norton to scan your disk and analyze the boot record, file allocation tables (FAT), analyze directory structure, analyze file structure, and check for lost clusters or cross-linked files. It then reads the FAT and stores a copy in a different place on the hard disk.

Reason for Smaller Logical Hard Disks

Early versions of DOS would not recognize a hard disk larger than 32Mb. DOS can now handle hard drive capacities up to several gigabytes. Most programs seem to be designed to be installed on drive C:. You could have a very large drive C: but if this large hard disk crashed, you might not be able to recover any of its data. DOS allows you to use the FDISK command when formatting your disk to divide it up and partition it into as many as 24 logical drives. If the same disk was divided into several smaller logical drives, and one of the logical sections failed, it might be possible to recover data in the unaffected logical drives.

PartitionMagic and Partition It

You can think of a partition much like a room with four walls. When the house was built, some of the rooms might have been very small. It is sometimes possible to knock out some of the walls and make the room larger. You can do something similar with the partitions on your hard disk.

You are probably using a hard disk that has already been formatted and has lots of data on it. Normally, the only way to change the size of the drive partitions is to backup everything, then use FDISK to resize it and then reformat it. Both Partition Magic and Partition-It will let you resize the partitions on your hard drive without having to back up all the data. It will automatically move the data, resize the partition, and move the data back into it.

A very fast way to back up is to copy the data from one logical drive partition to another. This type of backup is very fast and very easy. But it doesn't offer the amount of protection that a separate hard drive would offer. Still it is much better than no backup at all.

Head Crash

The heads of a hard disk "fly" over the disk just a few microinches from the surface. They have to be close in order to detect the small magnetic changes in the tracks. The disk spins at 3600 RPMs on some older drives and up to 10,000 RPMs on some of the newer drives. If the heads contact the surface of the fast-spinning disk it can scratch it and ruin the disk.

A sudden jar or bump to the computer while the hard disk is spinning can cause the heads to crash. Of course a mechanical failure or some other factor could also cause a crash. You should never move or bump your computer while the hard disk is running.

Most of the newer disks have a built-in safe park utility. When the power is removed, the head is automatically moved to the center of the disk where there are no tracks.

The technology of the hard disk systems has improved tremendously over the last few years, but hard disks are still mechanical devices. As such, you can be sure that eventually they will wear out, fail, or crash.

I worked in electronics for over 30 years and am still amazed that a hard disk will work at all. It is a remarkable mechanical device. It is made up of several precision components. The mechanical tolerances must be held to millionths of an inch in some devices, such as the flying head and the distances between the tracks. The magnetic flux changes are minute, yet the heads detect them easily and output reliable data.

Despite all of the things that could go wrong with a hard disk, most hard disks are quite reliable. Manufacturers quote figures of several thousand hours *mean time between failure* (MTBF). However these figures are only an average, so there is no guarantee that a disk won't fail in the next few minutes. I made a mistake in one of my earlier books and described the acronym MTBF as meaning *mean time before failure*. Several people wrote and pointed out my mistake, that it should be *between*, not *before*. If a disk should fail and you get it repaired, it should last as long as their guarantee says before it fails again. A hard disk is made up of several mechanical parts. If the disk is used long enough, eventually it will wear out or fail.

Crash Recovery

Despite the MTBF claims, hard drives do fail. There are lots of businesses that do nothing but repair hard disks that have crashed or failed. A failure can be frustrating, time consuming, and make you feel utterly helpless. In the unhappy event of a crash, depending on its severity, it is possible that some of your data can be recovered, one way or another.

There are some companies that specialize in recovering data and rebuilding hard disks. Many of them have sophisticated tools and software that can recover some data if the disk is not completely ruined.

OnTrack Data International

If it is possible to recover any of the data, the Ontrack Data Recovery can probably do it. They can send you a floppy disk that can help in the event of a crash or disaster. Here is some information from its website:

Diagnose a data loss directly on your computer!

When you lose your valuable computer data, every second that passes equals time, money, and effort lost to you or your company. Ontrack Data Adviser software reduces expensive downtime by providing you with an instant diagnosis of your data-loss situation. Ontrack Data Adviser software will investigate your desktop, laptop, or notebook computer to determine what is preventing you from accessing your data. This keeps your downtime to a minimum, helping you resume normal business functions as quickly as possible.

Powerful tools provide a comprehensive system analysis

Ontrack Data Adviser software includes a complete set of hard disk drive and system diagnostic tools. These tools assess the read abilities of your hard disk drive and determine if your drive is electromechanically stable. These tools also analyze your file systems and file structures, check your system memory, scan for computer viruses, and more. Contained on a bootable diskette, Ontrack Data Adviser software can even diagnose your system when it cannot boot on its own!

The first component of the patent-pending Ontrack Remote Data recovery process

Ontrack Data Adviser software is the first component of Ontrack Remote Data Recovery services, currently in development. This patent-pending process will allow Ontrack to perform remote data recoveries via communication link based on the test results provided by Ontrack Data Adviser software. It is yet another way to bring you the fastest data recovery services available.

OnTrack Data Recovery & Ontrack Data International
6321 Bury Dr.
Eden Prairie, MN 55346
800-872-2599
www.ontrack.com

DriveSavers

If your disk is crashed, you can try the following suggestions before you contact DriveSavers. This document covers a few of the many kinds of problems that can occur when data recovery might be necessary.

The "oops" Factor

Sometimes cables just wiggle loose. It's a good idea to check your cables when there's a problem accessing your drive. It's a good idea to do this anyway. Be sure to shut the system off and check both the power cable and ribbon cable(s). Make sure their connections are all secure. If need be, you can pull them off and then put them back on to be certain there's a secure connection.

The Disk Exhibits Unusual Noises (Clicking, Grinding, or Metal Scraping)

This typically indicates a serious hardware problem, such as a head crash or major media damage. In such a case it is best to copy all accessible data from the drive immediately. The longer the drive runs in this condition the more damage can occur making the data irretrievable. It is best to send the drive directly to DriveSavers so we might disassemble it in a special clean-room environment and extract the data for you.

Using Utility Programs

Use utility programs with caution. They are best used to clean up minor problems on drives that have already been backed up. These programs can do a fine job of helping you out of a tight spot...or they can "fix" your data beyond recoverability! If you do use one of these, please heed the following cautions.

Utility programs like Symantec's Norton Utilities and MS-DOS's Scandisk allow you the opportunity to save "undo" files if the repair doesn't work out. It's very important because saving an undo file can help you back out of a bad "fix." Save your undo file to a floppy disk, not your hard disk. It's a good idea to have a few formatted diskettes handy for the program to write to.

If your drive is sounding or acting "funny" in any way, it's extremely important that you avoid the use of these utilities altogether. These symptoms can include any rattling, buzzing, or scraping sounds the disk drive might be emitting. In these circumstances, it's best to backup your data immediately or shut the drive down as further use might cause damage. If the drive is completely crashed, your best chance for recovery is to contact us here at DriveSavers.

"Invalid Drive Specification" Error Message

A common problem that occurs, especially with older 386 systems, is a system's propensity to lose track of its CMOS drive setup. When you turn on your system, it goes through its memory countdown, etc., and then just sits there, asks for a system disk, or drops into BASIC (on true-blue IBM systems). When you put in a boot floppy, and ask for drive C:, you get the "invalid drive specification" message.

In such a circumstance, first check your CMOS setup. Most systems will allow you to enter the CMOS setup at startup time with a key stroke or two, such as [Del], [Esc], or [Cntrl]-[Esc]. Some systems, such as Compaq, NEC, Mitsubishi, and many laptops and notebooks, require a setup or diagnostic diskette to change the CMOS drive setting. Tab to the appropriate field for drive settings and enter in the correct settings for your drive. (It's a good idea to keep these settings on a note attached to your computer for future reference.) Most modern systems will let you "Auto" sense the drive. This will usually be successful. You should then reboot your PC. If this works, great! Back up your system and get a replacement battery from your dealer. If not, it might be time to give DriveSavers a call.

Removable Cartridge or other SCSI Drive Gives "Invalid Drive Specification" Error

If a removable cartridge (SyQuest, magneto-optical, or Iomega) or SCSI hard disk refuses to mount, the device driver might be damaged or the CONFIG.SYS file might have been changed. Look for lines in your CONFIG.SYS files that look something like "DEVICE=ASPIDISK.SYS".

If no such line exists, check the manual or README file on your installation disk for the cartridge drive or SCSI host adapter manual. Try another cartridge that is known to be good. This will help you identify whether the problem is with the cartridge or the drive mechanism. If the same problem occurs with another cartridge, check that your SCSI cables are firmly attached and the termination is correct.

You might also isolate the drive on the SCSI bus by disconnecting other devices. With most systems, the first SCSI drive must have a SCSI ID of 0 (zero), and the first removable media drive must have a SCSI ID of 2.

DriveSavers—Multi-platform Data Recovery
400 Bel Marin Keys Boulevard
Novato, CA, USA 94949
Phone: 800-440-1904
Phone: 415-382-2000
Fax: 415-883-0780
Internet: www.drivesavers.com

Another company that specializes in recovery is:

Total Recall
2462 Waynoka Rd.
Colorado Springs, CO 80915
800-743-0594

Cost of Recovery

The cost for recovery services can be rather expensive, but if you have data that is critical and irreplaceable it is well worth it. It is a whole lot cheaper to have a backup. There are several companies who specialize in data recovery. Look in the computer magazine ads.

Preventing Hard Disk Failures

During manufacturing, the hard disk platters are coated or plated with a precise layer of magnetic material. It is almost impossible to manufacture a perfect platter. Most all hard disks end up with a few defective areas after being manufactured. When the vendor does the low-level format, these areas are detected and marked as bad. They are locked out so that they cannot be used. But there might be areas that are borderline bad that won't be detected. Over time some of the areas might change and lose some of its magnetic characteristics. It might lose some of the data that is written to it. There are several companies that manufacture hard disk utilities that can perform rigorous tests on the hard disk. These software programs can exercise the disk and detect any borderline areas. If there happens to be data in an area that is questionable, the programs can usually move the data to another safe area.

The ScanDisk command in MS-DOS 6.2 basically does what some of the stand-alone utilities do. It does a surface test of the hard disk and will report on any areas that are questionable. It can move any data from those areas to safer areas. It will then mark the questionable areas as bad. The bad areas are listed in the FAT just as if they were protected files that cannot be written to or erased.

Why Not Backup

Here are a few of the lame excuses used by some people who don't backup their software.

Don't Have the Time   This is not a good excuse. If your data is worth anything at all, it is worth backing up. It takes only a few minutes to back up a large hard disk with some of the newer software. It might take just seconds to copy all of the files to a directory on another logical drive of the disk or to another hard drive.

Too Much Trouble   It can be a bit of trouble unless you have an expensive tape automated backup system or a second hard disk. If you backup to floppies it can require a bit of disk swapping, labeling, and storing. But with a little organizing, it can be done easily. If you keep all of the disks together, you don't have to label each one. Just stack them in order, put a rubber band around them and use one label for the first one of the lot.

It is a bit of trouble to make backups. But if you don't have a backup, consider the trouble it would take to re-do the files from a disk that has crashed. The trouble that it takes to make a backup is infinitesimal.

Don't Have the Necessary Disks, Software, or Tools   If you use floppy disks, depending on the amount of data to be backed up and the software used, it might require 50 to 100 disks. But it might take only a few minutes and just a few disks to make a backup of only the data that has been changed or altered. In most cases, the same disks can be reused the next day to update the files.

Failures and Disasters Only Happen to Other People   People who believe this way are those who have never experienced a disaster. There is nothing you can say to convince them; they just have to learn the hard way.

Outside of ordinary care, there is little you can do to prevent a general failure. It could be a component on the hard disk electronics or in the controller system. Or it could be any one of a thousand other things. Even things such as a power failure during a read/write operation can cause data corruption.

Theft and Burglary   Computers are easy to sell so they are favorite targets for burglars. It would be bad enough to lose a computer, but many computers have hard disks that are filled with data that is even more valuable than the computer.

Speaking of theft, it might be a good idea to put your name and address on several of the files on your hard disk. It would also be a good idea to scratch identifying marks on the back and bottom of the case. You should also write down the serial numbers of your monitor and drives. I heard of a story where a man took a computer to a pawn shop. The dealer wanted to see if it worked, so he turned it on. A name came up on the screen that was different from the name the man had given to the dealer. He called the police and the man was arrested for burglary. The owner of the computer was very happy to get it back. He was also quite fortunate; most burglaries don't have a happy ending.

Another good idea is to store your backup files in an area away from your computer. This way there would be less chance of losing both computer and backups in case of a burglary or fire. You can always buy another computer, but if you had a large database of customer orders, files, and history, how could you replace that?

An article in a recent *Information Week Magazine* says that PC theft has increased over 400% in the last few years. (*Information Week Magazine* is free to qualifying subscribers. See Chapter 17 for their address.)

Archiving

Another reason to backup is for archival purposes. No matter how large the hard disk is, it will eventually fill up with data. Quite often, there will be files that are no longer used or they might only be used once in a great while. I keep copies of all the letters that I write on disk. I have hundreds of them. Rather than erase the old files or old letters, I put them on a disk and store them away.

Data Transfer

There are often times when it is necessary to transfer a large amount of data from one hard disk on a computer to another. It is quite easy to use a good backup program to accomplish this. Data on a disk can be used to distribute data, company policies and procedures, sales figures, and other information to several people in a large office or company. The data can also be easily shipped or mailed to branch offices, customers, or to others almost anywhere. If more companies used disks in this manner, we could save thousands of trees that are cut down for paper.

Types of Backup

There are two main types of backup: the image and file oriented. An *image* backup is an exact bit-for-bit copy of the hard disk copied as a continuous stream of data. This type of backup is rather inflexible and does not allow for a separate file backup or restoration. The *file oriented* type of backup identifies and indexes each file separately. A separate file or directory can be backed up and restored easily. It can be very time consuming to have to backup an entire 40 megabytes or more each day. But with a file oriented type system, once a full backup has been made, it is necessary only to make incremental backups of those files that have been changed or altered.

DOS stores an archive attribute in each file directory entry. When a file is created, DOS turns the archive attribute flag on. If the file is backed up by using DOS BACKUP or any of the commercial backup programs, the archive attribute flag is turned off. If this file is later altered or changed, DOS will turn the attribute back on. At the next backup, you can have the program search the files and look for the attribute flag. You can then backup only those that have been altered or changed since the last backup. You can view or modify a file's archive attribute by using the DOS ATTRIB command.

There are several very good software programs on the market that let you use a $5\frac{1}{4}$ inch or $3\frac{1}{2}$ inch disk drive to backup your data. Again, you should have backups of all your master software, so you don't have to worry about backing up that software every day. Because DOS stamps each file with the date and time it was created, it is easy to backup only those files that were created after a certain date and time.

Once the first backup is made, all subsequent backups need only be made of any data that has been changed or updated. Most backup programs can recognize whether a file has been changed since the last backup. Most of them can also look at the date that is stamped on each file and back up only those within a specified date range. So it might take only a few minutes to make a copy of only those files that are new or have been changed. And of course, it is usually not necessary to backup your program software. You do have the original software disks safely tucked away, don't you?

Windows 95 Backup Accessory

Windows 95 has a very good built-in backup program. To use it, push the Start button, then choose Programs, then Accessories, then System Tools, then Backup. The Microsoft Backup Wizard will be displayed. Then just follow the simple directions.

Windows 3.1 and DOS Backup.Com

Early versions of MS-DOS included a Backup.Com that was very slow and rather difficult to use. MS-DOS 6.0 and later versions have MSBackup for DOS and Windows Backup that are fast and easy to use. The MS-DOS backup can now compete with some of the commercial backup programs. The MSBackup and Windows Backup can let you make full, incremental, or differential backups. DR DOS and IBM PC DOS also have backup commands that are as good as or better than the MS-DOS commands.

The XCOPY command can also be used for backup. There are several switches that can be used with XCOPY. (A switch is a /.) For instance, XCOPY C:*.* A:/A will copy only those files that have their archive attribute set to on. It does not reset the attribute flag. XCOPY C:*.* A:/M will copy the files, then reset the flag. Whenever a disk on A: is full, you merely have to insert a new floppy, and hit F3 to repeat the last command. This will continue to copy all files that have not been backed up. XCOPY C:*.* A:/D:01-15-96 will copy only those files created after January 15, 1996. There are several other very useful switches that can be used. Check your MS-DOS, DR DOS, or IBM PC DOS manuals for more details on backup. All of these systems have built-in, on-line help for all commands.

The MSBackup, Windows Backup, and Xcopy commands cannot be used with most tape backup systems. Tape backup systems usually have their own proprietary backup software. There are several commercial backup programs available.

XTree

XTree is an excellent shell program for disk and file management. It has several functions that make computing much easier. You can use it to copy files from one directory or disk to another very easily. I often use it to make backups when I only have a few files to backup. XTree is now a division of Central Point and PC Tools, which is now a division of Symantec; their phone number is (408) 253-9600.

Tape

There are several tape backup systems on the market. Tape backup is easy, but it can be relatively expensive, $250 to over $500 for a drive unit and $10 to $20 for the tape cartridges. Some of them require the use of a controller that is similar to the disk controller. So they will use one of your precious slots, but there are some SCSI systems that can be daisy chained to a SCSI controller. There are also enhanced IDE tape systems that can be controlled by an EIDE interface.

Unless the tape drives are external models, they will also require the use of one of the disk mounting areas. Because it is only used for back-up, it will be idle most of the time.

There are some tape systems that run off the printer parallel port. These systems don't require a controller board that takes up one of your slots. Another big plus is that it can be used to back up several different computers by simply moving it from one to the other. Figure 9-1 shows a tape drive at the top and a 120Mb cartridge below.

Like floppy disks, tapes have to be formatted before they can be used. But unlike a floppy disk, it might take over two hours to format a tape. You can buy tapes that have been preformatted, but they cost quite a bit more than the unformatted tapes.

Tape systems are very slow, so the backups should be done at night or during off hours. Most systems can be set up so that the backup is done automatically. If you set it on auto, you won't have to worry about forgetting to backup, or wasting the time doing it.

Another disadvantage of tape is that data is recorded sequentially. If you want to find a file that is in the middle of the tape, it has to search

Fig. 9-1
A quarter-inch
tape drive and
120Mb tape
cartridge.

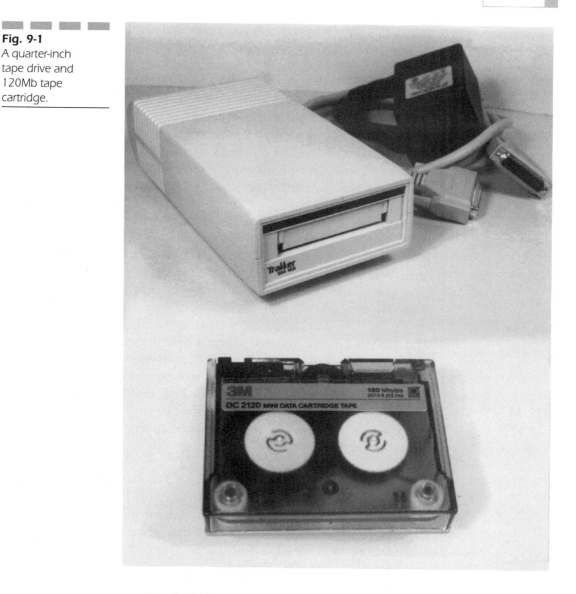

Fig. 9-1
A quarter-inch
tape drive and
120Mb tape
cartridge.

until it finds it. Because disk systems have random access, they are much faster than tape both in recording and reading.

DAT

Several companies are offering the digital audio tape (DAT) systems for backing up large computer hard disk systems. DAT systems offer storage capacities as high as 1.3 gigabytes on a very small cartridge. The DAT systems use a helical scan type recording that is similar to that used for video recording. The DAT tapes are 4 millimeters wide, which is about 0.156 inches.

Removable Disks

One of the better ways for data backup and for data security is to backup to a disk that can be removed and locked up. There are several different systems and companies that manufacture such systems.

The Iomega Zip Drive   The Iomega Zip drive uses a $3\frac{1}{2}$ inch disk that is similar to a floppy. But this $3\frac{1}{2}$ inch disk can store 100Mb. This system is much less expensive than the Bernoulli. At this time, the Zip drives cost less than $200 and the disks cost less than $20. With a few disks, you would never have to worry about running out of hard drive space. The Zip system is ideal for backup or for any type of data storage.

The 120Mb Floppy System   Chapter 5 mentioned that Compaq, 3M, and Matsushita-Kotubuki Companies are developing a 120Mb floppy system. The very high-density drives will be downward compatible so that they can also read and write to the 720K and 1.44Mb format. These drives will be ideal for backup. At the time of this writing, they are still not generally available, but they should be on the market by the time that you read this.

SyQuest Corp.   The SyQuest Corp., at 800-437-9367, manufactures drives with removable disks that can store up to 1.5Gb. Of course, data compression can be used to almost double this amount of storage. Each cartridge is actually a single hard disk platter.

Syquest also has a 230Mb EZ230 drive that costs less than $300. Each removable cartridge costs about $40. Any of these drives could be used to make an excellent backup system.

Magneto-Optical Drives   The magneto-optical drives (MO) are rather expensive, but the removable cartridges are fairly low cost. They are a good choice for use as a normal hard drive and for backup.

Pinnacle Micro, at 800-553-7070, has a 4.6Gb removable M-O drive system they call the Apex. It is almost as fast as a standard hard disk. The cartridges can be erased and rewritten up to 10 million times. A standard magnetic disk begins to deteriorate almost immediately after it has been recorded. It should be refreshed every two or three years. M-O disks have a minimum lifetime of more than 30 years without degradation of data. The Apex system would be ideal for backing up or archiving a large amount of data.

Recordable CD-ROM   When they first came out, the recordable CD-ROM systems were very expensive at about $10,000. Many companies are now selling recordable CD-ROM systems for less than $500 and the prices are still dropping. If you have a lot of data that needs to be permanently backed up, a CD-ROM can store over 650Mbs. An advantage of CD-ROM over magnetic systems is that data on a CD-ROM will last for many years. Magnetic data deteriorates and might become useless within ten years. Unlike the magnetic systems, the data on a CD-ROM cannot be erased, changed, or altered. If the data needs to be changed, just record it onto another disc. The blank discs cost about $6 each.

WORM   Write once read many (WORM) are laser optical systems that are similar to the recordable CD-ROMs. One difference is that the WORM systems usually have larger discs and can store up to several gigabytes. They are great for backing up and archiving data.

With a good document management system and a scanner, vast amounts of paper files can be stored on a WORM. This type of system even has earned an acronym, COLD, which means computer output to Laser Disc. A WORM recording should last for over 100 years. Ordinarily, even paper will deteriorate in less time.

Second Hard Disk   The easiest and the fastest of all methods of backup is to have a second hard disk. It is very easy to install a second hard disk. An IDE interface can control two high-capacity hard disks; the EIDE interfaces can control up to four hard drives. You can add as many as seven hard drives to a SCSI interface.

A good system is to have an IDE drive for the C: boot drive and one or more SCSI drives. You can backup several megabytes of data from one hard drive to another very easily and quickly. The chances are very good that both systems would not become defective at the same time. So if the same data is stored on both systems, it should offer very good RAID-like protection.

At one time tape backup systems were less expensive than a hard disk, but the cost of hard disks have come way down. One of the advantages of using a hard disk for backup is that, unlike tape, any file is available almost immediately.

LapLink   LapLink allows you to connect two computers together and access either one. It is very simple to use the parallel port cables that come with the package and transfer files from one computer to the other. LapLink allows you to update only those portions of a file that have changed. If you are updating or backing up files that are already on the disk, it takes very little time. See Fig. 9-2.

LapLink can also be used over a modem. If you are on the road and need to back up a laptop, you can easily send the data back to the desktop.

RAID Systems   RAID is an acronym for redundant arrays of inexpensive disks. There are some data that is absolutely critical and essential. In order to make sure that it is saved, data is written to two or more hard disks at the same time. Originally, five different levels were suggested, but only three levels, 1,3, and 5, are in general use today.

Some RAID systems will allow you to hot swap or pull and replace a defective disk drive without having to power down. You don't lose any information because the same data is being written to other hard disk drives.

Fig. 9-2
LapLink software and cables for connecting two computers. It can be used for back-up or transfer of data between computers. It also works over modems. It is great for transferring data and files to new hard disks or computers.

To prevent data losses due to a controller failure, some RAID systems use a separate disk controller for each drive. A mirror copy is made of the data on each system. This is called *duplexing*. Some systems use a separate power supply for each system, but all systems use uninterruptible power supplies.

RAID systems are essential for networks or any other area where the data is critical and must absolutely be preserved. No matter how careful you are and how many backup systems you have, you might still occasionally lose data through accidents or some other act of God. You can add more and more to the backup systems to make them fail-safe, but eventually you will reach a point of diminishing returns. Depending on how much is spent and how well it is engineered, the system should be system fault tolerant (SFT); that is, it will remain fully operational regardless of one or more component failures.

Uninterruptible Power Supplies

Uninterruptible Power Supplies (UPS) were discussed briefly in Chapter 2. They are mentioned here again because they are so important to backup. If you have a power failure or brownout while working on a file, you could lose a lot of valuable data. In areas where there are frequent electrical storms, it is essential that you use an UPS. The basic UPS is a battery that is constantly charged by the 110-V input voltage. If the power is interrupted, the battery system takes over and continues to provide power long enough for the computers to save the data that might happen to be in RAM, then shut down.

There are several companies who manufacture quite sophisticated UPS systems for almost all types of computer systems and networks. Of course for a single user, you only need a small system. On a network or for several computers, a system that can output a lot of current is required. There are several UPS companies. Here are just a few:

American Power Conversion
888-289-APCC, ext. 8172
www.apcc.com

Best Power Technology
800-356-5794

Sola Electric
800-289-7652

Tripp-Lite Mfg.
(312) 329-1777

Again, if your data is worth anything at all, it is worth backing up. It is much better to be backed up than to be sorry.

10

Monitors

You can't beat quality. Good monitors usually have long lives. I am still using an early NEC Multisync color monitor that is almost ten years old on one of my computers. I first used it on one of my old XTs with a digital adapter. But NEC was ahead of most monitor manufacturers and included a switch so that it can be used with analog input. Almost all monitors today are analog. It would be difficult to find a monitor that accepted digital input.

I recently bought three low-cost color monitors for systems that I set up for my grandchildren. Two of the three monitors failed within weeks of use. Of course the vendors replaced them. I bought them through mail order. The small amount of money I saved on the monitors was more than offset by the cost of packing them up, sending them back, and the downtime of the computers while waiting for the replacements. I still think you can get some real bargains through mail order. My experience with those monitors was an isolated case and is not typical.

It is possible to run some applications on a monochrome monitor, but most applications look much better in color. I spend a lot of time at my computer. Most of that time I am looking at the monitor. I like color, so even if I am just doing word processing, I want color. Most other people feel the same way. The monochrome monitors are now obsolete. It is difficult to even find a dealer who sells them today.

There are many different types of monitors with many different qualities and, of course, many different prices. A few monitor basics are discussed to help you understand how a monitor operates and to help you make a better decision in buying your monitor.

The CRT

A monitor is similar to a television. The main component is the cathode ray tube (CRT) or picture tube. In some respects, the CRT is like a dinosaur that is left over from the vacuum tube era. Before the silicon age of semiconductors, vacuum tubes operated almost all electronic devices. Like all vacuum tubes, the CRTs use enormous amounts of power, and generate lots of heat.

Vacuum tubes have three main elements: the cathode, the grid, and the plate. These elements correspond to the emitter, the base, and the collector of the transistor. In a vacuum tube, the cathode is made from metallic material which causes electrons to be boiled off when heated. The filament is made from resistive wire similar to that used in light bulbs. Also, very much like light bulbs, the filaments burn out which causes the tube to fail. Burned out filaments are the single greatest cause of failure in vacuum tubes. The filaments of computer CRTs are designed a bit better now, so that they don't burn out as often as in the early days.

If a positive direct current (dc) voltage is placed on the plate of a vacuum tube, the negative electrons boiled off from the heated cathode will be attracted to the plate. A control grid is placed between the cathode and plate. If a small negative voltage is placed on the grid, it will repel the negative electrons and keep them from reaching the plate. Zero voltage or a small positive voltage on the grid will let them go through to the plate. As the analog voltage swings up and down on the grid, it acts as a switch that allows a much larger voltage to pass through the vacuum tube. A voltage as small as a millionth of a volt on the grid of a vacuum tube can create a much larger exact voltage replica on the output of the plate. With the proper voltages on the emitter, base, and collector, a transistor operates much like a vacuum tube, acting as a switch or as an amplifier. In Chapter 1, Fig. 1-5 shows how a vacuum tube can take a small signal and amplify it. A vacuum tube can be quite large, require a lot of space and energy, and produces a lot of heat. Figure 1-5 also shows how a transistor can amplify the same signal, but it requires much less power and space. The Pentium II has 7.5 million transistors in a very small enclosure. If you had 7.5 million vacuum tubes, it would fill a large warehouse.

Like the vacuum tube, the CRT has a filament that heats up a cathode to produce electrons. It also has a grid that can shut off the passage of the electrons or let them pass through. The corresponding plate of the CRT is the back of the picture screen, which has about 25,000 volts on it to attract the electrons from the cathode. The back of the screen is coated with a phosphor. Because of the high attracting voltage, the electrons slam into the phosphor and cause it to light up and glow.

A very small thin beam of electrons is formed. This electronic beam acts very much like a piece of iron in a magnetic field. If four electromagnets are placed around the neck of the CRT, one on top, one on the bottom, and one each side, the beam of electrons can be directed to any area of the screen by varying the polarity of the voltage fed to the electromagnets. If you wanted the beam to move to the right, you could increase the plus voltage on the right magnet. If you wanted the beam to move up, you could increase the plus voltage on the top magnet. With these electromagnets, you can move the beam to any spot on the screen.

The small input signal voltage on the grid of the CRT turns the electron beam on and off to cause portions of the screen to light up. The beam can be caused to move and write on the screen just as if you were writing with a pencil. Alphabetic characters or any kind of graphics can be created in an exact replica of the input signal.

The present-day CRTs are like an ancient dinosaur. Many laptops and notebook computers have excellent color screens using transistors. The active matrix type uses thousands of transistors to light up each individual pixel. Other less costly systems are being developed. Eventually we will have large low-energy flat screens that can produce a good high-resolution picture. Even the television CRTs will be replaced with flat screens that can be hung on a wall.

Monochrome versus Color

In a monochrome television or a monitor, there is a single "gun" that shoots the electrons toward the back of the screen. Color televisions and color monitors are much more complicated than monochrome systems. During the manufacture of the color monitors, three different phosphors (red, green, and blue—RGB) are deposited on the back of the screen. Usually a very small dot of each color is placed in a triangular shape. If you use a magnifying glass and look at a color monitor or color television you can see the individual dots.

The different phosphors used to make color monitors are made from rare earths. They are designed to glow for a certain period of time after they have been hit by an electron beam.

In a color television or monitor, there are three guns, each shooting a beam of electrons. The electrons from each gun have no color. But each gun is aimed at a particular color, one to hit only the red dots, one the blue dots only, and one the green dots. They are very accurately aimed so that they will converge or impinge only on their assigned color dots. To make sure that the beams hit only their target, the beam must go through the holes of a metal shadow mask. Being hit by stray electrons causes the shadow mask to heat up. The heat might cause fatigue and loss of focus. Many of the newer monitors use shadow masks made from Invar, an alloy that has good heat resistance.

By turning the guns on or off to light up and mix the different red, green, and blue dots of phosphor, any color can be generated.

The Sony Trinitron monitors and televisions, use a system that is a bit different. Its three guns are in a single housing and fire through a single lens. Instead of a shadow mask, the Trinitron uses a vertical grill that allows the beams to pass through. The Trinitron system was actually invented in this country, but no one in the television industry was interested until Sony adopted it.

Dot Pitch

If you look closely at a black-and-white photo in a newspaper, you can see that the photo is made up of small dots. There will be a lot of dots in the darker areas and fewer in the light areas. The text or image on a monitor or a television screen is also made up of dots very similar to the newspaper photo. You can easily see these dots with a magnifying glass. If you look closely you can see spaces between the dots. This is much like the dots of a dot matrix printer. The more dots and the closer together they are, the better the resolution. A good high-resolution monitor has solid, sharply defined characters and images.

The more dots and the closer together they are, the more difficult it is to manufacture a CRT. The red, blue, and green dots must be placed very accurately and uniformly in order for their specific electron beam to hit them. Most standard monitors will have a dot pitch of 0.28 millimeters (mm). The better monitors will have dots that are as close as 0.24 mm. Some of the low-cost color monitors might have them from 0.39 mm up to 0.52 mm. Such monitors might be alright for playing games, but they wouldn't be very good for anything else.

Pixels

Resolution is also determined by the number of picture elements (pixels) that can be displayed. A *pixel* is the smallest unit that can be drawn or displayed on the screen. A pixel can be turned on or off with a single bit. But to control the intensity and color depth, it might take several bits per pixel.

The following figures relate primarily to text, but the graphics resolution is similar to the text. Most monitors are designed to display 80 characters in one row or line across the screen. By leaving a bit of space between each row, 25 lines of text can be displayed from top to bottom. The old color graphics monitor (CGA) could display 640 × 200 pixels. If you divide 640 by 80, you find that one character is eight pixels wide. There can be 25 lines of characters, so 200 divided by 25 = 8 pixels high. The entire screen will have 640 × 200 = 128,000 pixels. The EGA has 640 × 350, so each cell has eight pixels wide and 14 pixels high. The Video Electronics Standards Association (VESA) chose 640 × 480 to be the VGA standard and 800 × 600 to be the Super VGA (SVGA) standard. For SVGA it is 800 divided by 80 = 10 pixels wide and 600 divided by 25 = 24 pixels high. Many of the newer systems are now capable of 1024 × 768, 1280 × 1024, 1664 × 1200, and more. With a resolution of 1664 × 1200, you would have 1,996,800 pixels or almost 2 million pixels that could be lit up. We have come a long way from the 128,000 pixels possible with CGA.

Painting the Screen

To put an image on the screen, the electron beam starts at the top-left corner. Under the influence of the electromagnets, it is drawn across to the right of the screen lighting up a very thin line as it moves. Depending on what the beam is depicting, it will be turned on and off by the grid as it sweeps across the screen. When the beam reaches the right side of the screen, it is turned off and sent back to the left side. It drops down a bit and begins sweeping across the screen to paint another line. On a television set, it paints 262.5 lines in 1/60th of a second. These are all of the even numbered lines. It then goes back to the top and interlaces the other 262.5 odd numbered lines in between the first 262.5. It does this fairly fast, at a frequency of 15,750 Hz. (15750 divided by 60 = 262.5.) So it takes 1/30th of a second to paint 525 lines. This is called a *frame*, so 30 frames are written to the screen in one second.

When you watch a movie, you are seeing a series of still photos, flashed one after the other. Due to our persistence of vision, it appears to be continuous motion. It is this same persistence of vision phenomenon that allows us to see motion and images on our television and video screens.

Scan Rate

It is obvious that 525 lines on a television set, especially a large screen, leaves a lot of space in between the lines. If there were more lines, the resolution could be improved. As I was writing this, the FCC and the television industry was trying to decide on a standard for a high definition television that would have from 750 to about 1200 lines at 30 frames per second. At 750 lines, it would paint 375 lines in 1/60th of a second and 750 in 1/30th of a second. For 750 lines, the horizontal frequency would be 22,500 Hz. For 1200 lines, the horizontal frequency would be 36,000 Hz.

The Vertical Scan Rate

The time that it takes to fill a screen with lines from top to bottom is the *vertical scan rate*. This might also be called the *refresh rate*. The phosphor might start losing some of its glow after a period of time unless the vertical scan refreshes it in a timely manner. Some of the multiscan, or multifrequency, monitors can have several fixed or variable vertical scan rates. The Video Electronics Standards Association, (VESA) specifies a minimum of 70Hz for SVGA and 72Hz for VGA systems.

Multiscan

The multiscan monitors can accept a wide range of vertical and horizontal frequencies. This makes them quite versatile and flexible. Many of the early multiscans could accept both digital and analog signals. Almost all monitors sold today are the analog type.

The VGA system introduced by IBM on their PS/2 systems in 1987 used a fixed frequency instead of a multiscan adapter and monitor. A multiscan design costs more to build, so many of the low-cost VGAs are designed to operate at a single-fixed frequency. They are not as versatile or flexible as the multiscan, but the resolution might be just as good.

Many companies are manufacturing monitors with multifixed frequencies with two or more fixed frequencies. Again, they are not quite as flexible as the true multiscan, but they can cost less. I am using a 19-inch Sampo TriSync that has three different frequencies. For my purposes, it does everything that I need to do.

The multiscan monitors might sell for as little as $250 and up to as much as $3500 or more for some of the large 19- to 30-inch sizes.

Adapter Basics

You can't just plug a monitor into your computer and expect it to function. Just as a hard disk needs a controller, a monitor needs an adapter to interface with the computer. Our computer monitors are a bit different than televisions. A television set usually has all of its controlling electronics mounted in the TV console or case and is assembled and sold as a single unit. A computer monitor might have some electronics within its case, but its main controller, the adapter, is usually on a plug-in board on the PC motherboard. This gives us more versatility and utility because we can use different or specialized adapters if needed.

Televisions are usually much less expensive than a comparable-sized computer monitor. One reason is because they don't provide the resolution that a computer monitor does. Panasonic has developed a 36-inch TV/computer monitor that has the very good resolution. These monitors would be very good for presentations to large groups. See Fig. 10-1.

Fig. 10-1
A 36-inch Panasonic
television and
computer monitor.

There are several manufacturers that make monitor adapters so there is quite a lot of competition. This has helped to keep the prices fairly reasonable. Most monitors can operate with several different types of adapters. Adapters might cost as little as $40 and up to $1000 or more. Monitors might cost as little as $200 and up to $3000 or more. It would be foolish to buy a very expensive monitor and an inexpensive adapter, or vice versa. You should try to match the capabilities of the monitor and the adapter.

Most monitor adapters have text character generators built onto the board, which is similar to a built-in library. When you send an A to the screen, the adapter goes to its library and sends the signal for the preformed A to the screen. Each character occupies a cell made up of a number of pixels. The number of pixels depends on the resolution of the screen and the adapter. In the case of the VGA, if all the dots within a cell were lit up, there would be a solid block of dots 10 pixels or dots wide and 24 pixels high. When an A is placed in a cell, only the dots necessary to form the outline of the A will be lit up. It is very similar to the dots formed by the dot matrix printers when it prints a character.

With the proper software, a graphics adapter can allow you to place lines, images, photos, normal and various text fonts, and almost anything you can imagine on the screen. Almost all adapters sold today have both text and graphics capability.

Analog versus Digital

Most all monitors and adapters sold today are analog systems. Up until the introduction of the PS/2 with VGA, most displays used the digital system. The digital systems have severe limitations.

The digital signals are of two states, either fully on or completely off. The signals for color and intensity require separate lines in the cables. It takes six lines for the EGA to be able to display 16 colors out of a palette of 64. The digital systems are obsolete.

The analog signals that drive the color guns are voltages that are continuously variable. It takes only a few lines for the three primary colors. The intensity voltage for each color can then be varied almost infinitely to create as many as 256 colors out of a possible 262,144. To display more than 256 colors requires the true-color adapters.

Video Accelerator Boards

The fixed-function cards have accelerator chips with several built-in graphics functions. Because they have built-in functions, they can handle many of the Windows type graphics tasks without having to bother the CPU. Because they don't often have to go back and forth to the CPU over the I/O bus at the slow speed of 8MHz, they are usually much faster than the dumb frame buffer type. There is a wide price range for these cards. Examples of the graphics chips used in these cards are S3 86CXXX, IIT AGX014, and the ATI 68800. Some that have a limited fixed-function might cost as little as $50 up to $400.

Another type of adapter has its own coprocessor chip on board such as the Texas Instruments 34010 or the Hitachi HD63483. By using an on-board coprocessor, it frees up the CPU for other tasks. The coprocessor boards are usually more expensive than any of the other types of boards.

Newer and better boards are being developed every day to meet the strenous demands of multimedia for digital video, 3D technology, and full motion. Most of these boards are available for the VLB or PCI bus. One of the boards that has received some of the highest ratings by magazine laboratories is the Diamond Multimedia Stealth 64. It can play digital video from several different formats such as Indeo, Motion JPEG, and MPEG. (JPEG is a set of standards set up by the Joint Photographers Expert Group; MPEG is a similar set of standards set up by the Motion Picture Expert Group. Both standards concerns compression of video and motion pictures.)

An optional daughterboard can be added to the Diamond Stealth 64 Video Multimedia Accelerator to provide hardware MPEG decoding of both audio and video. The module provides capabilities to accept both NTSC (the American television standard) and PAL (the standard used in many European countries) signals. It will accept a camcorder, VCR, and several other input devices. The board comes bundled with Corel Draw, Turbo DLD, and PanaStation CAD accelerators. These software accessories alone are worth the cost of the board.

This Diamond adapter has a S3 Vision969 controller, 2Mb of VRAM, upgradeable to 4Mb VRAM, horizontal sync 31.5KHz to 96.6KHz, vertical refresh of 43.5Hz to 120Hz. It comes with several software utilities.

Diamond also manufactures the DTV 1100 that is a hardware option for their Stealth64 Video 2001 series. The hardware provides a 125 channel television tuner and the MPEG Video Player. This board can accept broadcast video or a television signal from a camcorder, VCR, laser disc, or camera. It also provides video capture capability.

3D Adapters

Much of the newer software for games and animation is now 3D. There are several companies that are manufacturing special adapters for 3D. At the present time there are no standards for 3D software or hardware, but Microsoft, Creative Labs, and several other companies are working to create a standard. Here are a couple of 3D software companies:

Lightwave 3D

NewTek

800-847-6111

Microsoft

3D Movie Maker

800-426-9400

A couple of 3D adapter companies are:

Creative Labs

3D Blaster

800-998-1000

Diamond Multimedia

Edge 3D

800-468-5446

Here are a couple of virtual reality products:

Stereo Graphics

SimulEyes VR

800-746-3937

Virtual I-O

Virtual I-Glasses

800-646-3579

There are many other companies that are working on 3D hardware and software. There are usually articles in several magazines, such as the *New Media Magazine, CD-ROM Today,* and *Virtual Reality*. See Chapter 17.

PCI Bus Adapters

You could use an old 8- or 16-bit ISA adapter on your Pentium Pro, but it would be about like hitching up a horse to pull a Cadillac. Many of the 486 and Pentium motherboards have either a VL bus or a PCI bus. The PCI offers some advantages over the VLB, so the VLB is obsolete. Most Pentium-class motherboards now have three or four PCI connectors and three or four ISA plug-in slot connectors. The PCI bus adapters are much faster than the older graphics and accelerator boards because they have a 32- or 64-bit path that is used to directly communicate with the CPU. This direct path also allows them to communicate at the CPU speed or frequency. The ISA I/O systems are limited to the 8- or 16-bit bus and operate at a speed of 8MHz to 10MHz no matter how fast the CPU is.

Some Windows, most graphics, and many other applications, require a lot of interaction with the CPU. So many of the true-color adapters are made for motherboards with a PCI bus. Most of the newer adapters are now designed for 64 bits and a few even operate at 128K, such as the Number Nine Imagine 128 Pro. Figure 10-2 shows a Diamond Edge 3D 3400XL adapter with 4Mb of VRAM.

Video Memory

Having memory on the adapter board saves having to go through the bus to the conventional RAM. Some adapter boards even have a separate plug-in daughterboard for adding more memory. With the older dumb frame buffer type cards, even with a lot of memory, the adapter had to go back and forth over the 16-bit bus to communicate with the CPU. Many of the applications, especially under Windows, might be painfully slow. An accelerator card with lots of on board memory and a VESA local bus (VLB) or Peripheral Component Interconnect (PCI) bus system can speed up the processing considerably.

You should have at least 1Mb of memory to display 256 colors in 1024 × 768 resolution. Of course, the more colors displayed and the higher the resolution, the more memory is required. To display 64,000 colors at 1024 × 768 requires 2M, and for 24-bit true color, it takes about 4Mb.

Fig. 10-2
A Diamond Edge 3D 3400XL monitor adapter with 4Mb of VRAM.

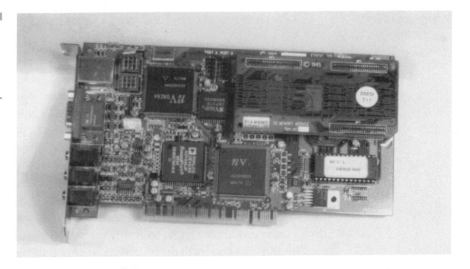

Adapter Memory Chips

Many of the high-resolution adapters have up to 4Mb or more of Video RAM (VRAM) memory on board. The VRAM chips look very much like the older DRAM DIP memory chips, but they are not interchangeable with DRAM. The DRAM chips have a single port; they can only be accessed or written to through this port. The VRAM chips have two ports and can be accessed by one port while being written to in the other. This makes them much faster and a bit more expensive than DRAM. Some of the less expensive adapters use DRAM memory.

Many of the less expensive adapter boards are sold with only 512K of DRAM or less. They often have empty sockets for adding more memory. Some cards have space to install as much a 40Mb of DRAM. It is not likely that you would need that much for ordinary use. It is very easy to install the memory chips in the sockets. Just be sure that you orient them properly. They should be installed they same way as other memory on the board. Make sure that all legs are fully inserted in the sockets.

If you expect to do any high-resolution graphics, then you should have a minimum of 1Mb of VRAM on the adapter; 2Mb would be even better.

Installation

Installing a monitor and adapter is usually fairly easy. Just plug the adapter board into an empty slot and plug in the monitor cable. Then run whatever software drivers that might have come with the board.

A new plug-n-play (PnP) standard should be available by the time you read this. The monitors and adapters that conform to the PnP standard will have a special connector that will include a display data channel (DDC) that can be used by the system to automatically choose the optimum settings for highest refresh rates and resolution.

The Video Electronics Standards Association (VESA) is also working on a new enhanced video connector (EVC) that will support higher bandwidths and let the monitor accept multimedia input devices such as cameras and microphones.

Windows 95 lets you easily customize your display. Just click the right mouse button anywhere on the desktop, then choose Properties. Display Properties has four different tabs: Background lets you set or change the desktop's pattern or wallpaper; Appearance lets you modify the color scheme; Screen Saver and Settings, let you change the color depth, resolution, and drivers for the monitor and adapter.

SVGA Colors

The number of colors that a SVGA card can display is dependent on the resolution displayed. Here are the numbers for a low-cost SVGA: 16.7 million colors at 640×480, only 64,000 colors at 800×600, and only 16 colors at 1280×1024.

Of course there are adapters that can display a much greater number of colors than those just listed, but they are also more expensive.

True Colors

Most of the standard low-cost VGA cards are capable of only 16 colors. True colors or pure colors requires video boards with lots of fast memory, a coprocessor, and complex electronics. *True color* means that a video board can drive a monitor to display a large number of shades in separate, distinct hues or pure colors. Remember that a pixel can be turned on or off with a single bit, but for color intensity or shades and depth, it might take several bits per pixel. A good adapter for true color might cost more than the monitor. Table 10-1 explains.

Table 10-1

Pure Color

Bits	Shades	Depth
4 or 2^4	16	
8 or 28	256	
15 or 2^{15}	32,768	5:5:5
16 or 216	65,536	5:6:5 or 6:6:4
24 or 2^{32}	16.7 million	8:8:8

Depth

True color usually refers to displays with 15-, 16-, or 24-bit depths. Depth means that each of the individual red, green, or blue (RGB) color pixels will have a large amount of information about each color. The 15-bit system will have five bits of information for each of the three colors. The 16-bit system might have six bits for red, six bits for green, and four bits for blue, or a combination of 5:6:5. The 24-bit system has eight bits for each color. Table 10-2 can give you an idea of how much memory is needed for the various resolutions and colors.

Bits/Pxl	Color	640 × 480	800 × 600	1024 × 768
4	16	150Kb	234Kb	386Kb
8	256	300Kb	469Kb	768Kb
16	35,536	600Kb	938Kb	1.536Mb
24	16,777,216	900Kb	1.406Mb	2.304Mb

Table 10-2

Memory and
Resolution

Dithering

If a board doesn't have enough power to display the true distinct colors, it might use dithering to mix the colors to give an approximation.

Dithering takes advantage of the eye's tendency to blur colors and view them as an average. A printed black-and-white photo uses all black dots, but several shades of gray can be printed depending on the number of black dots per inch. A mixture of red dots with white ones can create a pink image. Gradual color transitions can be accomplished by using dithering to intersperse pixels of various colors.

Antialiasing

Some low-resolution systems have a "stair-step" effect when a diagonal line is drawn on the screen. Some adapters have the ability to use anti-aliasing to average out the pixels so that a smooth line appears.

Sources

There are hundreds of adapter manufacturers. I hesitate to mention models, because each manufacturer has dozens of different models with different features and resolutions. And they are constantly designing, developing, and introducing new models. I have used several different models of the Diamond adapters and I think they are one of the best. Several computer magazines have tested and rated the following to be among the best. Call the companies for brochures and more information.

ATI Technologies
(905) 882-2600
www.atitech.ca

Boca Research
(561) 997-6227
www.bocaresearch.com

Diamond Multimedia Sys.
800-468-5846
www.diamondmm.com

Orchid Technology
(510) 683-0300
www.orchid.com

Matrox Graphics
800-361-1408
www.matrox.com

STB Powergraph 64
(214) 234-8750
www.stb.com

Number Nine Imagine 128
800-438-6463
www.nine.com

Adapter Software

Most adapter cards will work with any software that you have. But many adapter vendors provide special software drivers that are necessary for high resolution and speed with certain applications. Make sure that the adapter has drivers for all popular graphics type software.

MPEG Boards

The Motion Pictures Expert Group (MPEG) devised a specification for compressing and decompressing graphics and video. Ordinarily, a single frame in a moving picture requires about 25MB to digitize and store. The MPEG system allows a compression up to 100 to 1 so that it is possible to store as much as 72 minutes on a 650Mb CD-ROM. Several companies have developed plug-in boards that will allow you to capture and playback video from several different sources such as a VCR, Camcorder, CD-ROM, television, laser disk, and others. Some cards have built-in sound systems and some can even be supplied with a television tuner so that you can watch TV on your monitor.

There are a few feature movies that have been compressed to the MPEG specifications. With a MPEG board, you can watch the movies on your high-resolution monitor. It is possible that as the MPEG system becomes more widespread, the PC might become the home entertainment center.

Here are a few companies who manufacture MPEG boards. Call them for brochures and information:

Diamond Multimedia Sys.
800-468-5846
www.diamondmm.com

Orchid Kelvin MPEG
(510) 651-2300
www.orchid.com

Genoa GVision DX
800-934-3662
www.genoasys.com

Sigma Real Magic Rave
(510) 770-0100
www.realmagic.com

Choosing a Monitor

The primary determining factors for choosing a monitor should be what it is going to be used for and the amount of money you have to spend. Try to get a good 15-inch as a minimum. If you can afford it, buy a large 21-inch monitor with super high resolution and a good SVGA board to drive it. Look for monitors with a refresh rate of at least 72Hz or higher. Look for a dot pitch of at least 0.28 mm; 0.26 mm, or 0.24 is even better but more expensive. The resolution should be at least 800 × 600; 1024 × 768 is better. Make sure the controls are near the front and easily accessible.

The stated screen size of a monitor is very misleading and almost fraudulent. The stated size is a diagonal measurement. There is a border on all four sides of the screen. The usable viewing area on a 14-inch monitor is about 9.75 inches wide and about 7.75 inches high. One reason is because the screen is markedly curved near the edges on all sides. This curve can cause distortion so the areas are masked off and not used.

If you expect to do any kind of graphics or CAD/CAM design work, you will definitely need a good large screen color monitor, with very high resolution. A large screen is almost essential for some types of design drawings so that as much of the drawing as possible can be viewed on the screen.

You will also need a high-resolution monitor for close tolerance designs. For instance, if you draw two lines to meet on a low-resolution monitor, they might look as if they are perfectly lined up. But when the drawing is magnified or printed out, the lines might not be anywhere close to one another.

Most desktop publishing (DTP) is done in black-and-white print. The high-resolution paper white monochrome monitors might be all you need for these applications. These monitors can usually display several shades of gray.

Many of these monitors are the portrait type; that is, they are higher than they are wide. Many of them have a display area of $8\frac{1}{2}$ by 11 inches. Instead of 25 lines, they will have 66 lines, which is the standard for an 11-inch sheet of paper. Many have a phosphor that will let you have black text on a white background so that the screen looks very much like the finished text. Some of the newer color monitors have a mode that will let you switch to pure white with black type. Most of our monitors are wider than they are tall. These are called *landscape* styles.

What to Look for

If possible, go to several stores and compare various models. Turn the brightness up and check the center of the screen and the outer edges. Is the intensity the same in the center and the outer edges? Check the focus, brightness, and contrast with text and graphics. There can be vast differences even in the same models from the same manufacturer.

Ask the vendor for a copy of the specs. Check the dot pitch. For good high resolution, it should be no greater than 0.28 mm, even better would be 0.26 mm or 0.24 mm.

Check the horizontal and vertical scan frequency specs. For a multi-scan, the wider the range, the better. A good system could have a horizontal range from 30KHz-40KHz or better. The vertical range should be from 45Hz-70Hz or higher.

Controls

You might also check for available controls to adjust the brightness, contrast, and vertical/horizontal lines. Some manufacturers place them on the back or some other difficult area to get at. It is much better if they are accessible from the front so that you can see what the effect is as you adjust them.

Glare

If a monitor reflects too much light, it can be like a mirror and be very distracting. Some manufacturers have coated the screen with a silicon formulation to cut down on the reflectance. Some have etched the screen for the same purpose. Some screens are tinted to help cut down on glare. If possible, you should try the monitor under various lighting conditions. If you have a glare problem, several supply companies and mail-order houses offer glare shields that cost from $20 up to $100.

Cleaning the Screens

Because there are about 25,000 volts of electricity hitting the backside of the monitor face, it creates a static attraction for dust. This dust can distort and make the screen difficult to read.

Most manufacturers should have an instruction booklet that suggests how the screen should be cleaned. If you have a screen that has been coated with silicon to reduce glare, you should not use any harsh cleansers on it. Usually, plain water and a soft paper towel does fine.

Monitor Radiation

Almost all electrical devices emit very low frequency (VLF) magnetic and electrical fields. There have been no definitive studies that prove that this radiation is harmful to a person. In some cases, the emissions are so weak that they can hardly be measured. However, the government of Sweden developed a set of guidelines to regulate the strength of emissions from video display terminals (VDTs).

Several people in this country are also concerned that the VDT radiation might be a problem, so many monitor manufacturers now add shielding to control the emission. If you are worried about VDT emissions, look for monitors that are certified to meet MPR II specifications. Incidentally, if you use a hair dryer, you will get much more radiation from that than from a monitor.

Green Monitors

The monitor might use 100 to 150 watts of energy. The EPA Energy Star program demands that the energy be reduced to no more than 30 watts when it is not being used.

I sometimes sit in front of my monitor for 10 or 15 minutes, doing research, or more likely having writers block. All this time the monitor is burning up lots of watts of energy. Many of the new monitors meet the Energy Star specifications, so when there is no activity, they go into a sleep mode where they use very little energy. A small amount of voltage is still applied to the monitor and it will come back on-line almost immediately.

None of my monitors comply with the Energy Star specification, but I am saving energy by using the PC ener-g saver from the NEI Company at (800) 832-4007. The PC ener-g saver acts as an on/off switch for the monitor and printer. The keyboard cable connector is removed from the motherboard connection and plugged into the box. A cable from the box replaces the keyboard connection to the motherboard. Using software that comes with the unit, you can set the PC ener-g saver to shut down your monitor and printer if there is no activity from the keyboard. You can set the time interval for no activity from just a few seconds up to several minutes. As soon as any key on the keyboard is pressed or the mouse is moved, the monitor comes back on. It comes back to the same place where you were working when it shut down. To reactivate the printer, just send it a print command.

Software for Monitor Testing

If you are planning to buy an expensive high-resolution monitor, you might want to buy a software program called DisplayMate for Windows from Sonera Technologies at (908) 747-6886, www.displaymate.com. It is a collection of utilities that can perform several checks on a monitor. It lets you measure the resolution for fine lines, the clarity of the image, distortion, has gray and color scales, and a full range of intensities and colors. The software can actually help tweak and fine-tune your monitor and adapter. The setup also helps a person set the controls for the optimum values. About 40 percent or more of the cost for a computer system is for the monitor. It could be well worth it to test the monitor first.

The following are statements from the DisplayMate website at www.displaymate.com:

> The DisplayMate Utilities are designed to help you achieve the highest possible image quality and picture quality on any computer monitor, LCD display, video projector, television, HDTV, or any type of display

device that can be connected directly or indirectly to a computer. DisplayMate guarantees to improve the image and picture quality on any display.

You can use DisplayMate to compare and evaluate displays you're thinking of buying. Our video diagnostic products will thoroughly test including your entire video system for performance and compatibility, the monitor, video board and video BIOS.

DisplayMate's rich set of color and gray-scale patterns are also essential for accurate printer setup and calibration.

DisplayMate is the only utility in the world that is devoted to monitors and video boards. The product is easy to use. There is no learning time.

DisplayMate works by presenting a slide show of special highly sensitive test screen images. You simply look at them and follow the easy step-by-step instructions and expert on-line advice and guidance. The result is a complete video system Tune-Up with your display performing at its absolute best.

Here are some monitor tips that can be found at the DisplayMate website:

- How picky are you?
- No video display is perfect, including the best and most expensive monitors, so be prepared to accept some compromises in image and picture quality.
- Remember, you might be looking at that monitor for several thousand hours. Every single major computer magazine in the USA uses DisplayMate to test and evaluate monitors.
- You can gain similar insight into monitor performance and capabilities by taking along a copy of DisplayMate when you go monitor shopping.
- Know what bothers you the most.
- Different people are bothered by different image quality imperfections. It's important to identify the ones that bother you, and then prioritize them. The most common problems that bug people include color misregistration, fuzzy image, Moiré patterns in the image, geometric distortion, tilted image, flicker, glare, and screen reflections.

■ Look for monitors with controls that can adjust the imperfections that bug you the most. For example, look for convergence controls if color misregistration is at the top of your list.

■ The more controls on your monitor, the better.

■ Monitors are now coming with more and more end-user accessible controls that allow you to adjust and correct problems in the image. Besides the mandatory brightness, contrast, size, and position controls, you might find focus, convergence, tilt, pincushion, keystone, moire, color temperature, RGB color drive and cutoff, and manual degaussing controls.

■ Advanced controls found on only a few monitors include: dynamic focus, dynamic convergence, color purity, pincushion phase, and pincushion balance.

■ They're all very useful. The more controls you have, the better the image and picture quality on your monitor will be. Don't worry if you don't know how to adjust some of the more obscure controls, DisplayMate can show you how.

■ The more controls on your video board the better.

■ Controls on the video board can be used to correct some problems in the monitor's image. For example, as demonstrated within DisplayMate, certain combinations of video board and monitor control adjustments might be able to reduce or eliminate certain forms of geometric distortion. Controls that are especially helpful in a video board are: vertical and horizontal size, vertical and horizontal position, horizontal scanning frequency, and vertical refresh rate.

■ Some of the video board controls might only be accessible using obscure DOS utilities that came on the video board's drivers disk, so look over the list of files carefully. In other cases the controls are only accessible through supplementary utilities available from the manufacturer's BBS.

■ Watch out for sample-to-sample variations.

■ There is generally a significant sample-to-sample variation between monitors of the same make and model, even among the best brands. Monitors are actually delicate precision analog instruments. They are affected by variations in components, assembly, and factory calibration. They are also particularly affected by how much they bounce around during shipment and handling. If you're buying from a store rather than mail order, then checkout the actual monitor you're getting with DisplayMate before you pay for it and take it home. If you're buying mail order, then try to get an exchange capability in case there is a problem.

- Carefully set all the controls on your monitor and video board.

- Many users don't know how to adjust some of the controls on their monitor or video board. If you don't take the time to properly set every control, then they'll actually make matters worse rather than better. DisplayMate includes specialized test patterns to precisely adjust every one of the controls to its optimum value.

- Detailed on-line information and instructions explain what to look for and what to do. For example, setting the brightness and contrast controls is straight forward, but requires four separate test patterns in DisplayMate to do it accurately. The payoff is obtaining an optimum gray-scale with optimum contrast.

- Take advantage of the inherent image quality trade-offs between controls.

- Most of the monitor's image parameters are interdependent. Changing one control will often directly or indirectly affect another. While this is a complication, it's also an opportunity, because some things can be improved at the expense of others, based on your own preferences. For example: the higher you set the refresh rate, the lower the image flicker, but the fuzzier the image is likely to appear due to limitations in video bandwidth. Setting the refresh rate to the highest values allowed by your monitor and video board is not likely to be the best visual compromise setting.

- DisplayMate tells you which are the important trade-offs and provides test patterns that let you decide what the best overall visual compromises are. There are hundreds of suggestions on improving image quality.

- Make sure you get a sharp video board.

- Image quality and image sharpness vary significantly among video board brands and models. Try out different boards with the same monitor to compare the differences.

- If you need good color accuracy and color matching, get a good video board.

- The color matching controls found on most high-end monitors can only adjust the monitor's white point or color temperature. To perform detailed color matching or to correct color tracking errors you need a video board that lets you adjust the RGB color transfer functions, sometimes incorrectly referred to as the Gamma correction curves. This can be accomplished by downloading new RGB tables into to the board's hardware RAMDAC, or alternatively performed in software by the Windows driver.

■ Check for these capabilities. If you need them but don't understand the terminology or how to calibrate the colors and gray-scale, DisplayMate explains how and leads you through the calibration procedures in a detailed step-by-step fashion.

■ Keep the monitor in good tune.

■ Many users will set the controls as best as they can when the monitor and video board are first installed, and then forget about them. Monitors drift as they warm up, they'll drift a bit during the day, and they'll age over a period of weeks and months.

■ Environmental factors such as room lighting are also important, and can vary because of changing sunlight. How often you need to adjust the monitor controls depends upon how stable your hardware is, the nature of your application, and how discriminating you are. Once you become aware of image quality issues, you'll become sensitized to them. Things that you glossed over or tolerated before will no longer be acceptable.

Other Resources

A monitor is a very important part of your computer system. I couldn't possibly tell you all you need to know in this short chapter. One of the better ways to keep up on this ever-changing technology is to subscribe to one or more computer magazines. They frequently have articles about monitors. Of course, they also have many ads for monitors and adapters. I have listed several computer magazines in Chapter 22.

11

Input Devices

Before you can do anything with a computer, you must input data. There are several ways to input data, such as from a keyboard, a disk, by modem, mouse, scanner, barcode readers, voice recognition input, FAX, on-line from the Internet or a bulletin board, main frame, or a network. This chapter discusses a few of the ways to input data to a computer.

Keyboards

By far the most common way to get data into the computer is by way of the keyboard. For most common applications, it is impossible to operate the computer without a keyboard.

The keyboard is a personal connection with your computer. If you do a lot of typing, it is very important that you get a keyboard that suits you. Not all keyboards are the same. Some have a light "mushy" touch, some heavy. Some have noisy keys; others are silent with very little feedback.

A Need for Standards

Typewriter keyboards are fairly standard. There are only 26 letters in the alphabet and a few symbols, so most QWERTY typewriters have about 50 keys. I have had several computers over the last few years and every one of them has had a different keyboard. The main typewriter characters aren't changed or moved very often, but some of the very important control keys like the ESC, the CTRL, the PRTSC, the \, the function keys, and several others are moved all over the keyboard.

For the last few years, most keyboards had 101 keys. Windows 95 and multimedia functions have caused several more keys to be added. Keyboards now have 109 or more keys. The extra keys provide application shortcuts for Windows 95 and other task functions.

There are well over 400 different keyboards in the U.S. Many people make their living by typing on a keyboard. Many of the larger companies have systems that count the number of keystrokes that an employee makes during a shift. If the employee fails to make a certain number of keystrokes, then that person can be fired. Can you imagine the problems if the person has to frequently learn a new keyboard? I am not a very good typist in the first place; I have great difficulty using different keyboards. There definitely should be some sort of standards.

Innovation, creating something new that is useful and needed and makes life better or easier, is great. That type of innovation should be encouraged everywhere. But many times changes are made just for the sake of differentiation without adding any real value or functionality to the product. This applies not only to keyboards, but to all technology.

How a Keyboard Works

The keyboard is actually a computer in itself. It has a small microprocessor with its own ROM. The computerized electronics of the keyboard eliminates the bounce of the keys, can determine when you hold a key down for repeat, can store up to 20 or more keystrokes, and can determine which key was pressed first if you press two at a time.

In addition to the standard BIOS chips on your motherboard, there is a special keyboard BIOS chip. Each time a key is pressed, a unique signal is sent to the BIOS. This signal is made up of a direct current voltage that is turned on and off a certain number of times, within a definite time frame, to represent zeros and ones.

Each time a 5-volt line is turned on for a certain amount of time, it represents a 1, when it is off for a certain amount of time it represents a 0. In the ASCII code, if the letter A is pressed, the code for 65 will be generated, 1 0 0 0 0 0 1.

Reprogramming Key Functions

Most word processors, spreadsheets, database, and other software programs usually designate certain keys to run various *macros*. A macro is a word, or several words, that can be input by just pressing one or more keys. By pressing a certain key, or a combination of one or two keys, you could input your name and address or any other group of words that you use frequently. These programs also use the function keys to perform various tasks such as moving the cursor, underlining, bolding, and many other functions. The problem is that there is no standardization. Changing from one word processor or software program to another is like having to learn a new foreign language. It sure would be nice if you could go from one program to another as easily as you can drive different automobiles.

Keyboard Sources

Keyboard preference is strictly a matter of individual taste. The Key Tronic Company of Spokane, (509) 928-8000, makes some excellent keyboards. They are the IBM of the keyboard world. Their keyboards have set the standards. The Key Tronic keyboards have been copied by the clone makers, even to the extent of using the same model numbers.

Quality keyboards use a copper-etched printed circuit board and keys that switch on and off. The keys of quality keyboards have a small spring beneath each key to give them a uniform tension. Key Tronic offers several models. On some models, they even let you change the little springs under the keys to a different tension. The standard is 2 ounces, but you can configure the key tension to whatever you like. You can install 1, 1.5, 2, 2.5, or 3 ounce springs for an extra fee. They can also let you exchange the positions of the CapsLock and Ctrl keys. The Key Tronic keyboards have several other functions that are clearly described in their large manual.

Many of the less expensive keyboards use plastic with conductive paint for the connecting lines instead of an etched copper-printed circuit board. Instead of springs beneath each key, they use a rubber cup. The bottom of each key is coated with a carbon-conductive material. When the key is depressed, the carbon allows an electrical connection between the painted lines. The keys are part of, and are attached to, the main plastic board by strips of flexible molded plastic. These low-cost keyboards might have as few as 17 parts. The keyboards work fairly well.

I recently saw new clone keyboards being sold at a swap meet for $10 each. The keyboards looked very much like the Key Tronic 101 key types. The assembly snapped together instead of using metal screws. They also had several other cost-saving features. There is quite a lot of electronics in a keyboard. I don't know how they can possibly make a keyboard to sell for $10. At that price, you could buy two or three of them. If you ever had any trouble with one, just throw it away and plug in a new one.

There are several keyboard manufacturers and hundreds of different models with many different special functions. Prices range from $10 up to $400 or more. Look through any computer magazine.

Specialized Keyboards

Several companies have developed specialized keyboards. I have listed only a few of them here.

Quite often I have the need to do some minor calculations. The computer is great for calculations. Most of the word processor, database, and spreadsheet programs have built-in calculator functions. But in order to use the calculator, most of these programs require that the computer be on and be using a file. There are some keyboards that have a calculator built into the number pad. It has a battery so that it can be used whether the computer is on or not.

All newer keyboards now have the extra Windows 95 keys, even the $10 clones that I saw at the swap meet. You don't really need the extra keys to run Windows 95. I have several older keyboards that work just fine with Windows 95.

The Maxi Switch Company, at (520) 746-9378, NMB Technologies, at 800-662-8321, and SC&T International, at 800-408-4084, have multimedia keyboards that come with a microphone, speakers, input, jacks and volume control.

Another Key Tronic model has a bar code reader attached to it. This can be extremely handy if you have a small business that uses bar codes. This keyboard would be ideal for a computer in a point-of-sale (POS) system.

If you have been in the computer business for a while, you might remember the PCjr from IBM. It had a wireless keyboard that used an infrared system similar to a television remote control. The Casco Products Company, at 800-793-6960, thinks it is still a good idea. They have developed the LightLink, which is a wireless keyboard that communicates by infrared with a small receiver that plugs into the motherboard keyboard socket. One use for this keyboard is for presentations. The person can operate the computer from across the room.

Carpal Tunnel Syndrome

Businesses spend billions of dollars each year for employee health insurance. Of course the more employee injuries, the more the insurance costs. Carpal tunnel syndrome (CTS) has become one of the more common complaints. CTS causes pain and/or numbness in the palm of the hand, the thumb, index, and ring fingers. The pain might radiate up into the arm. Any movement of the hand or fingers can be very painful. CTS is caused by pressure on the median nerve where it passes into the hand through the carpal tunnel and under a ligament at the front of the wrist. Either one or both hands can be affected. Treatment often requires expensive surgery, which might or might not relieve the pain.

CTS most commonly affects those people who must use a computer for long periods of time. Keying in data is a very important function in this computer age. That is the job of many employees, eight hours a day, every day. CTS is usually caused by the way the wrist is held while typing on the keyboard. There are several pads and devices to help make the typing more comfortable. I have a foam rubber pad that is the length of the keyboard and is about four inches wide and three quarters of an inch thick. I can rest and support my wrists on this pad and still reach most of the keys. Many of the vendors give them away at shows like COMDEX.

Repetitive strain injury (RSI), is about the same as CTS. Many employees are asking for workers compensation insurance and taking companies to court because of RSI. At the time of this writing there are several cases in court against IBM, Apple, and several other large computer manufacturers. CTS and RSI injuries have cost millions of dollars in lost work days. It has become a serious problem.

Workers compensation programs in California were costing millions of dollars. In 1997, a law was passed requiring all employers with more than 10 employees to provide special training to injured workers and others doing similar work. The employers must try to identify and combat potential injury hazards with corrective action. Possible steps are adjusting desks for typists with sore wrists or more rest breaks. The law also includes those who might be lifting heavy weights or other repetitive tasks that could cause injury.

Before the computer revolution, thousands of people, mostly women, sat at a typewriter eight or more hours a day typing on keyboards that are similar to computer keyboards. Yet there were few, if any, cases of CTS or RSI ever reported. It is a disorder that has become prevalent only in the last few years. Last year 308,200 cases were reported. It could be that typewriter keyboards have more slant and were usually placed at a different height. Another factor might have been that the typewriter limited the typist's speed and repetition. With the computer, some data-input workers can do as many as 13,000 keystrokes per hour.

Some of the things that are suggested to help prevent RSI and CTS include pausing frequently and stretching your hands and upper body. Also adjust your desk and chair so that both feet rest easily on the floor.

Ergonomic Keyboards

The Key Tronic Company, at (509) 923-8000, has an ergonomic keyboard that breaks in the middle and each half can be elevated from the center. The center can be separated and angled to fit the angle of your hands. The B and N keys might be separated by as much as an inch or more, while the Y and T keys might be touching. The elevation and the angle should help prevent CTS and RSI. This Key Tronic keyboard is rather expensive at about $300. The Key Tronic company developed the ergonomic keyboard for Microsoft. Like most products with a brand name, it is a bit expensive at $99. Several other companies have also developed similar ergonomic keyboards for less than half that price.

ALPS Electric, at 800-825-2577, Cirque Corp., at 800-454-3375, and Northgate, at 800-548-1993, all have glidepoint keyboards with pads that can take the place of a mouse. They have a square pad below the arrow keys. You use your finger on the pad to move the cursor. To click, just tap the pad with your finger or press one of the three nearby buttons. The Northgate OmniKey is ergonomically shaped with the keys separated and angled similar to the Microsoft Natural keyboard. Mitsumi, at 800-648-7864, also has a low-cost ergonomic shaped keyboard.

Figure 11-1 shows a clone ergonomic keyboard with a touch pad. It is quite similar to the keyboards just mentioned. The main difference is that those keyboards are listed at this time for $139 to $149 each. I paid $49 for this clone. It has a PS/2 type keyboard connector, which is much

Fig. 11-1
An ergonomic keyboard that is similar to Microsoft's. It cost about half what the Microsoft keyboard costs.

smaller than a standard AT keyboard connector. It comes with an adapter so that it can be used on either system. See Fig. 11-2. The touch pad must be connected to one of the serial ports, just like a normal mouse. This port connector and cable are part of the keyboard cable. One of the advantages of the touch pad is that it does not have the mouse cable on the desktop and it does not require desktop space for a mouse pad. The keyboard has a switch that will allow you to switch off the touch pad and use a standard mouse if you want to.

This clone keyboard has the new Windows 95 extra keys. It also has extra Tab and Backspace keys. Most of the other keys are the same as the standard 101 keyboard, but they are angled, separated, and raised in the center. It has taken me a bit of time to become accustomed to it.

Even though some of the ergonomic keyboards are a bit expensive, they are a lot less expensive than having to go to a doctor for a painful operation that might or might not be successful. Other than surgery, the other alternative is to rest the hands and miss several months of work. If you work for a large company, the company might save money by installing these ergonomic keyboards. Many people are now suing companies for CTS and RSI injuries. Of course, the insurance companies are increasing their rates to help pay for any damages that might be awarded.

Fig. 11-2
The ergonomic keyboard comes with a PS/2-type cable.

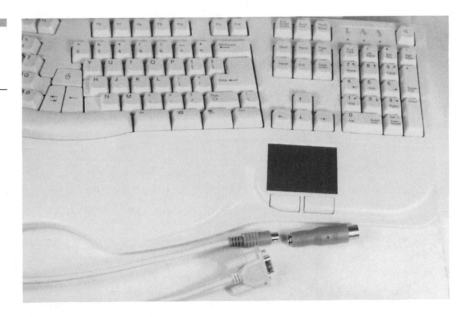

Mouse Systems

One of the biggest reasons for the success of the Macintosh is that it is easy to use. With a mouse and icons, all you have to do is point and click. You don't have to learn a lot of commands and rules. A person who knows nothing about computers can become productive in a very short time. The people in the DOS world finally took note of this and began developing programs and applications, such as Windows, for the IBM and compatibles.

There are now dozens of companies that manufacture mice. There are some mice that cost up to $100 or more; others cost less than $10. What is the difference in a mouse that costs $100 and one that costs $10? The answer is $90. The low-cost mouse does just about everything that most people would need from a mouse. After all, how much mouse do you need just to point and click. Of course if you are doing high-end drafting, designing, and very close-tolerance work, then you definitely need one that has high resolution.

The Ball-Type Mice

Most mice have a small round rubber ball on the underside that contacts the desktop or mouse pad. As the mouse is moved, the ball turns. Inside the mouse, two flywheels contact the ball, one for horizontal and one for vertical movements. The flywheels are mounted between two light-sensitive diodes. The flywheels have small holes in the outer edge. As the flywheels turn, light shines through the holes or is blocked where there are no holes. This breaks the light up into patterns of 1s and 0s which then control the cursor movement. On most mice, the ball can be easily removed and cleaned because it picks up dirt.

Mouse Interfaces

You can't just plug in a mouse and start using it. The software, whether Windows, WordPerfect, or a CAD program, must recognize and interface with the mouse. So mouse companies develop software drivers to allow the mouse to operate with various programs. The drivers are usually supplied on a disk. The Microsoft Mouse is the closest to a standard, so most other companies emulate the Microsoft driver. Most mice drivers are now included in Windows. Most mice today come with a small switch that allows you to switch between the Microsoft emulation or the IBM PC. If the switch is not in the proper position, it might not work.

The mouse plugs into a serial port, COM1 or COM2. This might cause a problem if you already have two serial devices using COM1 and COM2. DOS also allows for COM3 and COM4, but these two ports must be shared with COM1 and COM2, so they must have special software in order to be shared.

Many of the newer Pentium Pro and Pentium II motherboards now have PS/2 connectors for the mouse and keyboard. You can use either connector to plug in the keyboard or the mouse. The PS/2 connector saves having to use one of the COM ports.

The serial ports on some systems use a DB25-type socket connector with 25 contacts. Others use a DB9 socket with nine contacts. Many of the mice now come with the DB9 connector and a DB25 connector adapter. The DB25 connector looks exactly like the DB25 connector used for the LPT1 parallel printer port, except that the serial port connector is a male-type connector with pins, the LPT1 printer port is a female with sockets.

There might be times when you have a cable that is a male when what you need is a female, or vice versa. (A male connector is one that has pins; a female connector has sockets.) You can buy DB25 "gender bender" adapters that can solve this type of problem. See Fig. 11-3. If you simply need an extension so that you can plug two similar cables together, straight-through adapters are also available. There are many different kinds of combinations. The Cables To Go Company, at 800-225-8646, has just about every cable and accessory that you would ever need. The Dalco Electronics Company, at 800-445-5342, also has many types of cables, adapters, and electronic components.

Before you buy a mouse, you might check the type of serial port connector you have and order the proper type. You can buy an adapter for about $3.

Wireless Mice

One of the disadvantages of operating a keyboard such as the wireless LightLink mentioned earlier is that you also need a wireless mouse. Several companies have developed wireless mice. They operate with infrared rays similar to the remote control of a television. Some operate using a radio frequency, such as the wireless mouse made by Mitsumi Electronics, at 800-648-7864. Logitech, at 800-231-7717, also has wireless models. Even though they are wireless, they still need a receiver and an interface to connect to a serial port.

Fig. 11-3
A gender-bender. An adapter for DB25 sockets or pins.

Trackballs

A trackball is a mouse that has been turned upside down. Like the mouse, the trackballs also require a serial port.

One advantage of the trackball is that you don't need the square foot of desk space that a mouse requires. The trackballs are usually larger than the ball in a mouse, so it is possible to have better resolution. They are often used with CAD and critical design systems.

Constant use of a mouse can also lead to CTS and RSI. The Itac Systems, at 800-533-4822, claim that their ergonomically designed trackball Mouse-Trak can help prevent those injuries.

There are several companies who manufacture trackballs. Look through the computer magazines for advertisements.

Touch Screens and Light Pens

Some fast food places now have a touch screen with a menu of several items. You merely touch the item that you want and the order is transmitted to the executive chef, who is usually a high school kid. The same type of system is sometimes found in kiosks, in shopping malls, and large department stores. Some systems use an image of a keyboard so that you can touch the various keys almost as if you were typing. The touch system is accurate, saves time and money, and is convenient.

The touch screen operation is similar to using a mouse and pointing. Most of them have a frame installed on the bezel of the monitor. Beams of infrared light criss-cross the front of the monitor screen. For ordinary text, most monitors are set up so that they have 80 columns left to right and 25 rows from top to bottom. Columns of beams originate from the top part of the frame and pass to the bottom frame. Rows of beams originate from the left portion of the frame and pass to the right frame. If one of the beams is interrupted by an object, such as a finger or pencil, the computer can determine exactly whatever character happens to be in that portion of the screen.

Joysticks

Joysticks are used primarily for games. They are serial devices and need an interface. Many of the multifunction boards that have COM ports also provide a game connector for joysticks.

Joysticks are fairly reasonable costing from $10 up to $30. There are usually several advertisements for them in magazines such as the *Computer Shopper.*

Digitizers and Graphics Tablets

Graphics tablets and digitizers are similar to a flat drawing pad or drafting table. Most of them use some sort of pointing device that can translate movement into digitized output to the computer. Some are rather small; some are as large as a standard drafting table. Some cost as little as $150 up to over $1500. Most of them have a very high resolution, are very accurate, and are intended for precision drawing.

Some of the tablets have programmable overlays and function keys. Some work with a mouse-like device, a pen light, or a pencil-like stylus. The tablets can be used for designing circuits, for CAD programs, for graphics designs, freehand drawing, and even for text and data input. The most common use is with CAD type software. The Wacom Technology Corp. also has a digitizer pad that uses a cordless, batteryless, pressure-sensitive pen.

Most of the tablets are serial devices, but some of them require their own interface board. Many of them are compatible with the Microsoft and mouse systems.

The CalComp Company, at 800-932-1212, has developed several models. These tablets use a puck that is similar to a mouse except that it has a magnifying glass and cross-hairs for very high resolution. They have both corded and cordless pucks. Call CalComp for a brochure and more information.

Signature Capture

It is very easy to generate a fax with a computer, but most letters and memos need a signature. The Inforite Company, at 800-366-4635, has a small pad and a stylus that will let you input a signature into a file. The signature can then be attached to a fax or to other documents. With the Inforite you can add notes, comments, or drawings to other documents in the computer.

Pressure-Sensitive Graphics Tablets

Several companies have developed pressure-sensitive tablets. Wacom has developed several different models. The Wacom tablets use an electro-magnetic resonance system. This allows the use of a special stylus that requires no wires or batteries. The tablet has a grid of embedded wires that can detect the location of the stylus and the pressure that is applied. The tablets sense the amount of pressure and draw a thin line or a heavy line in response. The tablets can be used with different graphics software programs to create sketches, drawings, designs, and art.

Here are some of the companies that manufacture pressure-sensitive tablets:

Wacom Technology
800-922-6613

Kurta Corp.
(602) 276-5533

Communication Intelligence
800-888-9242

Summagraphics
800-337-8662

You can call the companies for brochures or more information.

Scanners

Scanners with optical character reader (OCR) software can scan a line of printed type, recognize each character, and input that character into a computer just as if it were typed in from a keyboard. A beam of light sweeps across the page and the characters can be determined by the absorption and reflection of the light. One problem with the early scanners was that they could only recognize a few different fonts. They could not recognize graphics at all. The machines today have much more memory and the technology has improved to where the better scanners can recognize almost any font or type.

Scanners have been around for several years. When they first came out they cost from $6,000 to more than $15,000. Many full-page flat-bed scanners are now fairly inexpensive, starting at about $500. Scanners now have the ability to recognize a large number of fonts and they can copy and digitize color graphics and images. Many of the early scanners had a 100 dot per inch resolution (dpi). Later ones had 300 to 400 dpi. Many of the newer high-end ones now have a dpi as high as 800.

Some of the early low-cost color scanners had to make three passes, one for each primary color. Most of the newer and more expensive ones can now scan all three colors in one pass.

Many of the flat-bed scanners have a resolution of 24-bit color. Some of the newer ones now have 30 to 36 bit resolution. The 36 bit resolution means that 12 different bits of information are possible for each of the three primary colors. Some high-end, very high-resolution scanners that are needed for color graphic image processing and publishing might cost from $12,000 up to $95,000.

The flatbed scanners have a glass panel that is similar to those found in copy machines. The sheet to be scanned is laid on the glass panel and the machine sweeps the scanning heads across the sheet from top to bottom. Scanners have a lot in common with copy machines, printers, and fax machines. Many companies are now manufacturing multifunction machines that include the capability to scan, copy, print, and fax. These machines are discussed in more detail in Chapter 13.

Personal Scanners

Several companies are manufacturing small-page pass through compact scanners, such as the Logitech PageScan shown in Fig. 11-4. This scanner is quite versatile. It attaches to the parallel port of the computer so it doesn't need a separate board. It can scan in text, drawings, or even pho-

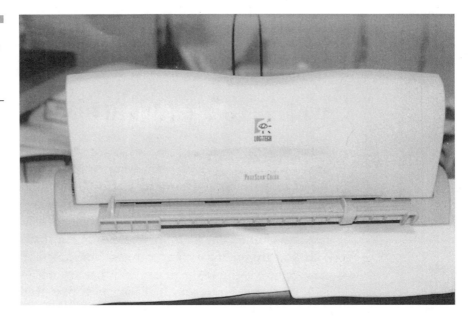

tos into the computer. If you need a copy of a page, scan it into the computer, then print it out. It can input printed text, signatures, drawings, or graphic images to a fax/modem board or to a hard disk.

Here are a few of the compact scanner vendors:

Delrina WinFax Scanner
800-268-6082

Microtek Lab PageWiz
800-654-4160

Envisions Personal PageVacuum
800-365-7226

Plustek USA PageReader 800
800-685-8088

Epson Personal Document Station
800-626-4686

Umax Technologies PageOffice
800-562-0311

Logitech ScanMan PowerPage
800-231-1717

Visioneer PaperPort
800-787-7007

The IRISPen Company, at 800-447-4744, has a small pen that can scan a single line at a time. There are times when you don't want or need to scan in a whole page, so the IRISPen is very handy for those occasions.

The Envisions, Epson, Microtek, and Umax companies previously listed also manufacture several other models and the higher quality flat-bed scanners. The Umax Mirage D-16 is a 12 by 17 inch format with 30 bit resolution and 800 dpi. There are many other scanner companies. Look for advertisements and articles in the computer magazines listed in Chapter 22.

Compaq Computer Systems and several other companies have developed a small feed-through scanner that is a part of the keyboard. It is very handy if you must do a lot of scanning.

What to Look for When Buying a Scanner

What to look for depends on what you want to do with your scanner, and of course, how much you want to pay. There are several manufacturers of scanners and hundreds of different models, types, resolutions, bus types, and prices. A monochrome scanner is fine for text. Many of the monochrome scanners are relatively inexpensive. They can recognize text and graphic images in up to 256 different shades.

If you are buying a color scanner, there are a lot more options to consider. Some of the lower priced ones have to make three passes, once for each color red, green, and blue. For each pass, the light is sent through filters that can recognize 256 levels of red, green, or blue.

The less expensive scanners might have a resolution of only 300 or 400 dots per inch. But they might use interpolation software that fills in the spaces between the dots to give two or three times the true resolution. As you might expect, some ads list the interpolated resolution in large letters and the true resolution in small letters, if it is mentioned at all.

The more expensive color scanners can capture all three colors in one pass. They might also scan at a true 24-bit color depth to yield 16.7 million colors. That means that there can be eight bits of color information about each of the red, green, or blue colors.

You should try to find a system that conforms to the TWAIN specification. The word *TWAIN* is an acronym for technology without an interesting name. (Mark Twain would have appreciated this acronym.) It is an application programming interface (API) specification that was jointly developed by Aldus, Caere, Eastman Kodak, Hewlett-Packard, and Logitech. A different device driver is needed for each of the hundreds of different printers. Before TWAIN, you needed a different device driver from every manufacturer for each model and type of scanner. TWAIN helps to standardize some of the device drivers. We really need something like TWAIN for printers.

Some of the less-expensive scanners use a proprietary interface board. It is much better to buy one that uses the SCSI interface. There are many manufacturers of scanners and of course many different prices.

OCR Software The OCR capabilities of a scanner allow it to recognize each character of a printed document and input that character into a computer just as if it were typed in from a keyboard. Once the data is in the computer, a word processor can be used to revise or change the data, then print them out again.

Faxes are received as graphical documents. It requires a lot of disk space to store a fax. But a scanner can convert them to text, which takes up much less disk space. Some of the OCR software programs, such as OmniPage Pro, supports over 100 different scanners. In most cases it can match text to the original fonts. It can read degraded text by reading it in context. It has a large internal dictionary that helps with this. It yields excellent OCR accuracy. OmniPage Pro can automatically convert scanned text into any of the most popular word processor formats. It has the Image Assistant, an integrated 24-bit color editor for graphic editing. OmniPage Pro 6.0 is one of the better OCR packages available. If you have any earlier version of OmniPage or WordScan, you can upgrade for a nominal sum.

Surplus Software, at 800-753-7877, advertises earlier versions of many software packages for a very low price. If you are an owner of a previous version of software, many of the companies will let you upgrade to the latest version for a very reasonable price. A software package that might cost as much as $600 originally, as an upgrade, might cost less than $100. (See Chapter 19 for details on surplus software and other low-cost early versions of software that can be traded in for current versions.)

Once data is entered into a computer it can be searched very quickly for any item. Many times I have spent hours going through printed manuals looking for certain items. If the data had been in a computer, I could have found the information in just minutes.

Several companies have developed advanced software to work with their scanners, and in some cases, those manufactured by other companies. Here is a brief list of the companies that have OCR software:

Caere Corp.
OmniPage Professional
800-535-7226

Recognita Corp.
Recognita Plus
(408) 241-5772

Logitech Corp.
Catchword Pro
(510) 795-8500

Delrina Company
WinFax PRO
(408) 363-2345

Ocron, Inc.
Perceive
(408) 980-8900

COLD

About ten years ago, just about everyone began installing computers in their offices. There was lots of excitement about the forthcoming age of the paperless office. But instead of reducing the large stacks of paper, the amount of paper increased. The reason was that most people insisted on having paper printouts along with the files on disk. A discouraged vice-president of a large company made the observation that we would probably see paperless offices at about the same time we had paperless bathrooms. He was right, but we are making a bit of progress.

Most large companies have thousands of file cabinets overflowing with memos, manuals, documents, and files that must be saved. Most of the documents will never be needed again. But from time to time, a few items stored in these files must be retrieved. Even with a good indexing system, it takes time to find a particular item. A good filing system and document management system using scanners, OCR, and a computer to laser disc (COLD) can be very helpful. Acres of file cabinets can be replaced by just a few small optical discs. As an added bonus, a good COLD system can help you find and retrieve any document within seconds.

Business Card Scanners

If you depend on business cards to keep in contact with prospective buyers or for other business purposes, you might have several Rolodexes full of cards. Or you can take each card and enter the information into your computer database. There is an easier way. Some companies have developed card scanners that can read the information off a business card and input it to a computer.

At this time they are still a bit expensive, but if you depend on business cards, they are well worth it. Like most computer products, the prices will come down very soon. Here are three of the companies that offer business card scanners:

CypherTech, Inc.   Cognitive Technology
CyperScan 1000   *Cognitive BCR*
(408) 734-8765   (415) 925-2367

Microtek Labs   Pacific Crest Tech.
Scan-in-Dex   *CardGrabber*
800-654-4160   (714) 261-6444

Large Format Scanners

Several companies manufacture large format scanners that are similar to the large plotters. They might be up to four feet wide and stand about three feet high. The scanners can be used to copy and digitize blue prints, CAD, architectural drawings, and even large signs and color images. These type scanners are rather expensive and are often used with high-end workstations. Here are a few companies who manufacture them:

ANAtech
(303) 973-6722

Scangraphics
(610) 328-1040

Ideal Scanners
(301) 468-0123

The WideCom Group
(905) 712-0505

Intergraph
(205) 730-8008

Vidar Systems
(703) 471-7070

Installing a Scanner

Most of the scanners, especially the high-end type color scanners, use a SCSI interface. You should get some sort of installation documentation and driver software with your scanner.

Some scanners might come with a plug-in board and software drivers. Some of them are serial-type devices, so they require the use of one of your COM ports and one of your motherboard slots. You might have to set switches or jumpers to configure the board so that it does not conflict with other devices in your system.

Voice Recognition Input

Another way to input data into a computer is to talk to it with a microphone. Of course you need electronics that can take the signal created by the microphone, detect the spoken words, and turn them into a form of digital information that the computer can use.

The early voice data input systems were very expensive and limited. One reason was that the voice technology required lots of memory. But the cost of memory has dropped considerably in the last few years, and the technology has improved in many other ways. Eventually, the voice input technology will replace the keyboard for many applications.

Voice technology usually involves "training" a computer to recognize a word spoken by a person. When you speak into a microphone, the sound waves cause a diaphragm, or some other device, to move back and forth in a magnetic field and create a voltage that is analogous to the sound wave. If this voltage is recorded and played through a good audio system, the loudspeaker will respond to the amplified voltages and reproduce a sound that is identical to the one input to the microphone.

A person can speak a word into a microphone, which creates a unique voltage pattern for that word and that particular person's voice. The voltage is fed into an electronic circuit, and the pattern is digitized and stored in the computer. If several words are spoken, the circuit will digitize each one of them and store them. Each one of them will have a distinct and unique pattern. Later when the computer hears a word, it searches through the patterns that it has stored to see if the input word matches any one of its stored words.

Of course, once the computer is able to recognize a word, you can have it perform some useful work. You could command it to load and run a program, or perform any of several other tasks.

Because every person's voice is different, ordinarily the computer would not recognize the voice of anyone who had not trained it. Training the computer might involve saying the same word several times so that the computer can store several patterns of the person's voice. Some of the new systems will now recognize the voices of others who have not trained the computer.

Uses for Voice Recognition

Voice recognition can be used for letters, reports, and complicated business and technical text. Voice recognition can be used by doctors, nurses, lawyers, reporters, loan officers, auditors, researchers, secretaries, business executives, in manufacturing, language interpreters, and by writers.

Computer voice recognition is very useful whenever you must use both hands for doing a job but still need a computer to perform certain tasks.

Voice recognition is also useful on production lines where the person does not have time to manually enter data into a computer. It can also be used in a laboratory where a scientist is looking through a microscope and cannot take his eyes off the subject to write down the findings or data. There might be times when the lighting must be kept too dim to input data to a computer manually. In other instances, the person might have to be several feet from the computer and still be able to input data through the microphone line or even with a wireless mic. The person might even be miles away and be able to input data over a telephone line.

Voice recognition and a computer can help many of those who have physical limitations to become productive and independent.

The Carnegie Mellon Institute is working on a system that would allow a person using English to call someone in Germany and the spoken conversation could be understood. The spoken English would be translated into German and the spoken German would be translated into English. The system would recognize the spoken word, then use computerized speech to translate it for the parties. So the parties would actually be talking to a computerized mechanical interpreter. Similar systems are being developed for Japanese and other foreign languages.

The same type of system can be built into small hand-held foreign language interpreters. Speak an English word into the machine and it gives you the equivalent spoken foreign word.

Many luxury automobiles now come with cellular phones with voice activated dialing. This lets the driver keep his or her eyes on the road while the number is being dialed.

The designers of computers are constantly looking for new ways to differentiate and improve their product. In the very near future you can be sure that many of them will have voice recognition built in.

Chips that use very large scale integration (VLSI) are combining more and more computer functions onto single chips. They are making computers smaller and smaller. We now have some very powerful computers that can fit in a shirt pocket. One of the big problems is that there is not room for a decent keyboard. To fit them all on a keyboard, the keys have to be very small. Some of them use a stylus to press each key. Some might let you use a single finger to type on the keyboards. Even then if your fingers are very large, you might end up pressing two keys at once. A solution would be to build in voice recognition so that the keyboard would not be needed.

Limitations

For most systems, the computer must be trained to recognize a specific discrete individual word. So the computer vocabulary is limited to what it is trained to recognize, the amount of memory available, and the limitations imposed by the software and hardware.

There are many basic systems available today that are very good at recognizing discrete words. But ordinarily, when we speak, many words blend together. There are not many systems around that can recognize continuous speech.

Another problem is homonyms, or words that are pronounced the same, and sometimes spelled the same, but have different meanings. For instance, him, hymn, and hem are all pronounced the same but have very different meanings. Another example is the words to, too, and two. Many people misspell and confuse the words there and their, your and you're, and it's and its. A lot of our words have many different meanings such as the word set, run, round, date, and many others.

One of the solutions to this problem would be to have software and hardware with enough intelligence that it could not only recognize the words but recognize the meaning due to the context in which they are used. That requires more intelligence than some human beings have.

Security Systems

The voice of every person is as distinct and different as fingerprints. Voice prints have been used to convict criminals. Because no two voices are alike, a voice recognition system could be used to practically eliminate the need for keys. Most automobiles already have several built-in computerized systems. You can be sure that sometime soon you will see autos that have a voice recognition system instead of ignition keys. Such a system could help reduce the number of car thefts and carjacking instances.

A voice recognition system could also be used for any place that required strict security. If they installed voice recognition at Fort Knox they could probably eliminate many of their other security measures.

In most of the older systems, the computer had to be trained to recognize a specific word. Memory limitations and computer power was such that the vocabulary was quite limited. Today we have computers with lots of memory and power. Because every word is made up of only 42 phonemes, several companies such as IBM, Verbex Voice Systems, and Dragon Systems are working on systems that will use a small sample of a person's voice that contains these phonemes. Using the phonemes from this sample, the computer could then recognize any word that the person speaks.

Basic Systems

The Verbex Voice Systems, at 800-275-8729, has developed a fairly sophisticated system that can almost make the keyboard obsolete. Their Listen for Windows uses special software and a 16-bit plug-in board with a digital signal processor (DSP) on it. After a bit of training, this system can recognize continuous speech. Of course it is still not perfect so there are times when you will have to slow down to discrete words and make corrections for words it does not understand. Call Verbex for more information and current pricing.

The Covox Company, (503) 342-1271, has several less expensive voice recognition systems. Call the Covox Company for a brochure and current prices.

Computers and Devices for the Handicapped

Several computer devices have been developed that can help the disabled person live a better life. Just because they have a physical impairment doesn't mean that they have a brain impairment. Nature often compensates. For instance, the hearing and tactile senses of many blind people are much more acute than those who can see.

There are devices that allow the blind, the deaf, the quadriplegic, and other severely disabled victims to communicate. There are special braille keyboards and keyboards with enlarged keys for the blind. The Eye-Typer from the Sentient Systems Technology of Pittsburgh, PA, has an embedded camera on the keyboard that can determine which key the user is looking at. It then enters that key into the computer. Words Plus of Sunnyvale, CA, has a sensitive visor that can understand input from a raised brow, head movement, or eye blinks.

The Speaking Devices Corp., (408) 727-5571, has a telephone that can be trained to recognize an individual's voice. It can then dial up to 100 different numbers when the person tells it to. The same company has a tiny ear phone that also acts as a microphone. These devices would be ideal for a person who can speak, but cannot use their hands.

Devices for the disabled allow many people to lead active, useful, and productive lives. Some have become artists, programmers, writers, and scientists. These communication devices have allowed them a bit of freedom from the harsh prison of their disabilities.

IBM has a number of products they call the Independence Series, which are designed to aid people with physical disabilities. They have a DOS-based utility, AccessDOS, that can be used to add functions to the keyboard, mouse, and sound boards. Call IBM at 800-426-4832 for more information.

Windows 95 has a bit of help for disabled persons. Click on the Start button, highlight Settings, click on Control Panel, then double click on the Accessibility Options. You will see five window tabs: (1) StickyKeys lets you press one key at a time instead of having to press two or three such as Ctl, Alt, Del. FilterKeys tells Windows 95 to disregard keystrokes that are not held for a certain length of time. (2) The SoundSentry lets you substitute a visual cue for an audible alert. ShowSounds can be used with programs that use digitized speech to display captions on screen. (3) Display is an option that allows you to select colors, fonts, and high contrast. (4) MouseKeys lets you control the cursor with the numeric keypad instead of a mouse. (5) The SerialKey option makes it easy to attach special equipment to the serial port.

Braille

I correspond frequently on the Internet with a friend who has been blind since early childhood. He has a computer with a braille reader and printer. He has not ever considered his blindness to be a handicap. He figures that he can do almost anything that anyone else can do. Here is his signature: Bud Keith Ph.D., blind cross-country skier, tandem biker, returned Peace Corps volunteer, and retired civil servant, currently surviving prostate cancer in Arlington, Virginia.

Despite all of his problems, he has never lost his sense of humor. Sometimes he becomes a bit philosophical about how his blindness can allow him to see things so much better and differently than others. He is a delightful person to know.

Here are some other companies that supply devices for the handicapped:

Wrist and arm support:	Miniature keyboards:
Bucky Products	InTouch Systems
800-692-8259	800-332-6244
DeRoyal/LMB	TASH
800-541-3992	800-463-5685

Programmable keyboards
Don Johnston
800-999-4660

IntelliTools
800-899-6687

On-screen keyboards
Don Johnston
800-999-4660

Words+
800-869-8521

Wands and pointers
Extensions for Independence
(619) 423-1478

North Coast Medical
800-821-9319

Electronic pointers
Ability Research
(612) 939-0121

Madenta
800-661-8406

Switches
AbleNet
800-322-0956

Toys for Special Children
800-832-8697

Touch screens
Edmark
800-426-0856

MicroTouch Systems
800-642-7686

Voice recognition
Dragon Systems
800-825-5897

Speech Systems
(303) 938-1110

Speech Technology Magazine is a free magazine to qualified subscribers. If you are in any kind of business that involves speech, you can probably qualify. Call (203) 834-1430 for information and a qualifying form, or E-Mail: Speechmag@AOL.COM.

Several organizations can help in locating special equipment and lend support. If you know someone who might benefit from the latest technology and devices for the handicapped, contact these organizations:

AbleData
800-344-5405

Accent on Information
(309) 378-2961

Apple Computer
(408) 996-1010

Easter Seals Systems Office
(312) 667-8626

IBM National Support Center
800-426-2133

American Foundation for the Blind
(212) 620-2000

Closing The Gap, Inc.
(612) 248-3294

Trace Research and Development Center
(608) 262-6966

Direct Link for the Disabled
(805) 688-1603

National ALS Association
(818) 340-7500

Some of these organizations will be glad to accept your old computers. Of course you can write it off on your income tax as a donation. You will be helping them and yourself, and it feels good helping someone else.

CHAPTER 12

Communications

Even if you had several large books on communications, it still wouldn't begin to cover this far-reaching industry. The marriage of computers to the telephone technologies has brought about a tremendous increase in functions, utilities, services, and applications.

Infoglut

At one time, long-distance communications was limited to as loud as you could yell, to beating on hollow logs, and to smoke signals. Today, we have more means of communicating than at any time in history.

The reason for communications is to share information. We need information for pleasure, for health, for business, and for every aspect of our daily lives. Some people think that today we have too much information, that it is overwhelming. Someone coined the term, *infoglut*. Whether you like it or not, the infoglut is going to continue to grow. What we all need is enough information to be able to determine what we need without being overwhelmed.

Telephones

Telephones are one of the most important communications devices ever invented. They can be a critical part of our personal life as well as for almost all business. By adding a modem to your computer, you can make the telephone even more useful and important. You can use your computer and the telephone line to access on-line services, bulletin boards, for telecommuting, for the Internet, and to communicate with anyone else in the world who also has a computer and modem.

Many of the modem boards are now integrated with fax capability. A modem board with a fax might not cost much more than the modem alone. Communicating by fax is fast and efficient.

Reaching Out

There are over 100 million personal computers installed in homes, offices, and businesses worldwide. About half of them have a modem or some sort of communications capability. This capability of the computer is one of its most important aspects.

If your computer has a modem, you can access over 10,000 bulletin boards in the U.S. You can take advantage of electronic mail, faxes, up-to-the-minute stock market quotations, and a large number of other on-line services, such as home shopping, home banking, travel agencies, business transactions, many databases, data services, and even dating services.

For some types of work, a person can use a modem and work from home. Someone has called this *telecommuting*. It is a whole lot better than commuting by auto and sitting in traffic jams on crowded freeways.

Communications covers a wide range of activities and technologies. Many books have been written that cover all phases of communications. Just a few of the many technologies are discussed in this chapter.

The Internet and World Wide Web

One of the hottest topics at the moment is the Internet and World Wide Web (WWW). The Internet started off as a government project in 1973 with the Advanced Research Projects Agency (ARPA), an agency of the Department of Defense (DOD). It was a network designed to facilitate scientific collaboration in military research among educational institutions. ARPAnet had some similarities to peer-to-peer networking. It allowed almost any system to connect to another through an electronic gateway.

The ARPAnet is no longer primarily concerned with military research. It is now known as the Internet. It is possible to access the Internet or WWW from several of the larger on-line services. Here are some voice numbers:

CompuServe 800-848-8990	America Online 800-827-6364
Prodigy 800-776-3449	Microsoft Network 800-386-5550

Besides these large on-line service providers, there are hundreds of smaller Internet service providers (ISPs). The larger on-line companies might have a higher hourly or monthly rate than the small ISPs, but the larger companies might offer more utilities. You can access anyone on the Internet or WWW from any of the on-line providers or ISPs.

Many books have been written about the Internet. Three very good ones, published by Osborne/McGraw-Hill at 800-227-0900, are *Internet Essentials and Fun List; Internet, the Complete Reference*; and the *Internet Yellow Pages*. If you are just getting started, the *Internet Complete Reference* would help you immensely. It has over 800 pages of information about getting on the net. It has addresses and numbers of hundreds of local, state, national, and international access gateways. There are valuable, helpful hints on almost every page. There are several other books about the Internet published by companies other than McGraw-Hill.

There are now millions of people who access the Internet. There is something on the Internet for everyone. There are encyclopedias, up-to-the-minute news, people chatting with one another, on-line romance, and X-rated photos and talk. You can post notes or send e-mail. You can send a message to anyone in the world for just the cost of the dial-up connection and your hourly rate from the ISP. I recently sent several e-mail messages to friend in England for less than it would have cost me to send a letter. There are several companies who are now making software and hardware that will let you use voice over the Internet. The telephone companies are a bit worried. If a person can make a long-distance call to anywhere in the world by just dialing a local access number, then the telephone companies would lose money. One of the software packages for Internet voice is WebTalk from Quarterdeck, at (310) 309-3700.

Because there is such a large amount of information on the Internet, search and browsing software is essential. The most popular navigational software at this time is NetScape. Microsoft also has a browser. Prodigy and CompuServe provide browsers as part of their service.

The vast majority of people are good and honest, but when you get a lot of people communicating with one another, there will always be a few who will try to take advantage of others. There are a lot of people who are now using the Internet for business purposes. Most of them are honest and have something of value to offer. But again, there are a few who will do or say anything in order to get their hands in your pocket. Just be careful and watch your wallet. More about the Internet in Chapter 14.

Modems

A *modem* is an electronic device that allows a computer to use an ordinary telephone line to communicate with other computers that are equipped with a modem. Modem is a contraction of the words *modulate* and *demodulate*. The telephone system transmits voice and data in analog voltage form. Analog voltages are sine waves that vary continuously up and down. Check back to Fig. 1-6 to see what a sine wave looks like. Computer data is usually in a digital voltage form which are a series of on and off voltages.

The modem takes the digitized bits of voltage from the computer and modulates, or transforms, it into analog voltages in order to transmit it over the telephone lines. At the receiving end, a similar modem demodulates the analog voltage and transforms it back into a digital form.

Transmission Difficulties

Telephone systems were originally designed for voice and have a very narrow bandwidth. A person with perfect hearing can hear 20 cycles per second or hertz (Hz), all the way up to 20,000 Hz. For normal speech, we only use about 300 Hz up to 2000 Hz.

The telephone analog voltages are subject to noise, static, and other electrical disturbances. Noise and static take the form of analog voltages. So does most of the other electrical disturbances, such as electrical storms and pulses generated by operating electrical equipment. The analog noise and static voltages can be mixed in with any analog data voltages that are being transmitted. The mixture of the static and noise voltages with the data voltages can corrupt and severely damage the data. The demodulator could be completely at a loss to determine which voltages represent data and which is noise.

Baud Rate

These problems, and the state of technology at the time, limited the original modems to about five characters per second (CPS), or a rate of 50 baud.

The term *baud* came from Emile Baudot (1845—1903), a French inventor. Originally, the baud rate was a measure of the dots and dashes in telegraphy. It is now defined as the actual rate of symbols transmitted per second. For the lower baud rates, it is essentially the same as bits per second. Remember that it takes eight bits to make a character. Just as we have periods and spaces to separate words, we must use one *start bit* and one *stop bit* to separate the on/off bits into characters. A transmission of 300 baud would mean that

300 on/off bits are sent in one second. For every eight bits of data that represents a character, we need one bit to indicate the start of a character and one bit to indicate the end. We then need another bit to indicate the start of the next character. So counting the start/stop bits, it takes 11 bits for each character. If we divide 300 by 11 it gives us about 27 CPS.

Some of the newer technologies might actually transmit symbols that represent more than one bit. For baud rates of 1200 and higher, the CPS and baud rate can be considerably different.

There have been some fantastic advances in the modem technologies. A few years ago, the 2400 baud systems were the standard. Today they are obsolete. The industry leaped over the 4800 and 9600 baud systems to the 14.4K systems. These units incorporate the V.42bis compression standard. This allows them to use 4:1 data compression and thus transmit at 57,600 bps. The 14.4K systems are now obsolete, but a lot of vendors are still selling them at very low prices. I would recommend that you spend a little more and get a 28.8K V.34 system.

When communicating with another modem, both the sending and receiving unit must operate at the same baud rate and use the same protocols. Most of the faster modems are downward compatible and can operate at the slower speeds. If you use a modem frequently, a high-speed modem can quickly pay for itself. We have sure come a long way since those early 50 baud standards.

How to Estimate Connect Time

You can figure the approximate length of time that it will take to transmit a file. For rough approximations of CPS, divide the baud rate by 10. For instance a 14.4K modem would transmit at about 1400 CPS. Look at the directory and determine the number of bytes in the file. Divide the number of bytes in the file by the CPS to give a rough approximation. For instance to transmit a file with 144,000 bytes at 1400 bytes per second, it would take 103 seconds.

Data Compression

One way to reduce modem phone charges is to use file compression. Bulletin boards have been using a form of data compression for years.

There are several public domain programs that squeeze and unsqueeze data. The newer modems take advantage of compression using the standard V.42bis for 4 to 1 compression. Using a 4 to 1 compression, a 14.4K modem can send at 57,600 bits per second (bps). With a 14.4K baud modem, and 4 to 1 compression, a 40K file that takes 3.6 minutes when transmitted at 2400 baud, can be sent in less than one second.

At this time, the 56K is the fastest modem available unless you have a digital ISDN system. Cable modems can operate at up to 10Mb per second.

Protocols

Protocols are procedures that have been established for exchanging data, along with the instructions that coordinate the process. Most protocols can sense when the data is corrupted or lost due to noise, static, or a bad connection. It will automatically resend the affected data until it is received correctly.

There are several protocols, but the most popular ones are Kermit (named for Kermit the frog), Xmodem, and Ymodem. These protocols transmit a block of data along with an error-checking code, then wait for the receiver to send back an acknowledgement. It then sends another block and waits to see if it got through okay. If a block does not get through, it is resent immediately. Protocols, such as Zmodem and HyperProtocol, send a whole file in a continuous stream of data with error checking codes inserted at certain intervals. They then wait for confirmation of a successful transmission. If the transmission is unsuccessful, then the whole file must be resent.

Both the sending and receiving modems must use the same protocol and baud rate. You cannot send a file at 28.8K to someone who only has a 2400 baud modem. However, the faster modems are able to shift down and send or receive at the lower speeds.

ITU Recommended Standards

The communications industry is very complex, so there have not been many real standards. There are many different manufacturers and software developers. Of course, all of them want to differentiate their hardware or software by adding new features.

A United Nations standards committee was established to help create world-wide standards. If every country had different protocols and standards, it would be very difficult to communicate. The original committee was called the Comite Consulatif International de Telephone et Telegraphique (CCITT). The name has now been changed to International Telecommunications Union (ITU). This committee has representatives from over 80 countries and several large private manufacturers. The committee makes recommendations only. A company is free to use or ignore them, but more companies are now adopting the recommendations.

All ITU recommendations for small computers have a V or X prefix. The V series is for use with switched telephone networks, which is almost all of them. The X series is for systems that do not use switched phone lines. Revisions or alternate recommendations have bis (second) or ter (third) added.

The V prefixes can be a bit confusing. For instance a V.32 modem can communicate at 4800 or 9600 bits per second (bps). It can communicate with any other V.32 modem. A V.32bis can communicate at 14,400 bps. The V.32bis standard is a modulation method and is not a compression technique. The V.34 standard is for 28.8K modems.

A V.42bis standard is a method of data compression plus a system of error-checking. A V.42bis can communicate with another V.42bis at up to 57,600 bps by using compression and error-checking.

Communications Software

In order to use a modem, it must be driven and controlled by software. There are dozens of communication programs that can be used. Crosstalk, (404) 998-3998, was one of the earlier modem programs.

ProComm Plus from DataStorm, at (314) 474-8461, is an excellent communications program. Qmodem from Mustang Software Company, at (805) 873-2500, is another very good program. At one time both ProComm and Qmodem were low-cost shareware programs. They were among the most popular communication programs available. Both of them are now commercial programs, but are still reasonably priced.

Mustang Software also provides software for setting up bulletin boards. If you would like to start your own BBS, contact them for details.

One of the most comprehensive communications programs is the Delrina WinComm PRO from Delrina, at 800-268-6082. It operates under Windows and handles both modem and fax communications. It can be used to access all of the on-line services, other modems, and can even be set up as a mini-BBS to let other users log on to your computer. You can set up passwords and access privileges. Because it works under Windows, a mouse can be used to point and click on the many icons and buttons. WinComm PRO is much like the plug-n-play software in that it can automatically detect and avoid port conflicts. Call Delrina and ask for a brochure. It is one of the better communication software packages available.

Low-Cost Communication Software

If you buy a modem or modem/fax board, many companies include a basic communications program. If you subscribe to one of the large on-line services, such as Compuserve or Prodigy, they provide special software for their connections.

You can get copies of communication shareware programs from bulletin boards or from any of the several companies who provide shareware and public domain software. Shareware is not free. You can try it out and use it, but the developers ask that you register the program and send in a nominal sum. For this low cost, they will usually provide a manual and some support. Some of the shareware companies are listed in Chapter 17. You should be very careful and check for viruses when downloading or using any public domain or shareware.

Basic Types of Modems

There are two basic types of modems: the external desktop and the internal. Each type has some advantages and disadvantages.

A disadvantage is that the external type requires some of your precious desk space and a voltage source. It also requires an external cable from a COM port to drive it. The good news is that most external models have LEDs that light up and let you know what is happening during your call.

Both the external and the internal models have speakers that let you hear the phone ringing or if you get a busy signal. But the internal modem could have a very small speaker and you might not even be able to hear the dial tone and the ringing. Some of the external models have a volume control for the built-in speaker.

The internal modem is built entirely on a board, usually a half or short board. The good news is that it doesn't use up any of your desk real estate, but the bad news is that it uses one of your precious slots. It also does not have the LEDs to let you know the progress of your call. Of course, not being able to see the LEDs flashing might not be that important to you. The only thing most people care about is whether it is working or not. The fewer items to worry about, the better.

Even if you use an external modem, if your motherboard does not have built-in COM ports, you will need an I/O board that will require the use of one of your slots for a COM port. Most all motherboards now have the COM ports built in.

The external modems might cost up to $50 more than an equivalent internal modem. By far, the most popular modems are the internal types.

Hayes Compatibility

One of the most popular early modems was made by Hayes Microcomputer Products. They became the IBM of the modem world and established a de facto standard. There are hundreds of modem manufacturers. Except for some of the very inexpensive ones, almost all of them are Hayes compatible.

Installing a Modem

If you are adding a modem on board to a system that is already assembled, the first thing to do is to check your documentation and set any jumpers or switches needed to configure the board. There are usually jumpers or small switches that must be set to enable COM1, COM2, COM3, or COM4. Most new modems are plug and play, no jumpers. Once the switches and jumpers have been set to configure the modem, remove the computer cover. Find an empty slot and plug the board in.

Normally, most systems only allow for two ports: COM1 which uses IRQ 4 and COM2 which uses IRQ 3. But COM1 and COM3 can share IRQ 4 and COM2 and COM4 can share IRQ 3 if the software or hardware will allow it. One of the biggest problems of installing serial type hardware such as network cards, mice, modems, fax boards, sound cards, serial printers, plotters, and other serial devices, is that there just aren't enough IRQs.

The ISA machines only have 16 IRQs and most of them are reserved for other uses.

The interrupt requests cause the BIOS and CPU to stop whatever it is doing and give its attention to the current request. The IRQs have a hierarchical arrangement so that the lower numbered IRQs have priority. If you would like to see how your IRQs are arranged, if you have DOS 5.0 or later, just type MSD (for Microsoft Diagnostics) and it will show you several things about your computer, including your IRQ uses. Table 12-1 shows how my IRQs are arranged:

TABLE 12-1

IRQ Arrangement

IRQ	USER
0	Timer Click
1	Keyboard
2	Second 8259A
3	COM2: COM4
4	COM1: COM3
5	LPT2
6	Floppy Disk
7	LPT1
8	Real-Time Clock
9	Redirected IRQ2
10	(Reserved)
11	(Reserved)
12	(Reserved)
13	Math Coprocessor
14	Fixed Disk
15	(Reserved)

It is permissible to use any of the IRQs marked *reserved* for things like sound boards and network cards, but serial devices such as mice and modems must be connected to one of the COM ports.

If you have an I/O board in your system with external COM ports and you have built-in COM ports on your motherboard, you can only use two of them. You must set the switches or jumpers to configure your system for whichever port that will be used by the modem and the port used by a mouse or other device. Any port on the motherboard or on a plug-in board that is not being used should be disabled. Ordinarily jumpers are used to enable or disable the ports.

If you are installing an external modem, you must go through the same procedure to make sure the COM port is accessible and does not conflict. If you have a mouse, a serial printer, or some other serial device, you will have to determine which port they are set to. You cannot have two serial devices set to the same COM port unless you have special software that will allow them to share the port.

A Simple Modem Test

It is often difficult to determine which COM port is being used by a device. You can use the AT command to determine if your modem is working with this simple test:

Switch to your communications software directory. At the DOS prompt C:> type the following using upper case: ECHO AT DT12345>COM1:. The AT is for modem attention, the DT is for dial tone. If you have a pulse phone system, the command would be AT DP12345. If the modem is set properly, you will hear a dial tone, then the modem will dial 12345. The modem will then emit a continuous busy signal. You can stop the busy signal by invoking the command ECHO ATHO. The HO tells it to hang up.

If two devices are both set for the same COM port, there will be a conflict. The computer will try for a while, then give an error message and the familiar "Abort, Retry, Ignore, Fail?" If the modem is connected to COM1 and you invoke the command ECHO AT DT12345>COM2, you will get the message, "Write fault error writing device COM2. Abort, Retry, Ignore, Fail?"

You might not get any message and not hear the dial tone if the COM ports on both the I/O board and motherboard are enabled. You must disable those ports that are not used.

A diagnostic program, such as Check-It Pro from TouchStone at (714) 969-7746, can determine which ports are being used. It also does several other very helpful diagnostic tests. Another good program for finding port conflicts is the Port Finder from the mcTronic Systems, at (713) 462-7687.

It is very important that you keep any documentation that you get with your various plug-in boards. Many of the I/O boards have dozens of pins and jumpers. If you don't have the documentation, you might never be able to determine how it should be configured. It is also necessary that you write down and keep a log of which ports and addresses are enabled. It can save a lot of time.

The Pentium-class motherboards usually will have a plug-n-play (PnP) BIOS. If you buy a modem that was manufactured to the PnP specifications, it will be very easy to set up your system. When you plug in a modem board, the BIOS will check to determine which IRQs are free and automatically set itself so that there is no conflict.

Plug in the modem board and hook it up to the telephone line. Unless you expect to do a lot of communicating, you might not need a separate dedicated line. But you will need some sort of switching device such as those from Command Communications, at 800-288-6794. They have several different devices that can recognize an incoming voice, modem, or fax signal, and route the call.

There should be two connectors at the back end of the board. One could be labeled for the line in and the other for the telephone. Unless you have a dedicated telephone line, you should unplug your telephone, plug in the extension to the modem and line, then plug the telephone into the modem.

After you have connected all of the lines, turn on your computer and try the modem before you put the cover back on. Use the simple test that was mentioned above.

Make sure you have communications software then call a local bulletin board. Even if you can't get through, or have a wrong number, you should hear the dial tone, then hear it dial the number.

Fax/Modem Software

Most fax/modems come with several communication software packages. The fax/modem that I had been using for the last couple of years died on me. I bought a new one and installed it along with some communication software that came with it. It screwed up my system completely. I could no longer access Prodigy or CompuServe. I sweated for half a day before I discovered that the software that was included is terminate and stay resident (TSR). It loads itself into memory each time I boot up. With that software in memory, I could not access CompuServe or Prodigy.

You can find out if there any TSRs loaded into memory on your computer when in Windows by pressing the Ctrl+Alt+Delete once. (If you do it twice, it will shut the computer down.) This will show you a list of any TSR programs in memory. You can then highlight them or point to them with the mouse, then press enter and they will be closed. You will always see Explorer in the list. If you close it, it will shut your computer down.

After closing the TSR programs, I was able to access Prodigy, but I could not access CompuServe. After several hours of frustration, I called CompuServe Support. They determined that somehow the modem initialization string software had become damaged. I re-installed the CompuServe software and everything now works.

That was a 14.4K modem. I have since scrapped it and bought a 28.8K faxmodem with voice mail. See Fig. 12-1. A couple of companies have introduced competing systems for 56K modems. Several companies are now selling them. At this time, there is still no standards and we don't know which system will eventually be accepted. I would like to get one, but I will wait until a standard is announced.

There are thousands of little things that can go wrong. PnP will go a long way to help solve some of the problems, but it can't possibly solve all of the thousands of little things that can go wrong.

Bulletin Boards

If you have a modem, you have access to several thousand computer bulletin boards. At one time most bulletin boards were free of any charge. You only had to pay the phone bill if they are out of your calling area. But there has been a lot of low-life scum who have uploaded software

Fig. 12-1
A 28.8k faxmodem with personal voice mail. I dislike voice mail, but if you can't beat them, join them.

with viruses, pirated commercial software has been loaded onto some of them, stolen credit card numbers have been posted, and many other loathsome and illegal activities. Because of this, the Sysops (systems operators) have had to spend a lot of time monitoring their BBS. Many of the bulletin boards now charge a nominal fee to join, some just ask for a tax deductible donation.

Some of the bulletin boards are set up by private individuals and some by companies and vendors as a service to their customers. Some are set up by user groups and other special interest organizations. There are over 100 boards nationwide that have been set up for doctors and lawyers. You probably won't be surprised to know that there are gay bulletin boards in the San Francisco area and other areas. There are also X-rated boards and several for dating.

Many of the bulletin boards are set up to help individuals. They usually have lots of public domain software and a space where you can leave messages for help, for advertising something for sale, or for just plain old chit-chat.

If you are just getting started you probably need some software. There are all kinds of public domain and shareware software packages that are equivalent to almost all of the major commercial programs. And the best part is that the public domain software is free and the shareware is practically free. Another good source of software is from the Surplus Software Company, at 800-753-7877. Call them for a free catalog. You can save hundreds of dollars on essential software.

Viruses

A few years ago, you could access a bulletin board and download all kinds of good public domain or shareware software. You never had to worry about the software destroying your data. Because a few sick psychopaths have created computer viruses, you now have to use safeguards. You now must be quite selective and very careful about where you get your software and who you get it from.

A computer virus is not a live thing, it cannot harm you, only the data in a computer or on a disk. But you might have invested a large part of your life creating that data. A computer virus is usually a bit of program code, hidden in a piece of legitimate software. The virus is usually designed to redirect, corrupt, or destroy data. The computer virus might resemble an organic virus in that it can cause a wide variety of virus-type symptoms in the computer host.

The virus code can be written so that it can replicate or make copies of itself. When it becomes embedded on a disk, it can attach itself to other programs that it comes in contact with. Whenever a floppy disk is inserted into the drive, it can come away with a hidden copy of the virus.

Infected software can appear to work as it should for some time, but eventually, it can contaminate and destroy many of your files. If a virus gets on a workstation or network, it can infect all of the computers in the network. The McAfee Associates, at (408) 988-3832, has one of the best shareware anti-virus programs available. McAfee has a bulletin board, at (408) 988-4004, from which you can download the latest version. They constantly revise the program to try to keep up with the latest viruses.

Where to Find the Bulletin Boards

Several computer magazines devote a lot of space to bulletin boards and user groups. In California, the *MicroTimes* and *Computer Currents* magazines have several pages of bulletin boards and user groups each month. The *Computer Shopper* Magazine has the most comprehensive national listing of bulletin boards and user groups of any magazine. The *Computer Shopper* alternates each month with a listing of User Groups one month and Bulletin Boards the next.

If you have a bulletin board or belong to a User Group and want them listed in the *Shopper*, use your modem and submit your entry to (913) 478-3088, 8NI at 2400 bps.

Online Services

The bulletin boards are not nearly as popular today as the Internet and online services. The online services provide forums for help and discussions, mailboxes, and a large variety of information and reference services. A caller can search the databases and download information as easily as pulling the data off his own hard disk.

They have phone service to most areas in the larger cities so that there is not even a toll charge. They have an impressive list of services including home shopping, home banking, airline schedules and reservations, stock market quotations, a medical bulletin board, and many others.

Banking by Modem

Many banks offer systems that will let you do all your banking with your computer and a modem from the comforts of your home. You would never again have to drive downtown, hunt for a parking space, then stand in line for a half hour to do your banking.

Intuit, at (415) 322-0573, developed Quicken, an excellent financial software program. Intuit offers CheckFree, a service that allows one to pay all of their bills electronically. Or it will allow you to print your checks from your computer on a laser printer. This requires special checks that are imprinted with your account number in magnetic ink.

CheckFree costs about $10 a month. But if you spend about 4 hours a month paying bills, the $10 is not very much compared to the time spent. Another advantage to CheckFree is that the bills are paid automatically, but not until they are due. This lets your account accrue interest until the last moment. If you ordinarily write a lot of checks, CheckFree and Quicken can quickly pay for itself.

Intuit is now merged with ChipSoft, at (602) 295-3070. ChipSoft is the developer of TurboTax, one of the better software packages for doing your taxes. The marriage of these two companies means that they can offer the most complete financial software available for your computer system. With a good financial program, you can get rid of the shoe boxes full of canceled checks. The data which is in your computer can automatically flow onto the TurboTax forms. It can make the onerous task that occurs on April 15 each year a bit easier to accomplish.

Facsimile Machines

Facsimile (fax) machines have been around for quite a while. Newspapers and businesses have used them for years. The early machines were similar to the early acoustic modems. Both used foam rubber cups that fit over the telephone receiver-mouthpiece for coupling. They were very slow and subject to noise and interference. Fax machines and modems have come a long way since those early days.

A page of text or a photo is fed into the facsimile machine and scanned. As the scanning beam moves across the page, white and dark areas are digitized as 1s and 0s, then transmitted out over the telephone lines. On the receiving end of the line, a scanning beam sweeps across the paper. The dark areas causes it to print as it sweeps across the paper. The finished product is a black and white image of the original. When a text file is sent by modem, the digitized bits that make up each character is converted from digital voltage to analog voltage. A modem sends and receives bits that make up each character. A fax machine or board sends and receives scanned whole pages of letters, graphics, images, signatures, etc. Because a modem recognizes individual characters, a computer program can be sent over a modem, but not over a fax. A fax sends and receives the information as digitized graphic data. A modem converts the digital information that represents individual characters into analog voltages, sends it over the line, then converts it back to individual digital characters.

There are times when a modem or fax is needed. Both units cannot be in use at the same time on the same phone line. Otherwise a single phone line can be used for both fax and modems.

There are millions of facsimile machines in use today. There are very few businesses that cannot benefit from the use of a fax. It can be used to send documents, that includes handwriting, signatures, seals, letterheads, graphs, blueprints, photos, and other types of data around the world, across the country or across the room to another fax machine.

Express mail costs from $8 to $10 or more. A fax machine can deliver the same letter for about 40 cents and do it in less than three minutes. Many of the software programs will let you delay sending a fax until late at night to get the best rates. Depending on the type of business, and the amount of critical mail that must be sent out, a fax system can pay for itself in a very short time. If you have a fax/modem board, it might be even less expensive to send e-mail.

Most of the fax machines use thermal type paper for printing, especially the lower cost machines. The thermal paper does not provide very good resolution and it fades when exposed to light. The better and more expensive fax machines use ink jet or laser technology and print on plain paper.

They are usually a bit slow, but almost all of the fax machines can be used as a copier. Fax machines have a lot in common with copy machines, scanners, and printers. Several companies have added these features to their machines so that one machine can do the work of several. More about these combo machines in Chapter 13.

Fax/Modem Computer Boards

Several companies have developed fax systems on circuit boards that can be plugged into computers. Most of the fax boards are now integrated with a modem on the same board. The modem and fax combination costs very little more than either board separately. This combination also saves having to use an extra plug-in slot.

For some time the standard baud rate for fax was 9600. But many of the newer fax-modem boards are now capable of a 14,400 speed for both modem and fax. However, just like the modem connections, both the sender and receiver must be operating at the same speed. Also, like the modem, the fax can shift down to match the receiver if it is slower.

Special software allows the computer to control the fax boards. Using the computer's word processor, letters and memos can be written and sent out over the phone lines. Several letters or other information can be stored or retrieved from the computer hard disk and transmitted. The computer can be programmed to send the letters out at night when rates are lower.

The computer fax boards have one disadvantage. They cannot scan information such as signatures, graphics, or drawings that are not in the computer. But with a scanner this information can be stored as a file on a hard disk then added to a document that is to be faxed. There are several scanners that can be used to input data.

With the proper software, a computer can receive and store any fax. The digitized data and images can be stored on a hard disk, then printed out.

Fax-On-Demand

Several companies have set up fax machines that can supply information to you 24 hours a day. You simply call them with your voice phone, tell them what documents you want, give them your fax number and the documents will be sent immediately.

Most of the companies have a catalog that lists all of their documents and the document number. You should first ask to have the catalog faxed to you. You can then determine which documents to order.

The FaxFacts Company, at (708) 682-8898, publishes a small booklet that lists several companies who have the Fax-On-Demand or Faxback capability. They list things such as medical, computers, travel, trade shows and many more.

Most Faxback information is free, but some companies such as Consumer Reports, at 800-766-9988, ask for a credit card number and charges a fee for articles you request.

Here are just a few of the other companies who offer Faxback or Fax-on-Demand: (When you call, ask for their new users instructions and navigation map.)

Borland TechFax
800-822-4269

Novell Support Line
800-638-9273

Cyrix Direct Connect
800-215-6823

Symantec Corp.
800-554-4403

IBM
800-426-4329

WordStar Fax Support
(404) 514-6333

If you prefer, most will send the information to you by mail rather than by fax.

Fax/Modem/Phone Switch

Having the modem and telephone on the same line should cause no problems unless someone tries to use the telephone while the modem is using it. Life will be a lot simpler though if you have a switch that can detect whether the incoming signal is for a fax, a modem, or voice. Fax and Modem signals transmit a high pitched tone, called the CNG (calling) signal. A fax/modem switch can switch and route the incoming call to the proper device. Figure 12-2 shows my ComShare phone line switcher.

You should be aware that there are a few old fax systems that do not use the CNG signals. My command communication system will let me manually transfer the call in that case. If I know the incoming call is a fax, I can press 1 1 and it will be switched to the fax machine. If it is a modem call, I can press 2 2 and it will be switched to the modem.

Of course I have to be there to answer such a call. One solution to this problem for those people who have machines without the CNG signal is to have them punch in the 1 1 or 2 2 on their end after they dial the number. I can also put this instruction on my answering machine if I am not available. Fortunately, not many of the old systems without the CNG signals are still in existence.

There is another solution for the problem of those people who have machines without the CNG signal. The telephone company can set up two or more numbers with different and distinctive rings on a single

Fig. 12-2

My phone line
switcher. It lets
me use a single line
for my telephone,
fax, modem, and
answering machine.

line. The Command Communications switchers can be programmed
to recognize the distinctive ring and route the call to the proper
device. The South Tech Instruments Company, at 800-394-5556, has a
FoneFilter device that can recognize the distinctive rings and route the
call to a fax, modem, or answering machine. Of course there is a charge
by the telephone company for the extra numbers added to your line.
At this time, in the Los Angeles area, it costs $7.50 to set up a separate
distinctive ring on your line and then $6.00 a month thereafter. This is
still less expensive than adding a second line.

If you still have one of the older fax machines, I would suggest that
you scrap it and buy a later model. Most of them are now very inexpensive, but they are faster and handle the paper much better. If you
do a lot of faxing, they will pay for themselves quickly.

Command Communications, at 800-288-6794, has several different
model switchers that are suitable for homes, small offices, and up to
large businesses. They have connections for a telephone answering
device (TAD), telephone extensions, a fax machine or fax board, and a
connection for an auxiliary or modem. The alternative to a switcher

would be to install a dedicated telephone line for the fax machine and another line for the modem and another line for voice. If you don't do a lot of transmissions by fax and modem, you can get by with a single telephone and a good switcher. It can pay for itself many times over.

Many of the stand-alone fax machines have a built-in detector that can determine if the incoming call is for voice or fax.

Telephone Outlets for Extensions

You need a telephone line or extension to hook up a computer modem or a fax. You might also want telephone outlets in several rooms, at one or more desks, or at another computer. You can go to almost any hardware store, and even some grocery and drug stores, and buy the telephone wire and accessories needed. But you might have trouble running telephone wires to the computer, desks, and other rooms. It can be a lot of work cutting holes in the walls and running the wires up in the attic or under the floor.

There is a much simpler way. Just use the 110 volt wiring of the building. The Phonex Company, at (801) 566-0100, developed special adapters that plug into any wall plug outlet. It requires at least two adapters, one for the telephone input line, then another adapter for where you want the extension. More adapters can be plugged into any other 110 volt outlet to provide as many telephone extensions as needed. Or if you need an extension in another location, just unplug an adapter and plug it into another nearby wall outlet. You could even use a standard electrical extension cord and a Phonex adapter to provide a telephone extension. Electronic circuitry in the adapters blocks the ac voltage from getting into the telephone lines, but allows voice and data to go through. The device is being marketed and sold by Comtrad Industries, at 800-704-1211.

Combination Devices and Voice Mail

The fax machines, copiers, printers, and scanners all have a lot in common. Several companies are now taking advantage of this commonality and offering combination devices.

Some companies are starting to use color for fax. If you have one of the combination devices with a color scanner, the Laser Today International, at (415) 961-3015 has software that will let you send and receive color faxes.

The Compex International Company, at 800-626-8112, has an all-in-one fax, scanner, printer, and copier.

The Speaking Devices Corporation, at (408) 727-2132, has a unit with a fax, fax/phone switch, scanner, voice mail, and caller ID.

Boca Research, at (407) 997-6227, has a Multimedia Voice Modem that has up to 1000 password protected voice and fax mailboxes, has private and public fax on demand, remote message and fax retrieval, professionally recorded greetings and voice prompts and personalized greetings for individual mailboxes.

Tiger Software, at 800-888-4437, publishes a catalog that has hundreds of software and hardware items. They advertise the Vomax 2000 which is a Fax, voice, and modem system. It has one megabyte of digital storage which can store up to 20 minutes of voice mail messages or up to 50 sheets of faxes. It has message forwarding so that it can call another number and play your messages. It can also call your pager and relay messages. Call Tiger Software for a catalog and more information.

I recently upgraded my 14.4K fax/modem to a U.S. Robotics Sportster Vi 28.8K v.34 system. This system has Personal voice mail that can be used as an answering machine. It also came with a book on the World Wide Web and several software packages for exploring the WWW. See Fig. 12-1.

The AnyWhere Associates, at (617) 522-8102, has software that allows you to send e-mail to faxes. Delrina's WinFax 7.0 integrates fax, e-mail, and voice mail. Cylink, at (408) 735-5800, and Syntel Sciences, at (800) 499-1469, has software that lets you encrypt faxes so that your nosey neighbor will not be able to read them.

Telecommuting

Millions of people risk their lives and fight frustrating traffic every day. Many of these people have jobs that could allow them to stay home, work on a computer, then send the data to the office over a modem or a fax. Even if the person had to buy their own computer, modem, and fax, it might still be worth it. You could save the cost of gasoline, auto maintenance, and lower insurance. Thousands are killed on the highways; telecommuting can be a life saver.

Being able to work at home would be ideal for those who have young children, for the handicapped, or for anyone who hates being stuck in traffic jams. It is expected that about half of all PCs sold in 1996 will be for home use. A large percentage of those computers will be used for telecommuting.

There is one other very big plus for working at home in that he or she can be an "open-collar worker" unlike a "blue collar worker or a white collar worker." Many women spend thousands of dollars buying new outfits so that she can wear a different one to work each day of the week. They can save that money if they work at home. Men won't save as much because few people notice if they wear the same clothes more than once a week. A man can wear the same shirt two or three times in the same week if he wears a tie so that no one can see the ring around the collar. This is one of the best reasons I know of for wearing a tie. If you are working at home you can wear any old clothes as often as you like. If you are living alone, you don't have to wear anything at all. But you probably should remember to put on a robe or something when answering the door for the UPS or Fedex man.

There are several technological tools such as the new fast modems/fax/voice/whatever machines, remote access software, conference calling software, cellular telephones, and many other goodies that can make working from home almost like being at the office. A telecommuter can have a first class virtual office in a bedroom or den. A plus for the company is that they will be saving office space, parking space, and less wear and tear on the coffee machine.

There are a few disadvantages. You might miss the face to face interaction of your co-workers. In some cases, you might be overlooked when it comes time to hand out raises and perks. Out of sight, out of mind. On the other hand, you might be required to wear a beeper and stay close to a telephone or computer. You might feel like you are on a short leash, but the advantages far out weigh the few disadvantages. Telecommuting or virtual offices will be adopted by more and more companies.

Remote Control Software

If you are on the road or working from home and have a computer at the office, it is often necessary to access the data on that computer. There are several software packages that will allow you to connect from remote locations. You can be sitting in a distant hotel room or at a PC at home and dial up a computer at the office. You can take control across a phone line or across a network and work just as if you were sitting in front of the office computer. You can review documents, update files, edit reports, do print outs, or download files.

LapLink

For many years LapLink, at 800-343-8088, has had one of the best ways to connect a laptop to a desktop or to connect any two computers together. Their software usually comes with a cable for linking computers together. LapLink for Windows 95 still does all the good things it did in the past, in addition it is now one of the better ways to remotely access and connect two or more computers. It has SmartXchange and will let you transfer only those files that have been changed. You can also update a file by sending only that portion of it that has changed which can save a lot of connect time. You can connect via cable, modem, Internet, a network, or even with infrared. It comes with a cable for the parallel port or for a serial port.

Here are a few other software packages for remote control:

- Reachout, from Ocean Isle at 800-677-6232
- Norton pcAnywhere from Symantec
- Carbon Copy from Microcom
- Close-Up from Norton Lambert
- CO/Session from Triton

You should be able to find the above software at most software stores or find them listed in software catalogs such as the MicroWarehouse, at 800-367-7080, or DellWare, at 800-847-4051.

All of these packages will only work if the computer is turned on and booted up. Server Technology has Remote Power On/Off + AUX. This device plugs into the power line between the computer and the wall plug. The telephone line plugs into this device. When the device detects an incoming call, it will automatically turn on and boot up the PC. When the call is ended, it can turn off the PC. It can even let you re-boot if the computer hangs up for some reason. Some companies bundle the Remote Power On/Off with the pcAnywhere and other remote software. It is available from Dellware, Microwarehouse, and other discount catalog stores.

Telephony

There have been some important advances in computers and telephones in the last few years. Even greater changes can be expected soon. All of the items listed below can be used in a large business or a small office or home office (SOHO). The SOHO has become a very important element of business today.

Computer Telephony is a magazine that is devoted entirely to telephone computer technology and computer telephone integration (CTI). The magazine is free to qualified subscribers. If you work for a company, for yourself, use a telephone or computer, then you can probably qualify for a free subscription. Call 800-677-3435 and ask them to send you a qualifying form.

The telephony business has become so important and widespread that computer telephony conferences and expositions are being held twice a year. The conferences are sponsored by the *Computer Telephony Magazine*. At these shows they have hundreds of vendors displaying and demonstrating the latest computer and telephone technology plus dozens of informative seminars. For the next show date and location, call 800-677-3435.

Another free magazine that deals with telephony is *InfoText*, at (218) 723-9437. A free catalog that is devoted to telephone products is *Hello Direct*. A current issue has 72 pages full of descriptions of telephone related products such as all kinds of telephones, headsets, computer and telephone integration products, and many other items. A couple of items actually does away with a standard telephone. The telephone line is plugged into your computer, then with a headset and microphone, you can use a mouse to point to an address list or to dial the number by pressing the keys of the keyboard. There are several different models with different features.

The products handled by Hello Direct are rather expensive, but they have many items that are difficult to find elsewhere. Hello Direct is at 800-444-3556. Call them for a catalog.

Universal Serial Bus (USB) is a new standard that will allow telephones and other telephone technologies to be connected to computers and operate, at up to 12M bits per second.

Several companies provide hardware and software for Interactive Voice Response (IVR) that can be used in many different business functions.

The computer industry is rife with hundreds of acronyms. The CTI portion of the industry has greatly increased the number.

Telephone Conference

It is very simple to have a telephone conference with as few as two persons, or as many as several hundred. In the conference calls, everyone is on the line can talk to anyone else on the line. You can do teleconferences from any where—home, a small office, a large office, or even a pay telephone booth.

U.S. Robotics, at 800-949-6757, has developed a PC-adaptable conference speakerphone, the ConferenceLink CS 1500. It can be connected to a computer, as a speakerphone for teleconferences or for videoconferencing, or for use on Internet telephony applications.

Fax Conferences

If you have a fax machine, you can send out a graphics design, plans, or any number of business papers to have other people review the document, make changes, or sign it and return it. You can have an interactive meeting with others in the same building, or almost anywhere in the world, over a simple telephone line. One disadvantage is that it is not in real time. You have to send the fax then wait for a reply.

Modem Teleconferences

With a computer modem you can have a desktop conference. You send data, graphics, and other materials over the telephone line to other computers over a local area network (LAN), in the same building or almost anywhere in the world. Other persons sitting at the computer, can view the text data, spreadsheets, graphics, and other materials. The persons can change the material or interact with the other persons on the line in real time.

One of the better products that can help with a desktop conference is called TALKShow, from Future Labs, at (415) 254-9000, fax, at (408) 736-8030. This small, simple program works under Windows. Each person in the conference must have a copy of TALKShow installed on their computer. TALKShow connects everyone together and automatically handles all of the computer communications.

The same data appears on all the computer screens that are on the line. Many live conferences use a large white board in front of the conference room. The leader writes on the board while the attendees watch, and perhaps make comments for changes. With TALKShow, each computer screen becomes a white board. Each individual can suggest changes, or additions, to the material on the screen. Of course, if it is the president of the company who is leading desktop conference, you might have to be careful of what you suggest.

With TALKShow, anything that appears on the screen can be saved on the hard disk or printed out.

Educational

Several universities, colleges, and specialized training facilities are using telecommunications to offer many different courses. Some courses might lead to degrees, others might be for specialized training for a large company. You could sit at home in front of your computer and take a course from a college or training facility on the other side of the country.

National Telephone Directories

I live in the Los Angeles area. In Los Angeles and Orange Counties, there are over 100 suburban cities with over 12 million people. Can you imagine a single telephone directory that would list all of these people? Or how about a telephone directory that would list all of the millions of people in New York? Or Boston or San Francisco? Believe it or not there are such directories. And these directories are smaller than one that you might find in a small town. These national directories are small because they are on CD-ROM discs.

The ProPhone, from New Media Publishing, at (617) 631-9200, has seven CD-ROM discs, 6 discs for the "white pages" and one disc for businesses in the U.S. There is over 600Mb of data on each disc which lists the telephone numbers, the address, and zip codes. The separate disc for business makes it very easy to look up a company anywhere in the country.

The PhoneDisc, from Digital Directory Assistance, at 800-284-8353, only has five CD-ROM discs. See Fig. 12-3. It has over 90 million listings of residential and businesses. It does not have a separate business disc, but lists businesses along with the general population in the white pages.

Not every person in the country is listed on the discs. And of course, many people move and change phone numbers. Most phone companies only update their directories once a year. But these CD-ROM disc directory companies do quarterly updates. Once you are a registered owner, the updates are very reasonable.

If you are in a business where you have to contact a lot of people, then you need these two directories. You might also need them if you live in the Los Angeles area.

ISDN

ISDN is an acronym for *integrated services digital network*. Most of the ISDN networks are made up of fiber optic cable. Eventually the whole world will have telephone systems that use this concept. It will be a system that will be able to transmit voice, data, video, and graphics in digital form rather than the present analog. When this happens, we can scrap our modems.

Fig. 12-3
A national telephone directory with over 90 million listings.

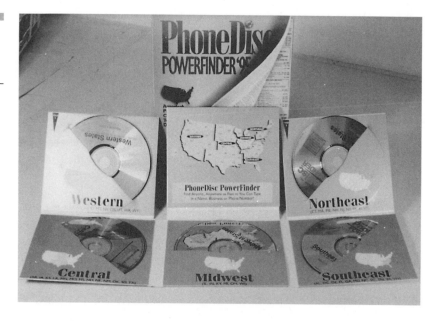

ISDN is already installed in several cities, but don't throw your modem away just yet. The new service might not be available at all locations for some time. It will be rather expensive.

Cable Modems

At the present time, ISDN allows modems to operate at up to 128K bits per second which is more than four times faster than a 28.8K modem. But it is not nearly as fast as communicating over coax cable, which can operate at up to 10M bits. Many of the Internet Web sites have lots of graphics. It might take several megabytes to create a good graphic image. Over the plain-old telephone service (POTS) it might take several minutes to download a graphic. With a cable modem it would only take seconds.

At the time of this writing, Congress has just passed a law giving cable TV companies the right to enter the phone business and vice versa. You can expect to see a lot of competition from the cable and telephone companies for your business. Motorola and several other companies are busy making new cable modems.

Sources

I have not listed the names and manufacturers of modems and faxes because there are so many. Look in any computer magazine and you will see dozens of ads. A recent copy of the Computer Shopper had ads for about 200 modem/fax boards from several different companies.

One modem company that we do want to mention is USRobotics. They manufacture a large variety of modems, especially the high end, high speed type. They will send you a free 110 page booklet that explains about all you need to know about modems. For a free booklet, call 800-342-5877.

I suggest that you subscribe to several of the computer magazines listed in Chapter 21. A good magazine that is free to qualified subscribers is *Telecommunications.* Almost anyone can qualify, especially if you fudge a little on the questionnaire form. For a qualification form, call them at (617) 769-9750, or write to *Telecommunications,* P.O. Box 850949, Braintree, MA 02185.

13

Printers

For the vast majority of applications, a computer system is not complete without a printer. There are several manufacturers of computer printers and hundreds of different models. You will have a vast number of options and choices when choosing a printer. This chapter discusses some of the features and functions of those different types.

Printer Life Expectancy

Printers usually have a long life. I have a HP LaserJet III that I bought in May, 1990. It has a self-test utility that tests and prints out all of the various fonts and graphics that it can do. It also prints out a record of how many pages it has printed. Up until now, it has printed out 26,590 pages.

Here is an approximate cost for those 26,590 pages. The original cost of the printer was $1,600. (The LaserJet III is no longer being manufactured. An equivalent printer now costs about $500.) The toner cartridge for the LaserJet III lasts for about 3,000 copies. The originals cost about $75, but several companies rebuild cartridges and sell them for about $30. I have spent about $300 on cartridges. So my cost has been $1,600 for the printer and $300 for cartridges for a total of $1,900. I buy my paper at a discount warehouse. It costs about $20 for 10 reams or about 2.5 cents per sheet. In the last seven years, I have spent about $120 on paper. So my total cost has been about $2,020 to print 26,590 sheets or about 13 cents per sheet. Of course, I should add the cost of electricity into that cost.

Just as I was bragging on how well this printer has held up, it started leaving a wide dark line down the center of the page. I tried a new cartridge, but it didn't help. I then noticed that a section was missing from a roller in the fuser assembly. See Fig. 13-1. I started looking in the magazines for new printers, but just in case, I called several numbers and finally talked to a person at Hewlett-Packard. This person told me that the fuser assembly could be replaced. A rebuilt assembly costs $228, but I would get $150 of that back if I sent in my old unit in exchange. I ordered it without giving it a second thought.

Figure 13-2 shows the rebuilt fuser. The fuser is held in place with four screws. It was very simple to remove the old one and replace it. My old LaserJet III now works every bit as good as it did the day I bought it on May 17, 1990. Figure 13-3 shows my old LaserJet III.

I had thought that it would cost me several hundred dollars to get my old LaserJet III repaired. To tell the truth, I was just a little bit disap-

Fig. 13-1
A large defect on the
fuser roller from my
Hewlett-Packard
LaserJet III.

pointed that it didn't cost more to repair it. Deep down, I was looking for an excuse to buy a new printer. There have been some fantastic advances in the last few years. The new lasers are faster, have much better resolution, and are much less expensive.

Although printers usually last a long time, like most other industries, the printer manufacturers constantly work to obsolete the printer that you might already have so that you will buy a new and improved model. There are dozens and dozens of printer companies. Each company produces dozens of different models. Because the models change so frequently, when I mention a product, I don't usually mention the model name.

Dot Matrix Printers

Except for a few specialized applications, the dot matrix is practically obsolete. The dot matrix is fairly low priced, but they are limited in fonts and graphics capability. The laser printer speed is measured by the average number of pages per minute it can print. Dot matrix printers speed is measured by the characters per second (CPS) they can print. They can print much faster in the draft mode than in the near letter

Fig. 13-2
A rebuilt fuser assembly. It takes only four screws and just a few minutes to remove and replace it.

quality (NLQ) mode. There are some high-end dot matrix line printers that can print a whole line at a time. Some of them can print up to 1,000 lines per minute. In order to get the high speed, some dot matrix printers have four or more heads, with each head printing out a different line.

Advantages of Dot Matrix

One of the distinct advantages that dot matrix printers have over the lasers is the low cost. Some dot matrix printers cost less than $150. Of course there are some high-end dot matrix printers, such as the very fast line printers, that might cost close to $10,000.

There are many applications where a dot matrix printer is needed to accomplish a task. Wide, continuous sheets are necessary for some spreadsheet printouts. My LaserJet can't handle anything wider than $8\frac{1}{2}$ inches. With the wide carriage on my Star dot matrix, the wide sheets are no problem.

Another advantage is the number of sheets that can be printed. Most lasers have from 100- to 250-sheet bins. The dot matrix can print up to a whole box of 5,000 sheets of fanfold, continuous sheets. (It has been my experience though, if you start a job that requires a lot of printed sheets, as long as you stand there and watch the printer, it will work perfectly. If you walk away and start doing something else, the printer will immediately have a paper jam or some other problem. This is probably one of Murphy's many laws. This sort of problem seldom ever happens with my LaserJet III.)

Many offices and businesses still use multiple-sheet forms. A laser printer can't handle these forms, but a dot matrix can easily print them.

The dot matrix can also print on odd sizes, shapes, and thicknesses of paper. There are many times when I use mine to address large manila envelopes.

The U.S. Post Office has adopted a Postnet bar code that helps sort and speed up mail. If you look at some of the envelopes that you receive in the mail, you might see the Postnet bar codes below the address. Many of the companies that send out bulk mail use this code. Several of the dot matrix printers have the Postnet bar code built in, some others offer it as an option. If you do a lot of mailing, the Post Office might give you a discount if the envelopes have the Postnet code on them.

Maintenance Costs   Maintenance costs of dot matrix is usually much less than that for lasers and inkjets. The main costs for a dot matrix is to

Fig. 13-3
My old LaserJet III, now as good as it was when I bought it on May 17, 1990.

replace the ribbon about every 3,000 sheets. A dot matrix ribbon might cost from $3.00 to $10.00. A laser toner cartridge also lasts for about 3,000 sheets, but it might costs from $30.00 to $75.00 to replace.

Number of Pins There are still a few nine-pin dot matrix printers being sold today, but most people are buying those with a 24-pin print head. The 24-pin head has much better resolution and might cost only a few dollars more. The 24-pin printer forms characters from two vertical rows of 12 pins in each row.

There are small electric solenoids around each of the wire pins in the head. An electric signal causes the solenoid to push the pins forward. Dot matrix printers are also called *impact printers* because the pins impact against the ribbon and paper. The solenoids press one or more of the various pins as the head moves in finite increments across the paper so that any character can be formed.

Here is a representation of the pins if it were a 7-pin print head and how it would form the letter A:

```
1 O                    O
2 O                  O   O
3 O                  O    O
4 O                 O      O
5 O                O O O O
6 O               O          O
7 O              O            O
```

Print head moves in this direction ==>. The numbers on the left represent the individual pins in the head before it starts moving across the paper. The first pin to be struck would be number 7, then number 6, then 5, 4, 3, 5 and 2, 1, 2 and 5, 3, 4, 5, 6, then 7.

A 24-pin head would be similar to the 7-pin representation above, except that it would have two vertical rows of 12 pins, side by side in each row. The pins in one row would be slightly offset and lower than the pins in the other row. Because the pins are offset, they would overlap slightly and fill in the open gaps normally found in a 9-pin system. There is a lot of competition between the dot matrix and laser companies for your dollar. Some vendors are now selling laser printers for about the same price as some of the dot matrix printers. This low cost of the lasers has forced the dot matrix people to lower their prices. In addition to lower prices, many dot matrix companies are also adding more features, such as more memory and more fonts, in order to attract buyers.

Some Disadvantages of Dot Matrix

Some of the disadvantages is that the dot matrix can't come close to the quality printing of a laser. In the draft mode, if the printer has a 24-pin print head, only half of the pins will be hit. There will be noticeable spacing between the dots. For NLQ all of the pins will be hit. In draft mode with a 9-pin head, all of the pins will be hit, but there will be spaces between the dots. For NLQ on a 9 pin system, the printer makes a second run with the head slightly displaced so that the pins will hit different spots and fill in the open spaces. So in draft mode, the printing can be fairly fast but has poor quality. In the NLQ mode, they slow down considerably but have much better quality.

Most 24-pin dot matrix printers have a resolution of 360×360 dots per inch (dpi). Until recently, the standard laser was rated at 300×300 dpi. But if you compare the dot matrix output to the laser, you will see that the laser has a much higher resolution. The reason is that the laser produces a much smaller dot than the dot matrix dot. So if an A is printed out on a dot matrix, the jagged edges from the large dots are very apparent.

Most lasers can use scalable type fonts; only a very few of the high-end dot matrix printers can use scalable fonts.

Most dot matrix printers have only 8K or less of memory. A few of the high-end dot matrix printers might have as much as 64K, or even up to 128K. The memory on a dot matrix can be used as a print buffer. The computer can download a file to the printer, then go about its business doing other things. Laser printers use memory a bit differently. They take the file and format the whole page in memory before they start printing. Most lasers come with a minimum of 512K and you have the option to add more. For higher speed and graphics, the laser should have a minimum of 2Mb.

If you can get by with a dot matrix, you should be able to find one at a very good price. Look for ads in the *Computer Shopper* or any of the other computer magazines.

Ink Jets

Hewlett-Packard developed the first inkjet printer. Now there are many companies, such as Brother, Canon, Epson, Texas Instrument, Lexmark, and several others who are manufacturing inkjet printers. Some of the companies call them by a different name such as Canon's Bubble Jet, but they are all basically inkjets. The inkjet printers have a print output that approaches that of the laser, but at a lower cost. Most of the inkjet manufacturers have one or more color models. Those models that can print in color usually have a C in the model number such as the HP DeskJet 660C or the Canon Bubble Jet BJC-70.

The inkjet printers use a system that is similar to the dot matrix printers. Instead of pins that press a ribbon onto the paper, however, they use a matrix of small inkjets that sprays dots of ink on the paper. They also have a much larger number of inkjets; the dot matrix might have from 9 to 24 pins, the inkjet might have from 48 to 128 small jets. The head moves across the paper much like the dot matrix system and dots of ink are sprayed onto the paper to form text or graphics. To print color, they have three or more color inkjets. Of course, those with a larger number of jets produce more and smaller dots that yields higher resolution.

Most of the inkjet printers come with one or more fonts but they might be able use several more that are available on plug-in font cartridges. Some of the inkjets can use scalable fonts.

Like the dot matrix, the speed of the inkjets is measured in characters per second. Depending on the type of print, the average speed is about two pages per minute.

Inkjet Color

Most inkjet printers sold today are color. Because black is used most often, most of them have a large black cartridge along with the three primary color cartridges. It is now possible to buy color inkjet printers for less than $200. Some of the color machines can be very slow. About the best they can do is two pages per minute just printing black text. Lasers can print 4 to 8 pages per minute. A color graphics printout might take several minutes on an inkjet machine.

The inkjet color printers use a system of three different colored ink cartridges (cyan, magenta, and yellow) to print color. Some systems also have a black cartridge for standard text, some use the mixture of the three colors to make black. Some low-cost systems use a single cartridge with three colors. I recommend that you look for a printer that uses a separate cartridge for black and each of the primary colors.

As the head moves across the paper the software can have any of the various colors sprayed onto the paper. The three colors blend to produce any color of the rainbow.

The black inkjet cartridges are good for about 700 pages of text. The color cartridges might yield about half as many pages. They must then be replaced or refilled. The Signal Computing Company, at 800-454-2288, has refill kits for most inkjet printers.

If you do any presentations using an overhead projector, the inkjets can handle transparencies very well. The color inkjet printers are ideal for creating low-cost colored transparencies for presentations, for graphs, and for schematic plotting and drawings. Figure 13-4 shows a low-cost Canon inkjet printer.

Compared to the less-than-$300 inkjets, there are some inkjet printers that are rather expensive such as the HP DeskJet 885C, the Epson Stylus Pro, and the Canon BJC-610. These printers are about equivalent in speed, graphics capabilities, and cost. The HP DeskJet 1200C is a more sophisticated machine, has more memory, and can print faster. HP also has a 1200C-PS which has PostScript. The IBM Jetprinter PS 4079 is also a PostScript printer and about equivalent to the HP 1200C-PS. There are several options and features that I haven't listed. Many of the companies have several different models of their products. Models and prices listed

Fig. 13-4
A low-cost color inkjet printer.

are for comparison only and might be different when you read this. Check through the advertisements in computer magazines.

Here are some of the color inkjet companies and their numbers:

Canon Corp.   Lexmark International
800-848-4123   800-232-2000

Hewlett-Packard   Okidata Okijet
800-752-0900   (609) 235-2600

Call the companies for brochures and specifications.

Multifunction Machines

There are many times in a small office or home office (SOHO) when you needs to make one or more copies or to scan something. A large office can afford to have high-end copiers, scanners, plain-paper fax machines, and printers. But each of these items is rather expensive, and if not used very often, the cost cannot be justified. Besides in a SOHO, especially one like mine, there just isn't room for all of these separate machines. Several companies have noted the fact that most of these machines have a lot in common. There are now many multifunction machines that can copy, scan, fax, and print. Most of them are fairly reasonable in cost when you consider what they can do. Another big plus is that this four-in-one machine takes up very little space. Figure 13-5 shows a Canon color inkjet printer, a fax, a copier, and a scanner. I use it mostly for faxing and copying.

The scan utility of most of these multifunction machines operates like the copy utility. The scan can be sent to a computer, but unlike most scanners, these do not have optical character recognition (OCR) ability. Still, they are very handy to have. Many of the machines come with several software packages, such as document management, that can help you organize scanned data. Some of them come with business card readers and organizers, with OCR software, and faxing software.

Many of the multifunction machines print and copy in black and white only. Here are few:

Canon MultiPASS 2500   Lexmark Medley 4x
800-828-4040   800-358-5835

Epson Personal Document Station   Xerox Document WorkCenter 250
800-289-3766   800-832-6979

Fig. 13-5

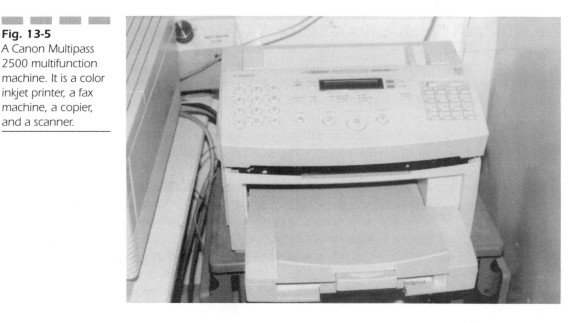

A Canon Multipass
2500 multifunction
machine. It is a color
inkjet printer, a fax
machine, a copier,
and a scanner.

Hewlett-Packard OfficeJet LX
800-752-0900

All of these machines use inkjet technology. Brother International, at
(800) 284-4357, has a multifunction laser machine, model MFC-4500ML.
The Panasonic Company, at (201) 348-9090, also has a laser multifunction
unit, model KX-SP100. Of course, the laser provides a bit better resolution
than the inkjet. It is comparably priced to the inkjet machines. There are
a few that can print and copy in color, such as the Scanpaq Color Scan
FX, at (800) 335-5533. It has high-resolution 24-bit true color and comes
bundled with several software packages.

The Hewlett-Packard CopyJet is a high-end color copier-printer combination. It has a flatbed glass panel surface that is similar to standard
copy machines and can copy originals up to $8\frac{1}{2}$ by 14 inches. It also has
the ability to reduce the size of the originals. It provides 300×300 dpi
full-feature color copies. The printer part of the combination is Hewlett-
Packard's 1200c, which provides good color resolution. It would have
been great if they had added a scanner and fax to this machine. There
are several inkjet and color inkjet printers that I did not mention.
There are many different models, from different companies with different features, functions, and prices. Look for advertisements in the major
computer magazines.

Wide-Format Printers

There are several companies that make wide-format color printers that can print such things as large posters, signs, banners, point of sale (POS) displays, trade show materials, advertisements, business and presentation graphics, and billboards. Most of the printers can print on 36-inch wide cut sheets or roll sheets as long as 50 feet. Usually the paper has to be specially coated. Most of the printers use a high-resolution inkjet technology. The cost of these printers range from $6,000 up to $20,000.

Using standard silk-screen techniques or large four-color printers to make a large poster or banner might cost from $1,000 up to $6,000 or more. The same poster can be printed on a wide format inkjet printer for $200 to $300 or less.

Another type of wide-format printer uses an electrostatic process with special cyan, magenta, yellow, and black (CYMK) toners. The special paper is electrostatically charged and the toners adhere to the charged areas. The high-speed printers have a very high resolution that is suitable for life-size posters, banners, or for several types of signs. The signs and posters can be used in exterior areas where they can withstand temperature changes, sun, and rain. The electrostatic printers are rather expensive at $30,000 to $100,000.

Most of the wide-format printers use a raster image processor (RIP) and a software controller. The RIPs act as color and ink control managers, handle enlargement, rotation, tiling and paneling, previewing, screening, and other tasks. The RIP software is made by several different companies, so it is not all the same. Here are just a few companies:

CalComp
(714) 821-2100

Houston Instrument
(512) 835-0900

Hewlett-Packard
800-367-4772

Encad
(619) 452-0891

Inkjet Supplies

The original cost of a printer is not the end. If you do much printing, the cost of supplies might be more than the cost of the printer. Ink cartridges might cost from $30 to $35. Some cartridges only last for about 300 pages. It is possible to refill some of the cartridges.

Laser Printers

The Hewlett-Packard LaserJet was one of the first lasers. It was a fantastic success and became the de facto standard. There are now hundreds of laser printers on the market. Most of them emulate the LaserJet standard. Even IBM's laser printer emulates the HP standard. Laser printers are a combination of the copy machine, computer, and laser technology. They have excellent print quality, but they have lots of moving mechanical parts and are rather expensive.

Laser printers use synchronized, multifaceted mirrors and sophisticated optics to write the characters or images on a photosensitive rotating drum. The drum is similar to the ones used in repro machines. The laser beam is swept across the spinning drum and is turned on and off to represent white and dark areas. As the drum is spinning, it writes one line across the drum, then rapidly returns and writes another. It is quite similar to the electron beam that sweeps across the face of a television screen or computer monitor one line at a time.

The spinning drum is sensitized by each point of light that hits it. The sensitized areas act like an electromagnet. The drum rotates through the carbon toner. The sensitized areas become covered with the toner. The paper is then pressed against the drum. The toner that was picked up by the sensitized areas of the drum is left on the paper. The paper then is sent through a heating element where the toner is heated and fused to the paper. Except for the writing to the drum, this is the same thing that happens in a copy machine. Instead of using a laser to sensitize the drum, a copy machine takes a photo of the image to be copied. A photographic lens focuses the image onto the rotating drum, which becomes sensitized to the light and dark areas projected onto it.

Engine

The drum and its associated mechanical attachments is called an *engine.* Canon, a Japanese company, is one of the foremost makers of engines. They manufacture them for their own laser printers and copy machines, and for dozens of other companies, such as Hewlett-Packard and Apple. There are several other Japanese companies who manufacture laser engines.

Low-Cost Laser Printers

Because of the large number of companies manufacturing laser printers, there is lots of competition, which is a great benefit to consumers. The competition has driven prices of both lasers and dot matrix printers down. It has also forced many new improvements. Until recently, most laser printers had a resolution of only 300 × 300 dots per inch (dpi). Most lasers now have a resolution of 600 × 600 and some have a 1200 × 100 dpi. Some laser printers are now selling for $500 or less.

Memory

If you plan to do any graphics or desktop publishing (DTP), you will need to have at least one megabyte of memory in the machine. Before it prints the first sheet, the printer loads the data into its memory and determines where each dot will be placed on the sheet. The more memory, the faster and better.

Not all lasers use the same memory configuration. For some machines, you must buy a special plug-in board for the memory. Check the type of memory that you need before you buy.

Several companies offer laser memories. Here are a couple:

ASP   Elite
800-445-6190   800-942-0018

Look in computer magazines for ads from other companies.

Page-Description Languages

If you plan to do any complex desktop publishing, you will need a page-description language (PDL) of some kind. Text characters and graphics images are two different species of animals. Laser printer controllers are somewhat similar to monitor controllers. The monitor adapters usually have all of the alphabetical and numerical characters stored in ROM. When we press the letter A from the keyboard, it dives into the ROM chip, drags out the A, and displays it in a precise block of pixels wherever the cursor happens to be. These are called *bit mapped characters.* If you wanted to display an A that was twice as large, you would have to have a complete font set of that type in the computer.

Printers are very much like the monitors and have the same limitations. They have a library of stored discrete characters for each font that they can print. My dot matrix Star printer has an internal font and two cartridge slots. Several different font cartridges can be plugged into these slots. But they are still limited to those fonts that happen to be plugged in. With a PDL, the laser printer can take one of the stored fonts and change it, or scale it, to any size you want. These are scalable fonts. With a bitmapped font, you have one typeface and one size. With scalable fonts, you might have one typeface with an infinite number of sizes. Most of the lasers printers accept ROM cartridges that have as many as 35 or more fonts. You can print almost anything that you want with these fonts if your system can scale them.

Speed

Laser printers can print from four to over ten pages per minute depending on the model and what they are printing. Some very expensive high-end printers can print over 30 pages per minute. A dot matrix printer is concerned with a single character at a time. The laser printers compose, then print a whole page at a time. With a PDL, many different fonts, sizes of type, and graphics can be printed. Because the laser must determine where every dot that makes up a character or image is to be placed on the paper before it is printed, the more complex the page, the more memory it will require and the more time needed to compose the page. It might take several minutes to compose a complex graphics. Once composed, it will print out very quickly. A PDL controls and tells the laser where to place the dots on the sheet. Adobe's PostScript is the best known PDL.

Resolution

Most lasers now print 600×600 dots per inch (dpi) resolution, which is very good. But it is not nearly as good as 1200×1200 dpi used for typeset in standard publications. The LaserMaster has models that can print at 1200×1200 and some that go as high as 1800 dpi. They also have upgrade kits for the HP LaserJet III and LaserJet 4 that can increase the resolution to 1200 dpi. Call LaserMaster, at 800-327-8946, for details and brochures.

Most lasers print in the $8\frac{1}{2}$ by 11 inch A-size format. CalComp, a division of Lockheed at (714) 821-2000, has developed a 600×600 high-resolution laser that can print in the $8\frac{1}{2}$ by 17 inch B-size format. QMS, Xerox, and several other companies have also developed large-size format printers.

Maintenance

Most of the lasers use a toner cartridge that is good for 3,000 to 5,000 pages. The cost of an original cartridge is about $75. Several small companies are now refilling the spent cartridges for about $30 each. It might be a good idea to keep an extra cartridge as a spare. The toner cartridge is sealed, so it will last for some time on the shelf. I had a cartridge go out on a weekend when I was working on a tight deadline. Most stores that sell cartridges were closed. Since then I keep a spare on hand. Most laser printers keep track of the number of sheets that have been printed. If you have a HP LaserJet, you can use the front panel buttons to run a self test. This tells you the configuration, how much RAM is installed, font cartridges installed, type of paper tray, how many pages have been printed, and several other tests.

When the toner gets low, most lasers will display a warning message in the digital readout window. Or if the print is very light, the toner might be low. If you remove the toner cartridge and turn it upside down and shake it vigorously, sometimes you can get a few more copies out of it. This might help until you can get a replacement.

There are other maintenance costs. Because these machines are very similar to the repro copy machines, they have a lot of moving parts that can wear out and jam up. Most of the larger companies give a mean time between failures (MTBF) of 30,000 up to 100,000 pages. But remember that these are only average figures and not a guarantee. Most of the lasers are expected to have an overall lifetime of about 300,000 pages. In the last seven years, I have printed out 26,950 sheets. I still have a long way to go.

Paper

There are many different types and weights of paper. Almost any paper will work in a laser, but if you use a cheap paper, it could leave lint inside the machine and cause problems in print quality. Generally speaking, any bond paper or a good paper made for copiers will work fine. Colored paper made for copiers will also work fine. Some companies are marking copier paper with the word "Laser" and charging more for it. The lasers will accept paper from 18 pound up to 24 pound easily. I have even used 67 pound stock for making up my own business cards. It is a bit heavy for wrapping around the drums and it jams once in a while. Some lasers use a straight-through path, so the heavier paper should not cause any problems in those machines.

Many of the laser printers are equipped with trays to print envelopes. Hewlett-Packard recommends envelopes with diagonal seams and gummed flaps. Make certain that the leading edge of the envelope has a sharp crease.

Labels

The Avery Company, at (818) 858-8245, and a few other companies make address labels that can withstand the heat of the fusing mechanism of the laser. There are also other specialty supplies that can be used with your laser. The Integraphix Company, 800-421-2515, carries several different items that you might find useful. Call them for a catalog. Here are some other companies that make small special printers for labels:

Brother International   CoStar
P-Touch PC   *LabelWriter*
800-284-4357   800-426-7827

Seiko Instruments
Smart Label
800-688-0817

Color Laser Printers

There are several color printers that are available. They might cost from less than $1,000 up to $15,000. These printers are often referred to as laser color printers, but at this time only a few actually use the laser technology. The other companies use a variety of thermal transfer technologies using a wax or rolls of plastic polymer. The wax or plastic is brought into contact with the paper, then heat is applied. The melted wax or plastic material then adheres to the paper. Very precise points, up to 300 dpi, can be heated. By overlaying three or four colors, all of the colors of the rainbow can be created. The Fargo Electronics Company offers a color printer for less than $1,000. Of course it does not have all of the goodies that you would find on the Tektronix Phaser or the CalComp ColorMaster.

Another type of color printer uses *dye-sublimation,* also called *thermal dye transfer* or *dye diffusion.* These systems use a ribbon with a continuous series of four different color ink stripes across the ribbon. The paper that is to be printed is forced against the ink ribbon. Dots of heat are applied to the various colors, which causes the color to diffuse onto the paper. The higher the temperature, the more color that can be diffused. The dots of heat can be accurately controlled for up to 256 different shades for each color. The dye-sublimation provides the best resolution and can provide prints that are near photographic quality. But as you might suppose, these printers are also the most expensive. Again, the least expensive dye-sublimation printer is the Fargo.

There are several companies who now make digital cameras. The photos taken with these cameras can be down loaded directly onto a hard disk and viewed on the monitor. But what if you wanted a copy of a photo for an album or to sit on your desk? Fargo Electronics has developed the FotoFUN, a small personal color printer that uses the thermal dye-sublimation technology. It can print 4 × 6 photos, postcards, or even use a transfer system to put a photo on a coffee mug. The photos are very near to the photo quality of film. At the present time the Foto-FUN printer costs $399. But you need separate kits for print film, postcards, or FotoMug. The print film kits cost $35.95 for 36 prints. A kit for 36 postcards costs $39.95, and a kit for four FotoMugs costs $29.95. The prices might be different by the time you read this. They are listed to give you an idea of what it costs for color printing.

The QMS ColorScript Laser 1000 was one of the first true laser color printers. It blends four different color toners, black, cyan, magenta, and yellow to print out color. The drum is sensitized for each color and that color toner is transferred to it. Once all of the colors are applied to the drum, it then prints out on ordinary paper or on transparencies. The QMS ColorScript is still rather expensive.

The Hewlett-Packard LaserJet 5M was introduced a couple of years after the QMS. Basically the technology is about the same as the QMS, but it is a bit less expensive.

The Xerox Corp. also has a true laser color printer. Call them for a brochure and pricing information.

Most of the color printers have PostScript, or they emulate PostScript. The Tektronix Phaser CP can also use the Hewlett-Packard Graphics Language (HPGL) to emulate a plotter. These color printers can print out a page much faster than a plotter.

One disadvantage of the color printers is the cost. Thermal wax might cost up to 45 cents per page; dye-sublimation might cost up to $2.75 per page. Most of this cost is for the ribbons and wax rolls that are used by the color machines.

The color printers are rather slow but the technology is improving. There will be several other color printers on the market soon. There is lots of competition so the prices are coming down.

Here are just a few of the companies who have color printers:

CalComp, Lockheed   Tektronix
800-932-1212   800-835-6100

Fargo Electronics   GCC Technologies
800-258-2974   800-422-7777

General Parametrics   Kokak
800-223-0999   800-344-0006

Hewlett-Packard   Xerox
800-257-3783   800-248-6550

QMS
800-523-2696

General Parametrics has a desktop film recorder attachment for their printer. This enables you to make 35mm color slides for presentations. Some of the other companies also provide features such as this. Call them for a brochure.

Color Photo Printers

Digital cameras are now becoming quite reasonable in cost and many people are buying them. Besides storing these photos on a hard disk or CD-ROM, many people would like to have hard copies.

Nikon Electronic has developed a dye-sublimation color photo printer they call the Coolprint. It also is limited to about 4×6 prints. It is much more expensive than the Fargo at about $2,000.

Plotters

Plotters can draw almost any two dimensional shapes or designs under the control of a computer. Plotters are a bit like a robot. An arm selects a pen. The pen can be moved from side to side, while at the same time the sheet of paper is moved from top to bottom. The computer can direct the pen to any point across the paper and can move the paper up or down for any point on an X-Y axis. The motors are controlled by predefined X-Y coordinates. They can move the pen and paper in very small increments so that almost any design can be traced out.

Values can be assigned for perhaps 1 to 1,000 for the Y elements and the same values for the X or horizontal elements. The computer can then direct the plotter to move the pen to any point or coordinate on the sheet. Some of the newer plotters use inkjet technology instead of pens. This makes them faster. The different colored ink cartridges can be activated much quicker than moving an arm to a rack, selecting a pen, then replacing it and selecting another.

Some less expensive plotters use a thermal paper such as that used by fax machines. An advantage is that it might be much faster than the pen-type plotters. A disadvantage is that this system does not provide any color and the resolution might not be very good. The thermal paper also fades when exposed to light.

Plotters are ideal for such things as printing out circuit board designs, for architectural drawings, for making transparencies for overhead presentations, for graphs, charts, and many CAD/CAM drawings. All of this can be done in many different colors. The different colors can be very helpful if you have a complex drawing such as a multilayered motherboard. A different color could be used for each layer.

A plotter might have from one up to eight or more different colored pens. There are several different types of pens for various applications, such as writing on different types of paper, or on film or transparencies. Some pens are quite similar to ball-point pens, others have a fiber-type point. The points are usually made to a very close tolerance and can be very small so that the thickness of the lines can be controlled. The line thicknesses can be very critical in some precise design drawings. The plotter arm can be directed to choose any one of the various pens. There are several different sized plotters. Some desk-top units are limited to only A and B sized plots. There are other large floor-standing models that can accept paper as wide as four feet and several feet long. Many of the floor standing models are similar to the wide format CalComp inkjet printer/plotter, shown in Fig. 12-3. There are many very good graphics and computer aided design (CAD) programs available that can use plotters.

One of the disadvantages of the early plotters was that they were rather slow. There are now some software programs that allow laser printers to act as plotters. Of course they are much faster than a plotter, but except for the colored printers, they are limited to black and white. Most of the laser printers are also limited to the A-size, or $8\frac{1}{2} \times 11$ inches.

Plotter sources

Here are a few of the plotter manufacturers. Call them for a product list and latest prices.

Alpha Merics
(818) 999-5580

Houston Instrument
(512) 835-0900

Bruning Computer
(415) 372-7568

Ioline Corp.
(206) 775-7861

CalComp
800-225-2667

Roland DG
(213) 685-5141

Hewlett-Packard
800-367-4772

Printer and Plotter Supplies

It is important to keep a good supply of toner cartridges, plotter pens, special paper, film, and other supplies on hand. Plotter supplies are not as widely available as printer supplies. A very high-priced plotter might have to sit idle for some time if the supplies are not on hand. Most of the plotter vendors provide supplies for their equipment. One company that specializes in plotter pens, plotter media, accessories, and supplies is the Plotpro Company, at 800-223-7568. Another company that has all kinds of printer, plotter, and office supplies is the Numeridex Company, at (800) 323-7737. Call these companies for a current catalog.

Installing a Printer or Plotter

Most IBM-compatible computers allow for four ports: two serial and two parallel. No matter whether it is a plotter, dot matrix, or laser printer, it will require one of these ports. Most printers use the parallel port LPT1; most plotters use a serial port. Some printers have both serial and parallel connections.

If the serial port is used, the printer can be up to 50 feet from the computer. If the parallel is used, normally the cable can only be about 10 feet long. There are special devices that allow longer cables to be used. The serial printers use a RS232C connector. The parallel printers use a Centronics-type connector. When you buy your printer, buy a cable from the vendor that is configured for your printer and your computer.

Printer Sharing

Ordinarily a printer will sit idle most of the time. There are some days when I don't even turn my printer on. There are usually several computers in most large offices and businesses. Almost all of them are connected to a printer in some fashion. It would be a terrible waste of money if each computer had a separate printer that was only used occasionally. It is fairly simple to make arrangements so that a printer or plotter can be used by several computers.

Sneaker Net

One of the least expensive methods of sharing a printer is for the person to generate the text to be printed out on one computer, record it on a floppy diskette, then walk over to a computer that is connected to a printer. If it is in a large office, an old 286 or 386 clone could be dedicated to running a high-priced laser printer. It doesn't matter whether the person carrying the floppy disk is wearing sneakers, brogans, or wing tips, the sneaker net is still one of the least expensive methods of sharing printers.

Switch Box

If there are only two or three computers, and they are fairly close together, you can use a simple switch box to switch between the computers. If you use a simple switch box, and the computers use the standard parallel ports, the cables from the computers to the printer should be no more than 10 feet long. Parallel signals will begin to degrade if the cable is longer than 10 feet and could cause some loss of data. A serial cable can be as long as 50 feet.

If an office or business is fairly complex, then there are several electronic switching devices available. Some of them are very sophisticated and can allow a large number of different types of computers to be attached to a single printer or plotter. Many of them have built-in buffers and amplifiers that can allow cable lengths up to 250 feet or more.

Printer Sharing Device Sources

Here are a few of the companies who provide switch systems. Call them for their product specs and current price list:

Altek Corp.
(301) 572-2555

Arnet Corp.
(615) 834-8000

Belkin Components
(310) 515-7585

Black Box Corp.
(412) 746-5530

Buffalo Products
Buffalo XL-256
800-345-2356

Crosspoint Systems
800-232-7729

Digital Products
PrintDirector
800-243-2333

Fifth Generation
Logical Connection
800-225-2775

Server Technology
Easy Print
800-835-1515

Quadram
Microfazer VI
(404) 564-5566

Rose Electronics
(713) 933-7673

Western Telematic
800-854-7226

Wireless Connections

Many of the Pentium-class and later motherboards now have an infrared (IrDA) built-in port. The IrDA systems are similar to television remote controls. The IrDA ports can be used to connect keyboards, notebook computers, and printers. The JetEye from Extended Systems Company, at 800-235-7576, is two small devices: one plugs into the parallel printer port on the computer and the other plugs into the printer connector.

The Merrit Computer Products Company, at 800-627-7752, has a wireless printer sharing kit. Instead of IrDA, it uses a radio frequency. The system can support up to 16 computers and four printers.

Network Printers

Almost any printer can be attached to a network and called a network printer. But several companies make fast, high-end, heavy-duty laser printers specifically for networks. The prices range from $3,000 up to $30,000. Many of the printers come bundled with special network printer management software and internal network interfaces. The print speed can range from 12 pages per minute (ppm) up to 32 ppm. Some of them are capable of duplex printing, or printing on both sides of the paper. The resolution can be from 300 dots per inch (dpi) up to 1200 dpi. They come with several different page description languages (PDLs), such as Post-Script, Hewlet-Packard HPGL, Intellifont, or True Image. They have paper trays that can hold as many as 3,000 sheets. Here are some of the companies:

Dataproducts Corp.
800-980-0374

Lexmark International
800-891-0331

Digital Equipment Corp.
800-777-4343

QMS Inc.
800-523-2696

Hewlett-Packard
800-752-0900

Xerox Corp.
800-349-3769

Kyocera Electronics
800-232-6797

Call the companies for more information.

Green Printers

The entire industry is under pressure to produce energy-conservation products. The Federal government will no longer buy computer products that do not meet Energy Star standards. Printers, especially laser printers, are notorious for being energy hogs. Hewlett-Packard and most of the other manufacturers are designing newer models that go into a "sleep mode" after a period of inactivity. Ordinarily it takes from 20 to 30 seconds for a printer to warm up. Some of these models maintain a low-voltage input so that they can warm up almost instantly.

Progress

If you mention Johann Gutenberg, most people think of the first printed Bible. Actually Gutenberg developed the movable print and started the printing of the Bible, but he ran out of money. He borrowed from Johann Fust and when he couldn't repay the loan, Fust took over the printing press and completed printing the Bible. So it was Fust who was first to print the Bible. There is a copy of this Bible in the British Museum.

If Gutenberg were around today you can bet that he would be quite pleased with the progress that has been made in the printing business. We have come a long way since 1436.

The Internet

Never before in the history of the world has there been so much information available. Almost all of it is no further away than your fingertips. The one thing that makes it possible is the Internet and the World Wide Web. The Internet started off as a government project in 1973 with the Advanced Research Projects Agency (ARPA), an agency of the Department of Defense (DOD). It was a network designed to facilitate scientific collaboration in military research among educational institutions. ARPAnet had some similarities to peer-to-peer networking. It allow almost any system to connect through an electronic gateway.

The ARPAnet is no longer primarily concerned with military research. For a while it was known as the Information Super Highway. Now it is just the Internet. There are four major providers: CompuServe, at 800-848-8990; Prodigy, at 800-284-5933; Microsoft Network, at 800-386-5550; and America Online (AOL), at 800-827-3338. Besides the large on-line service providers, there are hundreds of smaller Internet service providers (ISPs). The Los Angeles, California edition of the *Computer Currents Magazine* lists several local ISPs each month. They have an overall listing of over 200 ISPs in the greater Los Angeles area. There are several thousand in the entire country. The ISPs link to a network of a number of National Service Providers (NSPs).

At one time the larger on-line companies had a higher hourly or monthly rate than the smaller ISPs. The smaller ISPs began cutting their rates in order to attract customers. The larger companies began cutting their rates to match the small companies. Most of the small ISPs in the Los Angeles area charge $20 a month for unlimited hours. Some are as low as $10 or $12 per month. Now almost all of the large companies offer a flat rate of $19.95 per month for unlimited usage. This is an excellent example of competition working to our benefit.

The lowered rates and unlimited time has caused some problems. Before the unlimited time was instituted, you had to watch the clock and get on and get off as quickly as possible. Now you can log on and chat or surf for hours because of the flat rate.

AOL instituted a very aggressive advertising campaign and signed up over 8 million subscribers. Unfortunately, this was more than they could handle. Many people spent hours trying to get on-line, only to get a busy signal. They have since increased the number of phone lines, but it can still be difficult to get on at certain times of the day. Many people go on-line after they have their dinner, so it might be almost impossible to sign on during the hours from 5 P.M. until 10 P.M. This usually isn't too much of a problem with most of the other ISPs.

Modems and Access Numbers

At the time when there were only three or four major providers, most people were using 1200- and 2400-baud modems. It took quite a lot of time for downloads or to send messages. When the 14.4K modems came out, the companies figured that they would be losing a lot of money because the people would not be on line as long. To make up for the lost revenue, if you used a high-speed modem, they charged you extra. Now there is no difference in the charge for faster modems. The access numbers that you call must be able to handle the faster modems. Most companies have been very good at providing numbers for the faster modems. Of course, they also still provide numbers for the older 14.4K and even the old 2400-baud systems. Most faster modems will drop down and operate at the lower speed. Because you pay a flat monthly rate, it might be advantageous to use a 14.4K number. It might be easier to get on during the busy hours. If you are just chatting or sending a short e-mail, it won't make much difference what speed you use. But if you are browsing the Web sites, especially if there is a lot of graphics, then you definitely need a fast modem.

When you sign up with most of the companies, they will ask for your telephone area code and number, then provide a list of numbers in your area. They will list them by speed, such as 28.8K, 14.4K, and even 2400-baud. You are usually allowed to choose two numbers, a primary number and an alternate number. If the primary number that you choose is busy, then usually the software will have the modem try the alternate number. Hopefully, the numbers offered are toll free. If the numbers offered require a toll charge, you have to pay it. Unfortunately, there are some parts of the country that do not have local service. It might be in your best interest to check with several ISPs to find out if there are any local numbers available.

AOL has been very good at providing most of the country with the faster modems. But they don't always do it where the most people live. AOL has announced that they will support the new X2 56K modems made by 3Com/U.S. Robotics. Los Angeles is the second largest city in the country, but as of this time, there is no X2 support. However, they have set up a site at Anaheim, a suburb of Los Angeles, best known for Disneyland.

At the present time, there are two companies who have developed 56K technology. The International Telecommunications Union (ITU) has not yet decided which technology to adopt. It will probably be a mix of the two. Both companies claim that their product will still be usable no matter which is adopted. If you do a lot of downloading of graphics or access a lot of Web sites with graphics, it might be a good idea to buy a 56K modem. If you are on AOL, to find out if the X2 or 56K is available in your area, go to AOL KEYORD and type in X2. You will then be prompted to type in your area code, state, and city. It will then display a list of access numbers in your area. Those that are 56K will have an X2 beside the number.

Modems operate by taking the digital signals from the computer, then turning them into analog signals for transmission over the phone lines. There are several factors that limit the speed of analog signals. One big factor is noise and static, which are analog-type signals. Digital signals are not affected by the noise and static. When using high-speed modems, the standard analog signal is sent to the main router. The signal is then broken up into packets and transmitted digitally to the next station, where it is again converted back to analog. This analog signal is then fed to your modem, which converts it back to digital.

So the signal is converted from digital to analog, then to digital, then back to analog, then back to digital. The Integrated Service Digital Network (ISDN) will make life a lot better. But it has been very slow to be installed in most cities and it is rather expensive. ISDN is discussed a bit more later on in this chapter.

Free ISP

Unlike the other Internet service providers, the Juno Online Services Company, at 800-654-JUNO, www.juno.com, provides Internet service without charging a monthly fee. They can do this because they have signed up several advertisers. If you are on a tight budget and don't mind a few commercials, Juno could be all that you need. They don't offer all of the goodies that you would find on AOL, but they provide e-mail and most of the other essentials.

You can access anyone on the Internet or WWW from any of the on-line providers or ISPs. Unfortunately, if you travel a lot, you might not be able to find a local number for a smaller ISP. The larger companies have local numbers near most cities.

Services

There is something on the Internet for everyone. There are encyclopedias, up-to-the-minute news, people chatting with one another, on-line romance, and X-rated photos and talk. You can post notes or send e-mail. You can send a message to anyone in the world for just the cost of the dial-up connection and your hourly rate from the ISP. I recently sent several e-mail messages to a friend in England for less than it would have cost me to send a letter. It is as easy to chat with someone in Australia, France, or England as it is to chat with your next door neighbor.

There are several companies that are now making software and hardware that will let you use voice over the Internet. The telephone companies are a bit worried. If a person can make a long distance call to anywhere in the world by just dialing a local access number, then the telephone companies might stand to lose some money. One of the software packages for Internet voice is WebTalk from Quarterdeck, at (310) 309-3700, www.qdeck.com.

Because there is such a large amount of information on the Internet, search and browsing software is essential. The two most popular navigational browsers at this time are NetScape and Microsoft Internet Explorer. Prodigy, AOL, and CompuServe provide browsers as part of their service.

Most of the Internet services provide search engines also to help you find specific items. A search utility that works with most of the browsers is the ZooWorks Research software. It can help you find almost any information on the Internet or on an intranet. One good feature is that it records keywords and tracks where you have been so that you can easily return. Contact Hitachi Computer Products (America), 408-986-9770, www.hitachisoft.com/research.

The vast majority of people are good and honest, but when you get a lot of people communicating with one another, there will always be a few who will try to take advantage of others. There are a lot of people who are now using the Internet for business purposes. Most of them are honest and have something of value to offer, but again, there are a few who will do or say anything in order to get their hands in your pocket. Just be careful and watch your wallet.

There are now millions of people who access the Internet. There is something on the Internet for everyone. Most sites have search software that can help you find almost anything on their site. Yahoo is a search engine that can search the whole net.

All of the major companies offer chat rooms, instant messaging, home pages, member searches, and many other services. Many offer private chat rooms where two or more people can go to chat or do almost anything they want to behind closed doors. One reason AOL is so popular is because of their many chat rooms and areas. They also offer a "Buddy List." You can add your friends to this list and whenever one of them signs on it will show up on the list. You can then send an instant message (IM) to the buddy and it will reach him or her wherever they are. You can even ask to locate the member. It will tell you if they are in a private room or a chat room or just on-line doing IMs. If they are in a chat room it will ask if you want to join them or send them an IM.

AOL has made this instant message utility available so that anyone on any other network can send and receive instant messages to any member of AOL. If you have a friend on another network, just have him or her point their browsers to www.aol.com and download the free software.

I have been a member of Prodigy for over ten years. It is fine for e-mail and a few business-type things, but it can't come close to America Online (AOL) for fun and games. To it's credit, Prodigy has changed quite a lot. They still have the old Classic Prodigy, but they now have Prodigy Internet. The old Classic has an old, very slow browser. The Prodigy Internet uses Netscape for a browser. They added a few features to Netscape that makes it look a little bit like AOL.

Most of the larger service systems offer either Netscape or Microsoft Explorer with their programs. They have more or less become the double standard. Most of the systems also include search engines, such as Yahoo, Magellan, and Lycos.

There are millions of people who are lonely, and have no one to talk to or to visit with. About 8 million of these people have discovered AOL. One person called Prodigy that stodgy old Prodigy, compared to AOL.

On Prodigy, without any input from me, any time that I make a post to one of the lists or send e-mail, my name is emblazoned at the top as MR. AUBREY PILGRIM. Because my name is in all capitals, which means to shout on the Internet, several people have written to me and asked if I was on an ego trip or something. I had nothing to do with it, Prodigy set it up that way. Hopefully, they will have made some changes by the time you read this. They are trying hard to catch up to AOL.

AOL, CompuServe, and several other services will let you choose a unique screen name. On AOL I am simply Apilgrm. If I get tired of using that name, I can have up to five aliases. I can log on as someone else, play out any fantasies, and do it anonymously. I don't have to worry that my dignity or reputation will be marred by something that I might say or do, because nobody would know it was me. No matter how mousy or wimpy you are in real life, you can assume any identity, persona, or personality you want and play out your wildest fantasies.

The downside of the anonymity is that there are always people who go too far. They might be crude and rude and disruptive. It can sometimes take all the fun out of it. Some of them will join a chat room and use special programs they have created that will completely take over the screen and prevent anyone from participating. The senior scene room on AOL seems to be a favorite target. It is suspected that it is younger people just showing off. AOL usually provides a host to facilitate the chat sessions. The host might remind the person of the rules of netiquette, but it might not dissuade some of them. Of course, these people can be reported to the AOL Terms of Service (TOS) Advisors and the culprit will be warned or even denied service. But the disruptive people usually hit and run so it is difficult to catch them. These people are a lot like those who write virus programs to harm other people. I believe that they are sick. They take great pleasure in causing problems to others who they have never met.

AOL has many different chat rooms for various topics. There is a senior scene room, a married with children, a lesbian room, twenty something, and many more. Often there are as many as 20 to 25 people in these rooms. When one fills, the host will open another one similar to the one that is filled.

It is not required, but members are invited to post a profile of themselves. This is a brief statement, whether you are male or female, your interests, and anything else you would like to say about yourself. Of course no one is going to verify the statements, so some of them might be just a bit exaggerated. The names of the members who are in a room is displayed in a box alongside the chat screen. You can double click on any member's name and a box comes up that will let you read their profile.

AOL also has an instant message (IM) utility. You can click on this button and type in a person's name. It will tell you whether the person is on-line and whether the person is available. It can even tell you if the person is in a particular chat room. You can type in a message and it will be sent to the person immediately. The person can then respond or ignore you. Many people just spend time chatting without going to a room. It is very private so that no one else can see what is going on. Maybe it is better that no one sees the typed words that are exchanged in these sessions, especially if you are easily shocked.

Sometimes the messages can be a bit humorous or whimsical. I logged onto a chat room one day and saw this conversation: "Hi, I have long blond hair and blue eyes. My measurements are 38, 26, 36. Would anyone like to chat?"

"Yes. My name is Eric. I would not only like to chat with you, I would like to take you aboard my magic space ship. We would travel to the edge of the universe, then stroll hand in hand, visit each of the stars, and make wild passionate love at each one."

"My, my, Eric. You type very well. Would you like to meet me in a private room and we can talk about your magic ship?"

There are private rooms where two or more people can go and chat behind closed doors. All kinds of things can happen behind these closed doors.

The Internet can be dangerous to some marriages. Although it is strictly fantasy, some spouses take a very dim view of their mate having a cyber affair with someone else. I heard of one woman who didn't trust her husband. She went next door and used her friend's computer. She signed on with an assumed name and made up a very sexy profile. She then sent IMs to her husband and enticed him into a private room. After leading him on to see just how far he would go, she stopped, went home, and confronted him. It very nearly led to divorce. I read once that someone had determined that there were 726 sins. But that was before cybersex. There must be many more than that now.

Lest you get the wrong idea, AOL and the Internet is not all just sex. Many lasting friendships are made on the Internet. It is a godsend to many of those lonely people, especially those who can't sleep at night. There are also informational and special interest groups who can meet on the Internet. There are some services that do require legitimate identification. One such place is the Well at www.well.com.

There is one other disadvantage of the Internet and that is addiction. The Canadian Medical Association and the University of Pittsburgh have defined a disorder they call the Internet addiction disorder, (IAD). They claim that it is a maladaptive pattern of Internet use that can lead to clinically significant impairments and increased levels of distress. They say it might be as serious as alcoholism.

In the news, a woman was recently arrested and charged with child endangerment. She had locked her three young children in a separate room while she chatted and surfed the Internet for hours. The children were dirty and hungry and neglected. Her ex-husband had often found them in this condition when he came to pick them up for his weekend visits. He finally turned her in for child neglect.

A support group, much like Alcoholics Anonymous, has been formed to help people. Of course, to participate, you have to be on the Internet. This is something like an AA member taking a bottle along with him to a meeting. If you would like to find out more about the Internet Addiction Disorder (IAD) Support Group, point your browser to: www.iucf.indiana.edu/~brown/hyplan/addict.html

House Wiring Intranet

I talked about the Phonex Company, at (801) 556-0100, in chapter 12. This company developed special telephone adapters that plug into any wall outlet. It requires at least two adapters, one for the telephone input line, then another adapter for where you want the extension. More adapters can be plugged into any other 110-volt outlet to provide as many telephone extensions as needed. Or if you need an extension in another location, just unplug an adapter and plug it into another nearby wall outlet. You could even use a standard electrical extension cord and a Phonex adapter to provide a telephone extension. Electronic circuitry in the adapters blocks the ac voltage from getting into the telephone lines, but allows voice and data to go through. The device is being marketed and sold by Comtrad Industries, at 800-704-1211.

The Adaptive Company, at www.adaptivenetworks.com or (617) 497-5150 has developed a similar system using ordinary house or factory wiring as cabling to form networks. Some of their products are operating at up to 100Kbps. Eventually these products should allow you to plug your computer or several computers and modems into any outlet in the house and be able to access the Internet or plug in a telephone extension.

E-Mail

To me, one of the most useful and worthwhile benefits of the Internet is e-mail. It is so much better than snail mail in dozens of ways. An e-mail message is almost instantaneous, and it is cheap. You can send hundreds of e-mail letters for the cost of one 32 cent stamp. E-mail that you receive can be answered immediately, saved to a hard disk, printed out, or deleted.

I subscribe to several health-related sites. Besides personal messages, I usually get 100 or so health messages in my mailbox every day. I have set up directories and files on my hard disk for the messages that I want to save. I usually save them in a word processor format. If I compose a message off-line with my word processor, I have to convert it to ASCII type format before it can be sent. Most word processors will let you do that.

Some of the e-mail programs designed for the Internet have several management tools. Eudora, at www.eudora.com, is a very powerful e-mail program. It can receive your messages, separate them, and automatically send them to various folders and directories. Eudora has multiple formatting tools to let you send or receive stylized text, fonts, graphics, sound bytes, videoclips, or any data file. Eudora lets you read and compose mail off-line. It also has a built-in spelling checker.

Eudora has a lot more utilities and functions than the e-mail that comes with AOL, Prodigy, or CompuServe. But unfortunately, Eudora will not work with these large companies. It works fine with most of the smaller ISPs, such as Juno.

J-Mail and Spamming

One of the disadvantages of the Internet is being bombarded with junk e-mail. Someone has called this *j-mail.* The reason there is so much j-mail is because it is so cheap and easy to do. There are organizations who are selling e-mail addresses. You can get over a million addresses for as little as $25 and up to $100. You could send a message to every one of those million people for less than the cost of a single postage stamp.

Boot Magazine is a new computer magazine that is rather irreverent and much like the old hippie-type stuff. One of their writers, Tom Halfhill, said in one issue, that if just 3% of the people who get the j-mail respond, it would be enough to give the direct-mail marketer an orgasm.

There are no laws against spamming. Even if there were, they would probably be unenforceable. The crush of spam material can clog a small ISP and even some of the larger ones. I have gotten unwanted mail on AOL, but when I reply and try to complain to the sender, it is sent back to me as undeliverable. They have ways of sending the stuff without revealing their whereabouts.

There are a few resources on the Web. First of all, http://www.compulink.co.uk/~net-services/spam/ This site says:

> ...Hit back at the Spammers! Get lots of e-mail offering you get-rich-quick schemes? Want to hit back? "Spam Hater" (Now at V2.03) is free Windows software that helps you respond effectively and makes it hot for these people. This program:

- Analyses the Spam.
- Extracts a list of addresses of relevant Postmasters, etc.
- Prepares a reply.
- Choice of legal threats, insults or your own message.
- Appends a copy of the Spam if required.
- Puts it in a mail window ready for sending.
- Tool to help keep you out of spammers databases.
- Analyses Usenet spam.
- Context sensitive help—right mouse click on the item concerned.
- Shows a sample of the spam it's analyzing.
- Generates a "WHOIS" query to help track the perpetrator.
- Generates a "TRACEROUTE" query to help track the perpetrator's upstream provider.

There's another site, which tells you how to do it yourself: http://www.cciweb.com/iway7/spam4.html or http://www.cciweb.com/iway7/spam5.html

One small ISP has sued one of the companies, but it has not gone to court yet. The spammers are making so much money that they will gladly pay any fine and continue doing business as usual. One way to stop them would be to ignore them and not buy their products.

Connections

You should try to find the fastest modem possible. Technology does not stand still. Newer and faster methods are being developed every day.

ISDN

Integrated Services Digital Network (ISDN) is about the fastest line available at the moment. But you need a special ISDN modem and the ISP must be able to interface with ISDN. Another disadvantage is that it is not available in all areas of the country. Even where it is available, it can be rather expensive and might cost from $25 to over $200 extra on your phone bill. If your business is large and does a lot of videoconferencing and other business over the telephone and Internet, it might be well worth it.

ADSL

Asymmetric Digital Subscriber Line is a very fast line that can provide data at a speed as high as 6.14Mbps (Megabits per second). That is about 200 times faster than a 28.8Kbps modem. It will be ideal for videoconferencing, video-on-demand, networking, fax, and voice. It is still being tested and developed, but it should be available in some parts of the country by the time you read this. The original hardware will cost about $300 to $500. The original service will cost about $100 a month.

Cable

Some companies have developed cable modems that can operate off the cable lines. They can operate as high as 10Mbps. The hardware cost might be $300 to $500 and cost an extra $30 to $40 a month on your cable bill.

Cable TV Internet

If you can't afford a computer and a modem, there are a few companies who have developed keyboards and set top boxes that will let you access the Internet over your cable TV. Instead of a computer monitor, it uses the TV screen. The keyboard uses a wireless infrared system similar to that used in the standard TV remote controls. These systems will do most of what you can do with a computer as far as the Internet goes. You can surf the Internet, access all the Web sites, send and receive e-mail, perform financial transactions, search for desired information, and visit chat rooms. Of course, you will not have all the advantages of a computer.

Most of the systems require you to purchase the set top boxes and keyboards for a nominal price. Then to access the Internet, it usually costs about $29.95 for unlimited hours.

Here are some companies who provide set top boxes:

Inter-Con/PC
(612) 975-0001

Interactive Media Systems
(408) 245-8283

Interlink Electronics
800-340-1331

NetLink Sega Saturn
800-733-7288
www.sega.com

Philips Magnavox Internet TV
888-813-7069
www.magnavox.com

Web-i
www.pmpro.com

WebTV
888-772-7669
www.sony.com

Distance Learning

The California State Universities, and I am sure several others, are using the Internet for teaching courses. It doesn't matter where you are, you can sign up for a course and receive college credit for it just as if you were sitting in class. Anyone can access the classes, but to receive credit, you might have to pay some fees and actually go to the class room for tests.

Quite often when I was attending the San Jose State University, I would try to get into a class, but if it was filled, I was just out of luck. It made it very difficult if that class was required for graduation. With the Internet, there will be no problem of denial because of filled classes.

Another problem that I faced was that I was working full time and had to take my classes when I could arrange them around my work schedule. I sure wish Internet classes had been available at that time. With the Internet, you can do your class work at any time that suits you.

McGraw-Hill World University, www.mhcec.com

You might be surprised to know that the company who published the book you are holding also provides significant distant learning opportunities. Point your browser to www.mhcec.com or call 888-649-8648, ext. 2621.

Here is some of the things you will find there:

McGraw-Hill World University is a unique distance education provider. The curriculum of the University's AAS degree program was written by experienced college professors and the unique CyberCampus was designed by a team of industry experts.

The educational, ethical, and business standards of McGraw-Hill World University have met the rigid requirements of the Distance Education and Training Council. McGraw-Hill World University is fully accredited as a distance education provider.

Online Catalog and Bookstore

The McGraw-Hill Online Catalog—Nearly 9,000 in-print titles in areas such as business, computing, engineering, science, and medicine from imprints such as Osborne, Schaum's, International Marine, and Ragged Mountain Press. The catalog includes all titles published by the McGraw-Hill College Division, with titles to be added from the recently acquired Irwin, Dushkin, and WCB publishing units.

The McGraw-Hill bookstore—professional books of all publishers with more than 30,000 titles in areas such as business, computing, technical, professional, and reference. The site puts the spotlight on a Book of the Week and features new arrivals, forthcoming titles, bestsellers, and special promotions—all available through secure electronic transactions.

McGraw-Hill has several good books on the Internet. Warning: The following is an unabashed commercial. Of course, you will find all of the books that I have written in the McGraw-Hill bookstore. Be sure to look for the *Save A Bundle* series such as the *Build Your Own Pentium, Build Your Own Pentium Pro,* and several others. Another good book about the Internet published by McGraw-Hill is *The Internet for Everyone: A Guide for Users and Providers* by Richard Wiggins.

Many books have been written about the Internet. Some very good ones can be found in the McGraw-Hill bookstore. Or you can contact Osborne/McGraw-Hill, at 800-227-0900 or www.osborne.com and they will send you a current catalog. Here are some of their books: *Internet Essentials and Fun List; Internet, the Complete Reference;* and *The Internet Yellow Pages; The Internet and Web Yellow Pages; The Internet Kids and Family Yellow Pages; Web Publishing with Netscape for Busy People; The World Wide Web for Busy People; America Online for Busy People; Official America Online Yellow Pages; The Official AT&T WorldNet Web Discovery Guide; Web Publish-*

ing with *Corel WordPerfect 8 Suite: The Official Guide*; *Internet Explorer 4.0: Browsing and Beyond*; *Great American Websites*; *The Webmaster's Toolkit*; *The McGraw-Hill Encyclopedia of Networking*.

If you are just getting started, the *Internet, the Complete Reference* would help you immensely. It has over 800 pages of information about getting on the net. It has addresses and numbers of hundreds of local, state, national, and international access gateways. There are valuable helpful hints on almost every page. There are several other books about the Internet, published by companies other than McGraw-Hill.

Internet Magazines

Most of the computer magazines have at least one article about the Internet in each issue. There are several magazines that are devoted entirely to the Internet. Most of the magazines have reviews and listings of Web sites. There are thousands of sites. The magazines can be very helpful in telling you where to look. Here are a few Internet magazines:

- *Boot Magazine*   Many of the *Boot Magazine* issues include a CD-ROM disc with lots and lots of programs and games. I enjoy the magazine for its new and fresh outlook. If you would like to subscribe, call (415) 468-4869 or send e-mail to: subscribe@bootnet.com. They have a website at www.bootnet.com.

- *NetGuide*   P.O. Box 420400, Palm Coast, FL 32142-9232. Tel. 800-829-0421 or send e-mail to netguide@palmcoastd.com. To access NetGuide on-line point your browser to www.netguidemag.com

- *Internet World*   P.O. Box 7461, Red Oak, IA 51591-2461, Tel. 800-573-3062, Internet customer service iwservice@iw.com, IW Online, www.iw.com.

- *The Web*   P.O. Box 56943, Boulder, CO 80323-6943, Tel. 800-932-6241. Subscription on line, www.webmagazine.com/webmag.html. The Web Online www.webmagazine.com

- *ZD Internet*   P.O. Box 55483, Boulder, CO 80323-5483. For subscription online go to http://subscribe.zdimag.com/service

The magazines are an excellent way to know what is available on the Web. They also have some very interesting and informative articles in each issue.

Your Own Web Page

Many of the large providers such as Prodigy, AOL, and CompuServe will give you space on their site for your own Web page. It is usually just a few megabytes. If you want more, it will cost you. Most of the large company Web pages have been constructed by professionals who are familiar with the hypertext markup language (HTML). There are books that can show you how to create your own professional looking site. WordPerfect 7 and Microsoft Word 97 can convert text to the HTML format.

Web Hosting

A recent issue of the *NetGuide Magazine* had dozens of advertisements from companies who will set up a site for you and give you 20 to 25Mb of space. Additional space is usually available in 5 megabyte blocks. They will take care of the business of registering you for one or more domain names. They will set up unlimited e-mail for you, setup anonymous FTP (file transfer protocol), and offer many other services. Most of the companies charge from $19.95 to $25.

If you have a company or larger business there are professional designers who will develop a complete site for you. For a large job, you might have to bring in an ISP representative, a graphics designer, a programmer, network integrators, and many others. It can be very expensive to set up a large site.

The Corel Company, at www.corel.com, has a WebMaster Suite that can be used to create a professional Web site. The suite contains Web Page Authoring, Web Site Management, Graphics, Database Publishing, Web Site Hosting Service, and much more.

Sex on the Web

There has been a lot of concern about young people accessing the many web sites that feature nudity and sex. Most of the sites ask if the person is over 18 or not. If they say they are under 18, they will not be allowed to access the site. But how many do you suppose will say that they are under 18?

In the Scandinavian countries, they don't worry too much about young people seeing depictions of the sex act. But they do ban young children from movies that have lots of killing and gore. Our children are exposed to an unbelievable amount of killings and blood and guts on television and in the movies. I think the Scandinavians are right.

The government is worried about pornography on the Internet and has spent a lot of time trying to come up with laws that would control it. They really shouldn't worry too much. Almost everyone of the sites will show a fairly modest teaser for free, but if you want to see anything more explicit, they ask for a credit card number. So unless your children have their own credit cards, you probably don't have to worry too much.

Future

The Internet is still in its infancy, but it is growing faster than the weeds in my front lawn. There are thousands of new sites put up every day. There are millions of Web pages. There is just about everything that anyone could possibly want on the Internet. Maybe even more than what you want. There will be even more tomorrow.

CHAPTER 15

Laptop, Notebook, and Hand-Held Computers

There can be a bit of confusion about these types of computers. Adam Osborne developed the first portable. It was the size of a large suitcase and had dual 5 $\frac{1}{4}$ inch floppy drives. The unit weighed about 40 pounds and wasn't too much fun to lug around. Adam became a millionaire selling them, then lost it all a short time later. (He lost most of his money paying lawyer and court fees in a dispute with Lotus over the "look and feel" of a software program he had developed. His program did not copy Lotus 1-2-3 code, but Lotus felt it had the look and feel of 1-2-3. After several years and much money, Adam lost.) There are still a few portables around, but they are considerably smaller and lighter than the original Osborne. They usually look like a large lunch box.

The advent of the large-scale integration of chips made it possible to design computers, such as the laptop, that are much smaller than the portables. With still greater integration, and by leaving out some of the utilities and functions, it became possible to shrink the size of the laptop to about the size of a notebook, hence the name. They have gone even further and shrunk the computer down to a palmtop size. These are called Personal Data Assistants (PDAs). The size and weight of the palmtops can vary from 5.7 ounces up to about 23 ounces.

Hand-Held Personal Computers

Microsoft created some specifications for palmtops or hand-held PCs (HPCs). HPC devices that met the specifications could run Microsoft's Window CE. The HPC standards call for a computer that can fit in a coat pocket and weigh less than one pound. It had to have a physical keyboard, 480 × 240 resolution touch screen, 2Mb of RAM and 4Mb of ROM, each of which could be upgraded. The devices should also include an IrDA (Infrared port), serial ports, a PC card slot, and a docking cradle so that it can be loaded or downloaded to a desktop. If the HPC meets all of these specifications, they can run a Win CE version of Windows 95. Win CE is a miniature suite that contains Explorer, Pocket Word, Pocket Excel, Inbox, Calendar, World Clock, and Tasks. These programs are all burned into the onboard ROM. The files can be transferred back and forth to a desktop very easily.

Here are some companies who manufacture HPCs that conform to the Microsoft specifications:

Casio, Inc.
(201)361-5400
www.casio.com

NEC Computer
800-632-8377
www.nec.com

Compaq Corp.
800-345-1518
www.compaq.com

Palm Computing (U.S. Robotics)
800-881-7256
www.usr.com/palm

Hewlett-Packard
541 757-2000
www.hp.com/handheld

Philips Mobile Computing
888-367-8356
www.velo1.com

Hitachi Home Electronics
800-448-2244
www.hitachi.com

Psion Software
800-997-7466
www.psion.com

LG Electronics
(201) 816-2098
www.lgeus.com

Sharp Electronics
800-237-4277
www.sharp.usa

Prices for the HPCs range from $399 up to $739. A lot of the variation in price depends on whether it has a modem, the amount of memory, and other features and goodies.

The keyboards on the HPCs are so small that, even if you had fingers the size of a baby, you would still have trouble doing touch typing. So most of them come with a stylus that can be used to tap each individual key.

There are some smaller sized palmtop computers. For these smaller sized ones, it would appear that they have gone about as far as they can go. But there are wrist watches and several other gadgets that are even smaller than the palmtops. Of course, the smaller the size, the less the overall function.

But still quite a lot of information can be stored in something as small as a wrist watch. I have a Timex Data Link that can store up to 70 entries, such as several phone numbers, birthdays, to-do lists, anniversaries, and appointments. To input data into the watch, I first type it into a computer. The special software converts the information into a series of lines that are similar to bar codes. I then hold the watch up in front of the computer screen and an electric eye on the watch picks up the signals from the screen and stores the information in the memory of the watch. You couldn't exactly call this a computer, but it does more than some of the early computer systems that filled a whole room.

Laptop Evolution

A short time ago, I paid $3,600 for a Toshiba laptop. It was the latest and greatest laptop available at that time. It came with an Intel 25MHz 486 CPU, Windows 3.1 and DOS 6.0, a floppy disk drive, and a 120Mb hard disk. It had PCMCIA slots for adding extra memory or any of the other cards that were available at that time. PCMCIA is an acronym for Personal Computer Memory Card International Association. It was a specification for the slots on the laptops for memory chips and other components. It is now known as the PC Card specification.

It had a 10-inch active matrix screen or thin film transistor (TFT). This means that there was a separate transistor for each of the several million pixels on the screen. If just one transistor became defective, it ruined the whole screen. Because of this, active matrix screens are much more expensive than the dual scan screens. The colors of the dual scan screens are not as bright as those of the active matrix. If you don't mind the brightness of the colors, the dual scan machines are usually considerably less expensive.

(Some companies have demonstrated 21-inch active matrix monitors for computers. At this time, a 21-inch active matrix screen costs about $5,000. As the technology matures and the cost comes down, larger screens will be available on laptops.)

I finally gave my old Toshiba laptop to my daughter and bought a new one for $3,600. This one came with a 2Gb hard drive, a floppy disk drive that plugs into the printer port, a 10 speed CD-ROM, a 33.6K modem, 16Mb of memory, an Intel 150MHz Pentium CPU, Windows 95, a 13.3-inch active matrix screen, and several other goodies. This laptop is more powerful than a couple other desktop computers in my office. My new laptop weighs about the same as the old Toshiba. It is a bit larger because of the larger screen. Figure 15-1 shows my AMS Travel Pro.

The main reason I bought it is because I do a lot of traveling. When I am on the road, I can plug into a telephone line and be on the Internet just like at home. I can use my spare time to write letters, notes, and work on my books. I have almost all of the conve-

Fig. 15-1
My AMS Tech Travel Pro laptop. It has a 2.1Gb hard drive, a CD-ROM, and an external floppy disk that plugs into the printer port.

niences of my office, except that the hotel rooms are not nearly as messy as my office.

If it were necessary, I could get by with this one laptop. I don't really need my desktops. But I have one 120MHz Pentium with a 19-inch monitor and another desktop with a 21-inch monitor for my new 266MHz Pentium II. So until it is necessary, at home I will continue to use my big guns.

Upgrading the CPU

I feel a bit sorry for my daughter that she doesn't have all the goodies on her laptop that I have on mine. But there are now several ways that an older laptop can be upgraded. One of these days when I get the time, I will upgrade it for her. The CPU can be replaced with an Intel Over-Drive CPU. This is a very simple upgrade that almost anyone can perform. It is not very difficult to remove the cover of a laptop.

Once the cover is removed, look for the CPU. Make a diagram. If you have to remove any cables or wires, make a note of how they were connected. Also note the orientation of the CPU. There might not be any indication on the board as to where pin one is. The CPU should have a small black dot on the top that indicates pin 1.

Many of the larger computer stores carry the Intel OverDrive CPUs. Look through some of the computer magazines such as *Computer Shopper*. They have a section near the back that lists products and tells you which of the 1000 pages have the CPU advertisements. You can also go to the Intel Web site at www.Intel.com and find out which distributors carry their OverDrive CPUs.

It is also possible to upgrade to a Pentium-class CPU with an Intel or Cyrix or AMD CPU. This type of upgrade might be a bit more difficult. The Evergreen Technologies, at 800-607-7333, has some excellent upgrade packages. They promise a 72-hour turn-around, using FedEx, depending on the pickup and delivery. They can upgrade the RAM, the hard drive, and CPU. They advertise an upgrade bundle that includes a 586 CPU and a 1Gb hard drive for $699. They have other upgrades that start as low as $399. Of course, these prices are subject to change and might be different by the time you read this.

The CMS Enhancements, at 800-988-1106 or www.cmsenhancements. com, also offers several hard drive upgrade options for a laptop. Some of the hard drives are on a cable connected to a PC Card. They offer capacities up to 3Gb.

Even if I had to pay $1,000 to upgrade the old Toshiba that I gave to my daughter, it would still be well worthwhile compared to paying $3,600 for a new one. I just wish I had known about this before I gave my old one away and bought this new one. I could have saved a lot of money.

Hard Disk Drive Upgrades

There are now several companies who make hard disks that can be plugged into the printer port. Many of them have removable disks. It makes it very easy to copy from the laptop to the external drive, then put it on a desktop.

Many of these printer port drives are fairly small, but most of them require a small ac adapter power transformer and to be plugged into a 110-volt source. One hard drive that does not require an external power source, and is very small, is the Avatar Shark 250. This drive and several others were discussed in Chapter 8.

PC Card Slot Components

It is almost impossible to operate computer now without a CD-ROM drive. Several companies now offer CD-ROM drives that can be plugged into the printer port. But like many of the external hard drives, they need a an ac adapter power transformer and a 110-volt source.

The EXP Computer Company, at 800-397-6922, has a CD-ROM and several other units that can be plugged into one of the PC Card slots. (The PC Card slots were originally called the PCMCIA slots). There are three different PC Card slot sizes, I, II, and III. The PC Cards are about the size of a credit card depending on the type, with type I being thinnest and type III the thickest.

There are a large number of components built into the PC Cards such as network cards, SCSI adapters, sound cards, fax/modems, even an ISDN fax/modem card, and many others.

The U.S. Robotics Company, at 800-525-8771 or www.usr.com/x2, has been the biggest driving force for 56K modem technology. Several of the larger computer stores carry their products. Call them for the nearest location. Other companies are the EigerCom Company, at (800) 653-4437 or www.eigerlabs.com, with a 56.6K fax/modem on a PC card. Apex Data Company, at 800-841-2739 or www.apexdata.com, also has the RapidTransit Data/Fax Modem.

Many of the components that can be added to a laptop come with a cable that plugs into one of the laptop PC Card slots. The CD-ROM is small and light weight and can be plugged into any of the PC Card slots. The PC Card system allows components to be plugged in or unplugged while the power is on.

Simple Technology manufactures hard drives in a PC Card format for the Type III slots. They have removable drives from 1.08Gb to 2.1Gb that will fit almost any model laptop. They are available from the CDW mail-order discount store, at 800-726-4239, www.cdw.com. Most larger computer dealers also carry them.

The Nikon Company, at 800-526-4566 or www.nikonusa.com, has a small digital camera on a PC Card. The Coolpix 100 can take full-color photos, then be inserted into the PC Card slot and downloaded for viewing. The digital photos can then be used to illustrate a document, sent as E-mail, or kept for a photo album. The small camera even has a built-in flash.

Barebones Units

Several companies sell barebones desktop computers. A barebones unit usually has only the minimum components in it. You can then add whatever you want to it.

The Ma Laboratories, at (408) 954-8188 offers a barebones laptop. The unit comes without a CPU. You can buy one from Ma Labs or elsewhere. They have a long list of components that can be installed in the laptop. You can pick whatever you want and install it yourself. They will give you an assembly manual and a VCR instruction tape.

Telephone Adapters and Accessories

It is not always possible to plug into a telephone outlet in some hotels. The Port Company, at 800-831-5824 or www.port.com, has adapters that they claim can let you attach to any telephone. At one time all modems used an acoustic coupler. The coupler fit over the mouthpiece of a telephone and transmitted the modem sound into the telephone. Port has a modern acoustic coupler for use in pay-phone booths or other places where it is not possible to connect directly. Port also has several other laptop accessories such as carrying cases, batteries, battery chargers, and security devices.

Theft

One study reported that over $2 billion worth of hardware, software, and irreplaceable data is lost to computer theft each year. Laptops are a prime target for thieves. They are very easy to carry, to hide, and to sell.

Several laptops have disappeared at airport terminals. When you go through the security check points, most people place their laptops on the moving belt so that it can be x-rayed. Then they might have to fumble around to empty all their pockets of any metal change, eyeglasses, pens, or even spiral pocket notebooks. Usually by the time you make it through the metal detector, your laptop has been sitting at the end of the conveyor belt for some time. It is quite possible that someone else might pick it up before you get there. It would be a good idea to empty your pockets first, then put your laptop on the conveyor belt so that you both arrive at the end at the same time.

Laptops can also disappear off a desk or from almost any place. The Kensington Company, at 800-535-4242, manufactures a MicroSaver locking system. Several of the larger laptop manufacturers have the slot built in. The lock has a hardened cable that can be looped around almost anything so that it cannot be easily stolen.

Magazines

Almost all of the major magazines usually have an article about laptops in each issue. There are hundreds of advertisements for laptops in the magazines. There must be a lot of profit in laptop and notebook computers. If you are thinking of buying a laptop or notebook, just look at the advertisements in any of the computer magazines. Most of the ads will list the company Web site if they have one.

Mobile Computing and Communications is one magazine that is devoted entirely to portables, laptops, and notebooks. To subscribe, call (800) 274-1218 or e-mail circulation@curtco.com. Access their web site at www.mobilecomputing.com

Need for notes

There is so much information today, you can be overwhelmed with information overload. It can sometimes be difficult to remember and keep track of all the dates and data that I need to. A small notebook or hand-held PC can be a marvelous personal data Assistant. I sometimes wake up in the middle of the night with an idea and reach for my laptop. Sometimes I even take it into the bathroom with me. Instead of reading a newspaper, I work on my laptop. If it was waterproof, I would take it into the shower with me.

Several of my friends have told me that I need to get a life. Of course, they have never owned a laptop.

Building the Dream Machine

This chapter is primarily about upgrading to a Pentium II or building a PC from scratch. Upgrading an older computer to a Pentium II is not much different than upgrading any other computer. It merely involves removing the old motherboard and installing a new Pentium II. You should be able to use most of your old components. Of course, you might have to buy new memory chips and perhaps a higher capacity hard drive. Building or assembling a dream machine from scratch is no different than assembling a 486 or Pentium-class machine. All PCs are very similar in the way they are assembled. They are all very simple.

Why the Pentium II

Many of us spend a lot of time using our computers for word processing, accessing the Internet, or other rather mundane tasks. For most of the simple tasks, a low-cost Pentium-class computer that runs at 75MHz would do fine. Most of us really don't need a computer that runs at 266MHz unless we are doing high-end graphics design, computer aided design (CAD), desktop publishing, or running large databases.

So why is it that everybody wants a bigger and faster computer, even though they might not need it. In case you missed it, here is something that I talked about in the Introduction.

The B-B gene Some people don't mind driving an older car, living in a modest home, or using an older computer. There are other people who must have the most expensive, the biggest, the most powerful, and the fastest of everything available, even if they have to hock the family heirlooms and take out a second mortgage on their home. Their lustful desires include cars, homes, fancy clothes, and even big and fast computers. I am convinced that there is a gene, as yet undiscovered, that influences and controls those people.

When this gene is finally discovered and documented, I suggest that it be called the Biggest-and-Best gene, or the B-B gene. There is little doubt in my mind that this gene exists in all of us, but it exerts a far greater influence over some than others.

Many of the people who are influenced by the B-B gene are also quite willing to pay exorbitant prices for goods that they perceive to be better than others, simply because of a brand name or because it is first on the market.

I hate to admit it, but I am also afflicted with the dreaded B-B gene when it comes to computers. I have never had much money, so I try to make sure that I get all of the value I can for my few dollars. That is why it is difficult for me to understand why a person would pay three or four times as much for such things as a purse, shoes, or jeans simply because the products have a well advertised brand name. The same goes for computers. I don't understand why some people will buy a high-priced computer just because it has an IBM or Apple logo. For the price of an IBM or Apple, you might be able to buy two or three equivalent compatible, no-name computers, or better yet build them yourself.

If you are also afflicted with the B-B gene don't feel guilty or ashamed. It is something that seems to be inherited. Just try to control it within reason and enjoy.

Minimum System Requirements

Here is a list of the major components that are needed for a minimum system. Later you might also want to add several other components such as a modem/fax board, CD-ROM drive, network card, and several other goodies. But it is best to start out with a minimum system.

- Case and power supply
- Motherboard with CPU
- Floppy drives
- Hard drives
- Keyboard
- Mouse
- Monitor and adapter board

These components were discussed in detail in previous chapters. They are also discussed a bit more later in this chapter.

Troubles

The Pentium II is quite a bit different from other systems in several ways. One difference is that the power supply fan is reversed. On the standard systems, the fan in the power supply draws air in from the grill in the front of the case and pulls it over the components, then exhausts it out the back to the system. The ATX power supply draws air in from the back of the computer and pushes it over the components and out of the front of the case. The newer cases have been redesigned so that the power supply fan is immediately over the CPU. Intel redesigned the Pentium II CPU. Unlike all CPUs until now, the Pentium II CPU is mounted on a board and plugs into a slot on the motherboard. Intel calls it slot 1. The board and CPU assembly rises about four inches above the motherboard when plugged into slot 1.

I bought a medium tower case at a computer show. When I tried to install the motherboard, there was not enough space to get the CPU under the fan on the power supply. Some of the cases have been redesigned to make them wider but not as tall. Figure 16-1 shows the new ATX medium-tower case beside a standard medium tower.

Figure 16-2 shows the fan on the power supply. I called the vendor who sold me the case and he said they had just learned of this problem. He said to bring the case back and he would exchange it for a full-tower case.

You have no doubt heard of Murphy's laws. I have discovered a law that Murphy overlooked. Pilgrim's law states that any time there is a good sale or something that you need, it is always on the other side of town. The vendor was about 40 miles away on the other side of Los Angeles. I drove over and when I got there he apologized and said that he had made a mistake and that he did not have any tower cases on hand. I asked that he give me my money back so I could look somewhere else. He said he would but there was a 20% restocking fee. I was already unhappy that I had driven 40 miles, only to find out that he had made a mistake. Then being told that I had to pay a restocking fee was too much. I was rather angry. He had assured me when I bought the case that it was the proper case. I stormed out and promised that I would never deal with him again.

I came back home and took the power supply apart. There was almost enough room in it to mount the fan inside the supply. All of the older power supplies have the fan mounted inside the power supply case. But there wasn't quite enough room in this ATX supply. I thought of mounting it inside anyway and then use duct tape to hold the supply cover on. After all, I would be the only one who would ever see it. But I changed my mind and finally got out my hacksaw and pliers and cut and bent the opening enough so that I could mount the fan halfway

Fig. 16-1
Fig. 16-1
The new ATX medium tower case on the left and a standard medium tower case on the right.

inside the supply. I used some large nuts as spacers and it gave me enough space to easily install my motherboard.

Figure 16-3 shows the fan after my modification of the power supply case. Figure 16-4 shows it and the CPU after I mounted the fan about halfway inside the power supply. I now have about one-quarter inch clearance.

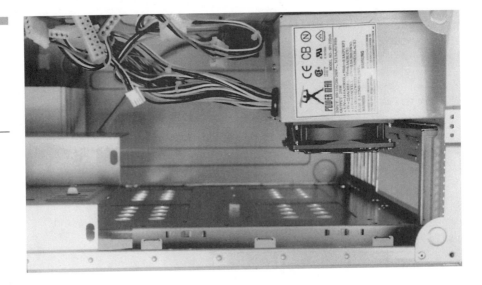

Fig. 16-2
The fan on the
power supply does
not allow enough
space to mount the
upright Pentium II
CPU assembly.

Tools

Before you start, gather all of your components and tools. You will need a Phillips and a flat blade screwdriver and a pair of long-nose pliers. The first illustration in Chapter 1 shows all the tools that you might need. That is, unless you need to modify the mounting of the fan on your power supply.

Caution: I mentioned electrostatic voltage earlier. Remember that you can build up thousands of volts on your body, so touch something to discharge yourself before touching any of the sensitive electronic components. A good way to discharge yourself is to touch some sort of metal object that is plugged into a wall socket. The object can be the metal part of a lamp, metal part of the computer case, almost anything that is plugged in. The object does not have to be turned on.

Assembly Steps

Detailed steps for assembly are listed below, but in a few words, here is a basic bench-top assembly. Plug the power supply cables into the motherboard. If you are using the old-style power supply, make sure that the four black ground wires are in the center. Next connect the keyboard, the floppy drives, hard disk drives, and the monitor. Then apply power, boot the computer up, and see if it works.

Fig. 16-3
The modified fan
mounting.

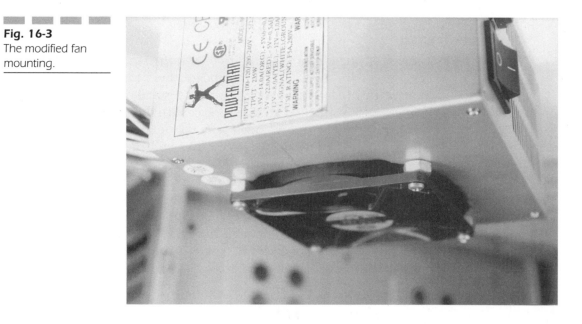

Fig. 16-4
After mounting the
fan partially inside
the power supply
case, I now have
about one-quarter
inch of clearance
space beneath the
fan.

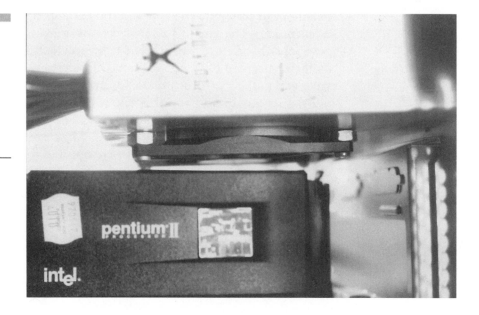

Installing the Motherboard

The old XT used brass stand-offs to mount the motherboard in the case. Beginning with the 286, all motherboards used white plastic stand-offs. Most of them also used one or two brass stand-offs to make sure the motherboard made good ground contact with the case.

When you buy a case, you will get a plastic bag with all of the stand-offs, screws, and other hardware that you will need. See Fig. 16-5. The white round items are rubber feet for the case.

There were several white plastic stand-offs in the bag. But there were no slots in the medium tower case for them. The only thing that would fit were the brass stand-offs except for one lone plastic one. The brass standoffs are a bit more substantial, but they do require a bit more time to install. They are not really necessary. The plastic standoff system is much easier to install. Refer back to Fig. 1-4.

Installing the Drives

When I started installing the drives, I noticed that there was no way to access the screw holes on the right side. It was completely blocked by the large metal panel that held the motherboard. I was quite unhappy, until I noticed that the large metal panel was designed so that it could be moved. If you pull up on the back panel, the panel allows you to slide the motherboard out so that you can easily add components or work on it. This is an excellent idea. The case had no instructions or manual of any kind to tell me about this feature. I discovered it by accident. Figure 16-6 shows the motherboard with the panel slid out. This offered plenty of room to work on or add to the motherboard or easy access to install drives.

Another good feature on this case is the fact that the wires that go to the front panel LEDs are in a ribbon cable. The connectors that plug into the motherboard are all clearly marked. Most earlier cases had twisted pairs of wires with connectors that were not well marked.

Ease of Assembly

You might think that because the Pentium II is so much more powerful than even some of the early mainframes that it would be more difficult to assemble. There is very little difference in the assembly of a Pentium

Fig. 16-5
A bag of hardware
that comes with the
case.

II and the assembly of any other computer, even the early XT. In fact, the Pentium II might be even easier to assemble than the old XT because it uses fewer screws and even fewer components. Your motherboard might have several integrated and built-in goodies, such as the serial ports, the EIDE and floppy drive interfaces, and sockets for memory modules that were not available a few years ago.

Some motherboards might be slightly different than others because of the built-in utilities and functions. They might also have the components placed differently on the motherboard. Usually the motherboards can operate at several different frequencies, depending on the CPU installed and how they are configured. So the different motherboards might have special jumpers for configuration.

It doesn't matter much how the board is laid out and designed. Every company tries to differentiate their product and add things to make it better than the competition. These differences usually have nothing to do with the assembly of the computer. They are all assembled into the system in the same basic way. Note also that they are still assembled the same way no matter whether the CPU on the motherboard is made by Intel, Cyrix, or AMD. The one big difference in the Pentium II, the Cyrix M2, and the AMD K6 is the socket for the CPU. The Cyrix and AMD CPUs use the standard socket 7. (See

Fig. 16-6
The motherboard
mounts on a panel
that can slide out for
easy access.

Chapter 4 for a desription of the different sockets.) Intel developed a new slot 1 nonstandard socket for the Pentium II. Because the slot 1 is proprietary to Intel, others such as AMD and Cyrix might not be able to use it. This means that even though the AMD and Cyrix CPUs might be equivalent, the motherboard manufacturers would have to design a new motherboard for their CPUs.

One reason Intel developed slot 1 is because the Pentium needs a very large amount of cooling. It needs a massive heatsink and fan as shown in Fig. 16-7.

A cradle is needed to support the heatsink and Pentium II CPU as shown in Fig. 16-8. It takes four screws to install the cradle. Figure 16-9 shows the heat sink and CPU assembly installed in the cradle and in slot 1.

At this time many vendors are wondering if slot 1 will become a standard or follow in the footsteps of IBM's Micro Channel Architecture (MCA). IBM developed the proprietary MCA slots, which was designed to lock out the cloners. But not as many people were loyal to IBM as it had hoped. The cloners developed their own systems and left IBM behind. For more about MCA, see Chapter 5.

I am sure that there are engineers who could design an adapter so that the Cyrix or AMD CPUs could be plugged into motherboards that have the slot 1 socket. It might be rather costly and might not be worth the effort because the Cyrix and AMD can use the standard socket 7.

Fig. 16-7
The large heat sink
and fan assembly
needed by the
Pentium II.

Fig. 16-8
A cradle that is need-
ed to support the
Pentium II CPU and
heat sink assembly.

Fig. 16-9
The CPU and heat
sink assembly
installed in the cradle
in slot 1.

Bench-Top Assembly

When I assemble a computer, I usually gather all of the components and assemble them on a bench-top or kitchen table. I then turn on the power and try it before I install it in the case. If there is any problem, it is fairly easy to find it while it is still open. The backside of motherboards and other plug-in boards have sharp projections from the cut and soldered component leads. I usually lay a couple of newspapers on the table or bench-top to prevent scratching or marring the table or bench. (If you scratch the kitchen table, you could be in big trouble with your significant other.) My Pentium II seemed so easy to assemble that I went ahead and assembled it in the case.

Figure 16-10 shows the connectors for the front panel LEDs. Figure 16-11 shows the installation of the DIMM memory. Just lay it in the slot and push down. There are catches on each end that snap in and lock the module in place. The modules are keyed so that they can only be installed properly. Figure 16-12 shows the PS/2 type cable connectors for the keyboard and mouse. You can plug into either of the connectors.

Fig. 16-10
The connections for
the front panel LEDs.

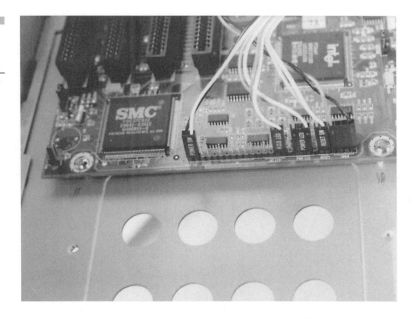

Fig. 16-11
Installing the DIMM
memory modules.

Fig. 16-12
The PS/2-type cable connectors for the mouse and keyboard. They can be plugged into either connector on the motherboard.

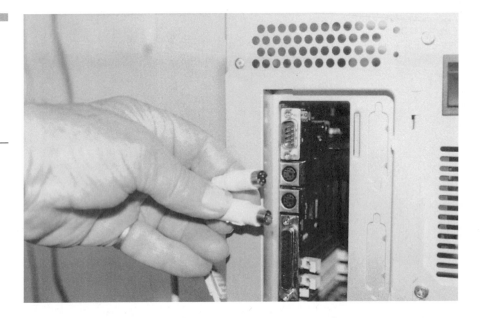

Figure 16-13 shows the back panel for the power connection and the on/off switch. The on/off switch is turned on, but the power is controlled from a soft switch on the front panel. Pushing this switch triggers the power supply to turn on the power to the motherboard and drives. Figure 16-14 shows the 266MHz Pentium II up and running.

If you bought a case, you probably received a small plastic bag with the necessary hardware, screws, and stand-offs. Your case might be different from the one that I bought. Yours might have the white plastic stand-offs and one or two small brass stand-offs that are needed to ground the motherboard to the case. There might be several extra holes in the motherboard for the standoffs. Determine which ones will be needed to match the holes or slots in the case. If you are using plastic stand-offs, push the stand-offs into place on the motherboard so that they lock in. Then line the motherboard up with the holes or slots in the case and install it.

Case and Power Supply

The power supply usually comes with the case. There are several sizes for cases, but for the Pentium II, I would recommend that you get a

Fig. 16-13
The back panel
showing the power
connector and the
on/off switch.

Fig. 16-14
The Pentium II up
and running.

full-tower case unless you want to modify the fan like I did. I am sure there must be other medium-tower ATX cases that don't have the problem with the fan that I had.

The power supply should be at least 250 watts. The older power supplies had the fan mounted inside the power supply case. It pulled air in from the front of the system and over all of the components, then exhausted it out the rear. The newer power supplies are just the reverse. They pull air in from the rear of the system and blow it over the internal components. The CPU is the one unit in the supply that is most in need of cooling. Most of the Pentium II motherboards position the CPU directly beneath the power supply fan so that it is first to have air blown over it.

You should look for a case and power supply that have the ATX form factor. The ATX cable for the motherboard power has a unique connector that can only be plugged in properly. The older system had two separate connectors and it was possible to plug them in improperly. If plugged in wrong, it could possibly ruin the motherboard. Some of the Pentium II motherboards have the old-style power connector beside the ATX connector. My Micronics Pentium II Stingray motherboard has both connectors.

Even if your motherboard has both connectors, it is better to use the newer ATX-type supplies. I would recommend that you spend a bit of money and get an ATX supply. The Pentium II uses 2.5 volts that must be regulated closely. You need a good power supply to help with the close regulation.

The ATX power supply and the Pentium II motherboard have electronics that allow the system to be turned on and off from the keyboard. The older power supplies had to have a switch, usually on the front panel for turning the 110 volts on and off.

Motherboard

Intel has gone into the business of manufacturing motherboards for the Pentium II. Some of the other manufacturers and vendors are a bit unhappy about this, but Intel figured that they were best suited to design a motherboard to fit their CPU.

There might be some slight differences in the motherboards manufactured by Intel, Micronics, ASUS, and some of the other manufacturers. Some of the differences might be the type of memory that can be used in the system.

I ordered 64Mb of 3.3v EDO DIMM memory. The company shipped me synchronous DRAM (SDRAM) modules. This memory will work in the Intel motherboards, but it is not supported in the Micronics motherboard that I have. Intel has special chipsets that allow the motherboard to use the SDRAM. Not all manufacturers have installed these chipsets. The SDRAM is very fast. The ones that were sent to me are 10 nanosecond (ns). Most DRAM is 60ns to 70ns.

Most of the Pentium II motherboards use a PS/2-type small connector for the keyboard and mouse. Many of the new keyboards have this small connector. If you are buying a new keyboard, make sure that it has the PS/2-type connector. The same type connector is used for the mouse. The two connectors on the motherboard are side by side and you can use either one for the mouse or the keyboard. If you already have a keyboard and mouse that you want to use, it is possible to buy adapters to change the standard sockets to the PS/2-type sockets.

Table 16-1 is a chart showing the difference in the wiring in the standard keyboard and mouse connector pins and the PS/2 connector pins. As you can see there is a difference in the pin assignments for the two systems. An adapter will have the wires crossed and wired so that the proper signal will be present on the proper pin.

The adapters are available from most major computer stores or from several of the companies who specialize in cables and connectors. The adapters cost from $3 to $5 each. Here are some companies who carry the adapters:

Cables to Go
800-506-9605
www.cablestogo.com

ABL Electronics
800-726-0610
e-mail sales@ablcables.coms

QVS Computer Connectivity
800-622-9606

There are several other similar companies. Look for advertisements in computer magazines. Call for a catalog.

The motherboard might also have a socket for the universal serial bus. This bus can theoretically allow up to 128 components to be daisy chained and attached. At the present time, there are not too many USB components and peripherals available. But there will be lots of them in a very short time. The USB has many advantages over the SCSI bus. The cable companies listed above also carry cables and connectors for the USB system.

Floppy Drive

You will only need one $3\frac{1}{2}$ inch floppy drive. The $5\frac{1}{4}$ inch floppy drive is obsolete. If you have a lot of stuff on $5\frac{1}{4}$ inch floppies, you could install a $5\frac{1}{4}$ inch drive. It is very easy to install and it attaches to the same ribbon cable as the $3\frac{1}{2}$ inch drive. You might consider just hooking a $5\frac{1}{4}$ inch drive up temporarily and downloading all the stuff that might be important onto your hard drive or onto 1.44Mb floppies. I have a couple of old $5\frac{1}{4}$ inch drives in my junk box. I am in and out of

TABLE 16-1

The difference in wiring in the standard keyboard and mouse connector pins and the PS/2 connector pins.

Signal	Std. Pin	PS/2 Pin
Clock	1	5
Data	2	1
Ground	4	3
+5 Vdc	5	4
Not used	3	2 and 6

my computers so often that I never install covers on them. So it is very easy to attach a $5\frac{1}{4}$ inch drive if I have to.

The 34-wire ribbon cable has a different colored wire on one edge that indicates pin one on the drive. If you intend to install a second floppy, you will find a twist in the ribbon cable. There might be several connectors on the ribbon cable. There might be two connectors for direct pin connections on the drive, or connectors for edge connections.

The connector nearest the end has a slit and some twisted wires. This connector should be attached to the floppy that is to be the A: drive. The B: drive attaches to the middle connector. The motherboard has some upright pins for the connection to the floppy drives. There are other pins there for the IDE hard drives and CD-ROM. The floppy drive has 34 pins, there are 40 pins for the IDE drives. There will usually be markings on the motherboard for the different cable connections.

It is very important that you look for pin one and match it to the colored wire on the ribbon cable. It is possible to plug the cable in backwards. If you then put a floppy disk in a drive that is conected backwards, it will destroy the information on the disk.

There are several four-wire cables from the power supply for the power to the various drives. The $3\frac{1}{2}$ inch drives use a miniature connector. The $5\frac{1}{4}$ inch drives, hard drives, and CD-ROM drives use the standard four-wire connector. The connectors can only be plugged in properly.

The A: Drive

The ideal floppy drive is the A: drive. It can read and write to the $3\frac{1}{2}$ inch 1.44Mb and 720K floppies. It can also read and write to special 120Mb floppy disks. The A: drive was discussed in a bit more detail in Chapter 7.

IDE Hard Drives and CD-ROMs

The IDE hard drives and CD-ROMs each have 40-wire ribbon cables. Like the floppy system, the ribbon cable has a different colored wire on one edge that indicates pin one. Some of the connectors have an elevation that fits in a cutout on the drive connector so that they can only be plugged in properly. But some cable connectors do not have this elevation so the connector can be plugged in backwards. Make sure that the colored wire side goes to pin one on the drive and to pin one of the upright connector pins on the motherboard.

There are usually two sets of IDE pins. They are usually marked primary and secondary. The IDE hard drive that will be the boot drive will go to the primary set. You might also have a second IDE drive on the same cable. There are pins on the drives with jumpers so that the first drive can be configured as the master and the second drive as a slave.

The secondary set of pins are used for one or two CD-ROMs or a CD-ROM and another IDE-type component, such as a tape drive. Just like the hard drives, the CD-ROMs have pins that can be jumpered to configure them as master or slave.

Assembly Instructions

Here are detailed instructions for the assembly.

Step 1: Set All Switches and Jumpers Motherboards from different manufacturers might have several alternate options and different ways that they can be configured. The many different possible configurations is one of the things that makes the computer so versatile and valuable. Some of the Pentium II motherboards are a bit different. You might have to set some configuration jumpers on the motherboard, on plug-in boards, disk drives, and other components. If you are new to computers and electronics, a jumper is usually a small block or cap that is placed over a set of pins. The jumper creates a short or solid path between the two pins. The jumpers are very small. It is almost impossible for someone with large fingers to handle one. That is one of the reasons you need the long-nose pliers. Long-nose pliers can be used to set the jumpers on an IDE hard drive to configure the drive as a master or slave. If you don't have long-nose pliers, you should be able to use a pair of tweezers. The jumpers are usually numbered from JP1 on up.

You should have received some sort of documentation with your motherboard and each of your components. Check the documentation and determine if there are any switches and jumpers that should be set to configure the component.

Jumpers and switches are often used on plug-in boards to set them for a specific interrupt request (IRQ) lines or the system memory address. Jumpers can be used to set the COM ports for the mouse, modem, sound card, and other peripherals.

Your motherboard will have built-in utilities, such as on-board COM serial ports. If you plug in an I/O board with COM ports, you must set jumpers to disable the COM ports either on the motherboard or the ones on the plug-in board. You can't have both of them enabled.

The improper setting of jumpers and switches is the source of a large number of problems when assembling a system or upgrading one. All of the Pentium II and most other motherboards and plug-in boards are now manufactured to the plug-n-play (PnP) specifications. This eliminates many of the problems that we suffered previously. PnP will cause most of the configurations to be done automatically by software and built-in firmware on the components.

Step 2: Install Memory   The 486 and Pentium-class motherboards, such as the Cyrix and AMD, usually have L2 SRAM cache memory on board. The Pentium Pro and Pentium II CPUs have L2 SRAM caches built into the CPU enclosure.

Many of the Pentium II motherboards have sockets for both 72-pin SIMMS and 168-pin DIMMS. The Stingray motherboard that I have from Micronics can accept up to 1Gb of memory. It is possible to mix both SIMMS and DIMMS. It would be preferable to use the DIMMs. They have a 72-bit wide data path. The SIMMs use a 36-bit wide data path.

If the SIMM memory chips have not been installed, you should install them now. Again, they are very susceptible to damage from electrostatic electricity, so make sure that you discharge yourself before handling them. Check your documentation. There should be a diagram of the motherboard showing how the memory is to be installed. You will probably have to install them in pairs. For instance, for 16Mb of memory, you will need to install an 8Mb single inline memory module (SIMM) in bank 0 and an 8Mb SIMM in bank 1. Make sure that your SIMMs are fast enough. Your documentation should tell you what speed to use. Depending on your system, you might be using dual inline memory modules (DIMMs) instead of SIMMs. There are several different types of memory and new types are being introduced almost daily. Some motherboards are designed for extended data out (EDO) memory or burst EDO (BEDO), others for fast page mode (FPM) or synchronous DRAM (SDRAM). Check your documentation to make sure that you buy the proper memory chips.

The SIMM and DIMM memory modules are very easy to install. See Fig. 16-11. Just place the SIMMS in the proper slot on a slant, then lift them to an upright position and they will lock in. There is a cutout on one end of the SIMM module assembly so that they can only be installed the proper way. But it is possible to have one end of the SIMM not inserted fully. The DIMM sockets have a couple of keys that match cutouts on the DIMM modules. So they can only be installed properly. If a SIMM or DIMM is not completely seated, or if they are not in the proper bank, the computer might not boot up.

Step 3: Connect the Power Supply to the Motherboard The old-style power supply will have two six-wire cables that are plugged in side by side to the 12-pin motherboard connector. These cables are sometimes marked P8 and P9.

Caution: It is possible to install these cables improperly. Each of the cables have two black wires for ground. When installed properly, the four black wires are in the center of the connector. If installed improperly, you could severely damage the motherboard components. You can see the four black wires in the center of the white connector in Fig. 10-5.

The Stingray motherboard from Micronics has both connectors for the ATX and the old-style power supply. The ATX connector can only be plugged in properly.

Step 4: Install Floppy Drives The older floppy drives have edge connectors for the 34-wire ribbon cable. Newer floppy drives have pins, but many of them come with an edge connector adapter or a universal floppy cable that has both edge connectors and pin connectors. Your cable might have pin connectors only. One end of the cable will have several wires that were split and twisted. The connector on this end goes to the drive that you want to be your drive A:. Be careful because these connectors can be plugged in backwards. The floppy ribbon cable will have a different color wire on one edge. This wire might be red, blue, or black, or it might have intermittent red marks on it. This indicates that this wire goes to pin one on the connectors. Make sure that this side goes to pin one on the floppy drive connectors. If you are installing two floppy drives, the connector in the middle of the cable goes to floppy drive B:. This connector can also be incorrectly plugged in. Make sure the colored wire side goes to pin one on the drive connector.

Make sure that the colored wire of the ribbon cable goes to pin one on the board. There should be some marking or indication on the board as to which is pin one. If the floppy drive cable is plugged in backwards, when you try to boot up from floppy drive A:, the disk will spin and it will erase the boot system from the floppy. (Never use your original software floppies except to make disk copies of them. Even then you should make sure that the originals are write protected.)

It is also possible to plug these connectors in so that only one row of pins are plugged in or have it shifted so that two pins on one end are not plugged in. Some boards will have a square outline around the pins. It is easy to see if the connector is within the outline.

Connect the power cable to the floppy drive. The white plastic shell of the power connectors are shaped so that they can only be plugged in properly. The same type of power connectors are used on the hard drives and CD-ROM drives. The small fan that sits on the CPU also needs power. My Stingray has a small connector on the motherboard fan power. The $3\frac{1}{2}$ inch drives use a miniature power connector. It can only be plugged in properly.

Step 5: Install Hard Disk Drives and CD-ROM Drives If you install an IDE hard drive, it will have a 40-wire ribbon cable that is similar to the 34-wire floppy disk cable. Unlike the floppy disk cable with twisted wires at one end connector, the three connectors on the IDE cable will all be the same. Like the floppy and SCSI cables, it will have a colored wire on one edge that indicates pin one. Most connectors on the drives have a plastic shell around them with a square notch on one side of the shell. The connectors on the cable have a square elevation that fits the notch on the drive connector plastic shell. This keys the connector so that it can only be plugged in properly. The 50-wire cable and connectors for the SCSI devices have the same type keying. If the connectors are not keyed, then look for some indication of pin one on the drive and connect the cable so that the colored wire goes to that side. Then plug in the power cable to the hard drive. If you are installing a second IDE hard drive, it will be plugged into the center connector.

IDE Drive Configuration The configuration instructions are similar whether you are installing IDE or EIDE drives. You should have received some instructions with your drive documentation. If you are only installing a single IDE drive, the installation might be very simple. The drive will probably have jumpers set at the factory that makes it drive one or master drive. Check your documentation and the jumpers, then just plug the 40-wire cable connector into the drive connector and the other end into a board interface or into a set of pins on the motherboard. You must make sure that the colored side of the ribbon cable goes to pin one on the drive and on the interface.

There will probably be two sets of EIDE pins on the motherboard or interface. One will say "Primary" and the other "Secondary." The cable from the master and slave IDE goes to the primary pins. If you are installing an IDE CD-ROM, tape drive, or other device, the cable will go to the pins marked secondary.

Even though you have an EIDE interface on the motherboard, you might want to install a fast EIDE interface that plugs into one of the PCI connectors. One reason to install a PCI interface is because you can have a disk cache on the board that will make the system much faster. Again, if you use a plug-in board, you must use the jumpers to disable the built-in interface.

If you are installing a second IDE drive you will need to set some jumpers so that the system will know which drive to access. When two IDE drives are installed, the IDE system uses the term *master* to designate the C: or boot drive and the term *slave* to designate the second drive. You will have to place small jumpers on the drives to configure them. If the drives are not configured properly, you will get an error message that might tell you that you have a hard disk or controller failure. You will not be able to access the drives.

Ordinarily, you will have to do a setup when you first turn on your computer. You will have to tell the system what kind of drive you have, the number of cylinders, sectors, and heads it has. But your Pentium II will probably have a plug-n-play (PnP) BIOS that will recognize the IDE drive and automatically configure it.

You should have received some documentation with your drive. If you don't have the configuration information, call the company or dealer.

Hard Drive Activity Indicator   The older hard drives used a stepping motor head actuator and they could be easily heard as they stepped from track to track. The newer drives use the voice coil technology. They are usually very smooth and silent. If you did not have some sort of indicator, you might not know that they are working.

Your front panel will have a small light emitting diode (LED) that will flash on and off to indicate hard disk activity. There will probably be a small two-wire cable that plugs into a set of pins on the motherboard for this LED. Note that the LEDs are sensitive to plus and negative voltage. The motherboard might be marked with a plus sign near one of the pins or one set of pins might have a 1 nearby. The two wires will be different colors, usually red and black, yellow and white, or blue and white. Usually the colored wire will go to pin 1 and the black or white wire will go to the negative pin. There will be several other sets of pins near the front of the motherboard for front panel LEDs for power, reset, and speaker connection. Check your documentation.

Installing SCSI Drives   If you are installing one or more SCSI drives, you need to check your documentation to set any switches or jumpers. Because the SCSI interface can handle up to seven devices, the drive will probably need to be set to a logical unit number (LUN) between 0 and 6. In Fig. 10-14, the pen points to the jumper pins for setting the LUN on a Seagate 1.05Gb drive.

The SCSI hard disk and CD-ROM drives have a 50-wire ribbon cable that is similar to the 40-wire IDE cable. Like other cables, it will have a different color wire on one edge that indicates pin one. The cable will have three connectors that will probably be keyed with elevations so that they can only be plugged in properly. If they are not keyed, then look for pin one and make sure that the colored wire goes to that side. The connector on the other end of the 50-wire cable is connected to the SCSI card. Again, this connector is usually keyed so that it can only be plugged in properly. The pen in the photo points to jumpers that might have to be set. Check your documentation.

If you are installing more than one SCSI device, such as a second hard drive or a CD-ROM drive, check your documentation and set any necessary jumpers for the correct LUN. You might also have to remove or install termination resistors if you have more than one SCSI device.

Install the power cable to the SCSI devices. They can only be plugged in properly. Most power supplies have only four cables. If you install more than four devices, you will need a small Y cable that allows two devices to be attached to one cable. The ATX power supply that came with the Micronics motherboard had six standard and two miniature power connectors.

Step 6: Connect Mouse and Printer Cables   Most of the Pentium II motherboards have two of the PS/2-type of small round connectors on the back of the motherboard. The PS/2 mouse does not need to use one of your precious COM ports. The two PS/2 connectors will be side by side or one on top of the other. The mouse can be plugged into either one. The other one is for the keyboard.

Most of the Pentium II motherboards also have a COM port connector if you insist on using a serial mouse. Many of the Pentium II motherboards will have a COM port connector on the back of the motherboard. The motherboard might also have a printer connector on the back of the motherboard. If it does not have these connectors, there might be a set of upright pins on the motherboard for the COM ports and the printer. You might have received a bracket with two short cables for the printer and serial mouse that can be plugged into the upright pins.

Again, look for colored wire and make sure that side of the cable goes to pin one. The bracket will be mounted on the rear of the case.

Step 7: Install the Monitor The next step is to plug your monitor adapter into a slot and connect the monitor cable to the adapter. You will probably have PCI slots. But you might use one of the older ISA adapters and plug it into any ISA slot. You might also have a VLB motherboard and adapter.

Step 8: Plug in the Keyboard Most of the Pentium II motherboards will have the PS/2 connector for the the keyboard. If you have one of the older keyboards, it is possible to get an adapter for it. Plug the cable into one of the PS/2 connectors on the back of the motherboard. It is keyed so that it can only be connected properly.

Step 9: Turn on the Power and Boot Up Before installing Windows, the hard disk must be partitioned and formatted as explained in Chapter 8.

If every thing was connected properly, the system should boot up. You will need a floppy disk that can boot up your system. If you are using Windows 95, you have a $3\frac{1}{2}$ floppy boot disk. Once you have booted up, it leads you into installing the CD-ROM drive so that the Windows program can be copied onto the hard disk.

I had a bit of a problem when I tried to start my new Pentium II. The CMOS setup screen allows you to make many different choices. One choice that I wasn't aware of is that the Award BIOS allows you to enable or disable floppy disks with 40 tracks, such as those on the $5\frac{1}{4}$ 360K floppies. The $5\frac{1}{4}$ inch 1.2Mb floppies and the $3\frac{1}{2}$ inch floppies are all 80 tracks. I tried several times to boot up from my $3\frac{1}{2}$ floppy drive but to no avail. I tried a spare drive that I knew was good. Each time I got a message that said floppy drive failure (40). As a last resort I looked in the manual that came with my motherboard and it said very plainly that the BIOS could be enabled or disabled to look for a 40-track drive. I reset it and it worked perfectly. There are lots of utilities and helpful functions that should be in the BIOS. I cannot imagine why they added the very obsolete 360K 40-track function.

Step 10: Install in Case If you have assembled your computer on the bench-top and everything works okay, turn the power off and install it in the case. Turn the power on and check it again to make sure it still works, then install the cover.

Step 11: Congratulations Go ask your spouse or somebody to pat you on the back and congratulate you. You deserve it.

CD-ROM

Today, a CD-ROM drive is an essential part of a computer. Almost every computer sold within the next year will have a CD-ROM as standard equipment. It has become almost as necessary as a hard disk drive.

A CD-ROM offers some very important benefits to the individual end user for entertainment, education, business, and for industry. There are thousands of CD-ROM disc titles that cover just about every subject imaginable are available.

CD-ROM Titles

A short time ago, CD-ROM disc titles were very expensive, but every day there is more and more competition. There are just too many titles to even try to review them in a book like this. There are several CD-ROM magazines and PC magazines that can help you be aware of what is available. Here are just a few:

New Media Magazine
800-253-6641
e-mail: vanessas@newmedia.com
www.hyperstand.com

This magazie is sent free to qualified subscribers. Almost any person with a business connection can qualify.

EMedia Professional
800-806-7795
e-mail: emediasub@online.com
www.online.com/emedia

The CD-ROM Today Magazine
(415) 696-1688

CD-ROM Power Magazine
800-328-6719

CD-ROM Multimedia
800-565-4623

Mr.D-ROM (Catalog)
800-444-6723

Because of the thousands of companies who are producing CD-ROM titles, the enormous amount of competition is forcing the prices down. Some CD-ROM titles that cost as much as $100 a few months ago can now be bought for as little as $5 to $10. And the prices are still going down. It is great for the consumers.

I have not had to buy any $3\frac{1}{2}$ inch floppy disks for some time. I just erased the ones that I got from AOL and other companies and reused them. I subscribe to several magazines. For some time, every magazine would have one or two disks with the AOL sign up software. But now CD-ROMs are so inexpensive that AOL and many of the other companies are sending out their sample software, ads, and demos on CD-ROMs. Looks like I might have to start buying floppy disks again.

Home Entertainment

A large number of the CD-ROM titles are designed for entertainment for both young and old. There are titles for arcade-type games, chess, and other board games. There are titles for music, opera, art, and a large variety of other subjects to entertain you. Many of the titles are both educational as well as entertaining.

Home Library

At the present time, only one side of the CD-ROM discs are used for recording, but this single side can hold over 650Mbs of data. You can have a multitude of different programs on a single CD-ROM disc and a world of information at your fingertips. More books and information can be stored on just a few CD-ROM discs than you can find in an entire library. A 21-volume encyclopedia can be stored in just a fraction of the space on one side of a single CD-ROM disc. When data compression is used to store text, several hundred books can be stored on a single disc.

It might take only seconds to search through an entire encyclopedia or through several hundred books to find a subject, sentence, or a single word.

Easier Way to Learn

Text, graphics, sound, animation, and movies can be stored on CD-ROM discs. We have several avenues to the brain. The more avenues used to input information to our brain, the easier it is to learn and to remember. We can learn by reading. But we can learn much better if sound is added to the text. We have all heard the old saying that a picture is worth a thousand words. It is so very true. We learn much better and retain more if graphics and motion are added. Rather than trying to remember just dry text, the many advantages of CD-ROM can make learning fun and pleasurable. Schools can use CD-ROM for teaching. Businesses can use CD-ROM to train their personnel.

Lawyers

Lawyers have to spend hours and hours going through law books to find precedents, to find some of the finer points of the law, or to find loopholes. A few CD-ROM discs could replace several law clerks.

Health and Medicine

The human body is a fantastic machine. There is more written about medicine and computers than any other subject. There are several CD-ROMs published for the home user such as the *Family Doctor*, published by Creative Multimedia Corp., (503) 241-4351, the *Mayo Clinic Family Health Book,* published by Interactive Ventures, (507) 282-2076, and several others.

A doctor must keep abreast of all of the scientific advances, new drugs, and treatments. A busy doctor can't possibly read all of the published papers. A CD-ROM can help. *The American Family Physician* is the official journal of the American Academy of Family Physicians. It is available from the Bureau of Electronic Publishing at 800-828-4766.

The A.D.A.M. (for Animated Dissection of Anatomy for Medicine) Software Company, 800-755-2326, has developed several discs that show the various parts of the anatomy, both male and female. This CD-ROM is very good for students and families to learn about the human body. If you are a bit prudish, you are given an option to cover certain parts of the anatomy with fig leaves.

How CD-ROM Works

CD-ROM is an acronym for compact disc-read only memory. The system was first developed by Sony and Philips using lasers for recording and playing back music. (LASER is an acronym for light amplification by stimulated emission of radiation.) Almost all CD-ROM drives can also play the music compact discs. Most of the drives have a plug for earphones and an audio connector on the back so that it can be plugged into a sound card. You can set up a very good hi-fi system using a CD-ROM and a computer. Basically, the music compact disc systems are quite similar to the CD-ROM systems, but the CD-ROM drives are usually more expensive.

When a CD-ROM disc is created, a powerful laser is turned on and off in response to data 0s and 1s, which burns holes in the disc material. When the beam is switched on to create a hole it is called a *pit*; when left off, the area of the track is called a *land*. When played back, a laser beam is focused on the track. The pits do not reflect as much light as the lands so it is easy to distinguish the digital data.

High Sierra/ISO 9660

The Philips and Sony companies developed the audio CD in 1982. It wasn't long before the importance of the technology was recognized and adopted for CD-ROMs.

It was a fast growing technology, but there were no standards. Every company wants to make their products a bit different, so there were several different formats. In 1985 a group of industry leaders, including Microsoft, met at a hotel in Lake Tahoe to hammer out a set of standards. The standard that they devised defined the table of contents and directory structure. It also defined the logical file and record structures. Microsoft provided their Microsoft Compact Disc Extensions (MSCDEX) software, a driver that allows DOS to access the CD-ROM through conventional DOS commands. All CD-ROMs used in PCs use the Microsoft MSCDEX driver.

There were several other specifications adopted at this meeting. Because they met at Tahoe, which is in the Sierra mountain range, they called the new standard the *High Sierra Specification*. The specification was later adopted, with minor modifications, by the International Organization for Standards as *ISO 9660*. Unless otherwise stated, most all CD-ROM drives and discs conform to the ISO 9660.

Besides the standards set forth in ISO 9660, several other standard specifications have been developed. There are thousands of pages of specifications in each of four books. Some books are more than 1 foot thick. The specifications were originally issued in books with different colors. The standards have been named for the color of the original book. Sometimes a disc will have specifications from two or more books. For instance if the disc contains text, audio, and graphics it might conform to specifications from the Red Book, the Yellow Book, and the Green Book. Here is a brief explanation of what each book covers:

- The Red Book sets forth the standards for audio or compact disc digital audio (CD-DA).

- The Yellow Book sets forth the ISO 9660 standards for storing files that can be translated to DOS, Apple, or Amiga files. The Microsoft MSCDEX drivers are used to accomplish the translation. Of course every time someone uses the MSCDEX drivers, they make Bill Gates a little bit richer.

- The Green Book covers CD-Interactive (CD-I) and CD-ROM extended architecture (CD-ROM/XA).

- The Orange Book covers write once read many (WORM) drives and magneto-optic (MO) type drives. It also covers the multi-session Photo CD type drives.

How the Discs are Made

Data that is to be stored on a CD-ROM disc is usually assembled and organized, then copied onto a large-capacity hard disk. The data can be copied onto the large hard disk from floppies, hard disks, tape, or almost any medium. A table of contents, an index, error detection and correction, and retrieval software is usually added to the data.

A *One-off* disc can be made from the organized data. A CD-ROM recorder similar to the Philips CCD 521 can be used to make this first test disc. The disc can be tested and tried and if it meets the clients specifications, then the data is laser etched onto a glass master disc. All of the duplications come from this disc.

All CD-ROM discs are pressed much like the vinyl phonograph records. But a disc that is pressed from the original master would be a mirror image of it. The pits and the lands on the copy would be just the reverse of those on the master. To make it identical to the master a copy of a copy is made. The pits and lands are then in the proper order.

The first copy of the master is called a *mother*. Then a working copy of the mother is made which is called the *father*. *Virgin* blank discs are pressed against the father to make all of the commercial discs. The blank discs are 120 millimeters, about $4^3/_4$ inches in diameter, and are made from a polycarbonate plastic. Each blank disc costs less than one dollar. After being pressed, the discs are coated with reflective aluminum. This coating is 1 micron thick. The discs are then coated with a thin layer of lacquer to prevent oxidation and contamination. The same process is used for both audio compact discs and CD-ROM discs.

Laser Color

White light encompasses all of the colors of the rainbow. Each color has its own frequency of vibration; the slower frequencies are at the dark red end. The frequencies increase as the colors move toward the violet end.

The particles that make up ordinary light are incoherent; that is, they are scattered in all directions. Lasers are possible because a single color of light can be sharply focused and amplified. All of the particles of one color are lined up in an orderly coherent fashion.

The laser effect can be obtained from several different gases and materials. Most of the present CD-ROM lasers use light at the lower frequency dark end of the spectrum, such as the red or yellow. The Samsung Company has developed a green laser, which has a shorter wave length and higher frequency. They claim that by using this laser and their proprietary compression techniques, they can store up to 110 minutes of the MPEG 2 video on a disc, five times as much as usual. (MPEG is an acronym for Moving Pictures Experts Group, who developed a set of methods for video compression.)

An experimental blue laser has also been developed. It will have an even higher frequency than a green laser. At the time of this writing, neither the green nor the blue have been incorporated into available units.

A hard disk might have several thousand separate concentric tracks with each track divided into several sectors. Usually each sector can store 512 bytes. A CD-ROM disc has a single spiral track that begins in the center and winds out to the outer edge. If the track was stretched out, it would be several miles long. The track is similar to the groove on a phonograph record, except that the groove on a phonograph record begins on the outer edge and winds to the center. An old question is how far does the needle on a phonograph travel when it plays a large record? The answer is about six inches. The needle moves from the outer edge to the center while the record spins beneath it.

The long, spiral track of a CD-ROM disc is divided into about 270,000 sectors, each sector with 2048 bytes. The sectors are numbered and given addresses according to the time in minutes, seconds, and hundredths of a second. For instance, the first sector starting from the center is 00:00:00, the second sector is 00:00:01.

Remember that the hard disk has a head actuator motor that moves the head to the various concentric tracks. The CD-ROM has a similar small motor that moves the laser beam to whatever sector on the spiral track that is to be read. Figure 17-1 shows a CD-ROM drive with the cover removed. The round object in the center is the spindle from the main motor that spins the disc. At the left is a black object with the white laser head assembly. This assembly has a small motor that moves it back and forth in the slot to read the various sectors of the track as the disc spins.

Rotational Speed

The CD-ROM uses a system that constantly changes the speed of the drive. The drive electronics speed the disc up or slow it down depending on what area of the disk it is reading. The original 1× drive spins at about 200 RPM and up to 530 RPM. This is called *constant linear velocity* (CLV).

Fig. 17-1
A CD-ROM drive with the cover removed. The round object in the center is the spindle motor. The small white round object to the left is the laser head assembly. A small motor moves it on a track so that it can access any sector as the disc spins above it.

The double-speed 2× CD-ROMs rotate at 400 RPM to 1060 RPM; the Quad speed drives double these figures again from 800 to over 2,000 RPM; 6× ranges from 1200 to over 3000 RPM; 8× ranges from 1,600 to over 4000 RPM. At 4000 RPM, there might be a lot of vibration from the spindle motor. The plastic disc is somewhat flexible. At the higher speeds, a slight imbalance can cause the spinning disc to wobble and vibrate. Even if the label is not properly placed on the disc it can cause an imbalance at the high speed. This might cause errors in reading the small pits and lands.

Because of its importance, several companies have developed label printing machines and installers. Many people are now using the CD-recordable machines to make their own CD-ROMs. Here are some companies who sell CD labeling kits:

Mediastore
800-555-5551
www.mediastore.com

The Mediastore also sells CD-R recorders, CD-Blanks, and other electronic products.

One-Off Label System
800-340-1633
www.oneoffcd.com.

NEATO CD Labeler Kit
800-648-6787

CD-R Gold Label Applicator
800-255-4020

PressIT CD Labeling Kit
800-203-6727

Prosource
800-903-1234

Look in several CD-ROM magazines for other dealers and other components.

The Speed Limit

Because of the vibration and other problems, when they came out with the 8× speed, many people thought that this was the absolute speed limit. But technology does not stand still. I have just bought a 24× speed Panasonic for $115. By the time you read this there will probably be 32× units available.

Actually the discs will not rotate much faster than the 12× speed. They achieve the transfer rate of a higher speed without spinning that fast by using a combination constant linear velocity (CLV) and constant angular velocity (CAV).

The 1× and 2× speed drives are as obsolete as the 360K floppy drives. Just a short time ago, the double-speed drives were selling for over $400. No one is even making 2× speed today.

Here are just a few companies who make CD-ROM drives. In many cases they make all of the faster speeds.

Diamond
800-468-5846

Samsung
800-726-7864

NEC
800-632-4636

Sony
800-352-7669

Panasonic
800-742-8086

TEAC
800-888-4293

Pioneer
800-444-6784

Toshiba
800-678-4373

Plextor
800-886-3935

UMAX
800-562-0311

Call these companies for brochures and spec sheets.

Transfer Speed

The *transfer speed,* or the amount of time that it takes to read a track on the original 1×, and all of the audio CDs, was 75 sectors per second. A sector is 2048 bytes (2K) times 75 are equal to 150K bytes per second.

Doubling the speed of the 1× drive doubles the transfer rate to 300K bytes per second. A quad-speed drive transfers data at 600KB/S; the 6× speed drives transfer data at 900KB/S. The faster transfer times allow video and motion to be displayed in a smooth fashion. The faster drives can read all of the CD-ROM discs that the slower drives can read, but read them faster.

The audio files must still be played back at the 150K rate. When playing audio, the speed must drop down to the original speed of 200 to 530 RPMs.

Data Buffers

The faster drives usually have a fairly large buffer system that also helps smooth out video and motion and speeds up the transfer rate. The buffer memory is located on chips on the drive. The firmware (software embedded on chips) portion of the buffer system decides which information will be used most often and stores it in the buffer. For instance the contents of the disk directory might be stored in the buffer. Many of the newer drive systems have from 128K up to 2Mb of DRAM for cache memory buffers.

Access or Seek Time

The access or seek time is the time necessary to move the laser head to find a certain block or sector on the spiral track and begin reading it. The original MPC specification was that the drive should be able to find any block in 1000 milliseconds (ms) or one second. Most of the older drives had access times of 300 to 400 ms.

You would think that the faster rotational speed would yield faster access speed, and it does, but not in direct proportion. For instance, some of the better double-speed drives have access speed of 200 ms. You might think that the quad-speed drives would double that, but they don't. The best quad-speed drives have an access rate of 150 ms. The best eight-speed drives still have a rate of 150 ms. The best 12-speed drives are a little better at 130 ms.

Generally speaking, the transfer rate or speed is more important than the access speed. In most cases, the transfer rate is proportional to the rotational speed.

CD-ROM Differences

There are several different types of CD-ROM drives. Some mount internally, some are external, some use SCSI for an interface, some use an enhanced IDE interface, and of course the various speeds. There are also a lot of different prices. The external drives might cost up to $100 more than an internal because they need a power supply and cables. What you should buy will depend on what your needs are.

Interface Systems

Some of the earlier systems had their own proprietary interface. Often the interface was built-in on sound cards. Almost all drives today are either SCSI or EIDE. The EIDE interface is built-in on many of the Pentium-type motherboards. If your EIDE interface is not built-in or you are buying an SCSI drive, the interface card and cable might not be included in the price of the system. Read the ads carefully if you are buying by mail order.

The interface card is plugged into one of the bus slots. Before plugging the card in, make sure that any jumpers or switches on the board are set properly. The board must be configured so that it does not conflict with the address or interrupt (IRQ) of any of your other devices. Check your documentation. Always turn your computer off before unplugging or changing the settings of any card. Never plug-in or unplug a card, cable, or device while the power is on.

If your system does not conform to the plug-n-play specification, a CD-ROM drive interface might be difficult to set up and configure. It must be set to a specific IRQ and memory address location. If the board conflicts with any other device in your system, it will not work.

Enhanced IDE Interfaces

The enhanced IDE (EIDE) interface can handle up to four devices. This can be any combination of EIDE hard drives and EIDE CD-ROMs or EIDE backup tape drives. The IDE CD-ROM systems are considerably less expensive than the SCSI. Your motherboard will probably have a built-in EIDE interface. If not, you will have to buy one. They are fairly inexpensive costing from $20 to $60. The interface can be plugged into any one of the 16-bit ISA slots. Remember that the ISA system operates at 8 to 10MHz. For high-end work, you might want to buy a PCI IDE interface, which would be considerably faster but, of course, more expensive. IDE CD-ROM drives might cost from $50 to $100 less than an equivalent SCSI CD-ROM drives.

SCSI Interfaces

More companies are now manufacturing drives for the SCSI interface. If you have other SCSI products, such as a SCSI hard drive or tape back-up, you already have an interface card. The SCSI interface cards can drive up to seven different devices. It is amazing how quickly the slots get used up. The SCSI can save having to install a separate interface for up to seven different devices. Most SCSI devices have two connectors: one for the input cable and an identical connector for the next item.

There are also several sound boards that have SCSI interfaces built in such as the Diamond Sonic Sound and the Adaptec Audio Machine. Not all SCSI interfaces are the same. Some of them are made for special-purpose SCSI devices and might not be able to completely control a hard disk. The Adaptec Audio Machine has complete control functions for hard disks and most other SCSI devices.

If you don't already have an SCSI interface, you might have to pay $100 to $200 extra for the interface. Again, these interfaces would plug into the 16-bit ISA slots and operate at 8 to 10MHz. If you are doing high-end work, you might want to buy a faster and more expensive PCI SCSI interface.

Parallel Printer Port

The parallel printer port has become a popular method to attach peripherals. It all started with tape backup drives that could be attached to one system, then removed and used on another. Soon many hard disk drives were doing the same thing. It saves time and saves not having to open the system, not having to buy an interface board or controller, and the peripheral can be used on multiple machines. Some companies are now using the parallel printer port for attaching CD-ROMs. It is a very easy way to go.

Multidisc Systems

Even though you have over 600Mb on a disc, there will be many times when a particular disc doesn't have the programs or information that you need at the moment. For instance, I have a telephone directory of the whole country on five discs from PhoneDisc at 800-284-8353. Each disc covers a certain section of the country. Ordinarily, to change discs, you have to eject the disc, unload the caddy, and put the new disc in. To solve this type of problem, several companies have developed multidisc systems. The MultiSpin 4×4 from NEC, at 800-632-4636 can hold four discs. The 4× drive is rather inexpensive and fits in the same half-height space as a standard drive. The DRM 624X from Pioneer, at 800-444-6784, can hold six discs and is fairly reasonable in cost. Alps Electric, at 800-825-2577 has a multidisc changer that can hold four discs. The CDJ 7004 changer from the Smart & Friendly Company, at 800-959-7001 can hold seven discs. There will probably be many more companies who offer multidisc systems by the time you read this.

Multidrive Systems

There are several companies that manufacture multidrive systems for network servers and other high-end users. Anything that is high-end is usually highly expensive. They have four to 14 drives or more and cost from $2,000 up to $18,000 or more. Here are some of the companies that offer multidrive systems:

JVC	SciNet
800-828-1582	800-653-1010
Logicraft	TAC HotSwap
800-308-8750	(205) 721-1976
Meridian	Plasmon Data
800-755-8324	(408) 956-9400
Microtest	
800-526-9675	

JVC, at (714) 261-1292, has several changers and network devices. Their CL-100 CD-Library gives you access to 100 different discs. The NSM Mercury Jukebox, at 800-238-4676 gives you access of up to 150 discs.

Build Your Own Multidrive/ Multidisc System

You can build your own system and save a bundle. The cost of CD-ROM drives are coming down every day. I just bought a 24× drive for $115. They will be less than that by the time you read this. If you have a fairly late Pentium-type motherbord with the built-in IDE interfaces, you can easily install two of these in your system. If you have an older system, you can buy an IDE interface that will support two hard drives and two CD-ROM drives for less than $20.

If you need even more drives, you can set up a SCSI system and have up to seven drives. By plugging a second SCSI adapter into the first adapter, you could have six drives on the first adapter, then seven on the second adapter. Theoretically, you could have up to 49 units on SCSI adapters.

There aren't any CD-ROMs available at the moment for Universal Serial Bus (USB), but there will probably be several by the time you read this. The USB system will allow up to 128 peripherals to be attached. That would probably be all that you could possibly need, especially if you have a small office, home office (SOHO).

Some of the multidisc drives are selling for just a little more than $300. (Prices quoted are for comparison only and will be less by the time you read this.) With an enhanced IDE interface, you can install up to four multidisc drives, or up to seven or more with an SCSI interface. You would need a tower case with several bays. You can put together a system with three or four of the multidisc drives for a whole lot less than $18,000, or even less than $2000.

Caddies

Some of the CD-ROM drives just have a tray to hold the disc. You push a button and tray comes out, you drop the disc in with the label facing up, and push the tray back in. (One of the computer magazines reported about a person who had just bought a new computer. A short time later the person called the company and complained that his coffee cup holder had broken. The technician finally deduced that the person had thought the CD-ROM disc tray was a coffee cup holder. It would be a good idea to have coffee cup holders on the computer somewhere. I have spilled my coffee several times and ruined some perfectly good keyboards.)

You should be very careful in handling the discs to prevent fingerprints, scratches, coffee stains, or other damage to the bright side of the disc. Try to handle them by the edge.

Some of the CD-ROM drives use a caddy to hold the disc. The caddy has a clear plastic hinged cover. The caddy encloses the disc and protects it from dirt, dust, and unnecessary handling. When the caddy is inserted into the drive, a metal sliding door moves to one side for the head access. It is similar to the $3\frac{1}{2}$ inch floppies. If your CD-ROM drive uses a caddy, you can buy several caddies, load them up, and not have to handle the discs thereafter. The caddies cost about $3.00 each and are available from several places. Look in the computer magazines.

CD-ROM Recorders (CD-R)

There are several companies that are now manufacturing CD-ROM recorders. When they were first introduced, they were very expensive at around $10,000 for a system. Some companies are now offering the CD-recorders for less than $500. The blank discs cost from $5 to $7 at this time.

In 1989, Taiyo Yuden of Japan developed an organic dye that could be combined with a reflective gold plating on a blank disc. A laser could then be used to burn pits in the disc and it would have the same qualities of a standard CD-ROM disc. In addition, this disc offered the capability of multisession; that is, data can be added from time to time. When a disc is stamped out at a factory, nothing further can be added. The data on the recordable disc has the same reflective characteristics as that of a standard CD-ROM.

There are several advantages of recordable CD-ROMs. If only one or two discs are needed, they can be made for the cost of the media. The disc is available immediately. You might have to wait for a week or more to have a disc made up at a factory. Of course, if a large number is needed, then it would be better to have a factory master made to replicate them. Even then, it would be advisable to record a single disc, check it for accuracy and content, then have a master made. Another reason to record the disc in-house is to guarantee the security of the data. Recording a small number of discs in-house from time to time is much less expensive than having them mastered and replicated.

Some large businesses have huge databases of customers, invoices, prices, and other information. Businesses might also have large parts catalogs that must be updated frequently. They can use a single disc to replace parts catalogs. A CD-ROM disc can store millions of part numbers, descriptions, drawings, cost, location, and any other pertinent information.

In addition to paperwork records that are stored, some businesses keep important records on backup tape and floppy disks. Tape and floppy disks are good for less than 10 years before they start to deteriorate. A CD-ROM disc should last for 75 to 100 years or more. It is much easier to search and find an item on a CD-ROM disc than on a backup tape or in a stack of paperwork.

Large organizations might have acres of file cabinets overflowing with paper. Some studies have shown that 90% of the files are never looked at again after they are stored. What a terrible waste of space and paper. If businesses replaced the millions of file folders and cabinets with CD-ROM discs, they could regain millions of square feet of office space. We could save thousands of trees if businesses saved documents electronically or on CD-ROM discs instead of putting everything on paper.

CD-ROM recordings are ideal for data that should never be changed. CD-ROM discs are an excellent way to make backups, and to store and archive data. CD-ROM makes it very easy to share large files with other computers, across the room, across the nation, or anywhere in the world. It can be shipped for a very nominal price and you won't have to worry too much about it being erased or damaged. The CD-ROM discs can be read by any standard CD-ROM drive.

Most of the CD-ROM recordable systems record at 2× or 4×. Faster systems are being developed and will be available by the time you read this. They can usually record at a fairly low speed but play back at a higher speed. With a 2× CD-R, you could record 74 minutes of music in 37 minutes. With a 4× CD-R it would only take half that time or about 18½ minutes.

Most of the CD-R systems will let you have multisession recording. If you don't have enough data to completely fill a disc, you can record as much as you have, then come back later and record more. This is also the system used for photo CDs.

When you send data to CD-R it will probably be from a hard disk. Either the hard disk or the CD-R should be SCSI. If both drives are IDE, there might be some conflict and slowing of data transfer. There won't be as much of a problem if both of them are SCSI.

Organizing Data

There are systems that can be used to scan information into a computer and then compress it. It can then be indexed, so that any item can be quickly found and accessed. The data can then be stored on a CD-ROM disc, a write once, read many (WORM) disc, or other storage device. COLD is a recent acronym for computer output to laser disk. With a good COLD system and the proper hardware and software, millions of documents can be placed on a few small discs. To learn more about this technology, subscribe to the following imaging magazines. They are free to qualified subscribers:

Imaging Business Magazine
(301) 343-1520

Advanced Imaging
445 Broad Hollow Rd.
Melville, NY 11747-4722

Managing Office Technology
1100 Superior Ave.
Cleveland, OH 44197-8092

If you are registered as any kind of business at all, you should be able to qualify. There are several other magazines listed in Chapter 21.

Here are just a few of the many companies who offer recordable CD-ROM systems:

Alos
800-431-7105
www.alosmc.com

MicroNet Tech.
(714) 453-6100
www.micronet.com

CMS Enhancements
800-327-5773
www.cmsenh.com

Optima Tech.
800-411-4237
www.optimatech.com

Consan Storage
800-229-3475
www.consan.com

Philips Proffesional
800-235-7373
www.pps.philips.com

Creative Labs
800-998-5227
www.creativelabs.com

Pinnacle Micro
800-553-7070
www.pinnaclemicro.com

DataDisc
800-328-2347
www.datadisc.com

Pioneer New Media
800-444-6784
www.pioneerusa.com

DynaTek Automation
800-461-8855
www.dynatek.ca

Plasmon
800-451-6845
www.plasmon.com

Eastman Kodak
800-235-6325
www.kodak.com

Smart & Friendly
800-366-6001
www.smartandfriendly.com

Hewlett-Packard
800-810-0134
www.hp.com/go/storage

Sony
800-352-7669
www.sel.sony.com

JVC
(714) 261-1292
www.jvcinfo.com

TEAC America
(213) 726-0303
www.teac.com

Microboards Tech.
800-646-8881
www.microboards.com

Several companies manufacture blank discs for the CD-R systems. The ProSource Company, at 800-903-1234, offers blank discs from several companies. The discs cost from $6 up to $9 each. They also have several other items that are needed, such as labels and label applicators. A group of hardware manufacturers, led by Philips and IBM, is working on a CD-erasable (CD-E) format.

Kodak Photo CD

Eastman Kodak, at (716) 742-4000, www.kodak.com, has developed a system that displays photos on a television set or on a computer monitor. A person can take a roll or film to a photo developer and have the photos copied onto a CD-ROM disc. The Kodak CD recorder is much too expensive for most small photo finishing labs, so they have to send them out to be done. It usually takes about a week to get the disc back. It costs about $20 for a disk and the cost for putting 24 photos onto a

CD disc is about $20. If later you decide to add more photos to the disc, just take it back to the lab and they will load them on.

Some of the advantages of the Photo CD system is that the photos can be recorded at a resolution of 128×192 and up as high as 4000×6000 pixels. There are no televisions or even computers that would allow you to view the photos at 4000×6000. At this resolution, less than 100 photos in the 4×5 inch format can be recorded on a disc. The lower the resolution and the smaller the photo, the more photos that can be stored on a disc. Most photos are stored at 480×640. At a resolution of 128×192 as many as 6000 small thumbnail size photos can be stored on a disc. The 128×192 format is often used to make a small copy of each photo on the disc. These small copies are then used as an index or catalog for all photos on the disc. If you are using a computer, you can use a mouse to point and click on any of the small images to bring up the large photo.

The Kodak Photo CD player can be connected directly to a television or to a computer. The photos can be displayed and enlarged on a television screen, they can be rotated, mirrored, flipped, cropped, copied to a computer file, and printed out or exported.

The Kodak Photo CD player is a great tool for business presentations. It would be much more versatile than using a slide projector. The Kodak Photo CD player is also a high-fidelity player for audio CD.

Multimedia Upgrade Kits

Many companies are offering multimedia upgrade kits or bundles. Many of them sport the MPC logo, which means that they conform to the MPC specifications for any of the products in the kit. Some of the kits are a very good bargain, but you should check them out carefully. Be aware that some of the kits might have older CD-ROM drives and components. At the minimum, the kit should have a late-model eight-speed or faster CD-ROM drive, a 16-bit audio sound board, a 22KHz mono playback and 11KHz recording (44KHz stereo playback and recording is better), Multivoice MIDI synthesizer (boards with the Wave Table are better), internal audio mixer for CD audio, MIDI and digitized sound, and MIDI and joystick ports.

In addition to the hardware components, some vendors include several multimedia titles. In some cases, the list price of the titles alone exceed the cost of the entire bundle. Some kits might even include speakers and a microphone.

Digital Videodisc (DVD)

It takes a tremendous amount of memory to store digital images. Just one digitized frame of a movie might require over 25Mbs to store. At this rate, you could only store a few seconds of a movie on a standard CD-ROM disc. But it is possible to store up to three hours of movies on the digital videodisc (DVD) systems. The discs for this system will be the same size as the present CD-ROM discs; however, instead of 650Mb, the new disc will be able to store up to 17Gb.

At this time not very many titles are available. The film industry has held up the production of DVD because of their insistence that absolute copy prevention be installed on all units. The copy prevention must be built into the hardware, which is rather expensive because of engineering and manufacturing problems.

Besides being able to store complete movies, the new system will be great for business use. There is always the need for more information. Though chances are great, even with 4.7Gb of data, what you are looking for will be stored on some other disc. Several companies have developed systems that can have four or more discs loaded in the drive. If what you want is on another disc, it can easily and quickly switch to that disc. These companies should be able to do the same with the DVD system.

The DVD system will be able to read all of our present CD-ROM discs, but our present CD-ROM drives will not be able to read the new DVD discs. There will be several companies manufacturing DVDs by the time you read this. Here are just a few:

Creative Labs
800-998-5227
www.creativelabs.com

STB
888-234-8750
www.stb.com

Quantex
800-896-4898
www.quantex.com

Toshiba
(714) 457-0777
www.tais.com/taisdpd/

Rewritable DVD

Several companies are working on DVD-R (write once), but the Hitachi Co., at 800-448-2244, www.hitachi.com, has developed a DVD rewritable system that can be erased and rewritten several times. They call it

DVD-RAM. The discs can store 2.6Gb on each side. They are available as IDE or SCSI units. They are backward compatible with DVD systems.

Installing CD-ROM Drives

Step 1: Remove the Computer Cover There are two main types of CD-ROM drives at this time: IDE and SCSI. The first step in installing any of these drives is to remove the cover from your computer. Then make sure that you have a standard $5\frac{1}{4}$ inch bay that is accessible from the front panel. Use two small screws on each side to mount the drive.

Step 2: Set any Jumpers or Switches You should have received some sort of documentation and installation instructions with your drive. If you are installing more than one IDE CD-ROM drive or an IDE hard disk on the same cable, they must be configured as master and slave.

IDE CD-ROM Drives Most Pentium-type motherboards have a secondary EIDE interface built in. If not you will have to buy an EIDE interface. The EIDE interface can support up to four devices. Set any jumpers or switches necessary, then follow instructions below for plugging in cables and boards. The IDE CD-ROM drives come with driver software, so they are fairly easy to install.

SCSI CD-ROM Drive You might have up to seven SCSI devices installed, but each device must be assigned a logical unit number (LUN) between 0 and 6. The LUN is usually determined by a set of jumpered pins. Check your documentation. If you already have other SCSI devices installed, you must determine which LUNs are assigned to them and configure the CD-ROM drive for a number not being used.

Step 3: Install the Interface Board If you have a newer motherboard, there should be two sets of upright pins for IDE devices. One set will be marked primary and one set secondary. The primary set is used for the hard disk that will be the boot drive and a second hard drive if you have one. The CD-ROM will use the secondary pins. They can be plugged in backward, so make sure that the colored wire on the ribbon cable goes to pin one on the motherboard. If you have an older motherboard, find an empty slot on the motherboard and insert the board.

Step 4: Install Cables For proprietary and IDE CD-ROM drives, you should have a flat 40-wire ribbon cable. For IDE drives, you might have to use the middle connector on the cable that is connected to your IDE hard drive.

For SCSI drives, you will have a 50-wire ribbon cable that connects to the back of the CD-ROM and then to an SCSI interface board. Most SCSI interface boards have provisions for two cable connections. If you have more than two SCSI devices, you might need to buy a cable with two or more connectors in the center.

The flat ribbon cable will have a different colored wire on one side. This wire will go to pin 1 of the connectors. Some connectors might have a shell with a square slot on one side. The cable connector will have a square elevation that fits in the slot so that they can only be plugged in correctly. Otherwise, look for an indication of pin one on the CD-ROM drive and on the interface board.

Plug in one of the four wire power cables to the drive. Most computer power supplies only have four cables. If all four cables are already being used, you might have to buy a small Y power cable.

If you plan to use your CD-ROM drive with a sound card, and I strongly recommend that you do, you will have to install a small audio cable. There is no standardization for the audio cables and sound cards. Because the CD-ROM drives and sound cards are made by different manufacturers, you must tell the vendor which sound card you are using to get the proper audio cable. Because there are so many variations, many vendors don't include the audio cable unless you specifically ask for it. The cable might cost an additional $5. Figure 8-6 shows the 50-wire ribbon cable being attached. To the left of this connector are pins for setting the logical unit number (Lun) of the drive. There is also a small connector for attaching the audio cable.

Step 5: Install Software Drivers All of the drives should come with some sort of installation and driver software, usually on a floppy disk. The vendor might not provide it unless you ask for it.

If you have other SCSI devices already installed, then you probably have SCSI driver software such as the Corel SCSI. If not, then you should contact your vendor for SCSI driver software. Once the SCSI software is installed, it will automatically recognize the new drive when you boot up.

Step 6: Test the System Test the system with a CD-ROM disc. If every-thing works, then reinstall the computer cover.

Sources

There are several companies and vendors for CD-ROM drives and CD-ROM disc titles. Just look in any computer magazine and you will see dozens of ads. Check the magazines listed earlier.

CHAPTER 18

Computer Sound and Music

Sound can be an important part of your computer system. You can run your computer without a sound board and speakers, but you will be missing out on a lot good stuff. Sound can add a lot more fun, function, and utility to your computer. There are some Windows applications that make great use of sound. The Windows Sound Recorder is an included utility that lets you record, edit, insert, mix, and play sound files that are in the .WAV format. You can add sound annotations to documents such as spreadsheets or to programs that support object linking and embedding (OLE). It is possible to run applications with sound with most 386 or later computers, but it works best if you have a Pentium-class computer.

Teleconferencing

One important reason to have a sound board and speakers in your computer is for voice and data conferencing. Two computers can be linked together on a network in an office, a large campus, or by modem anywhere in the world. Several modems and faxes are now capable of sending and receiving voice and data. A couple are WinFax Pro 7.0 from Delrina, at 800-268-6082, and Fax Center PC Server from SoftLinx, at 800-899-7724.

My 28.8K Sportster Vi Fax/Modem from US Robotics with voice mail lets me play and record voice messages. Here are a few others that do about the same thing:

Aztech Labs
Aztech Audio Telephony 2000
800-886-8859

IBM PC
Options Multimedia Modem
800-426-2968

Best Data
ACE 5000
800-632-2378

Prometheus Products
CyberStereo
800-477-3473

Boca Research
Sound Expression
(407) 997-6227

Reveal Computer
Decathlon XL
800-738-3251

Creative Labs
Phone Blaster
800-998-5227

US Robotics
Sportster
800-342-5877

Diamond Multimedia
TeleCommander 2500XL
800-468-5846

The OfficeF/X from Spectrum Signal Processing, at 800-667-0018, is a modem/fax, Sound Blaster compatible sound card, voice mail, and speaker phone. It can distinguish between incoming voice, modem, or fax and routes the call appropriately.

Microsoft has developed MS Phone, a telephony application for Windows 95 that functions as a telephone, speakerphone, answering machine, PBX, interactive voice response (IVR), and personal assistant. With this application you can use several voice commands to operate your computer.

The AT&T Computer Telephone 8130 connects to a serial port on the computer and provides several functions such as contact management, logging of incoming and outgoing calls, and Caller ID.

Music

Computers have made enormous contributions to the creation and playing of music. It has been said that music is the universal language. Everybody likes music of one kind or another. There are many different kinds of music and it can be used in many different ways. Music can be used to express just about every emotion known to man. There is music that makes us happy, elated, excited, and exhilarated. There is patriotic and marching type music that can make you want to stand up and salute. There is passionate music that can arouse you and make you feel amorous. There is music that can make you feel joyful, merry, and cheerful. There is music that is touching and sad and sorrowful. There is music that makes you feel sentimental and reminiscent. There is heartbreaking music of unrequited love that can make one feel sad and forlorn. There is serious music that is solemn and sedate and dignified. And then there is rock-and-roll and heavy metal music. All of this music can be played on your computer.

Not only can you play music through your computer, but even if you know nothing at all about music, you can use your computer to compose and create music. A computer is very good at converting text and graphics into digital data. Music can also be represented as digital data just as easily. Once music is digitized, you can edit it, re-arrange it, add new sounds to it, remove certain sounds, or change it in hundreds of different ways. The Pentium-class computer, along with the proper software, is an excellent tool for this purpose.

Music software is available from most of the software discount companies. Egghead, at 800-344-4323, has several music software packages. Rhapsody lets you compose, edit, and print your music score. The low-cost Concertware lets you enter music, play it back, edit it, or change it. They have instruction software for the piano and for guitar.

American Music Supply, at 800-458-4076, has Cakewalk Professional which is one of the most complete prorgams for music. They have several versions of Cakewalk. It can let you record up to 16 tracks. It lets you create music, edit it, print it, and control it in MIDI sequences.

American Music also has several other software packages, such as Band in A Box, Sound Forge, Steinberg Cubase Score, and Music Ace. American Music Supply also has just about every kind of musical instrument known. Call them for a catalog.

There are lots of articles and ads for music software in the music magazines and catalogs listed near the end of this chapter.

Sound Boards

A good audio board should be able to digitally record narration, sound, or music and store it as *.WAV files. You should have the option of recording in mono or stereo and be able to control the sampling rate. The board should have chips to convert the stored digital signals for analog conversion, digital-to-analog converters (DACs). It should also have chips to convert analog sound to digital signals, analog-to-digital converters (ADCs).

A good board will have a musical instrument digital Interface (MIDI). With MIDI capabilities, you can use the board with MIDI instruments such as piano keyboards, synthesizers, sound modules, and other MIDI products.

The board should have a FM synthesis chipset that duplicates the 128 different MIDI voices and 46 percussion instruments. Instead of the synthesized sound, some of the more expensive cards might have samples of actual instruments and use a wave table for synthesis.

The board should have an audio mixer function that allows you to control the source and level of the audio signals. The better boards have tone controls for the bass and treble ranges. The board should also have a joystick port connector, a microphone input, and a speaker output jack.

Figure 18-1 shows a Creative Labs Blaster Awe 64. It comes with microphone and several excellent software bundles. Figure 18-2 shows an excellent speaker system from Altec. The large object in the center is the woofer.

Sound, Microphones, and Speakers

Sound is made by the pressure on air created by a vibrating object. The pressure of the vibrations causes the air to move back and forth, creating sound. If a microphone is placed in the vicinity of the sound, it can capture an image of the sound and turn it into electrical impulses. There are several different types of microphones. One basic type has a diaphragm that vibrates due to the pressure of the sound waves. The diaphragm is attached to a coil of wire that moves in and out of the field of a permanent magnet. The movement of the coil of wire in the magnetic field produces an analog voltage that varies according to the vibration of the sound. You can record the electrical pulses, then using electronics to amplify the small signals, you can cause a loudspeaker to reproduce the original sound.

Fig. 18-1
The fantastic Blaster Awe 64 sound board.

Fig. 18-2
A very good speaker
system from Altec.

Basically, a loudspeaker is quite similar to the microphone. The speaker has a coil of wire that is attached to the speaker cone. The coil of wire is surrounded by a strong permanent magnet. Moving a coil of wire through a magnetic field produces a voltage; passing voltage through a coil of wire produces a magnetic field. The polarity of the magnetic field thus created will vary plus or minus depending on the polarity of the voltage. As the positive and negative pulses of voltage are passed through the coil of wire, it alternately attracts and pulls the coil into the magnet or repels it pushing the coil and cone outward. The movement of the speaker cone produces pressure waves that are a replica of the original sound.

Digital Sampling

Some large mainframe network computers operate by giving each person on a network a small slice of time, or *time sharing*. If the time was divided into millionths of second, a person might receive a couple of slices, then the next person would get a few slices, then a few millionths of a second later the first person would get a few more slices of data. It would be done so fast that the person would not realize that the data was being received only part of the time. Hundreds or even thousands of people could be on a single line, all receiving different data, at the same time.

Digitizing an analog voltage is somewhat similar to time sharing. *Digital samples,* or slices, are taken of the analog waves. If the number of digital samples per second is rather low, then there can be a lot of unrecorded space between each slice. When played back, the unrecorded space can usually be electronically reconstructed to some degree. But if the sample rate is fairly low, with wide spaces between each sample, the output sound will be somewhat less than high fidelity. The higher the frequency of the sample rate, the more closely the output sound will match the original. Then why not take higher frequency samples? Because the higher the frequency of the digital sample rate, the more space it requires to be stored or recorded. High-fidelity digital sound requires a tremendous amount of disk space to store.

Sampling Rates and Bits

Sound can be digitized using 8-bit samples or 16-bit samples. An 8-bit system can chop a wave form into a maximum of 256 steps or 2^8. A 16-bit system (2^{16}) can save up to 65,000 pieces of information about the same wave form. As you can imagine, the 16-bit system offers much greater fidelity, but at a greater need for storage space.

Using an eight-bit mode with a sample rate of 11KHz, you will be recording 11,000 bytes of data each second × 60 seconds or 661Kb per minute. If you were recording in 8-bit stereo at the same rate, the storage requirement would double to 1.6Mb for one minute. To record in 16 bits at 11KHz, it would be twice the bits per second, or 22,000 × 60 seconds would require 1.6Mb for one minute.

Most speech has a frequency range from about 300Hz up to about 6KHz. Sampling at 11KHz and 8 bits is good enough for speech, but it would not be very good for high-fidelity music. Most systems are capable of sampling at 22KHz and 44.1KHz in both monaural and stereo modes. A sample rate for 44.1KHz in monaural would be 82.2K bytes per second × 60 seconds = 5.292Mb. In stereo it would be doubled to 10.5Mb per minute. One hour of recording at this sample rate would require over 630Mb. Most audio CDs have about 630Mb of storage space and can play for about one hour. Standard digital sampling rates in the audio industry are 5.0125, 11.025, 22.05, and 44.1KHz.

Why 44.1KHz Sample Rate

If we had perfect hearing, we could hear sounds from 20 Hertz (Hz), or cycles per second, up to 20KHz. Most of us, especially the older people, have a much narrower hearing range. So why should we worry about a 44.1KHz sample rate? This is more than twice the frequency that we could hear even if we had perfect hearing.

Many instruments and other sounds have unique resonances and harmonics that go beyond the basic sounds they produce. These resonances and harmonics are what makes a middle C note on a piano sound differently than the same note on a violin or trumpet. Many of the harmonics and overtones of sound are in the higher frequencies. In digital recording, the upper frequency must be at least twice of what you can expect when it is converted to analog. So 44.1KHz digital signal will produce a 22KHz analog signal.

Resolution

We often speak of the *resolution* of our monitors. The more pixels displayed, the sharper the image and the higher the resolution. We also use resolution to describe digitized sound. The higher the sampling rate and the more bits of information about each sound wave, the higher the resolution and the better the fidelity. There is a limit to the resolution of an 8-bit system no matter how fast the sample rate. The maximum samples of a waveform that can be captured by an eight-bit system is 2^8, or 256. Some might think that a 16-bit system would only provide twice the resolution of an 8-bit system. Actually, a 16-bit system can provide 256 times more resolution, or 2^{16}, or 65,536. It is apparent that a 16-bit system can give much better resolution and fidelity than an 8-bit system.

Signal-to-Noise Ratio (SNR)

Analog audio is made up of voltage sine waves that vary up and down continuously. Noise and static are also made up of similar sine waves. Noise and static are everywhere. Noise and static are in the air, especially during electrical storms. They are in our electrical lines and in almost all electronic equipment. It is very difficult to avoid them.

The signal-to-noise ratio is the ratio between the amplitude of the audio or video signal as compared to the noise component. The SNR is measured in dB, usually a minus dB. The larger the negative number, the better.

Most sound boards, CD-ROMs drives, and other sound systems list the SNR on their specifications. Most of the better systems have at least —90 dB SNR. Because noise is analog voltage, a good digital system usually has less noise than the analog systems.

Digital Signal Processors (DSP)

One of the things that helps make it possible to get so much music from the sound board is a digital signal processor (DSP). It can be a very large task just to assemble and determine which notes to output from a single instrument. But it can be mind-boggling to try to do it for several instruments.

The central processor unit (CPU) is the brains of your computer. Ordinarily, almost everything that transpires in your computer has to go through the CPU. But there are certain things, such as intensive number crunching, that can be accelerated with a coprocessor.

The digital signal processor (DSP) chips are quite similar in function to math coprocessors. A DSP can take over and relieve the CPU of much of its burdens. DSP chips can be configured and programmed for several specific tasks, such as high-quality audio, or complex graphics and video. The DSP can be used for musical synthesis and many special digital effects.

At one time the DSP chips were rather expensive, but now the chips are quite reasonable. Because they add very little to the cost, more manufacturers are adding DSP chips to their sound boards. Before you buy a sound board, check the specifications.

Turtle Beach Systems was one of the first to design and implement the DSP technology on their MultiSound boards. Creative Labs followed soon after with their Sound Blaster 16 ASP. Figure 18-1 shows their latest, Awe 64. Several other companies are now manufacturing boards with the superior DSP technology. These chips add so much more function and utility to the sound board that eventually every manufacturer will be using them.

What Sound Board Should You Buy

It all depends on what you want to do and how much you want to spend. If you can afford it, I would suggest that you look for a 16-bit card with a DSP chip. For sources, look in any computer magazine such as *Computer Shopper*, the *New Media Magazine*, *PC World*, *PC Computing*, *PC Magazine*, and any of the several other computer magazines.

Installing a Sound Board

The CPU of your computer is always busy and can only be interrupted by certain devices that need its attention. The obvious reason for this is to keep order. If all of the devices tried to act at the same time, there would be total confusion. So computers have 16 interrupt or IRQ lines, and each device is assigned a unique number. They are given a priority according to their ranking number. For instance if the CPU received an interrupt request from the keyboard, which is IRQ 1, and a request from a mouse on IRQ 4, the keyboard request would be answered first.

If two devices are set for the same IRQ, it will cause a conflict. You might have to set one or more jumpers or switches on your board before you install it. If it has been designed and manufactured to the plug-n-play (PnP) specifications, you might not have to worry about setting switches and jumpers.

Just as your house has a unique address, areas of RAM memory have distinct addresses. Certain devices use a certain portion of RAM to perform some of their processing. So you might have to set jumpers or switches for the input/output (I/O) address of the sound card. The default address, the one set by the factory, will probably be set to 220. This is the Sound Blaster standard and it is used by many others.

There might also be a set of jumpers to set the direct memory access (DMA) channel. On most PCs there are three or more DMAs and they don't usually cause a conflict if two or more devices are set to the same channel.

Most of the newer audio boards now meet the PnP specification. If so, your computer BIOS will recognize these boards and automatically configure them. Many of the older boards have built-in diagnostics that can detect a conflict with the IRQ or I/O settings. But you might have trouble determining which other device is causing the conflict. If you have DOS

6.0 or later, you can use the Microsoft Diagnostics (MSD) command. It can show all of the IRQs and which components are using them.

One of the benefits of CD-ROM is that they can play sound and music along with the text, graphics, and motion. You can play CD compact audio discs on most CD-ROM drives. Most CD-ROM drives have a small audio connector on the back panel. A special cable is used to connect to the sound board. Unfortunately, there are no standards for the audio connector for the CD-ROM. It might be different on sound boards from different companies. Because there are so many variations, the audio cable is often not included with the sound board or with the CD-ROM drive. You might have to order it special. They cost about $5. The audio cable plugs into a miniature connector on the back of the CD-ROM drive. The other end plugs into a small connector on the sound board.

Speakers

Most of the sound cards have an output of about four watts. That isn't very much, but you're not trying to fill a concert hall. You really don't need much for your computer. You can attach any small speaker, but several companies manufacture small speakers with a built-in amplifier. The speakers are powered by batteries or by a power supply. They cost from $20 up to $100 for the larger ones. There are also high-end, high-fidelity systems available. Of course, high fidelity usually means high cost. Figure 18-2 shows an Altec speaker system.

Just a few of the many companies who offer small computer speakers are Labtec, Media Vision, Koss, and Roland. Look through computer magazines for others. If you use good sound boards and speakers, your computer can be a major component in an excellent high-fidelity system.

Microphones

Many of the sound boards come with a microphone. The type needed for just voice annotations can be very inexpensive, such as those available from Radio Shack for about $5.

If you expect to do any kind of high-fidelity recording, then you definitely need a good microphone. A sound system is only as good as its weakest link. A good microphone might cost from $35 up to $500 or more.

There are two basic types of microphones. The dynamic type uses a diaphragm and a coil of wire that moves back and forth in a magnetic field. The other type is the condenser, or capacitor, microphone. A capacitor is made up of two flat plates. When voltage is applied to the plates, a charged field, or a *capacitance*, will exist between the plates. The capacitance will depend on the voltage, the size of the plates, and the distance between the plates. If the plates are moved toward or away from each other, the capacity will change. In a capacitor microphone, one plate is fixed and the other is a flat diaphragm. Sound pressure on the flexible diaphragm will move the one charged plate in and out, which causes a change in the capacity. Capacitor microphones can be made very small, such as the lapel microphone.

Many professional-type microphones sold today are wireless. They have a small transmitter built into the microphone that feeds the sound to a small receiver, which is connected to an amplifier or recorder.

Microphones are also classified by their pickup directionality. The *omnidirectional* picks up sound from all directions. The *bidirectional* picks up sound from opposite sides of the microphone. The *cardiod* picks up sound in a heart-shaped unidirectional pattern (cardi is a prefix for heart). The *unidirectional supercardiod* picks up sound on a very narrow straight in path. Unlike what you might see rock stars do to a microphone, you don't have to stick it in your mouth to have it pick up your voice.

Musical Instrument Digital Interface (MIDI)

Electronic circuits can be designed to oscillate at almost any frequency. The output of the oscillating circuit is a voltage that can be amplified and routed through a loud speaker to reproduce various sounds.

In the early 1970s, Robert Moog used voltage-controlled oscillators (VCOs) to develop the Moog Synthesizer. With a synthesizer, you can create synthetic musical sounds that imitate different instruments. The sounds from the early systems didn't sound much like real musical instruments.

Also in the early 1970s, John Chowning, of Stanford University, developed Digital FM synthesis. The Yamaha Corporation licensed the technology from Stanford and introduced the first FM digital synthesizer in 1982. Since that time, there have been some tremendous technological advances. Today a person might not be able to distinguish whether a sound was synthesized or if it came from a real instrument.

In some instances, the music from a sound board does come from real instruments. Sample notes are recorded from instruments. Under computer control, any of the stored samples can be joined and played back. The notes can be held for a half note, or shortened to a quarter note or for whatever the music requires. Samples from several instruments can all be playing at the same time. The music can sound as if it is being produced by a live hundred-piece orchestra. And it all comes from a chip that is about one-inch square. It is absolutely amazing.

The early voltage-controlled oscillators (VCOs) were rather crude. The electronic industry was still in its infancy. There were no integrated circuits. As the electronic industry and technology evolved, newer and better VCOs were developed and incorporated into musical instruments.

The MIDI Standard

There were no standards for the VCOs and new musical instruments. As usual, each vendor's product was a bit different than all others. In 1983, a group of companies got together and adopted a set of standards, which they called the *musical instrument digital interface*. This was truly a historic agreement for the music industry. MIDI and the advances in electronic technology has made it possible to generate more new music in the last ten years than was generated in the last 100 years. Synthesized music is not only used for rock-and-roll, but for television commercials, for movies, and for all types of music.

How MIDI Operates

MIDI itself does not produce music. It is only an interface, or controller, that tells other devices such as a synthesizer or a sampler which particular sound to produce. In some respects, MIDI is similar to the old style piano players that used a punched roll of paper to play.

Briefly, the MIDI specification says that a MIDI device must have at least two MIDI connectors: an input and an output. (These are DIN connectors that are the same type as that used for the computer keyboard connector on the motherboard.) A MIDI device might include adapter cards, synthesizers, piano-type keyboards, various types of instrument pickups, digital signal processors, and MIDI controlled audio mixers. One of the great advantages of MIDI is that it allows many different electronic instruments to communicate with each other. When two MIDI instruments are connected, the devices exchange information about the elements of the performance such as the notes played and how loud they are played. A master keyboard can be connected to two or more MIDI electronic keyboards, or other MIDI devices. Any note played on the master can be also played on the connected MIDI "slaves." The electronic keyboards can emulate several different instruments. One person playing the master can use the slaves to make it sound as though a very large orchestra is playing. There are many options available, such as allowing you to record the notes played, then play them back or edit and change them.

General MIDI Standard Signals

There are 128 common instrument sound signals for MIDI control, each signal is numbered 1 to 128. (You might also see them numbered 0 to 127.) The standard was originated by the Roland Corporation and is now coordinated by the MIDI Manufacturers Association (MMA).

If the MIDI receives a signal and it is connected to a synthesizer, keyboard, or any MIDI instrument, it will trigger the device to play a note corresponding to the signal number. For instance, a signal on number 3 would cause a honky-tonk piano sound, number 40 would be a violin. There are 16 different instrument classifications. Every eight numbers represent sounds from a basic class of instrument. For instance, the first eight sounds are made by piano-type instruments, the next eight are made by chromatic percussion instruments, then organs, etc.

There are an additional 46 MIDI note numbers for nonmelodic percussion instruments. These numbers include such things as drums, a cowbell, wooden blocks, triangles, and cymbals.

Synthesizers

The MIDI specification was primarily designed as a standard for controlling synthesizers. It did not specify how a synthesizer should create a sound or what sounds should be created.

The word *synthesize* means to combine or put together. Synthesizers can combine two or more wave forms to form new sounds. There are several types of sound waves or oscillations. Each musical note has a basic oscillation frequency. For instance A2 has a frequency of 220 oscillations per second, or 220Hz. Note E3 vibrates at 330Hz, A4 at 440Hz, and E6 at 660Hz. You could generate pure single-frequency sine waves of each of these notes, but they would be rather dull and uninteresting. The actual notes are a combination of oscillation frequencies.

Even though it has the same basic frequency, if a note is played on different instruments, there will be a distinct difference in the sounds. The note A4 played on a trombone sounds quite different than A4 played on a guitar. They all sound differently because they are not pure single sine wave frequencies. The vibrations of a basic note cause other vibrations in the metal of a trombone or the wood of a guitar. These extra vibrations are the *timbre* that adds tone color to a sound and distinguishes it from a note played on another instrument.

Harmonics

An important cause for difference in sounds is the *harmonics* created. A guitar string that is plucked to play A4 will vibrate at 440Hz. If you photographed the vibrating string with a high-speed movie camera, then slowed it down, you could see a primary node of vibrations. But there would also be several smaller sized nodes on the string. These smaller nodes would be vibrating at twice the frequency of the primary node and some would even be vibrating at four times the primary frequency. The sounds made at the higher frequencies blend with the primary sound to give it tone and color. These higher frequencies are called harmonics. Harmonics are even multiples of the fundamental oscillation of a note or its basic pitch.

Envelope Generator

Bob Moog determined that there were four main criteria in each sound. He identified them as *attack, decay, sustain,* and *release* (ADSR). The attack determines how fast the initial sound rises. It might hold at the initial height for a while, then start to decay. Sustain determines how long the sound is audible while a key is held down. Release is the rate at which the sound intensity decreases to zero after the key is released. The ADSR electronic envelope is used in synthesizers to describe almost any sound.

Wave Tables

The FM synthesized sounds are usually not as good as the sound generated from an actual instrument. The more expensive sound cards and many of the better MIDI instruments use digital samples of real sounds. This requires some memory to store the samples, but actually not as much as you might think. For instance, a piano has 88 notes or keys. But it is only necessary to sample a few notes. Because they are all piano notes, the main difference is the pitch. Middle A or A4 has a frequency of 440Hz, A2 has a frequency of 220Hz. A sample of a single A can be electronically altered to make it sound like any A on the piano keyboard. So they only need a sample of an A, B, C, D, E, F, and G. With a small sample of each of these notes, any note of the 88 on the piano can be created. It also would not matter whether the note was a quarter note, half note, or whole note. Once the note is simulated, it can be held for as long or as short a time as necessary.

The same type of system would be used to sample notes from other instruments. It would be a little simpler to store notes from other instruments, because most of them don't have as many notes as a piano. A piano is one of the few instruments that allows more than one note to be played at the same time.

The samples are stored in ROM. When a note is called for, the sample is read from ROM, placed in RAM, electronically adjusted for whatever note is needed, then sent to an amplifier and loudspeaker.

The more instruments sampled and the more samples that are stored, the more memory that is required, both ROM and RAM. Some high-end keyboards might have 10Mb or more of ROM and about 4Mb of RAM.

Sequencers

Sequencers are a type of recorder that use computer memory to store information about a performance. Like the MIDI, they do not record the sound itself, but just the information about the sound.

Even if you know nothing at all about music, you can write and compose music with a sequencer that is connected to a synthesizer or other electronic instrument. If you know a little bit about music, you can become an expert composer with a sequencer. Most sequencers are software programs that allow you to create, edit, record, and playback on a hard disk musical compositions in the MIDI message format.

A sequencer memorizes anything you play and can play it back at any time. They are similar to multitrack recorders, except that they are much faster because the tracks are on a computer. The computer also lets you do hundreds of things better, quicker, and easier than a tape recorder. A sequencer lets you edit music in thousands of ways that are not possible with a tape machine. With a single MIDI instrument, an entire album could be recorded.

A sequence can be part of a song or a single track of a song or the whole song. The sequences are laid down in tracks. Several tracks of different instruments can be laid down separately, then all played back together. A single track can be played back and edited or changed. Tracks can be recorded at different times, then blended together. A song or an album can be created by a group even though one member might be in New York, one in Los Angeles, or others scattered all over the country. Each member of the group could record their part on a disk, then ship it to a studio where all of the tracks could be edited and blended together.

Some sequencers allow you to record channels while playing back existing channels. Tracks can be laid down over another track without erasing what is already there. Portions of a track can be erased and new material inserted. The editing capabilities are almost unlimited.

Some synthesizers and keyboards have a built-in hardware sequencer. The built-in sequencer allows you to do many of the same things that sequencer software allows. But a hardware sequencer would not have the capabilities of a computer.

Sequencer software, such as Cakewalk, lets you record in real time as an instrument is being played. Or you can use the step-entry mode and enter one note at a time. The notes can be entered from a computer keyboard or a piano-type MIDI keyboard that is connected to the computer.

The software is intelligent enough to take step-entry notes, combine them with the proper staff notation and timing. Some software will even add the proper chords to the step entry.

Some Windows sequencer software programs are Cakewalk Professional, Cadenza, Master Tracks Pro, and Midisoft for Windows. Many of the music software programs also print out music scores.

When you consider the modern technology that allows the editing and re-editing of a song until the cut is perfect, you just have to admire the works of some of the early recording artists. They usually didn't get the opportunity to go back and change a mistake or to improve a lick here and there.

Piano Keyboards

It is possible to use a computer keyboard to edit or create music, but it is a lot easier to work with an electronic piano keyboard. Many of the electronic keyboards have built-in synthesizers and MIDI connections.

If you are interested in music, one of the magazines that you should subscribe to is the *Electronic Musician,* at 800-843-4086. They have excellent articles about music and new devices. This magazine is of interest to professional musicians as well as amateurs and anyone who enjoys music. They also publish an annual *Digital Piano Buyer's Guide* that is available from the Mix Bookshelf, at 800-233-9604. The Mix Bookshelf specializes in books for musicians. One book that they carry is *The Musical PC.* It is an excellent book for anyone who wants to learn more about music and computers. Another book they carry is *Making Music With Your Computer.* It would be very helpful to anyone just getting into music. There are also articles in the book that would be of interest to the old pro.

Another magazine for musicians and anyone interested in music is called *Musician* at 800-347-6969. It is published primarily for the professional musician, but it is of interest to anyone who enjoys music and wants to keep up with what is happening in the music and entertainment field.

Music Software and Hardware

There are several software packages that you can use with your computer to make music. Listed here are just a few:

The Cakewalk Company
800-234-1171

Has some of the most comprehensive music software in the business. They also have Cakewalk Pro Audio which is a MIDI sequencer. Call them for information and a Demo Pack.

The Kurzweil Company
800-421-9846

Also has an extensive line of music products.

Digidesign
Pro Tools III
800-333-2137

Lets you record, edit, process, mix, and master your music.

Soundtrek
Jammer
800-778-6859

Allows you to enter a few chords then choose from over 200 band styles to create professional sounding songs.

The EMAGIC Company   The Free Play Company
(916) 477-1051   (310) 459-8614

This company has World Music Menu that can help you create music similar to that of countries from around the world.

The PG Music Company
800-268-6272

This company has Band-In-A-Box that lets you type in a few chords and it will supply the rest. It will automatically generate professional quality accompaniment instruments. PG Music also offers several other music software programs.

There are many other companies who offer software that can let you make beautiful music with your computer. To find out more about these companies, subscribe to the *Electronic Musician* and the other music magazines and catalogs listed.

Catalogs

You will need music software for your PC. The *Soundware Catalog*, at 800-333-4554, lists hundreds of music software programs. They have a comprehensive and detailed description of each program listed. Even if you don't intend to order the program, the descriptions in the catalog can give you a good idea of what is available. Call them for a catalog.

The *Musician's Friend Catalog*, at 800-776-5173, the *American Musical Supply Catalog*, at 800-458-4076, and *Manny's Mailbox Music*, at 800-448-8478 all have hundreds of musical instruments, supplies, videotapes for training, and books. Call them for catalogs.

Musician Trade Shows

Partly due to the success of the COMDEX shows, there are now lots of trade shows. Here are a couple that you might be interested in.

The National Association of Music Merchants (NAMM) has two large shows each year, usually one near Los Angeles in the winter and one in Nashville during the summer. There are usually hundreds of exhibitors at these shows. You will find just about every imaginable musical product at these shows. They have dozens of rooms where they demonstrate amplifiers and loudspeakers. There are hundreds of electronic keyboards on the floor, everything from the small toys up to the very expensive grand pianos. They also have several old-fashioned, nonelectronic pianos all the way from the spinet up to the concert grand. If you are at all interested in music, this is the place to see all that is available. To find out when and where the next NAMM show will be held, you can call (619) 438-8001.

The Consumer Electronics Show (CES) also presents two large shows each year, a winter show held in Las Vegas during the first week in January and a summer show held in Chicago during the first week in June. This show also has several music and musical instrument exhibitors. To find out more about this show, call (202) 457-8700.

If you are interested in multimedia, you can order my book *Build Your Own Multimedia System and Save a Bundle* from McGraw-Hill at 800-262-4729. It is also available from most bookstores.

CHAPTER 19

Essential Software

This chapter can save you hundreds of dollars on software. You cannot operate a computer without software. It is equally as necessary as hardware. Software is merely instructions that tell the hardware what to do. Computers are dumb. Computers will only do what the software tells them to do.

Off-the-Shelf and Ready-to-Use Software

There are a few basic programs that you need. I can't possibly list all of the software that is available. There is more software, already written and immediately available, than you can use in a lifetime. The software companies are constantly revising and updating their software. There are off-the-shelf programs that can do almost everything that you could ever want to do with a computer.

There are several categories of programs that you will need. Just a short time ago, we all needed a separate Disk Operating System (DOS), but Windows 95 has eliminated the need for that. Windows 95 does a lot, but we still need word processors, databases, spreadsheets, utilities, shells, communications, and graphics. Depending on what you intend to use your computer for, there are hundreds of others for special needs.

List Price versus Discount Price

Prices are listed several times in this chapter for comparison only. They will be different by the time you read this, no doubt lower.

Surplus Software

One of the best ways that I know of to save on software is to buy it from Surplus Software at 800-753-7877, or www.surplusdirect.com. Quite often there are quite a lot of software packages that have not been sold when a new version is released. The software business is somewhat like the soap business. The software and soap companies have to come out with a new and improved version every year. Quite often the new and improved versions don't perform much better than the old ones did. Or it may do things that you have no need for. Like most people, I never use all of the capabilities of my software.

If you would like to save some money and don't mind using an older software version, call the Surplus Software, at 800-753-7877, and ask for a copy of their free catalog. They have hundreds of surplus software packages still in their original shrinkwrap. Unfortunately, they don't have space to list them all. If you don't see a package that you need, call them and ask for it.

The Surplus Software Company also carries several low-cost hardware components, just about everything you would need to upgrade. They also have upgrade kits and offer bare-bone systems that can be used to build your own.

Software Upgrades

Most of the computer and software stores, such as Egghead and Comp USA, participate in upgrade discounts. These discounts can save you a considerable amount of money. There are two different types of upgrades: live upgrade and competitive upgrade.

Live Upgrade Discounts

The software packages mentioned here are only listed as an example. As you might imagine, store stock changes frequently as new products or later versions are released. There is no guarantee that stores they will have the packages listed by the time you read this. Call Surplus Software and ask for their latest catalog.

Software Surplus also has an academic program that enables eligible consumers to buy a large number of brand-new software packages and save a fantastic amount of money. These packages are offered to accredited K—12 schools, colleges, universities and current term students, faculty, and staff.

To place an order, students must have a student ID, current term class registration, or a schedule. Faculty and staff must have ID, a college or university pay stub, or a photocopy of their current teaching contract. Credentials can be faxed to (541) 386-4227. Or you can mail copies to P.O. Box 2000, Hood River, OR, 97031-2000.

Here are just a couple of examples of what you can save on brand-new software if you qualify: you can buy Corel WordPerfect Suite 7 for $36.99. A discount magazine lists it for $287. You can buy Office Professional 7 from Surplus for $123.99. A discount magazine lists it for $499.

A few other examples are Microsoft Office Pro 7.0 for $189, Microsoft Standard 7.0 for $149.99. A discount magazine lists Microsoft Office Pro for $579; the Microsoft Office Standard is only $449.

These are just a few of the fantastic bargains you can get from Surplus Software. The company has also branched out into low-cost systems and hardware components.

Competitive Upgrade Discounts

You might get an even better deal if you trade in an older copy of one of Microsoft Word's competitors, such as WordPerfect or AMI Pro or any of several other packages. The Software Surplus catalog offers earlier versions of several packages.

Microsoft is not the only one who plays this game. You can trade in any previous version of WordPerfect or any competitor of WordPerfect. Many other companies will also accept competitive trade-ins for upgrades.

Proof of Purchase for Upgrade Discount

Before you buy a major software product, you might call the software company and ask what would qualify for a competitive package to trade in for what you want to buy. There is usually quite a bit of latitude.

Often they ask for the title page from the original manual for proof of purchase. The software companies have no use for the older, used copies. They would just clutter up their stores. You can keep the old software and the rest of the manual. You might even be able to get a title page from a friend who has an older copy of a software package you want to buy. (This is another good reason why you should belong to a user group.)

The proof of purchase varies among the different software publishers. You might be required to provide one or more of four general types of proof of purchase or ownership:

- The title page of the user manual

- A copy of a sales receipt or invoice

- The serial number of the software program

- A photocopy of the original program disk

Most of the larger software vendors participate in these programs, such as Egghead, CompUSA, and others. If you are buying through mail order, you might mail or fax a copy of the required items. Call the companies and ask what their requirements are. Call the catalog companies and ask for a copy of their catalogs.

CD-ROM Discs and Multimedia

The Surplus Software Company also lists hundreds of low-cost CD-ROM discs. The discs have hundreds of different kinds of software for business, graphics, education, science, games, entertainment, and other subjects. If you like beer, they even offer a CD that tells you how you can brew your own.

Shareware and Public Domain Software

Also remember that there are excellent free public domain programs that can do almost everything that the high-cost commercial programs can do. Check your local bulletin board, user group, or the ads for public domain software in most computer magazines. There are also some excellent shareware programs that can be registered for a nominal sum.

Try Before You Buy

The Software Dispatch Company at 800-289-8383 can send you a CD-ROM disc that has several software programs on it. You can look at them and try them. If you find one that you would like to buy, just give them a call. Have your credit card ready. They will give you a password that you can use to unlock that particular program and down load it to your hard disk. It has just about all the software that a person in a small office or home office (SOHO) would ever need.

Software Catalogs

There are several direct-mail discount software companies. If you are undecided about what you need, call the companies for a catalog, then decide. Many of the companies who send out catalogs sell both software and hardware. They usually have very good descriptions of the software and hardware along with prices. In a book like this, I don't have the available space to describe the software and hardware like the catalogs do. Catalogs are an excellent way to get the basic facts about software.

Be aware that some of the companies are not exactly discount houses. You might find better prices at your local store or in some of the computer magazines.

Also notice, some of the catalogs do not have a date on them. They usually have some sort of unintelligible code near the mailing address. If you order from one of the catalogs, they will ask you for the code. They will then charge you the price listed in that particular catalog. Prices of software and hardware change almost overnight. So if you don't have the latest catalog and you order, you might not be paying the latest price. Here are just a few of the companies that will send you their software catalogs:

Computer Discount Warehouse (CDW)
800-330-4239

Insight CD-ROM
800-488-0002

DellWare
800-847-4051

MicroWarehouse
800-367-7080

Egghead
800-344-4323

PC Connections
800-800-5555

Desktop Publishing (DTP Direct)
800-325-5811

The PC Zone
800-258-2088

Elek-Tek
800-395-1000

PowerUp! Direct
800-851-2917

Global Software & Hardware
800-845-6225

Shareware Express
800-346-2842

J&R Computer World
800-221-8180
(Mostly Macintosh)

Software Spectrum
800-787-1166

JDR Microdevices
800-538-5000

Tiger Software
800-888-4437

Essential Software

I can't possibly list all of the thousands of software packages available. The computer magazines listed in Chapter 22 often have detailed reviews of software. And of course, they usually have many advertisements for software in every issue. Briefly, here are some of the essential software packages that you need.

Operating Systems Software

If you are using an older system, you might still be using DOS and maybe Windows 3.1. *DOS* is an acronym for disk operating system, but it does much more than just operate the disks. In recognition of this, OS/2 has dropped the D.

One of the problems with DOS is that it is hard to learn. DOS has over 50 commands, but chances are you will never need to know more than 15 or 20 of the commands. One reason that the Macintosh is so popular is that you don't have to remember a lot of commands. Just use the mouse and point and click.

You don't need DOS with Windows 95. But Windows 95 can only be used on 386DX systems and up. There are millions of people with older XTs, 286s, and 386SXs that still need DOS. There are many people who will not move up to Windows 95, so Microsoft will continue to offer MS-DOS. It is doubtful that they will update it as often as in the past.

IBM PC DOS

PC-DOS 7.0 also has support for the PCMCIA technology, for PenDOS, CD-ROM support, and much more.

OS/2 WARP

OS/2 Warp breaks the 640K barrier and can seamlessly address over four gigabytes of RAM. It can do true multitasking and run several programs at the same time. If one program crashes, it does not affect the other programs. It can run all DOS software and any of the software that has been developed for Windows.

OS/2 also has Adobe Type Manager (ATM) that allows scalable fonts for Windows and for printing. It has several other excellent utilities and goodies. Version 3 has BonusPak that allows Internet connection, fax software, multimedia, and much more. They even include a few games such as solitaire and chess if you have nothing else to do.

OS/2 Warp is a 32-bit system. It can be run on 16-bit 286 systems, but they recommend a 386SX or higher. They also recommend at least 4Mb of RAM; better would be to have 8Mb or more.

OS/2 Warp is very easy to install and comes with an on-disk tutorial for easy learning. It is rather sad, but OS/2 is now obsolete.

Windows 95

One of the problems with DOS is that often you had to type in arcane commands. Many of the commands were difficult to remember. On the Macintosh, you only have to point to a command with a mouse and click. Windows 95 is now very much like the Mac in that respect. It does everything that DOS and Windows 3.1 did and more. Windows 3.1 could be run on the 16-bit 286 and 386SX, but some of Windows 95 is 32-bit software, so it requires a 386DX as a minimum. It will run with only 4Mb of RAM but 8Mb is recommended and at least 16Mb is better yet.

Windows 95 makes plug-n-play a reality for most components being produced today. Components that carry the Windows 95 logo are supposed to meet the plug-n-play specifications set out by Microsoft.

Word Processors

The most-used of all software is word processing. There are literally dozens of word processor packages, each one slightly different than the others. It amazes me that they can find so many different ways to do the same thing. All of the major word processor programs come with a spell check and a thesaurus, which can be very handy. They usually also include several other utilities, such as a calculator, communications programs for your modem, outlines, desktop publishing, print merging, and many others.

WordStar

I use WordStar. I am almost ashamed to admit it, because I am afraid that people will laugh at me behind my back. At one time, WordStar was the premier word processor and number one in its field. But it has lost a lot of its luster and has been displaced by others such as WordPerfect and Microsoft Word.

I have several other word processors that I use once in awhile because I have to write about them. But when I write about them, I usually use WordStar to do it. WordStar has both DOS and Windows versions. But WordStar is now as obsolete as the 360K floppy drive. Alas, how the mighty have fallen.

WordPerfect

WordPerfect has the ability to select fonts by a proper name, has simplified printer installation, the ability to do most desktop publishing functions, columns, import graphics, and many other useful functions and utilities.

WordPerfect also has several other software products such as Word-Perfect Presentations, WordPerfect Office for e-mail, scheduling, and calendaring, DataPerfect, a database, and WordPerfect Works, an integrated software package.

WordPerfect is now part of the Corel Corporation. This should make it a bit easier for them to compete with Microsoft Word.

Microsoft Word 7.0 for Windows 95

Microsoft Word for Windows lets you take advantage of all of the features and utilities of Windows. If you have previously learned a different word processor, such as WordPerfect, Word For Windows can let you use the WordPerfect commands. Besides an excellent word processor, Word for Windows does just about everything that is needed for such things as desktop publishing, generating reports, making charts, drawings and presentations. It does columns, imports graphics, can import data from databases, spreadsheets and other files. It even has a corrector for people like me who constantly type teh instead of the. It has many more features than I would ever use, even if I could learn them all.

Lotus Word Pro 96

Lotus Word Pro 96 has all the tools you need to create professional-looking documents. It has several preformatted templates and intuitive tools such as Revision Marking, Highlighter, and Comment Notes. There are several other very good word processor programs.

Database Programs

Database packages are very useful for business purposes. They allow you to manage large amounts of information. Most programs allow you to store information, search it, sort it, do calculations, and make up reports and several other very useful features.

At the present time there are almost as many database programs as there are word processors. Some of them allow the interchange of data from one program to another. The average price for the better-known database packages is almost twice that of word processors.

dBASE

dBASE II was one of the first database programs for the personal computer. It has gone through several revisions and improvements. It is a very powerful program and has hundreds of features. Previous versions were highly structured and could be a bit difficult to learn. The new Windows version is very easy to use, in many cases, just point and click or click and drag. You can create forms or design reports very fast and easy. It has excellent built-in help and tutorials. dBASE is downward compatible, so the 7 million users who have databases generated by the older versions can still use their old data.

It is now possible to buy Visual dBASE 5.5 and Visual dBASE Compiler bundled together so that you can easily create and distribute database applications.

Paradox

Paradox is fairly easy to learn and use, and it is fast and powerful. It is designed for both beginners and expert users. It is a powerful full-featured relational database that can be used on Windows 95 or Windows NT, on a single PC, or on a network.

The query-by-example is very helpful for beginners and experts alike. Paradox has a very powerful programming language, PAL. Experienced programmers can easily design special applications. For more information, call Borland International, at (408) 438-5300.

askSam

The Windows version even has a spell checker and hyperlink. A hyperlink in a document can link up with other parts of a document, open a new document or report, and several other useful functions.

They also have a discount program for students. Students can get a very good discount when they buy the program when the order is placed by an instructor. Any instructor who places an order for 10 or more copies will get a free copy. They also have a very low price to upgrade from a previous version. For more information, call Seaside Software, at 800-800-1997.

High-End Database Programs

There are several high-end database programs for networks and network servers such as Oracle and Sybase SQL. Most of these databases are 32-bit programs that will suit the Pentium Pro very well.

Spreadsheets

Spreadsheets are primarily number crunchers. They have a matrix of cells in which data can be entered. Data in a particular cell can be acted on by formulas and mathematical equations. If the data in the cell that is acted on affects other cells, recalculations are done on them. Several of the tax software programs use a simple form of spreadsheet. The income and all the deductions can be entered. If an additional deduction is discovered, it can be entered and all the calculations are refigured over automatically.

In business, spreadsheets are essential for inventory, for expenses, for accounting purposes, for forecasting, for making charts, and dozens of other vital business uses. There are a large number of spreadsheet programs.

Lotus 1-2-3

Lotus was one of the first spreadsheets. It is still one of the most powerful and popular spreadsheets. The discount price listed in several catalogs is $309.95. The upgrade price is $95.95. Any previous version of 1-2-3 can be used for a live upgrade.

Competitive spreadsheets such as Excel, Quattro, Quattro Pro, or SuperCalc can qualify for a competitive upgrade. Prices listed are for comparison only and will probably be different by the time you read this.

Check through any of the catalogs listed earlier or call Lotus Development, at (617) 577-8500. Lotus is now a division of IBM.

Microsoft Excel

Microsoft Excel is a very powerful spreadsheet program, with pull-down menus, windows, and dozens of features. It can even perform as a database. It has a long list of other features. Excel is one of the products that makes up Microsoft Office.

Several catalogs have a discount price for Excel of $299.95. A live upgrade is only $89.95; competitive upgrade is $119.95.

Quattro Pro

The Quattro Pro spreadsheet looks very much like Lotus 1-2-3. In fact Lotus sued Borland because it has the "look and feel" of 1-2-3. After dragging through the courts for several years and costing hundreds of thousands of dollars, a judge has ruled against Lotus.

Quattro Pro has better graphics capabilities for charts, calculates faster, has pull-down menus, can print sideways, and has several features not found in Lotus 1-2-3. It is fully compatible with Lotus 1-2-3 spreadsheet files. It is very easy to learn, it has Object Help, Interactive Tutors, and Experts.

Like most of the other major software packages, earlier versions of Quattro is available from Surplus Software for a very low price. There are many other spreadsheet programs. Check the ads and reviews in computer magazines.

ACT! for Windows

ACT! for Windows from Symantec, at (408) 253-9600, is a business contact database program that lets you store names, addresses, phone numbers, and other information about your customers, accounts, notes, or other types of data. It has a history log that automatically records all completed activities for each contact. The information and records can be easily accessed in seconds.

Suites

One of the best ways to buy software now is to buy a suite. A suite usually costs much less than buying each package separately.

The suites usually have the most important items such as a word processor, a spreadsheet, and a database. They might also have items such as presentation software, personal information manager (PIM), financial managers, Groupware, e-mail, and web tools. The software in the suite packages are integrated so that they will all work together.

Sometimes, a whole suite of programs will cost the same price as a single program. It is also possible to trade in old software for an upgrade price.

Some of the new programs, such as Office 97, have so many utilities and goodies that you could easily get lost trying to find and use them all. Comparing WordStar and Office 97 is about like comparing my house to Bill Gates' new home. I live in a modest little 1,500 square foot home. It has three bedrooms, a large family room for my pool table and exercise equipment, a kitchen, and living room. It is all I need. Bill Gates' new home has 50,000 square feet. That is 5,000 square feet larger than a football field. They could fit 33.33 of my houses in Bill's house. I just wonder if Bill ever gets lost.

Most word processors come with a dictionary and thesaurus, but they are usually quite limited. Most of them have a spell checker. In Microsoft Word 7.0 that came with Office for Windows 95, if you type in a word that isn't in the dictionary, it will offer one that it thinks is what you meant. If you type in *zzzz*, Microsoft Word will tell you that it isn't in the dictionary and offer the suggestion of *sex*. This was posted on the Internet and a lot of people thought it was rather funny. I just checked Word for Windows that came with Office 97. It still offers the same suggestion. Evidently Bill didn't see the Internet post.

Some of the most popular suites are Microsoft Office 97, Lotus SmartSuite 97, and CorelWordPerfect Suite 8. Microsoft Office has several different versions.

Microsoft Home and Small Business Value Pack

This is another version of Microsoft Office. It has Microsoft Word, Microsoft Excel, Microsoft Publisher, and Microsoft Bookshelf.

Microsoft Works

Microsoft Works could be called a poor man's suite. It has a word processor, a spreadsheet, data base, communications, charting, and drawing all in one package. It also includes Microsoft Bookshelf. A discount house is offering this software package for $73. The same discount house offers other suites for prices from $279 up to $559. So you know that the Microsoft Works package cannot be nearly as powerful or have as many goodies as the full-featured suites. Depending on what you want to do, the Microsoft Works may be all you need.

Utilities

Utilities are essential tools that can unerase a file, detect bad sectors on a hard disk, diagnose, unfragment, sort, and do many other things. Norton Utilities was the first, and is still foremost, in the utility department.

WINCheckIt 4.0

Norton Utilities for Windows 95 Ver. 2.0

The Norton Utilities are constantly being upgraded and new, improved functions are added. The latest Norton Utilities is a program that everybody should have. It has several excellent utilities that can help you run Windows 95 better and save you time and money. One new feature helps to resolve software conflicts when you install a new program. It has a new Norton System Genie that can help you customize Windows 95 to work the way you want it to. Its new SMART Sensor can alert you of potential hard drive problems.

The Norton Disk Doctor (NDD) file can automatically repair disk problems, both hard and floppy. The Norton Disk Editor lets you explore and repair sectors of a hard disk. The File Fix lets you repair data files. The Unerase command is great for recovering accidentally erased files.

The latest version of the Norton Utilities for Windows 95 improves many of the old standard features and adds several new ones. It has added several new utilities that can help in diagnosing, troubleshooting, and repairing.

Norton can automatically check all of your hard drives for cross-linked files, will fix any corrupted files, and ask if you want to make out a report. It will then make a mirror image of the FAT and store it in a second location. If the primary FAT is damaged, you will still be able to access your data from the second FAT.

Norton AntiVirus is a simple and easy-to-use package that detects, destroys, and prevents virus infections. It has automatic virus removal. It works with files downloaded from the internet.

The no-good #$%@&^'(&^# people who write viruses are always coming up with new ones. In a family book like this, I can't tell you what I really think about people who stoop so low as to write viruses that harm others. They are sick individuals. Solitary confinement for life without any possibility of ever seeing a computer might not be punishment enough.

To keep up with the new viruses being created, Norton AntiVirus has free LiveUpdates on the Internet each month. The free virus information can be obtained from the Virus Hotline, at 541-9VIRUS9, the Symantec BBS, America Online, CompuServe, or the Microsoft Network.

To find out more about Norton and other Symantec products, call their FaxBack number at 800-554-4403. Ask for their catalog directory to determine which numbers to order. Or check their Web site at www.symantec.com.

Directory and Disk Management Programs

There are dozens of disk management programs that help you keep track of your files and data on the hard disk, find it, rename it, view it, sort it, copy, delete it, and many other useful utilities. They can save an enormous amount of time and make life a lot simpler.

XTree for Windows

XTree was one of the first and still one of the best disk management programs available. I use it to view my files then delete unnecessary ones. I also use it to copy and backup files from one disk or directory to another. It also lets you order the files by date or alphabetically. I often look at the date stamp so I know which files are the latest. It has many other excellent features. I don't know how anyone can get along without XTree.

XTree is a part of the Symantec Companies. Symantec has a large number of excellent software products. If you have a fax machine, you can call their automated fax system, at 800-554-4403, and have them fax you information about any of their products.

Turbo Browser for Windows 95

Turbo Browser is similar to Windows 95 Explorer, except that it does much more. You can drag and drop files, cut, copy, paste, delete, and rename files. You can also backup files to removable media in zip format (it has built-in PKZIP), convert graphic files from one format to another, extract text from document or spreadsheet files, and much more. It is a great companion for word processor, spreadsheet, and graphic authoring tools. You can contact Turbo Browser, Pacific Gold Coast (516) 759-3011, www.turbobrowser.com, e-mail: 74777.3450@compuserve.com.

TurboZip

TurboZip is a Zip/Unzip utility from the Pacific Gold Coast Company who makes the Turbo Browser.

PKZIP

PKZZIP is one of the most-used and useful tools that has been around for several years. PKZIP allows you to compress files so that they take less space on a floppy disk or hard disk. A ZIP file takes much less time to download or upload to the Internet. PKZIP lets you save or archive files that are not used very often in compressed form to save hard disk space.

PKZIP is the de facto standard for most all software today. Call PKWARE, at (414) 354-8699, www.pkware.com.

CleanSweep

CleanSweep can find and give you the option of removing duplicate and unwanted files. When a program is installed, it might have several files. Some of them might even be hidden. If you decide later to delete one of these programs, it might have several files left on your disk just taking up space. CleanSweep can find these files and let you delete them or archive them.

DiskMapper

DiskMapper can visually show you how much space each program is using on your hard disk. It will then give you the option to remove it, compress it, or archive it. The visual "road map" helps you decide where to free up space on your hard disk. It is a great utility. Call MicroLogic, at 201-342-6518, www.miclog.com.

Computer-Aided Design (CAD) Programs

Most CAD programs are high-end programs that require very good high-resolution monitors and powerful computers. The Pentium is an ideal computer for computer-aided design.

AutoCAD

AutoCAD from the Autodesk Company is a high-end, high-cost design program. It is quite complex with an abundance of capabilities and functions. But it is also rather expensive at about $3,000.

Autodesk is the IBM of the CAD world and has more or less established the standard for the many clones that have followed. Contact Autodesk, Inc., at (415) 332-2344, www.autodesk.com.

Generic CADD

Autodesk has several modules and other programs that cost less than the full-blown AutoCAD. One of them is Generic CADD 6.0. call 800-228-3601, Ext. 803.

Home Series

Autodesk has a set of five low-cost programs they call the Home Series. These programs are Home, Kitchen, Bathroom, Deck, and Landscape. You don't have to be an architect to design your dream home, design an up-to-date kitchen bathroom, draw a deck, or plan your landscape. Each of the five programs has a list price of $59.95. The programs come with a library of professional symbols such as doors, outlets, furniture, fixtures, and appliances which you can import and place in your drawing. The program tracks the materials specified in your drawing and automatically creates a shopping list.

3D PLAN

Autodesk recently added 3D PLAN, a program that will let you look at any of the plans that were created in the Home, Kitchen, Bathroom, Deck or Landscape programs in three dimensions. Surfaces are shaded to add a realistic appearance.

I would recommend these programs for any one who plans to design their own home or do any remodeling on an older home. They can save you hours of time and lots of money. You can contact Autodesk at 800-228-3601.

DesignCAD 2D and DesignCAD 3D

These CAD programs will do just about everything that AutoCAd will do at a lesser cost. DesignCAD 3D allows you to make three dimensional drawings. Call American Small Business Computers at (918) 825-4844. There are several other companies that offer CAD software. Check the computer magazines.

Miscellaneous Software Programs

There are many programs for things such as accounting, statistics, finance, graphics, and many other applications. Some are very expensive; some are very reasonable.

CorelDRAW

CorelDRAW can be used for such things as drawing, illustration, page layout, charting, animation, and desktop publishing and presentations. It has word processing, OCR, over 5000 drag and drop symbols and shapes, over 18,000 clipart images, over 750 fonts, and many other features and utilities.

Corel has several other excellent software packages. Call them for a brochure at (613) 728-3733, www.corel.com.

CorelSCSI

CorelSCSI is a program that has software and several SCSI drivers that work with most major SCSI host adapters such as Always, DPT, Ultrastor, and Adaptec. It also has SitBACk, a software program for unattended backup and Corel Tape Backup software. It also has several other programs and utilities. Contact Corel Corp. at (613) 728-3733, www.corel.com.

Uninstaller for Windows

The Uninstaller from MicroHelp can track down all of the different parts of a Windows program and delete them. Even if you are a Windows pro, the Uninstaller can save you time. Contact MicroHelp, Inc. at (770) 516-0899, www.microhelp.com.

CleanSweep 95

Cleansweep 95 can check all of the files on your hard disks. If it finds two or more files with the same name in different directories, it will display them. It will also show the date the file was created, the number of bytes in the file and how often the file has been accessed. You then have the opportunity of backing up or archiving one or both of the files. You are also given the option of moving the file and all of its associated components to another directory or to a network. Or it will let you delete one or more files and its associated components. Cleansweep 95 from Quarterdeck (310) 309-3700, www.qdeck.com.

StreetSmart

StreetSmart from Charles Schwab Company, at 800-334-4455, lets you use your computer and modem to trade stocks, options, mutual funds, and bonds. It lets you research Dow Jones News and Dow Jones databases, use MarketScope for S&P database and news, stock ratings, and buy/sell recommendations, and use Company Reports to do comprehensive research on earnings and financials. You can create your own performance graphs, import and export critical financial data, and customize your portfolio reports. If you have any interest in the stock market, than you should have a copy of StreetSmart.

Money Counts

This is a very inexpensive program that can be used at home or in a small business. With it you can set up a budget, keep track of all of your expenses, balance your checkbook, and several other functions. It is very low in cost. Contact Parsons Technology at 800-223-6925, www.parsonstech.com.

It's Legal

This software helps you create wills, leases, promissory notes, and other legal documents. Parsons Technology has several other very good low-cost software packages. You can contact them at 800-223-6925, www.parsonstech.com.

WillMaker

WillMaker from Nolo Press, at (510) 549-1976, www.nolo.com, is a low-cost program that can help you create a will. Everyone should have a will, no matter what age you are or how much you own. Many people put it off because they don't want to take the time. Or they don't want to pay a lawyer a large fee. This inexpensive software can help you easily create a will that can prevent many family problems. Most people don't like to think about this sort of thing, but it happens to everyone sooner or later.

Living Trust Maker

Living Trust Maker is also from Nolo Press, at (510) 549-1976. It is a program that every family should have. Even if you have a will, it is possible that it could end up in probate court. You might have heard some of the horror stories about how probate can take several years to settle and the costs can completely eat up all of a large estate. A living trust can avoid probate and its lengthy and costly processes.

Ordinarily, a living trust requires a lawyer and can be relatively expensive. With the Nolo Press Living Trust Maker, you can create your own living trust without a lawyer. The program allows you to fashion the trust to your unique needs. The software guides you through the process, but it comes with a large user guide and legal manual that can explain and answer most of your questions. Nolo Press has free technical support if you have any problems.

Nolo Press has several other books and software. Call them for a catalog, or access them online at www.nolo.com.

Software for Kids

One of the big reasons to have a home computer is for the kids. If you have children and you don't have a computer, then they are being handicapped. In today's society, a child needs all the help he or she can get in order to make it as an adult. A computer is absolutely essential to help in the very important early training. There are thousands of software programs (commercial, shareware, and public domain) that have been developed for children. Most of the software catalogs listed have children software listings.

A good example of a children's educational program is the Smithsonian Institution Dinosaur Museum from the Software Marketing Corporation, at (602) 893-2042. Many educational programs come on CD-ROMs. This one comes on five 1.44Mb floppies. The program is in 3-D so a pair of plastic 3-D Video Glasses comes with it.

The *KidSoft Magazine*, at 800-354-6150, has reviews of dozens of reviews of software for kids.

Software Training

Most software manuals are very poorly written. You can usually tell how bad the manuals are by the number of books written telling you how to use the software. Microsoft is the largest software publisher in the world. They also have a very large book publishing house, the Microsoft Press. They publish hundreds of books each year to help people learn to use the software they publish.

There are also several companies who conduct training classes and seminars for learning some of the most popular software. These seminars might cost several hundred dollars for a one- or two-day session. I can't learn enough in one or two days to justify the cost of some of the seminars. If you pay five or six hundred dollars for a software package, you shouldn't have to spend another five or six hundred dollars to learn how to use it.

One of the better ways to learn software is by using videotapes. The ViaGrafix Company, at 800-842-4723, has about 200 different videotape courses. They have tapes on all of the most popular software and even some that are not so popular. You should be able to find a tape for almost any program imaginable. They even have instructional tapes on networking, telecommunications, programming, and much more. You can view the tapes at your leisure and learn at your own pace. Call them for a catalog. ViaGrafix now has several training programs on CD-ROM which is even better than a videotape.

There is one company that takes out full-page ads in local newspapers and offers a free videotape of any of several programs. They ask for a credit card number to pay a nominal sum for shipping. When you receive the tape, there will be notice in very small print that says they will ship additional videotapes on a regular basis for a cost of $39.95. I get a lot of mail, so I don't read everything as closely as I should. I began getting a new videotape every month. I finally read the small print.

LapLink for Windows

You can connect PCs with the supplied cables by using the LPT1 parallel printer ports, the COM serial ports, by modem, by wireless devices, or over a network such as Novell. Using the cables and software, two computers can be tied together in a very low-cost type of network. If you own a laptop, or work in an office with two or more computers, you could probably save a lot of time with LapLink for Windows.

Summary

I can't possibly mention all of the fantastic software that is available. There are thousands of ready-made software programs that allow you to do almost anything with your computer. Look through any computer magazine for the reviews and ads. You should be able to find programs for almost any application.

CHAPTER 20

Some Applications

There are many applications and ways to use your computer. I can't possibly list them all, but here are just a few uses.

For the Kids

One of the better reasons to have a home computer is for children. If you don't have a computer and you have kids, then you should be ashamed of yourself. You are depriving them of one of the greatest learning tools of all time.

There are lots of software for the kids. One of the better magazines that offers and reviews this type of software is *KidSoft*, at 800-354-6150. Check other computer magazines for advertisements as well.

Resume

There are few people who can't use a good resume. It is one of the better ways to get your foot in the door if you are looking for a job. Many of the larger companies are now using scanners to create databases of all the resumes that are sent to them. They can then have the computer search for whatever qualities they are looking for at the moment. To make sure your resume gets into their computer, you should use a good printer or typewriter with a standard font to create it. In order to find out what the companies are looking for, look in the want ads from major companies to see what keywords are used. List your strongest and best skills first. Don't hide them in the middle of a long list.

There are several books and software programs that can help you create a good resume. Here are a couple of books: *Be Your Own Headhunter Online* by Pam Dixon, published by Random House and *Electronic Resume Revolution* by Joyce Lain, published by John Wiley & Sons.

The WinWay Resume 4.0 from WinWay Corp., at 800-4WINWAY, or www.winway.com is a low-cost program. With an estimated street price of $39.95, it comes on a CD-ROM that is full of good information. It will not only help you write a good resume, it will also help you find a job.

Some of the features are automatic resume and letter writing, contact management, interview simulation, and salary negotiation. The CD-ROM has over 12,000 job descriptions to help you tailor your resume and cover letter. You can even use the program to link to the Internet, send your resume as e-mail, and help you to find jobs via the Internet.

If you are looking for a job, the cost of this program may be one of the best investments you can make. They even offer a 30-day, money-back guarantee.

According to a recent Careers edition of the *Los Angeles Times,* the top jobs at this time are for computers and technology. Here are some of the jobs: computer graphics designers, computer network builders, financial information technologists, Web page designers, multimedia designers, and Internet security.

Many of these jobs require a degree in computer science. Most local colleges and universities now offer many computer courses. There are several colleges and universities that now offer home study courses or distance learning over the Internet. Check the courses offered by the McGraw-Hill World University at www.mhcec.com, or call 888-649-8648, ext. 2621.

Some colleges and universities offer college credit courses over local television channels, usually the Public Broadcasting System channels (PBS). This type of learning can be a fantastic alternative to driving to class, trying to find a parking spot, then sitting in class at a certain time. If the class is offered on TV, you can use a VCR to record it, watch it when you have the time, or watch it several times in order to learn it. If it is on the Internet, you can usually download the lessons to your hard disk and study when you have time. It is a great way to learn and get a college or university degree.

Home Office

SOHO, a new acronym has recently been created. It means small office, home office. Many businesses can be operated from a home office. With a home office there is no commuting, no high office rent, no possibility of elevating daycare expenses, and the ability to set your own hours. More businesses are allowing their employees to work from home and telecommute. There are some jobs that can be done from home as easily as at a big office.

There is one other very important savings if you work at home. You don't have to spend a lot of money for clothes. This is especially so for women. I might get in trouble for this, but it seems that women are a lot more sensitive as to not only what they wear, but what other women wear. It is almost unthinkable for a woman to wear the same outfit more than once a week. Men are much better off. We can even wear the same shirt twice a week if we wear a tie to hide the ring around the collar.

Another excellent reason for working at home, is not having to sit in traffic jams for hours. The Los Angeles freeways are choked 24 hours a day. Many people have cellular phones and do business while sitting still in the middle of a 70 mile per hour freeway that doesn't have a stop sign for a hundred miles. Some people have even installed fax machines in their cars.

And of course you know that about 60,000 people are killed each year on our highways. Telecommuting or doing business from home could save your life.

There are several computer programs that let you connect your home computer to an office computer. A modem and the Internet might be all you need.

You should be aware that the IRS looks very close at any deductions for a home office. I have been audited twice, and each time I had to pay more becuase they disallowed some of my deductions. I didn't mind so much having to pay more, although I still think my deductions were legitimate. But what really cost me was the large amount of time and trouble. The next time they audit me, and I am pretty sure they will, I am going to ask them how much. If it is within reason, I will just write out a check. It will be much less expensive than having to go through the hassle of trying to explain and justify my deductions.

Deducting the Cost of Your Computer

If you have a home office for a business, you might be able to deduct part of the cost of your computer from your income taxes. You might even be able to deduct a portion of your rent, telephone bills, and other legitimate business expenses.

Some IRS Rules

I can't give you all of the IRS rules for a home office, but there are several deductions available if you use a portion of your home exclusively and regularly to operate your business. These deductions might include portions of your real estate taxes, mortgage interest, operating expenses (such as home insurance premiums and utility costs), and depreciation allocated to the area used for business. You might even be able to deduct a portion of the cost of painting the outside of your house or repairing the roof.

You should be aware that the IRS looks very closely at home office expenses. Before you deduct these expenses, I would recommend that you buy the latest tax books and consult with the IRS or a tax expert. There are many rules and regulations, and they change frequently. For more information, call the IRS and ask for publication no. 587, *Business Use of Your Home.* Look in your telephone directory for the local or 800 number for the IRS.

Here is another recommendation, whether you have a home office or not, keep good records. I have been rather sloppy in keeping records in the past, but after being audited twice for a home office, I am a changed man. I now use the askSam database program to keep track of all my expenses. The askSam for Windows system is very easy to use. Information can be entered as structured data or it can be entered much like if you were using a word processor. The askSam systems software is available from most large software companies or you can call them at (904) 584-6590.

Another excellent program for record keeping is Quicken from Intuit. The data from Quicken can be imported into TurboTax, which can help make the onerous tax time task a bit easier.

Be aware that the latest versions of Quicken come with the Netscape browser. I already had Netscape installed. When I installed Quicken, its Netscape conflicted with the one already installed and I couldn't use either one. I reinstalled Quicken and when it asked if I wanted to install Netscape, I just said no and it cured all my problems. It only took me a day and a half to find the problem.

Home Office as a Tax Preparer

Congress and the IRS changes the tax rules every year. Every year they become more and more complicated. It is almost impossible for the ordinary person to be aware of, comprehend, and understand all of the rules and regulations. Some of the rules are even difficult for the IRS. If you call several IRS offices with complicated questions, about 50% of the answers you get will be completely opposite.

If a person works at a single job and has a single source of income, the forms are fairly simple. But if you have several sources of income or a small business, preparing your taxes can be a nightmare. It is an impossible task for many people and they must hire a tax preparer. Many of the tax preparers charge from $50 to over $100 dollars an hour.

Because the tax rules change so often, and are so difficult for the average person to comprehend, being a tax preparer is almost like having a guaranteed income.

If you have any inclination for accounting and tax preparation, then you might consider taking a course to become a CPA or tax preparer. Many community colleges offer courses in accounting, but the H & R Block Company is probably the best place to learn tax preparation; they conduct several classes throughout the year in various locations. Just to give you an indication of how profitable tax preparation can be, the H & R Block Company owned CompuServe, but recently sold it to AOL.

Accountant

It is not absolutely necessary to be an accountant in order to be a tax preparer, but it helps a whole lot. Another reason to learn accounting is that many small businesses can't afford to hire full-time accountants. Many of them hire accountants on a part-time basis to keep their books and accounts in order. There are several good software programs that can be used for accounting. The ACCPAC accounting package from Computer Associates Company, at (516) 324-5224, is very good accounting program for both small and larger businesses. Call them for brochures. Another low-cost accounting package is Peachtree Accounting for Windows. This program is available from most software companies or from PC Zone mail order, at 800-258-2088. Other accounting packages available from PC Zone are StageSoft Accounting for Small Business and One-Write Plus Accounting. Call them for a current catalog.

M.Y.O.B. Accounting is designed for small businesses. It has general ledger, sales, inventory, checkbook, purchases and card file. It is available from Egghead, at 800-344-4323, or most other software stores. Egghead and most other software stores also carry QuickBooks Pro from Intuit. It has several modules that are ideal for small businesses such as time tracking, estimating, project costing, payroll, and accounting.

Tax Programs

Because you have a computer, it might not be necessary for you to pay a tax preparer to do your taxes. There are several tax programs that can do the job for you. Unless you have a very complicated income, it can be done quickly and easily. In many cases, the cost of the program would probably be less than the cost of having a tax preparer do your taxes.

Besides doing your own taxes, most of these programs allow you to set up files and do the taxes of others. Many of the software companies offer tax preparation programs for professional tax businesses, but usually at a much higher price.

All of the programs operate much like a spreadsheet, in that the forms, schedules, and worksheets are linked together. When you enter data at one place, other affected data is automatically updated. Most of them have a built-in calculator so that you can do calculations before entering figures. Many of them allow "what if" calculations to show what your return would look like with various inputs. Most of the companies also have software for state income taxes. Most of them allow you to print out IRS forms that are acceptable.

Here are brief reviews of just a couple of the better known programs.

TurboTax

TurboTax is unique in that it offers modules for 41 states. It is an excellent program and is fairly easy to install and learn. It starts out with a personal interview about your financial situation for the past year. It then lists forms that you might need. Based on the present year's taxes, it can estimate what your taxes will be for next year.

Quicken, from TurboTax, is a financial software program that is an ideal adjunct to TurboTax. You can use Quicken to keep track of all of your financial records, then at the end of the year, the records can be directly imported into the TurboTax program.

ChipSoft Inc.
5045 Shoreham Pl. #100
San Diego, CA 92122-3954
Tel. (619) 453-8722.

J.K. Lasser's Your Income Tax

It has several state modules. It has a scratch pad, calculator, and a next-year tax planner. The popular *J.K. Lasser's Tax Guide*, is included with the package.

J.K. Lasser's Your Income Tax
1 Gulf + Western Plaza
New York, NY 10023
800-624-0023
800-624-0024 in New York.

Electronic Filing

The IRS is now accepting electronic filing from certain tax preparers and companies. Eventually you should be able to complete your taxes from one of the above listed programs, then use your modem to send it directly to the IRS. This, of course, saves you a lot of time and will save the IRS even more. Ordinarily the IRS has to input the data from your return into their computers by hand. Can you imagine the amount of time saved if they can receive it directly into their computers. So the IRS encourages electronic filing.

Electronic filing also offers advantages to you. Here are just a few:

- Faster refund (up to three weeks faster)
- Direct deposit of the refund
- More accurate return resulting in fewer errors
- IRS acknowledges receipt of the return
- Reduces paperwork
- Saves IRS labor, therefore taxpayers money

Some people have used electronic filing to file false claims for refunds. You can be sure that from now on the IRS agents will be checking to make sure that no one is filing refund claims for their cat or dog.

There are still some limitations. For more information call 800-829-1040 and ask for an Electronic Filing Coordinator, or check with your local IRS office to see if electronic filing is possible in your area.

Other Tools of the Trade

The following items are some other tools that can go very well with your computer in business uses.

Point of Sale Terminals

Point of sale terminals (POS) are a usually a combination of a cash drawer, a computer, and special software. It provides a fast customer checkout, credit card handling, audit, security, reduced paperwork, and efficient accounting. By keying in codes for various items, the computer can keep a running inventory of everything that is sold. The store owner can immediately know when to order certain goods. A POS system can provide instant sales analysis data as to which items sell best, buying trends, and the cost and profit or loss.

There are several POS systems. A simple cash drawer with a built-in 40-column receipt printer might cost as little as $500. More complex systems cost $1500 and more. Software might cost from $175 up to $1000. But they can replace a bookkeeper and an accountant. In most successful businesses that sells goods, a POS system can easily pay for itself.

Here are a few of the POS hardware and software companies:

Alpha Data Systems (404) 499-9247	Indiana Cash Drawer (317) 398-6643
CA Retail 800-668-3767	Merit Dig. Systems (604) 985-1391
Computer Time 800-456-1159	NCR Corp. 800-544-3333
CompuRegister (314) 365-2050	Printer Products (617) 254-1200
Datacap Systems (215) 699-7051	Synchronics (901) 761-1166

Bar Codes

Bar codes are a system of black and white lines that are arranged in a system much like the Morse code of dots and dashes. By using combinations of wide and narrow bars and wide and narrow spaces, any numeral or letter of the alphabet can be represented.

Bar codes were first adopted by the grocery industry. They set up a central office that assigned a unique number, a Universal Product Code (UPC), for just about every manufactured and prepackaged product sold in grocery stores. Different sizes of the same product have a different and unique number assigned to them. The same type of products from different manufacturers also have unique numbers. Most large grocery stores nowadays sell everything from automobile parts and accessories to drugs and medicines. Each item has its own bar code number.

When the clerk runs an item across the scanner, the dark bars absorb light and the white bars reflect the light. The scanner decodes this number and sends it to the main computer. The computer then matches the input number to the number stored on its hard disk. Linked to the number on the hard disk is the price of the item, the description, the amount in inventory, and several other pieces of information about the item. The computer sends back the price and the description of the part to the cash register where it is printed out. The computer then deducts that item from the overall inventory and adds the price to the overall cash received for the day.

A store might have several thousand items with different sizes and prices. Without a bar code system the clerk must know most of the prices, then enter them in the cash register by hand. Many errors are committed. With bar codes, the human factor is eliminated. The transactions are performed much faster and with almost total accuracy.

At the end of the day the manager can look at the computer output and immediately know such things as how much business was done, what inventories need to be replenished, and what items were the biggest sellers. With the push of a button on the computer, he or she can change any or all of the prices of the items in the store.

Bar codes can be used in many other ways to increase productivity, keep track of time charged to a particular job, track inventory, and many other benefits. There are very few businesses, large or small, that cannot benefit from the use of bar codes.

There are several different types of bar code readers or scanners. Some are actually small portable computers that can store data, then be downloaded into a larger computer. Some systems require their own interface card which must be plugged into one of the slots on the computer motherboard. Some companies have devised systems that can be inserted in series with the keyboard so that no slot or other interface is needed. Key Tronic has a keyboard with a bar code reader as an integral part of the keyboard.

If you are interested in the bar code and automatic identification technology, there are two magazines that are sent free to qualified subscribers. They are as follows.

ID Systems
174 Concord St.
Peterborough, NH 03458
(603) 924-9631

Automatic I.D. News
P.O. Box 6158
Duluth, MN 55806-9858

Call or write for subscription qualification forms. Almost everyone who has any business connections can qualify.

Bar Code Printers

There are special printers that have been designed for printing bar code labels. Labels can also be printed on the better dot matrix and on laser printers. There are several companies who specialize in printing up labels to your specifications.

Networks

The term *network* can cover a lot of territory. There are some networks that are worldwide. The telephone system is a good example of a worldwide type of network. There are some computer networks that connect only two or three computers, others that have thousands tied together.

Networks are made up of two major components: hardware and software. The hardware might consist of boards, cables, hubs, routers, and bridges. There are several different companies who supply network operating software (NOS). The main ones are Novell, Microsoft, and IBM.

There are a few standards so that the hardware and software from the major companies are compatible. For instance, software from either Novell or Microsoft will work on boards and systems from several different vendors and manufacturers.

Types of Networks

There are several different types of networks such as zero slot types, proprietary systems, peer-to-peer types, local area networks (LANs), and wide area networks (WANs). A local area network is usually a system within a single building, plant, or campus. A LAN might include several different types of systems.

A zero slot network is usually two computers tied together with a cable through their serial or parallel ports. Special software can allow access of the hard disk of each unit. Files can be viewed, copied, and transferred between computers. It is a very inexpensive way to share resources. A disadvantage is that it might be limited to a maximum of 115,000 bits per second, which is relatively slow. Another disadvantage is that the distance between the two computers might be limited to about 50 feet.

LapLink from Traveling Software, at 800-527-5465, is very good if you need to tie a couple of computers together in a small office.

There are some companies who have proprietary systems for small networks and peer-to-peer systems. Moses Computer, at (408) 358-1550, has several systems that are ideal for small networks. I have a MosesALL! IV! Computer network system in my office.

For small businesses or small groups, a proprietary system might be all that you need. They are usually inexpensive, yet can have many of the utilities and functions of the large systems.

I also have two other types of network interface cards (NICs) in my office. They are both Ethernet boards. I have several software programs that these boards will work under such as Microsoft LAN Manager, Novell's NetWare Lite, Windows for Workgroups, Windows 95, and Windows NT.

A disadvantage with using the proprietary systems is that they have their own nonstandard software and hardware. These proprietary systems might not work with the standard network operating software and hardware.

A peer-to-peer network can be rather sophisticated. It requires a network card in each computer and requires special software. Depending on the type of system, it might operate from 1MHz up to 10MHz or more.

A peer-to-peer network is distinguished from a client server network in that the computers on this type of network communicate with each other rather than with a large file server. They can share and transfer files and utilize the resources of all the computers on the network.

In a file server network, one computer is usually dedicated as the server. A Pentium Pro type computer is ideal as a file server. It can have a very large hard disk that contains all of the company's files and records. The individual computers attached to the server are called *workstations.* The workstations can access the files and records and change or alter them as necessary.

A file server network offers several advantages to the company. You only have to buy software for one machine. You do have to pay for a license for each of the networked computers, but it costs much less than having to buy software for each machine.

A network can keep all of the records and data in one place. This can allow close control of the updating and revisions of the data. A network can allow communication between each of the networked computers. It can also allow the users to share a single printer, fax, modem, or other peripherals.

RAID

One disadvantage is that if the main server goes down, the whole system is down. The data and records must also be routinely backed up. For critical data, it might be necessary to have a redundant array of inexpensive disks (RAID) that would automatically make two or more copies of all data. A less expensive type system would be to use a couple of large IDE hard disks and a couple of SCSI hard disks. Because they use different interface controllers, there is less chance that both of them would fail.

UPS

For critical data, it is also necessary that the server be supplied with an uninterruptible power supply (UPS). A UPS is essential in areas where there is frequent lightning and electrical storms. It is also necessary in areas where there are wide variations in the electrical supply where there might be "brownouts." The American Power Conversion (APC) Company has some excellent UPS systems. They can supply you with a system for a single user or for a fairly large network.

Wiring faults are possible in some older houses and even in businesses. When an outlet is wired, if it is a two-wire outlet, it should have a long slot and a shorter slot. If you look at how the outlet is wired, it should have a white wire going to the longer slot and a black or other colored wire attached to the shorter slot. The white wire is ground and should be attached to a water pipe or some other ground at the fuse box. If it is a three-wire outlet, which should be standard for all newer installations, the long slot should have the white ground wire and the short one the hot black or other color wire. The U part of the outlet might have a single bare copper wire that is also attached to ground at the fuse box.

If the outlet is miswired, it can be dangerous and deadly. A miswired outlet can also cause grounding problems among your systems.

NOS

A company needs network operating software (NOS). Novell is the leader in both software and network interface cards (NICs) hardware. The Windows NT can also be used as a NOS. There are several companies that provide NOS and NICs for small networks. Lantastic from the Artisoft Company, at (602) 670-7326, is one of the better known suppliers. Novell also has Novell Lite for small networks. Microsoft Windows 95 can also be used for small networks.

There are three main methods, or topologies, of tying computers together: Ethernet, Token Ring, and Star. Each system has some advantages and disadvantages. The Ethernet system is the most popular.

Desktop Publishing

If a company has to depend on outside printing for brochures, manuals, and documents, it can be quite expensive. Desktop publishing (DTP) can save the company a lot of money. There are some high-end DTP software programs, such as PageMaker and CorelDRAW Ventura, that are necessary if you expect to do a lot of DTP. But for many projects, Word for Windows 95, WordPerfect for Windows, or any other good word processing program might be all you need.

One of the better high-end packages is CorelDRAW Ventura, which has several good graphic and drawing packages. They have clip art and just about everything else that is needed for desktop publishing.

You might also need a good laser printer and scanner for DTP. If you plan to do any color work, you will need a color printer and scanner.

DTP Direct, at 800-395-7778 or 800-325-5811, is a desktop publishing catalog. They list several DTP software packages. They also list several hardware DTP products. The ads in many of the computer magazines don't have much information about the product because the space is expensive. But many of the catalogs such as the DTP have a fairly good summary of the various features of the products. Call them for a copy of their catalog.

There are several good books on DTP. McGraw-Hill publishes several. Check the online McGraw-Hill Bookstore at www.mhcec.com.

There are also several magazines that are devoted to DTP. Almost every computer magazine often carries DTP articles.

Presentations

The word *presentation* as used in this chapter has several meanings. A presentation can be used for sales and promotions, for training employees, for informing employees, and other persons, of policies, benefits, events, changes, updates, news, and many other messages.

Presentations are not only for businesses. Almost any communication is a presentation. Even a discussion with your spouse about upgrading your computer is a presentation. Every time you have a conversation with a person, you are usually presenting ideas that you want the other person to "buy." There might be no monetary reward if a person buys your ideas, but there might be a substantial reward and sense of satisfaction to your ego. Whether we realize it or not, most of us are nearly always presenting and selling our ideas. Usually for this type of presentation, we don't need a lot of software and hardware.

For an old-fashioned type of presentation where a person stands up before a group with a projector and pointer, you might need software and hardware for text, graphics, sound, and video. A few years ago software and hardware to accomplish all of this would have required large studios full of equipment and would have cost many thousands of dollars. Today it can be done relatively inexpensively with a desktop multimedia PC.

The Need for Presentations

Presentations are very important business tools for sales, contract proposals, and all of the other things listed earlier. Business presentations are also used for reports. Businesses spend billions of dollars each year on presentations trying to get their message out. But a poor presentation can be a terrible waste of a company's valuable resources. Quite often, it is not the message that is at fault, but the messenger.

Designing a Good Presentation

It is not always the presenter's fault for giving a bad presentation. He or she might not have the proper tools to make a good presentation. There are several new electronic tools, but one of the more important tools is proper training. There are a few people who are born with the charisma that makes them the perfect silver-tongued orators. They don't need to be trained. But if you are like most of us, you might need to learn a few basic rules to become a better presenter.

The AskMe Multimedia Center, at (612) 531-0603, has an excellent software package, Super Show & Tell, for developing presentations. Michael O'Donnel, the company president, has written a booklet called *Making Great Presentations Using Your PC.* The AskMe Company has also produced *A Guide To Multimedia On The PC,* a 52-page spiral-bound book that has a wealth of information. Call them for copies of these very helpful books.

Presentations are so important that there is a magazine devoted solely to presentations. It is free to those who qualify. Almost anyone in business can qualify. For a qualification form, write to:

Presentations
Lakewood Building
50 South Ninth Street
Minneapolis MN 55402-9973.

Whether you ever expect to do any professional type presentations or not, you should know how to give them. You should know the basic principles of public speaking. One of the best and least expensive ways to learn is through a Toastmasters group. There are usually chapters in most cities. Look in the phone book.

Electronic Notes

If you are giving a talk and need notes, put them on a laptop computer. Use a large type. Have the notes arranged so that each time you press page down new notes roll up. Pressing page up would let you easily go back and review. Set the computer on the podium, then glance down now and then at your notes.

Laptops have now become very inexpensive unless you are looking for one with color and an active matrix display. If you do much public speaking, notes on a laptop are much better than handwritten notes.

Displaying the Presentation

The slides and the overhead projectors are still the most popular and most used. Of course there is no sound or motion on these systems.

With an LCD panel, any image that appears on a computer screen can be projected onto a wall or a large theater-type screen. The output of a computer is plugged into the LCD panel, which is then placed on the bed of an overhead projector system. Whatever appears on the computer screen, appears on the LCD panel which is then projected onto the screen. If the computer has a soundboard and speakers, a complete presentation with color, sound, and motion is possible.

Some of the LCD panels can be connected to a TV, VCR, or a camcorder and project the output onto a large screen. Some of the LCD panel systems might be rather expensive. They have an active-matrix type screen, the same type of screen used in the more expensive notebook computers. The active-matrix means that they require a separate transistor for every pixel in the panel, which can be several hundred thousand. One reason the active matrix panels are so expensive is that a single defective transistor makes the whole display panel defective.

There are some less expensive LCD panels that are monochrome, but can display several shades of gray. The list prices for the LCD panels start at about $1,000, but the color active-matrix might cost from $4,000 and go as high as $10,000 or more.

Here are a few companies that manufacture LCD panels.

In Focus Systems	Sayett Technology
800-327-7231	800-678-7469
nViwew Corp.	Sharp Electronics
800-736-6439	(201) 529-9636
Proxima Corp.	3M Corp.
800-447-7694	800-328-1371

Projection monitors

The NEC Company, at 800-632-4636, has a couple of MultiSync Projection Monitors. This system takes the output from a computer, VCR, or other video source and projects it onto a large screen. The system uses a red, green, and blue projection lamps such as those used on very large screen television sets.

There are several other companies that make similar screen projection monitors.

Large Screen TV

Several companies have developed small devices that allow the output of a computer to be plugged into a large screen TV. The Advanced Digital Systems, at (310) 865-1432, has the VGA to TV Elite. Panasonic has developed a 36-inch television screen that is also a computer monitor. It is a SVGA monitor with a resolution of 800 × 600 pixels. Call W. Pritchard at Panasonic at (201) 348-7182, e-mail pritchardw@panasonic.com., or www.panasonic.com.

The Consumer Technology, at 800-356-3983 has The Presenter and The Presenter Plus, small pocket-size devices that can connect a computer output to a TV. These devices can be used with a desktop PC or a small laptop. You can carry your presentation with you on a laptop and display it on a large television. The devices work with standard TVs or with the S-Video TVs.

The Comedge Company, at (818) 855-2784, has the Audio/Video Key, a device that is similar to those listed above. It can be used to connect a computer to a TV, a VCR, or a camcorder. It has both standard video and S-VHS outputs.

Ordinarily there is a lot of loss and degradation when a video signal is copied. If you have ever seen a video tape copy of a copy you can see just how much is lost. Many of the newer VCRs and television sets are now equipped with the S-VHS or super-video option. This option separates the chrominance signals from the luminance signals of composite video. The resulting signals are much cleaner with a lot less signal loss. If you are thinking of buying a new TV or VCR, look for the S-video input and output types.

Camcorder Presentations

All three of these devices can also be used to record a presentation from the computer to a VCR or camcorder. If you record your presentation on an 8mm tape recorder, you can easily take it with you. The palm-sized camcorders are small, relatively inexpensive, and can be connected to any TV. The 8mm tape cartridges can hold up to two hours of text, graphics, speech, or music. The cartridges are small enough to fit several in a coat pocket. The camcorders can run off a small battery so they don't have to have an external power source.

The Gold Disk Company, at 800-465-3375, has VideoDirector. This software comes with cables that plugs into your computer, camcorder, or video recorder. You can use the software and cables to edit and record clips of your tapes. It works under Windows so it is very easy to use. The VideoDirector is ideal for editing home video tapes or for professional editing for presentations. They have both DOS PC and Macintosh versions.

A camcorder can be an excellent presentation tool. Sony and several other companies are now manufacturing digital camcorders.

Snappy is a small device that lets you capture a single photo from a camcorder, VCR, or TV. Once the single frame is captured on disk, it can be edited, or changed or morphed. For a free demo disk and more information, call Snappy at 800-306-7529.

Digital cameras

Several companies are now making digital camcorders and still cameras. There are lots of opportunities for business use of this type of cameras. Photos taken with a still camera can be downloaded directly to a hard disk. The photos can then be printed out with a color printer. For some applications, even a low-cost color inkjet printer would do.

Several realty companies in my area take color photos of houses that they have listed. They then have four-color brochures printed up and they mail them to potential buyers. Four-color printing can be very expensive. Besides by the time the brochures are printed, the house might have already been sold. It would be a lot less expensive and take a lot less time if a person used a digital camera to take photos of the houses for sale, then use an inkjet printer to print up color brochures. Rather than using an inkjet printer, you might want to use one of the more expensive dye-sublimation or color laser printers.

Some of the digital cameras and printing systems are now film quality. The one-hour photo shops are not yet shaking in their booths, but eventually, the convenience and less cost will have an impact on the film business. Many of the photo shops have started to recognize this fact. Many of them now have printers that can print out your digital photos. And of course many of them will put your photos on a CD-ROM for you.

There are many other business uses for digital cameras. At this time, they are a bit expensive, but they will be coming down in price very soon.

Here are a few companies who make fairly inexpensive digital cameras that cost from $500 to $1,000 at this time.

Apple QuickTake   Kodak DC40
800-538-9696   800-235-6325

Casio QV-10   Logitech FotoMan Pixtura
800-962-2746   800-231-7717

Chinon ES-3000   Dycam DC-10
800-441-0222   800-883-9226

These companies have several different models. There are several other companies who manufacture very expensive professional digital cameras that cost from $3,000 up to $40,000. Here are just a few.

Dicomed Digital Camera   Leaf Lumina, Leaf DCB II
800-888-7979   (508) 836-5500

Kodak DCS 420, DCS 200   Nikon E2
800-344-0006   800-526-4566

We are all presenters and salespersons in almost everything we do. We can sell our ideas much better if we communicate better.

Another Resource

Intel has a Business Guide that has several good suggestions at their site at http://www.intel.com/businesscomputing/. They offer some business solutions for business users. Of course, they want you to use their technology, but they have some suggestion for reducing the total cost of PC ownership, network management, and business video conferencing products.

Summary

There are thousands of different applications for your upgraded computer. I can't possibly list them all. It is a most versatile and fantastic tool.

21

Digital Cameras and Imaging

Digital cameras might someday replace standard cameras and film. After all, you don't have to buy film for them or pay to have them developed. You don't have to wait to view them. Many digital cameras have a small LCD screen that lets you preview the photos. If you don't like it, just erase it and shoot again.

You can download the photos onto your computer hard disk for viewing or print them out if you have a good-quality color printer. They make it very easy to add a photo to a presentation or just for an album. Because they are digitized, you can also send the photos as e-mail to anyone on the Internet. Even though she is on the other side of the country, just imagine how happy grandma will be to see the new baby on her computer. She can save the image to her hard disk and call it up at any time.

At this time digital cameras and the printers still don't have the resolution that is possible with film. Film captures the large range and gradation of tones and colors much better than charge-coupled devices (CCDs). But the CCDs can capture enough detail to make them invaluable in many cases. Insurance company claims adjusters can take photos of automobiles at the time they are being insured, then later if there is a claim for an accident. Real estate agents can have several shots of houses they have for sale. They can show them to the prospective buyer on a computer in the office before driving around for miles. Law enforcement agents often need to record and document accidents, crime scenes, and evidence. Many officers now carry digital cameras and laptop computers in their patrol cars as part of their standard equipment.

How Digital Cameras Work

Digital cameras use the lens technology of standard-film cameras combined with the technology of scanners. Of course the better ones use the better lenses. The better the lens, the higher the cost. The lens focuses the image onto a charge-coupled device (CCD) such as those used in scanners and camcorders. When light falls on a charge-coupled device, it causes an electrical output. Filters are used to capture the various colors. A big difference between film and charge coupled devices is that film can have a resolution of up to 2500 lines per square inch. A medium-priced digital camera (about $600) has a resolution of only 300 lines per square inch.

The initial image is in an analog form. It is passed through an analog-to-digital converter (ADC) chip and converted to digital form. A digitized image can require an enormous amount of memory, up to 25Mb for a single image. Compression systems are used so that several images can be stored in built-in memory or on flash memory PC Cards. Most of the cameras give you an option for the amount of compression you want to use. With a lot of compression, you can store more photos in the camera memory, but as compression increases, some detail is lost. The number of images captured and stored in a camera depends on the amount of compression and the amount of memory available. The medium-priced cameras store as few as eight images and up to 96. Some of the cameras accomodate a type III PC Card slot. There are small hard disks that can be installed in a type III slot. Up to 900 images could be stored on one of these systems. Figure 21-1 shows a type II PC Card on top of a credit card. Figure 21-2 shows the thickness of the type II compared to credit card. This view also shows the connector end of the PC Card.

Most of the cameras operate much like the standard-film point-and-shoot cameras. Just point the camera and click the shutter. Most of them are autofocus so you don't have to worry about f-stops or shutter speeds. Because lighting is as important with digital cameras as it is with standard cameras, many of them come with a built-in flash.

Fig. 21-1
A type II PC card on top of a credit card.

A disadvantage is that the initial cost of the cameras are rather high, especially for the better ones. It is expected that the costs will come down as more vendors enter the market. Here are a few of the manufacturers of digital cameras. (Prices listed are for comparison only and might be different by the time you read this.)

Agfa ePhoto 307
800-227-2780
www.agfahome.com
$600

Apple QuickTake
800-776-2333
www.apple.com
$600

Cannon PowerShot 600
800-848-4123
www.cssi.canon.com
$950

Casio QV-10A Plus
800-962-2746
www.casio.com
$699

Dycam Digital 10-C
800-883-9226
www.dycam.com
$799

Epson PhotoPC
800-289-3776
www.epson.com
$400

Kodak DC20, 40, 50
800-235-6325
www.kodak.com
$300, $600, $900.

High-End Professional cameras

There are several high-end digital cameras that produce an image that approaches that of film, but at this time they cost from $3,500 up to $28,000. These cameras use the very expensive lenses and CCDs. Here are just a few:

Agfa ActionCam	Minolta RD-175
800-227-2780	800-964-6658
www.agfahome.com	www.minoltausa.com

Quite often one company might manufacture cameras, VCRs, and other equipment for other companies. Both of these cameras are made by Minolta. They use three CCDs for resolution up to 1528×1146. They come with a type III PC Card slot and a 131Mb hard disk. Approximate price at this time is about $6,000 to $7,000.

The Kodak DCS 410 has a 1.5 million pixel CCD and provides a resolution of 1523×1012. Approximate price is about $7,000. The Nikon E2N is built for professionals. It is quite versatile and has a long list of features. It has a type II slot for PC Card flash memory. The approximate price is $10,000.

Eastman Kodak	Nikon E2N
800-235-6325	800-526-4566
www.kodak.com	www.nikonusa.com

Digital Movie Cameras

Connectix QuickCam, at 800-950-5880, www.connectix.com, is a small, low-cost camera that plugs into your computer. It can give you still pictures or movies. It can be set up as a surveillance camera with images stored on a hard disk.

Sony and several other companies now manufacture digital camcorders. They are still rather expensive. They also use a rather small cartridge that is limited to less than an hour.

Photo Capture

The Snappy from Play Inc., at 800-306-7529, www.play.com, is a small device that lets you grab a still photo from a camcorder, a VCR, or TV.

Snappy plugs into the printer port of a computer and you can capture and send to disk any scene that you want. Figure 21-3 shows the small device.

PhotoSuite Software

PhotoSuite from MGI Software Corp., at 888-644-7638, www. mgisoft.com, lets you capture, edit, transform, and catalog your photos. You can create your own photo greeting cards, turn a photo into an oil painting, retouch photos, view a photo album, and print your photos.

You can use it to make professional business presentations, or put photos in real estate flyers or business documents. It can be used for special effects on photos to emboss, swirl, mosaic, splatter, reverse, blur, sharpen, and much more.

PhotoSuite supports all major image file formats including BMP, GIF, JPG, DIB, Kodak Photo CD, TGA, and TIF. PhotoSuite can be used to send photos over the Internet as e-mail.

It has many other features. Considering its many features, it is a very low-cost package at a list price of only $49.95.

Fig. 21-3
Snappy is a device that lets you capture a single frame from a VCR, TV, or camcorder.

Presto!Print Suite

The Presto!Print Suite, at (510) 252-0267, www.tophat.com, has a suite of six different utilities, Presto! Photo Album, Presto! ImageFolio, Presto! PageManager, Kai's Power GOO SE, Presto! ClipArt, and Presto! Print-Magic.

The Presto! PhotoAlbum lets you organize photos in to albums with text. The photos can be shared over the Internet.

The Presto! ImageFolio allows true-color image editing. It has tools to adjust brightness, hue, contrast, and saturation. It can also be used for retouching and creating special effects.

Presto! PageManager lets you scan images directly to your printer, fax, e-mail, or Windows application. You can drag and drop images to Presto! Folio or Kai's Power GOO SE for editing.

Kai's Power GOO SE lets you stretch, stir, smear, and morph photos.

Presto! ClipArt is a collection of over 1,000 clip art images. They can be used to decorate album pages, greeting cards, or stationery.

Presto! PrintMagic lets you design personalized calendars, greeting cards, letterheads, and then print them.

Imaging for Windows

Imaging for Windows comes from Eastman Software Products at www.eastmansoftware.com/imaging. This software from Kodak lets you turn paper documents and faxes into electronic files that you can view, annotate, edit, publish one the Internet, distribute, or file. It lets you capture process and distribute scanned and faxed documents. It lets you convert an image into a HTML document or save a scanned or faxed document as a TIFF file, which can be posted directly to a Web site.

If you would like to find out more about digital imaging, you might order the book *Digital Imaging for Visual Artists* by Daniel and Sally Grotta, published by McGraw-Hill.

Digital cameras and imaging software is still in its infancy. You ain't seen nothing yet!

22

Component Sources

How much you save by upgrading your own Pentium Pro depends on what components you buy and who you buy them from. You have to shop wisely and be fairly knowledgeable about the components in order to take advantage of good bargains. It is very difficult to keep up and know what is going on in this ever-changing industry. One of the best ways to do this is to subscribe to some of the many computer magazines. You can look through the magazines and do price comparisons of the various components and systems.

Computer Shows and Swap Meets

Another good way to keep up is to attend the many computer shows and swap meets. I have done a lot of my buying at these events. There is a computer show or swap almost every weekend in the larger cities. Sometimes there are two or three in the Los Angeles area on the weekends. If you live in or near a large city, check your newspaper for ads.

To set up a computer swap, an organizer usually rents a large building, such as a convention center or a large hall. Booth spaces are then rented out to various local vendors. Most of the booths have good reputable local business people. Most of the shows have a circus-like atmosphere about them and I often go just because of this.

One of the best features of the swap meets is that almost all of the components that you need are there in one place on display. Several different booths will have similar components for sale. I usually take a pencil and pad with me to the shows. I walk around and write down the prices of the items that I want to buy and compare prices at the various booths. There can be quite a wide variation in the prices. I bought a good printer at one show. One dealer was asking $995 for it in one booth. About 50 feet away, another dealer was offering the same printer for $695.

You also can haggle with most of the dealers at the shows. Especially when it gets near closing time. Rather than pack up the material and lug it back to their stores, many will sell it for a lower price.

The Softbank Company, at (617) 433-1500, sponsors the Computer Dealers Exposition (COMDEX). They put on the two biggest annual computer shows in the country. The Spring show is usually held in Atlanta or sometimes in Chicago. Then a much bigger Fall COMDEX is held during November in Las Vegas. The attendance goes up every year. When I first started attending in 1984, they only had about 60,000 people at Las Vegas. They now attract over 200,000. Every hotel room in Las

Vegas is usually sold out six months before the show. They have now started a New Media Expo, which will be held in Los Angeles in the Spring. The Interface Company also puts on international shows in several foreign countries.

Your Local Store

Most of the vendors at the swaps are local business people. They want your business and will not risk losing you as a customer. But there might be a few vendors from other parts of the country. If you buy something from a vendor who does not have a local store, be sure to get a name and address. Most components are reliable, but there is always a chance that something might not work. You might need to exchange it or get it repaired. Or you might need to ask some questions or need some support to get it working.

Again, computers are very easy to assemble. Once you have bought all of the components, it takes less than an hour to assemble a computer. But it is possible to make a mistake. Most components are now fairly reliable; however, there is a possibility that a new part that you buy and install could be defective. Most of the dealers give you a warranty of some kind and will replace defective parts. If there is something in the system that prevents it from operating, you might not be able to determine just which component is defective. Besides that, it can sometimes take a considerable amount of time to remove a component, like a motherboard, and return it to someone across town, or even worse, someone across the country. So if at all possible, try to deal with a knowledgeable vendor who will support you and help you if you have any problems.

Magazines and Mail Order

Every computer magazine carries pages and pages of ads for compatible components and systems that can be sent to you through the mail. If you live in an area where there are no computer stores, or shows, you can buy by mail.

One of the biggest magazines in size and circulation is the *Computer Shopper*. It usually has over 1000 tabloid-sized pages. About 90% of the magazine is made up of full-page ads for computer components and systems. They do manage to get a few articles in among the ads. For subscription information, call 800-274-6384. The *Computer Shopper,* and some of the other magazines, have a categorized list of all the products advertised in the magazine and what page the product is on. This makes it very easy to find what you are looking for. Sometimes they have several vendors offering the same product. This makes it easy to determine which one offers the better price.

Another reason to use mail order is because it might be less expensive than the local vendors. Local vendors usually have their stores in a fairly high-rent district; the mail-order people might work out of their back bedroom. Most local vendors have to buy their stock from a distributor. The distributor usually buys it from the manufacturer or a wholesaler. By the time you get the product, it might have passed through several companies who each made some profit. Most of the direct marketers who advertise by mail have cut out the middleman and passed their profit on to you.

Still another reason why I do a lot shopping by mail is because of state taxes. In California, the state sales tax is 8.0 to as much as 8.50 percent. If I buy a computer system in California for $1,000, it will cost me over $80 just for sales taxes. Even if I have to pay shipping charges for mail order, it is usually much less than the sales tax. States have tried several times to eliminate this loophole and make you pay taxes no matter where you buy, but so far they have been unsuccessful.

Without computer magazines, there would be no mail order, and without mail order there would be no computer magazines. Advertisements are the lifeblood of magazines. The subscription price of a magazine doesn't even come close to paying for the mailing costs so they must have advertisements to exist.

Most mail-order vendors are honest, but a few bad advertisers can ruin a magazine. *PC World* has a regular Consumer Watch column. If you have a problem with a mail-order vendor that you can't resolve, write to them. They can usually get it resolved. For *PC World* subscription information, call 800-234-3498. The magazines have formed the Microcomputer Marketing Council (MMC) of the Direct Marketing Association, 6 East 43rd St., New York, NY 10017. They have an action line at (212) 297-1393. They police the advertisers fairly closely.

You should be sure of what you need and what you are ordering. Some of the ads aren't written very well and might not tell the whole story. Ads are expensive, so they might abbreviate or leave out a lot of important information. If possible, call them up and make sure. Ask what their return policy is for defective merchandise. Also ask how long before the item will be shipped. And ask for the current price. The ads are usually placed about two months before the magazines are delivered or hit the stands. The way prices are coming down, there could be quite a change in cost at the time you place your order. Of course, if you send them the advertised price, I am sure that they will not refuse it. A two or three dollar phone call could save you a lot of time, trouble, grief, and maybe even some money.

Ten Rules for Ordering by Mail

Here are some brief rules that you should follow when ordering by mail:

■ Rule 1: Look for a street address.

Make sure the advertiser has a street address. In some ads, they give only a phone number. If you decide to buy from this vendor, call and verify that there is a live person on the other end with a street number. Before you send any money, do a bit more investigating. If possible, look through past issues of the same magazine for previous ads. If the vendor has been advertising for several months, then the vendor is probably okay.

■ Rule 2: Compare other vendor prices.

Check through the magazines for prices other vendors are selling the product for. The prices should be fairly close. If it appears to be a bargain that is too good to be true, then...you know the rest.

■ Rule 3: Buy from MMC members.

Buy from a vendor who is a member of the Microcomputer Marketing Council (MMC) of the Direct Marketing Association (DMA) or any other recognized association. There are now about 10,000 members who belong to marketing associations. They have agreed to abide by the ethical guidelines and rules of the associations. Except for friendly persuasion and the threat of expulsion, the associations have little power over the members. But most of them realize what is at stake and put a great value on their membership. Most who advertise in the major computer magazines are members.

Members of the Post Office, the Federal Trade Commission, the magazines, and legitimate businesses who advertise have taken steps to try to stop fraud and scams.

■ Rule 4: Do your homework.

Read the ads carefully. Advertising space is very expensive. Many advertisers use abbreviations, and the ads might not be entirely clear. If in doubt, call and ask. Know exactly what you want, state precisely the model, make, size, component, and any other pertinent information. Tell them which ad you are ordering from, ask them if the price is the same, if the item is in stock, and when you can expect delivery. If the item is not in stock, indicate whether you will accept a substitute or if want your money refunded. Ask for an invoice or order number. Ask the person's name. Write down all of the information, the time, the date, the company's address and phone number, description of item, and promised delivery date. Write down and save any telephone conversations, the time, date, and the person's name that you spoke with. Save any and all correspondence.

■ Rule 5: Ask questions.

Ask if the advertised item comes with all the necessary cables, parts, accessories, software, etc. Ask what the warranties are. Ask about the seller's return policies and refund policies. With whom should you correspond with if there is a problem.

■ Rule 6 Don't send cash.

You have no record of cash once it leaves your wallat. If possible, use a credit card. If you have a problem, you can possibly have the bank refuse to pay the amount. A personal check might cause a delay of three to four weeks while the vendor waits for it to clear. A money order or credit card order should be filled and shipped immediately. Keep a copy of the money order.

■ Rule 7: Ask for delivery date.

If you have not received your order by the promised delivery date, notify the seller.

■ Rule 8: Try the item out as soon as you receive it.

If you have a problem, notify the seller immediately, by phone then in writing. Give all details. Don't return the merchandise unless the dealer gives you a return material authorization (RMA). Make sure to keep a copy of the shipper's receipt, packing slip, or some evidence that the material was returned.

■ Rule 9: What to do if it is defective.

If you believe the product is defective or you have a problem, reread your warranties and guarantees. Reread the manual and any documentation. It is very easy to make an error or misunderstand how an item operates if you are unfamiliar with it. Before you go to a lot of trouble, try to get some help from someone else. At least get someone to verify that you do have a problem. There are many times when a problem disappears and the vendor is not be able to duplicate it. If possible, when you call try to have the item in your computer and be at the computer so you can describe the problem as it happens.

- Rule 10: Try to work out your problem with the vendor.

If you cannot, then write to the consumer complaint agency in the seller's state. You should also write to the magazine and to the DMA, 6 E. 43rd St., New York, NY 10017.

Federal Trade Commission Rules

Here is a brief summary of the FTC rules:

- Rule 1: Must ship within 30 days.

The seller must ship your order within 30 days unless the ad clearly states that it will take longer.

- Rule 2: Right to cancel.

If it appears that the seller cannot ship when promised, the seller must notify you and give a new date. You must be given the opportunity to cancel the order and have your money refunded if you desire.

- Rule 3: Must notify if order can't be filled.

If the seller notifies you that your order cannot filled on time, the seller must include a stamped self-addressed envelope or card so that you can respond to the notice. If you do not respond, the seller might assume that you agree to the delay. He or she still must ship within 30 days of the end of the original 30 days or cancel your order and refund your money.

- Rule 4: Right to cancel if delayed.

Even if you consent to a delay, you still have the right to cancel at any time.

- Rule 5: Must refund money if canceled.

If you cancel an order that has been paid for by check or money order, the seller must refund the money. If you paid by credit card, your account must be credited within one billing cycle. Store credits or vouchers in place of a refund are not acceptable.

■ Rule 6: No substitutions.

If the item you ordered is not available, the seller might not send you a substitute without your express consent.

Sources of Knowledge

There are several good magazines that can help you gain the knowledge needed to make sensible purchases and to learn more about computers. These magazines usually carry interesting, timely, and informative articles and reviews of software and hardware. They also have many ads for computers, components, and software.

Some of the better magazines that you should subscribe to are the *Computer Shopper, Byte, PC Computing, PC World,* and *PC Magazine.* Most of these magazines are available on local magazine racks, but you will save money with a yearly subscription. Besides they will be delivered to your door.

If you need a source of components, you only have to look in any of the magazines listed above to find hundreds of them. If you live near a large city, there will be several vendors who advertise in your local paper.

Another source of computer information can be found in the several good computer books published by McGraw-Hill.

There are hundreds of computer and computer related magazines. If you read every one of them, you still will not be able to keep up with the flood of computer information.

Recommended Computer Magazines

Here are just a few of the magazines that will help you keep abreast to some degree:

Computer Shopper
P.O. Box 51020
Boulder, CO 80321-1020

Byte Magazine
P.O. Box 558
Highstown, N.J. 08520

KidSoft Magazine
718 University Ave. #112
Los Gatos, CA 95030-9958
800-354-6150

EMedia Professional
462 Danbury Rd.
Wilton, CT 06897-2126
800-806-7795
e-mail:emediasub@onlineinc.com

CD-I World
P.O. Box 1358
Camden, ME 04843-1358

CD-ROM Multimedia
720 Sycamore St.
Columbus, IN 47201
800-565-4623

Compute!
P.O. Box 3245
Harlan, IA 51593-2424

Computer Life
P.O. Box 55880
Boulder, CO 80323-5880

ComputerCraft
76 North Broadway
Hicksville, NY 11801-9962

Computer Currents
5720 Hollis St.
Emeryville, CA 94608

Computer Graphics World
P.O. Box 122
Tulsa, OK 74101-9966

High Color
P.O. Box 1347
Camden, ME 04843-9956

Computer World
P.O. Box 2044
Marion, OH 43306-2144

Home Office Computing
P.O. Box 51344
Boulder, CO 80321-1344

LAN Magazine
P.O. Box 50047
Boulder, CO 80321-0047

MicroTimes Magazine
5951 Canning St.
Oakland, CA 94609

Nuts & Volts
430 Princeland Ct.
Corona, CA 91719-1343

PC Computing
P.O. Box 50253
Boulder, CO 80321-0253

PC World Magazine
P.O. Box 51833
Boulder, CO 80321-1833

PC Magazine
P.O. Box 51524
Boulder, CO 80321-1524

PC Today
P.O. Box 85380
Lincoln, NE 68501-5380

PC Novice
P.O. Box 85380
Lincoln, NE 68501-9807

PRE-
8340 Mission Rd. #106
Prairie Village, KS 66206

Imaging Magazine
1265 Industrial Highway
Southampton, PA 18966
800-677-3435

Internet
P.O. Box 713
Mt. Morris, IL 61054-9965

Publish!
P.O. Box 51966
Boulder, CO 80321-1966

Desktop Video World
P.O. Box 594
Mt. Morris, IL 61054-7902

Video Magazine
Box 56293
Boulder, CO 80322-6293
800-365-1008

Videomaker Magazine
P.O. 469026
Escondido, CA 92046
800-334-8152

Voice Processing Magazine
P.O. Box 6016
Duluth, MN 55806-9797

Open Computing
P.O. Box 570 Highstown
NJ 08520-9328

Digital Video Magazine
P.O. Box 594
Mt. Morris IL 61054-7902

Windows Magazine
P.O. Box 58649
Boulder, CO 80322-8649

Computer Pictures
Knowledge Industry Publications
701 Westchester Ave.
White Plains, NY 10604

*National Association of Desktop
  Publishers*
P.O. Box 11668
Riverton, NJ 08076-7268

Desktop Video World
P.O. Box 594 Mt.
Morris, IL 61054-7902

Repair, Service & Remarketing News
P.O. Box 670
Joplin, MO 64802-0670
(417) 781-9317
Fax (417) 781-0427

International Spectrum
10675 Treena Street, Suite 103
San Diego, CA 92131

MicroComputer Journal
Classified Dept. 76
N. Broadway
Hicksville, NY 11801

Insight Direct Inc.
800-796-1111

MUSICIAN'S Friend
P.O. Box 4520
Medford, OR 97501

Electronic Musician
P.O. Box 41525
Nashville, TN 37204-9829

AUDIO-FORUM
96 Broad Street
Guilford, Connecticut 06437

Black Box Corporation
P.O Box 12800
Pittisburgh, PA 15241

HOME & STUDIO RECORDING
Music Maker Publications Inc
7318 Topanga Canyon Blvd.
Suite 200
Canoga Park, CA 91303

CD-ROM Today
Subscription Department
P.O. Box 51478
Boulder, CO 8032-1478

CD-ROM Multimedia
P.O. Box 2946
Plattsburgh, NY 12901-9863
800-565-4623

Digital Imaging
MIcro Publishing
21150 Hawthorne Bld. #104
Torrance, CA 90503

Virtual Reality
P.O. Box 7703
San Francisco, CA 94120Tel.
(415) 905-2563

Virtual City
P.O. Box 3007
Livingston, NJ 07039-9922

Free Magazines to Qualified Subscribers

The following magazines are sent only to qualified subscribers. The subscription price of a magazine usually does not come anywhere near covering the costs of publication, mailing, distribution, and other costs. Most magazines depend almost entirely on advertisers for their existence. The more subscribers that a magazine has, the more it can charge for its ads. Naturally they can attract a lot more subscribers if the magazine is free.

PC Week and *InfoWorld* are excellent magazines. They are so popular that the publishers have to limit the number of subscribers. They cannot possibly accommodate all the people who have applied. They have set standards that have to be met in order to qualify. They do not publish the standards, so even if you answer all of the questions on the application, you still might not qualify.

To get a free subscription, you must write to the magazine for a qualifying application form. Or if you attend one of the larger computer shows, such as COMDEX, they will have free samples and qualifying forms. The form will ask several questions such as how you are involved with computers, the company you work for, whether you have any influence in purchasing the computer products listed in the magazines, and several other questions that gives them a very good profile of their readers.

I wouldn't tell you to lie, but it might help you qualify if you exaggerate just a bit here and there. Especially, when it asks what your responsibilities are for the purchasing of computer equipment. I am pretty sure that they will not send the FBI out to verify your answers.

One way to qualify for most of these free magazines is to become a consultant. There are very few rules and regulations as to who can call themselves a consultant. (You should be particularly aware of this fact if you decide to hire a consultant.)

The following list of magazines is not nearly complete. There are hundreds of trade magazines that are sent free to qualified subscribers. The Cahners Company alone publishes 32 different trade magazines. Many of the trade magazines are highly technical and narrowly specialized.

PC Week
P.O. Box 1770
Riverton, NJ 08077-7370

InfoWorld
P.O. Box 1172
Skokie, IL 60076

New Media Magazine
P.O. Box 1771
Riverton, NJ 08077-7331
(415) 573-5170

Multimedia Merchandising
P.O. Box 99400
Collingswood, NJ 08108-9972
Fax (609) 488-6188

ec.com
14407 Big Basin Way,
Saratoga, CA 95070-9905
Sub. Req. 847-291-5212

AV Video Production &
Presentation Tech.
701 Westchester Ave.
White Plains, NY 10604
(914) 328-9157

Data Communications
P.O. Box 477
Hightstown, NJ 08520-9362

Datamation
P.O. Box 7530
Highlands Ranch, CO 80163-9130

Electronic Publishing
P.O. Box 3493
Tulsa, OK 74101-9640

Network Computing
P.O. Box 1095
Skokie, IL 60076-9662

The Network Journal
600 Harrison St.
San Francisco, CA 94107
800-950-0523

Client/Server Computing
Sentry Publishing Company
1900 West Park Dr.
Westborough, MA 01581-
3907

Computer Design
Box 3466
Tulsa, OK 74101-3466

Computer Systems News
600 Community Dr.
Manhasset, NY 11030

Communications Week
P.O. Box 2070
Manhasset, NY 11030

Computer Reseller News
P.O. Box 2040
Manhasset, NY 11030

Computer Telephony
P.O. Box 40706
Nashville, TN 37204-9919
800-677-3435

*InfoText, Interactive Telephone
  Applications*
Advanstar Communications
P.O. Box 6490
Duluth, MN 55806-6490

Speech Technology Magazine
CI Publishing
43 Danbury Rd.
Wilton, CT 06897-9729
(203) 834-1430

InterActivity Media Magazine
P.O. Box 1174
Skokie, IL 60076-8174

Computer Products
P.O. Box 14000
Dover, NJ 07801-9990

Computer Tech. Review
924 Westwood Blvd. #65
Los Angeles, CA 90024

Communications News
2504 Tamiami Trail North
Nokomis, FL 34275
(813) 966-9521

Advanced Imaging
445 Broad Hollow Rd.
Melville, NY 11747-4722

Imaging Business
P.O. Box 5360
Pittsfield, MA 01203-9788

Advanced Imaging
445 Broad Hollow Rd.
Melville, NY 11747-4722

Micro Publishing News
21150 Hawthorne Blvd. #104
Torrance, CA 90503

California Business
P.O. Box 70735
Pasadena, CA 91117-9947

*Beyond Computing, An IBM
  Magazine*
1133 Westchester Ave.
White Plains, NY 10604

Software Magazine
Westborough Office Park
1900 West Park Dr.
Westborough, MA 01581-3907

Designfax
P.O. Box 1151
Skokie, IL 60076-9917

EE Product News
P.O. Box 12982
Overland Park, KS 66212

Electronics
P.O. Box 985061
Cleveland, OH 44198

Electronic Manufacturing
P.O. Box 159
Libertyville, IL 60048

Elect. Publish & Print
650 S. Clark St.
Chicago, IL 60605-9960

Federal Computer Week
P.O. Box 602
Winchester, MA 01890

Identification Journal
2640 N. Halsted St.
Chicago, IL 60614-9962

ID Systems
P.O. Box 874
Peterborough, NH 03458

Automatic I.D. News
P.O. Box 6158
Duluth, MN 55806-9870

Lan Times
122 East, 1700 South
Provo, UT 84606

Network World
161 Worcester Rd.
Framingham, MA 01701
(508) 875-6400

Lasers & Optronics
301 Gibraltar Dr
Morris Plains, NJ 07950

Electronic Design
P.O. Box 985007
Cleveland, OH 44198-5007

Machine Design
P.O. Box 985015
Cleveland, OH 44198-5015

Enterprise Systems Journal
P.O. Box 3051
Northbrook, IL 60065-3051

Manufacturing Systems
P.O. Box 3008
Wheaton, IL 60189-9972

Medical Equip. Designer
29100 Aurora Rd., #200
Cleveland, OH 44139

Mini-Micro Systems
P.O. Box 5051
Denver, CO 80217-9872

Modern Office Technology
1100 Superior Ave.
Cleveland, OH 44197-8032

Managing Office Technology
1100 Superior Ave.
Cleveland, OH 44197-8092

Office Systems
P.O. Box 3116
Woburn, MA 01888-9878

Office Systems Dealer
P.O. Box 2281
Woburn, MA 01888-9873

Photo Business
1515 Broadway
New York, NY 10036

Photo Lab Management
P.O. Box 1700
Santa Monica, CA 90406-1700

The Programmer's Shop
5 Pond Park Rd.
Hingham, MA 02043-9845

Quality
P.O. Box 3002
Wheaton, IL 60189-9929

Reseller Management
Box 601
Morris Plains, NJ 07950

Robotics World
6255 Barfield Rd.
Atlanta, GA 30328-9988

Scientific Computing
301 Gibraltar Dr.
Morris, Plains, NJ 07950

Surface Mount Technology
P.O. Box 159
Libertyville, IL 600048

CD-ROM News Extra
462 Danbury Road
Wilton, CT 06897-2126

Sun Expert
P.O. Box 5274
Pittsfield, MA 01203-9479

STACKS
P.O. Box 5031
Brentwood, TN 37024-5031

Telecommunications
P.O. Box 850949
Braintree, MA 02185

Mobile Office
Subscription Department
P.O. Box 57268
Boulder, CO 80323-7268

MrCDRom
MAXMEDIA DISTRIBUTING
 INC.
P.O. Box 1087
Winter Garden, FL 34787

*Document Management & Windows
 Imaging*
8711 E. Pinnacle Peak Road, #249
Scottsdale, Arizona 85255

NewMedia
P.O. Box 10639
Riverton, NJ 08076-0639

Component and Software Catalogs

Several companies publish special catalogs for components and software through direct mail. Even IBM has got into the act. You should be aware that most of these companies charge a bit more than those who advertise in the major magazines. But ads cost a lot of money so there usually isn't too much information about an advertised product in the major magazines. The direct-mail order companies usually have room in their catalogs to give a fairly good description and lots of information about the product. The catalogs are free. Here are just a few:

IBM PC Direct
800-426-2968

Power Up!
800-851-2917

KidSoft Software Catalog
800-354-6150

Software Spectrum
800-787-1166

Egghead Software
800-344-4323

ELEK-TEK
800-395-1000

DataCom Mall
800-898-3282

PC Mall
800-555-6255

Data Comm Warehouse
800-328-2261

Bull Express
800-343-6665

MEI/Micro Center
800-634-3478

PCs Compleat
800-385-4522

Digital PCs Catalog
800-642-4532

PrePress
11 Mt. Pleasant Ave.
East Hanover, NJ 07936-9925

Mr. CD-ROM
800-444-6723

CompuClassics
P.O. Box 10598
Canoga Park, CA 91309

Data Cal Corp.
800-842-2835

Processor
800-334-7443

United Video & Computer
800-448-3738

Software Labs
100 Corporate Pointe #195
Culver City, CA 90230-7616

Global DataCom
800-440-4832

Global Industrial Equipment
800-645-1232

System ID Warehouse
Barcode Catalog
800-397-9783

Pasternack Enterprises
P.O. 16759
Irvine, CA 92713

Paper Catalog
205 Chubb Ave.
Lyndhurst, NJ 07071

Compute Ability
P.O. Box 17882
Milwaukee, WI 53217

PC Connection
6 Mill Street
Marlow, NH 03456

Multimedia World
P.O. Box 58690
Boulder, CO 80323-8690

JDR Microdevices
2233 Samaritan Drive
San Jose, CA 95124

DAMARK
800-729-9000

Edutainment Catalog
(Mostly Kids Software)
800-338-3844

T2 Tech Squared
800-890-9375

Digi-key Corporation
701 Brooks Ave. South
P.O. Box 677
Thief River Falls, MN 56701-0677

Personal Computing Tools
90 Industrial Park Road
Hingham, MA 02043

Hello Direct (Telephone Products)
800-444-3556

Arlington Computer Products
800-548-5105

DTP Direct
800-890-9030

MicroWarehouse
1720 Oak Street
P.O. Box 3014
Lakewood NJ 08701-3014

TENEX Computer Express
56800 Magnetic Drive
Mishawaka, IN 46545

MOMENTUM GRAPHICS INC.
16290 Shoemaker
Cerritos, CA 90701-2243

Dell Network & Communications
800-509-3355

DellWare
800-449-3355

Image Club Graphics
800-387-9193

MAILER'S Software
970 Calle Negocio
San Clemente, CA 92673

Computers & Music
647 Mission St.
San Francisco, CA 94105

Global Computer Supplies
2318 East Del Amo Blvd. Dept. 64
Compton, CA 90220
800-845-6225

QUEBLO
1000 Florida Avenue
Hagerstown, Maryland 21741

One Network Place
4711 Golf Road
Skokie, IL 60076

Projections
P.O. Business Park Drive
Branford, CT 06405

Soundware
200 Menlo Oaks Drive
Melo Park, CA 94025

TigerSoftware
800-888-4437

Edmund Scientific Company
101 E. Gloucester Pike
Barrington, NJ 08007-1380

South Hills Datacom
760 Beechnut Drive
Pittsburgh, PA 15205

Tools for Exploration
4460 Redwood Highway, Suite 2
San Rafael, CA 4903

Presentations
Lakewood Building
50 South Ninth Street
Minneapolis, MN 55402-9973

UNIXREVIEW
P.O. Box 420035
Palm Coast, FL 32142-0035

Public Domain and Shareware Software

There are several companies who provide public domain shareware and low-cost software. They also publish catalogs listing their software. Some might charge a small fee for the catalog.

PC-Sig 1030D
800-245-6717

MicroCom Systems
(408) 737-9000

Public Brand Software
800-426-3475

Software Express/Direct
800-331-8192

Selective Software
800-423-3556

The Computer Room
(703) 832-3341

Softwarehouse
(408) 748-0461

PC Plus Consulting
(818) 891-7930

Micro Star
800-443-6103

International Software Library
800-992-1992

National PD Library
(619) 941-0925

Computers International
(619) 630-0055

Shareware Express
800-346-2842

PsL News
800-242-4775
(cost $24 year)

MMI Corporation
800-221-4283

Computer Discount
 Warehouse
800-330-4CDW

The PC Zone
800-258-2088

PrePress Direct
800-443-6600

Numeridex
800-323-7737

Industrial Computer Source
800-523-2320

J&R Computer World
800-221-8180

Jameco Electonic Components
(415) 592-8097

Zenith Data Systems
800-952-3099

Computer Books

There are several companies that publish computer books. One of the larger companies is McGraw-Hill, at 800-262-4729. Another good source for computer books is Osborne/McGraw-Hill, at 800-227-0900. Call them for a current catalog listing of the many books that they publish. You might also access and search the thousands of books at the McGraw-Hill online bookstore at www.mhcec.com. I admit that I am a bit prejudiced, but I recommend them highly.

CHAPTER 23

Troubleshooting and Repairing Your PC

This is one of the longest chapters in this book, but I must tell you that you might not be able to find the answer to your problems in this chapter. There are a thousand and one things that can go wrong in a computer, in both hardware and software. This chapter could be ten times as long and still not cover every possible problem. However, this chapter will cover most of the major problems that you might experience.

When speaking of troubleshooting, most people think of hardware problems. But I have had far more trouble with software problems than with hardware. Software problems might be even more difficult to solve than hardware problems.

Windows 95 can help solve some problems. When I built my 200MHz Pentium Pro, rather than buy all new components, I just upgraded my old 60MHz Pentium. I had two hard disks in the unit: a Maxtor 540Mb IDE and a 1.05Gb Seagate SCSI. When I attached all of the components to the Pentium Pro motherboard on the bench top, they all worked perfectly. But when I installed the components in the case and tried to boot up, the Windows 95 screen came up and froze. I rechecked all of my cable connections, made sure that the boards were seated, then tried again to boot up. Again, it got as far as the Windows 95 screen, then froze.

I turned off the power and this time pressed F8 as it was booting up. Out of the options that came up, I chose number 5, step-by-step confirmation. This displays each line of the Config.sys and asks whether you want to load it or not. When it got to the line that loaded my SCSI driver, the system hung up again. So I knew that it must be either my Toshiba CD-ROM or my Seagate hard drive. I disconnected them both and the system booted perfectly. I then reconnected the CD-ROM and it booted perfectly. I then switched the connector from the CD-ROM to the hard disk and it hung again. So evidently, something happened to the hard disk during the time I disconnected it on the bench and installed it in the case.

Of course I was disappointed. I had paid over $700 for this SCSI drive a couple of years ago. I wasn't too concerned about the data on the drive because I had it all backed up on the Maxtor IDE drive. That is the beauty of having at least two large hard drives.

I called the Seagate customer service center, at 800-468-3472 and was pleasantly surprised to learn that I had a five-year guarantee on this drive. All I had to do was send it in and they would either repair or replace it. A couple of weeks later, they sent me a new drive. Of course, because it was a different drive, none of my data was on it. There was no note or indication as to what the problem was.

Finding the cause of the problem is the first step in fixing it. There are several hardware and software diagnostic tools available that can help you find and fix problems. A few of them are discussed here.

Computer Basics

Troubleshooting is a little easier if you know just a little of the electronic basics. Computers are possible because of electricity. Under the control of software and hardware, small electric on/off signal voltages are formed when we type from the keyboard or when data is read from a disk or other means of input. This voltage is used to turn transistors on and off to perform various tasks.

An electric charge is formed when there is an imbalance or an excess amount of electrons at one pole. The excess electrons will flow through whatever path they can find to get to the other pole. It is much like water flowing downhill to find its level.

Most electric or electronic paths have varying amounts of resistance so that work or heat is created when the electrons pass through them. For instance, if a flashlight is turned on, electrons will pass through the bulb, which has a resistive filament. The heat generated by the electrons passing through the bulb will cause the filament to glow red hot and create light. If the light is left on for a period of time, the excess electrons from the negative pole of the battery will pass through the bulb to the positive pole of the battery. Electrons will continue to flow until the amount of electrons at the negative and positive poles are equal. At this time there will be a perfect balance and the battery will be dead.

A computer is made up of circuits and boards that have resistors, capacitors, inductors, transistors, motors, and many other components. These components perform a useful function when electricity passes through them. The circuits are designed so that the paths of the electric currents are divided, controlled, and shunted to do the work that we want done. The transistors and other components can force the electrons to go to the memory, to a disk drive, to the printer, or wherever the software and hardware directs it to go.

If an electronic circuit is designed properly, it should last several life times. Unlike an electron tube that has filaments that burn out, there is nothing in a semiconductor or transistor to wear out. But occasionally, too many electrons might find their way through a weakened component and cause it to heat up and burn out. Or for some reason the electrons might be shunted through a path or component where it shouldn't go. This might cause an intermittent, a partial, or a complete failure.

Electrostatic Voltage

Before you touch any electronic component or handle them, you should ground yourself and discharge any electrostatic voltage that might have built up on your body. It is possible for a person to build up a charge of 4000 volts or more of electrostatic voltage. If you walk across a carpet and then touch a brass door knob, you might see a spark fly and get a painful shock. If you should touch a fragile electronic component, this high voltage can be discharged through the component. It might weaken the component or possibly ruin it. Workers on most electronic assembly lines have to wear a ground strap whenever they are working with any electrostatic discharge sensitive components. You can discharge yourself by touching an unpainted metal part of the case of a computer or other device that is plugged into a wall socket. The computer or other grounding device does not have to be turned on in order to discharge yourself.

Document the Problem

Chances are, if a computer is going to break down, it will do so at the most inopportune time. This is one of the basic tenets of Murphy's immutable and inflexible laws.

If it breaks down, try not to panic. Ranting, cussing, and crying might make you feel better but these reactions will not solve the problem. Instead get out a pad and pencil and write down everything as it happens. It is very easy to forget. Write down all the particulars, how the cables were plugged in, the software that was running, and anything that might be pertinent. You might get error messages on your screen. Use the PrtSc (for Print Screen) key to print out the messages if possible.

If you can't solve the problem, you might have to call someone for help. If you have all the written information before you, it will help. Try to call from your computer, if possible, while it is acting up. If it is a software problem, have your serial number handy. Most organizations ask for that before anything else.

Instruments and Tools

For high levels of troubleshooting, you need some sophisticated tools and expensive instruments to do a thorough analysis of a system. You need a good high-frequency oscilloscope, a digital analyzer, a logic probe, and several other expensive pieces of gear. You also need a test bench with a spare power supply, spare disk drives, and plug-in boards.

It would be very helpful to have a diagnostic card, such as the POST-PROBE or the Ultra-X, and several of the diagnostic and utility software programs such as those discussed later in this chapter.

It would be helpful to have a known good computer with some empty slots so that you could plug in suspect boards and test them. You would also need a voltohmmeter, some clip leads, a pair of side cutter dikes, a pair of long-nose pliers, various screwdrivers, nut drivers, a soldering iron, and solder.

You need a good work bench with plenty of light over the bench and a flashlight or a small light to light up the dark places in the computer case.

Besides the expensive tools and instruments needed for high-level troubleshooting and repair, you need quite a lot of training and experience.

Fortunately, we don't need the expensive and sophisticated tools and instruments for most of our computer problems. Just a few simple tools and a little common sense is all that is needed for the majority of the problems. Here are some tools that you should have around. It is good to have these tools even if you never have a computer problem:

- You should have a pad and pen near your computer so that you can write down all of the things that happen if you have a problem.

- You should have several sizes and types of screwdrivers. A couple of them should be magnetic for picking up and starting small screws. You can buy magnetic screwdrivers, or you can make one yourself. Just take a strong magnet and rub it on the blade of the screwdriver a few times. The magnets on cabinet doors will do, or the voice coil magnet of a loud speaker. Be very careful with any magnet around your floppy diskettes. It can erase them.

■ You should also have a small screwdriver with a bent tip that can be used to pry up ICs. Some of the larger ICs are very difficult to remove. One of the blank fillers for the slots on the back panel of the computer also makes a good prying tool.

■ You should have a couple pairs of pliers. You should have at least one pair of long-nose pliers.

■ You should have a set of nutdrivers. Many of the screws have slotted heads for screwdrivers as well as hexagonal heads for nutdrivers. Using a nutdriver is usually much easier to use than a screwdriver.

■ You might need a pair of side cutter dikes for clipping leads of components and cutting wire. You might buy a pair of cutters that also have wire strippers.

■ By all means, buy a voltohmmeter. There are dozens of uses for a voltohmmeter. They can be used to check for the wiring continuity in your cables, phone lines, switches, etc. You can also use a voltohmmeter to check for the proper voltages in your computer. There are only two voltages to check for: 12 volts and 5 volts. The newer CPUs may require 2.5 to 3.3 volts, but usually have a voltage regulator on the motherboard or on the CPU socket that reduces the 5-volt supply to the required voltage. You can buy a relatively inexpensive voltohmmeter at any of the electronic stores.

■ You need a soldering iron and some solder. You shouldn't have to do much soldering, but you never know when you might need to repair a cable or some other minor job.

■ You should also have several clip leads. Clip leads are insulated wires with alligator clips on each end. You can use them to extend a cable or for shorting out two pins or hundreds of other uses. You can buy them at a local electronics store.

■ You need a flashlight for looking into the dark places inside the computer or at the cable connections behind the computer.

The chances are very slim that you will ever need these tools unless you are in the repair business. Even then there will be very few times when you will have to use some of them, especially if you are working on a Pentium Pro system. Still it is nice to have them available if you ever do need them.

Solving Common Problems

For many of the common problems you won't need a lot of test gear. Often a problem can be solved by using our five senses: eyes, ears, nose, touch, and taste. (Actually we won't be using our taste very often.)

- Eyes: Look closely, you might see a cable that is not plugged in properly, or a board that is not completely seated, or a switch or jumper that is not set properly. You might see other obvious things such as smoke.

- Ears: Listen for any unusual sounds. Ordinarily, those little electrons don't make any noise as they move through your computer at about two-thirds the speed of light. The only sound from your computer should be the noise of your drive motors and the fan in the power supply.

- Smell: If you ever smell a burned resistor or a capacitor, you will never forget it. If you smell something very unusual, try to locate where it is coming from.

- Touch: If you touch the components and some seem to be unusually hot, it could be the cause of your problem. Except for the insides of your power supply, there should not be any voltage above 12 volts in your computer, so it should be safe to touch the components, even when the power is on. Before touching a component, be sure that you have discharged yourself of any electrostatic voltage.

The Number One Cause of Problems

If you have added something to your computer or done some sort of repair and the computer doesn't work, something might not have been plugged in correctly or some minor error was made in the installation. If you have added a component, remove it to see if the computer works without it. Never install more than one item at a time. Install an item, then check to see if it works, then install the next one.

By far the greatest problem in assembling a unit, adding something to a computer, or installing software, is not following the instructions. Quite often it is not necessarily the fault of the person trying to follow the instructions. I am a member of Mensa, and have worked in the electronic industry for over 30 years. But sometimes I have great diffi-culty in trying to decipher and follow the instructions in some manu-als. Sometimes a very critical instruction, or piece of information, might be inconspicuously buried in the middle of a 500-page manual.

The Importance of Documentation

You should have some sort of documentation or manuals for all of your computer components and peripherals. You should have a written record of the switch and jumper settings of each of your boards. It is also very important that you have the drive type and the CMOS infor-mation of your hard disk drives written down with your records or on a special floppy disk. If for some reason your system fails, you might not be able to access your hard drive and its data if you don't know the drive type listed in your CMOS configuration. You should know what com-ponents are inside your computer and how they are configured. The plug-n-play components now make it a lot easier, but there are still a lot of items that do not conform to the PnP specifications.

Nortons Utilities lets you make a Rescue disk that has a copy of your CMOS, boot record, partition tables, autoexec.bat and config.sys. This disk is bootable, so it can be used any time that you might lose your CMOS or any of the other vital information. PC Tools alsos let you make an emergency disk similar to the Norton Rescue disk.

What to Do if It is Completely Dead

There are several software diagnostic programs. They are great in many cases, but if the computer is completely dead, the software won't do you any good. If it is completely dead, the first thing to do is to check the power outlet. If you don't have a voltmeter, plug a lamp into the same socket and see if it lights. Check your power cord. Check the switch on the computer. Check the fan in the power supply. Is it turning? The power supply is one of the major components that frequently becomes defective. If the fan is not turning, the power supply might be defective. However, the fan might be operating even though the power supply is defective. Does any of the panel lights come on when you try to boot up? Does the hard disk motor spin up?

If there is a short anywhere in the system, the power supply will not come on. The fan won't turn and none of the drives will come on. The power supply has built-in short circuit protection which shuts everything down when the output is shorted. The power supply has four or more cables for the various drives. Unplug the drives one at a time and try the system. If the system works after a drive is unplugged, then you have found the problem. (I hate to say this, but I am pretty sure that one of Murphy's laws dictates that a problem will never be this easy to solve.)

If a SIMM or memory chip is not completely seated, the computer might not boot up. You might not get any kind of error message or warning.

You can check any of the cables from the power supply with a voltohmmeter. The power supply will not work unless it has a load, so have at least one disk drive plugged in. There should be +12 V between the yellow and black wires and +5 V between the red and black. If there is no voltage, then you probably have a defective power supply.

If you hear the fan motor and the panel lights come on, but the monitor is dark, check the monitor's power cord, the adapter cable, and the adapter. The monitor also has fuses, but they are usually inside the monitor case. Check the documentation that came with your monitor. You should also check the monitor's brightness and contrast controls. If you have just installed the monitor, check the motherboard or adapter for any switches or jumpers that should be set. Check the documentation of your adapter board. You should also check your CMOS setup to make sure that the BIOS knows what type of monitor you have.

Remove all of the boards except for the monitor adapter and disk controller. Also disconnect all peripherals. If the system works, then add the boards back until it stops. Be sure to turn off the power each time you add or remove a board or any cable. If you have spare boards, swap them with suspected boards in your system.

Config.sys and Autoexec.bat

In the DOS era, you could see your autoexec.bat working during boot-up. In Windows 95 it is now usually hidden, but it is still working just as it did before. If you have just added a new piece of software and your system doesn't work or it doesn't work the way it should, check your autoexec.bat and config.sys files. Many programs change these files as they are being installed. These files might have commands and statements that conflict with your new software or system. I try out a lot of different software and systems. I have had problems where a statement or command was left in the autoexec.bat or config.sys file from a system no longer being used. It might ask the computer to perform a command that is not there. It will go off in never-never land and keep trying to find the command or file. You will usually have to reboot to get out.

You might get an error message that says, "Unrecognized command in config.sys." It might then have an additional message: "Bad or missing file, driver, or path." You could have a misspelled word in the config.sys file, or you might have left out a back slash or forward slash. It is quite easy to type in the wrong slash such as a / instead of a \. The structure of the config.sys is rather strict and doesn't provide much room for error.

You can use the EDIT command to change, add to, or delete portions of your autoexec.bat or config.sys files. Whenever you make a change to them, always keep the old one as a backup. You can rename them with the DOS REN command. You can call the old files, config.old, autoexec.1, or whatever. If your new autoexec.bat or config.sys doesn't work, you can always rename the old files back to their original names.

If you have a long autoexec.bat file that doesn't work, you might try editing out parts of it, then reboot and retry it. (Use the DOS EDIT command which uses ASCII text. Don't use a word processor because it adds symbols and characters that will confuse the system.) You can temporarily change lines in your autoexec.bat or config.sys files by adding a REM (for REMARK) at the beginning of a line that you don't want to be executed.

By pressing F8 while booting up, DOS 6.2, PC-DOS 7.0, and Windows 95 will let you look at each line of the autoexec.bat and config.sys file and ask if you want to load it, yes or no. If you say no to a certain line, and the system then works, you have found the problem. You can then use the EDIT command and put a REM in front of the offending line in your autoexec.bat or config.sys file.

You should always have a "clean" boot disk that has a very lean autoexec.bat and config.sys on it. There might be times when you don't want any TSRs or anything in your 640K in order to run a special program. If you have a lot of TSRs or other things in your 640K of memory, you might not be able to run some programs. Use the DOS MEMMAKER or the IBM PC-DOS 7.0 RAMBOOST program to create more free memory.

Clearing TSRs from Memory

Windows 95 often loads lots of things in memory and you might not even know it. Quite often when you install a new program, it sets itself so that it will be loaded automatically in memory. Sometimes the name of the program or its icon is displayed on the bar at the bottom of the screen. To see what programs are loaded in your memory, press the CTRL-ALT-DEL keys. A list of anything loaded in memory will be displayed. Use the arrow keys or mouse to highlight anything that you don't want to be loaded, then press the enter or return key and it will be deleted from memory.

The Microsoft Explorer is always loaded. You cannot delete it; if you do the system will shut down.

Drive C:

Every program that you install on your computer will try to load on drive C:. That is the default built into most software. Often you are given the option to install the program on another drive, but a newbie might not realize this. (A newbie is someone new to computers, to the Internet or almost anything new. It is not meant as a putdown.) If you allow the programs to load on C:, it will soon be completely filled.

If you install Windows 95 on your C: drive, it will take up about 80Mb, but it doesn't stop there. Every time you load in a new program, even on another drive or in another directory, a large amount of Windows control data is added to the Windows 95 directory. It is much like the old story about the Arab and his camel. It was a cold night on the desert, but the Arab was nice and warm in his tent. The camel asked his master if he could just put his nose in the tent. The master agreed. But then the camel complained that his head was cold, and could he please put his head in the tent. Again the master agreed. The camel kept it up and soon his entire body was in the tent and the master was outside.

I have a scan program that will not run unless I have at least 10Mb of free space on my C: drive. There are times when Netscape will not let me access some Web sites because I do not have enough free space on one of my computer's C: drive.

When you set up and format a new drive, make sure that you have a large C: drive. If you have a hard drive of 1Gb or more, I would recommend a C: drive of 500Mb.

If your system is already set up and you are running out of free space, you can try to copy some of the programs to another drive or directory. It will work best if you are able then to uninstall the program and reinstall it. Many of the later programs now come with the uninstall feature. The uninstall clears out all of the hidden portions of the program that is intertwined with Windows 95. Not many of the older programs had the uninstall feature.

Beep Error Codes

Every time a computer is turned on, or booted up, it does a power on self test (POST). It checks the RAM, the floppy drives, the hard disk drives, the monitor, the printer, the keyboard, and other peripherals that you have installed. If everything is okay, it gives a short beep then boots up.

If it does not find a unit, or if the unit is not functioning correctly, it will beep and display an error code. It might beep two or more times depending on the error. If the power supply, the motherboard, the CPU, or possibly some other critical IC is defective it might not beep at all.

You can check the beep system by holding a key down while the system is booting up. You might hear a continuous beep. After the boot is complete, the system might give two short beeps and display the message, "Keyboard error. Press F1 to continue."

There are several other beep error codes that are in the system BIOS. Each BIOS manufacturer uses slightly different codes for some of the errors it finds. Some of the beep codes are for fatal errors that cause the system to hang up completely. The beeps are arranged so that you might get a beep, a pause, another beep, then three beeps close together or 1-1-3. This code would indicate that there was a failure in the CMOS setup system. One long and two short beeps, accompanied by a POST code of 400, 500, 2400, or 7400, could mean that there is an error in the CMOS RAM, a motherboard switch setting, or defective video card. A 1-1-4 would indicate that there was an error in the BIOS itself. A continuous beep or repeating short beeps could indicate that the power supply or the motherboard had a fault.

Here are some of the AMI BIOS fatal error beep POST codes:

- 1 short   DRAM refresh failure.
- 2 short   Parity circuit failure.
- 3 short   Base 64K RAM failure.

- 4 short   System timer failure.
- 5 short   Processor failure.
- 6 short   Keyboard controller Gate A20 error.
- 7 short   Virtual mode exception error.
- 8 short   Display memory read/write test failure.
- 9 short   ROM BIOS checksum failure.
- 10 short   CMOS shutdown read/write error.
- 11 short   Cache memory error.

Here are a couple of nonfatal error beep POST codes:

- 1 long, 3 short   Conventional or extended memory failure.
- 1 long, 8 short   Display/retrace test failed.

Displayed POST Codes

Besides the beep POST codes, there are hundreds of POST codes that might be displayed. The POST codes start with 100 and go up to as high as 200,000. This does not mean that there are actually 200,000 separate codes. Most of the BIOS designers arrange the codes in blocks. For instance, the 100s have to do with the motherboard errors; 200s are RAM errors; 300s are keyboard errors; and 600s are floppy drive errors. Many of the code numbers were designed for systems that are now obsolete such as the 286 and PS/2. Ordinarily the codes will not be displayed if there is no problem. If there is a problem, the last two digits of the code will be something other than 00s. Each BIOS manufacturer develops their own codes so there are some slight differences, but most of them are similar to the following:

- 101 Motherboard failure.
- 109 Direct memory access test error.
- 121 Unexpected hardware interrupt occurred.
- 163 Time and date not set.
- 199 User indicated configuration not correct.
- 201 Memory test failure.
- 301 Keyboard test failure or a stuck key.
- 401 Monochrome display and/or adapter test failure.

- 432 Parallel printer not turned on.

- 501 Color graphics display and/or adapter test failure.

- 601 Diskette drives and/or adapter test failure.

- 701 Math coprocessor test error.

- 901 Parallel printer adapter test failure.

- 1101 Asynchronous communications adapter test failure.

- 1301 Game control adapter test failure.

- 1302 Joystick test failure.

- 1401 Printer test failure.

- 1701 Fixed disk drive and/or adapter test failure.

- 2401 Enhanced graphics display and/or adapter test failure.

- 2501 Enhanced graphics display and/or adapter test failure.

POST Cards

Several companies have developed diagnostic cards or boards that can be plugged into a slot on the motherboard to display the POST codes. If there is a failure in the system, it tells you immediately what is wrong.

If you have eliminated the possibility of a defective plug-in board or a peripheral, then the problem is probably in your motherboard. If the power supply is okay, you could use a diagnostic card, such as the POST-PROBE from Micro 2000, at (818) 547-0125, the R.A.C.E.R. II from Ultra-X, at 800-722-3789, or the RACER II from Microdata, at 800-539-0123. These three cards are quite similar in the tests that they perform. They can be plugged into a computer that is completely dead except for the power supply, and they will check every chip and component on the mother-board. Each card has a small digital display that lights up a code for the condition of each component. These cards work on any ISA or EISA machine, XT, 286, 386, 486, or Pentium.

R.A.C.E.R. is an acronym for Real-time AT/XT Computer Equipment Repair. There are several other POST cards on the market, but some of them are not very sophisticated. The Ultra-X R.A.C.E.R. II has several ROMs that can run over 70 diagnostic tests. Besides displaying the test codes on the plug-in board, the progress of the tests can be displayed on a monitor. If there is a failure in one of the tests, a fault tree will be displayed that lists in order which chips might be at fault. In a computer where several chips interact, it is often difficult to determine exactly which chip might be at fault. The Ultra-X can narrow it down to a very few. At the end of the test, a report can be printed out.

Businesses can lose a lot of money when a computer is down. These diagnostic cards are tools that every professional repair shop and every computer maintenance department should have. It might also be well worth the money for an individual to buy one. If you have to take your computer to a repair shop, at $50 to $100 an hour, the repair could be rather expensive. You will also have to give up some of your time and some trouble just to take the computer in to the shop. If the shop is busy, it might be some time before you get your computer back.

Diagnostic and Utility Software

There are several excellent diagnostic software programs available. Some of the utilities and tests are quite similar in some of the programs. Most of them test and report on your system configuration and your system memory. Many of them do a test on your hard drives. Some of them, such as SpinRite and Disk Technician, are primarily designed for hard disk tests and preventive maintenance.

Most BIOS chips have many diagnostic routines and other utilities built in. These routines allow you to set the time and date, tell the computer what type of hard drive and floppies that are installed, the amount of memory, the wait states, and several other functions. The AMI and DTK BIOS chips have a very comprehensive set of built-in diagnostics. They can allow hard and floppy disk formatting, check speed of rotation of disk drives, do performance testing of hard drives, and several other tests.

MSD Command

If you own a copy of MS-DOS 6.0 or later, you have a MSD (Microsoft Diagnostics) command. This utility can be used to search for files or subjects, and it also gives you a wealth of information about your computer. It can show you the IRQs, the memory usage, your autoexec.bat and config.sys, and many other useful bits of information. You can view the information or have it printed out. Depending on what you have in your computer, it might take up to 20 pages to print it all out.

Norton Utilities

Norton Utilities, from Symantec Corp. at (408) 253-9600, www. symantec.com, includes several diagnostic and test programs and essential utilities. One of the programs is Norton Diagnostics (NDIAGS). This tests the memory, the CPU, the DMA controllers, the real time clock, performs CMOS tests, and tests the serial and parallel ports.

Software cannot recognize and test the serial and parallel ports unless you have a loopback plug installed. These are 9- and 25-pin connectors that plug into the serial and parallel sockets. Some of the pins in these connectors are shorted out so that the software can recognize them. Figure 23-1 shows some loopback plugs for checking serial and parallel ports. A couple of them are shown with the cover removed so that you can see the wire that shorts out a set of pins.

Norton Utilities has all of the standard utilities, most of which are periodically updated and improved with new releases. Some of the standard utilities are Unerase, Disk Doctor, Disk Test, Format Recover, Directory Sort, System Information, and many others.

Fig. 23-1

Some loopback plugs for checking serial and parallel ports.

MicroScope

MicroScope, from Micro 2000 at (818) 547-0125, www.micro2000.com, is an excellent diagnostic software tool. It can test the CPU, IRQs, DMAs, memory, hard disk drives, floppy drives, video adapters, and much more. It can search for Network cards and display its I/O and node address. It shows IRQ and I/O addresses. It tests memory and displays available memory space. It displays CMOS contents and will let you run CMOS setup. It can run video tests for memory and character sets. It can do a read, write, and random seek test of the hard drives. It even allows you to edit sectors of the hard drive. It can be set up to run any or all of the tests continuously. It can be set to halt on an error or to log the error and continue.

QAPlus/FE

QAPlus/FE from DiagSoft, at (408) 438-8247, www.diagsoft.com, is a very sophisticated software program. Among its many functions is the ability to diagnose problems on the disk systems, memory, video, IDE and SCSI drives and interfaces, interrupts, BIOS, and serial and parallel ports. In order to test the serial and parallel ports you need loopback plugs. The loopback plugs come free with QAPlus/FE diagnostic software.

If a semiconductor or system is going to fail, it will usually do so within the first 72 hours of use. Many vendors do a burn-in on their products to find any such systems before they are shipped. But many vendors might not have the time or the software to properly exercise the units. The QAPlus/FE can perform rigorous and continuous tests on systems for burn-in. If you buy an expensive system or component, it might be well worth the cost of buying a copy of QAPlus/FE just for the burn-in capability. If you find a defective component early, it can usually be sent back to the dealer or replaced at no cost.

WINCheckIt and CheckIt PRO:Analyst

WINCheckIt from TouchStone, at 800-531-0450, www.checkit.com, was discussed in Chapter 19 as an essential piece of utility software. It is also very useful as an essential piece of diagnostic software. Touch-Stone has been developing diagnostic and utility software for some time. Their first product, CheckIt, was developed several years ago. They then improved it and called it CheckIt PRO. They improved it again, added several new features, and called it CheckIt PRO: Analyst for Windows. It is a comprehensive analysis tool that can be used by ordinary personnel as well as advanced users. It can collect configuration and performance data, test hardware integrity, evaluate a system to compare performance with other systems, determine upgrade needs, and assess compatibility of hardware and software.

They are constantly improving their products and should have a new one on the market by the time you read this. Call them for the latest.

The Troubleshooter

The Troubleshooter from AllMicro, at 800-653-4933, www.allmicro.com, has its own self-booting operating system that bypasses DOS. It can test the motherboard, run memory tests, test the hard disks and floppy disk drives, check and test the serial and parallel ports, test the video adapter, keyboard, and mouse. It can identify the system hardware and print out a report. It is a good low-cost software tool.

WinSleuth Gold Plus

WinSleuth Gold Plus from Dariana Software, at (714) 236-1380, is another good low-cost diagnostic software tool. They have a BBS number for technical support. WinSleuth Gold Plus can check hardware configuration, give you BIOS information, check CMOS settings, perform CPU tests, keyboard tests, and many more tests. It is a very good tool to have in your library.

WINProbe

WINProbe is now a part of the Quarterdeck Company, at 800-683-6696, www.qdeck.com. The PC Certify program that comes with WINProbe can save a lot of time and trouble. PC Certify can also be used to test all types of hard drives, floppy drives, and the controllers.

Besides the drives, PC Certify does complete diagnostic tests on the whole computer. It tests the memory, the serial and parallel ports, the BIOS, the video adapter, the monitor, keyboard, and printer. The tests can be run continuously for as many times as you desire. These tests are ideal for burning in a computer. The PC Certify program will even print out a form for a technician to fill out. The form shows what tests were run and has a space for the technician to verify and sign.

The WINProbe portion also has the following diagnostic utilities: Audio for sound tests, Communications for serial ports, Floppy Drive RPM test, Floppy Drive Surface Analysis, Hard Drive Surface Analysis, Keyboard tests, Math Coprocessor, Motherboard CPU function tests, Mouse driver tests, Printer cable test, RAM chip test, and Video mode tests.

FIXIT

FIXIT is another diagnostic and repair tool from Quarterdeck. It detects and repairs potential conflicts before you install new software. It also has a list of over 1700 hardware and software companies, which includes the phone numbers and URL addresses. If you can't fix it yourself, maybe you can find someone who can.

First Aid for Windows Users and PC 911

First Aid for Windows Users from CyberMedia, at 800-721-7824, is a low-cost program that can spot problems, diagnose them, and then fix most of them automatically. For those it can't fix automatically, it can help you fix them manually. It fixes problems with printing, multimedia, bad INI files, Path problems, missing application components, network problems, and many others. The software is optimized for several of the well known brand name programs, such as Microsoft Office, Word, Excel, Corel Draw, Quicken, Paradox, and many others. In addition, they offer free upgrades to the program that can be downloaded from Compuserve.

PC 911 is a low-cost companion program to First Aid for Windows from CyberMedia. PC 911 keeps track of all changes made to your PC's set-up files. Several times in the past, I have installed programs that automatically changed my autoexec.bat and config.sys files so that my system would no longer operate. Recently, a program changed my files so that I was not able to use my word processors. It took me a couple of hours to find the problem. PC 911 could have saved me that time. PC 911 can also help you with conflicts in IRQs, DMAs, and other problems when installing multimedia and other cards.

First Aid and PC 911 can be bought separately or you can save about one-third by buying them as a bundle. They have several other good diagnostic programs and they offer frequent upgrades. Call them for the latest.

Which One Should You Buy

If I could only afford one program, I would be hard pressed to choose one. They are all good tools. Many of them have a few similar utilities, but there are also different utility features in every one of them. I can't possibly list all of the features of the products here. I suggest that you call each company and ask for literature on their products.

I can't even list all of the diagnostic products that are available. New ones are being developed daily. Check computer magazines for ads and reviews.

Spares

One of the easiest ways to check a part is to have a good spare handy. If you suspect a board, it is very easy to plug in a known good one. If your computer is critical to your business and you cannot afford any downtime, then you should have a few spares handy. I would suggest that you have a spare floppy disk drive, a monitor adapter, and a spare keyboard. These items are all fairly inexpensive. Depending on how critical your business is and how important your computer is to it, you might even want to have spares of all your components, such as a motherboard, power supply, and all of your plug-in boards.

You might have some very expensive video adapters, PCI bus interfaces, or other boards that might cost hundreds of dollars. But there are usually some equivalent, inexpensive boards for all of the boards in your system. For instance, a good PCI IDE interface with caching might cost from $150 to $200 or more. You can buy a simple ISA IDE interface for less than $10. A good PCI graphics, high-resolution monitor adapter might cost as much as $500, but you can buy an ISA adapter that doesn't have all of the goodies for about $30. A low-cost board can help pinpoint the problem. If your monitor doesn't light up but it works with a replacement adapter, then you know the probable cause of the problem.

DOS Error Messages

Even with Windows 95, you will still have DOS running in the background for many programs. DOS has several error messages that display when you try to make the computer do something it can't do. But many of the messages are not very clear. Don't bother looking in the MS DOS manual for error messages, they are not there. If you are using the IBM PC-DOS and you get an error message, just type help n, where n is the first letter of the error message, and an explanation will pop up.

I have dozens of books on DOS, but few of them make any reference to the DOS error messages. One of the better books I have is *DOS, The New Complete Reference* by Kris Jamsa, published by Osborne-McGraw-Hill, at 800-227-0900. Another of his books, *DOS Secrets, Solutions, Shortcuts,* explains the DOS commands in great detail along with the DOS error commands and what to do about them. These reference books should be in your library.

Some Common DOS Error Messages

Here are a few messages you might come across.

Access Denied

You might have tried to write on or erase a file that was protected. The file might have been hidden or protected by an Attribute command. Use the Attribute command to change it.

Bad Command or File Name or File Not Found

You might have made a mistake in typing in the command, or the command or file does not reside in the current directory.

CHKDSK Errors

You should run CHKDSK often. Some people put CHKDSK/F in their autoexec.bat so that it is run every time the system is booted up. (Disk Technician can do it for you.) The CHKDSK might give you an error that says nnn lost clusters found in n chains. Convert lost chains to files Y/N. Reinvoke CHKDSK with the /F (for fix) and the lost clusters will be converted to FILE000n.CHK. These are usually incomplete files. When you delete a file, sometimes portions of it might be left in a sector. Or something might have caused an error in the FAT and caused portions of two different files to be written in a single sector or cluster. The files created by CHKDSK/F are usually incomplete. In most cases they can be deleted. MS-DOS 6.22 and Windows 95 still have CHKDSK, but they also have ScanDisk, which does a better job than CHKDSK.

General Failure Reading or Writing Drive n:, Abort, Retry, Fail

The disk might not be formatted. It is also possible that track 0 on the disk, which stores the FAT, has become defective. It might be possible to restore the disk by using Norton's Disk Doctor (NDD) file on it.

Invalid Directory

If you do a CD (Change Directory) from the root directory, all you have to type is cd norton, or any directory you want to change to and it will change immediately. If you happen to be in the WordPerfect directory and you type cd norton, it will say that it is an invalid directory. If you are in any directory except the root directory, you have to type cd\norton, or whatever directory. If you type cd/norton, using the forward slash instead of the back slash, you will get the same error message.

Non-system Disk or Disk Error. Replace and Strike Any Key when Ready

You have a nonbootable disk in drive A:.

Not Ready Error Reading Drive A. Abort, Retry, Fail

You might have asked the computer to go to drive A: and it was not ready or there was no disk in the drive.

Software Error Messages

Most software packages have their own error messages. In many cases, the manual will not tell you what the error message means. You will probably have to call the software company to get an answer.

Glitches

There are times when something might go wrong for no apparent reason and the computer might hang up. Glitches can happen when you are running almost any kind of program. Sometimes you can get out of them with a warm boot (pressing Ctrl, Alt, Del). Other times you might have to turn off the computer, wait a few seconds, then turn it back on.

You should remember that anything that you are working on is in memory. If you are working on a file that is on your disk, then you still have a copy on the disk; however, if it is something that you have just typed in, when you turn off the computer or reboot, anything in memory is gone forever. It is a good idea to save your data to disk every so often while you are working on it. By all means try to save your work before rebooting, but quite often if the computer hangs up, there is nothing you can do except to grit your teeth and reboot.

Power Supply

The power supply is one of the most frequent causes of problems. Most of the components in your computer are fairly low power and low voltage. The only high voltage in your system is in the power supply, and it is pretty well enclosed. So there is no danger of shock if you open your computer and put your hand inside it. But you should **never** connect or disconnect a board or cable while the power is on. Fragile semiconductors can be destroyed if you do so.

Semiconductors have no moving parts. If the circuits were designed properly, the semiconductors should last indefinitely. Heat is an enemy and can cause semiconductor failure. The fan in the power supply should provide adequate cooling. All of the openings on the back panel that correspond to the slots on the motherboard should have blank fillers. Even the holes on the bottom of the chassis should be covered with tape. This forces the fan to draw air in from the front of the computer, pull it over the boards, and exhaust it through the opening in the power supply case. Nothing should be placed in front of or behind the computer that would restrict air flow.

If you don't hear the fan when you turn on a computer, or if the fan isn't running, then the power supply could be defective. Table 23-1 lists the pin connections and wire colors from the power supply:

The eight-bit slotted connectors on the motherboard have 62 contacts, 31 on the A side and 31 on the B side. The black ground wires connect to B1 of each of the eight slots. B3 and B29 have +5 Vdc, B5 has –5 Vdc, B7 has –12 Vdc, and B9 has +12 Vdc. These voltages go to the listed pins on each of the eight plug-in slots.

Most of the other contacts on the plug-in slots are for address lines and data input/output lines. They are not often involved in problems.

Intermittent Problems

Intermittent problems can be most frustrating and maddening. They can be very difficult to find. If you suspect a cable or a connector, try wiggling it to see if it goes away or gets worse. I once spent several hours trying to find the cause of a floppy disk problem. It turned out to be a loose wire in the connector. It was just barely touching the contact. A slight vibration could cause the disk drive to become erratic. A wire or cable can be broken and still make contact until it is moved.

You might also try unplugging a cable or a board and plugging it back in. Sometimes the pins might be slightly corroded or not seated properly. Recently I turned on one of my computers that hadn't been used for about a month. I got a message that the FDC (floppy disk controller) had an error. This board also controls my hard disks so I was a

TABLE 23-1

Power supply
connections

Disk Drive Power Supply Connections		
Pin	Color	Function
1	Yellow	+12 Vdc
2	Black	Ground
3	Black	Ground

Power Supply Connections to the Motherboard		
P8 Pin	Color	Function
1	White	Power good
2	No connection	
3	Yellow	+12 Vdc
4	Brown	-12 Vdc
5	Black	Ground
6	Black	Ground

P9 Pin	Color	Function
1	Black	Ground
2	Black	Ground
3	Blue	-5 Vdc
4	Red	+5 Vdc
5	Red	+5 Vdc
6	Red	+5 Vdc

bit concerned. I unplugged the controller board and cleaned the contacts and plugged it back in. (The copper contacts on a plug-in board might become corroded. You can clean them with an ordinary pencil eraser.) But I still got the FDC error message.

I got out another FDC and prepared to plug it in, but I had to change the setting of a shorting bar on the controller board. On a hunch, I slipped the shorting bar on and off my original controller a few times, then tried the board again. The floppy drives worked perfectly. The shorting bar on the jumper pins had become corroded during the time it was not used.

The contacts of the edge connectors on floppy drives and plug-in boards can also become corroded. Sometimes just unplugging and plugging them back in several times can wipe away the corrosion.

Before unplugging a cable, you might put a stripe on the connector and cable with a marking pen or nail polish so that you can easily see how they should be plugged back in.

You might even have a problem in the contacts of a DIP switch. You might try turning it on and off a few times.

Caution: Again, always write down the positions before touching any switch. Make a diagram of the wires, cables, and switch settings before you disturb them. It is easy to forget how they were plugged in or set before you moved them. You could end up making things worse. Make a pencil mark before turning a knob, variable coil, or capacitor so that it can be returned to the same setting when you find out that it didn't help. Better yet, resist the temptation to reset these types of components. Most were set up using highly sophisticated instruments. They don't usually change enough to cause a problem.

If too much current flows through a chip, it can get hot and fail. It might only fail at certain times when you are running a particular program. If you suspect a chip and it seems to be warmer that it should be, you might try using a hairdryer to heat it up. If it fails due to the extra heat, then you have found the problem. Be careful that you do not heat up a good chip and cause it to fail.

At one time we could spray a coolant on a component that seemed to be too hot, such as Freon. Because of environmental concerns, you may no longer be able to buy Freon. You might try using ice water in a plastic bagggie. This will cool it. If the component then works properly, you have found your defect.

Some of the diagnostic software will run a system in an endless loop to try to force the system to fail.

Serial Ports

Conflicts in setting up serial port devices can cause a lot of problems. Like the parallel ports, pins for the serial ports are available on any of the bus plug-in slots. The serial ports might be available as a group of ten pins on the motherboard. Or it might be on a multifunction plug-in board. The serial port might be a male DB25 connector with pins, or there might be a male DB9 connector. The original RS232 specification called for 25 lines, but most systems only use four or five lines, so the DB9 connector with nine pins is more than sufficient. Many of the mice sold today have the DB9 connector.

The serial ports are most often used for a mouse or other pointing device, for modems, FAX boards, for plotters, scanners, and several other devices. DOS supports four serial ports: COM1, COM2, COM3, and COM4. But DOS only has two interrupt request (IRQ) lines for the serial ports: IRQ4 for COM1 and IRQ3 for COM2. So COM3 and COM4 must share the IRQ lines with COM1 and COM2. You need special software in order to permit sharing. They can share because it is not likely that all four IRQ lines would be used at the same time.

If two devices are set for the same COM port, it causes a serious conflict. Neither device will operate properly. When installing a mouse, modem, or FAX board, the interface plug-in boards must be configured so that none of the devices use the same port. If you have devices already installed on your system, you might not know which port they are set for.

There are several programs that can help you determine which ports and IRQa are being used. In Windows 95, go to Control Panel, then System icon, then Device Manager, then double click on Computer to see IRQs that are being used.

Software Problems

I have had lots of problems with software. Quite often it is my fault for not taking the time to completely read the manuals and instructions. But I don't usually have the time to read and study every page in the manual when I install a program. Many of the programs are getting easier to run. Plug-n-play will eliminate a lot of problems, but there will still be lots of software problems that you will probably run into.

Many vendors have support programs for their products, hardware and software. If something goes wrong, you can call them. Some companies charge for their support. Some have installed a 900 telephone number. You are charged a certain fee for the amount of time on the phone. It can cost a lot of money to maintain a support staff.

If you have a hardware or software problem, write down everything that happens. Before you call, try to make the problem happen again. Carefully read the manual. When you call, it is best to be in front of your computer, with it turned on, and with the problem on the screen if possible. Before you call, have the serial number of your program handy. One of the first things they will probably ask is for your name and serial number. If you have bought and registered the program, it will be in their computer.

Many companies have set up Web sites with answers to frequently asked questions (FAQ). I have never been fortunate enough to find an answer to whatever question I have had. Many of them have also set up FAXBACK systems. You call a number, get a list of documents available, and they will automatically fax them to you. Again, I have had very little success in getting an answer to any of my problems. But it is a good way to get documentation and answers to the most FAQs.

It seems that everybody in business has now gone to automatic telephone answering machines. When you call, usually long distance, you will be given several options. It might take several minutes to list them all. Press button 1 if you want one service, 2 for another, 3 for another, then when you get to that number, there will be another five or six options. You might stay on the phone for half an hour and never get to speak to a live person. Or you will be put on hold to wait for the next available person. It can be very frustrating. One of the best investments I ever made was buying a speaker phone. I can call a number, then push the speaker button, go about my other business while I am on hold.

Most software programs are reasonably bug-free. But lots of things can go wrong if the exact instructions and procedures are not followed. In many cases, the exact instructions and procedures are not very explicit. It seems that most software manuals are written by people who know the software very well, but they seem to forget about the person using it for the first time.

Software companies could save millions of dollars if they produced manuals that were better written to make installation and usage easier. For every major program, there are dozens of books written to help you learn how to use it. Many training programs have been developed to teach people how to use "user friendly" software. If you spend a lot of money on a program, you shouldn't have to spend a lot more time and money to learn how to use it. Windows 95 is a step in the right direction in being fairly easy to use. But it is a very complex program and it will take some study, training, and time to learn all of its advantages and benefits.

User Groups

There is no way to list all of the possible software or hardware problems. Computers are dumb and very unforgiving. It is very easy to plug a cable in backwards, or forget to set a switch. There are thousands of things that can go wrong. Sometimes it can be a combination of both software and hardware. Often there is only one way to do something the right way, but ten thousand ways to do it wrong. Sometimes it is difficult to determine if it is a hardware problem caused by software or vice versa. There is no way that every problem can be addressed.

One of the best ways to find answers is to ask someone who has had the same problem. One of the best places to find those people is at a users group. If at all possible, join one and become friends with all of the members. They can be one of your best sources of troubleshooting. Most of them have had similar problems and are glad to help. Many local computer magazines list user groups in their area. The nationally distributed *Computer Shopper* alternates with a listing of bulletin boards one month and user groups the next.

Thank you for buying my book. I wish you all the best. I hope all your problems are easy ones.

GLOSSARY

active matrix LCD   System used for high-resolution *liquid crystal diode* (LCD) display panels used on color laptop and portable computers. This type of display is fairly expensive because it requires an individual transistor for each pixel. See *passive matrix*.

adapter card   A printed wiring board with digital circuitry that plugs into connectors on the motherboard of a personal computer, usually performing input/output functions.

ADC   An abbreviation for *analog-to-digital converter*. The electronic device converts conventional analog audio and video signals to digital form. The digital form can be processed by computer and stored as data on a computer's hard disk drive.

address   The numerical value, usually in hexadecimal format, of a particular location in a computer's random-access memory (RAM).

ADPCM   An abbreviation for *adaptive differential pulse code modulation*. A method of digital waveform sampling encoding the difference between successive samples rather than encoding their actual values ADPCM. The differences are assigned different values based on the content of the sample. ADPCM is the storage format used by CD-ROM XA and CD-1 discs.

ADSL   Asymmetric digital subscriber line; a digital phone line technology that supports high-speed connections using an ordinary phone. ADSL is asymmetric because the uplink speeds at about 64K is much less than the download speeds of up to 6 Mbps.

algorithm   (1) A digital set of instructions for solving a problem. (2) The configuration of operators in an FM synthesizer.

amplitude   (1) The strength or intensity of sound or signal. (2) The measure of a current's deviation from its zero value.

amplitude modulation   A term describing the interaction of two signals: a carrier and a modulator. The modulation signal varies the amplitude (intensity) of the carrier. In AM radio transmission, the carrier is a medium-frequency signal (550—1550 KHz), and the modulator is the sound signal. In sound synthesis, a low-frequency oscillator modulates a carrier that is the sound's fundamental frequency.

analog   A term describing a circuit, device, or system which responds to continuously variable parameters; generated by hardware rather than by software.

analog-to-digital converter   A circuit that periodically samples a continuously variable voltage and generates a digital representation of its value, also called an ADC, A-to-D, or A/D converter.

ANI   Automatic number identification, or caller ID.

ANSI   An abbreviation for the *American National Standards Institute*. ANSI, in the Windows context, refers to the ANSI character set that Microsoft uses for Windows.

API   An abbreviation for *application programming interface*. Generically, a method of accessing or modifying the operating system for a program. In Windows, the API refers to the functions provided by Windows 3.x allowing applications to open and close windows, read the keyboard, interpret mouse movements, and so on. Programmers call these functions hooks to the operating systems.

APM and SMM   Abbreviation for *advanced power management* from Intel and Microsoft. It allows certain programs and operating systems to slow down various hardware components, thereby saving power. SMM is *system management mode*, which is a group of instructions built into the CPU. .

ASCII   (Pronounced ask-ee.) It means *American Standard Code for Information Interchange*. It is the digital code for displaying alphanumeric characters. It originally consisted of 128 codes, but later it was extended to 254 characters. Some of the characters are smiling faces, playing cards, or music notes. You can see what some of them look like by using the Type command to view almost any .exe or .com file. Most word processors add control characters so that they display bold, underline, page formats, or other characteristics. Text generated on one word processor is usually quite different than that of another. It is almost like a foreign language, but most computers and word processors can handle pure ASCII characters. The control characters can be stripped off so that only ASCII characters are left.

artifact   An extraneous sound or affect on an image not present in the source signal and introduced by one of the components in the recording or reproduction chain.

aspect ratio   An image's ratio of width to height. Aspect ratio is usually expressed as $W{:}H$ (W representing the width and H representing the height of the image). The aspect ratio of digital images is expressed as the ratio of the number of pixels in each dimension (40:480 for VGA images).

ASPI An acronym for *advanced SCSI programming interface*. It is the industry standard for SCSI interface cards. If the card conforms to this standard, then several different peripherals from different manufacturers can be used with the card. The Adaptec Company was the original creator of this standard. See *CAM*.

ATM (1) *asynchronous transfer mode*, a wide-band, high-frequency protocol for data transmission. (2) *Adobe Type Manager*, Adobe's system for managing TrueType fonts. (3) *Automated teller machine*, a banking computer where you can withdraw money from your checking or savings accounts or do other banking transactions.

AVI An abbreviation for *audio video interleaved*. The Microsoft Application Programming Interface (API) designed to compete with Apple's QUICKTIME methodology. AVI techniques provide a software synchronization and compression standard for audio and video signals competing with DVI.

BitBlt Abbreviation for *bit block transfer*. An assembly-level function used for copying graphic images in Windows applications from a source to a destination graphic context.

buffer A section of RAM where data is stored temporarily, usually containing data to be edited or inserted.

CAM *Common access method* is a standard that was developed for SCSI devices. It is similar to the ASPI standard except that the interface cards have their own BIOS on-board.

camcorder A contraction of camera and recorder. The term describes a video camera and videocassette recorder combined into a single, hand-held unit.

Carpal tunnel syndrome (CTS) Pain and numbness in the hand, wrist, and arm along the path of the medial nerve. It is often caused by the repetitive action of typing on a computer keyboard. See *Repetitive strain injury (RSI)*.

CAV An abbreviation for *constant angular velocity* devices, such as computer hard disks and CAV video laserdiscs, depending on the distance of the read/write head from the drive spindle.

CCD Abbreviation for *charge-coupled devices*. An integrated circuit consisting of a linear array of semiconductor photoreceptor elements. CCDs are used to create a bit-mapped image. Each photoreceptor creates an electrical signal representing the luminance of one pixel. CCDs are primarily used in scanners, color xerographic printers, and video cameras.

CCITT An abbreviation for the *Consultative Committee International for Telephone and Telegraph* communication. CCITT establishes standards for telephone interchange and modems in Europe. Several CCITT standards for communication between modems over telephone networks have been adopted in the United States. The CCITT has been renamed the International Telecommunications Union (ITU).

CD An abbreviation for *compact disc.* CDs are the original format for distributing compact optical disks for audio reproduction (CD audio). This early format was jointly developed by Phillips N.V. and Sony Corporation and is described in Phillips *N.V.'s Yellow Book.* Control of Yellow Book CD-ROMs, such as starting and stopping the drive and file selection with your computer, requires Microsoft's. MSCDEX.DRV driver.

CD-DA An abbreviation for compact disk digital Audio, also called "Red Book" audio. CD-A requires compatibility with MPC specification 1.0. It enables interleaving of audio with other types of data, so recorded sound can accompany images. Playing CDs with CD-DA is not provided with Windows 3.1. It is usually supplied with the CD-ROM drive when purchased as a component of an MPC upgrade kit. The CD-DA format is defined in the International Electrotechnical Commissions' (IEC) Standard BNNI-5-83-095.

CD+Graphics A format in which the subchannel(s) of an audio CD contains graphic images that can be displayed on a computer or a television set.

CD-I An abbreviation for *compact disk-interactive.* CD-I refers to a class of CDs primarily designed to be viewed on conventional television sets by means of a CD-I player. CD-I players incorporate at least 1M of memory (RAM), special pointing devices, and remote-control systems. CD-I players also can be used for training and other commercial and industrial applications. CD-I formats are covered by Phillips N.V.'s Green Book specification.

CD+MIDI A format in which the subchannel(s) of an audio CD contain data in standard MIDI file format that can be routed to a MIDI OUT connector and played on external MIDI synthesizers or internally by audio-adapter cards.

CD-MO An abbreviation for *compac disk magneto-optical*; CDs and CD-ROMs that are capable of multiple use because they can be erased and re-recorded. The standards for CD-MOs are incorporated in Phillips N.V.'s "Orange Book 1" specification. CD-MO technology is used for high-capacity, 3-1/2-inch "floptical" floppy disks.

CD-ROM An acronym for compact disk read-only memory. CD-ROMs can incorporate both audio and graphic images as well as text files. Phillips N.V.'s documentation for this standard has a yellow binding, hence the term Yellow Book audio. MPC Specification 1.0 requires multimedia PCs to include a CD-ROM.

CD-ROM XA An abbreviation for CD-ROM extended architecture, jointly developed by Philips N.V., Sony Corporation, and Microsoft Corporation in 1989. CD-ROM XA provides storage for audio and other types of data interleaved on a CD-ROM, enabling access simultaneously.

channel message A MIDI command or data which is sent over a specific MIDI channel.

chrominance A term used in television broadcasting to describe the signal (a subcarrier of the basic black-and-white signal) containing the color information in a composite video signal. Chrominance has two components: hue (tint) and saturation (the degree to which the color is diluted by white light). Chrominance is also called *chroma* and abbreviated as *C*.

clipping Audible distortion of an audio signal, usually caused by overloading a circuit of transducer.

clock An electronic circuit that generates the pulses used to synchronize bits of information.

CLV An abbreviation for *constant linear velocity*. The recording technique used with CD-ROMs (and other CD devices) specifying that the velocity of the media at the point of reading or writing remains constant, regardless of the distance from the spindle. CLV devices have a constant data transfer rate. To achieve CLV, the rotational speed of the spindle motor must be inversely proportional to the distance of the read or write point on the media from the spindle Video. Laser disc drives are produced in CLV and constant angular velocity models.

codec Acronym for *compression-decompression* for video data.

coprocessor A processor support chip that can vastly improve intensive calculations and graphics. They can only be used if the software is written to take advantage of their capabilities. Coprocessors have the designation x87. For instance, the 386 CPU uses the 387 coprocessor. The 486DX CPU and all pentiums have the coprocessor built in.

CP/M *Control program for microprocessors* was the first operating system for personal computers. It was written by Gary Kildall in 1973. It was used by all of the early PCs such as Osborne, Kaypro, Merrow, and others. In 1980, IBM approached Gary to develop a system for the first IBM PC. IBM later went to Bill Gates and you know the rest of the story.

CPS (1) Abbreviation for *cycles per second* such as the frequency of an electronic circuit. (2) In speaking of printers, it means *characters per second* that the printer can produce.

CTI *Computer telephony integration.* Connecting a computer to a telephone switch.

cycle A single, complete wave; the basic unit of oscillation.

DAC An abbreviation for digital-to-analog converter. DAC is the electronic device used to convert digital audio and video signals stored on CD-ROMs, DAT, or in computer files to analog signals that can be reproduced by conventional stereo and television components.

daisy chain (1) The connection of several devices on a SCSI. (2) A network in which data flows from one receiving device's MIDI thru-port to another receiving device's MIDI in-port.

DAT Acronym for *digital audio tape.* DAT is a process of recording sound in helical bands on a tape cartridge. This process is similar to recording video signals.

default A parameter value that exists when hardware is turned on or an application is run.

Dhrystones A benchmark that measures millions of instructions per second (MIPS).

digital-to-analog converter A circuit that generates a digital representation of a continuously variable signal; also called a DAC, D/A converter.

DIN An acronym for *Deutches Institute fur Normalization.* DIN is an organization similar to ANSI that establishes and coordinates standards for Germany. It has become the de facto standards bureau for Europe.

DLL An abbreviation for *Dynamic Link Library.* DLL is a Frye containing a collection of Windows functions designed to perform a specific class of operations. Functions within DLLs are called (invoked) as necessary by applications to perform the desired operations.

drag-and-drop A Windows process whereby an icon representing an object, such as a file, can be moved (dragged) by the mouse to another location, such as a different directory, and placed (dropped) in that location. Visual Basic provides drag-and-drop capabilities for control objects.

DSP An abbreviation for *digital signal processing*. Although all synthesized sound involves DSP, the term is usually applied to the creation of electronic, acoustic effects such as reverberation, chorusing, flanging, and panning.

DTV The abbreviation for *desktop video*. The term describes the production of videotape presentations using the multimedia capabilities of personal computers. DTV implies the capability to edit videotapes by using the playback and record functions of VCRs that can be remotely controlled by a computer.

DVI An abbreviation for Intel's *digital-video interactive* standard.

DVI Simultaneously displays compressed video images and sound files. IBM has adopted the DVI standard for its Ultimedia product line. Microsoft adds DVI capability through its DVMCI extensions.

EISA An abbreviation for *extended industry standard architecture*. A bus specification used to interconnect adapter cards employing 32-bit memory addresses or providing multiprocessor capabilities. The EISA standard is now obsolete, although there are several systems still in existence.

Energy Star The EPA's requirement that PCs implement automatic sleep modes when the item is not being used so as to save energy. Many of the laptop computers have used similar systems for some time. Newer CPUs have a variety of power-saving options.

EPROM Acronym for *erasable programmable read only memory*. The type of chips usually used for ROM BIOS.

error correction code (ECC) A coding system that, in conjunction with an error detection coding scheme, can reconstruct erroneous data to its original value.

error detection code (EDC) A coding system that detects errors in a single byte or in blocks of data. Single-byte errors are caught by parity checkers, such as the ones employed in the PC's memory system. Errors in blocks of data are commonly determined by using techniques, such as the cyclic redundancy codes (CRC), used for data transfer by modem. More sophisticated EDC methods are employed when error-correction is required, such as with CD-ROMs.

FAQ *Frequently asked questions;* many of the technical support systems and online services list the frequently asked questions. Hopefully, you might find an answer to your question or problem without having to call on the telephone and switch through all the many options.

field In video terminology, one half of a television image. A field consists of either the even or odd lines of a frame. When used in conjunction with computer databases, a field is a single, distinct element of a complete database record.

filter A circuit or function that alters a signal's frequency spectrum by attenuating or accenting certain portions.

Firewire Apple Computer's proprietary implementation of IEEE-1394. IEEE-1394 is somewhat like the universal serial bus (USB). It is a high-speed bus that can accommodate several devices.

firmware Software that is embedded in the computer's ROMs or elsewhere in the computer circuitry. You cannot ordinarily change or modify firmware.

FM synthesis A method of generating complex waveforms by modulating the frequency of audio waveforms (carriers) with other waveforms (modulators); frequency modulation.

frame rate In film or video, the frequency at which single frames are shown, usually equal to 24, 25, or 30 frames per second.

frequency The rate of oscillation, which determines pitch, measured in cycles per second, or Hertz.

FTP *File transfer protocol;* a TCP/IP protocol for transferring files from one machine to another or from sites on the Internet.

fundamental frequency A sound's primary frequency; the first harmonic.

genlock A process for synchronizing the video display of a computer to the frame synchronization signal of NTSC, PAL, or SECAM video. This process allows computer-generated graphics to be viewed on a television set or recorded with a VCR. Genlock capability is required to add computer-generated titles to video productions.

GIF Acronym for *graphic interchange format.* GIF is the file format (and extension) storing most graphic images in the CompuServe forum libraries.

global Pertaining to a computer program as a whole. Global variables and constants are accessible to, and can be modified by, program code at the module and procedure level.

gray scale A description for monochrome (black and white) images displayed in various intensities of black. The most common format is an eight-bit gray-scale providing 256 shades of gray. Four-bit gray-scale images with 64 shades are also used.

harmonic A simple component of a complex waveform that's a whole-number multiple of the fundamental frequency.

HDTV Abbreviation for *high-definition television,* a form of television transmission that results in clearer images, especially on large screen sets. Our present standard is 525 lines swept across the screen from top to bottom. HDTV would increase the number and give much better resolution.

Hi 8 An abbreviation for *high band 8-mm,* a format developed by Sony Corporation for camcorder videotapes. His provides the capability of recording PCM digital audio, and time, code tracks in addition to conventional analog audio and enhanced-quality video information.

High Sierra format A name assigned to the predecessor of ISO standard 9660 defining the table of content and directory structure of CD-ROMs for computer applications. Microsoft's MSCDEX.DRV driver reads the table of contents and directory structure and converts the latter to the structure used by DOS. This function enables you to treat CD-ROM files as if they were located on a conventional hard disk drive.

HMS time Time expressed in hours, minutes, seconds, usually separated by colons.

HTML (hypertext markup language) A special language used to create Web pages.

http Hypertext transfer protocol is the World Wide Web text-based protocol.

Hz An abbreviation for hertz, the fundamental unit of frequency of audio and radio waves. Hertz was previously called cycles per second (cps). Most people can discern sounds that range in frequency from about 20 to 18,000 Hz.

icon In Windows, a 32-by 32-pixel graphic image, usually in color. An icon identifies the application in the program manager window when the application is minimized and in other locations in the application chosen by the programmer.

interlaced The method of displaying television signals on conventional TV sets and computer images on video display units. Alternative fields of images, consisting of the even or odd horizontal lines comprising the image, are displayed succession.

interleaved A method for containing sound and video information in a single file but in separate chunks, so digital images and audio signals can be transferred from a file to the computer's memory without delays incurred by CD-ROM seek operations.

IP Internet protocol; a protocol used to send packets of data over the Internet.

ITU *International Telecommunications Union,* formerly called the CCIIT. A United Nations committee that tries to convince nations and companies to standardize telecommunications devices and protocols. See *CCITT.*

ISA An abbreviation for *industry standard architecture,* the specification of the connections to plug-in adapter cards with 16-bit memory addressing capability. ISA is the bus structure used in conventional IBM-compatible computers using the 8088, 80286, 80386, and 80486 CPU chips.

ISDN *Integrated Services Digital Network;* a digital telephone network that allows much faster communications.

ISO An abbreviation for the *International Standards Organization.* The ISO is a branch of the United Nations headquartered in Geneva. ISO coordinates international standards for a wide variety of products and equipment. The CD-ROM standard for tables of contents and file directory entries, originally called the High Sierra format, has been established as the ISO-9660 standard.

ISP *Internet service provider;* A company that provides connections to the Internet. Larger ones include AOL, Prodigy, Compuserve, and Microsoft Network. But there are hundreds of small local ISPs. There are well over 200 in the Los Angeles area.

IVRU *Interactive voice response unit,* a system whereby the computer can play back digitized speech and can accept requests from a touch-tone telephone. These systems are now used by many companies to displace live human beings. It saves a lot of money for the companies because these systems never take a coffee break, go on vacation, or ask for a raise.

JPEG An acronym for the *Joint Photographic Experts Group* that has established an industry standard for photographic image compression.

.JPG The file extension for graphic image files stored with JPEG compression.

jumper A small, plastic-enclosed spring clip making an electrical connection between two adjacent square metal pins, usually in the form of a header. Jumpers are used to set device addresses, interrupt levels, and select other optional features of adapter cards. They are also found on motherboards.

karaoke A musical arrangement designed to accompany an added singing voice. Karaoke can be used to describe a consumer audio or audio-video component equipped with a microphone (and often with digital signal processing). The added singer's voice is combined with the accompaniment and heard through the same speakers.

LAN *Local area network;* a network where several computers can be tied together. The area served might be a single building or it might include several buildings, such as a campus.

luminance One of the characteristics defining a color in the hue-saturation-luminance (HSL) system. Luminance is the collective intensity (lightness) of the color defined by hue and saturation. In television broadcasting, the signal containing the black-and-white image is referred to as the luminance signal.

MIDI Musical instrument digital interface; a means of communicating musical information among computers and microprocessor-based devices.

MIME *Multipurpose Internet mail extensions;* a protocol for sending non-ASCII type data over the Internet. Such data can be sound, video, and graphics.

MIPS An acronym for million of instructions per second; a measure of how fast a CPU operates.

NAMM Abbreviation for the *National Association of Music Merchants.* NAMM is an industry association of music dealers and musical instrument manufacturers. NAMM holds a yearly exhibition where new MIDI devices and audio components are introduced.

nanosecond One billionth of a second, abbreviated ns. The speed of memory chips is measured in nanoseconds, usually ranging from about 30 to 100. Faster computer clock speeds require memory chips with lower nanosecond response times. For instance, 33-MHz computers use 70—80 ns memory chips.

NBT   The *next big thing;* what everybody is waiting breathlessly for. Time and time again, NBT has been rumored and hinted at. When it arrives, it will be a real killer application or component.

NLQ   *Near letter quality;* many printers, especially the dot matrix, can print fairly fast in a draft mode. In draft mode, there is usually spaces and jagged edges in the characters. For NLQ printing more pins in the head are struck so that the characters are better defined.

noninterlaced   The preferred method of displaying computer images, usually on a multisynchronous video display unit, in which the image is created by displaying consecutive rather than alternate scanning lines.

OCR *optical character recognition;*   System used in scanners to recognize printed text and convert it into digital data.

oscillator   A circuit or software that generates voltage signals.

PAL   An acronym for *phase-alternative line* system. PAL is the television transmission standard of Western Europe (except France). PAL displays 625 lines per frame at a rate of 25 frames per second.

palette   A Windows data structure defining the colors of a bit-mapped image in RGB format.

parallel interface   A connection between devices that transfers one or more bytes of information simultaneously.

parameter   A variable characteristic or value.

passive matrix LCD   A system used on the lesser expensive display panels for color laptops and portables. It uses a single transistor to activate rows and columns of pixels. It is much less expensive than active matrix, but the colors are not as bright as those in the active matrix systems. See *active matrix.*

PCM   *Pulse code modulation,* a means of digitally encoding and decoding audio signals.

PCI   *Peripheral component interconnect;* a system that allows plug-in boards and devices to communicate with the CPU over a 32- or 64-bit high-speed bus.

PCX   The file extension created by ZSoft Corporation for storing images created by its PC Paintbrush application. PCX bit-mapped files can monochrome or color and are used by many other bit-mapped image-creation (paint) and display applications.

photo CD   A trademark of the Eastman Kodak Company for its technology and CDs that provide copies of photographic color images in a format compatible with CD-I and CD-ROM XA drives. Photo CDs are produced from 35-mm film images by licensed photo-finishing facilities. These facilities have equipment that can write to the special photo CD media.

pipeline   In the Pentium, a pipeline is an arrangement of registers within the CPU. They are also called *execution units.* Each register performs part of a task, then passes the results to the next register. PCs such as the 486 computer have a single pipeline and can only process one instruction per clock cycle. The Pentium has two pipelines and can process two instructions per cycle.

POP *post office protocol;*   The protocol used to send and retrieve Internet e-mail messages.

presentation   Multimedia production consisting principally of still images or simple animation covering a single topic.

prosumer   A contraction of *pro*fessional and cons*umer.* Prosumer describes video components, such as camcorders and VCRs, bridging the gap between consumer-grade products and industrial-quality devices.

QIC   *Quarter inch cartridge;* magnetic tape used for tape backup.

RAM   *Random-access memory;* a computer's main memory in which data is temporarily stored, and which allows the user to enter and retrieve data at will.

RAID   An acronym for redundant array of inexpensive disks. When the data is critical, a RAID system of two or more hard disks can be used to mirror each other so that the same data is recorded on each disk.

RBOC   *Regional Bell operating companies* or telephone companies.

repetitive strain injury (RSI)   Pain and numbness to areas of the hand, wrist, and arm. RSI is similar to carpal tunnel syndrome, except that ordinarily, RSI can occur to any part of the body that is subjected to frequent motion or trauma. The injury usually occurs in tendons and in synovial sheaths that surrounds the nerves. This injury is sometimes called *repetitive motion injury,* which is probably a better term.

ribbon cable   A flat multiconductor cable having parallel individual conductors that are molded together. One side of the ribbon cable is marked with a printed line, usually blue or red. This line identifies the conductor corresponding to pin 1 of the attached connectors.

RIFF   An acronym for the Windows *resource interchange file format*. RIFF is used in conjunction with multimedia extensions. Depending on their definition, these files can contain MIDI sequence, sample dump, or system exclusive data, waveform audio files, or data to create graphic images. RIFF is the preferred file format for Windows multimedia files; however, few third-party applications currently create RIFF files, except in wave format (WAV files).

RTM   What you may hear when you call a company for support, or ask someone for help, *read the manual.*

RTDM   Same as above, but a bit more imperative, *read the damned manual.* Another version that can't be used in nice company is RTFM.

sample   To digitally encode an analog signal.

sawtooth wave   A waveform that contains every component of the natural harmonic series; also called a *ramp wave.*

scalability   Scalable, multiprocessing operating system that allows a user to run the same application on single-processor and multiprocessor computers .

SCSI   *Small computer system interface*, pronounced "scuzzy." An interface standard for connecting peripherals to a PC. The standard supports several different peripherals such as hard drives, CD-ROMs, scanners, and other devices. As many as seven different devices can be connected to one interface card.

SECAM   The acronym for *system couleur avec memoire.* SECAM is the French standard for television transmission (819 horizontal lines per frame displayed at 25 frames per second). SECAM is the standard for most of Eastern Europe, including the former USSR and in African countries where French is the most common second language.

seek   To locate a specific byte, sector, cluster, record, or chunk within a disk file.

square wave   A pulse wave with a 50% duty cycle, consisting of odd harmonics only.

SRP   *Suggested retail price;* sometimes it is MSRP or *manufacturers suggested retail price.*

streaming   The technique used to transfer information from a file structure, such as on a disk or CD drive, to the computer's memory. Streaming takes place in groups of bytes less than the entire file's length, usually processed in memory as a background activity.

stripe A synchronization signal recorded on one track of a multitrack tape recorder.

superscalar Refers to the fact the Pentium architecture has two parallel pipelines. It can process instructions in both pipelines simultaneously, or two instructions per clock cycle.

S-VHS A VHS-format videocassette recorder S-video capability.

S-video Abbreviation for *super-video*. S-video is a video signal with enhanced quality used for recording. S-video separates the chrominance signal from the luminance signals of composite video.

sync Abbreviation for synchronization.

TCP *Transmission control protocol*; usually seen as TCP/IP for transmission control/Internet protocol, it is used on LANs as well as on the Internet. It guarantees reliable delivery by resending any lost packets or corrupted bits and bytes.

.TGA The file extension identifying files created in the format used by Truevision's TARGA series of graphic adapter cards.

.TIF An acronym for *tagged image format*. TIF is a format for storing black-and-white, gray-scale, and color bit-mapped images developed by Aldus Corporation.

time code A method of identifying the time an event (such as a single motion picture or video frame) occurs in a format that can be understood by a computer.

time stamp The date and time data attributes applied to a disk file when created or edited. In MIDI files, a time stamp identifies the time MIDI events (such as Note On or Note Off) should occur, so the correct tempo is maintained.

triangle wave A waveform with a strong fundamental and weak overtones, comprised of odd numbered harmonics only.

trigger A control signal that indicates the beginning of an event.

truncate In sampling, to remove recorded data before or after a sample.

TrueType A trademark of Apple Computer, Inc. for its outline-based typeface design and display system that creates display and printer fonts in a manner similar to Adobe's PostScript. Microsoft Corporation has incorporated an improved version of TrueType technology in Windows 3.1.

TSR *Terminate-and-stay-resident;* A term describing software that loads itself into RAM and stays there. It is available at any time, but it can use up a lot of the much needed 640K.

twip Window's smallest unit of graphic measurement. A twip is a twentieth of a point or 1/1,440th of an inch.

typeface Print or display type of a single design. Typeface is often confused with the term *font,* which means a particular size of a typeface. A typeface might be a member of a typeface or type family including related designs with attributes, such as bold, Roman (regular), italic, compressed, or extended.

UART *Universal asynchronous receiver and transmitter;* It is a chip that processes data through the serial port. For example, it takes eight bits to make a character. The parallel port can send a whole eight-bit character over eight lines at one time. To send data over the serial port, the chip takes the digital data and sends it through the port one bit at a time in a serial string. The early UARTs used an 8250 chip which is rather slow. Newer devices use the 16550, which is much faster. Many of the less expensive multi I/O boards still use the older 8250. To find out what you have, use the DOS MSD command.

URC *Uniform resource locator;* the name of a site on the World Wide Web; for instance, http://www.pencomputing. com/dim. Ordinarily, the http:// can be omitted.

VESA An acronym for the *Video Electronic Standards Association.* VESA is a group of manufactures and software developers who create standards for graphic and video display adapter cards.

VLB VESA local bus, a system that allows plug-in boards or other devices to communicate with the CPU over a fast 32- or 64-bit bus.

WAVE file A RIFF (resource interchange file format) file containing PCM waveform audio data, usually with a .WAV extension. Microsoft and IBM have adopted .WAV files as their standard format for multimedia sound applications.

waveform audio A data type standard of the Windows multimedia extensions. Waveform audio defines how digitally sampled sounds are stored in files and processed by Windows API functions.

wavetable A term describing the synthesis technique of simulating the sounds of musical instruments with short digitized recordings (PCM samples) of their sounds.

whetstones Whetstones measures arithmetic operations. WinBench executes on top of Windows WinMark measures.

wild card   A character that substitutes for and allows a match by any character or set of characters in its place such as the ? and ˙ symbols.

WinBench   A benchmark for use with Windows.

WinMark   A benchmark for use with Windows.

WORM   An acronym for *write-once read-many*. The WORM system uses a laser to write on a special optical disc. CD-WO (the write-once CD standard) is a special type of WORM format.

Write-back cache   A write-back system that only writes data back to the main memory that has been modified.

Write-through cache   A system where all data is immediately written back to memory.

WWW   *World Wide Web*; the Internet that is made up of thousands of sites and millions of home pages.

YC   An encoding method used in S-Video. In YC, the luminance (*Y*) and chrominance (*C*) signals are separated. The chrominance signal incorporates both hue and saturation information.

ZIF   An acronym for *zero insertion force*. A 238-pin chip like the Pentium requires a large amount of force to insert and remove. It is a fragile device and the pins can be easily damaged. A ZIF socket has a lever that opens the socket contacts so that the device can be dropped in.

zoom   To magnify an image on a video display.

ABOUT THE CD

Along with the valuable upgrading and repairing information found throughout this book, we have included a CD-ROM with a small collection of useful PC diagnostic tools and utilities. Diagnostic tools are test programs used to study the "inside" of your computer. Diagnostics typically read status data from within the PC and translate that data into meaningful information that can easily be read. Utilities on the other hand are software programs intended to enhance or modify a specific function on your PC such as adding printing capabilities or enhancing graphics. This CD is by no means a complete collection of shareware diagnostics and utilities, but rather a sampling of the various tools that exist. For more shareware diagnostics and utilities, you can visit the Public Shareware Library at *http://www.psl.com.*

Shareware

All of the programs on the CD are fully functioning shareware evaluation versions. Shareware programs are copyrighted programs that are distributed freely to allow users to evaluate and use programs on a trial basis (usually 30 days). Keep in mind that shareware is not free. If you decide that you like the software and plan to use it, you're requested to register the software with the author. Registration usually involves a minimal fee, although some shareware only requires that you send your name and address to the author. After you register the software, you'll usually receive added benefits such as updates, a printed users manual, and technical support. To help ensure that software authors continue writing innovative new programs and distributing them as shareware, please support the shareware concept and register all programs that you plan to use. To assist in the registration process, we've included all prices and addresses for the shareware included on this CD.

Installing the Software

- Install the CD in your CD-ROM drive.
- Decide whether you wish to install the program to your hard drive or floppy diskette.

Hard Disk

Prepare a subdirectory on your hard disk. You can create a subdirectory from your DOS prompt with the following command:

C:\>md program name <enter>

Example: To create a directory for SNOOP330, type C:\md SNOOP330 <enter>

To switch to the new directory type:

C:\>cd\program name <enter>

Example: C:\cd\SNOOP330 <enter>

Floppy Disk

To prepare a subdirectory on a floppy disk, insert a clean floppy disk into the A: drive and switch to the A: drive by typing

C:\>A: <enter>

To create a new directory, follow the instructions above for creating subdirectories on your hard disk and simply substitute

A:\ for all C:\ commands.

- You can now copy programs to the new directories you have created.

Hard Disk

To copy a program from the CD to the subdirectory created on your disk, make sure you are in the desired directory (C:\program name) and type

C:\program name\>copy d:\program name\program name.zip c: <enter>

> Example: C:\SNOOP330\>copy d:\SNOOP330\SNOOP330.zip c:
> <enter>

If your CD-ROM drive uses a different letter, be sure to use that notation instead of D.

Floppy Disk

You can copy files to a floppy disk using the same command and replacing A: for all C: references.

■ Now that programs are copied to the desired directories, you can decompress the file. First, copy PKUNZIP to your hard drive or floppy disk using the steps above. Then, unzip the desired program by typing

C:\program name\>c:\pkunzip program name <enter>

> Example: C:\SNOOP330\>c:\pkunzip SNOOP330 <enter>

If the program is a self-extracting file (files with a .EXE extension), go to the directory that you've created for that program and simply type the file name.

> Example: C:\SNOOP330\>SNOOP330 <enter>

The Programs

Each table below contains a brief explanation of the program and its intended use. You can find more detailed information within the programs themselves.

BACKEE28.ZIP

The Backer provides users with a useful tool for backing up, restoring, and synchronizing files. Requires Window 3.1*x* or Windows 95 to run. Registration fee of $25 can be sent to

Bernd Cordes
Wiesingerweg 34
20253 Hamburg
Germany

BIOSR11.ZIP

BIOS Data Area Reader is a BIOS data area (BDA) information utility that will allow you to check your PCs hardware states and the memory that composes the BDA without having to run a full diagnostic. NO FEE REQUIRED.

DATA_REC

TIRAMISU is a software for reconstructing data from a crashed hard drive.

It helps when the drive is hit by a virus, scratched by a head crash, formatted, 'fdisk'ed, zapped by a power failure, or damaged by applications. Registration fee of $99 can be sent to

Uwe Gissemann
Plug 'n Play
Crellestr.6D-10827 Berlin
Germany

GUARD.ZIP

The Guardian is a software utility that encrypts the contents of your hard drive, thereby protecting the information from theft. Registration fee of $40 can be sent to

Marcor Enterprises
8857 Commerce Park Place, Suite D
Indianapolis, IN 46268

IRQINFO.ZIP

CTS IRQInfo is the most accurate software IRQ identification tool available. IRQInfo does a detailed analysis of the hardware to identify used and available IRQs. Unlike many other utilities, IRQInfo actually uses most hardware to accurately detect IRQs used by the hardware.

Registration fee of $24 for IRQInfo or $35 for IRQInfo Pro can be sent to

Computer Telecommunications Systems, Inc.
3847 Foxwood Road, Suite 100
Duluth, GA 30136-6100

JCBENCH.EXE

JC-Bench is a computer speed-testing program. It provides users with a tool that allows for evaluation of different PCs. JC-Bench focuses its testing on three areas of the PC: the CPU, video, and hard disk. Registration fee of $ 10 can be sent to

Jesse Bize
15 Yerba Buena Ave
San Francisco, CA 94127

Note: JC-Bench requires a clean boot of the PC for best results. You can boot your system with a blank bootable floppy disk, or you can boot clean under MS-DOS 5.0 to 6.22 by hitting <F5> when the message "Starting MS-DOS" appears.

MAXSPEED.EXE

The Clock Speed Checker can be used to determine the computer's effective CPU clock speed. No Registration fee required.

MEMSCAN.ZIP

Memory Scan is a utility that is designed to display raw memory contents on the first one-megabyte of RAM. Registration fee of $15 can be sent to

James B. Penny
Coastal Computer Consulting
415 East Beach Drive, Suite 506
Galveston, TX 77550

PCM140.EXE

POSTCode Master is a POSTcode cross-reference utility that will tell you what each POSTcode from every possible BIOS maker means. Registration Fee of $59 (includes POST board and latest software) can be sent to

MicroSystems Development
4100 Moorpark AVE, Suite 104
San Jose, CA 95117

PRINTGF.ZIP

Print Graphics Files is a handy utility that makes it easier to print .BMP, .DCX, .GIF, .PCX, and .PNG graphics files. It can be used in either DOS or Windows. Registration Fee of $34 can be sent to

Cary Ravitz
Ravitz Software, Inc
P.O. Box 25068
Lexington, KY 40524-5068

PSPS30.ZIP

PSPS is a versatile screen dump tool for PostScript printers. PSPS allows you to use the PrintScreen key (or Shift-PrintScreen) and capture screens into PostScript format. Registration Fee of $25 can be sent to

A.N.D. Technologies
P.O. Box 64811
Los Angeles, CA 90064

SNOOP330.ZIP

Snooper is a system information utility that "snoops around" your computer to report its configuration and operating characteristics. You can use Snooper to keep an eye on your memory and disk usage. Registration Fee of $39 can be sent to

John Vias
Vias & Associates
P.O. Box 470805
San Francisco, CA 94147

SRXTEST.EXE

Test For Cyrix Upgrade CPU allows you to test a 386SX CPU for upgrade capability. No Registration Fee required.

Cyrix
800-848-2979

Note: This test was designed to test older systems for upgrade compatibility. Running this test on Pentium class PCs may result in system lock up.

SYSCHK40.ZIP

SYSCHK is a program that provides valuable information about devices installed in your system. The following are some of the items SYSCHK will search for: Computer model type including manufacturer if known, Micro Processor including the Intel Pentium™, Complete IRQ listing including usage and availability, and Microsoft Windows setup information. Registration Fee of $29 can be sent to

Paul Griffith
Advanced Personal Systems
105 Sera Way, Suite 418
Milpitas, CA 95035

UPGRADEPRO '97

"Upgrade Pro '97 is the most comprehensive, accurate, and up-to-date guide to upgrading memory, cache and video RAM ever developed". It allows you to eliminate time consuming research and cross-referencing, conduct searches with only partial information, and view memory layouts and proper parts installation sequences. Upgrades are available from

GoldenRAM
8 Whatney
Irvine, CA 92618
800-222-88861
www.goldenram.com

INDEX

About the Author

Aubrey Pilgrim (Long Beach, CA) is the author of McGraw-Hill's highly successful Build Your Own series. He is a trusted name among computer do-it-yourselfers.

SOFTWARE AND INFORMATION LICENSE

The software and information on this diskette (collectively referred to as the "Product") are the property of The McGraw-Hill Companies, Inc. ("McGraw-Hill") and are protected by both United States copyright law and international copyright treaty provision. You must treat this Product just like a book, except that you may copy it into a computer to be used and you may make archival copies of the Products for the sole purpose of backing up our softw

By saying "just like a book," M ⬚ ay be used by any number of people and may be f ⬚ , so long as there is no possibility of the Product (o ⬚ on or on one computer while it is being used at a ⬚ rent people in two different places at the same time, ⬚ eople in two different places at the same time (unle ⬚).

McGraw-Hill reserves the righ ⬚ ny time.

This agreement is effective u ⬚ omatically without notice if you fail to comply wit ⬚ termination by reason of your breach, you will de ⬚ any computer system or made for backup purpos ⬚ rage facilities.

LIMITED WARRANTY

McGraw-Hill warrants the physi ⬚ materials and workmanship for a period of sixty d ⬚ written notification within the warranty period of ⬚ ation is determined by McGraw-Hill to be correct, M ⬚ equest to:

Customer Service
McGraw-Hill
Gahanna Industrial Park
860 Taylor Station Road
Blacklick, OH 43004-9615

The entire and exclusiv ⬚ shall be limited to replacement of defective ⬚ r right to cover any other damages, including ⬚ are, or special, incidental, or consequential ⬚ s been specifically advised as to the possibili ⬚ ty for any damages to you or any other pers ⬚ l price paid for the license to use the Produc ⬚

THE McGRAW-HIL ⬚ **LL OTHER WARRANTIES, EXPRESS OI** ⬚ **Y IMPLIED WARRANTY OF MERCHA** ⬚ **RPOSE.** Specifically, McGraw-Hill makes no r ⬚ ticular purpose and any implied warranty of ⬚ e Limited Warranty covering the physical disk ⬚ erwise expressly and specifically disclaimed.

This Limited Warrant ⬚ ich may vary from ⬚ to state. Some states ⬚ amages, or the limi- ⬚ long an i ⬚ o you.

⬚ use of the Product. ⬚ reement. Failure of ⬚ all not constitute a ⬚ d governed in accor- ⬚ contrary to law, that ⬚ ing provisions will ⬚ effe